BOOK I

The Annals Of Arrinor

GRYPHON'S HEIR

D.R. RANSHAW

*To Robyn,
with best wishes*

D.R. Ranshaw

FriesenPress

Suite 300 - 990 Fort St
Victoria, BC, Canada, V8V 3K2
www.friesenpress.com

Copyright © 2015 by D.R. Ranshaw
First Edition — 2015

All rights reserved.

No part of this publication may be reproduced in any form, or by any means, electronic or mechanical, including photocopying, recording, or any information browsing, storage, or retrieval system, without permission in writing from the publisher.

ISBN
978-1-4602-5763-0 (Hardcover)
978-1-4602-5764-7 (Paperback)
978-1-4602-5765-4 (eBook)

1. Fiction, Fantasy

Distributed to the trade by The Ingram Book Company

For Jane
Who was there from the Beginning

PROLOGUE

"From death and destruction shall the One deliver you; place your trust and faith in His Servants, and by them be led. Truly, although His paths may seem beyond understanding or endurance, the righteous Child of the Light reposes complete faith in the goodness and mercy of the One."

The Book of the One, 76:9:17-18
(Cantos 76, Chapter 9, Verses 17-18)

Acrid smoke, thick and heavy, drifted past the young woman pressed tightly into the stone wall's tiny alcove. Much of Tor Eylian was aflame by now, nearly all the wooden structures of the castle fully engulfed in the holocaust. It lit the darkness of the night sky in a crimson glow, fires casting ruddy light against billowing clouds of smoke. Sparks and glowing embers borne on the night winds brought peril even to the city beyond.

She quickly checked the small bundle held against her chest before glancing around desperately. It was nigh on impossible to see clearly through flame and fume, but the harsh voices and laughter of the brigands responsible for this night were plainly audible, and drawing nearer. They had not given up searching for her, then. Worse, they were not even bothering to be silent in their hunting, evidently completely confident their quarry could not escape.

With a small sob of fear, she edged from the alcove and continued, attempting unsuccessfully to locate exactly where along the outer wall she was. Darkness and smoke obscured normal landmarks that would reveal how close the postern gate was, and she felt utterly lost and alone. *Was* she truly alone, save for the bundle at her breast? Had all the loyal garrison soldiers really died in this treachery? It seemed certain her husband was dead. She had seen him earlier in the flames, frantically trying to win through to her. Then, through the reek, she thought she saw him cut down from behind by one of the cowards, employing the inferno they had started as a cover to effect the murder of the entire royal family. But she was unsure; it was almost impossible to be sure of anything.

A blazing beam crashed down, its massive bulk shaking the ground as it struck the spot where she stood mere moments before. By the light of the flames, she could at last determine her location, but it was not a good knowing. She was nowhere near where she needed to be; the postern gate was an impossible distance. She sank to her knees in despair. All was lost. That bitter certainty mingled with the sharp taste of ashes on her tongue.

The bundle in her arms shifted, a small whimper escaping from within folds of cloth, and she glanced down, reverie broken. Faint as it was, the sound was enough to kindle in her the resolve to make one last effort, however vain it might prove. If she could not save herself, there must be some way to save her son. Wearily, she stood and again cast her gaze about, searching for any hope.

She caught sudden movement out the corner of her eye: a man seemed to shimmer forth from the wall mere yards away, and, horrified, she shrank back. He saw her at once and extended a gauntleted hand, palm empty, shaking his head in denial as he observed her reaction to his sudden appearance.

"Be not afraid," he said urgently. "I am come to help you and yours escape this carnage. The way out is actually quite near. If you will trust to my deliverance, I can assist you."

She peered at him, suspicion uppermost in her mind. He was not a garrison trooper, she was certain. Tall, dark haired and handsome, with knowing eyes and a neatly trimmed goatee, he wore a long, flowing cloak closed at the throat with a gryphon-shaped broach. The tunic beneath, somehow unbesmirched in the reek, was snowy white, the Sign of the Three chased on it in large, crimson relief. At his belt, a long, slender sword glittered in the flames.

"Who are you?" she demanded, past caring about tact. "You are not of our guard. And the design on your tunic... it is of no Order I know. What do you seek here?"

He shook his head brusquely. "There is no time for lengthy explanation, and my name is unimportant. You need know only that I seek to save you and your child. Do you accept my aid?"

Wide-eyed, cowed by the terse man who dared to speak so to the Queen, she nodded mutely. He returned her nod with a curt one of his own. "Very well. Although you do not recognize me, I am friend to your family. And my comrade in arms brings you your own handmaiden, delivered from death even as we searched for you." He motioned into the murk, and from it stumbled her lady-in-waiting, whom she had thought dead in the night's evil. Their joyful reunion was cut off as another figure emerged slowly into the light. The Queen turned, staring curiously at the new arrival as her maid whispered animatedly in her ear.

He was much younger than the first — in fact, only slightly older than she. Evidently another member of the mysterious order with the insignia of the Three, he was identically clad to the first knight. His hair was dishevelled, but he was a handsome youth, even grimed from fire and smoke. He inclined his head, eyes downcast, unaccountably reluctant to meet her gaze. She felt inexplicable compassion for the brave but shy young man well up within her, and said softly, "Well met, sir. My maid informs me she owes you her life. You have her gratitude, and mine."

The young man nodded, but remained silent. He raised his eyes and met hers, and in that moment she experienced a dizzying flash of recognition. "Do I know you, sir? You seem familiar."

Oddly, the innocent question provoked a strange reaction, the two knights, appearing almost... alarmed: they stiffened and exchanged unreadable glances. After a moment, the younger shook his head and stammered, "No, Lady. We are not acquainted."

The elder knight roused. "Come, ladies. There is no time for idle talk. That murderous rabble still hunts you, and is nearby. We will require the Grace of the One to evade them. Follow and stay close." He turned and strode swiftly along the wall, not looking back to see whether they obeyed. They stood irresolute for several seconds, but a shout close behind made them jump in alarm, and they ran after the knight, nearly lost now in smoke.

Breathing hard, they caught up. He had halted, however, peering cautiously at the surroundings, head cocked to one side as though listening intently. Abruptly, he turned and headed in a different direction, away from the outer walls.

"We must change our route," he called over his shoulder. "I wish to avoid someone nearby."

The Queen frowned. "What—?" she began, but he had already moved on, and they were obliged to follow immediately or lose him.

Several seemingly endless minutes of twisting, laborious progress through flaming chaos brought them back to the outer wall. The Queen was about to demand explanation when the knight pointed.

"There!" he said in grim satisfaction, and as her gaze moved to the spot indicated, her eyes widened in shock.

In the midst of the wall — the *outer* wall — was a door where no door should be. Where no door ever had been. It was of ordinary size, like within a house, and could in no way be mistaken for the castle's postern gate. It appeared to have been there always: not somehow tacked onto the structure of the wall, but an integral part of it. The dark wooden door was polished and ornately carven with decorative figures, its craftsmanship in marked contrast to the surrounding plain grey stone. A gleaming pearl doorknob was halfway up one side.

"Go through yonder door, and leave this place of death. Beyond lies safety and the explanations you seek. Take maid and babe through, and live."

"But where —?" she began.

She was interrupted by a triumphant yell: soldiers charged into the area behind them. The knight muttered inaudibly, swung round and calmly drew his sword in one flowing movement; his young colleague did likewise. "Behind us!" he ordered as the soldiers fanned out in a semicircle to confront them. "Open the door and go through!"

The two women moved swiftly past the two knights, but even in such peril, the Queen could not bring herself to leave them. She watched her rescuers engage the enemy, their swordplay fluid and skilful. Several opponents were dispatched quickly, but more flooded into the area, drawn by the shouts of their fellows.

Glancing over his shoulder, the older knight snarled inarticulately and retreated several steps, forcing her to move also, until they were all bunched in a knot around the door. He motioned impatiently at it, but as more men entered the area, he stiffened, and puzzled, she followed his gaze.

The newcomers included archers and a richly dressed, unarmed man. He was dark haired, relatively youthful, only of average height, but there was a compelling manner to him, the aura of a person accustomed to being obeyed. He seemed oddly calm. There was something strangely unpleasant about his eyes, and the Queen shivered, but from twenty feet, with only flames giving uncertain illumination, she could not fathom the nature of that unpleasantness.

An archer raised his bow and loosed an arrow. His intended target was unclear, but it struck the Queen in the upper part of her left arm. As the arrow penetrated, she screamed at the pain, nearly dropping the child. Crying out, her maid steadied her.

Both knights whirled, eyes widening as they took in her wound. "Open the door!" the older one hissed. "I cannot do it for you. You must choose to do so!"

Through bright agony, she tried to make him understand, but could not give voice to her thoughts. How was she to open the door *and* hold her babe, one arm sorely hurt? But her maid realized. "Give me the child, and for love of the One, do as he says, Majesty!"

The older knight raised his arm, and the Queen thought *he* would take the baby. But to her surprise, he made a sweeping gesture with his palm in a semicircle before them. Immediately, the haze intensified. The air rippled and visibly thickened, hardening to a jelly-like consistency.

The women blinked and clutched each other, trying to decide whether their eyes were playing tricks. The maid wordlessly took the child, and the older knight turned to examine the Queen's injury. His concern was obvious as he placed a gloved hand on her brow. In the midst of the furnace in which they stood, she felt a sudden frosty wave of coolness and strength flood her mind, like a breeze through an open window on a scorching summer's day. It pushed back the darkness threatening to envelope her thoughts, and the pain in her arm.

"Who are you?" she whispered. "*What* have you done?"

"Friends, as I said. No time for more. Explanations will come once you pass through." He glanced hurriedly at the soldiers. "The door, Lady, if you please," he said gently. "My defences will not last long against the forces arrayed here. Your delaying endangers us all."

Dazed, she finally obeyed. The knob turned smoothly, and as the door opened, she saw, to her utter surprise, no opening in the wall leading from the castle, but a dark, enclosed corridor extending as far as she could see. Candlelight flared suddenly in the corridor, lighting the way even as she stared. Turning to her defenders, while her maid handed her the child, she looked suspiciously at the older knight.

"This is no ordinary door," she whispered. "Where would you have us go?"

"To safety," he said grimly. "And quickly. You must trust me. My shield weakens. Choose whether to enter or stay here. However, if you remain, you do so alone, for we will not linger. Then those soldiers will finish what they started, you and yours perishing." He glanced at her wryly. "I grant there is little choice. But I have your best interests at heart, as will a colleague of mine beyond that corridor. Come, my shield is almost spent. Choose."

A moment longer she stood, studying these strange saviours, by turns earnest and rude, but steadfastly anonymous throughout. Behind them was her home, reduced to ashes. The brigands responsible had nearly worked their way to them, through the very air turned to molasses, and she shook her head in resigned acceptance.

"Enough, Knight of the One. I yield, trusting you do not send us to a worse fate."

"I do not," he replied quietly. "Go with the One."

Their eyes met. "Will you not come also? I would not have you meet your deaths here."

He shook his head. "There is no danger of that. But we are needed elsewhere, and may not follow you."

"Will we meet again, sir? There is much I would know..."

He gave a small smile. "Who can say?" He glanced down at the bundle. "We may, if the One allows. Now stop delaying. Go."

She nodded solemnly. "My gratitude, Deliverers," she said, stepping over the threshold. Her maid followed, pulling the door closed. It clicked with an air of finality, melting into the wall, becoming wispy and indistinct before fading away completely.

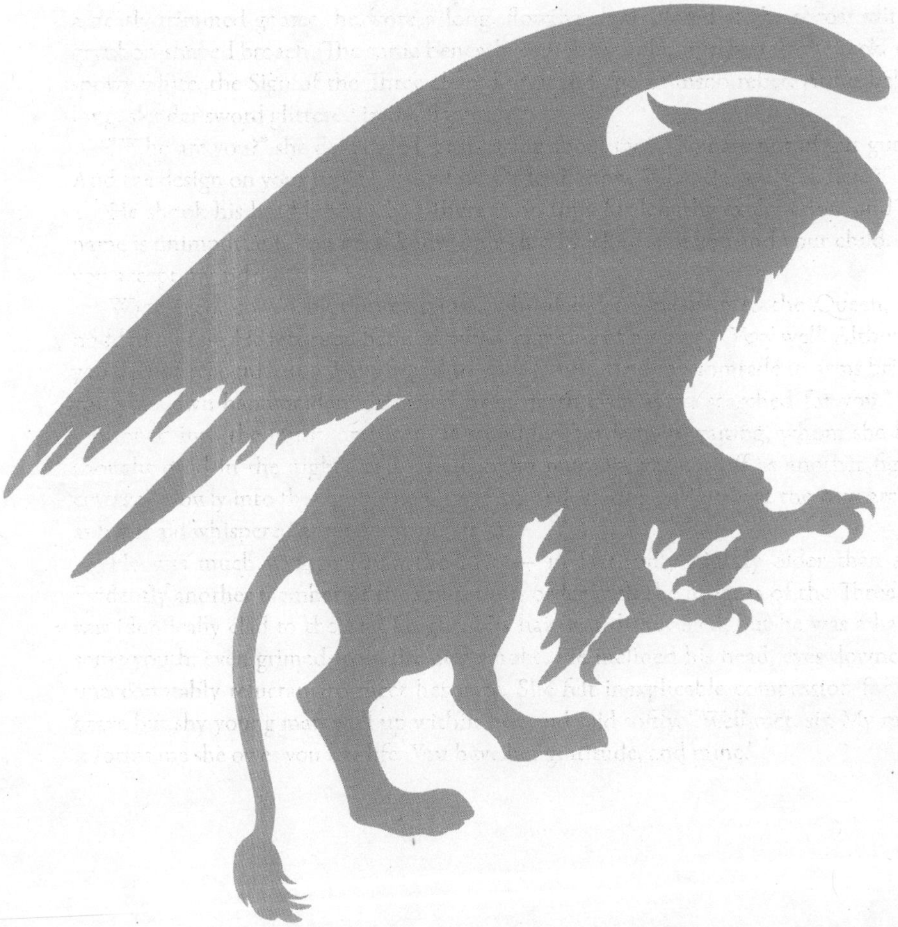

I

NOT FOR THE FAINT OF HEART

"Where, O my Essence, will I find my heart's desire and the justice promised by the One? I am denied that which I seek at every turn. My enemies conspire against me, and I am sick at heart. Where is my strength and salvation? It is in the Servant of the One who comes unlooked for."

The Book of the One, 85:3:4-6
(Cantos 85, Chapter 3, Verses 4-6)

The door to the classroom exploded open with a crash and a small boy hurtled through, skidding to a stop. The room's occupant spun around at the window to glare at the intruder.

"Please, sir!" gasped the child, chest heaving from his exertions. "Beg pardon disturbing you, but they're having a go at Colin again. Please, sir, come and sort them! They're hurting him this time!"

The man muttered an oath and strode quickly out the door without a word, the boy following at a run. Looking intently up and down the hallway, he sought the problem.

It was not difficult to find. Several rooms along, a knot of teenage boys gathered in a circle, cheering and catcalling, the object of their attention not immediately visible. Briefly wondering how he had not heard it, he ran to the commotion, pushing boys out of the way. "Right, then! Enough! Stand back, I say!"

A surly silence fell; Authority had arrived, with presence and resolve to halt the sport. Slowly, unwillingly, they stood aside. The master made his way through, jostling those who did not move quickly enough to suit him. As he did, he could have sworn he heard a derisive "Taffy" muttered somewhere in the crowd. He whipped his head around, but was met only by a sea of bland stares, and angrily returned his attention to the centre of the commotion.

A young boy with a bloody nose and a cut over one eye struggled to rise from where he cowered on the floor. Above him, an imperious youth with a badge stood ramrod straight, looking disdainfully at the student he had so obviously been tormenting.

Eyes flicking between the two, the master wordlessly gave the younger his handkerchief. Looking around, he spoke to the assemblage, words clipped and tightly controlled. "What is the meaning of this?"

No response. The master circled slowly, ending up facing the youth, who remained stock still. "Well, Talbot?" he said tonelessly.

The boy's gaze appeared fixed on a distant point over the master's shoulder. "Sir?"

"I seek explanation, Talbot. A good one. I presume you can enlighten me."

"An explanation? For what, sir?" The student's voice was smug, mocking.

"Do not take that tone with me, Talbot! An explanation for this appalling spectacle, as you bloody well know!"

The crowd edged back slowly at the fury in his voice. From personal experience, many knew the man was not to be trifled with, especially when it was plain he felt there had been injustice. Belatedly, Talbot appeared to realize he had gone too far; his expression lost its cockiness, and he said warily, "It was just a bit of fun with the new boy, sir. I didn't — that is, we didn't — mean any harm."

It was precisely the wrong thing to say. Talbot felt his arm gripped in an iron vise.

"No harm?" Mr. Griffith said fiercely. "Look at the boy, Talbot! Just what do you think you're playing at? You assaulted him! As Head Boy, you are supposed to set an example to the others — preventing this sort of thing, not causing it! And this is not the first time, is it? Is it?"

"No, sir." The response was muffled.

Eyes blazing, Mr. Griffith released Talbot's blazer. "Come with me, both of you." He looked around the motionless spectators. "The rest of you, clear out. This is no exhibition for your amusement." He turned, striding towards his classroom, motioning the two boys to follow.

"Just a moment, Mr. Griffith, if you please!"

The thin, reedy voice was all too familiar; Mr. Griffith raised his eyes to the heavens, silently cursing the ill fortune of the headmaster coming through the halls at that particular moment. The headmaster arrived and stood, rocking slightly back and forth.

"Would you be so kind as to explain, Mr. Griffith?"

"Nothing important to concern yourself with, sir." The tone was polite, but cold. "A minor matter of house discipline."

The headmaster, a small, slight man, frowned, catching the insubordinate tone. "I'll be the judge of that." He turned watery eyes to the two boys, appraising both. "Talbot, proceed to my study. I shall speak with you after having a word with Mr. Griffith."

The hint of a smirk reappeared on the youth's face. "Yes, sir. Very good, sir."

"And you, boy... uh—" the headmaster stopped, peering blankly, clearly at a loss.

"Lewis, sir. Colin Lewis," Mr. Griffith supplied acidly.

The headmaster glanced up sharply, hearing the implied rebuke. "Yes, of course. Thank you." He turned to the boy. "Lewis, report to matron and have her attend you. Off you go, now." The boy scampered off, casting an unreadable glance back as he went.

The headmaster cleared his throat. "All of you, on your way. Quickly, now." There was a rush as all except Talbot complied. Mr. Griffith had quietly laid hold of his arm again, although the headmaster had not registered it. "Mr. Griffith, let us return to your classroom."

"Would you be so kind as to go ahead, Headmaster, if you please? I should like to speak privately with Talbot."

"What? I see no need—" The headmaster stopped, squinting at Mr. Griffith. Whatever he read evidently caused him to rethink what he was about to say. "Oh, very well, if you must," he said ungraciously. "Join me when you are finished." The headmaster stalked off.

Mr. Griffith watched, then spun to face the youth. "Let me be perfectly clear, Talbot," he said, voice low and expression hard. "We both know the headmaster's appearance has provided you a very lucky escape, indeed. He will do nothing to chastise you, because he is perhaps too mindful that you are an earl's son, and fearful of the repercussions should he do what he ought, in good conscience."

The boy had regained a measure of his cocky demeanour. "But *you* aren't fearful of the repercussions for what you were about to do, are you, sir?"

Mr. Griffith slowly shook his head. "No, I am not, Talbot, as you know without needing to ask. Your behaviour today — and too often in the past, I might add — has been reprehensible. You are a bully, a cad and a coward, and we both are fully aware of that truth, even if others are too afraid to confront it." His eyes flashed as they narrowed. "But know this also: if ever you lay a hand on that boy again, or do anything to cause him grief, I *will* thrash you within an inch of your miserable life, earl's son or no. Because what you and others like you have either forgotten or never known is that the responsibility of the strong is to nurture and protect the weak, not take advantage. And if miserable cads like you only feel better about yourselves when tormenting someone weaker who cannot fight back, know that I or others like me — people who know what the right thing is and refuse to be intimidated by your wealth or status — will oppose you. You will not prevail. You *cannot* be allowed to prevail." He paused, wetting his lips. "Perhaps you need reminding of an aphorism I tried to teach you — apparently in vain: 'All that is required for the triumph of evil is that good men do nothing.' I will not be that man. Do you understand? Have I been crystal clear?"

The youth began to make arrogant reply, but stopped, locking eyes with the adult. For an endless moment, they stood engaged in silent struggle. However, Talbot broke contact first, involuntarily cowering as if expecting to be struck.

"Yes, sir," he muttered.

"Then get out of my sight," said Mr. Griffith calmly, releasing the boy's arm. "And meanwhile, I shall go to hear the startling but happy news of your exoneration."

An hour later, he sat at his desk in dark, solitary reflection. Another week was over and done, and, with its passing, the 1924 Spring term was that much closer to completion. It had been another in a long progression of somber, tedious days, leaving him beyond frustration. Apathetic, cynical — and, in thankfully few cases — utterly amoral students who could not appreciate learning, colleagues with no passion or skill whatsoever, a headmaster and senior staff completely out of touch with reality... it all made Rhissan Griffith — Rhiss to his closest friends — wonder why on earth he had ever chosen teaching, although he knew the answer perfectly well. It was, he reminded himself with a sigh, because he *did* have a gift and passion for it; but it was a gift that seemed singularly unappreciated. Twenty-five was far too young an age to be so cynical, he thought wearily. But there seemed naught to be done about it.

He rose slowly and wandered to the window. Located on the village outskirts, the school faced green fields and thickly forested lands. But even the sight of the lovely, verdant English countryside failed to lift his spirits as it usually did. His reflection, tall, slender and grim, stared back through the window panes, and Rhiss studied it critically. He was not wearing his master's gown: it lay discarded on the chair, thrown off in frustration as the last boy left at day's end and it was no longer required. Consequently, his brown serge suit, with tie, waistcoat and jacket, made for a rather drab image. His thatch of dark hair was usually carefully groomed, although rather longer than was really acceptable for someone in his position — a minor act of rebellion, he knew. But it was dishevelled from running his hands through it, the physical manifestation of his frustration. His hair crowned a face commanding respect, certainly. The slate grey eyes could travel swiftly from sympathetic warmth to icy fury, and his students had learned to keep a weather eye for when they provoked him. The mouth below the long, aquiline nose was framed by a pair of thin lips pressed firmly together in disapproval.

The late afternoon sun slid behind a grey cloud bank, plunging the land into shadow. He watched his reflection in the glass materialize like a melancholy grey wraith in the stronger light of the classroom, wondering if there was something symbolic in that. With another sigh, he slowly returned to his desk and sat heavily, staring disconsolately at the stack of unmarked essays piled untidily where the last scholars had left them.

Rhiss put head in hands and closed his eyes, utterly disheartened. It was difficult to remember the enthusiasm of arriving at Darkton School last summer to take his post teaching English literature at the exclusive boys' institution. While not Eton, admittedly, it had a fine reputation as a school catering to the children of the affluent — a reputation completely undeserved, Rhiss had quickly discovered. But how could he have known? Everything had seemed possible when the train from London pulled into the village that bright August morning. Unfortunately, disillusionment had not been long in manifesting.

How had things gone wrong? It was not that he lacked skill or knowledge. Nor did he have difficulty keeping a class of adolescent boys under control. It was just that there seemed no magic in his life. Had there been, once? He thought so, and wondered where it had gone.

Rhiss shook his head. What a fey state of mind to be in. Whatever had triggered such dark thoughts? Well, that was a daft question, of course: it had started with that supercilious bully Talbot, then the heated altercation with the headmaster. Heated?

That was an understatement. He had nearly struck the man in his rage. Rhiss glanced down at his hands. They still trembled from the intensity of his reaction.

It had been the boy. Lewis. Colin Lewis. Peering at the small form cowering on the floor, it had been as though he had looked at a younger image of himself. The bleeding nose, the cut above the eye, the surrounding crowd... all that was missing were the cruelly derisive taunts: *Taffy! Gog! Filthy taffy! Thieving gog!*

The door banged open for the second time that afternoon, breaking his reverie. Rhiss looked up angrily, but the biting words died in his throat. It was no student — they had all long since left — but a colleague. More, it was one of the few friends he had made amongst a staff whose defining characteristics were aloofness to younger masters and unwillingness to discard teaching practices straight out of Dickens.

Rhiss had found a kindred spirit in Alistair Bellamy, who was only a year or two older. They had quickly banded together as the fall term started, at first in mutual self-preservation, then in true friendship discovering common interests like Saturday walking tours of the countryside. Sometimes — in fact, more often of late — they borrowed horses from the local squire Alistair knew, and rode along narrow country lanes instead of walking. On Saturday evenings, they frequently headed to community dances — ostensibly, Alistair maintained, to sample the beers at surrounding public houses — but really, to meet and dance with pretty young girls at such functions. Alistair had met one on just such a weekend foray, and Jennie was now nearly his fiancée, Rhiss suspected. She was a winsome lass, and Rhiss thoroughly approved of Alistair's choice.

Alistair taught rugby, cricket and other physical pursuits, more than once loudly proclaiming bafflement with literature. But Rhiss knew the remark to be humourous rubbish, and Alistair a literate, articulate chap. On Fridays, after lessons, they frequently had grand discussions about history or philosophy over a pint or two in The Admiral Rodney, the quiet local pub where they retired after another week of attempting, as Alistair put it, to "knock some knowledge into the Great Unwashed." Rhiss was sure something of the sort would be Alistair's purpose now.

It was.

"Come along, Mr. Griffith," Alistair drawled cheerfully. "I say, I can't imagine for the life of me what you're still doing here — other than waiting to be rescued, perhaps. The weekend is upon us, and you're still at your desk with those idiotic papers, looking for all the world like a cantankerous old bear set to hibernate for winter. About as lively, too, I shouldn't wonder. But it is the weekend, and I'm officially letting you know that We Have Plans."

Rhiss smiled in spite of himself. Alistair felt the same frustrations, but was more adept at refusing to allow them to affect his mood. But Rhiss did not want cheering up or a night out. There was some idea in his melancholy train of thought about to wash to the surface of his mind — an important observation, he was sure, although he could not put his finger on it. He couldn't articulate *why* he was so sure, but he *was* sure that if he was left alone and allowed his mind some peace, the idea would eventually arrive, like a piece of driftwood making its way to shore on the tide.

"Not tonight, Alistair," he replied, shaking his head. "I've something on my mind, and I need quiet to sort it."

Alistair looked incredulous. "But it's a Friday night in May, old man! There's a dance Ilseby way, and Jennie promised to bring a friend for you. A sweet-looking girl, she says, with personality to match. Just the thing for a weary literature master who's had too much Shakespeare, don't you think? Because eventually, he'll make you feel that, let me see—" his brow furrowed in mock concentration — "'Life's but a walking shadow, a poor player that struts and frets his hour upon the stage and then is heard no more.'"

Rhiss made a face. "You can't *use* Shakespeare to *denigrate* Shakespeare, you silly clot." He sighed. "Another time. I had a bit of a run-in today with the headmaster and that bloody awful chief toady of his."

Grimacing, Alistair flopped his lanky frame over a student desk, all pretence of jollying vanished. "Talbot? Yes, I know... and so does the rest of the staff, I should imagine. I heard about it in the masters' common room. You were the subject of some very animated discourse."

Rhiss grunted. "I can just picture it. No doubt they were united in their vigorous defence of everyone's pet Taffy."

"Well, not quite, as I suspect you know jolly well. Not a very progressive lot, our colleagues, I fear."

"Or passionate about elementary concepts, like justice or morality," Rhiss interjected bitterly.

"However," Alistair added lightly, "believe it or not, there *was* admiration expressed for the way you took on the Old Man. Incredulity, too, and odds given for how long it will take him to sack you after the row the two of you had, but, on the whole—"

Rhiss interrupted, frowning. "Row? How on earth would they know about *that*?"

Alistair smiled crookedly. "Oh, come now, Rhiss, I should think the entire school heard the two of you going at it. You can't actually believe your flaming contretemps was private." He paused, then added thoughtfully, "Never knew the Old Man had it in him, actually — he's always struck me as a rather weedy old git."

"Hmm," Rhiss replied. "No argument there." He sighed again. "I'll correct papers a while, then head home for a late tea. Thank Jennie for me, and extend my apologies. Perhaps I can meet her friend another time."

Alistair stared in frank disbelief. "Look, you're my best mate in this asylum. You mustn't allow the inmates to get you down. If they *are* doing that, this is the last place you should be. Come with us, and forget your troubles. What say you?"

Rhiss was tempted, but rejected the idea. He managed a wan smile. "I think not. But thank you for trying."

"Well then, what about a quick session at The Blade and Bow? You could pretend I'm the headmaster and take out your frustrations on me. Come to think of it, you've been so good of late, I wouldn't even have to pretend you're better than me."

Rhiss smiled, genuinely amused. 'The Blade and Bow' was a private joke. The name, implying a pub to the casual listener, was a spartan, outdoor fencing area and archery range they maintained on the local squire's land, with his permission. Alistair was a keen fencer and archer, and master at both. It was an unusual combination of interests, so they coined the misleading name to prevent ridicule from colleagues prepared to provide it at the slightest provocation. Anyone overhearing would assume they were off for pints at some pub — as long as they didn't think too hard about it, which at Darkton was unlikely. But Rhiss accepted it as just a small eccentricity, and to their mutually surprised pleasure, they discovered he had an unexpected flair for both arts. They spent much of their free time at The Blade and Bow, Alistair transmitting his passion, practicing, instructing, critiquing — to the point where Rhiss was now, they both knew, the better of the two. But he displayed not the least resentment that the student had surpassed the instructor, a truly noble characteristic. Rhiss had learned early in their friendship that Alistair possessed ample measures of both grace and humility.

"Don't be daft. You've got your dance and there isn't time to have a go — anyway, I wouldn't want to carve you up before an evening with Jennie, would I, now? What would she say?"

Alistair laughed. "The dance isn't until later. Plenty of time for a quick bout."

Rhiss glanced out the windows. "But... what about the weather? It's going to rain before the day's much older."

"Then we'll get wet," Alistair said patiently. "It would hardly be the first time. Stop making excuses. You know jolly well a quick bout is the perfect thing after a day like this. What do you say?"

"Well..." Rhiss began uncertainly.

Alistair sensed his indecision, quickly pressing home the attack. "We can stop by The Admiral Rodney, have them pack sandwiches... and drinks." He raised an eyebrow. "Rhiss, you know you want to. Think of you trouncing me while I pretend to be the Old Man. Or Talbot, if you prefer. I'll even howl and beg for mercy."

"You would anyway," Rhiss joked, and threw his hands up in surrender. "All right, you win. But I shall hold you to your word: you'll be that frightful cad Talbot, and I warn you, I shall thrash you within an inch of your life!"

Two hours later, reclining at The Blade and Bow, they ate their sandwiches, washing them down with bottles of stout. The May sunset was fighting a losing battle with dark clouds, but the rain held off, for a change. Rhiss had to admit Alistair was right: his mood was much improved after time with bow and sword... although, he mused again, the blades they fought with had about as much in common with the slender foils of traditional fencing as rifles had with cannon. He reached over to the stand where the swords hung, hefting his gently.

"Alistair," he said, running his thumb carefully down the blade, "I've asked several times, and you've continually avoided a real answer, but it's always puzzled me: whatever possessed you about swords like this? These bloody great things are straight from King Arthur. I well remember the first time you invited me to fence. I nearly died of shock when I saw what you proposed. And the fighting we do with these... calling it 'fencing' hardly does it justice. It's not exactly the traditional back and forth for points."

Alistair grinned. "I suppose not," he admitted cheerfully. "But there's grace and artistry to this kind of swordplay too, you know, especially in the hands of a master." He eyed Rhiss appraisingly. "Like you, for instance."

Rhiss flushed. "Don't be ridiculous. I'm no expert—"

Alistair raised a hand. "Just a moment, if you please. You're the one being ridiculous. You've got a gift with the sword — and bow — and you know it as well as I. In fact, you're better than me now, and we both know that, too, so it might as well be said. It certainly doesn't bother *me*. And being left-handed makes you an even more formidable opponent — most swordsmen are right-handed, used to right-handed people."

Rhiss grimaced. "So, then tell me again why you insisted I learn to fight right-handed as well?"

Alistair spread his hands wide. "Because a man who can fight with either hand is a formidable opponent indeed — which is what you are definitely becoming. *And* an exceptional horseman, too."

Rhiss rolled his eyes. "Go on. Formidable? Exceptional? Tell us another one."

Alistair sighed in exasperation. "You know, Rhiss, you're modest to a fault. It's most annoying. For the life of me, I don't understand why you find it so difficult to accept the praise of others. You must be able to allow that you're good at things."

"Well, perhaps. But let's return to my original question. Despite your continued efforts at prevarication, Mr. Bellamy, we weren't discussing me. At least, I wasn't. I asked about these swords, and why you play with them instead of something traditional."

"Well, I suppose I just... like them," Alistair replied slowly. "I've done 'traditional' fencing, and found it wanting. Swords like these are far more... robust. More of a challenge. And well-handled, as I said, there's a speed and beauty to them almost like ballet. Also, speaking of King Arthur—" he snapped his fingers as though inspiration had just struck "—what about all that Malory you're always spouting? There's romance to those stories! Haven't you ever wanted to be Arthur or Lancelot? *I* have. And if that's the case, you can never tell when you might meet an evil Mordred needing a good thumping!" He paused and looked at Rhiss with a twinkle in his eye. "Although perhaps I'd rather be Arthur. And you could be Lancelot."

"Hang on a moment," Rhiss objected. "Why not the other way 'round?"

"Well, it's obvious, isn't it? Who was captain of the faculty cricket team? *And* led them to a resounding victory against the village team during the Squire's tournament? Just a natural leader, that's me." He laughed, but Rhiss only smiled half-heartedly.

Alistair noticed and gave up trying to jolly his friend along. "Come on, what is it, Rhiss? Even after several eminently satisfying bouts, you're still... contemplative. You have been all afternoon. It's not just that swine, Talbot — or even the foul headmaster, is it?"

Rhiss shook his head. "I... don't quite know." He didn't want to speak of his mood, wasn't even sure he could properly articulate it. "Never mind. You need to find your way over to Jennie's and take her to that dance. Look at the time."

"And you should—" Alistair began.

"—return to school," Rhiss interrupted smoothly, "and tackle those papers you dragged me from."

Alistair raised his eyebrows in shocked disbelief. "What? You can't be serious about heading back to that dungeon! Come with us. I guarantee a better time."

"No," Rhiss replied firmly. "I'm going back to the school. I really want to get some papers marked. And I need quiet time to think. The time there... will do me good."

"You old bugger. It bloody well won't, and you know it." Alistair paused, looking shrewdly at Rhiss. "You know, there's far more to this than a disagreement with the headmaster. You said before we left you were trying to work through something. Come on. What is it?"

Rhiss was silent a moment, but Alistair's question unlocked something deep within, and the words came tumbling out without conscious thought. "I don't quite know... but... something needs to change in my life. The incident earlier today... it's left me in a very odd mood. I'm not sure what needs to occur, or how, or when... but I can feel it. It's almost... I feel so damned restless. I can't adequately explain it, even to you, because *I'm* not sure what I'm talking about. But... something's out there, and I need to be ready for it."

Alistair was still, expression strange and unreadable. "And are you?"

"Am I what?"

"Ready for change. And before you reply, let me caution you: fate, or destiny, or God, or whatever you call it, has an uncanny way of supplying what you ask for. But the strangest thing is, often we don't consider the ramifications of our request. There's an old saying that warns some things in life are not for the faint of heart. So, I'll ask again: are you ready for this... this change? Even if it turns your life completely and irrevocably upside down?"

Rhiss considered, pursing his lips. "Do you know, after today, I just might be. It was almost the final straw. I came within a hairsbreadth of flinging my resignation at the headmaster... or at least flinging *something*."

Alistair sighed and stood. He seemed to be weighing whether or not to speak.

"I'll leave you to it, then, if you're sure I can't change your mind. But don't stay at school too long. The weather's going to be positively filthy before the day ends, and even if it wasn't, it's not good to spend an entire evening at hideous old Darkton. Go home before too long."

"I will," said Rhiss, meaning it.

"Can I leave you to put things away? I rather need to get to Jennie's. She'll be wondering where I am."

Rhiss felt a stab of guilt. "Of course. I'm terribly sorry to have delayed you. Don't bother about me. It's just a silly mood."

Alistair waved dismissively. "Don't talk rot. You're my friend." He hesitated, then stuck out his hand. Surprised, Rhiss stood to take it, and they shook firmly. "Lancelot and Arthur, indeed," mused Alistair, almost to himself. "I'd be there for you. And you'd likewise be there for me, wouldn't you? If ever I needed you."

"Of course I would," Rhiss replied. "I'm your man Lancelot, remember? You don't even have to ask."

"Yes," Alistair said thoughtfully. "I do believe you're right. You're that sort of chap." He released Rhiss' hand and began walking, Rhiss following. At the path leading to the village, Alistair stopped and turned. "I hope you find what you seek, Rhiss. I really do. In fact, I think you will." Then he turned abruptly and was gone, striding resolutely down the path. Rhiss stared after the receding figure, wondering what in the world had gotten into his friend.

After carefully stowing their gear, Rhiss returned to the school. It seemed deserted, but the main doors were unlocked, so someone must have been about. He entered his room and sat at his desk for half an hour, fully intending to buckle down on the discouraging piles of marking. Focus, however, proved maddeningly elusive. His mind kept returning to Alistair's last words. They were disturbing, the more so since Rhiss was sure Alistair would not have intended them as such.

Rhiss sighed. It was ridiculous. He was accomplishing nothing; worse, he was at school on a Friday evening, of all things. It was time to go — past time. What had he been thinking? Perhaps he should see if Alistair had yet left for the dance. He rose to don his coat, but before he could complete the action, two things occurred simultaneously: there was the sound of a door closing quietly but firmly, and the overhead lights flickered. Rhiss glanced at the classroom door before remembering that he had closed it himself on arriving.

It was still firmly shut.

Puzzled, he looked about, confusion turning to shock as his eyes took in the west wall. The windows at which he had stood hours ago were still there, the clouds outside darker and promising rain any moment. But the windowless part of the wall was what attracted his attention: bare, scuffed and rather dirty, it was normally unremarkable. *But no longer*.

Now it contained a door — one which hadn't existed seconds previously, one with absolutely no business being there. Incredulous, Rhiss rose to gain a better view.

It seemed quite ordinary, and to all appearances had been there forever. It did not look tacked to the wall's structure; on first glance, it looked to be an integral part. But on closer examination, the fine layer of grime coating most of the room's horizontal surfaces covered no part of the door. The door was dark, richly polished wood, ornately carved with decorative figures, its craftsmanship contrasting markedly to the drab institutional confines of the room. A gleaming pearl doorknob was halfway up the right side.

Before realizing what he was doing, Rhiss grasped the knob and, with a quick, almost convulsive movement, turned it. He did so with blank amazement such an action could be performed at all, when he knew full well it should be — and until mere moments ago, was — completely impossible.

The door swung smoothly inward on noiseless hinges. To his astonishment, the opening revealed not the grassy lawn outside the school, but an unlit corridor proceeding straight into darkness — a corridor that could not possibly exist.

It remained dark no more than a moment. Thick, ivory candles flared into light. The flames burned brilliantly vermillion, imbuing the corridor with a warm glow. Strange, grey sconces, four or five feet apart at shoulder height and shaped like closed human hands, held the candles as if they were the hilts of swords. The walls were deep sky-blue above waist-high wainscoting of some dark wood. It wasn't even the same material as the wall from which it appeared to extend. The corridor stretched fifteen to twenty feet before broadening into some kind of room. A smooth hardwood floor of the same colouring as the wainscoting was beneath his feet.

How could this happen? Why was this happening? *Was* it even happening?

That brought him up short, brow furrowing in consternation. *Could* this be some incredibly detailed hallucination? During the war, he had known people who imagined places or even whole lives apart from where they actually were. That was all he needed, he thought, distractedly touching the wall. It was silky-smooth. He moved hesitantly to the nearest candle sconce, cautious of its disturbingly realistic appearance. Initially reluctant to touch — his inner voice nervously insisting the hand might come to life and envelop his — he eventually mastered his fear and gently grasped the sconce. It was stone, finely sculpted and glossy to the touch. The candle smelled strongly of beeswax, and the flame warmed his cupped hand.

He passed through the door, slowly proceeding down the corridor. It took only moments to come to where the corridor opened into a large square room, illuminated by more of the strange candle holders. He stood in the entryway, gazing at a bizarrely inviting sight.

On the side opposite whence he had come was another corridor, twin to the one he had traversed. Currently unlit, it was in shadow, but he could see it appeared a similar length as the one he had come along, possibly ending at another door. The chamber's centre was occupied by a waist-high, four-sided bookcase filled with leather bound volumes of varying sizes and colours. A smooth, white, stone statue of a graceful, winged figure in flowing robes stood atop the bookcase. The figure held out its arms, facing Rhiss, a spear in one hand and a rolled up scroll in the other. The face was serene and ageless. A nameplate at the statue's base was inscribed in a graceful, flowing, completely unreadable script.

Against a wall unbroken by corridors were several finely carved wooden chairs with generous cushions, as though placed to accommodate anyone wishing to rest and avail themselves of the books. Set in the other wall was a fireplace. Strange, silvery-blue, smokeless flames burned within it, casting dancing shadows on the ceiling. An oak mantelpiece with several knick-knacks framed the fire. All very cozy and reassuring, or it would have been had he been able to convince himself that corridor, room, and furnishings were nothing more than what they seemed: natural and logical extensions of the school.

But they were not, he reminded himself fiercely, completing his examination and becoming aware again of what he was doing. The surroundings were neither natural nor logical. *None* of it could be happening. It was all utterly impossible. His strong inclination to sit, pull a book from the bookcase and read while enjoying the ambience of the strange chamber was inexplicable at best, sheer madness at worst. *Madness.* He turned on his heel and strode back along the corridor. At the door, he paused. Ahead lay his dreary classroom confines; behind, the extraordinary corridor and its richly inviting contents. The contrast could not be more pronounced. Ironically, the unreal felt more authentic than the real, the dreary schoolroom feeling nothing more than a bad dream. He stepped over the door's threshold, closing it quickly and firmly. As the door swung to, he noted, with a curious lack of surprise, the candles within the corridor dimmed and snuffed out on their own.

The door clicked shut. There was the faintest suggestion, at perception's limits and the furthest threshold of audibility, of a sigh from — he was not sure quite where. It was no physical sensation, not really a sound at all in that sense, but he knew it was not imaginary: it *was* there, as elusive as when a thought or name is almost recalled on the tip of the tongue, but momentarily irretrievable.

Tamping down the panic threatening to overwhelm him, Rhiss ran to the windows. Rain was beginning to spatter in fat drops from the heavens. Peering to his left out the windows, he struggled to view the construction he had stood in moments ago. But it was not there to view. He turned and ran to the door — the *real* exit, he reminded himself sternly, wondering what strange vista he might find as he opened it; but there was only the ordinary school hallway. He didn't know whether to be disappointed or relieved.

Was the door visible outside? Rhiss dashed down the hallway and exited the building. It was raining harder now, full-fledged downpour only moments away. Ignoring it, Rhiss made his way across the lawn to the point outside his own classroom. He looked up — but the exterior wall without windows had no door. There was simply ivy-encrusted brick; no break of any kind. Rhiss stood disbelieving, heedless of the rain soaking his clothes. It had been *so* real. Was the door still there, on the inside?

Retracing his steps, Rhiss stopped at the door into his classroom, frozen in shock: the ornate door was gone, the wall as it had always been. There was nothing to indicate his journey through door, bizarre corridor, and brief foray into the square room with the bookcase surmounted by the winged statue, had ever occurred.

Rhiss stood stock-still, mind in turmoil, trying to decide whether he was going mad, while outside, the heavens unleashed their full fury at last, and rain lashed the window panes.

II

DISCOURSE AND CHOICES

> *"It came to pass that Beltor, the second Companion, was appointed a mighty task. In a dream, a Servant of the One appeared and offered him a hard but fair choice. 'Why,' asked Beltor, 'is this task given unto me? For lo, I am unworthy and sore afraid.' And the Servant answered unto him, 'Fear not. For with the One all things are possible.'"*
>
> The Book of the One, 95:26:44-45
> (Cantos 95, Chapter 26, Verses 44-45)

Hours later, Rhiss again stood outside the school. The rain had lost its earlier fury and settled into a gentle, steady downpour. The night was chilly, and as Rhiss exhaled, his breath emerged in little white puffs. He halted irresolutely, wondering once more why he had come.

Following his fruitless exterior examination and return inside, Rhiss had searched the building for anyone to share his story with. He desperately needed reassurance he was not losing his mind, and such had been that need, he might even have been prepared to receive that assurance from the headmaster. But the school had well and truly emptied, and Rhiss could find no one. He briefly contemplated going after Alistair and Jennie, but he knew they would hardly want to leave the dance and return to school to confirm some fantastic tale. So, packing his satchel in a daze, he left, giving a final, disbelieving look around his classroom before closing the door firmly and locking it. Then it was home to the small but comfortable cottage on the other side of the village where he lived in simple bachelorhood.

The house was let from one Mrs. McDowell, a white-haired grandmother and formidable local presence. The cottage's chief advantage was that it was neither too distant from nor too close to school — a fifteen minute walk he invariably enjoyed, passing as it did through shady village lanes. Even on rainy days, the route had charm. But the walk's semi-rural English beauty was lost on Rhiss this day, preoccupied as he was with incredible events.

Mrs. McDowell, who was also housekeeper, had been and gone. All was neat and tidy; a meat pie — steak and mushroom, his favourite — warmed in the oven. But food was the last thing Rhiss fancied. He went into the sitting room, poured a brandy, and sat by the fire in his favourite chair, trying to sort things out. Doors, corridors and chambers could not just appear out of thin air, then vanish with no trace. It defied all sense...

He woke with a start much later. Somehow, despite the shock, or perhaps because of it, he had fallen asleep, and dreamt of running through endless, dimly lit corridors, calling someone's name. But that faded, replaced by a more vivid dream, quite unlike any he ever recalled: possessing none of the hazy, ethereal feel dreams often have, it had rather a hardness etched in stark clarity in memory even on awakening. In the dream, a tall, handsome, strong man in fine but strange, almost medieval clothes strode through wind-swept grasses on a barren moor. Holding a bright sword, the man moved swiftly and with grim purpose towards... Rhiss had been unable to see. Some... dark thing, shaggy and malignant, crouched just beyond his field of vision, and the man — who looked familiar in some intangible way — was saying something to it. Although Rhiss could not recall the words, he well remembered the clear, ringing tones. The man finished speaking, lowered his sword, the darkness disappeared... and Rhiss awoke.

A thought just below the level of consciousness nagged, but would not surface. The rain drummed gently on the roof, and the fire in the grate had died to embers. Rhiss rose stiffly; then, making up his mind, donned his overcoat before going back into the night without eating. He simply had to see his classroom again.

So there he was on a fool's errand, standing outside school on a miserably damp, drizzly night. He shook his head, unable to believe he was engaged in such silliness, when he could be warm and dry at home, reading by the fire. Or, come to that, at the dance with Alistair, Jennie and the winsome lass she had brought in a vain quest to draw Rhiss out. He sighed, knowing he should give up and go home. But as he turned, a quiet mental voice suddenly whispered that having come this far, it would take little effort to quickly peek and satisfy himself, once and for all, that he had simply imagined door, corridor and chamber that afternoon, most likely because of the awful day's stresses.

To his considerable surprise, the door remained unlocked and opened creakily, unlike the smooth phantom in his classroom. Rhiss stood in the vestibule, listening, raindrops falling off his coat into a glistening puddle on the floor. The rain made a gentle tattoo against the doors. He marshalled his resolve, trudging up the stairs and across polished tiles. Only a few of the corridor's electric lamps remained lit, creating small islands of light in a sea of darkness. The hall eerily resembled a subterranean tunnel, doors branching off to either side at regular intervals. Outside his room, he paused again, head cocked to one side, straining to hear anything out of the ordinary, but there was only the usual faint clanking and gurgling of water circulating through steam radiators, warding off the damp. He grasped the knob shakily and turned it, opening the door into the darkened room and flicking the lights on.

Everything was disconcertingly normal. The room had been swept after his flight, papers and other academic detritus whisked away, but otherwise it was exactly as he had left it. There were no extraneous doors, or anything else, for that matter. Although it was not exactly the change he had blithely discussed with Alistair, Rhiss felt a keen pang of regret that the finely carved and polished door did not punctuate the classroom's bland west wall.

So it *had* been a dream or, more worryingly, hallucination. Most disappointing, indeed. Come Monday morning, all would again be achingly normal, the torrent of young bodies thronging the halls and classrooms, casual disinterest all too manifest. Rhiss was not certain he could face that much longer, and realized he also felt defeat that the door was not there... not to mention what it implied regarding his own mental health: he must have simply imagined the entire episode. What would the door's reality have meant? Something completely out of the ordinary, humdrum existence that was his life. Something... magical. Never mind. It was time to go — wearily retrace his steps and return to his little home. Rhiss turned to the classroom's door — its only door, he reminded himself resignedly. As he walked, it came spontaneously — the train of thought he had been thinking that afternoon when the door appeared. He had wondered about a lack of magic in his life. But not literally, and certainly not in the form of magical doors opening onto corridors and rooms.

Outside, a tree branch scraped against a window, blown by a gust of wind. Rhiss whirled involuntarily at the unexpected sound; the lights went out as though someone had flicked the switches, leaving him in darkness dispelled only partially by gas lights in the street outside. His eyes, plunged into gloom, could discern nothing save those exterior lights casting strange shadows on the walls.

Then the lights blazed on, and he saw, with an odd sense of vindication, that the object of his quest had returned. The carved, polished door stood once more in the west wall, looking as though it had always been there — and would be as long as the building stood — not like the transitory, fickle visitor it really was.

The room was eerily silent. Rhiss cast for explanation, and found it. Outside, the rain was stopped, no hiss of water against the windows. But... how very strange: steady downpours tend to taper off, not end as though someone turned a switch. Inside, the large classroom clock, black hands framing the upper third of the clock face, had stopped along with the rain. His gaze absorbed that and moved on, but his eyes were drawn by something most unusual. The regulator pendulum was halted, but not in the middle of its swing, as it would if the clockwork mechanism had simply run down. No, the pendulum was frozen at the extreme end of its arc, and the sonorous ticking permeating the room was gone as though time itself had paused, surprised into submission by the door's reappearance.

Even as he absorbed these phenomena, Rhiss approached the enigmatic door, reaching for the knob and turning it. *Eagerly?* As before, the door swung silently inwards, opening into the darkened corridor that lit immediately, the candles in those strange sconces flaring into warm radiance. Then he was over the threshold, and into the corridor without hesitation. Leaving the door open, Rhiss swiftly covered its length, not stopping until he re-entered the room. It was as he remembered, right down to the winged statue on the bookcase and the fire burning in the fireplace. Had anyone tended it the last several hours? Rhiss halted, the fierce imperative bringing him thus far ebbing in confusion. He glanced around uncertainly. What to do? If he left to find someone, the afternoon's experience suggested that the capricious door and chamber would simply disappear again. A wry thought occurred: perhaps he should sit, remove a volume from the bookcase, and wait for someone to come along. He quashed the ridiculous thought: he had not ventured out on a wild and woolly night simply to read in an unearthly locale — hardly the British Museum Reading Room.

Scanning the room, he once again noted the corridor on the far side, twin to the one through which he had come. What lay at the end of *that* one, behind its closed door? Perhaps it was time to discover.

Rhiss moved purposely across the room, circumnavigating the bookcase in the centre, and walked down the corridor. Like its twin, darkness melted away as he advanced, candles flaring into light of their own volition. He was almost used to it by now, and scarcely jumped.

He stopped before the door, regarding it with trepidation. It looked a precise duplicate of the other. The knob was on the left, and plainly visible hinges on the right indicated this door swung inwards into the corridor. But now he was actually there, he was unsure whether to open it or not. Doing so could have profound implications: the second door could lead into another situation just as startlingly dramatic. An amusing thought occurred: what if there was a looking glass world on the other side, a world no more than a mirror image of this one? No, that, too, was ridiculous. This was not Lewis Carroll.

After only two encounters, the first corridor and room had assumed some familiarity, but there was none ahead; quite the reverse, in fact. Something about this door suggested finality — once the choice was made to open it, there would be no turning back. Rhiss was unsure why, but there was no denying it; the feeling was very strong.

He dithered for minutes, several times grasping the doorknob, then releasing it. But his mind cleared suddenly, and Rhiss felt if he didn't open the portal and find what lay beyond, he must leave the room and its contents forever. Assuming the door would even appear again if he failed to act, Rhiss doubted he would have courage or will to open that second door. It must be now. Either that, or return to those mountains of indifferent papers awaiting marking, and be satisfied with that uninspiring life forever. He grimaced with distaste, and clasping the knob firmly, turned it.

Disappointingly, and anticlimactically, nothing happened. The knob did not turn, merely slid smoothly beneath his grasp. He tightened his hold and tried again, with the same results. Frowning, he bent to examine the reluctant mechanism. It did not appear locked. In fact, there *was* no lock of any kind. There was just the door knob: white, smooth, and utterly uncooperative. He tried it once more, still unsuccessfully, and paused, lost in perplexed thought. Then, a quiet voice behind him said clearly, "I am afraid it does not work that way, young man."

Rhiss whirled, flattening against the door, fighting the sensation that his stomach sought to rise into his throat. Wildly glaring down the corridor revealed an extraordinary sight: someone sat in one of the chairs, regarding him calmly. Rhiss willed his pounding heart to slow, and, finding his voice, croaked hoarsely, "What?" It was neither a particularly intelligent nor articulate greeting, but considering he was speaking to someone who hadn't been there a moment ago, in a room that shouldn't exist... it was the best he could manage.

"What you attempt cannot work as things now are. Will you return and allow me to elaborate, without need to shout down the corridor? There is really no reason for you to remain pressed against the door."

Rhiss swallowed hard. There was no menace. The male voice was pleasantly melodious, and in spite of its assertion, nowhere near shouting. It seemed to contain a hint of amusement; but even so, Rhiss didn't fancy moving quite yet. He desperately needed to process the impossible becoming manifest in his world — a world that, until very recently, proceeded in an utterly predictable manner. The figure sat between Rhiss and the door to his classroom. He could just see it beyond, and at that moment, tedious or not, it also looked familiar and safe, not at all like this. After all, he was absolutely certain no one had been in the room when he passed through. The only other visible door into the chamber was the one connecting to his classroom. Somehow, Rhiss was quite sure the man had not strolled in *that* way.

As if reading his thoughts, the figure glanced at the open door, studying it before returning his gaze to Rhiss. "Fear not, Master Rhissan," he said levelly. "I am here only to make you aware of several matters, so you can ultimately decide your course with proper knowledge of what you do. It would be undesirable for you to decide hastily and without consideration. You have a choice before you, a most important choice." He indicated the classroom with a deliberate toss of the head. "And if, after hearing me, you decide you do, indeed, wish to return to the world beyond *that* door, I will not hinder your going." He paused. "Well? Will you join me in comfort here, or must we continue bellowing at each other like fishmongers in a marketplace?"

Still tightly pressed against the door, Rhiss took stock. His pulse had slowed from a gallop to a canter. The man was clearly not aggressive and would not hinder his return to his own world. Perhaps, in talking to this... person, he would get answers to the many questions plaguing him. He slowly pushed away from the door and walked tentatively to the chamber, keeping a careful eye on the figure, who regarded him with a quiet smile. What was so amusing, Rhiss could not fathom. As he re-entered the chamber, the last candles in the corridor noiselessly extinguished, leaving, as before, faint puffs of smoke and the strong aroma of beeswax. Rhiss halted at the entrance and remained there.

"Much better," said the figure approvingly, motioning the chair beside him. "Will you join me? We have matters to discuss. And there is fine refreshment in the decanter on the table if you feel in need of something."

Rhiss certainly did, but made no attempt to move. The figure sighed in faint annoyance, making a steeple of long, slender fingers. "Hmm. I think I understand. You cannot bring yourself to believe I really exist, can you, Master Rhissan?"

Rhiss swallowed hard. "No, sir. You cannot be here. Nor can any of this. You *weren't* here when I came through. I'd swear you weren't. This is all impossible. I'm... imagining it."

"Really? You have a most excellent imagination, then." The figure gazed appreciatively about. "And marvellous sense of detail, too, I see," he added dryly. "I congratulate you, or would, were I no more than an imaginary figment." He paused. "However, with no slight intended, I must inform you this is no fantasy. It is all very real, as am I. Now, while I understand this—" he waved an arm at the chamber "—must come as immense shock, the sooner you come to terms with its reality, the sooner we can move on to business. And... it is business of some import."

Rhiss shook his head violently, mute negation intended as much for himself as for the man, negation of the entire situation and all it represented. The man seemed to understand.

"Why would you doubt the evidence of your own senses?" he queried, sounding genuinely interested.

"Because they can lie, or be wrong. This is no reality. Rooms and corridors do not appear at random and attach to buildings, then vanish. And they do not contain people where moments earlier they did not! It's impossible!" Rhiss realized he was raising his voice, and stopped to draw a deep breath. "This is a delusion. I've..." He swallowed hard. "I've been under a great deal of stress. I'm experiencing some... hallucination. You are part of it. I argue with myself. It must be so. How can you refute the impossibility of this?"

The figure looked at him sharply, then suddenly struck a hand against his chair. It sounded loud in the confines of the chamber, like the crack of a whip. There was an edge to the soft voice. "I refute it *thus*, Master Rhissan. As you can, if you think rationally. Now let me make a few things clear. We *are* here, both of us, *physically* present in a room that *physically* exists. Its impossibility is frankly irrelevant, because its existence is irrefutable. And nothing is 'random' about the chamber's appearance, for nothing is random in the grand schemes of the One. I realize hallucinations will insist on their own reality, but *this is real*. Mark me, young man, for I do not intend to sit here all night, bandying fuzzy metaphysical concepts back and forth. The evening wears on. Time and tides wait for no one. Now, come. Sit, young sir, and let us commence business. The time for idle talk is past."

———◆———

Rhiss sat warily, getting a good look at the source of his consternation. It was not hard, despite the flickering illumination, because some trick of the light actually seemed to make the area around the figure brighter than the rest of the chamber. He was dressed in flowing robes of white and tan, a wide brown cord around his waist knotted at the front. Sandaled feet peeped out from the robes, while finely shaped hands were folded on his lap. Silvery hair, thick and lustrous, hung down to his shoulders, framing a clean-shaven face. The face... was handsome, but ageless, until one got to the eyes.

His eyes. They were a piercing sapphire, and in some manner impossible to explain, simultaneously conveyed immense age *and* youth, radiating life and vitality, and also enormous compassion. There was the impression of great joy, and great sorrow. In some respects, it was difficult to meet his gaze; as their eyes locked, Rhiss experienced an odd sensation, as though the other could see right into him — through him. It was not unpleasant, and as he met the man's gaze, Rhiss felt fears and doubts melt away in the absolute conviction that this person, whatever he was, would not harm him; was, in fact, someone in whom he could repose complete trust. *How* he knew, he could not say; but he would have confidently trusted the figure with his life. Then the man poured a ruby-red liquid from the decanter into an empty glass on the table; the moment ended, and the spell was broken.

Wordlessly, he offered the glass; Rhiss took it automatically, sipping cautiously. The drink was fruity and sweet, full-bodied, extremely pleasant, and quite unidentifiable. It was not wine and did not resemble anything Rhiss could remember drinking, but made him feel much better. He took another sip and put the glass down as the figure spoke again.

"So, young... Rhiss, I believe your friends call you," he smiled, "here we are. And we have matters of import to discuss. So let us begin. I take it you wish to pass the far door. Doubtless you have many questions. Some I may answer, some not, but I will tell what I can. What would you know first?"

Rhiss found his voice, looking plaintive. "If it truly is real... what is this place? Where has it come from? And why?"

The figure reflected. "You may call this... Berasheathe." He stopped and smiled, as if at an entertaining private joke. "Aye... that will do. As to how it came to be here... why, it has always existed. It is a bridge, and it has opened to you to provide another path." He held up a hand, as if to forestall the question he knew would follow. "Which will become clearer as we speak. Next?"

Rhiss considered. "You scared me to death moments ago. What are you, sir, and how did you come to be in this room, when I saw no one as I came through?"

"A friend, with only the best of intentions. That is all I may say for now. Later you will learn more. And I apologize for frightening you. That was not my intention."

"Forgive me, sir, but you have the advantage. You know my name, but I do not know yours."

The figure raised an eyebrow. "Of course. I beg your pardon. When one has achieved certain — notoriety, shall we say? — one assumes one is known to all. Ah, well. A lesson in humility. You may call me Brother Gavrilos," he said, emphasizing the second syllable. He considered briefly, and nodded. "Aye. That will suffice very well."

"Are you a monk?"

"It is one of my names," said Brother Gavrilos easily. "It will do for the present. It is the name I am known by through yonder door, which you futilely rattled moments ago. But I am no monk, having not withdrawn from the world. Quite the contrary. It would be more accurate to call me a servant — like you. Or, in this instance, a guide. But let's to the present: I said you appeared to wish to pass that door. Do you?"

"Pass through?" Rhiss said slowly. "I'm not sure I'd thought that far ahead. I *was* extremely curious about its other side, I don't deny it. I wanted to know what this was all about, yes, and where the door leads. But I'm not sure *what* I planned to do.

This is difficult. I live a simple, orderly, uncomplicated life. Random things do not just happen."

Brother Gavrilos nodded. "And random things did not. You did not stumble across this room any more than it randomly appeared. And while I appreciate how difficult this is, I am pleased you came to terms with it so quickly. It bodes well. All right, then. You were curious about what lies on the other side. I can tell you: difficulties, disorder, and complications." He smiled at Rhiss' confusion. "You said your life was simple, orderly and uncomplicated. I told you what you will find on the door's far side. The description of your life may be true, but it is not the full story. In fact, your description lacks other applicable adjectives."

"What adjectives?" Rhiss demanded defensively.

Brother Gavrilos gave that shrewdly penetrating glance, and Rhiss again had the oddest sensation the man had just seen straight to his soul's core. "Unfulfilled, unappreciated — words of that ilk," replied Gavrilos. He raised his eyebrows as if seeking confirmation, although his tone made it clear he did not ask a question.

Rhiss flushed, his first inclination being to heatedly deny it, but something kept him silent. It was, he realized glumly, a disconcertingly accurate summation. His life *was*, on several levels, uncomplicated, but also frustratingly unfulfilling, with an uneasy feeling, only lately and half-consciously acknowledged within, that the dreams of his youth were falling to the harsh realities of a world he had not made and was not enamoured with. He had thought that very thing that afternoon.

Brother Gavrilos seemed to read the truth as Rhiss sank in his chair. "There, my young friend, do not allow the truth to dismay you. Let it guide you, let it instruct you, but do not ever let it dismay you. Truth brings freedom. Now, you have a singular opportunity here, and the only issue is what you do with it. I said through that door lies difficulty, disorder, and complexity. Although that is true, I said it facetiously, and I ask your pardon for dismaying you. I do not lie or mislead you now when I say that through the door lies danger and a life as difficult, disordered and complicated as anyone could want. *However*, through that door also lies the possibility of a life as fulfilling, as adventurous, as full of great purpose and great deeds rendered in the service of the One, as any Child of the Light could possibly seek. *That* is your singular opportunity, my young friend. Will you seize it? Or return to that dusty classroom yonder, to be slowly buried under musty mounds of mediocre term papers and examinations, until you wake up one day to realize you have become one of those dreary old masters you despise? The choice is yours."

Rhiss could not reply. He felt queasy as it hit: this was no nebulous dream, but a real situation with life-altering alternatives. But he needed more. "Can you be more specific?" he finally managed.

Brother Gavrilos considered. "An entire world, different from this one, known as Arrinor," he replied softly, emphasizing the name's first syllable. He stared into the fire. "A world utterly unlike this in many ways, yet greatly alike in others. A world of magnificent beauty. It is also the world of a young king, unjustly deprived of his birthright, displaced by an evil usurper who seized the crown. That young king is in need of assistance in reclaiming his throne. I understand you are the type of man who would provide help to those needing it." Gavrilos looked up. "The door leads to that and much more, if you but open it. It will be difficult and dangerous, and I cannot say with certainty you will succeed, but it will be enormously fulfilling. I can say *that* with certainty."

Rhiss licked dry lips. "But... I tried opening the door. The knob wouldn't turn."

Gavrilos smiled, but instead of answering, gestured back towards the classroom. "You left *that* door open. Why?"

Rhiss thought. Why *had* he done that, anyway? The answer, not consciously registered until that moment, suddenly came. "I suppose... I didn't want to eliminate my only way of getting back," he admitted slowly.

"This chamber bridges two worlds, appearing on my command — rarely, and only to certain individuals. But both doors cannot open at the same time. When one is open, the other will not. The first must be closed before the second will open. In this way, crossing is an act of deliberate will and choice."

"But why?" Rhiss felt overwhelmed. "Why now, here, to me? What have I done to earn or deserve it? What possible help could I give this king you speak of? I truly think you have approached the wrong person. You make it all sound very difficult. And dangerous."

Gavrilos smiled sympathetically. "*Life* is difficult and dangerous. Anyone who says otherwise, lies. You could walk back into that classroom, trip and break your neck as you cross the threshold. And I never said this is without purpose. Quite the contrary, in fact. This place, this bridge has come to you — to *you* — at this time for a specific purpose. I may not discuss all details with you, but this is no random event. As to your question about what you could offer: I think you might be surprised at the assistance you can render. You have potentials and strengths you do not know, or at the least, acknowledge. As to your most important question relating to why... well, you already know the answer."

Rhiss looked blank, and raised his hands questioningly. Brother Gavrilos looked at the ceiling, as if searching his memory for something, before returning his gaze to Rhiss.

"*Taffy was a Welshman, Taffy was a thief. Taffy came to my house and stole a piece of beef,*" he recited softly. "*I went to Taffy's house, Taffy wasn't in; I jumped upon his Sunday hat and poked it with a pin.*" He grimaced with distaste. "And there is more to this so-called nursery rhyme, isn't there? All of it similarly uncomplimentary, as I recall, including one particularly ghastly version that concludes by encouraging violence on the Welsh."

Rhiss had gone pale and rigid, eyes furious. "Yes..." he eventually managed to reply in a strangled voice. "I've heard them all at one time or another, from students at boarding school right on up to fellow officers in the Navy."

"And masters at this school as well. Is that not so?"

Rhiss nodded impatiently. "Some of the cockier students, too. What does all this have to do with my question?"

"Do you recall Lewis, the small boy from this afternoon?"

Rhiss stared uncomprehendingly: the incident seemed so far removed from the fantastic events of the last few hours, he had almost forgotten. Then the details returned in a flash.

"Yes," he responded grimly. "He was bullied by older boys, and I came to his aid. What of it? How do you know about that?"

"What did you feel?"

"I guess... I was angry," said Rhiss slowly.

Gavrilos raised an eyebrow, smiling knowingly. "Angry? Just angry? You were far more than that, surely."

"Furious... icily, righteously furious," Rhiss allowed.

Gavrilos nodded. "And we both know why. The random cacophony of adolescent boys everywhere... the throng of boys clustered together... knowing Lewis was the small child within that crowd, tormented by a group of sneering boys much larger and older... the look of hopeless fear in Lewis' eyes as his gaze caught yours, the look of someone expecting no aid from anyone, anywhere. It was all too familiar, wasn't it?" He leaned forward. "Lewis was *you*, once upon a time. And in truth, not as long a time ago as you might like to think."

"How would you—?" There was silence. "Yes," Rhiss finally admitted in a whisper.

"And you came to his aid, even though many masters would have felt things were best left to sort themselves out."

"I know," said Rhiss bitterly. "But I couldn't stand by and do nothing. It would have made me no better than they."

"Precisely," agreed Gavrilos approvingly, "and you need not feel defensive. Quite the contrary, in fact. But you have answered your own question." At the slowly dawning realization in Rhiss' eyes, he nodded and elaborated, marking off reasons with his fingers. "You went to someone's aid for the only reasons there can be: you were capable; you were needed; you could make a difference; and because it was the right thing to do. *Those* are the motives for anything worthwhile, or should be. You may well wish life had been gentler, but experience is often a harsh taskmaster, I fear. However, the lessons learned are invaluable if one does not become irrevocably embittered or buckle beneath their weight — and you have not. Not yet, at least. While you may not appreciate it, your experiences as an orphaned child in Wales, and later as a young man struggling to make his way in England, have honed your moral sensibilities to a knife's edge." Gavrilos smiled with genuine compassion. "Which pleases me. So... now you know consciously what you knew instinctively all along. You have answered your own question as to why you should step through that door, rendering assistance where needed."

Rhiss hesitated, looking at the door to his classroom; the lights burned brightly in there, and strangely, it looked warm and reassuringly known. Then he swivelled his gaze to the other door, tightly closed, offering no reassurance, no hint of what wonders or terrors might lie on the other side. He had only the explanation of Brother Gavrilos to go on, vague and under-detailed as it was. Part of him wanted to go back to his classroom, picking up the threads of a life he at least knew and was known in; another part dreaded the very notion. He turned to face his guide.

"Brother Gavrilos," he began slowly, "this portal appeared, disappeared, and reappeared, all in the space of one day. If I went through that door into my classroom now, would I see it — would I see you — again?"

Those sapphire eyes once more probed the very depths of his soul, and Brother Gavrilos gently shook his head. "No. The time of decision is here and now. You have all the information I can give. There is nothing to be gained by waiting. In any event," Brother Gavrilos' lips quirked in a smile, "you already know what you want to do. At least, your heart does. Why not act?"

Rhiss felt doubts and hopes coalesce in two neatly opposed lists, pluses and minuses laid out for inspection like an exercise in a student's copybook. There was a split second of indecision before he realized it was true: he *did* know what he wanted. Brother Gavrilos' last question had been asked in an instant; it must be answered in another.

Silently, he rose. Brother Gavrilos watched with interest but said nothing. Rhiss walked purposefully to the corridor and proceeded toward his classroom. He noticed the strange candle sconces once more, marvelling at their realism. Then he was at the door. He peered in, careful not to cross the threshold: somehow, he knew that doing so, even accidentally, would make any conscious decision irrelevant.

He gazed calmly at the dusty light fixtures, rows of battered, empty desks, ancient bookcases, grimy texts lined up like silent, waiting soldiers; and his desk, strewn untidily with papers. Rhiss was unsurprised to see that the ancient clock, by which he and his students measured time in endless classes, had resumed, pendulum marching with the steady measure of a metronome. Outside, the rain again beat against the windows; muffled thunder sounded. Time's passage, briefly halted by the portal's reappearance, had resumed. It was the world he had known his entire life. All he had to do to reclaim it was step over the threshold; then it would be his again.

He slowly reached out and grasped the pearl door handle. With deliberate finality, he gently closed the door on his classroom and, it occurred to him, his life as he'd known it. It seemed to take a long time for the door to complete its noiseless arc, but then it shut, the noise reverberating loudly in the corridor's confines. Rhiss stood as the import of what he had done, what he was about to do, flooded through him. Who would miss him? Only Alistair, really. And would he understand? After their strange conversation that afternoon, Rhiss felt quite sure he would.

Rhiss sighed and returned to the chamber. He walked to Brother Gavrilos and indulged an inexplicable need to bow. "After hearing you, I believe I have been waiting for Arrinor quite some time. If what you say is true, then I think it also awaits me. This king you spoke of — if his cause is just, I will do what I can to help — although, as I said, I'm not sure what assistance I can provide."

Brother Gavrilos smiled warmly, and stood. "You will do wondrously. Well done, indeed. My heart is gladdened that you responded as you did."

Rhiss was startled. "Did you think I wouldn't?"

Brother Gavrilos shrugged. "You had the capacity to choose, and could have decided either way. Knowing you a fairish time, I *thought* I knew what your choice would be, although I could not be certain. But the One we serve is not interested in mindless drones, ever. And that is a good analogy. Think you of the honeybee. It is not valued by its collective or its queen as an individual. Why? *Because* it has no choice in what it does. All its instincts dictate that it *must* act to build and preserve the hive against all perils, often to its own detriment. That is all it knows, with no possibility of doing otherwise. Therein lies the lack of worth in what it does. It has no freedom of action, no choice in deciding its destiny. Deeds only assume significance when there is no external compulsion to performing them. It is choice that matters in all we do, and to the One. Without choice, there can be no service, love, or value to your actions. Remember that." He shook his head. "But enough of philosophy. I wish to prepare you. Time passes."

Brother Gavrilos moved to the bookcase in the chamber's centre. On one side, Rhiss noticed, was a set of shallow, inlaid drawers, each about six inches high. Brother Gavrilos opened the top one and carefully drew something from it that caught the firelight and glittered. Rhiss followed, seeking a better look at the object. Brother Gavrilos placed it on top of the bookcase.

It was a circlet, plainly meant to be worn on the head. Two inches or so in width, it was a steely silver colour that sparkled in the firelight. Fine black lettering, etched into the metal and written in an elegant cursive script Rhiss could not read, adorned its upper and lower rims. The workmanship was superb, and it would have been beautiful even if that was all; but a single gem, mounted at the circlet's front, took Rhiss' breath away as he gazed on it.

He first thought it must be an opal, albeit a very large one: it was oval and the size of a hen's egg. The gem had the same milky, misty characteristics as an opal, but there was something unusual that made Rhiss narrow his eyes and lean in for a better look. Something on the gem seemed to move.

There *was* movement, although he realized immediately it was *within* the gem, not *on* it. Involuntarily, he gasped at its incredible beauty: filaments of brilliant reds, blues, greens, yellows moved individually in graceful, leisurely striations through the milky gem. They rose toward the surface, then fell away into its depths, as though there was great distance within the stone. The overall effect was stunningly beautiful. He raised his eyes to see Brother Gavrilos watching intently.

"Magnificent," Rhiss breathed. "Strange and impossible at the same time. I have never seen a gem do that... that movement. Do you know what the inscription says?"

"I do. And when the time is right, you will also."

Rhiss smiled at the polite unhelpfulness, returning his gaze to the beautiful circlet reposing on its velvet bed. "Will you at least tell me its name?"

"Gladly: the Circlet of Araxis, after he who had it crafted, long ago. It is ancient, you see, and uniquely valuable."

Rhiss was intrigued. "How? And why show it me?"

"Its uniqueness will become apparent. I show it you, young master, because I would like you to wear it as you pass the portal."

Rhiss was startled again. "Me? Why? How do I deserve such generosity?"

"For the moment, let us simply say it will serve as token that you have come to Arrinor not only with *my* blessing, but of the One, also. It will dispel any doubts those you meet will have as to the rightness of your presence. You will not want to wear it all the time, nor should you — that would not be appropriate, as you will come to understand — but I charge you: keep it safe and take care of it. Let no one else wear it."

"Is it... is it a crown?"

Gavrilos smiled. "No, very old jewellery. Although it *is* ultimately for the King."

"And I am to convey it to him?"

Gavrilos nodded. "It is meant for the King," he repeated. He turned back to the inlaid drawers, opening the second. "And I have another gift. It is of a more immediately practical nature."

Taking a long, slender object at least a foot long and wrapped in blue velvet from the drawer, Brother Gavrilos carefully handed it to Rhiss, who unwrapped it and studied what lay in his palm.

It was a dagger, which, practical or no, was as much work of art as the Circlet. Not only was it obviously made by the same craftsman who fashioned the Circlet, but meant to match it. The metal of the hilt, visible above the rich, dark leather sheath concealing the dagger, was the same steely silver material as the Circlet. Rhiss drew the blade from its sheath, admiring the way the metal glittered in the firelight. It looked wickedly lethal. As with the Circlet, there was black lettering in finely cursive script etched on the blade, and in the hilt's centre was a blue gem. Then something else caught his eye and he looked closer. Below the gem was the outline of a creature, one he remembered in old heraldry books: a... gryphon, that was it. He remembered pictures of the creature with a lion's body and head and wings of an eagle. It seemed an unusual design for the dagger. Did heraldic devices normally go on such small weapons? He looked at Brother Gavrilos, who studied him even as he studied the dagger.

"It's also beautiful. Thank you for both. I don't know why I deserve them, but I will gladly take them."

The sheath had a wide leather loop riveted to the top so it could attach to a belt, yet pivot freely with the dagger inside. Looking inquiringly at Brother Gavrilos, who nodded, Rhiss quickly sheathed the dagger and attached the assembly to his own belt. Brother Gavrilos then lifted the Circlet off its velvet cushion and gravely placed it on Rhiss; it felt cool to his tentative, questing touch. He was gently steered to a previously unnoticed alcove to one side of the fireplace. A looking glass mounted on the wall showed Rhiss his own reflection, hair arranged untidily about the Circlet nestled on his head. It looked beautiful, although he felt sheepish: it seemed incongruous when set against his ordinary clothes — he had not changed from the day on arriving home, and still wore suit, vest and tie. The result was as if a character from one of the romantic poets he quoted in class had stepped into the modern world. "Like Ulysses embarking on his journey," he muttered.

Brother Gavrilos smiled again. "Well said. Perhaps a more accurate observation than you realize. You might wish to recall what Tennyson said about Ulysses, and take his words to heart. They are uniquely applicable at this time."

Rhiss well knew the poem Brother Gavrilos referred to, and had taught it many times; it had to be known by virtually every English student. "Which lines in particular?"

"There are several, but I refer specifically to the one which includes the phrase 'To strive, to seek, to find, and not to yield.' A noble sentiment indeed — worthy of being on a coat of arms, in fact. Take care to remember it."

"What do you think the admonition 'not to yield' applies to?"

Brother Gavrilos looked mildly surprised. "There are many vices and evil traits that could be applied. Too many, alas, are deeply ingrained in human nature. But all need not be lost. Notice he exhorts his reader to seek and strive. Seek truth and strive in the service of the Light; that is what Tennyson urges — as I exhort you. Now, again, let us to business. I do not begrudge these explanations, for you must understand as clearly as possible why and what you enter into, but time is passing." He turned and gestured down the corridor to Arrinor. "In an alcove by the door you will find my final gifts. They, too, are items of a very practical nature. Take them and use them well." He cocked his head to one side, and stared that penetrating stare again. "Is there anything else you would know — anything I may tell you, that is?"

"This king you speak of — how will I find him? Where should I go?"

Gavrilos paused, as if considering what to say. "I counsel you not to trouble yourself seeking the king. He will become known to you when you are ready. In the meantime, the best advice I can give is to go forth and, to paraphrase another poet, meet the slings and arrows of outrageous fortune by taking arms against them — sometimes metaphorically, sometimes literally, I fear. As of this moment, you are caught up in a most ancient conflict, older than you can possibly guess. You will find Arrinor has much to occupy you. Do not identify your quest to everyone you meet. Be circumspect. Most would simply find your tale the ravings of a lunatic... or worse, dangerously subversive and requiring silencing. You are simply a young traveller seeking adventure. When asked your name, say nothing of Griffith. Surnames are seldom used in Arrinor, except to identify noble houses. Instead, you may quite legitimately tell anyone you are Rhissan, son of Tovan." Rhiss nodded, curious how Brother Gavrilos knew, but said nothing. "A good, honourable name. If asked where you hail from, you may also truthfully say Dinas Mawr, your village in Wales. The name will be unfamiliar to Arrinorans, but if you explain it is far away, people will be satisfied. It is better you should be truthful in this, rather than inventing connections with places in Arrinor you are not yet conversant with."

Rhiss nodded thoughtfully. "Three final questions, if you don't mind."

Brother Gavrilos spread his hands encouragingly.

"Well, first of all, how am I to talk to people in Arrinor? Do they speak English there? Or Welsh? Because that is the limit of my linguistic achievements, I'm afraid, aside from some ancient Greek and Latin."

Gavrilos nodded. "An excellent point, and one I was just coming to." He extended his hand and placed it gently on Rhiss' forehead for several seconds. The touch felt warm and tingled oddly as though charged with static electricity, but there was no shock and Rhiss felt nothing else.

Gavrilos withdrew his hand. "English and Welsh are *not* the extent of your linguistic achievements, Master Rhissan, for you will find that you can understand and make yourself understood as well as any Arrinoran."

"Really? How did you—?"

"Hush, boy, and focus. That can hardly be the most amazing thing you have encountered today. What is your second question?"

"Well... will I see you again? You have set my feet on a path to somewhere, but I'm not sure exactly where or what. I would like to think we may meet again when this journey is complete — or even before."

Brother Gavrilos smiled warmly. "Who can say? Much may happen, and only the One knows with certainty how things will turn out. Yet we may meet again. And lastly?"

"If I am... successful... and this king is restored to his throne... will I be returned to—" he tossed his head back the way he had come "—that world?"

Gavrilos was still smiling. "A conversation to have when the king indeed sits on his throne. At that time you will have freedom to choose. I promise."

The smile faded, and Brother Gavrilos became serious. "Now go with my blessing, in the Name of the One, young Rhissan." He traced three vertical lines in the air, the centre line longer than the outside ones. "Go with confidence and faith you do the right thing, working in service of the Light. Above all, my young friend, *remember that Light* when darkness closes in about you. Without the One, you are nothing, and can accomplish nothing. Put your faith in the One, not in people or things. Call out your needs and desires to the One in faith and humility. With the Light, all things are possible, and help often comes from unexpected quarters."

Rhiss bowed his head, feeling the blessing as an almost physical thing. A great calm filled him. "Thank you for everything."

Brother Gavrilos also bowed his head, but said nothing more, and Rhiss understood he was dismissed. He turned to enter the corridor to Arrinor. As he walked, he glanced back to see Brother Gavrilos still standing, arms raised in silent benediction, a faint, luminous glow seeming to emanate from his person. Then Rhiss was in the corridor, the candles flaring into life at his coming even as the lights in the chamber behind began fading.

At the door, Rhiss halted. There was indeed a small alcove in the left wall. He frowned, sure it had not been there on his earlier foray, then shrugged and peered in the shadowy recess, eager to see the last gifts of Brother Gavrilos.

Two items hung from an ornate metallic peg. The first was a leather flask, complete with a long silver chain going over the neck and shoulder so the flask could hang by the waist. Rhiss lifted it off the peg and shook it gently; a sloshing noise indicated it was full. He unstoppered it and sniffed cautiously, then smiled with pleasure. It was the ruby drink given him in the chamber. Rhiss restoppered the flask, placing it over his neck and shoulder before looking for the next item.

A long cloak also hung on the peg. Carefully, Rhiss took it, marvelling that such a large garment — it fell to his calves when he put it on — could be so lightweight and comfortable. Its exterior was a coarse material, although the inside was finished with soft, smooth linen. Confusingly, the cloak both was and yet was not a steely grey colour inside and out; there was a strange iridescence to it, other colours seeming to shimmer just below the surface when his peripheral vision caught them. It troubled his eyes, as though they had to work hard to ascertain the reality of the cloak's very existence. It fastened closed with a simple clasp and chain at the throat; the clasp, Rhiss noted with interest, was fashioned in the shape of a gryphon. It appeared there was a common theme developing in his accoutrements.

The cloak came with a large hood that, when drawn full over his head, hid his face within. Rhiss tried it, put the hood down, and turned his attention to the other item still in the alcove, the last gift of Gavrilos. He sucked in his breath sharply as he realized what lay against the wall, and picked it up gently.

It was a bow, quite a long one. Made of yew, in the best tradition, it was a couple of inches thick at its centre, slimming to less than an inch at each end. The middle was reinforced with heavy blue yarn wound around, improving the grip. The bowstring was a fine, flax-like, waxed material, and rather unusually was already strung, each end snugly fitted in its blue coloured horn notch at the weapon's ends. Rhiss knew such bows were not generally strung until use was imminent; that this *was* could be no accident. Brother Gavrilos appeared in command of every detail. The only possible explanation was he foresaw Rhiss needing the bow very soon after proceeding through the door; which was unsettling.

Also leaning against the wall was a quiver with two types of long birch arrows Rhiss had come to know well. Alistair had whimsically nicknamed the lighter arrows 'marauders,' the heavier ones — which could pierce armour at close range — 'berserkers.' Rhiss examined the quiver more closely, and found what he knew he would need: a glove and a finely decorated leather vambrace. The glove would protect the fingers of his left hand from the force necessary to pull the string back, while the vambrace fitted on his right forearm to protect it from the slap of the released string — vital accessories for such a powerful bow. He tried on glove and vambrace, fumbling a bit with the latter, and found, to his delight, that they fit perfectly, as though crafted just for him.

The quiver hooked snugly onto his belt, and he stood before the door in his cloak, holding the bow in one hand. "Ulysses, meet Robin Hood," he muttered, glancing down. Truth to tell, he did not feel much like either. Now he was actually there, standing before the portal leading to another world, armed and — at least superficially — dressed for it, Rhiss hesitated, doubts and anxieties crowding in. What if this was some hallucination after all? And even if it wasn't, what colossal conceit made him think he had anything to offer, aiding some ragged, deposed king's struggle to regain his throne? He didn't even know this displaced king's name, where to find him, what to do once he did. He was just a simple literature master. Rhiss wondered whether to return and tell Brother Gavrilos he had made a grave mistake and should seek someone else. He even looked back to see whether Brother Gavrilos was there.

The corridor candles still burned brightly, but the chamber lights had extinguished, only the fireplace's dim glow providing illumination, casting strange, flickering shadows on the walls. Brother Gavrilos had vanished as suddenly, quietly and mysteriously as he had appeared. Rhiss realized returning to the chamber would be inappropriate, like re-entering a shrine after its guardian had left. He had made his choice, and second guessing it was wrong.

And if Brother Gavrilos, possessed of amazing abilities as he was, saw some quality in him suggesting an ability to — how had he phrased it? "work in the service of the Light" — that was sufficient. He must go forward in faith. It was the only way. What had Brother Gavrilos said? Those lines from Tennyson? "To strive, to seek, to find, and not to yield." That was it. What better commission to begin such an enterprise?

Rhiss laid his hand on the doorknob, resolutely turned it, and pulled the door open.

III

ALLIES AND FOES

"Behold, I am come unto a strange land. Whither shall I go, and with what manner of friend? The Servants of the Other surround me, and black fear gnaws at my heart. Yet will I gather the Gifts of the One and seek ever the Light."

The Book of the One, 87:12:62
(Cantos 87, Chapter 12, Verse 62)

Rhiss wondered what he would encounter as the door opened, revealing his first glimpse of Arrinor — would the view be sweeping vistas of emerald forests, barren deserts, snow-capped mountains, endless plains, heaving oceans... or something else completely?

The one thing he did *not* expect as the door soundlessly swung wide was... yet another corridor.

Perplexed, he entered slowly. This corridor was not like the one behind — which he could still glimpse. In fact, the candles from what he regarded as *his* corridor sent dancing shadows into this one.

The corridor was constructed mostly of stone — floors and walls were worn blocks of meticulously cut, dark grey rock. Only the ceiling was wood — and it was in poor condition, sagging noticeably in places, many of the heavy wooden boards splintered and cracked, obviously not maintained in years. All in all, the corridor showed no indications of having seen use in a very long time.

Rhiss became aware of something else: chill dampness in the air, and water dripping through the shattered boards overhead. It was raining lightly outside. He wondered whether it was night here as it was in his own world. The corridor was unlit, but a dim half-light came from the right. Rhiss decided to explore, and was about to set off when a thought occurred: close the door, or leave it open? Leaving the door open was safer. What if he had to retreat suddenly? Closing it might maroon him in this unknown world, especially given the door's capricious tendency to appear and disappear on a whim. He realized he still tightly gripped the pearl knob, and consciously forcing himself to release it, took several steps, leaving the door ajar, but then stopped.

Safe. Anxious. Were these descriptive of someone striding boldly to aid a beleaguered king? Leaving the door open also displayed lack of faith. Anyway, what conceit made him think this door would not vanish the moment his back was turned? He swallowed hard, faced the door, reached out and closed it firmly. Then he turned and resolutely advanced slowly along the corridor, shoes clicking as they echoed on the flagstones.

The corridor ended at an open arch, and going through, Rhiss found himself in a large, rectangular, grassy courtyard. He looked into the slate-grey sky; the rain was light, but the clouds threatened more of it. It appeared to be late afternoon. The place was obviously some kind of castle; stone walls rose at least four storeys, but empty windows revealed most rooms lacking floors and roofs. A multi-tiered, octagonal stone fountain sat in the courtyard's centre, ornately decorated and empty but for puddles left by the rain. There was no sign of gate or passage to the outside.

He scanned the scene, deep in thought. Why was he here, brought to a ruin obviously long uninhabited? An inauspicious beginning at best, downright pointless at worst. Certainly anticlimactic. He had half-expected immediate activity and battle; perhaps, Rhiss thought wryly, even a dragon to slay or a damsel in distress to rescue; not some long dead, ruined castle. But Brother Gavrilos must have his reasons. Rhiss would not believe he was abandoned in some cruel joke, and a mistake seemed unlikely. If the purpose for his arrival in that place at that time was unclear, then his first responsibility lay in making it so. Nonetheless, feeling rather let down, he decided to retrace his steps to where he had entered the dreary place, wondering if the door was still there. He pulled his cloak tighter, glad of its snug warmth.

Within minutes, he had his answer. As expected, the portal was gone, a blank, featureless wall in its place. He looked around, confirming the location. Yes, he recognized that severed beam hanging down in the corridor, marking the spot like a beacon where the portal should have been. While not totally unexpected, it was a little disconcerting, all the same. He was alone, in an utterly strange land, and his immediate objectives were a little hard to fathom. Brother Gavrilos had not, he reflected, been terribly specific about practical issues.

However, practicalities were not slow manifesting: he was cold, and his stomach rumbled dismally. Rhiss was acutely, regretfully aware he had not touched his dinner back home, hours previously. Food and shelter, proper shelter, were immediate imperatives, especially since neither appeared available here, and night approached. Well, since the first exploration had yielded little, perhaps it was time to go the other way and see what could be found.

Five minutes later, Rhiss stood in a rolling meadow several hundred paces beyond the castle, studying his surroundings. The rain had stopped, but fog was moving in to take its place, at once damp, chill and bitter, slowly wreathing all in a ghostly silvery blanket, fading visibility into a swirling nothingness. An icy breeze that somehow did nothing to lift the fog rippled the grasses. Water droplets lay everywhere, a dank, unpleasant coating covering all. The castle itself, he could just see, was situated in a good defensive position, perched on a low, rocky promontory projecting out into a dark lake. Fingers of white mist floated lazily over the water, like steam over a cauldron, while a clear, swiftly flowing brook rushed from a dense forest which halted at the meadow's edge. A packed dirt road ran through the meadow before disappearing into the trees. Going the other way, it met the brook and passed over a sturdy little stone bridge before twisting out of sight. An overgrown side path left the road before the bridge, leading to the remnants of the castle's main entryway, where Rhiss had emerged. The only sound was the brook gurgling over its slaty bed on the way to the lake, and even that seemed muffled by the encroaching mists. It had all probably looked very romantic at one time, he thought, and Byron might have had a field day with it, but Rhiss found the scene cheerless and unappetizing. With the fog moving in, none of it would even be visible in another fifteen minutes. There was obviously no real shelter in sight, and it was impossible to tell whether a village was nearby. Resigned, Rhiss turned back to the castle to seek what cover could be had.

But scarcely had he set foot on the overgrown path when the silence was shattered by a powerful, ululating wail. Horrified, Rhiss stood rooted. It went on and on, up and down the scale. The similarity to a hunting call was unmistakable, but a call filled with menace. It ended abruptly, and there was a pregnant silence during which Rhiss could hear his heart thudding in his chest. Then it sounded again, closer, and out of the mists, flying low and fast, came two repulsive creatures, vaguely batlike in form and colour, but hideously larger — easily thirty feet from wingtip to wingtip. Their elongated, podlike bodies were decorated on the underside with strange markings glowing with faint iridescence in unpleasant colours. Leathery, segmented wings flapped slowly and effortlessly, disturbing the mists. The creatures' faces, if they could be called such, were blank masks, yet managed to convey a terrible, implacable purpose. Small antennae on the heads pointed stiffly upwards.

Conflicting imperatives flashed through Rhiss: to run far away from this nameless horror, or to cower and hide before it. Before he could do either, however, the creatures glided swiftly over him, leaving a foul odour of decay in their wake. Somehow, they had not noticed him, although how they could have missed him standing in the open, he did not know.

There was no time to puzzle through that minor mystery, though. Even as he realized the creatures were not attacking *him*, Rhiss saw something in the greyness aloft, and strained his eyes to make it out. It appeared to be a large bird, but oddly shaped — he could not be sure of its exact form at this distance, with mists thickening. And there were two, he could now see, the second much smaller. Whatever they were, they fled from the creatures, but the smaller was not as fast and slowed the larger, which obviously was refusing to leave it. In a matter of seconds, the creatures would be upon them.

Even had the monstrous things not been so loathsome to the senses and as patently malign, there was something about the scenario that reminded Rhiss of Lewis at Darkton. Before he quite knew what he was doing, his limbs seemingly moved of their own accord and Rhiss ran after the creatures, one hand reaching into the quiver at his side. Given the apparent toughness of the creatures' hides, he selected one of the heavier berserker arrows.

By the time he closed on the creatures, a deadly battle raged above, barely visible. The smaller bird had vanished, but the larger had turned on its pursuers, screeching defiance as it swooped and feinted, attacked and dodged. The creatures rolled and banked ponderously in response, warbling hideously all the while. Rhiss could not see precisely what weapons they brought to bear — claws, beaks, something else entirely — but he had no time to study the situation carefully, for it was obvious the large bird was receiving the worst of it, despite its tenacious attacks. He stopped directly below the action, hastily donned vambrace and glove, fitted his arrow, and aimed, complex instructions from Alistair about wind velocities, trajectories and the like crowding up from memory. It would be an extremely difficult shot, for the creature was constantly on the move and he had to track with it. In addition, the bow's draw required far more force than most he had used before. "Not... to... yield!" he muttered through gritted teeth, sighting on one creature. If it would just roll and expose its underside... presumably a weak area...

It did. Instantly, Rhiss let fly with every ounce of strength he could muster, grunting reflexively as the bowstring slapped smartly against the leather with considerable force. A drawn out, terrifying shriek rent the very air, and the monster he had targeted careened over on one side before crashing into the meadow with a terrific impact that shook the earth. It wheeled end over end several times, stopping brokenly several hundred feet away, and was still.

The other creature turned, breaking off its attack on the large bird, which fell to the ground. The creature appeared to search, then fix its attention on Rhiss, antennae probing mutely. He felt, rather than heard, a venomous hiss as it switched its wrath to him, and groped for another arrow. But at that precise moment, a different ululating call reverberated in the distance. The monster hesitated, evidently caught between the desire to attack Rhiss, or obey what was plainly a summons. The call came insistently again, and, reluctantly it seemed, the creature broke off, flying slowly and noiselessly to be swallowed up into the mists whence it came.

Rhiss watched disbelievingly, wanting to ensure it did not return. Then he ran to the spot where the large bird had crashed to earth. Arriving, he saw the long grasses crushed and stained with blood. He stopped short and gasped as he came upon the torn body of the animal and took in an unearthly sight. Eagle's head, yes, but... lion's body? With wings?

The creature was beautiful even as it lay mortally wounded, but it was no bird. What it appeared to be — no, what it *was*, Rhiss corrected himself — was almost too incredible. He knew enough of heraldry and mythology to recognize it, artistic representations of which, he realized, decorated both weapons Brother Gavrilos had given him.

The animal before him was a gryphon.

It could not possibly be, but it was. The size of a pony, the gryphon lay on the ground, and Rhiss realized with a pang of remorse that it was clearly dying, lifeblood spilling onto the thirsty ground. For the moment, it still lived, great golden eyes regarding him calmly with surprising intelligence. Short-haired and tan in colour with white underbelly, it did indeed possess, as the mythologies said, the body of a lion and the head of an eagle. Rhiss studied it carefully. Contrary to what ancient tales might suggest, it did not look cobbled together by some crazed artist. Instead, the contradictory parts — lion, eagle, amazingly large wings — gracefully melded into a creature that, even mortally wounded, displayed nobility and might. The massive forelegs ended in razor sharp talons instead of forepaws, and paradoxically, the ears were almost horse-like, arching from the head in large, upstanding tufts. Great, feathery wings attached to the gryphon's upper back by powerful musculature. A long tail trailed behind.

There was a dignified aura to the creature: it was indeed, as legends said, a fascinating fusion of the King of the Beasts and the King of the Air, and Rhiss felt a surge of sympathy and compassion. Ignoring that as a wild animal, it could be dangerous — particularly when wounded — he dropped his bow and fell to his knees at its side, extending hands in supplication.

"I am so sorry I did not arrive sooner," he said softly. "Perhaps this could have ended differently." He paused. "I wish I could do something." Disregarding the talons and fearsome beak, he reached out and gently stroked its neck. The gryphon made no attempt to attack or pull away, surprisingly, even arching its neck slightly to allow better access. Rhiss looked carefully at the creature's wounds. There were numerous, jagged tears and slashes all over its body, far too many to bind, and most were hideously deep. There also appeared to be burns, as if the gryphon had been subjected to acid. But the blood loss alone, Rhiss thought, would be mortal.

A faint whuffling noise emanated from foliage by the gryphon's head, and Rhiss was staggered anew to see yet another gryphon, about as large as an Irish wolfhound, slowly emerge from the grasses to nuzzle the first. His jaw dropped as realization struck: *this was mother and cub*. The younger gryphon looked uninjured, although Rhiss did not approach, remembering how wild animals often take exception to anyone coming close to their young. Rhiss felt sure, based on the way he had seen monsters and mother gryphon flying, she would have had no difficulty outpacing her adversaries, had she been alone.

The mother turned her head to the cub, making soft chuckling noises. It snuggled close to her battered head, responding with little cheepings of its own. But her actions were steadily weakening, and it must have been as obvious to her as it was to Rhiss. In an unmistakable gesture, she lowered her head and gently butted her young towards Rhiss. The cub made no protest except for a tiny, almost soundless cheep as it was moved. The mother raised her head and gazed at Rhiss.

Wild animals do not generally make direct eye contact with humans, so it was disconcerting, to say the least, to have the full force of those enormous orbs turn directly on him. But Rhiss could not have torn his gaze away even had he wished. It was like staring into pools of liquid gold, and there was, unmistakably, a sharp intelligence there. He realized he was being handed a sacred trust, transcending the boundary between human and animal. Staring into the mother's eyes, he nodded slowly, moved over several paces, and knelt, enfolding the cub as best he could within his cloak in what he hoped was a clear gesture of acceptance and protection. It made no objection, settling immediately.

The mother gryphon seemed to sigh, head falling to the ground. A shudder ran through her frame; she raised her beak to the skies and emitted one last defiant, screaming cry. Her head sagged sideways, and her breath came out in a long, slow expiration. There was no intake to follow. The intelligent, golden eyes glazed over. She was dead.

The cub made no sound, but Rhiss glanced down to see the animal intently watching its mother's body. Rhiss crouched, wondering what he should do. He didn't fancy leaving the majestic creature in the chilly meadow, exposed to any and all carrion eaters. But he had nothing with which to dig a grave, and even building a cairn would be difficult; few suitable stones lay in the vicinity.

The decision was made for him. The gryphon's corpse emitted tendrils of steam, as though competing with the mists. The tendrils abruptly caught fire, blue flames running up and down the corpse. Rhiss involuntarily rose and stepped back in horrified amazement, the flames growing until the entire body was enveloped in a bluish conflagration that writhed and roared but gave off no heat whatsoever. Oddly, the flames were confined to the corpse, and Rhiss was relieved: there appeared no danger of them spreading to the lush foliage. Neither Rhiss nor the cub made any sound as the body was consumed. There was something almost reverential about the immolation — like standing at a Viking funeral pyre, witnessing the passing of a great warrior.

It was over in minutes. The flames lessened, flickered, and finally ceased. All that remained was a handful of ashes. Even the great bones had been consumed. The grasses underneath were blackened, but whether from flames or the gryphon's blood, Rhiss could not tell. He sighed and looked at the beast now at his side, peering gravely up at him.

"Well, my friend, here we are. A right pair, too... a motherless cub and a rank newcomer at a complete loss. What happens now?"

The cub eyed him alertly and cheeped quietly. It was amazingly tolerant of humans. By rights, a wild animal should be absolutely terrified after all that had transpired. This one could likely put up a fair fight, too, even at its tender age. Rhiss had briefly viewed the cub's talons, and, while obviously not as deadly as the mother's, they already resembled wickedly huge straight razors. He wouldn't care to argue with it.

Rhiss felt his stomach rumble again, quite audibly. The cub jumped in alarm, and Rhiss recalled what he had been about to do when the terrifying monsters floated out of the mists: find food and shelter for the night... which was even closer now.

"Right, then. I'm afraid that mourning must give way to practicalities. First things first: food. Do you know, I didn't eat my supper, and that was hours ago. Let's see what we can find to eat around here, little one. After that... a fire and a bed with a warm eiderdown would be nice, but I doubt we're going to find anything like that out here." He glanced down at the gryphon. The amber eyes watched him closely, an amazing spark of intelligence clearly present. He sighed. "Come on, then. Do you fancy anything in particular for dinner?"

He turned, meaning to go back, but a sudden thought struck. With the gryphon following, he made his way to the downed monster lying crumpled like a prehistoric nightmare. He had seen it careen upon landing and flip over at least twice, as the crushed grasses mutely testified. Rhiss stopped fifteen feet from the monster. It hadn't burst into flames, he thought — yet. The stench was nauseating, and the gryphon cub hissed at it. "Steady, young one," murmured Rhiss, and it subsided. The ebon creature was as horrific in death as it had been in life. The weird markings — it was impossible to discern whether they were natural or applied — still displayed obscene phosphorescence. One of the bristly antennae was broken and bent at a right angle, oozing dark ichor. Rhiss turned away in disgust. He had hoped to find the arrow with which he brought the creature down, but obviously its cartwheeling landing had snapped it clean off. A pity: aside from wanting to reuse it, he must have hit the beast in a spot both vulnerable and vital, and it would have been extremely useful to know where such a spot was — after all, at least one of the things was still alive out there, and it had not been at all pleased when this one went down. Rhiss shuddered as he recalled the second creature's hatred wash over him like a tidal wave as it fixed its attention on him, preparing to attack. But something had called it away. What manner of thing controlled such flying behemoths, and why had it recalled the second? Could it somehow have known the first had been downed? If so, how? It was altogether an unpleasant train of thought, and Rhiss could not even begin to guess the answers. A funny thought struck, and he laughed.

"Do you know, I've slain the Jabberwock. What a beamish boy I am."

He sighed and shrugged. On one hand, staying in the immediate vicinity was not the best idea — what if the surviving creature returned, to resume the attack interrupted by that summons? What if the beasts' *keeper* came looking for either the body or its killer? Rhiss wanted nothing to do with whoever controlled such monsters.

However, set against that was the fact that night and weather were closing in. To attempt to blunder through the forest — which could hold who knew what horrors — in the dark and the wet with a young animal which was *not* tame, despite how it currently was acting... well, weighing alternatives equally unattractive, Rhiss decided he would stay where he was. After all, there was shelter nearby, and he was somewhat familiar with the lay of the land. That had to count for something. He sighed again and, gryphon at his side, trudged slowly through the gloom back to the ruined castle. It was the only shelter in the vicinity, and even if it *was* crumbling, it would provide cover from the rain that was threatening to resume momentarily.

Rhiss re-entered the ruined castle, coming back to the courtyard. This time, searching more thoroughly, he found a neatly stacked pile of dry firewood someone had left on the courtyard's far side, under a large, arched, open doorway connecting with an area inside that had once been a stable: the remains of numerous stalls were very much in evidence.

Rhiss inspected the area. The same someone had even built a small fire away from the entryway and possible inclement weather, but close enough for the fire's smoke to be drawn out and up. There was a ring of blackened stones and ashes to indicate where it had been. It was impossible to tell how long ago the fire pit had last been used, but it did not appear recent. As he stood wondering how to make a fire, sudden inspiration struck. Rhiss dug in his pockets, searching for the box of wooden matches he used to light his stove. To his delight, he found them after a moment's fumbling. There were only a few remaining, but there were enough, and he showed them to the gryphon, smiling broadly.

"There, young one," he said proudly to the animal sitting on its haunches, watching him alertly. "No endlessly rubbing two sticks together for us tonight! We'll soon have a fire going with these. Now all we need is dinner, for I'm fair famished. I don't suppose you know a nice little pub close by? Steak and mushroom pie and a pint would go down nicely."

The gryphon stared fixedly as he spoke, head angled to one side. Absurdly, it looked as though it was listening carefully, hanging on his every word. When he finished, it stood, shook itself as a dog might, and flexed its wings. Rhiss was surprised how large they were for such a young animal. They must be for a gryphon as feet and ears are to a puppy. But it certainly was no puppy; the gryphon gave a harsh cry and without further ado, simply leapt into the air. Rhiss had quite forgotten seeing it fly earlier; he'd been so focused on the combat surrounding it that it came as a shock when the gryphon flew into the mists.

Distraught, Rhiss stood gaping, and then, recovering his wits, cried out. But it was already gone, and he rushed through the corridors to exit the castle, calling all the while. The sky was empty. A fine drizzle was falling, the greyness quickly darkening. It would be folly to stay there, with weather deteriorating and night coming on. The gryphon could have gone anywhere. He peered to the spot, barely visible, where the mother had died. The young gryphon was not there. It had not gone back to mourn, then. Whatever had made it dash off like that? He swore, hugely disappointed with himself, and turned back to the castle. His stewardship hadn't lasted long at all; a wonderful guardian he had turned out to be.

Back in the ruined stable, Rhiss focused on building a fire. He had no axe or hatchet, and didn't want to desecrate his fine dagger by using it to cut wood, but in the end it proved unnecessary: there was also a good supply of kindling. With care and determination, he soon had a good fire burning. The shadows created by the flames danced on the walls, turning the aged stones a warm bronze hue. Rhiss was glad of the warmth, but continued to reproach himself bitterly for losing the gryphon so soon after taking charge of it. He felt he had let the mother down. He slumped, kneeling on the ground before the fire, hands held out to warm them, and stared into the flames.

King, he thought disconsolately. Here in this land, he was supposed to find and come to the aid of some dispossessed king. How was he to do that? He couldn't even look after a creature placed into his care. In fact, he was like old Pellinore, on an endless hunt — except, he noted wryly, he had already slain his Questing Beast. Arthur and Pellinore... Arthur and — his train of thought screeched to a halt and he sat bolt upright as it struck him. *What* had Alistair said in relation to King Arthur, almost immediately before very strange things had begun to happen?

"Although perhaps I'd rather be Arthur. And you could be Lancelot... I'd be there for you. And you'd likewise be there for me, wouldn't you? If ever I needed you."

The sudden realization made him dizzy: King's Champion... what if *Alistair* was this king he was meant to aid? What if Alistair had come to Rhiss — God alone knew why Alistair would seek Rhiss out, of all possible people, but there it was — had come to Rhiss to *train* him to be Alistair's champion? Aye, it made sense! It could explain—

Suddenly, there was a rush of air and the sound of something large swooshing out of the night. The other of those vile beasts returned? Rhiss jumped to his feet, heart pounding as he fumbled for his dagger. But even as he did, a flying mass dropped in a blur from above, and then the young gryphon landed awkwardly before him, staggering as it did so. The source of its aerodynamic difficulties was immediately obvious: it rather inexpertly grasped two very large, dead hares in its claws, and their bloodied, limp forms made it difficult for the gryphon to keep its balance. It released them on landing, somersaulting once as it regained equilibrium. Then it peered up at Rhiss, cocked its head to one side as it had done earlier, and cheeped twice. It looked at the hares, then bent its head down and nudged them towards Rhiss. The gesture reminded him poignantly of the mother gryphon thrusting the cub towards Rhiss.

Rhiss laughed delightedly at several things: his mental epiphany regarding his role in Arrinor, the gryphon's unexpected return and its bounty. His world suddenly made sense again. His laughter resounded through the ruined stable, and for a few bizarre seconds, it seemed the flames leaped higher and the firelight was brighter. Rhiss frowned uncertainly, but the important thing was to express his gratitude for the provender.

"Well, I never did. A brace of hares!" Rhiss exclaimed. "So you heard me moaning and decided you'd go and secure dinner on your own, did you? And here I thought you'd just up and flown off. Forgive me, and thank you, my friend. This is most welcome." He squatted down, again eyeing the carcasses judiciously. "You did very well: plump, young and tender. They must have been a good weight, so they'll taste just fine, I warrant. Let's see, now. One for you and one for me, is that how it works?"

The gryphon soundlessly opened and closed its beak several times. Rhiss took that as assent, and pushed one over. The gryphon promptly lay down and, using its front claws to grasp the body, began tearing off chunks of meat with its beak. Rhiss watched a moment. He was glad for the gryphon, but didn't fancy raw meat himself. He rose and went over to the firewood, finding a slender stick to serve as a skewer, and two other sticks to function as crude supports. He planted the two sticks firmly in the ground at either end of the fire pit, then skinned and gutted the other hare with his dagger as well as he could — the gryphon eyed the steaming innards and, smiling, he pushed them over — before placing the carcass on the skewer over the fire. While the meat roasted, he went into the courtyard, cleaning his hands and dagger in the fountain, which by now was full from the increasing downpour.

Damp from his endeavours, Rhiss returned and carefully removed his cloak, shaking it to rid it of the wet before laying it to dry on one of the partitions demarcating the old stalls. He inspected the hare, rotating it so a different side was exposed to the flames. He was pleased to see it cooking nicely, although the finished meal would never meet gourmet standards.

Unconcerned with such things, the gryphon was still busy with its meal, enjoyment evident with every bite. While he waited for his meat to finish roasting, Rhiss sat cross-legged by the fire, studying the gryphon.

"You need a name," he mused aloud. "I can hardly keep calling you 'young one.' What would a gryphon like to be called?"

Rhiss mentally ran through names common and exotic, from his own experiences and from legends he knew. He didn't even know the animal's gender. But most gryphons were supposed to be female. Male gryphons were quite rare — what were they called in heraldry? *Keythongs*, that was it. He would assume his gryphon was female until shown otherwise, but it needed a neutral name, neither too male nor female. And it needed to be a noble name for an animal possessing characteristics of the eagle, king of the air and the lion, king of the land. The gryphon was also associated with Christian symbols. He strained to remember the Latin for eagle and lion. Eagle was... *aquila*, yes, and lion was *leo*. So... an animal that was both should be called... yes! Aquileo if male, and Aquilea if female. Rhiss was not really sure of the proper Latin, but looked around with exaggerated care. Not a single linguist in sight to make a fuss over incorrect usage, he thought, smiling. Anyway, both names sounded grand.

"Aquilea," he said, emphasizing the second syllable, savouring the word as it rolled off his tongue. "Aquilea," he repeated approvingly, this time louder, more clearly. The gryphon looked up with interest; Rhiss pointed at her. "That's it, my friend. *You* are Aquilea. A noble name for a noble beast. What do you think?"

The gryphon regarded him gravely, then emitted a single loud cry — almost as if indicating assent. Nonsense, he told himself sternly. He was shamelessly anthropomorphizing a mere animal, although undeniably a remarkably intelligent one. "Right, then," he said aloud, "Aquilea it is. We both like it."

He turned his attention to the hare. It was a bit unevenly cooked, and scorched in places. They would doubtless turn their noses up at it in The Admiral Rodney, he thought... and salt or spices wouldn't have gone amiss. However, hunger dulled any fussy epicurean fancies he might have had, and Rhiss fell to, although the meat turned out to be rather dry and not nearly as tender as he would have liked. Mrs. McDowell made it all look so easy, he thought ruefully; but obviously, there was more to the art of cooking than he had imagined. He stopped occasionally to wash it down with sips of the fruity red drink in his flask provided by Brother Gavrilos... how long ago that all seemed. It felt like years, but was only hours. And twenty-four hours ago... he had been, literally and figuratively, in a completely different world. He shook his head, amused. Only a day past, he was a young, disillusioned schoolmaster, craving change and adventure in his life. Less than a day later, he had come through an incredible doorway into another world, killed a nameless creature with gifts given him by a supernatural being, and sat eating his fill in a ruined castle, in the middle of nowhere, with a mythological animal staring calmly at him across the fire! He grinned. Who said life was devoid of magic?

By the time Rhiss finally finished, there was little left of the carcass, and he felt pleasantly full. The fire warmed the stables wonderfully, and despite their advanced state of decay, it was snug and cozy, particularly when he looked outside and observed the rain pouring in the pitch dark. Rhiss put more wood on the fire to keep it burning decently into the night. He got up and retrieved his cloak, now fully dry, and donned it again, wrapping it around him as he would a blanket. He yawned, feeling a delicious weariness, and sat with his back against one wall, legs stretched out. He pulled the hood over his head and said sleepily, "Aquilea, I'm all for bed. I don't know whether the good brother drugged that wine, or if it's just been a rather more adventurous day than I'm accustomed to, but I can't keep my eyes open. So good night. I doubt any creature is fool enough to be out in this weather, and I think these ruins will hide us and our fire from unfriendly eyes, in any case."

The hood came a good way over his face, masking most of the firelight, although with it on, Rhiss suddenly became aware he still wore the Circlet of Araxis. It was not uncomfortable, and he had quite forgotten it since entering Arrinor. He debated removing it, but in the end decided against it. It would not do to take it off, then have it stolen while he slept. Unlikely, but not worth the risk. That resolved, he pulled the hood well down over his face, closed his eyes, and began drifting off. As he was almost there, a warm body snuggled against one leg. He roused, opened his eyes, and smiled: Aquilea had moved across the floor to join him. An odd rumbling noise emanated from deep within her chest, and after a moment's puzzlement, he realized what it was: the gryphon was purring, in her own fashion. Rhiss laid one hand on her head, gently scratching between the tufted ears. The rumbling rose in crescendo, and he let his hand rest there as he fell asleep, still smiling.

<hr>

An unknown time later, Rhiss woke with a start. It was still blackest night; the fire had burned down to embers, and only a dull red glow lit the chamber. The rain continued steadily, but it was not that which had woken him. It took a moment to orient himself to the surroundings; for one fleeting second, he thought he was back in his own little cottage. Then recall flooded in, along with the reason for waking.

He had been having a nightmarish dream, running through endless grassy meadows. He could not have said what he was fleeing *from* until Brother Gavrilos appeared some distance ahead, pointing dramatically behind Rhiss. He turned to see a darkly gigantic, vaguely humanoid shape reaching across the sky, seeking him without quite being able to locate him. Somehow, Rhiss knew the shadow was the keeper of the monster he had shot the previous afternoon; it was searching for whomever had shot its pet. Brother Gavrilos called a warning, but Rhiss had already halted and turned to face it, holding a great sword that suddenly materialized in his hand. The

Circlet of Araxis chose that moment to blaze forth blindingly pure white light, and the shadow was aware of him. A wave of malice and hatred emanated from it, almost physical in its intensity, and Rhiss quailed, sick under its ferocity. But an undercurrent of something else radiated from the shadow, and amazed, Rhiss realized it was fear. Why something as vast and evil as the shadow should be afraid, he did not understand. Brother Gavrilos called again, and with great effort, Rhiss understood he was being told not to yield. He was about to — he could not recall what — when he suddenly awoke, and looked around uneasily.

Waking had not dissipated the dream's very real sense of foreboding — quite the opposite, if anything. He felt most uncomfortable — of being seen without actually being observed, of being sought without actually being found. He strained his ears, and fancied he could almost hear, at the very limit of audibility, an incredibly evil, small voice, continually whispering *where... where*. Shivering violently, Rhiss stood up quickly, casting wary eyes around the chamber. Aquilea, already awake and on her feet, took stock of her surroundings, stiff-legged, and hissed softly. It was apparent she, too, felt something she did not like at all, something frightening her. It was as though she could see something Rhiss could not.

Rhiss remembered his dream, reached up, and removed the Circlet of Araxis. No blazing light emanated from it, but the opaline colours *did* swiftly shift and move within the depths of the crystal. Rhiss recalled receiving the Circlet, and gently smoothed his hand over the crystal, wishing Gavrilos was present. There was a peculiar dual sensation within him, an irritating itch and unpleasant pressure on his spirit. He shook his head impatiently, feeling negation rising within. He would not yield to this feeling. Framing this thought, the crystal in the Circlet *did* glow a milky white for a few moments, suffusing the entire chamber with a cool, peaceful light.

The voice and the sensation of being sought abruptly ceased. Rhiss glanced up unbelievingly, but it was as though a switch had been turned off. Nothing looked or felt out of the ordinary, and the unpleasant weight on his soul was gone. He reached down, took wood and threw it on the embers, watching puffs of flame erupt as new fire took hold and ignited the seasoned wood. Feeling the need of some illumination, both literally and figuratively, Rhiss fed the fire, and it grew until the entire chamber was brightly lit.

Somewhat reassured, Rhiss donned the Circlet again and sat. Aquilea came and lay beside him, head draped on his lap. Rhiss scratched her between the ears. "*What* was that about, Aquilea? A nasty dream, and a nastier awakening. I've never felt anything like it, and I've had my share of nightmares. But this was much more real than anything I've ever dreamed." He sighed. "Too much wild hare, perhaps." He pulled his hood back up on his head and partially over his face before continuing. "Well, no, I don't believe that, not really. There are strange things in this land, Aquilea, not least of all you, begging your pardon." He yawned, and closed his eyes. "I don't know about sleep again after this, but the night's not done." Curious, he opened his eyes and reached for the chain on his pocket watch to check the time, before realizing belatedly it was still on his kitchen table. He shrugged and closed his eyes again. In spite of his doubts, he was asleep within minutes, and this time, his rest was dreamless and undisturbed.

Aquilea, however, did not drop off to sleep as quickly. She lay awake awhile, listening to the sounds of the rain without, and within, The Man's breathing as it again became slow, shallow and regular, signs of Essence rest. She was well content, all considered. It had been a truly terrible day, but was ending on a more hopeful note. Lying beside the sleeping Man, Aquilea recalled all that had transpired since dawn.

She had not understood the reason for the journey they undertook that day, and her mother either would not or could not reveal their destination. While she had been terrified by the sudden appearance of the Malmoridai and their unprovoked attack, the fight had happened almost too quickly to register for a youngling such as she. She remembered falling out of the sky. Then she hid in the grasses while her mother fought above, crying out, warning her to stay hidden. She watched as The Man came thrashing through the meadow, shooting his wooden stinger at one of the monsters. He killed it and somehow drove off its mate, but Aquilea's mother had also fallen from the sky, Aquilea rushing to where she lay. The Man arrived too, and even though Aquilea was only a cub and did not yet possess all the ancient wisdom of her people, she could see, like her mother, the Essence of this human burned clearly and cleanly and truly, lighting up the meadow with its radiance even without the magical stone set in metal on his head. He was a good man, truly grieving over what was shortly to be, and would be a worthy guardian for Aquilea when her mother was gone. That was why she travelled with him without protest after her mother went through the Fire of Cleansing to be with the One.

Afterwards, The Man proved unexpectedly resourceful, finding a dry place in the icy rain to shelter, even conjuring up and controlling the red tongues to warm them. She sensed his hunger and wanted to reciprocate his kindness, so she went on the hunt, returning with enough food for them both, although he had inexplicably scorched his in the red tongues — on purpose, it seemed. He also gifted her a name — a harsh, creaky-sounding noise when measured against the flowing, graceful names her own people bestowed upon each other in their thoughts. However, he meant well. It was acceptable and would suffice: she could answer to it. And when it was time for Essence rest, they shared warmth together, as was proper among those who knew kin trust. He was her kin now, a worthy guardian indeed, even if he lacked wings and was therefore peculiarly bound to the earth.

He also sensed the searching hand of the evil one in the night as she had, although not as quickly or clearly, for she woke to the threat before he did. But with that stone of his and force of will, he was also able to do something she could not: muddy the air around them, confusing and dispelling the grasping of the evil one. Precisely how he had accomplished it, she did not know; she suspected he did not, either. There was much of The Man's mind she could not see, which puzzled her, and other images were there that she could not comprehend. But she was not troubled; what she could see and understand pleased her. His Essence was a fine one.

So there they lay, an odd combination, to be sure, but a good one nevertheless; Aquilea was content. Her mother had given her over to this human. The choice was highly unusual, but not unpalatable. Aquilea nestled closer to The Man again to share warmth, and closed her eyes. In moments, she too slept.

IV

STEEL AND MIRACLES

"Child of the Light, attend: for hard choices lie before you. The forces of the Other are abroad and at work in the world, and you may yield to evil, or stand against it. Choosing the former may at first seem less costly, but be not fooled: for evil is never gentle, neither merciful nor just, and the cost of appeasing it is ruinous, always. Therefore, truly I say, stand fast, have courage, and take heart; for the One will not fail you, nor forsake you…"

The Book of the One, 76:61:89-91
(Cantos 76, Chapter 61, Verses 89-91)

When Rhiss awoke, the night's rains had ended and a pale, watery sun was visible through the arch, valiantly attempting to pierce the remaining fog. Beside him, Aquilea stirred and opened her eyes. Rhiss got stiffly to his feet, yawned and stretched. As his back cricked, he groaned softly and wiped sleep from his eyes. He had been on camping excursions, but was used to sleeping on more than just bare ground with only a cloak for warmth — although it possessed marvellous insulating qualities, and he had not been cold. The fire was merely warm ashes. Rhiss was tempted to rebuild it, but felt an urgent need to explore. They were still near the place where he had killed that monstrous creature yesterday. He wanted to put distance between them and it, particularly after that awful dream, or whatever it had been.

Going into a stall to relieve himself, Rhiss glanced around self-consciously, half-expecting someone to chastise him for such an unseemly breach of manners. He stepped into the courtyard, making his way over to the fountain. There was a great deal of clear, clean water in it from the night's rain, and he cupped his hands and drank before splashing water over his face. It was bracingly cold, but banished the last cobwebs from his mind, and he returned feeling refreshed. Aquilea was up and stretching, very much like a cat, back extended and first one pair of legs outstretched, then the other. It was odd to see such a feline gesture in a creature also possessing very avian physical characteristics, but Rhiss was slowly coming to terms with it, and it did not startle him as much as it had the previous day.

"Well, my girl, I think it's time we were out and about, don't you? Brother Gavrilos put us here for a reason, I'm certain, and I think we need to find what it is. We'll pick up breakfast on the way. Perhaps there'll be berries or something to nibble, as we don't have time to stop and build a fire, and I've no appetite for raw meat. In fact, a cosy little inn with hot baths and cooked breakfasts wouldn't go amiss, that's a fact. Although... hmm..." Rummaging through his pockets, he brought out a handful of coins. "There's a thing, now. How do you suppose I'd pay for a room? No innkeeper here is going to want English shillings." He shrugged. "Well, no sense worrying about it. We'll cross that bridge when we come to it. I guess I could sing for my supper." He grinned. "That was a joke, as you'd know if you'd heard me sing."

Rhiss paused to take inventory. He inspected his dagger to make sure it was clean and dry, and stowed it in its sheath. He still wore the Circlet of Araxis, and his flask, mostly empty, was at his waist. He did not fill it with water: there was still some cordial in it which he was reluctant to dilute. He retrieved the bow and quiver from the wall where he had leaned them the previous night, and strung it. "I wonder if this bow has any... unusual properties, Aquilea? It came from Brother Gavrilos, after all. And that *was* a pretty impressive shot yesterday if I do say so myself. I think even Alistair would have been impressed. But truth to tell, I'd like to think I managed it by myself. Maybe I actually do have some ability." He checked to make sure the fire was out, and drew his cloak about him. Aquilea watched with interest.

"Right, then," he nodded, "we're off. Stay at my side, lass. We don't want you flying off now... although it might be useful, later, to have some aerial reconnaissance. But first we'd better make sure none of those lumbering nasties are out there looking for a meal of young gryphon. I had a lucky shot yesterday, but I'm not sure I could repeat it."

Rhiss set off across the courtyard, pleased to see Aquilea fall in and trot alongside. They passed the fountain — Aquilea stopped, reared on her hind legs and drank — and then proceeded into the corridor that would take them out. At the spot where the portal had been, he halted, running his hand over the featureless stone.

"Right there, it was," he murmured. "Will it reappear? And if it did, would it show up anywhere, or only here—?"

Rhiss stopped and frowned; at the same moment, Aquilea pricked up her ears, looking down the corridor towards the outside. They both heard the clash of metal ringing on metal, and shouts of men. As one they turned and ran toward the sounds. When they burst into the open again, they skidded to a stop, assessing the situation.

Down in the meadow, perhaps two hundred paces distant, where the stone bridge carried the road over the brook, a carriage was stopped, the horses pulling it dead in their traces. A swirling melee was in progress, more than a dozen men at arms trying to protect the carriage and its occupants from a smaller but more heavily armed group, some of whom were on horseback. Aquilea glanced uncertainly at Rhiss; he noticed and looked at her. "Rest easy, girl," he said, as if responding to a verbal question. "I'm not sure who to support." He was tempted merely to watch a moment and puzzle out what was what, and which side he might want to assist, but he knew full well that was a callous thing to do, and he couldn't simply stand by while people were slaughtered. His instincts said the men attacking the caravan looked less than savoury, more like common hooligans.

However, within mere seconds, the fighting was over. The men defending the carriage lay dead, except one, who galloped madly toward the forest on a horse stolen from a dead attacker. Several victorious soldiers urged their horses in pursuit, but at least four remained behind, their attention on the carriage. They swaggered to the door in its side, flinging it open. A couple charged in, and a moment later exited, laughing uproariously, dragging the passengers onto the road.

There were only two, both women, one older than the other. Their flowing dresses were finely made. The younger was about twenty and extremely attractive, even from a distance. She had long hair streaming down her back in a golden cascade, but a soldier had his hand twisted in it as he dragged her to the road side. He threw her to the ground, doffed his sword belt, and straddled her, intentions frighteningly clear. All the while, she screamed and fought like a demented animal, but to no avail. The older woman, too, fought her captors, but one struck her full across the face, and, stunned, she subsided.

Rhiss had seen more than enough; he felt coldly furious. This was the small boy at school, or the attack on Aquilea's mother all over again: nothing more than cowardly bullying at its absolute worst, the casual brutality of conqueror against vanquished. In one smooth action, he swept his cloak back, plucked an arrow from the quiver, and was ready with glove and leather, arrowed nocked. He sighted carefully and let fly, deliberately aiming at the ground in front of the rapacious soldier. The entire procedure took less than three seconds, and an irrelevant thought flitted through Rhiss' mind: Alistair would have been proud. Even as he framed the idea, the arrow was in the air, and Rhiss selected another, fitting it in his bow.

The arrow, a heavy berserker type, buried itself in the ground a foot from the soldier, its feathers a brilliant scarlet against the emerald grasses of the meadow. It made an entirely satisfying thwocking sound and the men glanced in stunned surprise towards the castle, abruptly halting raucous laughter and crude comments. Spinning on their heels, attempting to determine the arrow's source, their eyes widened at what they saw: a tall, slim, youthful figure, apparently sprouted from the meadow where he stood, clad in a cloak of indeterminate colour that made it difficult to see him clearly. A silver circlet with a gem in its center glittered off the youth's forehead in the wan sun, framing the tousled mane of dark hair in a halo of light. A large animal, a dog or something, stood beside him. And the bow — one of the largest the soldiers had ever seen, arrow fitted and string drawn tautly — was aimed directly at their leader. A wild thought flashed through the targeted soldier's incredulous mind, that he beheld an angel of death, or at least, a reasonable earthly facsimile. But his men stared back and forth between him and the youth, waiting for him to take action, and revealing the fear he felt was not a luxury open to him. Even the women ceased struggling and looked towards the youth, expressions on their faces instantly running the gamut from terror to astonishment to cautious hope.

"That is absolutely enough, *gentlemen*," Rhiss called coldly. He made sure his voice was loud enough and pitched so it carried clearly across the meadow, noting with wry satisfaction at least one school master skill was still useful.

For several seconds, the scene in the meadow resembled a strange tableau, as though the participants had been transformed into stone by the unexpected turn of events. The only sound was water flowing swiftly and noisily over the rocks in the stream's bed. Interrupted before he could begin his act of rape, the soldier, tall and swarthy with thin lips and cruel eyes, stood slowly and stared at the youth materialized without warning.

Gazing at the man, Rhiss recalled the Roman historian Tacitus: "They terrify lest they should fear." Even from across the meadow, he could tell what went through the man's mind. Heart sinking, Rhiss realized he was probably going to have to do something he had never done, or imagined doing: kill a man, or at least, attempt it. If he did not, the man would kill *him*. No other course of action would suffice, because he knew, beyond any doubt, the soldier would not — could not — yield before his men without losing authority. Rhiss swallowed hard and waited for the response to his challenge, praying he would not have to see it through to its likely conclusion.

"Listen, whorespawn," blustered the leader, voice dripping with contempt. "We are Sovereign's Men. You don't dare interfere. Take your toys and crawl home to your mother, and be careful: you'll hurt yourself if you don't watch out. There are four of us, and only you. You also commit treason by threatening us. So I tell you once to be on your way. This doesn't concern you."

"But it does," Rhiss called back, tone still calm, betraying none of his inner turmoil. "Sovereign's Men, you say? Sovereign's *Brigands*, more like. Any Sovereign who employs such as you must be desperate for fighting men. What kind of pathetic Sovereign employs rapists and murderers? I will not leave these ladies to be violated and killed by the likes of scum such as you. And your numbers mean nothing in the face of this bow. It will pick you off before any of you can close with me, and will, too, unless you follow my instructions to the letter. Now lay down your weapons, and we'll wait patiently for the man who escaped to return with reinforcements. Or you can face summary justice at my hand. Your choice, sir."

For an endless, taut moment, no one moved. Then several things happened at once. One man, nerve breaking, flipped a wicked dagger from his tunic sleeve and foolishly made a run at Rhiss, who saw the movement from the corner of his eye. He shifted position to sight on the man, and the arrow left his bow without time for further conscious thought or regret. Before the man had come fifteen paces, the arrow struck him squarely in the chest and passed *through* him as though he was not there, spinning his body round to face his stunned companions. He was dead before he hit the ground. Incredibly, the bloodied arrow went on to find a *second* target in a man with the unbelievably bad fortune to be standing in a direct line behind his crazed compatriot. The arrow lodged in his neck, and he also fell like a stone, dying too quickly to do more than begin lifting his arms in a fruitless, instinctive attempt to remove the arrow which had inexplicably grown from his throat like a small tree. Guarding the older woman, the third soldier completely forgot his captive, spellbound at the sight of two comrades dying in the space of less than a heartbeat from the same arrow. She took full advantage of that, snatching the sword hanging limply in his hand, and slashed it with all her strength across his belly. He screamed harshly and went down, clutching his innards as they spilled out like sausage links from the gaping wound created by his own sword.

The lead soldier, apparently convinced his own moment of destiny was nigh, swiftly hauled the girl to her feet and, yanking his dagger from his belt, slashed it across her throat in a bid to distract Rhiss before throwing her to the ground and turning to run for his life. But as a diversion, it failed completely: Rhiss loosed the arrow he had retrieved from his quiver the moment the first left the bow. A lighter marauder arrow, it hit the soldier squarely in the back, penetrating but not passing through his body. The man swayed, swivelled to face Rhiss, began snarling a defiant comment, then fell dead.

Even as Rhiss realized what had been done, he cursed, running to the girl writhing on the ground. Aquilea bounded along at his side. He reached the girl at the same moment as the older woman, and they both fell kneeling beside her on the ground. A first glance confirmed her wound was every bit as lethal as it appeared from a distance. The soldier's knife had created a jagged tear stretching right across her neck, severing at least one major blood vessel. The girl's eyes were closed, her life force draining in a river of scarlet. It was obvious even to Rhiss' untrained eye she had but moments to live. She was in shock, gasping and choking, blindly clutching the hem of his cloak.

"You must *do* something!" The older woman's voice, half imploring, half commanding, drew Rhiss from his trance as she glanced at him, pure desperation in her eyes. "She will die otherwise!"

Rhiss did not respond. There was no time, he thought, no time to talk, no time to do anything. He feverishly tried to recall what he had been taught about tending casualties, but a hurt of this magnitude — it was utterly impossible. The wound was massive.

But he had to do something, so not knowing what else to do, he placed his hands firmly on the girl's neck to apply pressure and attempt to stanch the bleeding. The blood flowed over his hands, down onto the grass, staining both. Rhiss was suddenly, indelibly reminded of the mother gryphon yesterday as her lifeblood, too, leached into the cold, hard ground, the result of just such a terrible, unprovoked attack as this. *No*, he thought, *not again!* He would not allow another tragedy. He closed his eyes, trying to focus on a plan, some idea that would save the young woman's life before it was cruelly and prematurely ended.

Suddenly, the blood running under his fingers burned hot, almost scalding. He gasped in pain and involuntarily tried to pull away. But he could not force his hands to obey his will, and they remained firmly locked together over the frightful wound. Rhiss felt a burning, tingling sensation begin in his upper arms and spread into his hands. It mingled there with the heat from the girl's steaming blood, and as Rhiss opened his eyes wide in astonishment, he saw a golden haze or mist floating on and even *through* his hands. Then the pain faded, the haze pleasantly warm, not uncomfortable at all. For one endless, dumbfounded moment, he fancied he could see, through the mist, another pair of hands superimposed over his, simultaneously wispy and insubstantial, yet graceful and sturdy. There was a tangible sensation of pressure on his hands, warm and strong, and Rhiss felt a surge of well-being and glowing vitality pass through him like an electric shock. He gasped again, this time in reaction to the marvellous feeling.

Then it was gone, and his bloodstained hands lifted slowly as they once more obeyed his will. No new blood gushed forth. He rocked unsteadily back on his heels, glancing around. Aquilea watched intently with huge, liquid eyes, but made no sound. The girl gave a sudden, convulsive gasping intake of breath and opened her eyes. The older woman, face chalky white, gazed at the girl in rapt attention, then raised her eyes to Rhiss in stunned amazement, and made as if to speak.

But all at once, the world was spinning around him, out of control, and he licked dry lips. "Feel like I'm... I'm... about to..." He stopped, unable to go on. There was a roaring in his ears, and the ground rushed to meet him. He was falling, aware even as he did that the world was suddenly both shadowy and cold... very cold. Then, even that was gone. Dark oblivion gathered him in, and he knew no more.

Watching The Man crumple to the ground as one dead, Aquilea's thoughts were a bright jumble of disbelief, dismay and terror overlying amazement.

The young woman had lain on the cold, uncaring earth, life-force spilling out like a roaring cataract draining a deep lake. Even to Aquilea's inexperienced eye, it was obvious the woman had but moments to live before her Essence fled the cruelly shattered housing of her body to join the One. Aquilea bowed her head in reverence, acknowledging the inevitable, awaiting the Passing of the woman's Essence and the Fire of Cleansing. It was both sorrow and joy — privilege, too, of course — to witness such a thing twice within two sun-cycles.

But then the character of the very air around them changed in a penetrating, indefinable way. A deep thrumming assaulted her ears, and startled, she raised her head. The Man's hands were pressed on that hideous gash, anguish clearly written on face and Essence, the depth of his emotions creating a violent, coruscating pattern on it so different from the liquid calmness she had previously seen. Something else about his Essence was very strange, too: a golden stream of sparkling motes rained down from the sky, swirling around him, infusing his Essence, strengthening it and endowing it with a darker, richer hue.

Then a searing golden flash momentarily blinded Aquilea. When both inner and outer sight returned, she could blurrily see the woman's Essence steady and settle back in the body it had been on the verge of abandoning.

Even as The Man fell, and Aquilea's awe turned to horror, one thought hammered relentlessly through her mind...

To perform such an astounding, impossible deed — exactly what manner of human was this?

V

CLARITY AND CONFUSION

"Thus Lord Beltor came at last to the Gardens of Soran-gar-may. As he wandered, enthralled at their loveliness, he chanced upon a fair maiden of the Gardens. "From whence do you hail? Whither are you bound, on what errand?" asked she. "Lady," he replied, "I may not answer. For my tale is both surpassing strange, that none might believe it, and of needful secrecy. If I am found by the Servants of the Other, my destruction is certain."

The Book of the One, 97:72:18-21
(Cantos 97, Chapter 72, Verses 18-21)

Rhiss awoke cosily ensconced in bed, and kept his eyes closed, luxuriating in soft warmth as awareness slowly returned. A large hot water bottle, still giving off plenty of heat, made his feet feel toasty. What day was it? Saturday, of course. Strange... he didn't recall coming to bed last night. Had he and Alistair been to The Admiral Rodney, done a little too much tippling? He hoped not. The one time *that* happened, Mrs. McDowell voiced acerbic comments about drunken wastrels for weeks. It couldn't be that. What had Alistair said about a dance, with a pretty girl for Rhiss? Hmm... pretty girls... he had *dreamed* of a pretty girl... saving her life. *That* was it... an epic dream! Strange beings, portals to other worlds, mythical animals, fighting like a medieval knight... a dream straight from Malory. What absolute, romantic rubbish one dreamt at times. He stretched lazily. But it was time to be up; doubtless Mrs. McDowell had already let herself in to prepare breakfast. Smiling, Rhiss opened his eyes, a hand beginning to lift the covers — and froze in shock as he viewed his surroundings and realization struck. This was not his room; he was not even in his own home! Full recall flooded his mind. It was no dream, then. Where was he? What predicament was he in now? He sat up, taking in his surroundings. Fortunately, they were reassuring, which stilled the panicky mental voice starting to gibber.

Covered in richly embroidered bedclothes, the bed was much larger than his — large enough for two or three, come to that. Four ornately carved, dark wooden posts, one at each corner of the bed, wound their way in spiral patterns to the ceiling, which was crisscrossed by heavy wooden beams supporting the floor above. Small tables were at either side at the head of the bed.

A faint buzzing interrupted his observations, and he sat up, puzzled and searching for the source of the sound. Tucked at the foot of the bed was a slumbering animal (*not* a hot water bottle) that resembled a small lion except for one major anomaly. Seeing the neatly folded wings, Rhiss realized it was the young gryphon he had named Aquilea. Smiling at her flute-like snores, he studied his surroundings.

While not large, the room was well constructed and comfortably appointed. It was a corner room: a bay window with a built-in, maroon cushioned seat took up most of the wall to his left, while another opened in the wall before his bed. Polished hardwood floors were partially covered by intricately woven carpets. The walls were whitewashed plaster above waist height, wood panelling below. Brilliant sunlight streamed through both windows, catching on dust motes floating in the air. Judging by the sun's position, it was late morning. Two high-backed wooden chairs were set against the left wall. To his right, the wall was punctuated by a door, a low table and a fireplace. Although there was no fire in the grate, the room was comfortably warmed by the glorious sunshine. On the table lay his flask, dagger and cloak, neatly folded. The Circlet of Araxis, sparkling in the light, reposed in solitary splendour on a wine-red cushion. His bow and quiver leaned against the wall. In all, a comfortably tranquil scene. *But where was he?*

Rhiss got up, realizing abruptly he was not in his clothes: his sole garment was a long, finely woven linen nightshirt. Extending just above his knees, its creamy whiteness vividly offset his legs' darker colour. Involved, embroidered designs were worked in scarlet around the nightshirt's neck. Rhiss inspected his hands; they were clean, as was the rest of him. He felt across his face, and realized a trifle uneasily that someone had washed and shaved him as he lay unconscious. He had obviously been deeply out of it for somebody to do that without his waking. He looked around for his clothes, but whoever had undressed him had removed his clothing. There was, however, a pair of felt slippers on the floor beside the bed, and a dressing gown draped across a chair.

He put on slippers and dressing gown, which fit as though they had been custom tailored for him. He shrugged. Perhaps they had. Disturbed by his movements, Aquilea awoke, rolled over and stretched. She caught sight of him, making a small chirrup of recognition and pleasure as she rose and came to the edge of the bed. Rhiss scratched her between the ears.

"Well, lass, this is a bit different from that damp old castle, isn't it? But how many nights ago? I'd like to know where we are, who brought us here, and see about getting breakfast; aye, that'd be a start. And I need clothes. I don't suppose you have ideas about any of that, do you?" Aquilea evidently did not, which made Rhiss smile. He felt remarkably refreshed and clear-headed; his time unconscious had produced no ill effects. He walked slowly to the window and looked out.

The building was constructed of reddish-brown stone, built on a gentle hillside overlooking a valley through which passed a swiftly flowing river, clear and sparkling. Gardens and orchards surrounded his windows. Lush green trees, heavy with low-hanging fruit, waved in the late morning breeze. The area beyond was gently rolling, forested hills. It was all extremely pastoral, but provided no clues as to his whereabouts. How far he was from the castle where he had entered Arrinor, Rhiss had no idea. The terrain hereabouts was not as flat, although he realized his time at the castle had not been graced by good weather — in fact, the fog had precluded any proper read on the area at all. Rhiss came to the glum conclusion that he really had no clue where he was — the castle could be one mile away, or five hundred, especially as he did not know how long he had lain unconscious.

Which brought up another issue: why had he fallen unconscious? There was a recollection of ineffectually trying to assist the girl slashed by that swinish soldier. Somehow, if memory served, the bleeding had stopped... but how, given the wound's awful nature? It should have been lethal. Rhiss frowned, trying to pierce the veil drawn over his memories. He had felt very strange and then, on lifting hands from her throat... what? Perhaps she was dead? But the girl had opened her eyes. He recalled the ground rushing up to meet him. And that was all until here, wherever this was. He shook his head in frustration. He had never before been prone to fainting.

Rhiss sat in the cushioned window seat, leaning his back against the wall. Aquilea came and leapt up beside him, folding her legs under her and nudging his hand with her beak when he didn't scratch her head at once. Complying absently, mind far away, he mused that his introduction to Arrinor had not ended how he had expected; in fact, it was not much of a fairy tale at all. Almost immediately, he had battled a hideous monster, then was joined by a mythical creature. Their first night was spent in the stables of a dank, ruined old castle... well, *that* sounded like a fairy tale. But afterwards, he had had to fight malignant thugs, and had even... killed a man; three, in fact. He shivered, the enormity of his action registering fully for the first time. While there were murders in fairy tales — Rhiss had often thought it ironic how so-called 'children's literature' was frequently filled with ghastly imagery completely unsuitable for young ones — it was one thing to read in books, very different to actually see or perform the deed. Taking someone's life — he had never wanted or imagined that. True, late in the Great War, Rhiss had served in the Royal Navy. But even there, he had never, so far as he knew, killed anyone. In Arrinor, there had been no choice in what occurred — the men in question were about to commit vile crimes and stood ready to kill him for interfering; it was a clear case of kill or be killed — but *still*. He had taken three lives, and it was no easy thing to reconcile — it made him feel slightly ill, in fact. Not much of a fairy tale at all, Rhiss thought bleakly; hardly part of the job description given in a quiet room between worlds.

His reverie was cut short as the door opened. Aquilea looked up questioningly and swung her head, as did Rhiss. Standing in the entryway was a woman he recognized: she had been with the girl outside the castle. She was tall, dark-haired, elegantly attractive, regal in a dusky green dress falling to her ankles. Behind her was an older, white-haired man holding a tray with a large bowl and cloths. The woman saw the empty bed, swept her gaze around, and smiled radiantly as she spied Rhiss at the window seat. He rose awkwardly, leaving Aquilea on the spot he had just vacated.

"Thanks be to the One, at last you've returned to us," she said warmly, bustling across the room to stand before Rhiss. To his surprise, she curtseyed, then turned without waiting for response, motioning the man to put down his tray. "Dalys, refreshment for our guest, please. He will want to break his fast."

"Aye, my lady." The servant bowed low and left.

"Now then, young sir: are you feeling quite well?" Rhiss nodded cautiously, and she continued. "Then let us sit together and talk in the warmth." She gestured at the window seat he had just vacated, and sat. Wordlessly, he shooed Aquilea off the seat and joined her, at which the gryphon laid her head on his lap.

"We have been deeply concerned, as you lay unconscious a day and a half. You were not wounded and my physicians could find no reason for your collapse — no fever or sickness of any kind. Hence our anxiety." She paused. "But here you are now, awake and well — although seemingly mute. I would very much like to know your name, valiant hero. We are deeply indebted to you." Her eyebrows rose in enquiry as she smiled.

Remembering the instructions of Brother Gavrilos, Rhiss wondered how much to say, blushing at the lavish praise. "My apologies. I am Rhissan, son of Tovan... my lady," he said, adding the honorific used by the servant. "But those whom I count as friends usually shorten that to Rhiss."

"I am honoured to meet you, Rhiss, son of Tovan," she replied gravely, bowing her head in gracious acknowledgement, "and happy to hear you do, indeed, have a voice. I am Meranna of Tormere, your hostess." She smiled wryly. "I would normally add, 'your benefactor,' but I am not sure that is true. You fell and required care only after being *our* benefactor, rising from the mists like a guardian saviour sent by the One." She halted, eyes taking on the faraway look of someone recalling past memories. Then she shook herself lightly and returned to the present.

"Your pardon, young sir. You must have questions you wish answered, because I know *I* do. Shall we see if we can enlighten each other? To start with, whence have you come? You—" she stopped, appearing to search for the right words "—keep unusual company, and possess—" she halted again "—unique tokens."

Rhiss again recalled his instructions and decided, until he knew more, that the best tactic was to be as general as possible, to focus on answering her query's first part, avoiding references to 'unique tokens.' He waved a hand vaguely. "Oh, I am not from nearby, lady; I hail from a very small village named Dinas Mawr, a long, long ways distant. In fact," he added truthfully, "it is so far away, I am sure you will never have heard tell of it — or the country where it lies."

The tactic worked. Lady Meranna smiled. "Be that as it may, after meeting you, it must be a wondrous place to raise gifted warriors and healers like yourself. My daughter would never forgive me if I did not mention that latter, especially after the miracle you wrought." She seemed about to say more, but stopped when she saw his confusion. "Is something wrong, Lord Rhiss?"

Rhiss belatedly realized what she had said. "My lady, you say I... saved your daughter's life? Then... she *did* survive?"

"But of course." Lady Meranna smiled again, but it quickly faded. "How could you not know? That is one of the things I most wanted to ask about, for what I saw

— what appeared to occur — was something wondrous, and yet, at the same time, utterly impossible. However," she continued wryly, "there are several things about you fitting that category and begging explanation, if you will pardon my saying so."

Rhiss felt colour again rise in his cheeks.

"What things, my lady?"

She said nothing for several moments, appearing neither to have heard him nor be aware of his discomfiture. Her eyes were on Aquilea, but she seemed not to see the gryphon at all, and Rhiss realized her thoughts were again far away. In her reverie, she spoke in a low voice, almost musing to herself. "You materialized from the mists as though by magic, springing from the grass like a woodland sprite, but in appearance more like an avenging angel of the One. You challenged those brutes with a fearsome weapon, wielding it handily. You had a gryphon minor at your side — an uncommon thing in itself — and you wore strange tokens straight from legend. I saw my own daughter cut down by one of that murderous rabble." She shivered. "And I knew instantly I had just witnessed my child's death. A thing terrible beyond all imagining. She was dying, you were there at her side, laid hands on her, and..." She stopped, still playing the memory in her mind, unable to find words describing what she had seen. Rhiss leaned forward, keenly interested to hear what she would say next; he remembered some of it, but wondered how it had appeared to a bystander.

Abruptly, she resumed. "How did you do it, my lord?"

Question and title caught Rhiss off-guard. Attempting to avoid her question again, he focused on her manner of address.

"Lady, please, I beg you, do not bestow titles I do not deserve. I am no lord, just a simple man — a common wayfarer."

"You are too modest, *my lord*," she said, repeating and emphasizing the title. "You carry yourself with the bearing and assurance of one used to command. And simple travellers do *not* wear tokens bearing remarkable resemblance to the Circlet of Araxis." Rhiss started at the name, a reaction she clearly noticed, and she added softly, "Oh, aye. There is much more to you than you would have people believe, I think. Or it may be there is more to you than you realize." She scrutinized him. "Perhaps a combination of the two. And you have yet to answer my question."

Rhiss wanted to continue discussing the Circlet of Araxis, for it was clear she knew more than he. But he was unsure whether it was safe to reveal either his ignorance, or where and from whom he had received the Circlet.

He blinked. "I am sorry, my lady. Your question?"

"How did you do it, my lord?" she repeated.

He gave up trying to dissuade her from the title. "How did I do what?"

"Save my daughter. I have spoken of it with no one but her since our return, but I saw it with my own eyes and I must know. That terrible knife slashed across her throat and her life's blood was spilling onto the grass. The next moment, you placed your hands on the wound, and there was a brilliant golden flash piercing the very mists surrounding us. I felt its warmth. Then that hideous gash was simply... gone."

She paused, lifted her eyes to meet his, and said softly, "What are you? Man? Spirit sent by the One — or the Other?" She shivered again, making an odd gesture with one hand. Rhiss was startled; Brother Gavrilos had done the same when they parted: three vertical lines traced in the air, the centre much longer than the two flanking ones. But that had been a benison; Rhiss was quite sure this was a gesture warding off evil.

"The One?" he repeated uncertainly.

"Why, yes," she replied, looking at him narrowly. "Are you not a Follower of the One?" Rhiss looked blank, and she frowned. "How distant is this land of yours that you have not heard of He who is Three and Yet One? Who is Creator and Preserver of All?"

The titles were simultaneously different yet familiar, reminding Rhiss poignantly of St. David's, the small church which had been the spiritual hub of Dinas Mawr. He and his aunt had attended faithfully, and the rector, Father Llewellyn, had been a decidedly unconventional but positive force in his spiritual life as he grew up. And at Darkton, Alistair attended St. Michael's, so Rhiss naturally accompanied him. When you came right down to it, God was God, whether in Wales, England, or even Arrinor, he reflected philosophically. "Ah. I believe I understand. In my land we refer to... the One... by another name, but employ much the same titles. Yes: I am a Follower of the One."

Lady Meranna looked relieved. "I am glad to hear it. So I repeat my original question, which, I assure you, I do not ask lightly: what are you? Flesh and blood... or spirit of the One?"

Rhiss shifted uncomfortably. "Lady, I know little of such matters. I am not even clear what I did on the field, how I saved your daughter — if, indeed, I did much of anything. Perhaps her hurt was less than we assumed at her side. But I assure you again, I am no spirit — just a man, and, despite what you say, a rather ordinary one at that."

Lady Meranna looked at him shrewdly. "I very much doubt it. Ordinary men are not in the habit of performing miracles, and I witnessed one in the meadow. I know what I saw, and I think you do also. When you stood, if her blood was not still on the ground and your hands, I would have sworn the horror I witnessed was no more than a night terror. But my daughter was *dying*... and then she was *well*. There were no marks on her throat, then or now, not even the slightest scarring or redness. I have never seen aught like it. There is no doubt in my mind what occurred, and even if you will not or cannot explain, I am beyond grateful to the One for sending you. You shall meet my daughter shortly, and perhaps you may judge what you did or did not do. When you meet—"

They were interrupted by a muffled oath and the sound of crockery shattering in the corridor. Rhiss realized the door was ajar. The servant Dalys, face blotchy red, hastily entered, holding an empty tray, and bowed jerkily.

"A thousand pardons, m'lady," he said, flustered and trembling. "Most careless... must have slipped... I'll clean up the mess directly and return with more food and drink." He left quickly, glancing at Rhiss in agitation, this time closing the door completely.

"How strange," murmured Lady Meranna, obviously puzzled. "Do forgive him, please. It's most unlike him to be so clumsy." She straightened, dismissing him from her thoughts. "But no matter. We still have much to speak of. You will meet my daughter. She is most anxious to meet you, be assured."

Rhiss furrowed his brows. "I do not know whether or not to look forward to that; I am... not entirely sure what I would say. What does she remember of the... incident?"

"More than you, it seems," said Meranna dryly. "She has regaled me with detailed accounts since my soldiers arrived and brought you back here. And she has taken to your gryphon, a liking fortunately mutual, because the creature was most reluctant to allow us to move you until Rhyanna soothed it."

"Rhyanna?" Rhiss repeated.

"My daughter," smiled Meranna. "One of them, at any rate. She is the one you met and... worked with, if you recall."

"And she calmed Aquilea? Why? What did Aquilea do?"

"Aquilea?" Meranna repeated.

Rhiss smiled in turn and gestured at Aquilea, head still on his lap. "My gryphon... but she is, alas, the only one I have. The one you've met, if you recall."

Meranna laughed softly. "Well played, sir. Aye, we have met. Well, when you collapsed as one dead, Aquilea fiercely stood guard over you, suffering none to touch or even approach. No one was anxious to argue with her beak or talons. Except Rhyanna, that is, and she did not argue so much as gently persuade. Eventually, your... Aquilea relented, allowing us to carry you on a litter. Had she not, you might yet have been at Tor Linlith, and us, too, wondering what to do with you."

"Tor Linlith? What is that?"

Meranna looked surprised. "Why, the ruined castle. You were ignorant of its name? It is well known in these parts, with a long and colourful history. And that is another thing I wished to ask: why were you there? It is a fair distance from the nearest town. And you stayed there at least overnight, did you not? My soldiers found your campfire's remains inside the ruins... at least, they assumed it was yours."

"It was," said Rhiss, carefully attempting to be truthful without giving too much away. "And it *was* only overnight. I have not visited here before, although I felt a certain affinity with Tor Linlith. Aquilea and I took shelter there from the night's rain. I was... merely travelling. I have wished to see something of Arrinor for quite some time." That much was true, both figuratively *and* literally, he reflected, remembering his last conversation with Alistair. And Tor Linlith *had* literally been his doorway into Arrinor. "Aquilea and I are just simple travellers journeying through Arrinor; nothing more."

"I see," Meranna replied neutrally. She stood, crossed to the other bay window, and remained several moments, arms folded, regarding the view. Then she seemed to reach a decision, sighed, and turned. "Lord Rhiss, I appreciate that one must tread carefully when meeting new and untested acquaintances, and if you have been in Arrinor any time at all, you must be very aware that these are dark days indeed, requiring extreme caution and discretion. I can believe almost all you have said... save your last. There, I fear I must contradict you. You and your companion are *not* simple travellers. That much is obvious, so I ask: where do you travel, and to what purpose? You are no casual, sightseeing wanderer. And you are not telling the entire tale. That, too, is obvious."

"Lady Meranna," Rhiss began warily, "I know not how or why you could possibly make such assertions..."

She strode to the low table. "Several reasons, my lord. To begin... this," she said, indicating it without touching, "is I believe, as I have said, the Circlet of Araxis. As I also stated, common travellers do not 'simply wear it' casually travelling through Arrinor." Rhiss found that an extremely interesting statement, but she did not pursue it further. Intriguingly, however, she made that odd gesture of blessing again before moving on. "Your cloak, bow and dagger," she said, pointing at each in turn, "bear tokens of design and workmanship... both unique and unusual, to say the least. The beast who is your companion is uncommon enough to be worthy of comment. You turn up outside a ruined castle, miles from anywhere, a castle with an unsettling reputation. You are strangely garbed. Your gift of healing is miraculous. And finally, there is the thing my soldiers found when searching the area. What might you know of that?"

Rhiss licked suddenly dry lips. "I am... uncertain to what you refer."

"Really? Allow me to be more specific, then: the carcass of an enormous, hideous flying creature, blacker than the night, stinking to the high heavens, befouling the meadow where it was brought down. And it *was* brought down by someone -- or something. Its death was no accident. While it bore numerous wounds, my men were certain none would have been enough to cause its death. They could offer no explanation what *would* have done so. But I think *I* can." Her eyes strayed deliberately and obviously back to his bow. She stared at it before sighing. "If we are to assist each other — and since you do not yet seem to realize, I assure you that you *do* need my assistance — we must end this wary circling around the truth, and each other."

"Forgive me, Lady," Rhiss said slowly. "You have already done much, bringing me here and succouring me, and I am grateful, make no mistake. To be fair, though, as you already pointed out, that was *after* I had already come to *your* assistance, saving both you and your daughter's lives. How, then, am I still in need of your help? Frankly, it would seem we have settled our mutual debts."

"Indeed?" Lady Meranna raised her eyebrows. "Allow me to answer my own question, then, plainly. I think *you* brought down that obscene flying creature with your great bow. The creatures are extremely difficult to dispatch, and having personally seen you use your bow to extraordinary effect, I can think of nothing else that would account for one lying dead in the meadow."

She stopped and looked directly into Rhiss' eyes, nodding slowly at what she saw. "I thought so," she said quietly. "Know, then, that under the laws of this land, you committed a serious crime in killing one... as you also committed treason by killing Sovereign's Men."

Rhiss felt anger rise, and his eyes blazed. "*Sovereign's Men?*" he said contemptuously. "Aye... they threatened me with that title — but must have lied. What they were about to do to you and your daughter... they were worse than animals. What kind of Sovereign would employ such men — or condone such behaviour?"

Meranna looked grim. "Our present Sovereign, in fact, and you would do well in public to keep such sentiments to yourself. You will find, in Arrinor, that you gainsay Sovereign's Men at your peril. They have authority to do more or less as they please, and particularly in the last year or two, have grown more and more brazen in their cruelties — petty and otherwise — as they roam this realm. They answer only to the Sovereign and the Sovereign's Counsellor." She sighed. "As for the beast you slew... it and its kin are special servants of the Sovereign's Counsellor. All I need do — *must* do, by law — is report my suspicions to the Sovereign's Representative in the village nearby, and life would very quickly become... difficult for you. However," she said, lifting up a hand to stifle his reaction, "I said we must stop skirting the truth and trust each other. I am prepared to make the first gesture." She paused. "Before you reply, you would do well to know that those who control such creatures are no friends of mine. In fact, they are enemies of all decent folk, and I stand firmly against them, although, alas, not yet openly. You saw what the Sovereign's Men did to my soldiers, what they were about to do to my daughter and me. The Sovereign and the Sovereign's Counsellor have ruled Arrinor far too long, with increasing severity and cruelty. Maintenance of terror and control are their twin priorities. I count it no loss the world has one fewer of their terrible monsters flapping noisomely through it, and several fewer of those Sovereign's 'Brigands' striding through it — even though, as I said, legally, you have done great wrong in killing them." She paused again. "There. According to the law of this land, I have now committed a crime no less than yours with my treasonable utterings. Now, you need not tell me your entire tale if you still doubt me. I hope your trust will come. But I wanted to make sure you have no doubts regarding my position." She shrugged, adding, "Know, too, that I take personal risk telling you this without being better acquainted with *you*. But it is a risk I can bear, even with the little I know."

Rhiss was amazed. "How so? You know almost nothing of me."

She again gestured reverently at his possessions. "These are powerful tokens you bear; they mark you as a Champion of Right. Do you not realize that? And hearing you speak is nearly as powerful. You are worthy of my trust." She raised an eyebrow. "Well?"

Rhiss was unsure where to start. "I apologize for giving offence..."

"There is no need; I am not offended. The wise man does not pour open his heart to those whose hearts he does not yet know."

Rhiss sighed. "Aye. As you surmised, I shot and killed the beast with my bow. The creature was battling Aquilea's mother when I first laid eyes upon it, dealing her a lethal wound before I could kill it. There was... some form of communication between the mother and myself before she died... not words... in fact, I cannot really explain how I knew, but she made it plain to me I was to take the cub and care for her, so Aquilea accompanied me following her mother's death."

Meranna nodded, came back to the window seat, and sat again. "I have heard of such things. It happens rarely, because gryphon minors generally avoid humans, but when it does, the bond of loyalty between gryphon and its chosen companion is very strong. To the death, it is said. They have many abilities, it is also said. They are not pets, because they do not domesticate like dogs, for example. But 'tis said they make excellent companions."

"You have mentioned that term, 'gryphon minor,' before, Lady. What does it mean? 'Minor' as opposed to what?"

Meranna looked astonished. "You do not know?" Rhiss shook his head, wondering whether he had blundered in his honesty. But it was better to confess ignorance than to lay claim to knowledge of customs he did not know. "Truly," she went on, "you continually surprise me. Are there no gryphons in these far-off parts whence you come?"

Rhiss smiled. "Only on some of the emblems of my countrymen. But even there, they are regarded as no more than mythical animals. I assure you, I had never seen a live gryphon before, did not even suspect they existed until I encountered Aquilea and her mother."

Meranna said thoughtfully, "It must have come as quite a shock to you."

Rhiss inclined his head wryly. "Indeed. One of many in recent days."

"The gryphon minor is called thus because it is smaller cousin to the gryphon major. For all that she is a most impressive animal even now, when fully mature, Aquilea may be the size of a small pony, but no larger. The gryphon major, on the other hand, grows *very* large, its wingspan thirty to forty feet across, I am told, and body sized to match. In fact, they are large enough for humans to ride; legend speaks of people doing so, long ago. In addition, while you will find Aquilea an extremely intelligent companion, she is an animal, and therefore mute. Gryphon majors are as intelligent as humans — perhaps more so, in some ways — and use our speech to converse with us. Altogether, rare but remarkable creatures — possibly not the most unique or bizarre found in Arrinor, but good candidates for that honour."

Another thought occurred to Rhiss as he recalled the battle between Aquilea's mother and the monster. "What did your men do with the creature's body?"

Meranna shrugged. "Nothing, of course; there was no need. Shortly after they examined it, the Fire of Cleansing took place, and it was consumed." Something in his expression caught her attention, and she said slowly, "Why do you look thus? The Fire of Cleansing, I said. Surely you—" She paused, and then realization came. "You know nothing of the Fire of Cleansing, do you?" she said in a flat tone that was really more statement than question.

Rhiss understood he had committed another gaffe, this time perhaps more serious. However, he would not lie to escape an awkward situation. "Well," he began, ready to admit ignorance, but unbidden, the image of the body of Aquilea's mother bursting into flame flashed before him, "do you mean that blue fire destroying a body after death?"

Meranna looked relieved. "You *do* know," she breathed.

Rhiss gave an embarrassed shrug, not wanting to reveal his true ignorance. "I did not know what it was called, nor was I aware something so evil would undergo it."

"All living things in Arrinor — beasts and humans alike — perishing in conflict undergo the Fire of Cleansing, regardless of morality. A good thing in this case... I did not wish to give those seeking it more information than what its partner would provide."

"Partner?" Rhiss whispered.

"Of course. They always hunt in pairs. Did you not see the other? I thought it would have attacked straight away, especially as you brought down its mate."

"I did," Rhiss said, recalling the hatred he sensed in the surviving creature. "And it *was* about to attack, but was recalled before it could. It responded to some ghastly summons, flew off, and I did not see it again. Do you know these monsters, then, and who controls them? Why can it possibly be a crime to kill one?"

She looked grim. "I know a little. In time, I fear, you will know far more than I. The same goes for their handlers, but it is not something to speak of now." She nodded, as if confirming something to herself. "I have sent for my sister. When she arrives, she can tell you more. She is most knowledgeable about this and many related topics."

"Your sister?"

"My older sister, Arian." Meranna smiled affectionately. "More correctly, Seir-onna Arian."

Rhiss raised an eyebrow. "Seir-onna?"

Meranna looked at him oddly. "Why, of course. A lady Priest of the One. If she were a man, the title would be Seir-on. Are you not familiar with the names?"

"No," Rhiss admitted. "We do not use them in my land. And we do not have women priests at all."

"But, surely—" Meranna halted, shaking her head, a rueful smile on her lips. "Your pardon. Your country must be distant indeed, with many different customs. I would dearly like to know more of this place, but will not waste time with idle questions. Arian likely arrives today. The circumstances of your coming have given me cause for thought; but I realize most of it is beyond my ken, so I summoned her. Arian will know what needs doing." She smiled in reminiscence. "A good woman, my sister, knowledgeable and decisive. Oh, aye, decisive indeed. Not easy to get to know, either, but a very fine woman for all that. I will say no more... but I think you will like her."

A knock sounded. Meranna started and looked up. "That will be Dalys, hopefully this time with the food and drink he was originally sent for." She rose, motioning Rhiss back when he began rising. "I will leave you to eat and drink a little, and Dalys will bring clothes for you, clothing more suitable for a — how did you refer to yourself? — a 'simple traveller journeying through Arrinor?' Aye, that was it. Then Dalys will convey you to me and my daughter, who, as I said, is most eager to meet you." She looked at him, clearly amused. "Heroes who slay monstrous beasts and evil villains should not fear to engage fair maidens in conversation. But having admitted you have no idea what to say to a young woman, I suggest you spend time while eating and dressing composing suitable remarks for my daughter. I bid you farewell for now. Go you with the One."

She strode to the door and swung it open, revealing Dalys, obviously still ill at ease, and his tray, intact this time. She gave him quiet instruction, then swept past the old man without a backwards glance.

The tray contained an assortment of excellent fruits, cheeses and bread — no steak and mushroom pies, though, he thought wryly — and a tankard of cold ale with a pleasantly nutty flavour. Rhiss tucked in with a will, realizing he had not eaten since Aquilea provided dinner over two days ago. Presumably, their host had provided Aquilea with food and drink, but Rhiss shared with her anyway. Amusingly, she was willing enough to eat the fruits, but turned her beak up at the bread and cheese. No matter, he thought cheerfully: all the more for himself.

While he ate, the silent Dalys left, returning minutes later with clothes and a pair of boots. "I'll return shortly, after you've had a chance to eat, dress and rest, m'lord, and take you to her Ladyship," he said gruffly, clearly reluctant to engage in further conversation. Bowing, he left, closing the door.

Rhiss looked at Aquilea. "Something's not right about that chap, Aquilea. I'd even go so far as to say he doesn't care for us, though I can't imagine what we've said or done to offend."

Shaking his head, Rhiss rose, brushing the crumbs from his dressing gown, and walked over to inspect what Lady Meranna fancied a 'simple traveller' in Arrinor would wear. He was not displeased: breech clout and leggings, first, of course; a long sleeved, white linen shirt with red decorative needlework around the neck, similar to his nightshirt. The shirt's high, open collar made a plunging V down the front of the neck, the overall effect quite formal. Next, beige pants of plain woollen material, sturdy but soft, and long, supple black leather boots that reached almost to his knees; a steel grey, sleeveless leather tunic to be worn over the shirt; and a dark belt. Inspecting the buckle, Rhiss laughed aloud: he was not the least surprised to see the brass shaped in the form of a gryphon. Between the fashion choices of Gavrilos and Meranna, there was a common motif developing in his belongings. But he doubted a 'simple traveller' would wear such an emblem. He thought back to her talk of gryphon majors. Forty foot wingspans, he marvelled. Definitely not creatures to annoy. But surely a most impressive sight.

Sighing, he shucked off slippers and dressing gown, and was about to pull the nightshirt over his head when he became aware of Aquilea watching with interest.

"*Do* you mind?" he asked indignantly, motioning her to turn around. "I'll spell it out, since you seem to need it: you're a girl, I'm a boy, and I would therefore very much appreciate it if you find somewhere else to look while I dress."

She actually made a guttural noise that sounded very like disdain deep within her throat, but complied, making a great show of getting up and turning around several times before settling again, staring ostentatiously out the window.

"*Thank* you," said Rhiss to the back of her head. "I deeply appreciate your humouring me." He swiftly dressed, then stood admiring himself, rather wishing there was a looking glass so he could see his entire reflection. He noticed his belongings on the low table, and inspiration struck: in a moment, he had attached his dagger in its sheath to the belt on his right side — being left handed, it seemed the most logical location for the dagger. On a whim, he donned cloak and Circlet of Araxis, grinning.

"There!" Aquilea turned to regard him solemnly. "What do you think, lass? I wager I *do* look like Ulysses crossed with Robin Hood. If only Alistair could see me." He considered a moment, thoughts turning slightly sombre. "Of course, probably he'd just laugh and say I looked like a refugee from the pantomime. Dear old Alistair. I wonder what he's doing. I wouldn't mind having him here, Aquilea, and that's the truth. *He's* never at a loss to know what to do next."

Aquilea leapt from the window seat, made her way to Rhiss, and rubbed against his legs. He bent and scratched her head, and she made her rumbling, purring noise again. He straightened, carefully removed the cloak and placed the Circlet back on its cushion. "It's strange, you know," he observed, "this cloak looks an ordinary charcoal grey until you move, then it seems to shimmer with several different colours and makes my eyes feel funny. I can imagine how it was difficult to see me in the meadow." He folded the cloak neatly, placing it on the table. Then he sat in a chair. Aquilea came to him, and he sat for some time, rubbing her head and letting his mind wander, thinking over all Meranna had said — and *not* said. Her remarks had deftly skirted several things...

Rhiss woke with a start, realizing, to his surprise, that he had dozed off. There was another knock, and Rhiss called, "Enter!"

Dalys poked his head through as the door swung wide, and jumped as Rhiss stepped out from behind the door. "Oh, there you are, m'lord," he said stiffly. "If you're ready, I'm to take you to Lady Meranna." Rhiss nodded but said nothing, so Dalys continued. "Very well, m'lord, follow me. Oh, and the... uh... animal... is to come, too." He looked warily at Aquilea, flinching as she moved towards him. Retreating into the corridor, he gestured Rhiss to accompany him, then moved off without looking back to see whether Rhiss followed or not. Rhiss glanced down at Aquilea and shrugged, stepping into the corridor. Aquilea moved to his side, and he closed the door. Together, they struck out after the rapidly disappearing servant.

As Dalys led them through a maze of passages, Rhiss realized for the first time how truly massive the place must be. He had no idea of its name or location in relation to the ruined Tor Linlith. Of course, it probably wasn't particularly important to know where Tor Linlith was — if Gavrilos had anything to say, Rhiss was quite sure the good brother was perfectly capable of materializing his portal anywhere he wished. However, the ruined castle was a known landmark in an unfamiliar and as yet unexplored land.

Dalys eventually arrived at a large pair of heavy double doors, pushing them open to reveal a spacious dining hall facing south. He wordlessly motioned Rhiss and Aquilea through, closing the doors firmly behind them. The first impression Rhiss had was of a long, rectangular refectory table that could easily seat more than a score; but it was cleared and not presently in use. A number of colourful, intricately woven tapestries depicting battle scenes graced the walls. Over to one side, by large windows framing delightful gardens, was a smaller table for six, although only three seats were occupied. Meranna sat at the table's head, with two others on either side: an attractive young woman who looked familiar — he immediately surmised it was the daughter, Rhyanna, whose life he had somehow saved, and realized uneasily he had not composed any suitable remarks — and a regal looking, middle-aged man whom Rhiss thought might be Meranna's husband, although he was not at the head of the table. They were in the process of being served a meal, as a number of dishes and plates heaped with steaming food lay untouched. Meranna smiled as Rhiss and Aquilea approached. Sensing it was the right thing, Rhiss inclined his head and bowed.

"Lord Rhiss," said Meranna warmly, "may I present the two people in this household foremost in my heart? Master Tobias, the overseer of my estates, and my right hand; and, of course," she added, a mischievous glint in her eye, "one of my daughters, the Lady Rhyanna, whom I believe you have met. Please join us. We were about to begin with thanks for the meal." She motioned to the chair beside Rhyanna. "I know you broke your fast with light refreshments, but I do not doubt you will enjoy falling to again." Rhiss inclined his head and went to the seat indicated, but had no time to sit before the three stood. He remained standing behind his seat and waited, observing with interest.

Lady Meranna was quiet. Then, lifting arms in front, palms upturned, she began. "We give thanks unto the One. As the One is both Three and yet One, so are our thanks: for the great gift of Life, for the World harbouring it, for the Food sustaining it. Eternal is the One. We will Remember. In this we are One." She made the gesture of the three vertical lines, the center line longer than the two flanking, and Rhiss understood with sudden clarity that the gesture was indeed a blessing. She dropped her arms and all sat.

As Meranna had said, although he had eaten not long before, Rhiss found two days' privation, even if unconscious, had put an edge on his appetite. The food and drink were excellent, and he 'fell to' again with a will. To his relief, despite her playful warning, Lady Meranna had the good manners and social acumen as host to ensure the matter of the extraordinary events surrounding their initial meeting did not arise. The conversation was therefore not strained, ranging widely but on wholly innocent topics. Rhyanna and Tobias were charming conversationalists and put him at ease; they were also most interested in Aquilea and made a great fuss over her, to her obvious pleasure.

Seated beside Rhyanna, it was difficult to get a really good look at her. Rhiss had a certain fascination in seeing where her neck had been slashed... and healed, too, for he was still at a loss how the supposed miracle had been accomplished. And it was not just her neck that was interesting, either. Truth to tell, Rhyanna of Tormere was strikingly attractive, and proved both articulate and sensitive in conversation. Rhiss guessed she might be a year or two younger than he, in her early twenties. She was tall and slim, with flawless ivory complexion and deep blue, enchanting eyes. Her golden hair was, startlingly, quite short, not even reaching her shoulders. Evidently she had cut her hair in the intervening days since he had first seen her outside Tor Linlith. She was dressed simply but elegantly in a long white dress bearing the same red embroidery as his shirt.

Eventually, the leisurely meal ended and Tobias excused himself, laughingly saying there were accounts requiring checking before they could be submitted to the mistress of the Hall. Lady Meranna smiled, and when he had gone, she turned to Rhyanna. "My dear, I am occupied for the remainder of the afternoon, including those accounts Tobias mentioned, but why don't you take Lord Rhiss on a tour of our dear, rambling old Craggaddon Hall? There is much to see, and I think the gardens are particularly lovely now. A stroll among them in the fresh air may put some colour in his cheeks. But do not tax him too severely, and see he is allowed to rest afterwards before dinner; he has only today risen from his sick bed. By this evening, Aunt Arian should have arrived, hopefully in time to break bread with us."

Rhyanna turned an eagerly inquiring face towards Rhiss. "My lord? It would be a pleasure to be your guide this afternoon, if you wish."

Rhiss looked sideways at Meranna, wondering whether she was playing matchmaker; but her expression was guileless. It didn't really matter in the long run, he decided, and the only proper course was to capitulate gracefully.

"I would be delighted, Lady," he said, bowing. "Lead on, if you will."

Later, Rhiss would look back on that afternoon with wistful nostalgia as a last, pleasant calm before the storm. It was an idyllic day, the blue sky cloudless. The sun was warm but not unpleasant; a soft breeze prevented the heat from becoming too intense, and the air smelled fresh with growing things and the fragrance of flowers. Craggaddon Hall's gardens were every bit as magnificent as Meranna had said, and Rhyanna proved a most knowledgeable guide, pointing out plants, naming them and the places they were from — names which meant nothing to Rhiss.

When the flow of her presentation halted momentarily, Rhiss smiled and said, "And are these gardens as well known to others as they evidently are to you, Lady?"

"Everyone here is justifiably proud of them. But Tobias especially loves the gardens, and makes sure our groundskeepers tend them well."

"When I saw him prior to introductions, I thought he might be your father."

She laughed. "Oh, no, Lord Rhiss. You do not know this area or its people, do you? My father has been dead for a number of years, since I was a young girl."

"But your mother introduced Tobias as *her* overseer. Does *she* own and control this estate, then?"

"Yes," she replied, "and I understand your surprise, for I agree, it is somewhat unusual for a woman to do so alone. But when you have known my mother a while, I think you will agree she is an unusual woman. She possesses many amazing attributes, not the least a certain strength of will. My aunt is much like her, as you will see. Strong-willed sisters, the pair of them."

"And her daughters?" Rhiss smiled. "Are they also strong-willed?"

Rhyanna smiled back. "I leave that to your observations, my lord."

"Has your mother no sons, and you no brothers, then?"

Rhyanna hesitated for a moment. "Aye, she has," she admitted slowly, "but my brothers are... gone away... from here. I am sorry. It is a matter about which I would prefer not to speak."

"Of course," Rhiss replied contritely, wondering what he had stumbled upon. "I apologize for distressing you."

Rhyanna smiled. "I am not distressed, being with you. Very much the opposite. Please believe that."

They walked without speaking awhile, Rhyanna's hand on his arm, enjoying each other's company. Aquilea ambled a few paces behind, evidently content to do so. Eventually, Rhyanna broke the companionable silence.

"I noticed you gazing at me during midmeal. Were you searching for signs of your work?"

Rhiss coloured. "I was, but apologize for my clumsiness. I was under the impression I was more discreet than evidently was the case."

Rhyanna stopped and turned towards him. "Again, there is no need to apologize," she said evenly. "I am not offended, but, in fact, in awe of what you did. Look upon my neck now and behold your handiwork, if you wish."

She tilted her head up and examined the afternoon sky, surprising Rhiss with her lack of self-consciousness, although he was more shocked by the totally spontaneous and utterly irrational desire that took hold of him to lean over and kiss her alabaster neck, an impulse he hastily and sternly stifled. Instead, he contented himself with scrutinizing her smooth, flawless skin. Rhiss vividly recalled the hideous, jagged gash spanning from ear to ear, running bright scarlet with rivers of her blood, but there was absolutely nothing to suggest there had ever been so much as a scratch, much less a life-threatening wound. He wanted to reach out and touch her, but felt it prudent not to in light of his impulse a moment prior. He sighed in wonder, and she lowered her head to fasten lovely eyes upon him again.

"Can you tell me... what you recall of that afternoon?" he asked, as they resumed walking slowly along the path.

"A great deal," she replied softly, "although the memories are, understandably, somewhat fragmented. I was travelling with Mother; she was relating some strange story of Tor Linlith when all at once we were set upon by those terrible men. I was dragged from the carriage and thrown to the ground, and knew beyond doubt what was coming. I remember an arrow suddenly sprouting from the dirt mere inches from my face, and being astonished even in the midst of it. It was not there, and then it was, as if planted by magic. I heard your voice, low, clear and calm in the middle of madness." She paused, and when she resumed, her voice was slower, more hesitant. "But chaos broke out, and two soldiers went down. I was pulled to my feet, and... there was a shocking pain across my throat. Suddenly I couldn't breathe. My feet buckled and I fell. I could feel myself bleeding, choking; my eyesight failed, and I couldn't see my surroundings. It seemed as if night descended, and I felt very cold."

She stopped again and turned to gaze directly at Rhiss. "Then I recall a voice, calling. Your voice. You called my name. And—"

Rhiss interrupted. "Lady, with respect, it was not me. I said nothing to you, and even if I had, I did not know who you were. I could not have called you by name."

Rhyanna smiled. "My lord, with respect, it *was* you I heard." She held up her hand, forestalling another interruption. "I doubt not that you believe what you say, but hearing you today takes me right back. It was *you* calling. I opened my eyes, and there you were, a corona of white light behind you, so brilliant it almost hurt to look upon it. Almost, but not quite. And there was a star upon your brow. You looked at me with incredible compassion. You brought your hands down and laid them gently on my neck. There was warmth and great pressure, and I found I could breathe again. But when I sat up, you had fallen to the ground, lying as one dead. Fortunately, one of our soldiers escaped to return here and sound the alarm. More of our soldiers came and brought us back. The rest, you know." She surveyed Rhiss as he digested in silence for a moment. "You seem troubled. What is amiss?"

"Nothing, really. I am trying to make sense of something that twice defies rationality. First, as I said, I cannot recall those events quite as you do. Not that I dispute you experienced them as you say, you understand. Second, I still have no idea how I did what I apparently did. Nothing remotely like it has ever happened before. If there is anything I am troubled about, it is that."

"No, I beg you to see it for what it plainly is: a gift from the One. That is obvious. Rejoice, and be glad." She smiled again, shyly. "I know *I* am. I am glad beyond measure you were there, with your gifts, outside that ruined castle that day. Without them, I would not be here."

It was suddenly very still in the garden. Rhiss looked at her, feeling like he was drowning. Her eyes were a dazzling blue he could fall into and lose himself in. She gazed back with, clearly, the same intensity of feeling, and her gentle beauty was almost overpowering. The urge to take her in his arms and press his lips on hers came rushing, stronger than ever. He knew how utterly inappropriate that would be, but it took every ounce of effort not to yield. The moment went on endlessly, until they both read not only desire in each other's eyes, but wordless, tacit acknowledgement that it was neither the time nor the place. By silent agreement, they moved apart and began walking among the flowers and trees.

"Perhaps we should go inside now, my lord," she said quietly. "I will show you something of Craggaddon Hall, and then it might be wisest if we followed mother's instructions and gave you time to rest before dinner."

Rhiss nodded gratefully, but not without regret. "As you say, Lady."

Rhyanna looked keenly at him, apparently catching his tone. She started to speak, checked herself, then shook her head, smiling, and led him into the Hall.

The immense pile of brick, mortar, stone and wood that comprised Craggaddon Hall was no less impressive within than without. Built in the shape of an enormous 'U' and crossed at the top by a line that was the front of the building, there were rooms and passageways beyond count. Some chambers were small and intimate, others vast and impressive. Yet throughout, there was constancy of theme and a cosy, secure feeling belying the building's enormity.

Towards the tour's end, Rhyanna ushered Rhiss into a medium sized chamber, obviously a family chapel. Entering, she curtseyed and made the triple sign of blessing Rhiss now recognized. Carved wooden pews with maroon cushions filled most of the space, and at the front were beautifully fashioned choir stalls and an altar. Above the altar, strangely enough, hanging on a gold chain from the ceiling, was what could only be a Presence Lamp. Behind the altar were intricately wrought stained glass windows, letting in multi-coloured beams of daylight. Within the frames of several windows were the outlines of people, and Rhiss moved towards them, idly curious. With a shock, he realized that he recognized one of them. Turning to Rhyanna without thinking, Rhiss exclaimed, "How extraordinary! I know this one, Lady Rhyanna. Why, it's..." He was about to detail the circumstances of his meeting with Gavrilos, but the peculiar expression on Rhyanna's face caused his voice to trail off uncertainly.

"I hardly think it likely. That image is of the Exalted Herald, one of the Seven High Servants of the One. But then... of course... surely you know that," she finished hesitantly. It was more question than statement.

Mind whirling, Rhiss decided discretion was indeed the better part of valour right then. He swallowed and nodded carefully, saying nothing, and Rhyanna's expression changed to concern.

"You are pale, my lord. I apologize, for I fear I have taxed you, as my mother warned against, and now you are overtired. I had best convey you to your room, where you may rest until dinner. Aunt Arian will join us, and it would not do for you to be indisposed then. Come." She took him by the arm, gently steering him to the corridor. Rhiss allowed himself to go without protest, as there were actually several things he wished to reflect on in the privacy of his own room.

Once back, Aquilea curled up at the foot of the bed again. Rhyanna removed his dagger from his belt and had him lie on the bed while she closed the curtains against the late afternoon sun. Then she sat beside him. Seeing him relaxed, she tentatively extended a hand, gently touched his cheek, and said, "Rest now, and allow yourself to sleep this while. Then you may awaken refreshed for dinner this evening. I will come and rouse you when it is time. Until then, rest. Sleep."

Rhiss was startled by her gesture, but before he could make response, she rose swiftly, patted Aquilea softly, and went quietly to the door, passing through and closing it softly. Rhiss lay awake, his mind a confused tangle of thoughts. Rhyanna... what an attractive and enchanting girl. He was drawn to her beauty and gentle spirit, and glad beyond measure he had saved her life, even if he did not know just how he had done so. And Brother Gavrilos... was obviously far more than he had revealed during their time in the chamber. Rhiss turned both subjects over for a while, but his thoughts began to drift, and he fuzzily realized he really must have been more tired than he had known. Gradually, his breathing slowed and became more deliberate, until his mind washed into a silent sea of oblivion.

VI

BETRAYAL AND MEETING

> *"Beware the Servants of the Other. They are as coiled vipers in a cave, fleeing the Light, yet ever massed to do great evil at their Master's bidding. Be wary; be vigilant always; for while it is obvious that some are servants of the Accursed, others may be outwardly pleasing to look upon. For lo, the Other is also the Great Deceiver; and the hearts of men are too oft led easily astray."*
>
> The Book of the One, 120:4:6-8
> (Cantos 120, Chapter 4, Verses 6-8)

Swimming back to consciousness an unknown time later, Rhiss had the uneasy feeling all was not well. A low, rumbling noise was nearby, and for a fleeting moment he could not identify it. Then he realized it was Aquilea. But it was no sound of pleasure: it was deeper, ominous, full of disapproval.

He opened his eyes to find the room dimly lit from a single candle held by someone at the door. The sun had set behind the hills outside, and the evening was deep into twilight. Startled by the lateness of the hour, Rhiss turned his head to the person holding the candle, fully expecting it to be Rhyanna. But to his surprise, and, truth be told, disappointment, it was Dalys. At once, the cause of Aquilea's displeasure was obvious.

Rhiss yawned, sat up, and stretched. Dalys made no move to enter, but kept a wary eye on Aquilea, who regarded him balefully, continuing her bubbling discontent. She was still at the foot of the bed, but as Rhiss sat up she leaped lightly to the floor, watching Dalys keenly.

"What is it, Dalys? Where is Lady Rhyanna? She said she would awaken me when it was time for dinner. Is it not rather late? We are well into evening."

Dalys bobbed his head quickly. "A thousand pardons, m'lord," he said, actually attempting to sound regretful without much sincerity. "Lady Rhyanna has been detained by a... pressing matter. She apologizes for the hour, sir, and not coming herself, but the meal will be ready shortly, and she asked me to come and convey you to dinner."

Rhiss swung his legs over the side of the bed and stood. Something was still amiss, but he could not put his finger on anything specific. However, it spoke volumes that Aquilea was suspicious. Rhiss fervently wished he could put Dalys off while he confirmed the servant's account, but there was no reasonable way to do that. And it was just possible his suspicions were baseless, with all indeed as the man said.

"Right, then," Rhiss said slowly. "We can go more or less straight away. Give me a moment." He ran a hand through his hair, then took his dagger and began putting his belt on.

"Oh, you won't need that, m'lord," said Dalys brightly. "You can leave it here. In fact, probably better if you did, begging your pardon. Protocol and all, you know. Wouldn't do, bringing a weapon to a formal dinner."

Rhiss looked at the man with narrowed eyes; the suggestion was simultaneously odd and brazen, coming from a mere servant. "Thank you for the advice, Dalys," he said neutrally. "But I think I'll wear it, just the same."

Dalys tried smiling, but it was a half-hearted affair lacking warmth. "As you wish, m'lord. I apologize if I overstepped myself, just thought I'd make the suggestion. Oh, another thing... Lady Rhyanna *did* ask if you would wear your..." he indicated the Circlet, lying on its cushion, "...jewellery, if you would. She would be most pleased to see it on you."

"Very well." Rhiss couldn't imagine why Rhyanna would make such a request, but he finished donning his belt, the dagger in its scabbard, and lifted the Circlet off its cushion, carefully placing it on his head. Dalys nodded approvingly, then indicated Aquilea with his free hand.

"One final thing, m'lord: Lady Rhyanna, uh... specified the... the animal should remain here. Some of the guests at table tonight would feel unsettled having it there. She knew you'd understand." Dalys either would not or could not meet Rhiss' gaze, and dropped his eyes.

Rhiss stared. That did not ring true at all, given Rhyanna's demonstrated, obvious affection for Aquilea. His misgivings increased. Something was definitely wrong, very wrong indeed, although he still could not say precisely what, and could hardly refuse to accompany the servant over mere vague unease.

Dalys backed into the corridor, looked up, and actually did smile. This struck the falsest note yet, but Rhiss gave no outward sign of his suspicions, and motioned Aquilea to remain. She was plainly as unhappy with that as Rhiss, but he was relieved to see her reluctantly settle back onto the bed as he followed Dalys from the room. The door closed, and Rhiss said pleasantly, deliberately keeping his tone light, "Well, then, lead on, Dalys. I'm hungry once again, and more than ready for dinner. Will many join us?"

"Oh, no, sir, just a small gathering, I should think." The old man was already on the move.

Even though he had only been once to the dining hall from his room, Rhiss became aware after several moments that Dalys had deviated from the earlier route, heading in a different direction altogether.

"Dalys?" he called to the servant's retreating back. "This isn't the way we went this afternoon. Where are we going?"

"I thought I would... take you directly to Lady Rhyanna, m'lord, and you could proceed together. She's in the entry hall."

Rhiss vaguely recalled Rhyanna taking him through a large, open space, impressively majestic as befitted the place where visitors made their first entry into Craggaddon Hall. A great, wide, sweeping stone staircase leading from the main floor to the second was a chief feature, one that no doubt lent itself to grand theatrical entrances and exits. But Rhiss could not fathom why Rhyanna would be there, unless... perhaps her aunt had arrived, and she had gone to greet her. Aye, that was plausible. He shrugged and continued following Dalys.

Proceeding along the corridor, they passed a room whose door was open, unlike most. As they walked by, Dalys stopped dead in his tracks and straightened, as though addressed by someone. Rhiss nearly bumped into him. "Dalys? What is it?"

Strangely, Dalys ignored Rhiss completely. He turned his head to the open door and muttered, "The Other take her! What can *she* want?" Then he jumped, as if hearing a voice again, although Rhiss heard nothing. "All right, woman, all right, I'm coming!" Dalys snapped. "Hold your nagging tongue, you miserable old shrew!" He went through, closing the door heavily behind him.

Rhiss stood, baffled. What was *that* about? Was he going deaf, or had Dalys lost his mind? Should he follow the servant into the room and ascertain what was happening?

Before he could move, however, another door opened on the corridor's opposite side some distance back. Rhiss automatically turned to look, frowning at the sight.

It was a tall, armed fighting man, an officer by his bearing, not a common soldier. Rhiss assumed it was one of the Hall's household soldiers, although the man was cloaked and hooded in a mantle of grey. Consequently, it was difficult to see the face, but a sword's outline was clearly visible beneath his cloak. He strode along easily and was abreast of Rhiss within moments.

"Good evening, Lord Rhissan," he murmured, inclining his head courteously as he passed. Rhiss did not recognize the soldier, and blinked in confusion, wondering how the man knew him. Ten paces beyond Rhiss, the figure paused, then turned. As he did, the cloak swirled open slightly, revealing a brief, vertical flash of scarlet on the white of the man's tunic. Rhiss' confusion increased: Craggaddon Hall household troops wore Lincoln green with the Tormere badge; the man was obviously not one of them.

"My lord?" asked the man, evidently coming to a decision, throwing back his hood. He was dark-haired with gleaming eyes, handsome with a neatly trimmed goatee. "Perhaps I may be of assistance. You seem... bereft and alone."

"I... I am, sir," stammered Rhiss. "That is, I await a servant who seems... momentarily preoccupied."

The man flicked a grimly amused glance at the door where Dalys had vanished. "I daresay. However, his preoccupation will not last long, so I will not tarry." He fixed Rhiss with a penetrating stare, nodding. "Your impressions of that one are not in error. Be wary, but also remember you are not alone in what comes."

"'What comes?'" repeated Rhiss suspiciously. "What do you mean? Do you live here? I don't recognize you."

The man shook his head, and smiled coldly. "I am merely a guest... like yourself. A fellow traveller—" he raised an eyebrow "—from an unexpected quarter, you might say." He bowed slightly. "Lord Tariel, at your service. I must go, but I will be nearby. Call, if need arise."

"'Need—?'" Rhiss repeated again, but there was a sudden noise and he turned, startled. The door swung wide and Dalys came slowly through, eyes glassy and unfocused. Rhiss stared and waved a hand in front of the servant, but Dalys seemed unaware of his surroundings. Rhiss turned back to Lord Tariel, but the hall was empty. He growled an oath, pushing past Dalys to peer into the chamber. It was a small sitting room, quite empty, contents orderly and undisturbed. "There is something *very* peculiar going on," muttered Rhiss. He returned to the corridor to find Dalys blinking and looking around.

"Oh, *there* you are, m'lord. Don't wander off, if you please. Stay with me."

Minutes later, they arrived at the top of the entry hall staircase. It was brightly lit with torches, and Rhiss could indeed see a knot of people clustered on the ground floor, but Rhyanna did not appear to be among them. Then he was descending the staircase, several paces behind Dalys, footsteps echoing in the silence which fell as they were noticed.

The assemblage — all armed men in black and silver with an insignia not immediately clear, Rhiss noted with misgiving — drew apart left and right in two groups, leaving one man alone in the centre. Dalys broke away, and confused, Rhiss halted a dozen steps behind. It was to the man in the centre that Dalys skittered like a crab, falling to his knees. "Here is the one I spoke of, Master. I have brought him as instructed. He is the one you want," he said hoarsely, and Rhiss could see the servant trembling, although whether from fear, excitement, or something else altogether, it was impossible to tell.

"Aye. You have done well, Dalys," said the man absently in a voice nastily unctuous. But he reserved his attention for Rhiss, carefully studying him. Rhiss stood silently on the bottom step, returning the scrutiny. The man was dark haired, average height, but there was something compelling about him, the aura of a person accustomed to being obeyed. There was something strangely unpleasant about his eyes, but from twenty feet away, it was not possible to ascertain what it was. Their mutual inspections were suddenly interrupted by Dalys, too frantically impatient to remain silent. Wringing his hands, he entreated the man.

"What of my reward? Long have I faithfully watched this household. Finding this man is exactly what you commanded—"

His whining protestation was cut off in mid-sentence. The dark man, without even a glance, gestured dismissively with his left hand, a careless flick one would make when bothered by an irritating insect. Dalys was slammed by an unseen force to a stone pillar fifteen feet away and remained pinned there, feet dangling a yard off the ground, eyes bulging in terror as he tried unsuccessfully to scream. There was a ripple of unease among the assemblage, instantly silenced by another gesture from the man. Without turning his head or taking his strange eyes from Rhiss, the man said tonelessly, "I grow weary of your snivelling demands, Dalys. You forget yourself. Understand this: you have been a useful tool, but a tool is all you are, and I am occupied now. Dare to interrupt my thoughts again, and it will be the last error in judgement you ever make."

Leaving the unfortunate Dalys writhing silently on the pillar like a moth impaled on an invisible spike, the man stepped several paces forward, and said softly, contemptuously, "Well; the Circlet of Araxis reappears at last. But not boldly into the Light. Timidly, in a remote country house. So if it wishes to surface in the shadows, I say bravo. I say away with the light. Let the shadows grow." He waved his hand again, and while the torches did not die, the illumination they provided diminished somehow, and as the darkness grew, shadows in the hall increased. A renewed murmuring came from the assembled soldiers and a thrill of fear shot through Rhiss. The man ignored the whispering and continued, almost musing to himself. "So this is the little lordling whose foretold coming has aroused such intense interest. Gavrilos must grow desperate indeed if this is the best he can muster. Truly pathetic." He snorted and addressed Rhiss. "You've been very busy, haven't you, boy? Meddling in things that are none of your concern? Disrupting the natural order of things? Why, I am even given to understand you are responsible for bringing down one of my little pets a day or two ago. I find that alone extremely *vexing*. Tell me, boy: what is your name?"

Heart hammering, Rhiss realized this was grave trouble, much worse than the day outside Tor Linlith. This man, he sensed, was nothing like the Sovereign's Men in the meadow. This man was intelligent, dangerous, malignant, and obviously possessed terrifying abilities. If the frightful monsters responsible for the death of Aquilea's mother actually belonged to him, were controlled by him... then this was far beyond any trouble imaginable. It was... potentially lethal. Rhiss licked dry lips, glancing around. The other men on the main floor, eight all told, fanned out in a semicircle around Rhiss and the man, four to a side. Rhiss wondered about turning tail and retreating up the staircase, but a sudden rustling behind quickly made him turn his head to cast a wary glance up the stairs. Four more men clad in black and silver materialized from the shadows at the top of the staircase, ranged on the stairs behind, cutting off escape that way.

The smoothly venomous voice sounded again. "Well, boy? You *do* have a name, don't you? Or has fear silenced you?"

Rhiss turned to face the man, took a deep breath, worked deliberately to keep voice low and calmly insolent as he answered. "I have a name, sir. Do you? Or is it your habit to break into honest peoples' homes at night like a cowardly, nameless brigand and waylay guests?"

Several soldiers gasped; one strode forward angrily. "Impudent cub! You cannot speak thus to the Lord Mal—"

The man interrupted. "Peace, Feras," he said, quietly but coldly. "I need no one to speak *my* name for me. I answer for myself." He looked at Rhiss and smiled derisively.

"You are unaware who I am? Know me, then: I am Maldeus of Angramor, Chief Counsellor to our Most Gracious Sovereign. Now, one last time, say *your* name; and I advise you to take care answering. A little subservience might be in order."

"Rhissan, son of Tovan," replied Rhiss, trying to project confidence he did not feel. The man obviously served the Usurper who had denied the rightful king his throne. But it was vital to keep the man talking; Rhiss needed time to come up with a plan — any plan. "Although you already seem to know me. What do you want, Maldeus of Angramor? Why put a spy in this house to report my presence? What am I to you?"

"Much," said Maldeus coldly, for all to hear, turning to the men around. "This whelp preaches sedition. He advocates the overthrow of the Crown, therefore committing treason against your Sovereign. His life is forfeit." Then, lowering his voice, he added, "But above all else, boy, you are a threat to be eliminated at once, before you reach your full potential and do what you were sent to do. I have seen..."

Rhiss had heard enough. Obviously, keeping Maldeus talking was no successful strategy. There would be no negotiating with this man — his mind was already set on murder. Frustrated, Rhiss felt his course of action dictated. What could he do? Again, force was the only option — and this time, vastly outnumbered by soldiers with superior weaponry, the odds were heavily against him. Perhaps he could bluff long enough for help to arrive. Rhiss wanted to believe his absence from dinner would be noticed, and he hoped it would be sooner than later.

He thought of Aquilea back in their room. *If only you were here!* he thought fervently. It was obvious why Dalys had deceived him into leaving the gryphon behind: her razor sharp beak and talons would go far towards redressing the tactical imbalance. Without hope, but in one quick, sure movement, he swept his dagger from its sheath, and holding it before him, swivelled to meet threats before and behind. "Gentlemen, I warn you, stay back," he called. "I will harm any man coming within reach."

In response, a dozen blades rasped against scabbards. "Put that plaything down, boy," Maldeus said disdainfully. "Futile heroics will avail nothing. Your life hangs by a thread. If I command it, you will be cut down within a heartbeat. Thirteen to one are poor odds. You are alone." He smiled unpleasantly and licked his lips. "But I have a mind to show these fellows some entertainment. Perhaps your death is not immediately necessary. You may start by getting down on your knees and begging for mercy. Kneel to me, Rhissan, son of Tovan. Who knows? I might even be persuaded to spare your life for a time, at least. What say you, little lordling?"

Rhiss felt despair. The bleak reality was only too clear: he was outnumbered, armed with a completely inadequate weapon. There was to be no miraculous rescue, it seemed. Was this really how it would end? Before even beginning? How could a meaningless death like this be of any assistance to that unknown, displaced king? Rhiss bowed his head, utterly desolate; where was the mysterious soldier who had spoken in the corridor minutes ago? As he thought that, the words of Brother Gavrilos came unbidden: *"Remember the Light when the Darkness seems to close in about you... all things are possible, and help may often come from the most unexpected quarters."* Unexpected quarters. Rhiss suddenly realized: what had Tariel said minutes ago? *"A fellow traveller... from an unexpected quarter."* Rhiss raised his head and whispered softly, "Lord Tariel... I have need of you."

Looking around, Rhiss realized in startled hope there was a glowing light emanating... from *his own person*. He puzzled over it, then understood: he dared not remove it to check, but the Circlet of Araxis on his brow radiated a pure, cold, clear white light, pushing back the shadows, palely illuminating those around him. It occurred to Rhiss that above all, he must have faith — in Gavrilos, that his just cause would not be for naught, in this Tariel, who had promised aid, and above everything else, faith in the One. Rhiss thought he saw a flicker of uncertainty in several soldiers' eyes, and felt his heart grow a little lighter. He could almost feel an undercurrent of courage, circulating through the hall like a fresh breeze. In doubt, there is freedom, he thought. He turned again to face the figure waiting expectantly.

"No," he said, clearly audible.

Maldeus looked comically surprised. It was obviously not the answer he expected. "What? What do you mean, boy?"

"I will not kneel for your sport, Maldeus of Angramor — even for my life. At any rate, if you support the Usurper, I know what you stand for, and you are faithless. Your promises are worthless. I will not yield." He smiled, realizing what he had said. "And in spite of what you say, I am *not* alone."

One of the soldiers challenged him. "Do you not fear the greater numbers and weapons ranged against you?"

It was a strange question. Curious, Rhiss turned and tried to make out the man's face, but it was hidden in shadow. "I do," he replied quietly. "And I *am* afraid, I freely admit. Terrified, in fact. But I labour in a noble cause: the restoration of the true king, and I believe the One will not allow an ignominious death in mockery of such a cause." He looked around. "Is this justice?" he said, raising his voice to ensure all heard. "Creeping stealthily under cover of darkness, breaking into an innocent house to murder a man who has done no wrong, but seeks only the rightful king on the throne? Maldeus of Angramor supports one not entitled to wear the crown."

"What do *you* know of kings or who rightfully sits on the throne?" called another soldier, and Rhiss wondered if his words were making an impression. But his knowledge of the king was sketchy, based only on what Gavrilos had said, so he must speak carefully. Revealing his true ignorance of the whole story could lose him the small measure of support he now felt might be swinging to him.

"I know a true king is in Arrinor, even now; my life stands pledged to see him regain his rightful throne," Rhiss replied clearly. Maldeus snorted contemptuously.

The man who had asked Rhiss about fear looked at his comrades ranged on the stairs. "I have heard tell what this man speaks of, as have we all. It is whispered through the land that the Sovereign now on the Crystal Throne is there unjustly. And there are many still alive who recall events that took place when came the death of the old King." Maldeus looked up sharply, but the soldier continued. "I tell you, this man standing outnumbered speaks truth. He fears for his life — but will not beg for it. He does not cringe and whine. He speaks of justice. He will not give sport to those who would take his life. All that speaks of courage, and honour." He lowered his sword. "I say we have been misled. It is time to redress wrongs already committed, and those about to be."

Maldeus had been silent throughout this speech, but now angrily raised his hand at the soldier. A jet of orange flame erupted, roaring across the hall, and the man was instantly enveloped in a writhing, towering pillar of liquid fire that held him motionless. Oddly, no sound emanated from within the flames. The remaining soldiers fell to their knees, petrified, and Rhiss felt his blood turn to ice.

Eyes narrowing dangerously, Maldeus said softly, "I have wasted time enough." He gestured at Dalys. "Obviously, the spectacle of that wretch was not lesson enough." He glared around at the soldiers, none of whom dared meet his eyes. "Is there any other witless fool who disputes my will and wishes to be sent to the Shadows of the Other?"

The only sound was the flames crackling, and Maldeus smiled with satisfaction. "Very well, then. Back to the task at hand." He turned to Rhiss. "You, boy—"

A sudden cry interrupted him, and Maldeus spun around. A soldier extended a shaking hand, pointing at the unfortunate man being burned alive.

Something was happening to the flames: they went from orange to amber to white, before parting as though tent flaps were drawn aside, and the soldier stepped casually from them, quite unscathed. Rhiss gasped in recognition: it was the man who called himself Lord Tariel. Behind, the fires of Maldeus sputtered, flickered, and died.

"Good evening, Maldeus," said Tariel softly. "When we know each other as we do, introductions seem so unnecessary, don't you agree? And in answer to your question, *I* dispute your will. Oh, and I do not intend to be sent *anywhere* by you, least of all to the Shadows of the Other."

Rhiss darted a glance at Maldeus, whose face, incredibly, had paled visibly to the colour of whey. Was Maldeus afraid? Obviously he was well acquainted with the composed figure standing unharmed. There was a moment of complete silence, broken only as Maldeus spoke in a low-pitched, furious voice. "Why are you here? How *dare* you come?"

The retort was immediate. "I dare much in the face of your cowardice. I restore balance to a situation urgently requiring it." Not taking his eyes from Maldeus, Tariel pointed at Rhiss. "As you know, he is yet unready for this confrontation, and I will not permit you to force it as you would wish."

"So you would have him cower behind you like a cringing child," snarled Maldeus.

"He has not cowered," came the calm contradiction. "He stood before you, showing courage and spirit, even though there is much he is yet unaware of. The boy is worthy of my support. If there is cowardice here, it is yours alone, attempting this now."

"Gavrilos goes too far in sending you!" raged Maldeus.

"He did not send me. Nor is he privy to my plans," Tariel responded quietly. "I do not answer to him, as well you know."

Maldeus glared disbelievingly. The exchange might have gone on longer, but a sudden commotion at the stairs' far end interrupted. With a harsh scream, Aquilea leapt into the hall and took flight, alighting beside Rhiss, eyes furiously incandescent. Startled but pleased beyond all hope, Rhiss glanced at her, saying in a low voice, "Aquilea, how...? But welcome! Did you hear me?" In response, she butted her head affectionately against his leg, emitting her peculiar rumbling sound. There was alarm among the soldiers; one asked, "Whence came this beast?"

"She is my companion," replied Rhiss swiftly, "and most welcome, for she does much to even the odds here."

"She answers to you... will do your bidding?" queried another disbelievingly.

"Well... aye," Rhiss said, bemused that Aquilea's presence should cause so much comment.

Tariel called out, voice overriding the whisperings. "Gentlemen, I call you to witness: you have been sorely misled. This young man here," he gestured at Rhiss, "speaks truth. The current Sovereign wrested the Crystal Throne away from the rightful King, aided and abetted by this monstrous creature." He motioned at Maldeus. "I also call on you to right the wrong perpetrated this night. Abandon your support for the forces of Darkness, seeking forgiveness in the truth of Light."

For an endless moment, no one moved as men waited to see which way things would go. Then several on the stairs slowly lowered their swords. Another glanced around. "Lord Maldeus," he called, "As you can see, others like this not, and will support neither this travesty nor you. The odds have changed, sir, and are not as lopsided as before, even with your... abilities."

At this, a man at the base of the stairs strode to Rhiss, knelt, and offered his sword, hilt first. "My lord, I will join you."

Rhiss felt his heart leap, but gravely sheathed his knife, accepted the man's sword, and held it at the ready, looking directly at Maldeus. A crystalline moment of understanding passed between them; incredibly, in the space of minutes, momentum had passed from invader to intended victim.

Standing to the side, Tariel's eyebrow quirked upwards, and the merest hint of a smirk formed on his lips. "It would seem, my lord, you have not been as thorough in choosing your troops as you perhaps should have been."

"You may have snatched this encounter away," hissed Maldeus at Tariel, "but this is far from over!" He looked at Rhiss, hatred in those strange eyes. "And you, boy, look to our next meeting!"

With a snarl, he gestured at the unfortunate Dalys, who careened away from the stone pillar towards Rhiss. Soldiers rushed forward to shield him, taking the main force of the blow as the servant's body crashed headlong into them, but everyone, including Rhiss, went sprawling in a confused and tangled heap. Rhiss was knocked backwards onto the stairs by the force of the collision, where he banged into Aquilea, who screeched her alarm. Maldeus used the moment of confusion to signal his remaining loyal troops to withdraw. A dazzling flash of ruby light temporarily blinded those remaining, and before anyone could react, much less give chase, Maldeus and his remaining troops turned in a swirl of cloaks and disappeared through the huge doors into the night.

Those left behind quickly disentangled themselves, ready to pursue. Dazed, Rhiss rose to his feet to accompany them, first returning the soldier's sword. He looked around for Tariel, but the knight was nowhere to be seen. Rhiss frowned and swiftly counted. The number was what it should be, but Tariel was, impossibly, not among them.

Rhiss stepped over the prone body of Dalys: it was more important to give chase to Maldeus. He gestured, and they all clattered towards the doors. But as they crossed the threshold, a deep voice in the hall called strongly, "Hold!"

The entire contingent froze, heads whipping around to see who had given the order. Rhiss turned with the rest, reaching for his dagger. Then he stopped as he saw Meranna and Rhyanna accompanying Craggaddon Hall household soldiers. They noted Maldeus' men behind Rhiss, and seeing what they obviously thought was a kidnapping in progress, fanned out, menacing with their weapons in an ironic reversal of the situation minutes prior.

"Drop your weapons, scum!" called the household troops' leader. "Lord Rhiss! You may step away from that murderous rabble. You are safe now."

Rhiss smiled wryly, holding up a placating hand. "You are mistaken, sir," he replied easily. "These... ah... gentlemen are not abducting me. Far from it. In fact, they have seen the error of their ways, and have elected to join us. They were assisting me to pursue an uninvited guest when you intervened. Maldeus of Angramor has been here... and tried to murder me."

Rhiss noted curiously that there was instant agitation among all present at the name. Some actually made the three-fold sign of blessing; others made an odd gesture he had not seen before, holding the three middle fingers of their left hands splayed before their faces and muttering something too softly to hear.

From among them, an older woman in long, flowing robes strode forward. She was tall and slim, but exuded a palpable mantle of leadership. Her face was lean and spare, not truly attractive in a physical sense, but graceful and serene. Her long hair, braided in the back, was a dark brown shot through with silver. The resemblance to Meranna was unmistakable.

"Hold, gentlemen," she said clearly. "There is no need to invoke the protection of the One. I am sure we will have the full story in good time. It seems the assistance we thought Lord Rhiss in need of was not required, after all. But then, perhaps I should not be surprised, hearing his exploits of recent days. Suborning the Royal Counsellor's soldiers would appear no great task for the champion of Tor Linlith."

Rhiss moved towards her, but Meranna quickly intervened, stepping between them. "Lord Rhiss, I have the honour to present my sister, Seir-onna Arian, of the Order of the Militant Castellar Servanthood. You are both well met, and I am pleased you can acquaint yourselves at last."

Arian bowed her head, touching the three fingers of her right hand to her chest. Rhiss was surprised. When he had been told Meranna's sister was a priest, a mental image had formed of a stooped, overweight, scholarly old woman, not someone resembling a queen herself. Wondering whether he made the socially correct response, and flushing slightly in consequence, Rhiss returned the gesture. As he lifted his head, he was reassured that Meranna smiled in approval.

"Come," she said, "leave your new allies in the care of our household soldiers, and you can tell all. We are most anxious to know how the Royal Counsellor obtained admittance, and why. It is a tale I—"

Rhiss realized belatedly that he knew how Maldeus had gained entry, and held up a hand to forestall her. "My lady, I beg your pardon," he said breathlessly, "but you have reminded me of he who assisted the Royal Counsellor this evening, paying a high price in consequence. Accompany me." He ran to the stairs.

Rhiss knelt on the third step beside the broken body of Dalys; Meranna, Rhyanna and Arian were close behind, and he gave them a brief account. "I fear Dalys was rather thrown about by the Counsellor, and is badly hurt. Perhaps you should summon a physician?"

Meranna shook her head slowly. "I do not think this one has even the few minutes left it would take," she replied, kneeling beside Dalys. Shaking her head disbelievingly, she put a hand to his forehead, sighing. "And you, Dalys?" she murmured sadly. "You betray this House after so many years' service? I would have trusted you with my life once; it grieves me to see how you repay that trust."

Dalys gasped and moaned. He opened his eyes, and licked his lips. "M'lady, I am sorry," he croaked. "I was misled by envy and greed. Forgive me."

"Forgive you?" she repeated. "You must first tell me what you have done, before I can forgive deeds committed."

"I was deceived," Dalys managed painfully. "I was approached, months ago, by the Royal Counsellor's agents. Truly, they had bewitching tongues of honey, Lady... said all my service had not been rewarded as it should, but they knew well how to reward faithful conduct. They offered much to be their eyes and ears in this Hall. Gold... and..."

"And what?" said Lady Meranna softly. "Tell all, for it is clear your time draws to a close. The One will not look kindly on prevaricating now when you stand in judgement a short time hence. It is time for complete honesty."

"The Lady Rhyanna," replied Dalys, almost inaudibly. Behind Rhiss, Rhyanna gasped, hands flying to her mouth as she flushed.

Lady Meranna nodded grimly. "I suspected as much. I have seen the way you eyed my daughter of late. Continue. What, precisely, were they expecting to find? This Hall has ever been a loyal servant of the Crown in word and deed at least, if not in thought."

Dalys groaned and stiffened. Rhyanna turned to Meranna, and said, in a low voice, "Mother, perhaps Lord Rhiss can do what he did for me. I am not sure whether —"

A thrill of panic ran through Rhiss, but Dalys clutched at Meranna's sleeve with a bony hand. "No, my lady," he said through clenched teeth. "I don't wish it, don't deserve it. I am punished for my transgressions. I wish only to tell my tale and make contrition before being summoned by the One."

Meranna said neutrally, "Very well, Dalys. If that is what you desire, we respect your wish." Rhiss felt shamed relief wash over him, and almost missed Meranna's next question. "Now, I ask again: what were they looking to find?"

"Lord Rhiss," Dalys replied faintly. As they looked at him, astonished, he shook his head slightly, grimacing with the pain it caused, and corrected himself. "Not by name, m'lady, but someone matching his description: appearing from nowhere, I was told, likely accompanied by strange happenings." He stopped and coughed. "Also, to look for someone wearing a circlet with a wondrous stone... a stone that moved and shifted colours within its depths. That would be a dead giveaway. And the man might have unusual abilities. When you brought Lord Rhiss here those few days ago, the Hall was full of all manner of rumours about events at Tor Linlith. I told my contact in the village that it might be what they sought. Then today, when I heard you talking to Lord Rhiss about what he had done — healed the Lady Rhyanna — I knew that was it. Gave me a fair turn, it did. So I sent word."

"To whom?" asked Meranna urgently, as Dalys closed his eyes.

Skin pale and waxy, breathing increasingly laboured, Dalys did not answer immediately. Then he said painfully, "I always went myself — no one I could trust. It was in the village. The Boar's Head Inn. The tap room. A tall man, always cloaked. I never saw his face. Nasty voice. At first, I just knew him by the silver brooch he wore on his cloak. A skeletal hand, holding a dagger. Later, I knew him because... well, I knew him. He was always alone. No one else talked to him. You wouldn't want to. He didn't invite conversation."

"Why did they seek me?" asked Rhiss quietly. "How would they even know I was coming? I didn't know myself until days ago. There's more to this than you tell us."

Dalys tried to shrug, but the effort cost him. Beads of sweat stood out on his forehead. "M'lord, I swear I've told all I know," he whispered harshly. "They didn't tell the why or the how. They just said —" He broke off, and shivered. "Why is it so cold?" he said, peering into the distance behind Rhiss. "Who is behind you?"

Startled, they swiftly turned. No one was there, and Rhiss felt the hairs on the back of his neck rise.

"What do you mean?" asked Meranna intensely. "What do you see?"

"A man," said Dalys slowly, "dressed all in white. He has a star on his brow, like Lord Rhiss, and stands behind him, a hand on his shoulder. He—" Dalys suddenly stiffened, and his eyes glazed. He exhaled softly, but there was no intake of breath. Meranna reached out and closed the staring eyes, while Rhiss shivered and glanced uneasily at his shoulder, wondering who or what had been there.

"Well," Meranna said meditatively, "that is that. We have learned several things, but wanted to know more. That is often the way of it." Then she seemed to realize where she was, and straightened. "Our brother has gone to the One," she said loudly, and the group performed the benediction. "He was guilty of treachery, but acknowledged that. Before he died, he repented of the evil he had done. May the One grant him grace in his time of judgement." She turned to the household soldiers standing a short way off, and motioned them to pick up the corpse. "Take the body and prepare it for the Fire of Cleansing." As they did so, silently carrying it away, Rhiss noted it was evidently not only animals who underwent the Fire, and wondered how long before the body was consumed; at least long enough to "prepare" it, obviously.

Meranna signalled to other soldiers of the Hall to take Maldeus' men in hand, and they all trooped out slowly. Finally, there was only Meranna, Rhyanna, Arian, Rhiss and Aquilea left, and Meranna sighed.

"Well," she said again, "a tragic evening, and no mistake. The treachery of Dalys grieves me greatly. But Tobias waits in the dining hall, likely fretting over the meal slowly going cold. Let us return. No doubt you are all famished." She turned to Rhiss and frowned. "I think — are you are all right?"

Rhiss realized he was trembling all over as reaction set in. He felt nauseous and shook his head. "It has been eventful, Lady. It belatedly dawns on me that I have just had a very narrow escape. I could not eat anything right now, in truth, but would be glad of something hot to drink."

Meranna nodded, smiling sympathetically. "Of course. You have had an exceedingly strange encounter, with nearly fatal consequences. You have not experienced anything like it, I take it?"

Rhiss grimaced. "If you mean complete strangers showing up with premeditated murder in their hearts... no."

"You are holding up well, then. Come, let us go. We need to consider and discuss what has happened tonight, and why. The ramifications of Maldeus spying on us are many, and there is much more that must be examined in light of what has taken place." She turned and walked down the stairs before proceeding through an arch and into a hallway with Arian at her side, Rhyanna and Rhiss behind. Aquilea brought up the rear.

Rhyanna put her hand on Rhiss' arm as she had done in the garden earlier. "I am immensely relieved you were not hurt or killed, my lord," she said quietly to Rhiss as they walked. "Rushing into the entry hall and seeing the soldiers, I feared for your life."

"How did you know I was in peril, and needed aid?"

"I went to fetch you, but your room was empty and the door open, so I swiftly returned to the hall, and related what I had found. We wondered where you were, and began searching. Then, as Mother and Aunt Arian summoned Household Guards, both heard Aquilea cry out nearby. She sounded enraged, so they came immediately."

"I see," said Rhiss absently, his mind on another question, one he did not speak aloud: they had responded to Aquilea's cry; but how had *she* known of his need? Had she somehow heard his thoughts? Could Aquilea sense men's thoughts... his in particular?

His train of thought was interrupted by their arrival at the dining hall. As they caught up, Arian was speaking to Meranna. "Sister, I wish to talk with the men who were with Maldeus, and gather their impressions before I eat. There is much of substance that occurred here today and the last several days, and it is vital to obtain as much information as possible. I will be only a little while, and will rejoin you presently."

"Arian, no," objected Meranna, clearly put out. "Attend first to family. Eat with us and talk to those men afterwards, if you feel it essential. This is your first visit in months."

Arian smiled. "This is important, little sister. I must do it now. But I will not be long, so do not eat all the venison!"

She turned and strode off. Meranna sighed in exasperation and motioned Rhiss and Rhyanna to chairs at the same table where they had eaten earlier. Tobias stood, looking at them expectantly. "We will begin, Tobias," Meranna said resignedly. "Save some for my stubborn sister; she will join us presently. So she says, at any rate."

Although a close call with death had blunted his appetite, the mulled wine given Rhiss soothed his stomach, and two of his companions were the picture of conviviality. Lady Meranna, however, was also visibly unsettled by the night's events. Rhiss noticed, as did obviously the others. He was unsure whether to raise the matter, but Rhyanna was not as reticent. "Mother," she said quietly during a lull in the conversation, "what troubles you? For something is plainly wrong. Will you share your concerns?"

Meranna smiled at her daughter, but it was strained. "Bless you for noticing, my dear. But I should not bring my burdens to place them before you."

Rhyanna made an impatient gesture with one hand. "Oh, come, Mother. Look around. I am no child, and you always say I need to learn the managing of a large household. Tobias is the senior servant on the entire estate. And Lord Rhiss has been our saviour twice these last few days. If you cannot confide in us, then in whom can you? Share your thoughts, I beg you. What is it?"

Meranna smiled again, this time more easily as she looked fondly at her daughter. "Very well, stubborn child, relax your tongue." She sighed. "As you may surmise, it is this evening that has me so concerned. In particular, two things alarm me." She looked at each of them. "First is the fact that Maldeus has had a spy in this household, possibly for a very long time. That he felt the need — that he clearly anticipated needing eyes and ears in this Hall, reporting the arrival of Lord Rhiss — is most unsettling. I ask myself: why would he expect Lord Rhiss? And why would he feel that arrival so urgent a threat that he himself would come and deal so precipitously with it?"

"But he could not have known I was coming," interjected Rhiss. "As I said, I myself did not know I would be here until several days ago. There is no possible way he could have known."

"You saw but the merest hint of Maldeus' abilities this evening," Meranna replied soberly. "He has many disquieting skills and powers, some of which are best left undescribed in present company. I believe you when you say you made the choice to come here only recently; but rest assured also, somehow or other, he knew. He was aware you would be at this Hall. Perhaps he did not know precisely when — after all, Dalys evidently spied for him for months — *but he knew you would come.* And as I said, why would he feel compelled to travel here quickly and deal with you as he did? To come so hastily, with only a small contingent of soldiers, some of whose loyalty was obviously, in hindsight, questionable... this is not the Sovereign's Counsellor I thought I knew. It speaks of ill-planned haste and agitation. It even speaks of... fear. While meaning no offence, Lord Rhiss, who are you to awaken such fear within him who never before has moved so speedily and without apparent plan? I must say, I do wonder mightily at the implications."

Rhyanna broke in. "Your second concern, Mother?"

"Simply this, child: the presence of Maldeus this evening. He fled with the remainder of his men when the situation left his control, but he knows Lord Rhiss is here. Would not his obvious course be to return as soon as possible with more men, more *reliable* men, and remedy his failure?"

Rhiss looked stricken and began rising. "You're absolutely right. I have put you all in danger and must leave immediately. I will gather my belongings and be off before I cause any more trouble."

Rhyanna made a soft, pained cry, also rising, but Meranna forestalled them, raising a hand firmly. "Peace, both of you. Sit, and let us think this through carefully. We will not make the same sort of hurriedly panicked decision that cost our enemy his easy victory." She sat, staring silently into space for several long moments. Finally, she stirred. "We may be able to determine a course of action to extricate ourselves from this quagmire, although not without cost, I fear. But I must first consult my sister. Let us hope her legendary appetite compels her to rejoin us at table soon."

She would say nothing further, although Rhyanna pressed her more than once. Clearly, Meranna was determined to discuss her idea only with Arian; however, they discussed the evening at length. But Arian did not join them, although they lingered some time over the meal and the sweets afterwards. Eventually, Tobias yawned hugely, prompting Rhiss to do the same, his eyelids getting heavy. Meranna noticed and stood, and they did likewise.

"My dears," she said, smiling ruefully, "it is regrettably plain that my boorish sister has not seen fit to join us. Obviously, she feels holding conversation with a group of common soldiers is more important than spending time with loved ones, so I think it meet we bid each other good night. It has been a most exciting day. I will try to locate my sister before I sleep. Rhyanna, please accompany me to my chamber. Tobias, would you escort our honoured guest to his?"

Tobias bowed acquiescence, and the ladies, with a soft chorus of good nights, departed in one direction, while Tobias smilingly indicated another. "This way, my lord. I hope to the One you find me a more trustworthy guide than your last."

"Indeed," said Rhiss, returning the smile. He found Tobias an extremely likeable man, good humoured, thoroughly efficient and mindful of Meranna's best interests. "That would be my prayer also, good Tobias, because I caution you to remember my gryphon neither tolerates nor appreciates being led astray."

Tobias laughed as they moved towards the corridor. "You are gracious to warn me, my lord, although I have always had a healthy respect for the creatures. As a child, I was often warned by my grandmother that the mountain gryphons near my home would come and spirit me off if I did not mend my ways. And they were huge — much larger than your gryphon — so I am sure they would have had no difficulty making off with a wayward child."

Rhiss was intrigued by the reference. "Were they gryphon majors, Tobias?"

"Possibly, my lord. I am not well versed in their lore, so could not say with certainty. We never saw them close up, but there were numerous occasions when, as a boy, I saw them flying in the mountain areas around my home at Brynteg. An incredible sight it always was, to be sure."

"I can imagine," replied Rhiss absently. He was curious about something else, but did not know quite how to broach the topic. "How long have you been in Lady Meranna's service?"

"Nigh on ten years, ever since the Lady's husband died in a tragic hunting accident. Poor Lady Rhyanna was only twelve at the time. It was a mishap no one expected. Indeed, it was Seir-onna Arian who arranged for my employ here following the memorial. I was to stay only temporarily, until her late brother-in-law's affairs could be set in order. But time stretched on, and Lady Meranna and I mutually reached the conclusion that our skills and abilities complemented each other, so she asked me to stay. I was delighted to do so and now regard Craggaddon Hall as my home. No one could have asked for a better employer."

"Lady Rhyanna mentioned brothers, but only in a very general sense. Why do they not administer this estate?"

Tobias hesitated. "My lord," he said apologetically, "that is a question perhaps best directed to Lady Meranna. It involves family matters that are delicate, if you take my meaning."

"Of course," replied Rhiss, although he didn't. "I am sorry to put you in a difficult position, Tobias."

"Not at all," said the older man easily. They turned a corner, and Rhiss recognized the corridor outside his room. "Here is your door, Lord Rhiss. Go you with the One." He bowed and left, retreating back along the corridor. Rhiss watched for a moment, then sighed and opened the door.

As they entered, Aquilea realized perhaps a second before Rhiss: someone was present. She opened her beak to issue a challenge, but stopped before any sound escaped, and Rhiss tensed, fumbling for his dagger. But whoever it was made no hostile moves. In fact, he could see the figure sitting comfortably in a chair; a vermilion glow emanating from the fire illuminated the room with flickering light and shadows. For one fleeting moment, he had the wild fantasy that it was Brother Gavrilos or Lord Tariel. Then he stepped further in, and realized his mistake. It was neither of them; Meranna's sister, Arian, sat waiting.

"Come in, my young friend," she said, rising and gesturing at them both. "We have a number of urgent things to discuss before I find my sister."

Rhiss felt the tension drain away, to be replaced by irritable lethargy. "My lady, or Seir-onna Arian, or however one addresses a woman who is both priest *and* noble-born — although I know not how that can be, begging your pardon, madam, and not wishing to offend you — but could this not wait until tomorrow?" he asked. "I am exhausted from the strain of nearly being murdered. The last thing I expected on reaching my room was someone else wishing to speak with me. Your sister is most anxious to talk with you; perhaps you could seek her out, if you wish lengthy discussion." He stopped, realizing his speech was becoming a rant and guiltily aware he sounded petulant. Arian did not stir, but gestured again, this time to a window seat.

"Sit, young man," she said in a tone that was level enough, but had steel in it. Her eyes glinted and she watched while Rhiss sat. Only then did she continue. "I am well aware this day has proven lengthy and adventurous, and I appreciate that you barely escaped with your life from the clutches of one of the most dangerous personages in this kingdom. I know it has likely produced its own special fatigue, but there *are* matters we simply must discuss. Dear to me as they are, I did not want my sister or niece listening to some things we need to speak of. I will go and find my sister when you and I have finished. Now, I have a jug of wine," she indicated the shadows by the floor, "and a pair of cups, so I suggest we make ourselves comfortable, and discuss what must be discussed before the night grows much older, so you may soon climb into that excellent bed and find the sleep you crave."

Rhiss sighed resignedly, wearily lifting his legs onto the cushions. "Very well. Your servant, Lady. I apologize for my intemperate remarks. In my defence, I have met a never-ending stream of people all day, some friendly, some not, but all popping up at odd moments when least expected, requiring split-second decisions in dealing with them... culminating in your presence."

Making no response, Arian reached down and poured wine into the cups. She passed one to Rhiss, who accepted it before leaning back against the wall at the side of the window seat. Arian also settled comfortably into her own chair. Aquilea came over and sniffed inquisitively at the jar. Arian laughed briefly, and gently pushed her away. "No, small one, not for you." The gryphon looked at Arian reproachfully, but turned away without argument, leaped up on the window seat beside Rhiss, and settled comfortably. Arian watched as she did so.

"A remarkable beast. You are most fortunate in having her companionship and loyalty." She paused. "But now, my lord, tell me your story from the *very* beginning, omitting *nothing*. I say it thus because I do not think you have done so with anyone yet; you have told parts to some, and others have inferred parts — more than you might imagine, I shouldn't wonder. I have spoken to several people about you — starting with my sister and niece, moving on to people in this Hall, such as our good Master Tobias, and finally with the servants of Maldeus, whom you somehow persuaded to turn against him. They are all elements which make it an impressive and fascinating tale, I willingly grant, but there are gaps and unanswered questions. I wish the complete picture, something even you may not have." She paused. "Let us begin here: the soldiers in the hall said you declared something about coming to Arrinor to assist the restoration of a true king, saying our current ruler is a Usurper. What do you know of this?"

"Very little beyond what I said earlier, lady," replied Rhiss carefully. Arian noted the reaction and smiled wearily.

"Lord Rhiss," she said, "I appreciate your caution. It is commendable when unsure of those around you. But you must be open and honest with *someone* in Arrinor who can help and advise you, and I offer myself as that person. To begin, I agree with your assessment: usurper is the term, perhaps the politest of many we could use. Now, please: the night grows older as we speak, and as you have noted, it has been a long day, not just for yourself. I, too, would like to see my bed before much more time passes. So I implore you, stop dancing around the truth, and let us hold frank and open discourse. I wish to help you. I *will* help you, if I can, but first I must know your story — all of it. Will you not trust me?"

Rhiss hesitated. "I would like to... but some of the things I would tell you I think you would find... fantastic and difficult to believe, lady."

Arian waved her hand impatiently. "There are many things about you and what you have done already that meet that description, Lord Rhiss. Do not fear on that account. I assure you I am not totally ignorant of things that cannot be readily explained. By the One, there are more things in this world than we sometimes dream of."

Rhiss smiled, and Arian looked at him sharply. "I was not aware of making a jest. Have I said something to amuse you?"

"No, your pardon," Rhiss replied hastily. "I meant no offence, but you paraphrased a famous playwright of my people. He spoke about there being all manner of unexplainable things present in the world."

"He was well versed in the ways of the world, then. Life changes little, no matter where or when one is. But enough. I ask again: will you trust me? Tell me your story."

Rhiss gazed at the older woman, reading the sincerity in her voice, realizing she spoke truth indeed: he must take someone into his confidence for there to be any chance of success. Rhiss had instinctively trusted Meranna and Rhyanna since meeting them, and this woman was kin to both. He sensed Arian was worthy of trust also, and decided he would place faith in this woman, sharing the story of his time in Arrinor, beginning with Gavrilos and the portal and telling all.

"Very well, lady," Rhiss said. "This is my tale."

When Rhiss had finished, Arian sat deep in silent thought for some time. The fire burned low, and Rhiss rose to place a fresh log. A shower of sparks erupted as the new wood settled heavily on the old, and Arian started as one waking from a dream.

"You spin a rare tale," she sighed. "An extraordinary tale, indeed. Had I not witnessed portions of it myself, and spoken to those who saw other parts — people, incidentally, whom I trust with my life — I would say that you had missed your calling, and should have been a wandering minstrel, singing for your supper, entertaining the gullible with fantastic tales of titanic struggles between good and evil."

That was unexpected, and Rhiss was disappointed. "You do not believe me?"

"Oh, quite the contrary. I find your story all too believable, for reasons of my own, especially in light of... various events of late. But," Arian smiled wryly, "it is not a tale I would tell just anyone, were I you. You are right to be wary about whom you share it with. It is obvious there are powerful forces — for both good and ill — at work in your life. Some would find your tale terrifying; others would call you liar or madman. 'Traitor' is the least of the labels you might receive."

"What do you believe, my lady?"

Arian gestured negatively with one hand. "Call me not 'my lady,' Lord Rhiss, if you please. I gave up such titles long ago. I am but a priest and servant of the One. For now, 'Seir-onna Arian' or merely 'Seir-onna' is more than sufficient."

Rhiss pursed his lips. "What do you believe, *Seir-onna* Arian?"

"There is an old saying in Arrinor: 'All are in Sight of the One; but some He merely glances at, while others are pinned by His gaze.' Plainly, you are one of the latter. Whether it is an *honour* is something you must ultimately decide for yourself. But I do not think your life will ever again be quite ordinary. Certainly, it will not be dull. This Brother Gavrilos you speak of, for example. You cannot be surprised to hear me say he is no ordinary priest, or even man, for that matter. Know you whom he really is?"

Rhiss looked uncomfortable. "I know your niece took me on a tour of this Hall earlier today, and we looked in on a chapel. Do you know it?"

Arian nodded. "Of course. Intimately."

"One of the windows had *his* likeness in it. When I started to say I knew him, Rhyanna was taken aback."

"As well she might be. Because, if I am not mistaken, your 'Brother Gavrilos' is one of the Seven, a member of the Arkos, a most high Order in the service of the One. He is known as the Herald of the One." She leaned forward to stare intently into his eyes. "Do you mark the significance, my friend? You have kept company with a powerful being high in the counsels of the One Himself, and he was ultimately responsible for your entry into Arrinor. What think you of that?"

"It takes some getting used to," Rhiss uncomfortably admitted, with considerable understatement, "and I am not at all sure whether I am, even now. As you say, I do not know whether to count it honour or no. To tell the truth, I am not convinced I am comfortable being part of such mighty affairs, nor am I sure I would choose to be, given the choice."

"But you *did* choose," Arian pointed out sympathetically. "Did you not listen to the Blessed Gavrilos, and his emphasis on the importance of choice? You had the choice to enter Arrinor, or return to your life. Yet you are here. You have freely and squarely placed yourself in the middle of 'mighty affairs,' as you refer to them, and it is consequently your task now to acquit yourself as well as you may."

Rhiss stared into the fire without speaking, trying to marshal his thoughts and what he wanted to say. Finally, he looked up and said slowly but earnestly, "But my lady — I'm sorry, Seir-onna — I am *not* the stuff of which heroes are made. As I told your sister, I am just an ordinary man."

Arian snorted with derision. "Stop trying to maintain that fiction. My sister did not believe it for a moment, and neither do I: it does not serve you well at all. You are no ordinary man. My niece would not have been with you at table tonight if you were."

"Seir-onna, I swear, I have no idea how I healed Lady Rhyanna. I doubt I could even do it again, which is why I was terrified when she suggested I heal Dalys."

Arian looked sceptical. "Perhaps... but *I* have no doubt. Just because it is a gift over which you currently have no control does not mean it will *stay* thus. In time, I, and others, may be able to help you learn to manage that gift — and others you might possess." She glanced at Aquilea. "The loyalty of that beast also argues against your being 'just an ordinary man.' It is a rare and valuable relationship you have with her, happening to only a fortunate few. And you have already experienced the value of that friendship." To his questioning look, she added, "Aquilea came swiftly to your assistance when you called her in your thoughts, did she not?"

Rhiss nodded slowly. "Can she read my mind, then?"

Arian shrugged. "I do not know. My first inclination is to say not, for she is but an animal. However, I only guess. For most people, knowledge of gryphons is limited. But she certainly sensed your danger; that is obvious. And I am sure, as time passes, she will grow to complement your attributes and skills even more."

Rhiss sighed. "But Seir-onna, I *have* no particular skills of value in this venture I am embarked on. I do not know what I possibly have to offer. Earlier tonight, I was absolutely, completely terrified before Maldeus. I was utterly convinced my death was nigh, that everything that had gone before was for naught. Do you understand? I was afraid, desperately afraid."

Arian looked unconcerned. "In such a situation, facing that creature, I would be astounded had you said you were not, for you would mark yourself as fool or liar, and contemptible either way. Mark me well, young man: I do not know from what tales you have formed your ideas of what heroes are like and how they act, but minstrels and poets everywhere romanticize unforgivably." She paused, considering. "Well, perhaps 'unforgivably' is too harsh. It is, after all, their task to romanticize things, so swooning maidens and naïve children can listen entranced at banquets, open-mouthed and wide-eyed, dreaming of noble exploits — most of which are grossly exaggerated. But fear is both natural and healthy. The most heroic will encounter situations where they experience fear — mind-numbing, hope-destroying fear — as you did earlier this evening. That is inevitable, unarguable, and ultimately of small importance. *But*," Arian went on, holding up an index finger as she warmed to her topic, "what is of *great* import is how you comport yourself when those moments arise. Do you allow that fear to overwhelm the ramparts of rationality in your mind, seeing them washed away as the tide obliterates a sand castle? Arrows and swords have killed uncounted innocents, but fear has killed more. Fear is the terrible daughter of the Other. Now, I have spoken with the men in that entry hall this night, and they told me of the courage with which you gazed at death, even while admitting your fear. Look within yourself, and understand that one of the reasons why you prevailed without lifting a hand was that honesty."

"But not the only reason, Seir-onna. Remember, there was this Tariel in the hall, who was not there later. He was the one who began the revolt against Maldeus. Without him, I would not be here now. His lead gave the others the courage to come to my side. As it was, I was stunned by their defection."

Arian nodded. "I, too. That is no slight to your courage, merely acknowledgement that Maldeus generally commands far greater loyalty from his troops than those men displayed tonight. It is one reason why I was so eager to hear their tale. I found the One certainly favoured your cause this evening, for those men were mostly older, freshly conscripted into the Sovereign's service, from one region in particular that has had no cause to love the Crown of late." Arian nodded again. "Aye, you were fortunate indeed, most fortunate their loyalty was much more tepid than Maldeus is accustomed to." Arian raised an eyebrow and said dryly, "You can safely wager that Maldeus will take vigorous steps to ensure the loyalty of those serving him after tonight, so I would not count on that stratagem again."

"I understand, Seir-onna. But what of this Lord Tariel? No other soldiers remembered him. I first met him as Dalys took me to his trap. Maldeus knew Tariel well, and was enraged at his presence. Tariel said he had come to bring balance, implying he was a counter to the threat posed by Maldeus. And Tariel knew of Gavrilos, as well, and displayed miraculous abilities. Do you know the name? What is he?"

Arian shook her head, perplexed. "Lord Rhiss, I have no idea who your Lord Tariel is. That name is not one of the seven Arkos as laid out in the Book of the One. We can try to learn more later, but for now, let us simply be glad he was there and brought assistance, unexpected as it was. He may well have played a vital part in the victory of the entry hall, but let us also acknowledge that your courage was a decisive factor, too."

Rhiss began to object again, but Arian held up a hand, silencing him. "Oh, by the One, stop it, young man. Modesty is well and good, but there comes a time when pragmatic realism is better, as long as it does not lead to swollen arrogance. Here are my final words, for I grow weary of listening to you arguing your own limitations: aye, you are raw and unschooled. Aye, you have much to learn. And you will make mistakes. *But* you will learn. There is much potential in you. Brother Gavrilos saw it, as I do. If you will accept me as guide, I swear by the One that I will do everything in my power to see you assume that potential and prove worthy of the hopes placed in you. I might add I know many others who will also wish the same." She paused, cocking her head to one side. "Well?"

Rhiss again looked into the fire, going over all that had been said. It was another decision, he realized, not unlike the one Brother Gavrilos had offered. Choice, he remembered. Choice was vital. He looked up to see Arian regarding him intently. 'A good woman,' the Lady Meranna had said. Rhiss found himself in agreement with that assessment, and nodded. "Aye," he said quietly, then louder, as he extended his hand, "Aye, Seir-onna!"

Arian held out her own hand to clasp Rhiss. Together, they shook hands, and Arian, greatly pleased, said simply, "Then we are well met, Lord Rhiss. Well met, indeed. And in this, we are One."

―――⋗⋄⋖―――

Although she had not bothered to pay close heed to most of the endless chatter the Lady Priest of the One had with The Man, if Aquilea had been physically capable of laughter, she might have laughed at the Seir-onna's silly assertion, tentative though it was — although she also found it rather insulting.

Only an animal, unable to see his thoughts? Ludicrous! Even recalling it, her indignation reared like feathers buffeted before the North Wind. Her sharp intelligence was at least the equal of any human; in fact, she thought disdainfully, greater than most of the shambling, slow-witted creatures — or would be in time, for she was still very young, she admitted. She reminded herself that her mother always warned that the One did not love arrogance, and was not shy in teaching those filled with it that humility was essential in all things.

But of course she could see his thoughts! (He had a Name, she knew; in fact, he possessed at least two — and that was in addition to various human titles meaning little to her. First, there was the short, silly sounding name other humans called him by — the one resembling the hissing of a snake — and, strangely, he also seemed to identify himself by. Then there was the name his Essence proclaimed him to be — and she rather liked that one, although its pure thought-form was verbally unpronounceable, and curiously, he seemed unaware of it. But she had first known him, through her mother, simply as The Man, and so The Man he tended to affectionately remain in Aquilea's thoughts.)

At any rate, he was Guardian to her now, just as she was Shield-Protector to him. Which meant that eventually, they must be able to hear each other's thoughts. Aquilea was unsure when or how this exchange would happen; for some reason she did not understand, it had not occurred yet — while she could see some of The Man's thoughts, it did not appear the process worked both ways. But then again, the role of Shield-Protector was new to her, and she had much to learn.

What mattered most, however, was she had clearly heard The Man's call in his need; more, she had been able to act upon it, the door to their room being carelessly secured. And although her assistance had not been required in any physical form — the ruffians threatening The Man having had at least the good sense to be afraid of her formidable natural weapons — her presence had been deterrent enough.

Of course, there had also been strange, powerful forces at work in that hall, she thought absently. Forces of Darkness and Light, of the Other and the One. Very strange... and most disconcerting. In the short time she and The Man had been together, it seemed these forces doggedly followed him wherever he went. Would this be the pattern all their days together? She rather hoped not, but something within her recognized, not without resigned acceptance, that The Man was bound up in some ancient, gigantic struggle between Darkness and Light. She sighed. No matter. He was her Guardian now, and she his Shield Protector. That meant Aquilea was bound up in it, too, until the End.

Was it really as simple as that?

Well... aye, it was. And that was enough.

She slept.

VII

INCARCERATION AND AFTERMATH

> *"Deceit and treachery abound, and my enemies seem ascendant. Yet will I remember, for good or ill, that things are not always what they seem. The One will not forsake me; He shall succour me in my hour of need; yea, therefore I place my trust in the One, and will dwell in His House forever."*
>
> **The Book of the One, 115:5:8-9**
> **(Cantos 115, Chapter 5, Verses 8-9)**

Rhiss was shaken from a dead sleep; not roughly, but not especially gently, either. It seemed his head had barely touched the pillow, and Arian only just gone. He was still exhausted and not happy at being woken. He was about to say as much as he opened his eyes, but things were amiss: people crowded into his room, including Lady Meranna and a number of household troops. Blinking in confusion, he looked around. It was either very late or very early, as it was still dark and two soldiers carried lanterns. All were armed, swords unsheathed, demeanour elaborately casual, weapons not *directly* menacing Rhiss, but he had a foreboding realization that he was the focus of attention.

Sitting up slowly, Rhiss turned to Meranna. She looked grim in the flickering light. "Lady Meranna?" he said, puzzled. "Is something amiss?"

"There is indeed," she said shortly. "Rise, and dress, if you please. I will wait outside. These men will stay. Be quick." She turned abruptly and left.

Mystified, fighting down a growing conviction something was very wrong indeed, Rhiss did as he was told. He glanced at the soldiers, but they were impassive and silent. Evidently they were not about to give him privacy, so he shrugged and dressed, shucking off the nightshirt, then putting on the same clothes he had worn earlier. Finishing, he sought his dagger, but it was not where he had left it. Casting his gaze about, he noticed at once it was not the only item missing: his bow and quiver with its arrows, his cloak, and the Circlet of Araxis were all missing.

Belatedly, Rhiss realized something else: Aquilea was nowhere to be seen, either. He stopped in the act of putting on his boots and looked around again. A soldier noticed. "What do you seek?"

"My belongings, and my gryphon. Have you seen aught of them? They were here when I retired."

The soldiers glanced at each other, expressions unreadable. "The Lady Meranna removed your weapons and other items before waking you. As for the animal, her daughter took it away."

Rhiss was relieved Aquilea was with Rhyanna, and that she had evidently gone willingly, since he had heard no commotion. However, he was alarmed, not fathoming why she had been taken in the first place. His weapons confiscated? The Circlet removed? It was as though he was some kind of criminal. He said as much, but the soldier merely shook his head. "My orders are not to talk, m'lord, merely to see Lady Meranna's commands carried out with dispatch. If you please, step into the corridor."

Following the soldier, Rhiss' confusion and misgivings grew. Armed men in the corridor formed a cordon around him. Lady Meranna said coldly, "Extend your wrists, sir." He did so, whereupon she added to the soldier nearest, "Bind him." Instantly, Rhiss found his hands securely and uncomfortably tied together with a thick leather cord.

Bewildered beyond measure, Rhiss looked at Meranna. "Lady, may I ask the meaning of this? Why am I treated as a common criminal? I do not understand."

She ignored Rhiss completely, and spoke to the soldier who had bound him. "Bring him to the Great Hall with the others. I shall join you shortly."

The soldier touched hand to forehead in salute, and she swept off in a swirl of rustling skirts. Rhiss was prodded into motion, none too gently, and nearly stumbled. He regained his balance, glaring at the soldier responsible, but said nothing.

Minutes later, they arrived at the Great Hall. To his astonishment, Arian was there, also bound, standing before a dais upon which rested two ornate chairs. The soldiers who had deserted Maldeus to stand with Rhiss in the entry hall were also present, similarly bound and confined. A crowd of servants stood to one side. Brought beside Arian, Rhiss turned to her and began, "Seir-onna, what—?"

Before he could finish, Rhiss was shoved again, as a soldier beside him growled, "You are not to speak."

Rhiss gave another angry stare, bit back the retort on his lips, and glanced at Arian. She stared forward, not looking at Rhiss, but shook her head slightly. He was unsure whether that meant she, too, could not understand their predicament, or Rhiss should not cause trouble, or something else entirely. He subsided.

After a short wait, during which the only noises were the creak of leather from men's armour, whisperings of onlookers and occasional sputters from torches lighting the room, Lady Meranna swept in, Tobias closely behind. She proceeded to the dais and sat in a chair; Tobias stood to one side. She looked at the erstwhile soldiers of Maldeus, at Arian, and finally at Rhiss. She broke the silence by asking in a clear, cold voice, "These are all the traitors who would rise against our gracious Sovereign, Tobias?"

Tobias stepped forward. "Aye, Lady. All are accounted for and in custody before you."

"Very well," she replied. She let her gaze roam over the assembled prisoners before halting on Arian and Rhiss. "I am grieved," she announced, "to see both my own sister and an honoured guest, only just invited into this Hall, standing accused with this other rabble. Grieved, but perhaps not as surprised as I might be. My sister, I have long suspected your true sympathies did not lie with the Crown. But for you to forswear the colours of your Order like this... truly, you are a disgrace to our House and your vows." She flicked her gaze over to Rhiss. "And you, sir. We took you in and treated you with honour. How do you repay that trust? You spread exaggerated tales of your exploits on our meeting, inflating your importance with wild stories that have not a shred of truth. We find you are nothing more than a common criminal, sought by Sovereign's Men. When they tried to bring you to justice, you preached sedition and treason, persuading several to abandon their sworn service and join in your disloyal and ultimately lost cause. You forced the Sovereign's Counsellor to retreat from this Hall and seek reinforcements in the form of loyal troops elsewhere. You are responsible for the death of a beloved servant who was with this family many years." She shook her head in apparent disbelief at the catalogue of crimes she had recited. "I am relieved to have uncovered the depth of your perfidy," she went on. "You will all be confined in our cells until the soldiers of the Counsellor return to place you under arrest and escort you to justice."

Rhiss had listened to Meranna's speech, open-mouthed and with growing, incredulous anger, unable to believe she could really mean what she was saying. At last, unable to contain himself any longer in the face of such vile falsehoods, he stepped towards her without warning. "Lady Meranna—!"

His guard must have been anticipating just such an action, because before he could take more than a couple of steps, Rhiss was expertly felled by a spear butt to his middle. He collapsed on the floor and curled into a ball, struggling to breathe, gasping with pain. Through blurred vision, Rhiss saw the hem of a red dress approaching, and from a great distance, he heard Lady Meranna's voice say disdainfully, "Stand him up."

Rhiss was hauled roughly to his feet, held tightly between two soldiers. Meranna's face, bereft of the slightest hint of recognition or warmth, leaned close to him. "You have something to say, traitorous scum?"

"Have you taken leave of your senses?" he panted. "I saved your daughter's life. You expressed your thanks, solidarity with my cause, said you stood firmly with me against the Sovereign. I seek to see the rightful King—"

She slapped his face with such force that Rhiss felt half his teeth had been loosened, and his vision blurred anew. "How *dare* you parade such despicable lies before decent people!" she hissed furiously. "I should have your tongue cut out for the uttering of them! Save my daughter's life? You attempted to dishonour her! And this House has ever been a loyal servant of the Crown! You will not cast doubt on our fealty to our beloved Sovereign!" Her face was contorted with rage, and Rhiss was so stunned that he could find no words to respond.

Meranna studied him a moment longer, then spat at his feet and addressed the guards. "The sight of them sickens me. Remove them. Long live the Sovereign." She stood and quickly left by a side door, Tobias following. Numb and in pain, Rhiss offered no resistance as he and the others were dragged away.

A short time later, Rhiss found himself locked with Arian in a dungeon deep in the Hall's stone cellars. A guard cut their bindings, explaining stonily that prisoners were being confined two or three to a cell only because there were far more than could be accommodated singly in the modest number the Hall possessed. As the door swung shut, they were warned against conspiring escape: the consequences would be severe.

Rhiss looked around morosely, gingerly holding his sore jaw. Here was another new experience — one of several questionable ones since setting foot in Arrinor, he thought sourly: incarceration in a real dungeon.

It was a narrow, rectangular chamber, no more than twenty feet by ten, completely shaped from stone. The room was bare but for a small wooden table and chair. A tiny, barred window high up in the wall opposite the door looked as if it would provide natural light once daybreak arrived. At the moment, however, the cell was dimly lit only by torchlight from the hallway, whose light filtered through the door's barred opening, an opening meant to provide jailers with means of observing the cell's occupant. A slot cut at the door's bottom allowed the serving of meals without needing to open it. In one corner, a stone font held a tiny pool to serve as washing and drinking water. A rough wooden bucket in another corner was, he had been informed, the toilet. There was no means of heat, and the stone room was dank and chill. Rhiss could imagine catching pneumonia if forced to stay long.

As the cell's door was secured by the rasping of a key in the lock, the sounds of jailers retreated into the distance, and Rhiss sat heavily in the chair, turning to Arian. She had lost no time reclining on a narrow stone bench cut into the wall, obviously meant to serve as the unfortunate occupant's bed. Incredibly, she somehow appeared comfortable. She returned Rhiss' gaze with an ironic lift of the eyebrows.

"Well, Lord Rhiss," she said thoughtfully, "that did not go too badly amiss, although you would have been the ruin of us all with your impassioned comments, had my sister had not saved the day with her swift, well-chosen response."

Rhiss could hardly believe his ears. "Saved the day with her response? I was assaulted by her and her soldiers! She threatened to cut out—" He stopped abruptly as he recalled the discussion the night before. "Ohhh... it was all a ruse, wasn't it?"

Amazingly, Arian laughed softly. "Indeed, young man." She rose and walked to the door, peering out to satisfy herself no guard eavesdropped. Then she returned and knelt beside Rhiss. "I offer my apologies, and more importantly, those of my sister. You have no idea how difficult it was for her to stand and mouth those foul lies in front of all assembled — and to assault you — but it was necessary. Your reactions needed not only to *appear* genuine, but *be* genuine, and they most certainly were. The look on your face during my sister's tirade will have convinced even the most cynical doubters you were in earnest. It was all I could do not to laugh, I fear, for which I also ask your pardon. I had to keep my head bowed for much of my sister's speech. I know, just as it was not easy for her to say those things, it was not easy for you to hear them." She paused. "And I did not wish to laugh when you were assaulted, I swear. That was an unforeseen but unfortunate necessity in light of your ill-chosen words."

"Sweet Light of the One! I very nearly was the ruin of everything she sought to accomplish!"

Arian shrugged. "You were being true to yourself and your convictions. No one can fault you for that. But you forced her to act in a manner that — well, knowing her as I do, it will have been one of the most difficult actions she has ever undertaken." She paused. "'Sweet Light of the One?' Rather a colourful expression, my lord, not generally used in polite company. Wherever did you pick it up? Not from my niece, surely."

Rhiss blushed. "No, Seir-onna, from one of the soldiers. My apologies. But I was horrified at my own stupidity. Will Lady Meranna ever forgive me? Can you?"

"Don't be silly, young man. There is no need for forgiveness. You acted as you had to, and so did she." Arian returned to the stone shelf and sat. "You obviously recall what my dear sister said at dinner after the evening's events. After leaving you, I met with her and we talked almost until the moment we set our plan in motion, resulting in your untimely awakening. There was much to discuss. To start, the conduct of Maldeus over this entire affair has been both inexplicable and alarming, raising all manner of questions. How did he know you were coming? Why should it matter to him as much as it evidently did? What goaded him into taking such hasty action?" She paused. "Because I can tell you, beyond doubt, he *erred* last night, erred most grievously in a fashion that may have saved us all, perhaps even laid the seeds of his own ultimate undoing. In rushing here without proper plan and only a small contingent of men — an act of either supreme arrogance or abject desperation — he failed to ensure your capture and elimination. In fact, with the assistance of your mysterious benefactor Tariel, you were able to vanquish Maldeus without physical action at all. Truly a remarkable performance on your part, a humiliating defeat on his — one I can tell you will not endear him to his Sovereign, who is singularly focused on results, always."

"I drew my dagger, and threatened men with it," objected Rhiss.

"Aye... but fought no one," rejoined Arian, waving a hand dismissively. "Nor would it have availed you if you had, and I say that intending no insult. A courageous gesture for one man to make against many — if not a particularly practical one. Do you not agree?" Rhiss considered, then nodded reluctantly.

"So. Some of the questions I posed we cannot answer, at least for the moment, but we are left with several thorny issues from the affair, issues urgently requiring resolution. Now we have time for reflection. Let us, therefore, give you your first lesson in tactics. The first and foremost thorny issue: Maldeus will return. That is a foregone conclusion. The only question is *when*. So... what think you? Speculate."

Rhiss was taken aback by the unexpected command. "I would imagine," he said slowly, "as soon as he can muster a force of sufficient size to prevent a repeat of last night's debacle."

"Excellent. Which raises a sub-issue for consideration: how large would such a force have to be?"

"Well... large enough to overpower the household forces here, if necessary. But I do not know how many soldiers Lady Meranna has at her disposal."

"No matter," said Arian briskly. "Maldeus will have made it his business to be aware of the size of all private levies in the kingdom against just such a possibility as this. I can tell you he will want several hundred men, which, fortunately for us, will take a number of hours to assemble. Now, the second thorny issue: what will he want?"

"That is simple. He will seek what he was denied last night: my capture and murder."

"True, but incomplete, leading us to the third thorny issue which resulted in our relaxing in these luxurious accommodations: what becomes of this House on his return?" Arian stood again, pacing the cell. "Maldeus called you traitor, which is really a wilful misnomer, because he is fully aware of the real reasons you are here. However, he cannot openly discuss those reasons before ordinary soldiers without admitting that the charges you made are true, so it is convenient merely to hang the label 'traitor' on you, a label you have unwittingly but conveniently handed him through your comments. Now, back to the issue at hand: he knows you have sheltered at Craggaddon Hall. If you were he, what would you ask yourself regarding that?"

"He would want to know whether Lady Meranna is aware of my quest and in league with me."

"Precisely. So the final thorny issue for your consideration, the one connecting all the others: consider these factors in reverse order, and you will have your explanation for the shameful charade you witnessed upstairs."

But Rhiss had already made the connection. "Aye, Seir-onna, I do see it. I am not always as dim as I appear. She needed it to look like she was unaware of my so-called 'treason' and to make it look, when she found out, that she immediately did what any loyal servant of the Crown would: she publicly discredited me, distanced herself from me, and ordered my arrest, so that she would be cleared of any wrongdoing or collusion with me."

"And when Maldeus returns, she can again feign the righteous indignation she displayed and, we hope, avoid catastrophe with him. You do show promise, Lord Rhiss. *If* you can learn to work through the possibilities and anticipate what your enemy is *about* to do, not merely what he *is* doing, you will have gained considerable advantage. My sister felt terrible keeping you ignorant of our intentions, but there was no time after finishing our deliberations, and as I already said, your reaction had to be genuine. Also, a measure of haste has been important, because the longer we delayed your arrest, the stranger it would seem to outside eyes. By the way, the very public spectacle you refer to had another purpose, also: to let any additional spies witness the sincerity of everyone's reaction."

"Additional spies?" Rhiss was startled. "Has something led you to believe Dalys had accomplices?"

"No," replied Arian, shaking her head before adding thoughtfully, "but where there is one rat, it is only prudent to suspect more."

"So... what happens now?"

"Anticipate the possibilities. Knowing what you do, what will likely occur?"

"In light of everything that has so far happened, I would be unsurprised if a situation arises fortuitously so our escape becomes somehow possible."

"Excellent. There you have it, then, my lord."

"But will it all work? Maldeus... he seems a master of deception. Will he see through our attempt?"

Arian sighed deeply. "There you hit upon the thorniest question of all, for you are quite right: we deal with a Prince of Lies. Will he be taken in by *our* lies, or is he astute enough to see through them? In truth, I know not. But my sister and I would not have done these things if we did not feel there was a possibility of success. Ultimately, you will learn that we do what we can, and then place ourselves into the care and protection of the One."

Troubled, Rhiss began speaking, but checked himself. Arian noticed. "You have a question?"

"Why are you and your sister doing all this for me? You have put not only yourselves, but this entire House at risk."

Arian sighed, considering. "Lord Rhiss," she finally said softly, "Arrinor has languished in the stranglehold of Maldeus and his foul, usurping Sovereign these twenty-five years. Uncounted numbers of innocents have suffered and died, and this fair realm has been despoiled and corrupted. Based on what has happened in the few short days since your arrival, my sister believes — and I concur — that your coming is ordained by the One. There is something both unique and special about you, your claims to the contrary notwithstanding. While we do not pretend to comprehend all that has happened, we believe we must do all we can to assist you. And there is the personal debt we owe in saving Lady Rhyanna's life, of course."

Rhiss coloured. "I... don't know what to say."

"Then have the wit to say nothing, and spare me your earnest protestations that you are unworthy. It is too late for second thoughts — we have set events in motion, and are now irretrievably swept up in them, like the river traveller's boat entering the rapids."

"I see. So... what is to happen now?"

"Now?" Arian yawned. "You will keep watch while I sleep a little. You, at least, have slept. I have not, and am bone weary."

"But, Seir-onna, the escape?" asked Rhiss in frustration. "How and when is it to happen? Should we not prepare for it?"

Arian already lay prone on the stone shelf, facing the wall. Her voice was muffled as she replied, "I *am* preparing, young man. *You* can also prepare by coming to inner peace. There is a time for action, and a time for reflection. As to the how and when of the escape, it is as I already said: anticipate the possibilities. Work them out, and when you have done so, you will have gained a—"

"—considerable advantage," Rhiss chimed in wearily. "I know. But could you not give your fellow fugitive some hint of what is to come?"

Arian sighed once more. "You may look for a friend to come to our cell, offering assistance in vacating the premises."

"Mortal assistance, or should I expect something rather more... spectacular?" retorted Rhiss.

Arian gave a short bark of a laugh, sat up and wrapped herself in her cloak. As she lay down again, she said, "Mortal, I should think. You have had remarkable assistance in your quest thus far, much of it not easily explainable, but I daresay you have had your quota of that sort of aid for some time to come. Be careful what you say. Do not take it lightly, and remember to keep a respectful tongue in your head." She turned once more to face the wall, and said, almost as an afterthought, "When you see the first, faint stirrings of dawn in the world through yon window, expect assistance, and call your gryphon to you in your thoughts."

"Call her? But Seir-onna, we cannot base a plan on that. I am not even sure she came before because of my wishing..."

The reply came back sleepily. "Then we shall find out, won't we? However, I think you may be surprised by the intricacies of the relationship developing with your gryphon, a relationship that is, to be fair, very much in its infancy at the moment. Now please, no more discussion, or I shall be tempted to throw our carefully laid plans in ruin by escaping early."

"How would you do that?" asked Rhiss, bemused.

"By using your head to break down the door to our cell, if only so I can get some peace and quiet for myself."

Even though it hurt to do so, Rhiss smiled, took the hint and fell silent. Within minutes, Arian's breathing was slow and even. Rhiss listened for a while, shrugged resignedly, and went to the door to keep watch as instructed, gingerly rubbing his sore stomach all the while.

———◆———

The sound of raised voices jolted Rhiss into wakefulness, and he realized guiltily that he must have dozed off. He had been so tired, and thought he would just sit a moment to rest. Evidently he had done much more than that. He glanced at Arian's motionless form, but the slow risings and fallings of her chest indicated the lady priest slept undisturbed. Rhiss looked at the window grille, but as yet no dawn glimmered, the sky still inky black. That was good: it meant little time had elapsed while he was derelict in his duty.

The voices faded; then a metallic clanking noise emanated from the door in their stead. Rhiss hastily stood, wondering who or what was responsible for the sound. He realized he had not seen or heard guards checking on them in some while, although he vaguely recalled hearing voices calling at some point — probably, he thought remorsefully, as he drifted into sleep. He had paid it no mind at the time.

The door into the cell swung wide, revealing a figure in the doorway. It was brighter in the corridor than in the cell, and Rhiss was forced to squint momentarily while his eyes adjusted. Then his vision was reconciled to the increased light, and he gasped.

The figure cocked its head to one side, and said, with a touch of irritation, "Exactly why do my features seem to have that effect on you, Lord Rhissan? Twice you have greeted my appearance in such manner."

Given the circumstances of those appearances, Rhiss thought the assessment rather harsh. But not wishing to antagonize his visitor, he bowed and said quietly, "Your pardon, Lord Tariel. Your comings have been unlooked for, but not unwelcome. And you are somewhat early. You are, I take it, the assistance Seir-onna Arian indicated would come to effect our escape?"

The reply was startling. "No," said Tariel shortly. "As before, I come at no one's bidding but my own."

"But why—"

The figure sighed impatiently. "The situation is thus: your colleagues planned to come to your rescue soon, but in such a way that I fear they would only reveal themselves and undo the subterfuge they seek to maintain against the Enemy. However, *my* coming is simpler; Maldeus already has seen my hand at work influencing events last night, so will not be surprised to see it again. He will be enraged for all that, but it does not matter. Paranoia is never as satisfied as when it can confirm its own worst fears. However, I warn you, do not look to me to be your saviour again in the near future. I want you to know that I do what I do of my own volition, but it is at some personal risk *and* cost, I assure you, and in any event, you need to learn to stand on your own two feet."

Rhiss was eager to learn what such cryptic remarks meant, but, given Tariel's testy nature, refrained from asking, and merely nodded silently.

"You may leave the cell," Tariel continued, backing away from the door and gesturing. "I have brought someone with me who is most anxious to see you."

Rhiss exited quickly, hoping for and expecting Rhyanna. However, to his surprise, he was greeted by Aquilea, who expressed her delight by rearing up and placing her front claws carefully on his body, rumbling pleasure and approval. Rhiss was glad to see she was aware of the damage she could inflict if she was careless. He scratched the top of her head, and the rumbling went up an octave. He smiled and gently shooed her down, then glanced into the cell.

"Forgive me. Arian is evidently a sound sleeper. I will wake her, as she is most interested to meet you."

Tariel held up a hand peremptorily. "No. Leave her be for the moment. I come to speak with you, not the good Seir-onna. Be not concerned, as she sleeps with my encouragement. Now, hearken, young man, for I do not have a great deal of time. First, I have brought the gifts you received from Brother Gavrilos." Rhiss looked with interest in the direction Tariel indicated, and sure enough, propped against the corridor wall were his flask, dagger, bow and arrows, while on the floor, resting on his cloak, was the Circlet of Araxis. Another cloak, well made but rather travel-worn, and a sword with a red jewelled pommel, secured in a long leather scabbard, lay beside his things. Evidently they were Arian's.

"I suggest you don them," continued Tariel, speaking swiftly, "although I warn you: you cannot practically wear the Circlet of Araxis in public. It is too easily identifiable throughout Arrinor and will bring unwanted attention; it needs stowing somewhere safe. Moreover, it is really something for the King to wear. I will say no more about it, but Arian will understand my meaning. She is a good woman, worthy of your trust. As you see, I have also brought her belongings." Rhiss opened his mouth, but Tariel held up his hand again and said imperiously, "Do not interrupt. You may speak when I finish. After I have gone, wake Arian. She will know the way out, and the most efficient route to the stables. You will need to ride hard, but should be able to escape the reach of Maldeus, as my information is he is at least two hours away at this moment. Travel by night if at all possible, and avoid towns or villages, at least in the immediate vicinity. If Arian is at a loss to where you should go, as I suspect she will be, recommend Pencairn House to her. Tell her it is my personal suggestion."

"Pencairn House?" Rhiss repeated blankly.

"Aye. And I know beyond doubt she will object, proclaiming it completely unsuitable. Tell her that is not so, and the grounds for her objection are no longer valid. The problem has been resolved, as she will see if the two of you go there. Use those exact words." Tariel paused. "I doubt until now she has had time or energy to plan how all this must play out, but impress upon her that it is vital you make detailed plans as soon as possible." He smiled coldly. "You have managed well so far by merely allowing events to unfold, but you cannot continue to rely on things going your way. Do not tax the grace of the One overmuch, or become complacent. You will quickly need to become proactive, not merely reactive." Rhiss looked puzzled, and Tariel sighed. "When you are reactive, your opponent has the initiative, and therefore controls the situation. Always keep in mind that the Sovereign did not come to power by being reactive, waiting for things to happen and fortuitous events to fall into the royal lap. You will find Maldeus and the Usurper together are formidable opponents, and you would do well never to grant them control of either the tactical or strategic situation, insofar as you can, of course. You will ultimately need to think and plan on both levels to experience success. And certainly, you would do well not to underestimate them. Now, what do you wish to ask?"

"How will our escape be explained?"

Tariel moved to the cell door, holding his right hand in front, splaying the fingers wide. He said nothing, but as Rhiss watched, fascinated, a reddish mist formed before Tariel's outstretched hand. The mist rapidly coalesced, and within seconds formed the solid crimson shape of a heraldic gryphon, two feet tall, standing unwaveringly at waist height in the doorway to the cell. Tariel turned to face Rhiss.

"This will last several hours, or until Maldeus destroys it in his wrath, which he will probably do as soon as he lays eyes on it. However, when he sees it, Maldeus will know at once the manner of your escape and my involvement. That will exonerate the good people of this Hall."

"And increase his rage against *you*," Rhiss pointed out.

Tariel shrugged. "Immaterial. Maldeus is a servant of the Other. I care not about his feelings for me."

Rhiss glanced down the empty corridor. The heavy wooden doors at either end were closed. "Where are the guards, Lord Tariel? I would have thought some would be here at all times to forestall precisely what we now do."

Tariel's expression did not change, but there was no mistaking the satisfaction in his voice. "They are occupied by a — diversion, let us say, also of my making. It is something involving much smoke and the appearance of great destruction, but I assure you it looks far worse than it actually is."

"What?" asked Rhiss, alarmed. "You have not set a—"

"A fire, aye," responded Tariel, "but it is relatively small and will cause very little damage. I have no more desire than you to see Craggaddon Hall reduced to ashes. However, the fire has caused much commotion, as I intended, and the guards are summoned to the granaries to assist in its quenching, thinking you locked safely in your cells, as of course you were until I arrived. They will succeed in dousing the fire shortly, but in the meantime, you and Seir-onna Arian will be able to slip away unnoticed and unchallenged." He glanced around. "I must leave. As soon as I am gone, awaken the lady; make your escape with all dispatch."

Seeing the locked cells, a sudden thought struck Rhiss. "Lord Tariel, what of the other prisoners — the soldiers of Maldeus who came over to our side?"

"They are in those cells. Why do you ask?"

"What do you intend to do with them?"

"*Do* with them?" repeated Tariel dourly. "I do not intend to do *anything* with them. We cannot be assured of their loyalty, and some may already regret their hasty decision in the heat of the moment last night. In any case, they cannot accompany you to your destination. Two travellers alone will not attract attention, but an armed troop certainly would."

"Well... but... my lord, we cannot simply *leave* them," said Rhiss disbelievingly. "Maldeus would surely take his vengeance on them, a vengeance I suspect will be made all the worse once he finds us escaped. They *must* be allowed to flee with us. I will not insist they accompany Arian and me, but I do insist they be permitted their escape and chance to live. They risked their lives last night, helping to swing the tide in my favour. I would not see their faithfulness rewarded with abandonment and death."

"You seem passionate about traitors whose loyalty is uncertain at best," observed Tariel evenly.

Rhiss thrust his jaw out stubbornly. "I tell you I will not leave them here. They deserve better."

Tariel regarded Rhiss expressionlessly, then actually gave a small, wintry smile. "Aye, they do. You are quite correct. Your passion speaks well of you, standing up to me as you did." Tariel nodded slowly. "I was going to release them, because what you have said is true. But I was curious to see whether you would think of their welfare, and if so, how far you would go to protect them. I find myself pleased. A true leader always has the welfare of his men at heart — as you obviously do in this instance.

Very well." He reached inside his tunic, withdrawing a pair of plain iron keys. "This," he gestured at one, "unlocks the cells containing your soldiers. The other opens the guardroom at the end of the passage, where their confiscated weapons are. Once you and they have escaped from this place, mind, I insist they go *their* way and you and Seir-onna Arian go *yours*."

Rhiss nodded gratefully. "I give you my word."

"Then I will be on my way. Until our next meeting — which, as I have said, do not look for. Go you with the One."

"Thank you, my lord," said Rhiss, bowing his head, "for all you have done. It was unlooked for, but no less timely for that. Do you know, Brother Gavrilos said I would find assistance from unexpected quarters, and you certainly meet that description."

Tariel smiled again. "Did he? It sounds very like him. Farewell, Lord Rhissan." He laid his hand on Aquilea's head. "Good bye, Small One. Keep this man safe." He looked at her for a moment, and some communication passed between them. She rumbled contentment and approval. Tariel straightened, walking quickly to the end of the corridor. He opened the door, looked back, then slipped through. It clicked into place solidly.

Rhiss looked at Aquilea. "Hmm. How very pedestrian. I was rather hoping for something more spectacular, a flash of light and a cloud of coloured smoke or something." He sighed. "Well, we had better wake Arian, lass, although I'll wager she won't be pleased to have missed Tariel. But those guards won't stay away forever, and someone's on his way here to see us, someone I don't particularly want to meet again. Come, off we go." He cautiously eyed, then tentatively poked the smoky red gryphon still hanging in the air. It seemed wispy and insubstantial. However, it did not dissipate at his touch, but remained solid, quite unchanged. Rhiss shrugged, and went to waken Arian.

As expected, Arian was vexed to learn she had slept through Tariel's visit. "I'm sorry, Seir-onna," said Rhiss contritely, "but he specifically said he came to talk to me, not you. He made it clear he was helping you sleep and I was not to wake you until after he left. Short of openly defying him, there was little I could do."

"Oh, very well," growled Arian, studying the smoky red gryphon still hanging motionless in the doorway. "But you *did* defy him about not leaving yon soldiers for Maldeus."

"But Tariel was only testing me, so it doesn't count as defiance," Rhiss pointed out. "He wanted to test my resolve."

"Hmm," grumbled Arian, moving into the corridor and buckling on her sword. "Very well, I'm convinced. I suppose we had best move, then. Where is this fire Tariel started? We must give it a wide berth."

"In the granaries. I don't recall where they are."

"No matter. I do. And I grant it is a good spot for a fire, if you wish to pose minimal danger to the Hall proper. It is close by a well, but some distance from the main building, so unlikely to spread and cause devastation. Those fighting the fire will have to travel a short distance, which will be time consuming." She gestured with one hand. "Come, then: release your soldiers, give them their instructions, and let us be on our respective ways."

Rhiss took up his belongings, then went along the corridor, opening the cells containing the men who had switched sides to join him. They emerged cautiously, watching as he went down its length unlocking doors, including the guardroom with their weapons. When all were freed and armed, he gathered them in a circle. Rhiss glanced at Arian, but she motioned him to go ahead. He licked dry lips and rubbed his chin, marshalling his thoughts.

"Gentlemen," he began, "beyond all hope we have again been delivered from what seemed certain disaster only a short time ago. Give thanks to the One. And because of your service to me, I have made sure your release goes hand in hand with mine."

"Aye, m'lord," one of the soldiers said unexpectedly. "I heard you insist to someone that we be released, too. I don't know who he was, but I thank you, because we know well what our fate would have been had you not argued our case." The other soldiers murmured agreement, nodding.

Rhiss smiled and raised his hand. "No, my friends, as I said, it is I who should thank you. But enough; it is sufficient our gratitude is mutual. Now, we must leave before the guards return and raise the alarm. Seir-onna Arian knows the route, and she will lead us from the Hall. Once outside, I fear our paths take us on different roads, because where we go, you may not follow. However, you have proven yourselves resourceful men of good heart, and I charge you to conduct yourselves honourably, not becoming common cutthroats and brigands preying upon the helpless, be they travellers in the forests or inhabitants of towns and villages. Rest assured I will remember the service you have done me, and with forethought and determination, I know you will make decent, productive lives for yourselves until the true King comes again. Have I your word you will do thus?"

Again there was assent. Several men even touched hands to foreheads respectfully, and the one who had spoken said, "It shall be so, m'lord. You'll not have cause for disappointment. In this we are One."

"Excellent," replied Rhiss. "Then let us away. Seir-onna, lead us out, please. Aquilea and I will bring up the rear."

Arian smiled cryptically at him, but said merely, "As you command, Lord Rhiss. It will indeed be my pleasure."

They met no one as they trekked quietly through the Hall in a winding, convoluted route along empty passageways and chambers. Arian seemed to know every last byway, nook and cranny of the immense building, and used that knowledge to ensure their escape was uneventful. Finally, they came to a short flight of stairs leading to a small oaken door. It was locked but not barred. Arian produced a key, then ushered them into the open. Rhiss had to duck to pass through. As he came out, Arian locked it again. Rhiss looked around to find they were only a short distance from the stables. On the other side of the Hall, a pall of bluish-white smoke was visible, curling lazily into the sky as the sun peeped over the horizon and night gave way to partially overcast day. Arian saw it too, and nodded.

"Ah," she said in satisfaction, "it is as your benefactor assured us. The fire is contained to the granaries, and will soon be out, I wager. Come, gentlemen: let's away to the stables, and secure mounts before the day becomes older."

They made their way purposefully but without blind haste, for as Arian pointed out, nothing would arouse suspicion where there was none like a large group moving with unseemly speed towards the place where horses were kept. Rhiss recalled Arian's reaction as they left the cells. "Seir-onna," he said as they walked, "what made you smile when we left the dungeons? Did I say something witless?"

Arian did not answer at once, evidently considering what to say. "No," she eventually replied. "It is only that, as I listened to you speak and make arrangements for our departure, it sounded like someone very much in command of the situation."

"Forgive me for trespassing on your authority. It must have been the school master in me. I did not intend —"

Arian interrupted, looking sideways at Rhiss. "It did not sound like a teacher dealing with immature children, not at all. I should say rather it was the authoritative voice of a man very comfortable commanding others. But it was pleasing to hear. I was not offended, and did not feel you trod on my leadership. Did you not notice how the men accepted your orders without question or demur? I am glad to see the first stirrings of leadership in you, and the concern you voiced for the well-being of these men. They are qualities you will need aplenty in the struggle ahead." Rhiss flushed, but did not reply. He was thoughtful for the minutes until they arrived at the stables, saying nothing as the group tramped steadily along.

They found the stables almost as deserted as the rest of the Hall appeared to be. Nearly everyone was evidently either fighting the fire, or gaping at it. Rhiss motioned Aquilea to remain outside, and they entered the lofty, airy building. A grimy young stable boy of twelve or thirteen was the only person in evidence. He held a pitchfork, but did not appear to have been using it to move hay, and from the boy's posture and hunted expression, Rhiss realized it was held as a weapon against all comers. While Rhyanna had taken Rhiss through the stables during their tour of the Hall, he did not recognize the boy. Arian plainly did, however, and spoke in a low, soothing voice.

"Arcan, lad, what ails you? You look as though you expect the Other to charge through these doors. But as you can see, it is only me and some gentlemen. We have had a fine visit at the Hall, but it is time for us to leave, so I seek my horse, and mounts for these men as well. There's naught to be afraid of, is there?"

Wide-eyed, the boy shook his head, lowering the pitchfork. Arian continued in the same reassuring tone. "Good lad. If you will see to the horsing of these gentlemen, I'll attend to my companion here." She indicated Rhiss with a casual wave of her hand. "All right, then? Good. Off you go. And Arcan: travellers' supplies, if you please. Blankets, saddle bags, dried food... standard fare from the stable stores. Did Lady Meranna happen to send any saddle bags down, by any chance? If so, you may bring them."

The boy nodded and set off down the wide passageway, the soldiers following. Arian turned to Rhiss. "Come," she said quietly, leading the way. "Judicious speed is appropriate at this juncture. We need to be well away with as much lead time as possible. I would not give Maldeus any more advantage than he already has."

"What advantage?"

Arian did not answer immediately. She stopped before a stall containing a lovely horse with a golden coat and white mane. "How well do you ride?"

Anticipating an answer to his question, Rhiss was caught off guard. "I beg your pardon?"

Arian looked impatient. "Your riding skills. Do you fancy yourself an expert horseman? We will ride for quite some time, I think, and how good a rider you consider yourself influences my choice of mount for you."

Rhiss grinned ruefully. "I can ride moderately well, and have gone on excursions with a friend in the countryside near my home, but by no stretch could I be called a master horseman. Please be generous making your determination."

"So be it," murmured Arian with a small smile, "although I suspect exaggerated modesty concerning your abilities is again in play. But no matter which horse you are given, you will be forced to learn your horsemanship quickly on the open road, not in a practice paddock... and it will not be painless, I fear. However, it cannot be helped. We have need of haste." She indicated the horse, slapping her hindquarters gently with obvious affection. "This is Aralsa. She is a quiet, steady animal who will not play you for a fool." She smiled. "And she is Rhyanna's horse, so will have been properly trained. You will do well by her."

Rhiss looked pained. "I cannot take Lady Rhyanna's horse and ride off like a common thief. She will be —"

Arian interrupted. "Lord Rhiss, spare me your disingenuous qualms. We have need of haste, and after seeing the way she looked at you, my niece will not be irremediably offended by your taking her horse, as I think you already know. She will understand the need, I am certain. Mount up, and let us be off."

Glumly, Rhiss prepared to obey. Aquilea peered around the door with bright-eyed interest, and a sudden thought struck him. "Seir-onna, what will Aquilea do while we are on horseback? She can hardly sit in the saddle with me."

"Nor do I think she would willingly do so. In legend, there is reputed longstanding animosity between horses and gryphons, so I do not think the issue will arise. And before you are tempted to ask: no, I do not know the reason why, so you may as well save your breath. Aquilea must either fly or run alongside, but I am sure she will easily be able to manage either. Now for love of the One, come along, and let's be off."

Arian feverishly saddled Aralsa even as she spoke. Finished, she backed the horse from the stall and handed the reins to Rhiss before moving to her own horse nearby, saddling it also. Arcan returned just as that task was complete, wordlessly handing Rhiss and Arian a pair of plain leather saddle bags and blanket rolls each. Arian put them on both horses, glancing down the passageway. Their soldiers waited at the entry doors, already mounted. Arian nodded approvingly, turning to Arcan.

"Well done, lad," she said. "I note you have seen to the needs of our friends, as asked. Now, after we have gone, if you are queried about your part in our leave-taking, it might be best if you told the truth and said you did indeed saddle horses for us, but you might add you felt you could not refuse such a large armed group. And that would be the truth, wouldn't it?"

The boy nodded mutely, wide-eyed, and Arian smiled as she ruffled his hair. "Good lad," she murmured. "Then we are off. Remain indoors so you cannot say which direction we took. Lord Rhiss, do you have anything to say to yon troop? Final instructions or farewells before parting company?"

Rhiss shook his head, wondering if Arian was gently teasing in light of her earlier comments about his asserting leadership. But she seemed serious, and nodded briskly. "Fine. But I will say a few words, if you have no objection."

"By all means. One moment, if you please." Arian said nothing, watching as Rhiss took off the Circlet of Araxis and carefully placed it in one of his saddle bags. She raised an eyebrow. "He said I should not wear it all the time, as it was too easily identifiable," Rhiss explained. "He also said it was for the King, not me."

Arian said sharply, "Lord Tariel said that?"

"Aye; well, words to that effect, I think." Seeing her face, Rhiss added, "Why? Is something wrong?"

"How..." Arian began, then stopped. "Nothing. We'll let it alone. Come along. Lead your horse out into the dawn."

They clopped along the cobble floor to the doors. The knot of mounted soldiers preceded them, then sat waiting outside. Arian and Rhiss stopped once in the open, and Arian faced the soldiers.

"My friends, the time has come for us to part ways. I add my thanks to those of Lord Rhiss, and charge you to remember and honour the words he spoke. Have you given any thought as to which direction you will take?"

One of the soldiers spoke. "Aye, Seir-onna. We ride east into the Forest of Marturin to allow the furore of recent days to die down before venturing from there. There is plenty of game in the forest. Eventually, we will seek our own homes."

Arian nodded. "As good a plan as any. I would not gainsay it. Ride then, friends; go you with the One." She made the now familiar blessing, at which the soldiers bowed their heads before turning their mounts in a swirl of dust, and were gone.

Arian turned to Rhiss. "Time we were on our way, also."

"Aye, Seir-onna." Arian began climbing into her saddle, but Rhiss cleared his throat, and she stopped, glancing at him with raised eyebrows.

"I assume you have a question." At his nod, Arian held up a cautionary hand. "Very well. But I will permit only one at this time. Be brief, as I do not have all day to satiate your seemingly endless curiosity."

"I will. Where do we ride, if you please?"

Arian gazed at him thoughtfully, then sighed. "You present me with a conundrum. When my sister summoned me, I originally thought we could examine the issue at leisure right here. You were a young man who appeared from nowhere with a rather unorthodox companion and tokens, and a very unusual gift. But then the entire affair with Maldeus occurred, and it seems you are more complicated an issue than I at first naively thought." She stopped, seeing his confusion. "It is a complex and lengthy story, and while you need to know, I fear we have no time to discuss it now." She sighed again. "I simply thought to put distance between Craggaddon Hall and us, hoping to think of a suitable objective along the way. Why? Have you a destination to suggest?"

Rhiss hesitated. "Well, as a matter of fact, I do. Or, at least, Lord Tariel did. His recommendation is Pencairn House."

"What?" Arian straightened, looking comically surprised. "Pencairn House? No, no, to go there — why, young man, that is foolishness. I cannot understand what nonsense he was thinking."

"Actually, he also said that would be your reaction. But I am to tell you your objection is no longer valid. The problem has been resolved, he instructed me to say."

"What do you know of this place?"

Rhiss shrugged. "Nothing beyond the name. And I had never heard that until Lord Tariel spoke it a short time ago."

Arian's face was a study in consecutive emotions, each new one supplanting the previous: disbelief, doubt, contemplation, and finally cautious hope. Arian stood musing by her horse, one hand stroking its nose.

"Pencairn House. A name I have not heard in a very long time. An interesting idea. And most unexpected, too. I deeply regret not having made the acquaintance of this Lord Tariel. But if he is right, perhaps it is not as preposterous as I first thought. As a matter of fact, I begin to see possibilities..." Her voice trailed off, and Arian seemed to make up her mind. She swung into the saddle, nodding decisively.

"Very well. Pencairn House it is. We shall follow the advice of your Lord Tariel. A decidedly eccentric suggestion, but the more I think on it, the greater potential it has. Come, then. We have far to travel, and Maldeus comes nearer all the time!"

VIII

FLIGHT AND WARDING

> *"I am come as a thief in the night, for lo, I employ a tool of the Other, letting darkness be my cloak, concealing me from unfriendly eyes. And I will reject always the blind groping of evil as it struggles to find me. Let it be repulsed by the strength of the One working through me."*
>
> The Book of the One, 78:12:21-22
> (Cantos 78, Chapter 12, Verses 21-22)

They were on the road for nearly an hour before the overcast burned off and the day warmed. Their route at first took them through well-cultivated fields, rich with aromas of growing things and the promise of an excellent harvest, come summer's end. The lands, Arian explained, were farmed by Lady Meranna's tenants.

Over the next several hours they gradually passed out of territory belonging to the Hall, and the terrain became wilder, the land obviously untamed. Fields gave way to thick forests with heavy undergrowth and brush by the roadside. The road itself, though, was in good repair, covered by stones and flanked on both sides by well-tended drainage ditches. Rhiss made mention of the fact, and Arian grunted noncommittally.

"It is no more than is required by the Crown throughout Arrinor. Highly maintained roads make easy the passage of military forces responding quickly to any emerging crisis." She glanced sideways at Rhiss. "They also make riding considerably easier. How are your legs after several hours?"

"I am in no pain." Rhiss cautiously flexed his legs in the stirrups. "Although I cannot vouch how well I shall stand when we finally dismount. When will that be, might one ask?"

Arian frowned thoughtfully. "We *will* stop soon, although more for the purpose of resting our mounts. I am pleased, though, that your gryphon shows no sign of exhaustion, despite her youth."

Rhiss glanced down at Aquilea, loping effortlessly a short distance behind Aralsa. Despite Arian's dire warning about mixing gryphons and horses, there were no signs of animosity between the two. Aquilea had several times flown for short distances, but more from curiosity to take in the countryside than any weariness of running on land, it seemed. Experimentally, Rhiss had tried communicating with her by thought, attempting to emphasize the importance of staying nearby when she flew, not straying from his sight. It was impossible to be certain whether she understood his thoughts, or even heard them at all, for she made no overt sign. But for whatever reason, she *did* stay close to Rhiss while flying, never more than fifty feet above. Rhiss had not discussed the matter with Arian, but decided privately it added to mounting anecdotal evidence that she did, somehow, hear his thoughts. Strangely, he also discovered the idea that another creature could sense his thoughts was not an alarming one, although he *was* interested to find out how much of his mind she could fathom. After all, some thoughts, by their very nature, were private, not meant to be shared. He wondered if he would ever find anyone who could help with this mysterious communication, and assist him to establish logical boundaries. Arian had no special knowledge in this regard. Arian... as he thought of her, he returned to the present with a start, aware she was speaking again.

"Forgive me, Seir-onna, I fear my mind was elsewhere," he confessed sheepishly. "What were you saying?"

Arian raised eyebrows, but said mildly, "Merely that we will be obliged to ride, with rests, throughout the night and into the morrow, but should be able to take our ease at an inn I know of the following night."

Rhiss recalled Tariel's instructions, and related them to Arian, who nodded agreement.

"Sound advice. We will do very much as he recommends: riding as far as we can, travelling by night, and avoiding towns in the immediate vicinity. This inn I spoke of, where I propose we stay two nights from now, is a goodly distance from the Hall, and in a quite unexpected direction for us. As a matter of fact, I have never stayed there." She paused before going on thoughtfully. "In truth, these last few hours, I have tried to think as Maldeus will when he arrives at the Hall to find us gone. He will discover what he believes is the method of our escape — and, of course, your friend, Lord Tariel, has neatly drawn a veil of confusion over that event. Maldeus will spend time wondering why Tariel has twice involved himself in your cause. I *know* he will, because I do — and unlike Maldeus, whom you say seemed to know Tariel, *we* are not privy to the nature or agenda of our mysterious friend, so we cannot even venture a guess as to his motives. The next and most obviously practical question to occupy Maldeus will be: where will that traitorous Seir-onna Arian of the Knights Castellar take her newly found protégé?"

"And what will be his conclusion?" Rhiss asked, absorbed by the older woman's musings.

"Do you know," said Arian thoughtfully, "I think he will be completely at a loss. He is well aware I should never have taken up your cause at all, of course, but handed you over to him or his men straightaway. Failing that, I should have taken you directly to my own chapter house and sent word to the capital I had detained you there. That I have done neither will leave him with several questions: whither would I take you? And why? To what purpose? Our saving grace is that the answer is... that there is no obvious answer. After all, before hearing Lord Tariel's suggestion, I was unsure what to do with you, and had no special destination in mind. That will be Maldeus' conundrum. Not knowing Tariel's instructions, Maldeus must needs divide his forces and look to all points of the compass, for there is no immediately obvious place to have taken you."

"Seir-onna," Rhiss said slowly, "I am very uncomfortable just leaving Meranna and her household while we make good our escape. Was there nothing else we could have done?"

Arian reined in and halted, looking sideways at Rhiss. "What would you have had us do, my lord?"

"Well," he began uncomfortably, "I do possess some knowledge of advanced military technology. Regrettably, my world wages war on a much more sophisticated level than seems the case here in Arrinor."

"By that, you mean it is diabolically inventive at butchering and destroying."

"Aye." Rhiss sighed. "A harsh but fair assessment, I suppose."

Arian grimaced in distaste and made the warding-off gesture. "Then it is cursed by the Other and you are well escaped from it. What is your point?"

"It did occur to me... while we sat in the dungeon... we could employ some of this advanced technology against the forces of Maldeus on their return."

"You did not mention this before."

"It is not something I am proud of, Seir-onna, believe me. Quite the contrary."

Arian frowned. "Then I do not understand: why not bring it up when we could have done something with the knowledge? If, indeed, we would have even desired to?"

"Exactly my point. My world has only recently seen the end of an unbelievably terrible war, on a scale you cannot begin to envision: millions dead or maimed, incredible destruction, and all for nothing. Looking at my world since the end of that conflict, I have found it terribly blighted, especially when compared to this one. In that dank dungeon, I decided I would not see my world's dark plague of spiritual and technological malaise transplanted here — and would rather die than be the source of that contagion. We will not defeat Maldeus by becoming like him, or using his methods — even at the risk of being defeated ourselves."

Arian stared, slack-jawed, for long seconds, and Rhiss grew ill at ease. "What is it? Did I say something witless or offensive?"

"You mean every word," Arian marvelled softly. Then she appeared to return to the present, and cleared her throat. "Aye, of course, 'tis obvious you do. I ask your pardon. No, no, I am not offended. Amazed and impressed, and in fact rather confounded, for it is long since I have heard such a principled declaration, from anyone. These days, you may find that circumstances in Arrinor tend to discourage principle." She cocked her head to one side. "Are you aware of the trust such conviction engenders? And for once in your life, do not respond by belittling yourself or your actions."

"Well," he began, swallowing hard. It was not easy. "It *is* how I feel, Arian."

Her lips quirked in a small smile. "I suppose we will count that as progress." She was about to urge her horse into motion, but another question evidently occurred to her. "Did you fight in this war you spoke of, my lord?"

"I did. Towards its end."

"How did you survive, if 'twas so terrible?"

"Through the grace of the One," Rhiss said dryly, but Arian did not smile, and despite his reluctance to discuss it further, he felt compelled to elaborate. "The most horrific battles were on land, but I was assigned to our naval forces instead. It could still be highly dangerous, and often was, but the odds of survival were much better."

Arian raised an eyebrow. "Then the grace of the One *was* full upon you, indeed."

"No." Rhiss shook his head. "Well, yes, of course, but I think more prosaic forces were also at work. I have often wondered... there were one or two hints..."

"What, my lord?"

"Well... my mother had a... a rather unique relationship with a man of power and influence — Lord Caerchester, his name was. They were quite close, but given their different circumstances, it was a very unlikely relationship, and there was much about it I was never privy to. It has occurred to me that he could have been behind my extraordinary good fortune, for I well know that ending up in the Navy instead of the Army might literally have saved my life."

"I see." Arian digested this. "Marvellous are the ways of the One." She looked around. "Very well. Shall we proceed?"

"A moment, Seir-onna. I wish to return to my original question concerning the safety of Lady Meranna and Craggaddon Hall, and whether there was anything we could have done to ensure their safety. Could we have evacuated the Hall, for example?"

Arian shook her head. "Pack up the entire household in the space of a mere hour and move out like some ragtag army? To where? Some five hundred people make their home in and around Craggaddon Hall. Since it is the primary seat of the Tormere earldom, a couple of hundred are soldiers, who could, 'tis true, muster relatively quickly; but the rest are just ordinary folk — servants, tenant farmers, artisans and their families, ranging from the very young to the very old, the frail and sick to those in the prime of life. And transport for them all? There are not nearly enough horses or carriages. Even if there were, can you imagine trying to move them through the countryside swiftly and unobtrusively? They might just as well have targets whitewashed on their backs. Leaving and proceeding across country, we would have witnessed a rout, not an evacuation, with corresponding loss of innocent life."

Rhiss felt foolish. "I suppose not. I had not thought it through properly. The idea was ridiculous, and I am embarrassed. It is just that—"

"Aye, the colour of your face is proof. A most fetching scarlet it is, to be sure." Arian smiled. "But look you here, there is no need for shame. Your heart was in the right place. I, too, am worried for those left behind. It is simply that there was nothing we could practically do but leave the people of the Hall and trust to the plot my sister and I hatched. When Maldeus returns, she will maintain that, as a loyal servant of the Crown, she tried to detain us, but we escaped and even now ride to parts unknown."

"Will it be enough, do you think? Will he believe her?"

Arian sighed. "I know not. He is a veritable Prince of Lies, so whether he will be taken in by the story my sister spins, I cannot say. I pray to the One he will." She urged her horse into a walk again, clearly not wanting to pursue that line of thought.

"What of this Pencairn House Lord Tariel recommended?" Rhiss asked, changing the subject. "I would know more of it."

Arian smiled. "I would rather not describe it now. Let it leave you full of amazement when you first encounter it, and then you will understand why it really would never occur to anyone to take you there. It never occurred to me, and will not to Maldeus. We proceed there purely trusting Tariel, who twice saved your life. I do not think he would send us on this journey simply to betray us once there."

"I see. Why will Maldeus call you 'traitorous'?"

Arian looked bemused at the sudden topic switch. "Most especially because I am Castellar, of course," she explained. Her bafflement grew as Rhiss looked blank. "Surely you are aware, that as a Castellar, my first task should have been to deliver you straight to the Sovereign's Counsellor, Lord Maldeus of Angramor. That I have failed to do so — more, that I have actively thwarted such action — immediately marks me as renegade and traitor to the Crown." She laughed humourlessly. "As he overcomes his rage, I imagine he will straight away call for pen and parchment to proscribe me outlaw."

Rhiss shrugged. "No, Seir-onna, I am not aware of that at all. Do you not recall my tale explaining the circumstances of my coming? I do not really even know the function of the Knights Castellar."

Arian looked vexed, then smiled grimly. "Of course. I ask your pardon. In the press of events, I forgot you are but newly arrived in Arrinor. It may not be the last time I make such a mistake, I fear." She drew herself up in her saddle. "Know this, then: the Knights of the Order of the Priests Militant Castellar is a most ancient religious order, dedicated for hundreds of years to the protection and maintenance of Arrinor's monarchy."

"But..." Rhiss halted in confusion. Something was not right. "Seir-onna, this cannot be reconciled with what Brother Gavrilos said, that the present ruler of Arrinor is evil and a Usurper. Is that not correct?" Arian nodded, and Rhiss continued, recalling the words of Gavrilos. "He said there is a young king in Arrinor, unjustly deprived of his throne, who requires assistance regaining it." He looked at Arian. "Now, it is to that end I am here, as you know, although as I have said, what difference I could possibly make remains a mystery to me. And yet, you sit there saying an organization already exists to protect the Crown; but everything you have said implies it supports this Usurper. Just what are the Knights Castellar doing? And why would one of their members surrender me to the Usurper's chief servants if she was doing her duty?" He stopped for a moment, and then added, "Forgive my thick-headedness, but it makes no sense."

Arian smiled once more, but bitterly this time. She halted her horse in the middle of the road again, and, surprised, Rhiss did likewise. "Your confusion is entirely understandable," she said quietly. "And you are absolutely right. What I described does sound a complete contradiction. But the answer is really very simple. The order I belong to, the Knights Castellar, this ancient and most noble order, dedicated to the ideals of truth and justice... has in reality, during and since the Coup, and even before, if what I have learned is true, been suborned and corrupted by the very forces it has sworn to fight against, to the point where it now upholds the Usurper as the rightful ruler of Arrinor." She shook her head, saying sourly, "Nearly all my brother and sister priests are blinded by the Other's deceits, obeying his servants now. It is into the very midst of this tale of crushing betrayal and defeat you have come. Ultimately, the evil truth is that the very organization which should be your first recourse for aid in this quest is the one standing implacably pledged against you. And I have long been an unwitting part of it." With that, she abruptly slid off her horse, let go of the reins, and walked to the roadside, where she sat down heavily. Rhiss watched, stunned, unsure what to do.

After a moment, he dismounted and, wincing, walked a little unsteadily to where Arian sat. Aquilea followed. Rhiss flopped down beside Arian and began massaging his cramping legs. To his amusement, Aquilea watched solemnly for a moment, then began kneading his legs with her own forelegs, being extremely careful to keep her claws from damaging his clothes or flesh. Their combined motion seemed to bring Arian from her reverie, although she said and did nothing.

"Arian," Rhiss began quietly, "I truly doubt anyone holds you responsible for the situation existing in Arrinor. I certainly do not, and you need to know that. If anything, it seems you have gone out of your way to assist me, to your own obvious detriment. As far as your membership in the Knights Castellar... have you known long of this displaced rightful king needing assistance in regaining his throne?"

"No," replied Arian somberly after a moment. "Only shortly before your arrival in Arrinor."

"And prior to that?" Rhiss asked. "Have you known long that the current ruler usurped the throne?"

Again, Arian did not answer right away. She was silent for several seconds. "No." She looked up. "The story is long and complex, and it is one you must know, but here, at this time, I cannot tell the full tale. Allow an abbreviated version. Years ago, the King of Arrinor died, along with, it has always been maintained, his entire immediate family. It was given out that the cause of their deaths was a tragic accident in a terrible fire. The real circumstances were known to only a very few. Few have ever questioned that ruling, and life went on with the current Sovereign, who, as the dead King's sibling, stepped forward when none of his children were found alive. But in very recent times, certain... irregularities in the official account have surfaced, at times in rather remarkable circumstances, leading some few members of my Order, myself among them, to doubt the official version's validity. And there have been... other signs indicating all is not as we have long believed it to be. It is best, for now, we not discuss these irregularities, but you have my word that one day, we shall. My little group of colleagues and I had only begun, in recent months, to make preliminary inquiries, always in discreet and careful ways, but we have uncovered enough evidence so we now refer to it as the Coup amongst ourselves. But we realized we had to be circumspect in our investigations, for the implications of our line of questioning..." Her voice trailed off, and Rhiss, aghast as he realized what Arian implied, finished the sentence for her.

"...point, at the very least, at conspiracy to commit regicide, and at worst, the actual commission of the deed," he said softly. "You obviously believe this regicide has, in fact, occurred."

Arian nodded, saying nothing.

Rhiss pursed his lips, and was likewise silent a moment. Then he sighed, and murmured, "Arian, whatever have I ensnared myself in by stepping through that portal?"

Arian looked sideways at Rhiss, and smiled crookedly. "Oh, Rhissan, I assure you, we have only just entered this snare."

They sat quietly for several minutes, Rhiss gradually relaxing under the patient ministrations of Aquilea as he took in all that had been said. Eventually, he drew the gryphon to him and, scratching her head, whispered, "Enough, Aquilea. Thank you, lass. My legs feel ever so much better." He turned to Arian. "It is truly a tale of terrible evil and injustice; we could linger here in disbelief and despair all day, or many days. But I say to you truly, we have lingered long enough. We have a destination in Pencairn House, a goal once we get there, and presumably time to discuss the realizing of that goal."

Arian roused, as one waking from a dark dream. "Well, aye, we *do*... if you hold sufficient hope to be willing to accept the challenge, after hearing such a sorry tale."

Rhiss smiled wryly. "And what should I do in rejecting it, Seir-onna? Travel the length and breadth of Arrinor, asking folk I meet if they have seen a door appearing where there should be none?" He stood slowly, still feeling the effects of the day's ride, nearly losing his balance as Aquilea butted her head against him. "No, I made a commitment to Brother Gavrilos before we parted. He said that with the Light, all things are possible, and help would come at times from very unexpected sources. I am learning that powerful forces for evil are in the world, and have seen some already. But I will put my faith in the Light of the One, because I learn, too, that there are powerful forces for good also abroad, and have seen some of those, as well." He paused. "You told me 'despair is the daughter of the Other,' so we will have no truck with her, will we? We move on in the service of the Light."

Still at the roadside, Arian watched Rhiss in dawning hope, then suddenly pulled herself to her feet and clasped Rhiss' hand. "Indeed, we will," she said warmly. "Indeed we will." She strode briskly to her horse, cropping the grass after wandering a short distance. She took the reins, and, looking back, watched critically as Rhiss hobbled slowly to Aralsa. "Come, my lord," Arian called. "One would think, by your slow gait, you have no enthusiasm in this enterprise we embark upon. Let us go!"

"Aquilea," muttered Rhiss, "could you, perhaps, massage the good Seir-onna — with talons extended?"

———⟞◆⟝———

Re-mounting was not as difficult as Rhiss had feared; their unscheduled rest had been beneficial in easing the knots in his legs, and he was able to carry on without incident until Arian called a halt hours later.

When they finally stopped to eat, the sun was descending behind the tree tops, a great ball of molten vermillion. The meal consisted of strips of salted meat, a handful of dried fruit, and drinks from their respective flasks. Rhiss had diluted the remaining cordial of Gavrilos with water, and found with relief it diminished neither the taste nor its restorative effects.

While eating, they allowed the horses to wander and graze nearby. Rhiss offered to share his meat with Aquilea, but she sniffed it, snorted with what could only have been disapproval, and disappeared into the brush. She returned later, licking her forelegs, evidently having satiated her hunger by dining on some unfortunate animal. Rhiss grinned, recalling their first night at Tor Linlith and the pair of hares that had appeared to his overworked imagination to be nearly as large as she. Doubtless she would have done the same this evening if asked. However, he knew a fire would be undesirable because the time it required, and the smoke produced would alert anyone nearby to their presence.

They rode on after resting, through the evening twilight that deepened steadily into darkness, a clear night illuminated by moonlight, which bathed the land in silver radiance. For a while, they spoke quietly back and forth, Rhiss generally posing questions, Arian answering. Then there came a time when they ceased speaking and rode in companionable silence, each wrapped in their cloaks and their own thoughts.

At length, as the eastern sky began to pale with the promise of oncoming dawn, and Rhiss was blinking owlishly, trying with increasing difficulty to remain alert, Arian halted, looking around. She dismounted and, leading her horse by the reins, indicated Rhiss should follow. Groaning, he dismounted and hobbled after as best he could, taking Aralsa on what proved a path through the undergrowth into the forest.

They stopped in a small clearing bisected by a noisy little brook, with clear, cold water rushing over a slaty bed. Arian yawned as she hobbled her mount, gesturing Rhiss to do likewise.

"This will do as a resting place for a few hours," said Arian as she took the rolled blanket from the rear of her horse's saddle, laying it on the ground. "I feel every bit as exhausted as you look, and the horses are likewise tired. Find a comfortable spot, lad, and surrender to sleep a while. I do not think we need mount watch. Aquilea can sleep along with us, but I am sure she will wake and raise the alarm, should anyone chance by."

Rhiss nodded sleepily and settled slowly to the ground. He did not bother to retrieve the blanket from his saddle, simply rolling himself in his cloak. Arian smiled at that, but made no comment, and Rhiss drowsily sank into the welcome relief of sleep. He dimly felt Aquilea snuggling against him, then knew no more as sweet slumber brought oblivion.

It was late afternoon when Rhiss opened his eyes; a fresh wind dappled patterns of shadow and light from the overhanging trees. Arian was still in her blanket, fast asleep, but Aquilea awoke as Rhiss stirred and sat, golden gaze fixed solemnly on him as he stood and stretched. Feeling quite recovered, he strolled casually to the brook and knelt by its banks, splashing cold water on his face before cupping his hands and drinking. Aquilea accompanied him and drank also. The afternoon was a fine one, and Rhiss could not suppress the temptation to wander along the brook a short way, delighting in the serene beauty.

When he returned, Arian was awake. She knelt on her cloak in the middle of the clearing, facing the warm, late day sun, arms outstretched in an attitude that spoke clearly of prayer. Rhiss motioned Aquilea to be still, and waited quietly for Arian to finish. When she did so, minutes later, she made the triune blessing and stood, picking up her cloak and brushing leaves off. She turned and smiled.

"So you return, Lord Rhiss. Were you taking Aquilea for a walk? You really should not wander on your own, but knowing she was with you eased my mind. Unaware which way you went, I thought I would take advantage of the solitude to say tar-merida."

"We were appreciating the beauty of our surroundings, Seir-onna. I apologize for interrupting you at... tar-merida? What is that? It looked like prayer."

"Aye, it was. Tar-merida is the office for the afternoon, one of the four Great Services of praise and thanksgiving said or sung to the One throughout the quarters of the day. The other three are at morning, evening, and night."

Rhiss looked around the clearing, considering. "Do we have time before setting out on our journey?"

Arian smiled knowingly. "I had thought for us to break our fast, then wait for the gloaming before proceeding. Why do you ask? Have you yet more questions? I would have thought you had asked everything possible these last twenty-four hours."

Rhiss nodded. "I have been in Arrinor but a short time, Seir-onna, and have heard numerous references to the One... and the Other. I would know something of them, of Brother Gavrilos and Lord Tariel and how they fit into everything. Since you *are* a priest, perhaps you could enlighten me."

"Truly, 'tis a subject deeper than the ocean. How much time do you have?" Arian shrugged ruefully. "Very simply, the One is Maker and Master of all. The Other..." she paused, making the Triune Sign, "rebelled against the One, and seeks to corrupt and despoil all Creation. Both have many servants; as an Arkos, Gavrilos is among the highest servants of the One. While we eat, I will speak to you about the act of prayer, and how to pray to the One." She smiled. "It is something that should be done regularly. Do not wait until you are in crisis."

Rhiss nodded, and they sat to eat. Arian said a blessing very similar to the one Lady Meranna gave, and that served as catalyst for their discussion when Rhiss commented. Their conversation was brief but instructive. While they talked, they chewed on more dried provisions. Rhiss was sorely tempted to send Aquilea hunting for fresh meat, and said as much. But Arian dissuaded him; they still had urgent need to put more distance between themselves and Craggaddon Hall.

"Allow me to illustrate," said Arian, drawing a circle in the ground with a stick. "At the centre is our dear old Hall. Maldeus will use it as the focal point from which to begin his search, and we should make sure we are well clear of this radius as quickly as we are able. At the moment, I should say we are this far—" she indicated a spot about a third of the way from the centre to the perimeter of the circle "—from where I would feel safe from his gaze or those of his spies. It could be another day or two before we reach the circle's edge. We must make for it with all haste."

"But, Seir-onna, that circle represents an extremely large area. I do not see how Maldeus and his forces can possibly cover it all, especially if they indeed travel to all four compass points. Do you not think we are safely beyond their reach by now?"

Arian looked sideways at Rhiss with an expression of polite disbelief that Rhiss was already beginning to recognize well.

"Hmm... well, if we merely count men on horseback, I agree. However, Maldeus has at his disposal other means of conducting searches. Many involve black arts. It has long been rumoured he can somehow send forth his will to search for that which he seeks. He also makes use of animals to spy for him, animals you might expect would be favourably disposed to assisting a servant of the Other..." Arian made the three fold gesture of blessing, "...and I am told you have seen, in fact, actually done battle with another of his other servants." Arian cocked a quizzical eyebrow at his blank look. "And killed it with that great bow of yours, no less."

Rhiss felt a chill. "Are they intelligent? What do you know of them?"

"Intelligent," Arian mused. "It would seem so. They are quite capable of spying and fighting and killing on his orders, at any rate. And somehow they convey information gleaned on their flights. But I know little of them. *Malmoridai*, they are called, an ancient name, so they have existed a long time. They hunt always in pairs — why, no one knows. It seems difficult and revolting to envision them as male and female, although that is one suggestion I have heard. Maldeus has kept a tight rein on them, literally and figuratively, so they have not been often seen in Arrinor. It is only in recent years that people have begun to realize Maldeus and these creatures are associated with each other."

"And you think he will use these creatures to look for us from the air?"

"Depend on it. They are too useful a tool to ignore in a situation like this. And in shooting one down, you have ensured any others Maldeus sends against us will be most diligent in searching for you, as they will have a score to settle."

"Wonderful," Rhiss breathed dismally. "Do you have any other good news to share?"

Arian laughed. "They are not as rare in number as Aquilea's kind, but neither are they numerous, I think, so you need not fear seeing the sun darkened by hordes in perfect formation. And as you say, even using them, Maldeus has much terrain to cover attempting to locate us. With the grace of the One, we may not encounter them at all. And if we do," she added lightly, "you have leave to impress Aquilea and myself with your amazing archery prowess." She sobered and continued. "I have seen these things. Truly, to bring one down as you did, especially in one shot... an amazing feat."

"One I should not care to have to duplicate," said Rhiss grimly. "It was luck, nothing more. I do not even know where I hit the beast."

Arian clapped him on the shoulder. "My lord, I know *very* few archers skilled enough to make such a shot. And you should know that there is no such thing as luck. Do not dismiss your gift." She sighed. "But let us hope your skill need not be put to the test. Come, daylight wanes, and we should have the moon lighting our way again this night. Make ready, and ride."

They rode steadily into the evening. It was a clear night once more, the moon providing limpid, silvery illumination. But after making good time for several hours, Rhiss gradually became troubled by an oppressive darkness that had nothing to do with night. He could see no obvious reason to feel as he did, and attempted to dismiss, or at least ignore, the sensation. However, it continued to grow, and he could not. Several times he found himself shaking his head, trying to clear a dark miasma slowly creeping into every thought.

Just as he was on the verge of saying something, Aquilea stopped abruptly, moaning deep in her throat. Startled and concerned, Rhiss reined Aralsa in. The gryphon was halted, crouched low in the road, clearly much distressed. Rhiss dismounted, flinching, and went to her. He knelt and looked in her eyes. Her luminous orbs stared pleadingly, and Rhiss knew instinctively the same burdensome feelings weighed on her. Arian, who had evidently been deep in thoughts of her own, suddenly stopped, looked back, and called softly.

"Lord Rhiss, what ails your gryphon? Has she some legitimate complaint, or is she merely truculent? This is no place to stop and admire the surroundings."

Rhiss said nothing as he tried to analyze what they both felt. His vague oppression was crystallizing into definite foreboding: they were being watched, or at least sought by some nameless malignancy in the ebon reaches of night. And it was edging closer. He glanced into the sky and suddenly realized the moon was, inexplicably, completely gone. He transferred his attention to the darkened lands, became aware they were hushed, normal night sounds extinguished. He pursed his lips, aware the feeling was not new. When had he felt it before? Realization dawned abruptly, and he gently enfolded the cowering Aquilea in his arms.

"Arian, dismount and bring the horses after me," Rhiss said urgently. He stood and strode swiftly to the side of the road, Aquilea following closely. Seeking some hollow they could retreat into, the dim outlines of one emerged after a few seconds, and he plunged off the road into thick underbrush. Rhiss could sense Arian's confusion at the sudden turn of events. However, to her credit, the older woman made no query as she led the horses. Rhiss was glad, feeling he could not articulate his insistent sense that it was important to be under cover of the forest and away from the exposed road.

Rhiss led them into the small clearing and knelt beside Aquilea, murmuring vague, reassuring noises to her. Then he motioned Arian to lead the horses to the side of the clearing furthest from the road. When Arian had done so, Rhiss quickly went over to Aralsa and rummaged in the saddle bags. This last action finally stirred Arian into speech.

"Why we have left the road and now hide in this undergrowth? What exactly—?"

Rhiss held up a hand, momentarily silencing Arian while continuing his search. Then his other hand closed on the object, and he pulled it triumphantly from the depths of the saddle bag. Arian narrowed her eyes as Rhiss lifted it reverently to the sky.

"The Circlet of Araxis? Why bring that forth?"

Rhiss placed it gently on his head, turning to Arian. "I do not believe we have much time. Let me explain by asking you a question. Have you not felt... well... darker thoughts in the last hour or so? As if an oppressive force weighed heavily upon you?"

Arian looked thoughtful, then nodded. "Aye. But I would not have been able to articulate the mood had you not mentioned it, so gradually did it come upon me. I would have thought exhaustion was merely manifesting itself." She looked at Rhiss sharply. "But you do not, I take it?"

Rhiss shook his head. "I am sure it is quite real. Aquilea and I have experienced this before, at Tor Linlith. But the sensation is much stronger this time, hence her distress." He looked directly at Arian. "What is the gem in the Circlet doing, Seir-onna? Is there movement within it?"

Arian peered at the gem, and involuntarily made the triune sign. "Aye," she said softly, wonder in her voice. She opened her mouth to say more, but Rhiss stiffened and held up his hand for silence again. The hushed forest seemed suddenly to come alive with that same hideous whisper he had heard at Tor Linlith, the wind and the trees all echoing a single word: *where... where...*

"Do you hear that voice?" he asked urgently.

Arian looked startled. "Voice?" she repeated blankly. "I hear only the night wind on the trees."

"It's coming nearer! Get down!" Rhiss hissed. Not waiting to see whether she obeyed, he closed his eyes and turned to face the direction from whence the darkness seemed to originate. He felt a groping malevolent presence, and automatically put his arms out in front, palms outwards in rejection and warding. He tried to project his will outwards, encompassing Aquilea, Arian and the horses, as two thoughts thundered through his mind: *I will not yield! Batter yourself against my will, but in the Name of the One, I am adamant you shall not find us!*

For several endless moments, he felt a very real assault on the barrier he envisioned around them, as though something physically strained against a tangible shield. There was a brilliant white flash visible even through his closed eyelids, and the sensation ceased abruptly. He staggered slightly and opened his eyes, aware he was covered in cold sweat from his exertions.

Kneeling beside Aquilea, Arian appeared to search her own mind even as she eyed Rhiss in shock. "It... feels like it is gone," Arian said hesitantly. "What did you do?"

Rhiss licked dry lips, seeking to analyze recent minutes. "Aye... it is gone. As to what I did... I am not entirely sure. What did you see?"

"You lifted your arms and shouted something about not yielding," said Arian carefully. "A dazzling light emanated from the gem, and a white, smoky wave raced outwards in all directions from it. It was... quite unlike anything I have ever seen." She paused, and got to her feet, brushing pine needles from her legs. "What have we just experienced?"

"I believe," replied Rhiss thoughtfully, "someone, or something, has tried to find us, just as you said might happen. In fact, I think it was... him." A slow smile spread across his face as realization sank in. "And the Circlet repelled the attempt."

"How?"

Rhiss frowned and removed the Circlet, examining it. The stone's lambent glow was fading. "I do not precisely know. Somehow, the Circlet seems attuned to my mind, and can..." he stopped, confused. What *could* the Circlet do? And how?

Arian appeared prepared to put the issue aside. "You are quite sure they do not know our whereabouts?"

Rhiss again searched the memory. "Aye. Although I do not really understand *how* I accomplished it, I am certain whoever searched for us *was* blocked."

"Hmm. Will they *know* they were blocked?"

Rhiss hesitated. "I cannot see how they would not. The entire process was rather... violent." He tried to articulate a rational explanation for something almost purely instinctive, and as difficult to vocalize. "It's like they were... in a darkened corridor with many doors, feeling their way by touch, seeking the right one... and I suddenly slammed them all shut. They won't know which I was behind, but they *will* know I closed them." He grimaced. "And forcefully, I'm afraid. I'm sorry. I should have been more subtle."

For a split second, Arian looked incredulous, then chuckled wryly. "I hardly think an apology is necessary. You have accomplished an amazing feat without any instruction, and in the process, likely saved our lives yet again. You need not regret lack of finesse now. Later, as your skills grow, I think you will witness increasing control in this — as with your healing gift, and any others that arise." She patted Rhiss reassuringly on the shoulder. "All in good time, young man. Like the child who has just learned to stand, you cannot run before learning to walk. The important thing is to buy you that time, and hone the skills you need."

Rhiss nodded silently, catching the offhand reference to 'other' gifts, wondering what they could possibly be.

"One other thing: was it Maldeus, do you think, or... something else?"

"I do not know, in truth. It did not feel much like my experience at Tor Linlith. It was far more... intense." He suddenly felt very tired, and glanced at the Circlet again. The gem was dark, quiescent, and he carefully returned the Circlet to his saddle bag. He looked around the clearing, unsurprised to see the moon once again casting its silvery light. He sighed and said resignedly, "It may well have been. We had best resume our journey."

Arian looked concerned. "Perhaps we should rest a while. You look and sound fatigued from your exertions."

Rhiss shook his head. "I am," he replied, with feeling. "But I would rather continue distancing ourselves from... whatever that was. Aquilea would concur, I know, and I think you do, too. Let us be on our way."

Aquilea did, indeed, concur — wholeheartedly. Were it solely up to her, she would have allowed her fear to drive her ceaselessly and without embarrassment on the cool back of Brother West Wind, flying until she was far away from the black, monstrous Evil pursuing them. There was no shame in fleeing an enemy who was, plainly, far more powerful than oneself — in fact, utterly, implacably, unstoppable.

Except... Aquilea was slowly coming to the thoughtful realization that this Enemy might not be unstoppable, after all. And that was a knowing hopeful beyond all hope, for two reasons. First, The Man obviously had a powerful ally in the Transcendent Servant of the One — who did not appear nearly often enough to suit Aquilea's taste, but who was obviously prepared to provide assistance some of the time. That was better than nothing.

And then, The Man himself was beginning to manifest unusual and interesting abilities; it was like watching a golden flower unfurling its glorious petals with the coming of the Sun. This time, The Man had not only dispersed the foul, searching Hand seeking them — he had somehow slammed it back on itself, in the process generating a psychic shriek of pain that had set Aquilea's nerves on fire in a manner she had not experienced in a very long time. It was reminiscent of the occasions when her older sibling would deliberately rake her talons over a sharp rock outcrop by their Nest to drive Aquilea to distraction with the awful scraping noise.

And even though The Man did not yet seem to know what he was doing, or how, the fact he appeared capable of summoning such abilities as needed was comforting, after a fashion; Aquilea just wished he would have more faith in himself and those abilities and hasten his explorations of them, so the Evil could be sent reeling back into the Shadows of the Other where it belonged. At times, The Man's own doubts, which came through clearly, made her impatient, and she wished she could show him the necessary steps and skills. But she remembered her mother's quiet counsel that all living things must learn at their own pace; for only when one is ready and willing can the learning proceed.

And Aquilea realized her earlier characterization of The Man was incorrect: he was no flower at all, but almost a strange kind of chrysalis. Having arrived in Arrinor a drab and listless shadow, fearful of his own reflection, he was now well on his way to becoming a beautiful and powerful source of Light. The transformation was both intensifying and accelerating, even as the Servants of the Other attempted to destroy him and so thwart the Will of the One. It was all really quite ironic, Aquilea mused: in trying to prevent The Man's success, the forces of Darkness were actually hastening his ability and will to succeed. And as Evil so often does, it failed even to realize it.

Interesting. Most interesting — as long as success was his in the end, of course.

For the alternative did not even bear thinking.

IX

SHELTER AND STRANGERS

"Above the raging storm, the arrival of friends unlooked-for gives comfort to the Essence and strength to the will. Such friends prove stalwart and welcome. Have courage, hold fast, and seek ye the will of the One in all things."

The Book of the One, 77:1:1
(Cantos 77, Chapter 1, Verse 1)

Two days later, as afternoon waned and a hard, cold rain fell, Rhiss and Arian arrived at The King's Arms, an inn nestled in the small village of Rontha, their first objective in the flight from Craggaddon Hall.

The extra day's delay beyond Arian's prediction was due to the fact that her concern for Rhiss following his confrontation in the night had been justified. The morning after the struggle, Rhiss felt exhaustion deepen into an illness characterized chiefly by a dull fever. Wanting to continue, he said nothing to Arian, but the sharp-eyed priest noticed the flushed complexion and lethargy of her charge the first time they stopped, and insisted they make camp immediately and rest. The fever was not life-threatening, but Arian's concern extended to making a small fire and hunting for game in order that Rhiss could have a hot meal and warm broth. Rhiss was too spent to argue against the delay or the cooking fire, although he made a feeble jest regarding Arian's about-face, saying he would have taken ill sooner had he known it would mean respite and a cooked meal.

They rested all during that day, and through the night which followed, Rhiss slept — a deep, restorative sleep untroubled by dreams. Aquilea appeared to know Rhiss was unwell, and spent almost all her time snuggled against him, providing her warmth, leaving only briefly to forage for food. Whenever Rhiss awoke, regardless of the time, it seemed Arian was always there, awake and sitting beside the small fire, sometimes staring meditatively at Rhiss, other times gazing deep into the flames, lost in her own thoughts. Fortunately, the weather remained fair, and his fever broke early on the following day. They mounted up that morning, riding through cool winds and increasing cloud, arriving outside Rontha at the time of evenmeal, and moments, it seemed, before inclement weather.

Rontha was the first real settlement of any size Rhiss had encountered in Arrinor, and consequently he was fascinated with everything as they approached. He was not disappointed, even from a distance. Located in the highlands bordering a majestic mountain range, Rontha was only a small village — Arian estimated its population at less than a thousand — but the cottages and prosperous businesses were generally neat and tidy. The buildings, many single-storied, some double, were constructed from wood or stone. Roofs were a varied mix of thatch, wooden shakes, or slate, depending on the owner's wealth. The village was surrounded by a wide, dry ditch about fifteen feet deep and as wide, and a sturdy wooden palisade wall on the ditch's inner side. A fixed wooden causeway passed over the ditch at two places, where the palisade was pierced by wooden gates that swung shut at night or when peril threatened. Rhiss was interested to see the village was fortified, and commented to Arian, who grunted sceptically.

"Fortified? Not really. That is exaggeration, like saying your dagger is a kingly sword. Yon wall is merely meant to exclude wild animals and the odd brigand. It would not repel determined invasion by trained armies. You will see true fortifications one day, I promise you, and then you will realize Rontha's walls are but a child's fence in comparison."

"Then why have them in the first place?"

Arian shrugged. "They have some use, not the least of which, I suspect, is to reassure the inhabitants." She yawned. "Come. It is time to put into action our plan for entering. I would very much like a hot bath and good food before the foul weather is upon us. Let us toss this coin to see who enters Rontha from the far gate."

During their ride, they had discussed the tactical situation, and decided it was best they not enter Rontha in company. Arian was sure Maldeus would have issued bulletins about the lady priest and the young man who escaped the Sovereign's justice at Craggaddon Hall, to be apprehended on sight. While any such bulletin would likely not yet have arrived in Rontha, there was no point in giving Maldeus eventual information as to their whereabouts. Therefore, they determined that one of them would detour around the village and enter by the far gate, arriving at the inn later. In this manner, they would merely be two solitary travellers, strangers to each other, both ending up at the inn, housed in separate rooms.

They flipped the coin, and Rhiss lost. He eyed the highlands with little enthusiasm, sighed and reconciled himself to the extra time his detour would take.

"Very well, Seir-onna. Aquilea and I will be on our way. We should be at the inn within the hour."

"But not in each other's company. Remember what I said."

Rhiss had wondered what was to become of Aquilea while they stayed in Rontha, and as they approached the village, he and Arian discussed her fate. Arian was insistent that Aquilea could not accompany Rhiss: her unusual presence would invite unwelcome attention and guarantee recognition. Humans and gryphons together were not unheard of, but were uncommon. Since Maldeus already knew of Aquilea's existence from the altercation at Craggaddon Hall, his bulletin would doubtless mention her. Rhiss admitted Aquilea's presence would be a dead giveaway, but had argued they could not simply abandon her at the village borders and tell her to fend for herself.

In the end, they agreed Rhiss was to impress upon her that she must stay outside the village until darkness fell and he called her with his thoughts. If he could secure a room on the second floor, it might be possible to smuggle her through a window without attracting attention. Rhiss was not sanguine he would be able to make his wishes clear to Aquilea, or that she would be able to psychically hear him over great distances, but there was no other alternative.

"One thing more. For obvious reasons, it would be better to use names other than our own while here. Have you any preferences?"

Rhiss thought. "How about that stable lad at Craggaddon Hall? What was his name? Arcan? Would that suffice?"

Arian smiled. "Indeed it would. 'Tis a common enough name and will elicit attention from no one. Say you hail from Follet, another village not far from here. Now... my name shall be..."

Rhiss was struck by inspiration. "How about Ardwyad?"

Arian blinked. "A strange name. Does it have any particular significance?"

Rhiss coloured faintly, hesitating before replying. "It is a name from my own people. In the language of my forefathers, it means 'protector.'"

Arian regarded Rhiss gravely, then inclined her head. "I am honoured. Seir-onna Ardwyad it is." She handed Rhiss some coins. "Use these to pay the inn keeper. And be careful, Lord Rhiss. Sovereign's Men are everywhere these days. I can hardly believe our good fortune in not meeting any thus far."

Arian gave Rhiss her blessing, and he steered Aralsa off the road. Slowly, he struck off cross-country to make his way around to the far gate. Despite the uneven terrain, Aralsa made her way confidently. As they approached the road on the far side of the village, Rhiss halted. Dismounting, he knelt before Aquilea, holding her great avian head in his hands, staring intently into her golden eyes, marshalling his thoughts. It was impossible to know whether she understood, but when he finished, she chirruped, rubbed her head against him in a very feline gesture, spread her wings, and flew silently into the gathering gloom. Rhiss experienced a twinge of misgiving, but there was nothing else for it but to go ahead with the plan as conceived.

Rontha appeared to owe its existence to the fact that it was built at a crossroads, and travellers arriving from one point of the compass could alter the direction of their travels dramatically if they chose. An hour after leaving Arian, Rhiss finally entered the village. Rain was falling as he came through the gate. Challenged by the warden who was about to close for the night, Rhiss identified himself as Arcan of Follet, supplying the plausible tale Arian had devised: he was travelling on his own from Follet to visit his mother's kin, who lay ill in the coastal village of Ansby, several days' ride away. The guard accepted the story with little interest and waved him on with directions to the inn, plainly more focused on closing the gate and returning to his small shelter to escape the rain.

The inn was at the village's centre, both literally and metaphorically, and was obviously the largest establishment, several buildings constructed around a muddy courtyard. The main structure, housing the guesthouse itself, was a two storey wooden affair finished with plaster, built in the shape of an L. The other buildings surrounding the courtyard included storehouses and stables for guests' animals.

As he dismounted and removed his bow and saddle bags, a watching groom emerged from a building, throwing on a cloak to ward off the wet as he came. The groom took charge of Aralsa with a friendly nod and a smile, motioning Rhiss to the side door of the inn even as he led the horse into the stables. A welcome glow of warm, yellow light emanated from the open door, throwing objects in the yard into stark relief. A large wooden sign hung over the door, displaying an improbably long sword with gilded hilt encircled by a bejewelled crown and the establishment's name; the legend beneath read, 'Belan Othwain, Owner and Proprietor.' Rhiss hesitated before entering. He was about to experience his first extended, peaceful contact with ordinary folk in Arrinor. He took a deep breath and stepped over the threshold.

The room he entered was plainly the main room, the tap room. Most of one wall was taken up by an enormous fireplace in which a fire roared. Scattered around the stone floor in no particular arrangement were numerous benches and tables. Many were occupied, and a low murmur of conversation filled the room like the somnolent buzzing of bees. A number of heads briefly turned his way in idle curiosity as he entered, but conversation did not waver. Sweeping the room with a quick glance, Rhiss saw Arian sitting alone, drinking from a tall tankard. She met his gaze briefly, but gave no sign of recognition. At that moment, a short, plump man came bustling over and planted himself before Rhiss, eyeing his clothes and summing up the prospective customer's wealth and status with a single, practiced assessment.

"Good evening, young sir," he puffed, bowing a balding head respectfully. "What can I be doing for you this nasty, wet night?"

"A room for one, if you please," replied Rhiss, faintly amused. The man's tone indicated he thought his customer well off. "I am Arcan of Follet. Are you the owner?"

"I am indeed, young sir," said the man, bowing his head again. "Belan Othwain, at your service. A pleasure to have you at our humble wayside house. Your horse has been taken care of?" Rhiss nodded, raising his saddle bags as evidence. "Very well, then, master, if you'll follow me, we'll see you to your room directly, and you can get out of those wet clothes before you catch your death of cold."

He led Rhiss from the tap room and along a corridor lit with candles in wall sconces, up a flight of stairs with a landing halfway up before reversing their direction to complete the climb to the second floor.

As they walked, Othwain said apologetically, "The ground floor is full tonight, master, but we have grand rooms on the upper floor, if that meets your approval."

"Perfectly," said Rhiss, thinking it would indeed be easier to smuggle Aquilea through an upper floor window. He added, more to politely maintain the conversation than from any real interest, "Your business prospers, then?"

The little man nodded enthusiastically. "Aye, young master, commerce is brisk and numerous travellers like yourself are on the road these days. With the foul weather this night, many will find it preferable, I wager, to spend the time indoors with a mug of good ale and a warm fire, instead of out there in the cold and the wet. Especially out on Byrn Moor." He stopped abruptly and shivered, making the triune blessing before resuming his progress.

Rhiss was intrigued by reference and gesture. "Byrn Moor?" he repeated. "What would be amiss on the Moor — aside from the cold and wet?"

Othwain halted, glancing sharply at Rhiss before laughing uncertainly and continuing down the hall. "Ah, now, young master, you should not play a simple man for a fool. I thought for a moment you were serious. Imagine a man of Follet not knowing of Moressin Venator's return! You tricked me proper there!"

"Indeed," Rhiss answered with a smile and conviction he did not feel. But there was no chance to add or ask anything else, for at that moment, Othwain stopped again, this time outside a plain wooden door. Taking out an iron key and turning it in the lock, he swung the door open with a flourish, gave Rhiss the key, and gestured him to enter.

Rhiss stepped into a spacious room. A fire already burned in the fireplace to his left, with several very comfortable looking stuffed chairs arranged around it. Before him, a table and more chairs were set against the wall, where a large window looked out into the night. To his right, there reposed a bed large enough for two or three. He turned to the innkeeper, who had followed and looked at him questioningly, nodding in approval.

"Splendid!" said Othwain, rubbing his hands. "Now then, young master, I imagine you'll be wanting a hot bath, and then a bit of supper. The baths are on the ground floor at the far end of the hall. Here's a robe for you. Get yourself out of those clothes and off there to take the chill from your bones, and then we'll see about food. Would you like to eat here, or in the common room?"

Rhiss vividly imagined Aquilea impatiently circling in the miserable night. "I think here would be best, sir innkeeper. A quiet meal before the fire sounds appealing."

Othwain bowed low. "As you wish, young master. I'll have a meal prepared directly and brought up so it's ready when you return after bathing. Have you any specific requests for food?"

Rhiss was inadvertently carried back to The Admiral Rodney. "Well... I have a great fondness for meat pies. Steak and mushroom, perhaps?"

Othwain looked apologetic. "Ah, what a shame. To my certain knowledge, young master, we've just run out. An older Seir-onna came in a short while ago and took the last two. Must have had a fairish hunger on her bony frame to want both, but there it is."

Rhiss wryly but silently offered up a pox on Arian's 'fairish hunger,' reflecting that, had the coin toss only gone the proper way, *he* could have been the traveller enjoying the culinary delights of not one, but two meat pies. Why couldn't she have been satisfied with one, this night of all nights?

But he smiled disarmingly. "Ah, well. Doubtless, the business of rescuing lost Essences inspires great physical as well as spiritual hunger, sir innkeeper, so we won't begrudge the Seir-onna her little overindulgence. I know you will provide a worthy meal. The reputation of your establishment's food spreads far beyond Rontha."

Othwain beamed. "I'll not disappoint you, young sir. And perhaps you might wish to come down to the tap room later to have a tankard or two with your fellow guests. In the meantime, go you with the One, young sir."

Nearly an hour later, Rhiss made his way back to his room, much refreshed, feeling the cares of the last few days removed along with the grime and dirt of travel. Going down to the baths, he was surprised and delighted to find that 'baths' meant several good sized sunken stone pools, not merely bathtubs. The water in them varied from tepid to almost scalding, depending on user preference. The stone floor was also wonderfully warm to his bare feet, and perhaps most amazingly, there was actually a steam room. He questioned the attendant and learned it was all made possible by a large furnace and hypocausts under the floor, heating waters, floor, and air. It was positively Roman in design, and he came away from the experience with a new appreciation for the combination of hot water and steam.

Back at the room, he found, to his surprised pleasure, his clothes had been brushed and neatly folded, cloak hung to dry by the fire. He had just finished dressing when a knock came softly, and a young serving girl entered. She carried a large tray with several dishes and flagons. Smiling shyly, she wordlessly brought the tray to a small table beside one of the fireside chairs, setting out food and filling a tankard with an amber liquid. Then, with a quick curtsey, she let herself out, closing the door quietly.

Rhiss looked around appreciatively, but seeing the rain still beating on the window, realized guiltily that while he had been enjoying himself, Aquilea waited out in the night. He immediately strode to the window and unlatched it, letting in the cold and wet. He closed his eyes, crossed his fingers, and concentrated on mentally calling her.

After two or three minutes, he was both rewarded and warned by the rushing sound of approaching wings, and stepped back hastily, eyes opening. Almost immediately, Aquilea came gliding smoothly in through the open window, landing gracefully on the floor. She shook herself, rather like a dog, and water flew everywhere. Rhiss went to the window, closing it and the drapes before turning. She looked at him with a distinctly jaundiced expression, and Rhiss got the feeling she appeared ready to make an issue of the fact she had been kept waiting in the filthy weather so long. However, he held out a clean, dry towel, the expression on his face contrite.

"There now, lass, don't look like that. I've been as quick as I could... well, nearly as quick, anyway. I'm sorry you had to wait in the cold and the rain. But I've not eaten yet, either. Let me make amends and rub you down, then we'll enjoy supper."

Mollified, she allowed herself to be coaxed over to the fire, where Rhiss gave her a thorough rubdown. When she was dry, he looked over the food and found several items he thought would appeal to her palate. The second flagon was filled with water, so he filled a bowl and set it on the ground. Once she was busy with her food, Rhiss ate his own. It was delicious, and the amber fluid was a honey-tasting sweet wine that blazed a fiery trail on its way down to his stomach.

After dinner, feeling considerably mellower, Rhiss decided he would go down to the common room and meet Arian. He almost invited Aquilea to rest on the bed, which was covered by a large, feathery down quilt; but a mental image rose unbidden of his aunt looking scandalized at the very idea of damp fur or feathers on the best eiderdown, and he gestured at the fire instead. Aquilea yawned hugely and settled agreeably before the warmth of the flames. Smiling, Rhiss said, "Right. I'll be gone a short while to speak with Arian and plot our next move. You have a lovely sleep, and I'll return at bedtime. It's like Craggaddon Hall, isn't it, lass? Although hopefully without sudden awakenings." He thought grimly of that rude surprise, and then unbidden, Meranna and Rhyanna's faces came to mind. He hoped they had successfully carried out their deception, and not landed in trouble on his account. Was there a way to find out? He must ask Arian... who, even now, probably waited impatiently in the tap room. Rhiss sighed. It seemed to be his evening for keeping friends waiting. He looked at Aquilea as she lay before the fire. Eyes half-closed, she was contentedly purring in its warmth. He smiled again, turned, and left, locking the door.

The tap room was fuller, noisier and hotter. Evidently it served as a social gathering place for local folk in addition to travellers passing through. On reflection, it made sense. Travellers brought news from far and wide, and people of the village who dropped in could have a companionable ale or two and pick up all manner of stories — some, doubtless, even true. Tonight was no exception, and there was much talk, laughter, song and drink. Rhiss again thought briefly of The Admiral Rodney, feeling the slightest twinge of homesickness. Then he spied Arian, and it subsided. He had chosen this, he reminded himself.

Arian was deep in conversation at a table with a young man; Rhiss decided not to be so obvious as to make straight for his mentor. Instead, he sat at one of the few other empty places in the room. After a look to see what the locals were drinking, he hailed a serving girl and indicated a rich, dark brown brew consumed by the man adjacent, thinking the drink at least looked like stout.

It was not, he discovered when handed his own tankard moments later, but it was obviously ale of some kind, and had a very pleasant flavour, vaguely nutty, very full-bodied. He tried a cautious sip, then approvingly took a deeper draught.

The man beside him noticed. "Yer enjoying yer browan, then, lad?"

Startled, Rhiss choked briefly, then recovered. "I beg your pardon, sir?"

The man gestured impatiently towards the tankard. "Yer browan, lad. Yer browan. Do ye not know yer drink?"

Rhiss self-consciously glanced down, wondering what to say. Was it reasonable to admit being a novice with various Arrinoran tavern beverages? He decided again that it was best to be honest and not make claims of association that could invite trouble later.

"This is actually the first I've ever had, sir. I chose it simply by looking at your choice, and decided it was just the thing. But aye, it is delicious, and I thank you for demonstrating its finer qualities." He held out a hand. "Arcan of Follet, at your service."

Placated, the man smiled a wide, toothy smile as he shook hands. He appeared very old, Rhiss suddenly realized, getting a good look: grey, fine hair extended to his shoulders, and a lined, weather-beaten face that had evidently seen the changing of many years. But the hazel eyes twinkling still danced with vitality. "Well, that's grand, lad. Nothing like looking to yer elders for guidance, I always say. Here's to a youth who listens to an old man." He raised his tankard in salute, and Rhiss, amused, joined him. Despite the fact that he had neglected to introduce himself, there was something charming about the old man, a rare quality or characteristic he exuded, prompting Rhiss to feel, somehow, that here was someone worthy of trust. They sat and chatted, and as the old man finally drained his tankard, Rhiss beckoned the serving girl to bring two more.

"Thank ye, lad," said the old man approvingly. "Obviously yer a gentleman. What brings a fine young man such as yerself to Rontha and our humble hostelry, may I ask?"

"Oh, I'm on my way to Ansby," Rhiss responded easily. "I have relatives there, my mother's kin, who have been ill, and I'm going to visit."

The old man rubbed a stubbly chin thoughtfully, looking keenly at Rhiss. "Ye'll be takin' the north road to Ansby, then? Across Byrn Moor?" Rhiss nodded. The old man lowered his voice. "Ye've been that way before?"

Rhiss hesitated. "No, actually. Again, it's my first time."

"And will ye be leavin' Rontha tomorra?"

"I believe so. Why?"

The old man was silent for a moment, appearing not to have heard. "Then I'll offer a word or two of advice, lad, seeing as how ye have been kind enough to sit and talk with an old man and buy him a couple of brews. Start only if the weather is fair in the mornin', and be across the Moor well before dark. If it be rainin', or worse, if there be fog, don't leave. Stay another day. T'would be best for yer own health."

"I've travelled in foul weather before—" Rhiss began.

"Aye, as may be. But strange things have been happenin' on the road over Byrn Moor recently, lad. Travellers like yerself have odd tales to tell."

Rhiss frowned. "What tales?"

The old man did not answer immediately. He stared at his newly filled tankard, but his gaze was far away.

"Tales of fogs and storms blowing in on the Moor faster than they've any right to. Tales of people followed... and pursued... when the day is done or the weather be soft. Travellers missin' and not turnin' up when they're supposed to."

"From what cause?"

"Well, there be the old legend about Byrn Moor, of course," said the old man softly. "How, in times of trouble or evil, a dark spirit roams the moor on a ghostly horse, with a pack of the Other's hounds, seeking the Essences of unwary men." He looked earnestly at Rhiss, voice dropping even lower. "Moressin Venator, Moressin the Hunter. There be quite a few who say troubled times are upon us again, so he's come back and is out on the Moor, doin' the Other's bidding." He made the sign of the triune blessing.

Whether by chance or design, it seemed to Rhiss at that instant that a chill swept the room, and he shivered. The fireplace flames burned low and lost their heat, the candles flickered momentarily as though the door to the outside had opened, and a shadow passed over the room. Then the sensation was gone as suddenly as it had come. Rhiss looked around uncertainly to see whether anyone else had experienced it, but it was difficult to say. No one was unduly alarmed. He noted, however, that the number of people had thinned considerably while he and the old man had been deep in conversation. Rhiss turned back to his companion and realized, with discomfort, that the old man gazed at him with a shrewdly knowing look.

"Felt somethin' didn't ye, lad? Aye, ye don't have to say anything, I can read it in yer face as plain as plain." He paused. "Are ye armed, lad?"

"Why... of course," replied Rhiss cautiously, taken aback by the abrupt topic change, wondering if he had broken a social taboo in bringing his dagger. But a quick glance showed most other patrons with swords or daggers at their belts.

"May an old man see yer weapon?"

It was a strange request, but Rhiss saw no reasonable way to refuse, and got his dagger out. Slowly, he handed it, hilt first, to the old man, who took it carefully and examined it. His eyes widened slightly at the gryphon emblem and the jewel in the hilt; then he saw the blade's cursive lettering and bent closer to examine it. The old man was quite absorbed: closing his eyes for several seconds, he nodded, straightened with a sigh, and handed the dagger back to a puzzled Rhiss.

"Where did ye say ye were from, again, lad?"

Rhiss cleared his throat and found his voice. "Follet."

"Hmm," said the old man, managing to place much scepticism in the single sound, although his expression remained carefully neutral. "Well, ye can say that if ye like, but I think yer from a long ways further off than that. Shall I show you a trick, lad? Tell ye a wee bit about yerself?" He didn't wait for an answer, but closed his eyes and began, his voice becoming curiously monotone. "Ansby is not really yer destination, is it? No, ye needn't answer. If ye have need to tell folk it is, I'll not gainsay it, nor let anyone else know. But ye have much further to go, that I can tell too, startin' with somewhere long forgotten and unlikely. Yer journey stretches a fair longish way. But be careful, lad, fer the gaze of the One is full on ye, and while that's not necessarily a bad thing in itself, it means the gaze of the Other is likewise on ye. Yer bound up in great events, I think, and how it all turns out, only the One knows." He opened his eyes, glanced briefly in Arian's direction, then returned his attention to Rhiss, bringing an eyelid down in a deliberate wink.

Rhiss was deeply uneasy by the references the old man had made, references uncomfortably close to the mark. "How are you doing this?" he asked huskily. "Who are you?"

His companion smiled, shaking his head in a deprecatory way. "Ah, ye needn't worry. I'll not let anyone know. I'm no one of any consequence… just an old man out for a quiet drink. Ye have answered a call, although I don't think ye know quite the full story just yet. But yer marked for greatness if it ends well. So I'm content, well rewarded for the evening and will take my leave. Just ye remember what I said about Byrn Moor. If ye must travel it, to reach Ansby or wherever, and things go sour, keep yer faith in the Light, and use yer gifts. Remember, the Sight is a gift of the One. Above all, don't doubt yerself — ye have strengths ye don't know. Go ye now with the One." He stood, drained his tankard, and touched hand to forehead in a gesture of respect. Then he was gone, swiftly for an old man, too swiftly for Rhiss to do more than gape in confusion, many questions racing through his mind.

"Lord Rhiss, you have a gift for all manner of strange things happening when I am not about," said Arian in annoyance. They were in his room on the upper floor, half an hour after his anonymous companion had abruptly left. Arian had eventually managed to catch Rhiss' eye, and with a slight nod, indicated to proceed upstairs. Rhiss did so, waiting in the upper floor corridor; Arian joined him a few minutes later. Rhiss earnestly related what had transpired as they proceeded along the corridor. Aquilea waited eagerly as Rhiss unlocked the door, and now he sat in a stuffed chair, stroking her as she nestled her head on his lap. Together they watched Arian pacing.

"Seir-onna, calm yourself," said Rhiss mildly. "I was taken aback by what he had to say, and he was remarkably spry for an old man. He just up and left before I could even consider stopping him or alerting you. I *did* ask Master Othwain, but he either could not or would not recall any regular patron matching the old man's description or abilities. He gave the matter some thought, too, seemed genuinely concerned I might have been upset by what he called the old man's 'harassment.'" Rhiss paused before adding thoughtfully, "In any event, I do not believe we have anything to fear. I am certain he posed no threat, despite his disconcerting knowledge of our purpose and plans. There was some quality about him, something almost indefinable. I felt I could trust him without danger of its being violated. He told me the Sight was a gift of the One. I do not think a servant of Maldeus or the Other would say such a thing, or even be capable of saying it."

Arian stopped and sighed, passing a hand over her face. "Aye, you may be right. But—" She looked sharply at him. "Some quality, you say? What manner of feeling?"

Rhiss was confused. "Well… it was… a… a feeling, Seir-onna, that's the only way to describe it," he floundered. "I just *knew*, within the depths of my being, I could trust him without fear. I do not know *how* or *why* I knew, only that I *did*."

"Curious," murmured Arian. "Would you say you are usually a good judge of character?"

Rhiss was on firmer ground, recalling the school. "Oh, definitely. Certainly, with most boys — and even the masters."

"Hmm. An intriguing trait, useful in many capacities. I wonder... what of this old man's countenance? Come, give me a description."

"Well... as I said, he was old. Quite old. Long grey hair, down around his shoulders. Bright hazel eyes. Tall, lean. A several days' unshaven face that has seen the turning of the seasons many times, I shouldn't wonder, and a long, thin nose."

"Was there a scar anywhere on his face? Think carefully, boy. This could be important."

Rhiss cast his mind back. "Aye, on his right cheek. Faded, quite long, probably very old." He stopped, seeing her look. "What is it? Do you know him?"

"I did, I think. But if it is indeed he... I thought him dead these many years. In fact, at the time, I was quite sure. I wonder..." She sucked in her breath and frowned into the fire. Rhiss kept silent while Aquilea 'purred' at his lap. Finally Arian roused.

"Another minor mystery. You accumulate them as a dog does fleas. However, it is one we cannot solve tonight, and it is high time we sought our beds, so we must drop the matter of your mysterious friend with the strange ability. We must needs be away early tomorrow, for I would like to arrive at Pencairn House by day's end. If I recall my cartography aright, that should be entirely possible, as long as we do not sleep the morning away." She stood and looked around, seeming to notice the room and its furnishings for the first time. "You have done well by arriving later than I did. This room is far more luxurious than my own simple lodgings on the main floor."

"And the baths," Rhiss replied enthusiastically. "I was most impressed with their luxury. I had not thought to find anything like them here."

Arian laughed. "Such facilities are hardly uncommon, even in smaller wayhouses such as this. But Craggaddon Hall has bathing and steam facilities that put these ones to shame. Was she overcome by modesty, or did my niece see fit to include those in your tour that day?"

"She did not, Seir-onna."

"Well, take my word that they are there. Now, meet me in the tap room at first light, and we shall break our fast together. It will not seem strange for early morning travellers to eat in company."

"Perhaps we should see what the morning weather is like before deciding to leave. What of the apparition on Byrn Moor my elderly friend spoke of in such dramatic terms?"

Arian shrugged. "I have not heard of this Moressin before, so whether you were told the truth or tap room tales to alarm the weak-minded, I cannot speculate. Locals often have favourite ghost tales to frighten gullible travellers. But I have heard tell of far darker things in the world than this, and seen some, too. So your friend either had too much ale, or may simply possess a strange sense of humour. We will take care, not setting out if the weather is anything less than promising; although I would hope your reluctance to leave in such case would have nothing to do with the baths and other enticements of this establishment. But unless the weather is undeniably foul, we must be on our way. I will rest easier when we finally have you—" she stopped, smiled and corrected herself "—*both of us*, safely tucked away at Pencairn House."

Rhiss marked the alteration, but did not comment on it, nodding slowly. "Very well, Seir-onna, I am guided by you." He remembered something else he had meant to ask. "What of provisions on reaching Pencairn House? Do you expect to find food and other necessities waiting for our personal use?"

"No, I doubt there will be much in the way of food or other items for our use."

"Well, then, should we not purchase what we need in Rontha, to take with us? Perhaps even buy a pack horse to carry supplies? It would be a prudent course of action."

Arian smiled approvingly. "Excellent... you are thinking ahead, not merely reacting to circumstances. Well, as to purchasing supplies in Rontha, I had already considered that, but had decided against it. I think it more important we make for Pencairn House with all haste, assessing the situation on arrival. We have simple fare in our saddle bags that will last us for days more, and can return here once we have a better idea what our needs are."

"You still do not wish to share what it is, exactly, we may expect to find at Pencairn House?"

Arian smiled again. "Not at the moment. I want you to experience Lord Tariel's recommendation without prior prejudice from me."

Rhiss sighed resignedly and nodded. He abruptly felt tired. "Very well, Seir-onna, I bow to your wishes in this also. If there is naught else to discuss, I will make for my bed."

He made as though to stand, but Arian waved him back. "No, Lord Rhiss. You are quite right, it is time we sought our rest, but you need not escort me out. I can see myself back to my room. Rest by the fire a while longer, if you wish. I will greet you in the morning. Good night. Go you with the One." She retreated to the door, opened and closed it softly behind her as she left.

Rhiss stared into the flames. "Did you catch that little slip, Aquilea? That's the second time. Her fears are for *my* safety, not hers. She would see me delivered like a valuable, fragile package to Pencairn House. The good Seir-onna is not sharing all her thoughts, I wager. Not that I suspect her of anything ill. I know I can trust her, in the same way I knew my unknown friend in the tap room was worthy of trust..." He sighed and looked down. Aquilea watched with rapt interest. He smiled. "Once we reach Pencairn House, it is high time Arian and I have a little chat where she shares her thoughts more fully." He snorted. "Had I not more faith in the combined insight of Gavrilos, Tariel *and* Arian than I do in my own, I would think them all mistaken or deluded for their interest in me. Or is it something as simple as the fact I was willing to answer when called, as my friend tonight said? Although how he knew that, I don't understand. And I really wish Arian would stop calling me 'Lord' Rhiss." He sighed, aware his thoughts were becoming random and disjointed. "Aquilea, my dear, it's time for us to settle down. Come, lass. Off you go." She stood lightly, but as soon as he rose, she jumped into the vacated seat, settling into the residual warmth from his body. Rhiss laughed. "All right, then. You stay there while I undress and get into bed. Then you can decide where you want to sleep."

He went to his saddle bags and rummaged through them, finding a nightshirt identical to the one he wore at Craggaddon Hall. Holding it, warm thoughts of Rhyanna arose. During their walk in the gardens, she had shyly confessed to embroidering the nightshirt he wore after being brought unconscious from Tor Linlith. Aye, she had been so gracious, so elegantly charming, and altogether alluring in an innocent sort of way. The shirt he held now was very much like the one he had worn then, and since the saddle bags had been sent to the stables by Lady Meranna, Rhiss wondered if it had been crafted by Rhyanna's patient skill. He slipped into the shirt, rather hoping such was the case. It smelled faintly of roses, and Rhiss inhaled deeply. It was her scent. He smiled wistfully and climbed into the roomy bed, watching the flickering shadows from the fire on the ceiling. A moment or two later, the bed creaked as Aquilea bounded onto it. She settled at his feet after fussing for a bit, a warm weight even better than a hot water bottle, and he let himself yield to the delicious sensation of falling asleep in a soft bed again after several nights curled up in his cloak on the unyielding ground.

X

SLINGS AND ARROWS

"Why are the hearts of the Children of the One so oft inclined to rebellion and waywardness? Truly, 'tis naught but sheerest folly. For mark well: such conduct leads to lessons always painful, sometimes lethal."

The Book of the One, 84:21:35-36
(Cantos 84, Chapter 21, Verses 35-36)

Rhiss woke to gentle knocking. He turned to the window, afraid he had overslept, but the curtains he had opened during the night revealed a slate grey sky, rain softly blurring the glass. He glanced at Aquilea; she was awake but unconcerned, so he rolled out of bed and went to the door to find Arian, already dressed.

"No need for alarm, Lord Rhiss. You are not overdue... but I thought I should come up, lest you were preparing to leave. I have been up some time, evaluating our day's plan. May I enter?"

Wordlessly, Rhiss opened the door wide, mind still fuzzy. Arian quickly looked both ways along the corridor to confirm no one watched, then came in, shutting the door firmly. She shook her head in exasperation.

"Unfortunately, it has been raining heavily, off and on, most of the night. No one I have spoken to expects the weather to clear anytime soon, and travel, especially over Byrn Moor, is definitely not recommended by anybody — and that has nothing to do with dark spirits that may or may not exist. It is simply that conditions are positively filthy out there." She paused. "It frustrates me no end, but I think we must remain here another night — unless you can think of some other feasible course of action."

Rhiss listened to Arian's assessment with growing dismay, then had to hide his delight at her sensible conclusion: it was exactly his inclination, but he had not expected her to be of like mind. "No, no, I am more than content. I can return to bed for a while, enjoy the baths again, have a leisurely breakfast, then we can explore the village—"

"We will do no such things," she interrupted tartly. "This is no pleasure excursion arranged for your entertainment. I remind you that we are fugitives from the Sovereign's Counsellor, fleeing for our lives. We will remain in our rooms and attract no notice."

His delight deflated as suddenly as a balloon pricked by a needle. "But—"

"We are not debating this further," she said tersely, cutting him off again. "We shall stay here, quietly, and there is an end. I came to instruct you to send Aquilea out before it lightens further. Even in these conditions, we risk someone seeing her—"

"Wait a moment. The weather is too nasty for *us* to venture into, yet you blithely exile *her* out there?" Rhiss asked in outraged disbelief, interrupting in his turn.

"She cannot stay indoors. How do you suggest she relieve herself? Or feed? Or exercise? I doubt an animal would be willing to settle down with a book to while away the time. Nor can she be expected to sleep all day. And servants are bound to enter the room at some point, if only to clean the grate or bring wood. They cannot be allowed to see her lounging here, and forbidding them entry would arouse the very suspicion we seek to avoid." Arian spread her hands impatiently. "Can you refute any of this?"

"Well, no, but—"

"Then, for love of the One, stop wasting precious time and send her on her way. After that, in any case, you are *not* going back to bed; only a sluggard would do so. Were you a novice Castellar, you would have already been up, engaged in your duties, for quite some time. Bathe, dress and come down to the tap room to break your fast. I will await you there." Abruptly, she turned and left, leaving the door ajar.

Rhiss said nothing as he closed the door after her with rather more force than necessary. What a curtly patronizing list of orders to give someone only just awakened, he thought sourly; like being confronted by a tyrant schoolmistress. While Arian's reasoning was unassailable on the face of it, Rhiss felt sure he could have found a way to keep Aquilea tranquilly in the room, had he been given a chance to think things through. He sighed and looked at her apologetically.

"I'm that sorry, lass, but the Seir-onna is adamant you've got to go out. I'll bring you back as soon as practical, rest assured. Go and have a good fly, find something to eat, and maybe you can find some shelter until I call."

He opened the window, reflecting how strange it was to be holding a rational conversation, even rather one-sided, with an animal. But Arian's comments moments ago notwithstanding, he no longer felt that way. Fortunately, Aquilea took it with remarkably good grace. She cocked her head to one side while he spoke before jumping from the bed, loping to the window and bounding onto the ledge. She paused a few seconds, testing the air, beak jutting out, before soundlessly launching into the drizzle. He gazed, fascinated, while she soared in lazy circles, gaining altitude. Eventually she levelled off, heading northwards. Rhiss watched wistfully until he lost her in the grey sky.

"And *I* will not be caged all day, either," he murmured. "Regardless of what the schoolmistress directs."

After bathing and dressing, he descended to the tap room, where Arian and several early morning guests sat, some alone, some in twos and threes. But the place was certainly emptier and quieter than the previous evening. The only real activity came from a bustling pair of serving girls. He looked around casually, disappointed but not really surprised that his elderly drinking partner was nowhere in sight. He made an elaborate show of introducing himself to Arian, asking if he might share her companionship. She responded graciously enough, and Rhiss thought with satisfaction it must have seemed to any observer that their meeting was pure chance. But Arian was still out of sorts and largely uncommunicative, which spoiled the meal. When returning to his room, it was with repeated instructions to remain there echoing in his ears. He muttered under his breath and rolled his eyes as he walked away.

Following a tedious morning, they met for midmeal. Arian indicated she would meditate until evenmeal, and did not wish to be disturbed.

By mid-afternoon Rhiss was bored, lonely, and had had quite enough. Surely a companionable pint would not be dangerous. After a seemingly endless time pacing back and forth in his room, Rhiss made up his mind and quietly stole down the stairs, pausing in the door to the mostly empty tap room. As he did so, his gaze moved absently to a window that gave onto the street outside, passed over it — and jerked back in surprise: the old man from the night before had just walked sprightly by.

Rhiss was out the door in a trice, scanning the pedestrians, seeking the man's familiar features. But the old codger was as swift as ever, Rhiss thought distractedly. He could see no sign— Wait! Moving down that thoroughfare! Aye, that was him! Rhiss set off at a brisk pace, almost running, arriving at the place within moments, then halted, perplexed. The old man was nowhere to be seen. He had vanished.

For the next hour or so, Rhiss felt as though he played a frustratingly fruitless game of hide and seek, although he was sure the old man was not aware of being pursued. Several times, in fact, he caught fleeting glimpses of his quarry, and finally thought he had the man dead to rights, only to wind up alone in a blind alley, staring disbelievingly at the walls around him.

The rain was starting to fall again, and Rhiss felt disgust rising as he stood there, realizing he was without his cloak. It was completely ludicrous, this frantic, futile pursuit. About the only thing he had discovered for certain was that Rontha was much larger than he had imagined. Time to head back — if he wasn't already hopelessly lost. It would be unpleasant if Arian discovered his absence before he could return.

Rhiss retreated from the alley, looking around uncertainly. He was at the deserted intersection of several streets, darkened buildings all around. Aye, it was... that way. Definitely. Well, probably. He started off slowly, then sped up as the rain began falling more heavily. By the time he rounded the next corner, he was striding along quite briskly — and collided with someone.

Or several someones. He had a quick, jumbled impression of a group of people, a younger pair, male and female, and two or three older men, one of whom he had run into. Paradoxically, they were all motionless, facing each other, as though the weather was not deteriorating with each passing moment.

His first instinct was to simply apologize for his clumsiness and move on. But something was most definitely wrong: swiftly scanning the group, he felt a razor-sharp tension present in all, and in blinding realization, understood he had unwittingly blundered into the midst of a nasty confrontation.

"I'm sorry," Rhiss said to no one in particular. "Is there a problem I could—?"

"No. No problem." The tallest man — there *were* three, Rhiss realized — cut him off curtly. He was a dark haired, ill-favoured fellow with a sallow face and a scar on one side of his mouth that twisted it permanently into a frightening leer. "Be on your way. Nothing here to concern yourself with."

Rhiss hesitated, glancing at the couple. They were younger than he, barely out of their teens, raggedly dressed, dishevelled — and terrified. It was especially evident in the girl's eyes.

He smiled placatingly at the men. "Now, gentlemen, no need for that tone. They hardly appear any threat—"

"Begone, whorespawn. I won't say it again. Or stand with the filthy Tavvies!"

Rhiss' gaze whipped around to Scarmouth, who had spoken. "What did you say?"

"You heard me. We'll show lying, thieving Tavvies what happens when they dare bring their dirty faces to our village. Look at them, the whore and whorespawn! We'll teach them a lesson they won't soon forget! Do you want to be included in it?"

Rhiss glanced at the couple again. The mute plea in the girl's eyes all but shouted at him. He experienced a dizzying flash of recognition: he had seen that look before, most recently at Darkton and Lewis cowering under Talbot's imperious disdain.

Two conflicting voices spoke in his head. *You need to leave, now, before this becomes ugly; it's not your fight,* whispered one. *Of course it is,* retorted the second acidly. *All that is required for the triumph of evil is that good men do nothing, remember? Are those just words?*

Rhiss shook his head and smiled apologetically at Scarmouth. "No, I don't think so, friend. They're only Tavvies, after all, and need educating. I'll be on my way."

The couple gasped sharply in dismay. Scarmouth grunted, relaxed slightly, and jerked his head in the direction Rhiss had been going. "Right, then. Off you go."

Rhiss nodded, and avoiding everyone's eyes, made as to leave. Forgetting him instantly, Scarmouth began to turn back to the couple—

—and crumpled to the ground with an agonized roar as the heel of Rhiss' boot caught him squarely in the crotch.

"Run!" Rhiss shouted at the couple, sweeping out his dagger and menacing the two men standing dumbfounded. The girl needed no further urging and dashed off down the street; the boy gave Rhiss a quick, unfathomable look before sprinting after her.

"You miserable scum," said one of the men disbelievingly, looking at Scarmouth still writhing on the ground. "Bad mistake, my friend."

Rhiss had no intention of fighting two — three, when Scarmouth recovered and could stand again. He turned to flee after the couple, but put a foot wrong on the rain-slick ground, lost his balance, slipped again in a muddy puddle and felt himself falling. He put a hand out, landed roughly in the wet, his dagger went flying... and the two were on him, quick as vipers.

They hauled him to his feet. While one pinioned his arms, the other smiled nastily but said nothing as he drove his fist into Rhiss' torso, followed by several quick punches to his face. Rhiss felt his lip and one cheek split open, and through a scarlet haze of pain, he heard a voice say hoarsely, "Let me."

It was Scarmouth. He had tottered to his feet and was still partly bent over, but he approached Rhiss, an animal glint in his eyes, waves of murderous rage radiating almost visibly from him. Rhiss suddenly knew, beyond a shadow of a doubt, his life hung by a thread. The icy realization cleared the mists threatening to engulf his thoughts, but he had no time to say anything before Scarmouth was on him, hammering away mercilessly all over his body. Speech of any kind was quite impossible; in fact, he could barely get in a breath, and felt like his lungs were exploding.

An indeterminate time later — seconds? minutes? hours? — the blows abruptly ceased, and Rhiss groggily heard a disembodied voice say from a great distance, "Sweet Light of the One, Malreck, that's enough! You'll kill him!"

"No!" said Scarmouth triumphantly. "I'll give him a taste of what he gave me!"

Rhiss felt what seemed like a red hot bar of lead crash into his crotch, and screamed involuntarily, waves of agony arcing through his body like lightning. He felt his arms released, and he dropped like a stone into the mud, feebly curling into a ball.

"Malreck, enough, I tell you! I think someone's coming! Let's away!"

"Filthy Tavvy-lover!" he heard someone else say derisively. "Let's find the other two." There was the retreating sound of feet splashing through puddles, and he became aware of staring at something glittering a foot or two before him. *An icicle?* he thought hazily. The dancing dark spots in his vision grew larger and larger until they merged together, and awareness drifted away on waves of pain in a bright red sea.

He was cold. And soaked. Because it was raining. And something was nudging him, sending warm exhales of breath that smelled vaguely spicy into his throbbing face. He struggled to integrate the disparate pieces of information.

With an enormous effort, Rhiss slowly opened his eyes to find two luminous, golden orbs staring fiercely at him. It was... it was... Aquilea. Aye, that was her name. Where had she come from? He was dimly aware that someone, somewhere, was extremely concerned. How did he know? He couldn't remember. He just knew. Nobody said anything, and he wasn't sure he was capable of speech, anyway. Bright lancets of pain radiated everywhere.

"Aquilea," he whispered, and stopped. The flat, metallic taste of blood in his mouth was so strong, he wanted to vomit. But he somehow knew that would mean even worse pain, so he willed himself not to. The effort greyed out his world, and his thoughts start to drift away again.

Then a voice was calling urgently. What was it saying? His name? He tried to croak an answer, but nothing intelligible came out. Someone else was less concerned and... relieved. Why?

He felt arms lifting him. He gasped with the pain, did cry out involuntarily... and then the blackness returned.

There was a rumbling, purring noise from somewhere. He had heard it before. And he was warm, covered by something soft and smooth. His entire body ached. He opened his eyes. Low firelight sent flickering shadows throughout a dimly lit room. What room? He had seen it before. It was...

He licked dry, puffy lips. His mouth tasted abominably of stale blood, and his tongue felt furry and swollen.

"I hurt. All over," he hoarsely announced aloud to the ceiling after a couple of failed attempts at speaking.

"I am not at all surprised," came a tart reply. "Although you do not look too bad for someone who has evidently fought a war single-handed. And lost, of course." It was an older female voice.

"Arian? I'm alive, then?"

Her familiar face hove into view. "Aye. Who else? As to your corporeal status, I grant that you look more dead than alive, but I think you need not concern yourself with the Fire of Cleansing just yet."

"The Fire of Cleansing might actually make me feel better." Rhiss tried to sit but had to fall back, panting. "Where are we?"

"Do *not* attempt to rise, you young cretin. We have worked too hard putting you back together to have you thwart our efforts now. In your room at the inn, of course."

"My room? How—?"

Arian sighed. "Spare me your usual endless litany of questions, Rhissan. I am far too vexed to endure it, but I *will* relate your sad tale insofar as we have been able to reconstruct it. We have been in Rontha for three nights, and are likely to be for at least thrice as long again, thanks to you. You have not been conscious since the first night. Sometime on the second day, you deliberately defied me and went out to explore the village. Somehow, you managed to get into an altercation with several vicious hooligans — Rontha appears to possess no shortage of them — and very nearly lost your life. When I discovered you absent at evenmeal, I searched the inn, hoping you were merely in the baths. But a serving girl recalled seeing you leave earlier. After combing almost all Rontha, I found you late that night, lying in a gutter on the village's seedier side. I know not how she came to be there, but Aquilea lay beside you, sheltering and warming, as she is now." She stopped and gestured, and lifting his head, Rhiss could just spot and sense the gryphon at his feet.

"You can thank the One she was," Arian resumed, "for we are sure her presence is the only reason you did not die from shock and exposure, as it was still raining heavily. Fortunately, I chanced on a solitary pedestrian nearby and had him scurry to Master Othwain to bring help. With difficulty, we brought you back here: you are no joke to carry, even with all the blood you lost. A husky lad you are, to be sure. Othwain says he has seen grisly results of spectacular fights among drunken patrons in his time, but without question, you win the prize. He was utterly horrified at the sight of you. Fortunately, an itinerant travelling physician is also lodging here, and Othwain fetched him immediately. Also fortunately, Master Lukarran is an outstanding physician. And here you are." She grimaced. "It is worth noting how many times in this narrative I have used the word 'fortunate.' The One looked on you with grace and compassion, indeed — far more than you deserved."

Rhiss gingerly lifted the covers to regard himself. What wasn't bandaged in clean white linens seemed a mass of bruises and lacerations. He turned a sceptical eye to Arian.

"Really? This is fortunate?"

"Oh, considering the alternative, without doubt. And rest assured, your face is every bit as colourful. In fact, you bear a remarkable resemblance to a raccoon, and will not be turning young maids' heads for some while, unless they are turning away in horror at your appearance."

"Thank you very much for that warm assessment, Arian." He stopped, struggling to re-integrate fragmented and confused recollections.

"Rhissan, in the One's Name, *why* did you disobey me?" she asked softly. "When I wasn't terrified you would die, I was so angry, I could have thrashed you within an inch of your life — except that someone had evidently already saved me the trouble."

Rhiss carefully thought back. "You were so... pre-emptory with all those orders you were barking. I felt a little... annoyed."

"Aye, well... I am sorry about that. I was desperately anxious that something precisely like this would happen. That worry perhaps sharpened my tongue overmuch."

"I am sorry, too. I should have heeded your sharp tongue. Anyway, I went down to the tap room... honestly, I didn't intend to leave the inn. But then..." He looked up, startled as the memory clicked almost audibly into place. "Aye, of course... I saw him, Arian! The old greybeard from last night — I mean, the first night. I ran out after him. I wasn't thinking of anything else."

"Exactly," she replied dryly. "That is the key phrase: you were not thinking. But enlighten me, pray: *how* did you run afoul of Rontha's citizenry? And *what* did you do to provoke them so?"

"I was lost," Rhiss said slowly, thinking back. "I was unsuccessful locating the old man, and was returning to the inn. I ran into a knot of people: three older men, one with a hideously scarred mouth, and a young couple. It was obvious something ugly was about to take place—" he stopped, puzzled. "Arian, what *are* Tavvies, anyway? And why are they reviled so?"

Comprehension dawned on her face. "The young couple were Tavnians?"

Rhiss looked uncertain. "Scarmouth — I think his name was Mal-something — he called them Tavvies. He made it sound like a dirty word."

"Aye, well, you more or less have the right of it. But that explains it, I am afraid. They are from Tavna, a coastal city-state region northwest of here. After being independent for centuries, the Sovereign forcibly annexed it twenty years ago in a short but sharp, bloody conflict. Tavnian customs and culture... differ in many respects from Arrinor, so they are frequently looked down on. Calling one a 'tavvy' is a calculated insult, a deliberate provocation—" She halted at his expression. "What is it?"

"I thought I heard... well, it sounded similar to a very insulting name describing people from the area where I grew up."

Arian's face took on a knowing look. "*You* have been called that name, haven't you? And suffered harassment?"

"Many times. And so, when I heard it — *thought* I heard it — it only reinforced my natural inclination to intervene." He looked defiant. "There is nothing quite like experiencing oppression to impress on one the need for fairness and justice."

Strangely, Arian's eyes widened slightly; she coughed, clearing her throat, but said only, "Aye, of course. So you tried to help the Tavnian couple. What became of them?"

"I don't know. I shouted at them to clear out, and they did, but whether or not they escaped, I have no idea. I *was* rather pre-occupied by that time, of course."

"Being thrashed within an inch of your life."

"Aye. Eventually I collapsed, and lost consciousness. I woke later to Aquilea's presence. How she got there, I am at a loss to explain. But grateful, of course."

"So, ultimately, your gallantry may well have been in vain."

Rhiss sighed, then winced as though drinking a cup's bitter dregs. "Aye. King's Champion, charging to the rescue, indeed. I failed, Arian, and accomplished naught except nearly getting killed."

She hesitated, then murmured gently, "Remember what I have said, Rhissan: poets romanticize heroic exploits unforgivably. In the war between Darkness and Light, good does not, in the short term, always prevail. But it is the long term that concerns us. 'Tis a prudent lesson to keep in mind."

"The problem with the long term is that we wind up dead." He saw the flash of annoyance in her eyes, and held up a placating hand. "I'm sorry. I know what you are saying. What about finding the whorespawn who did this and bringing them to justice?"

Arian shrugged fatalistically. "I think you already know the answer to that, my lord. We cannot involve the authorities without giving ourselves away. Even were we to use our false names, we would be exposed, sooner or later. Of that I have no doubt. In any event, if your description of the man with the scarred mouth is accurate, I think I know of whom you speak — and he happens to be the brother-in-law of the Sovereign's Representative in the village." She shrugged again. "So much for formal justice, I fear."

"Well... what about informal justice, then?"

Arian stared levelly. "Many would call such an act 'Sovereign's justice.' Is that really the sort of man you wish to be in Arrinor?"

Rhiss flushed and grimaced. "Of course not... but confound it, what is one to do when justice is denied? After what those scum did? Allow them to walk scot-free?"

"They *will* face justice. As a Follower of the One, you know that as well as I. It may not be in your desired time frame, but 'tis certain. That may be cold comfort at the moment, but must suffice. Not to mention the obvious fact that you are in absolutely no condition to wreak vengeance of any kind."

"But, the Tavnian couple's fate — I fear for them. And I lost the dagger Brother Gavrilos gave me. Scarmouth or one of his cronies must have stolen it."

She shook her head. "They did not take your weapon." She reached behind her belt and held up his dagger. It glittered redly in the firelight.

A measure of relief washed over him. "Where was it?"

"No more than a couple of feet from you. I assume it was knocked from your hand at some point. Somehow, they must not have noticed it lying in the mud."

He cast his mind back and yawned hugely, although it hurt to do so. "Aye. They were interrupted. There was something shiny. I remember now. I thought it an icicle."

Amused, Arian shook her head. "'Twas more valuable and less fragile." She placed a gentle hand on his brow. "As for the Tavnian couple, I will have Othwain make discreet inquiries: there appears to be no one in Rontha this innkeeper does not know. We may yet be able to glean good tidings from this. In the meantime, the vital thing is to get you hale and on your feet again as swiftly as we may. Sleep now, and fear no evil."

The next day, Rhiss was able to rise and, with assistance, hobble down to the baths. Once there, he waved off all offers of attention, saying he just wanted to soak quietly alone in hot water. The attendant nodded and threw several bunches of aromatic herbs in the water, explaining that they possessed remarkable healing properties. "I'll increase the steam in here, too, my lord," he said. "It'll help you to breathe deeply, and get the full restorative benefit of the herbs. Although... I will tell you that they may cause you to get a little... dreamy." Casting a sympathetic look at Rhiss, he bowed and left.

Rhiss painfully shucked off his robe and glanced down, took in the vivid purple and russet bruises, some starting to change to orange and yellow, and shook his head despairingly. Lukarran put it best when calling on Rhiss that morning. "Well, my lord," he had said crisply, "you *will* recover — but while healing, you'll resemble the most incredible sunrise ever seen in Arrinor."

He had catalogued the hurts he had tended: two black eyes; a swollen nose; numerous lacerations, several requiring stitching; and, of course, bruises too many to count. "You, my lord, are extremely fortunate: beyond bruising, it does not appear any bones are broken, nor is there any significant internal damage. But it will take time — a week to ten days, in all likelihood — before you are back to full strength. Until then, as your physician, I recommend you refrain from bar fights and brawls. In the meantime, to speed healing, there are techniques I can use to manipulate and massage sore muscles."

Rhiss had felt an immediate, instinctive liking for the physician, whose manner varied between refreshingly brusque honesty and cynical sarcasm. But he reflected glumly on the prognosis. A week! Arian had wanted them at Pencairn House as swiftly as possible. Rhiss doubted that in his current state he could even mount a horse, much less ride any distance. What to do? The experience had sharpened his awareness of the dangers facing them to a knife's edge: the longer they remained in Rontha waiting for him to recuperate, the more likely they were to be discovered and captured. But beyond *that* issue, Rhiss was uneasily aware of another that could not be lightly dismissed, something he had instinctively shied away from but which had to be faced.

Shakily standing naked and alone, leaning against the bath for support in the room's warmth, he gazed distractedly at the steaming water, and it struck him how there was something very symbolic in discarding his clothing and preparing to enter the balm of healing waters. Carefully, Rhiss climbed into the bath, sat down in the hot water up to his neck, slowly relaxing with a shallow sigh, and, breathing the steam and vapours in deeply as he had been instructed, tried to calmly take stock.

But it felt as though some internal spring, wound tighter and tighter ever since his encounter with Brother Gavrilos, was abruptly released. It was an almost audible thing, sickening in its physical intensity, and he actually stiffened slightly from the force of it.

A deep wave of emotion welled up, and he was unable to prevent the scalding tide of grief, shame, terror and relief from overwhelming the tight control he usually maintained over himself. Gripping the sides of the bath, he was wracked by deep sobs, ungovernable and unstoppable in spite of the terrible physical pain they caused his injured body. "I just don't think I can!" he cried aloud to the empty room, the anguished words ripped from his very core. "I'm not—!" His voice failed him, and he gave up trying to articulate or rationally manage it, sobbing uncontrollably as he had not done since he was a small child.

Eventually, after an eternity, his sobs lessened and subsided — not because the emotions causing them were in any way resolved, but because of simple physical exhaustion. Rhiss lifted his heavy head and looked about apathetically: the attendant had been as good as his word, and steam swirled thickly through the room as air currents eddied this way and that, making it difficult to see more than ten feet or so.

Sudden movement registered off to the left, and Rhiss automatically turned to look. But something was wrong with his vision: things were blurry and indistinct, and he squinted and widened his eyes several times, attempting to remedy his focus.

A young boy strode out of the steam, and Rhiss blinked in disbelief. "Lewis?" he whispered. But the boy was dressed in Arrinoran garb, not in student robes. And... it might not be the Darkton student... might, in fact, be a younger version of himself. The features seemed to waver back and forth, from Rhiss to Lewis and back again. The boy stopped at the left end of the pool, raised an accusing finger at Rhiss, and spoke, although his lips remained motionless.

Whatever were you thinking? You nearly managed to get yourself killed! You're out of your depth; in fact, far out of your league. This is no game you play, nor some child's fairy tale. You nearly died! People have died on your account! And you have killed, too, killed real people, by your own hand. How does that feel, Hero? King's Champion? What ridiculous conceit is that? What the hell do you think you're playing at? You should just go home before you do even more damage.

Before Rhiss could even begin to reply — the One alone knew what he might have said — there was answering movement on his right, and another figure walked serenely out of the steam. Rhiss caught his breath: it was Rhyanna, but her features, too, seemed to waver and morph into those of another, a dark-haired young woman he did not know. She also stopped, at the right end of the pool, and smiled radiantly.

But you can do this. You have already begun, rejoined her calm and reassuring voice softly through lips likewise motionless. *You can, you are, you must, because that is what is required of you. We are all afraid, Rhissan — for what we are and what we are not, for what may or may not come — and there is neither shame nor guilt in that. Those fears are part of what it is to be human. But to allow them to paralyze you into inaction and permit the triumph of evil... now there* is *the shame, a shame not to be borne.*

The boy shook his head vehemently. *No! Talbot, Scarmouth... they hurt us! Just like the others... in Dinas Mawr, and later, in England. There is so much evil in them, in all of them. We can't possibly stand up to those people. There are too many, and they are everywhere. It's best to keep clear of them, to give in. They'll win, anyway.*

The young woman shook her head too, but gently, in rebuke. *That's not true. There is also great goodness in people... in you. And ability. There is more ability in you than you are willing to admit. You cannot give up or just go back home. You are caught up in it now, and must do your utmost... to strive, to seek, to find... and not to yield.*

"I don't know," Rhiss murmured dully. "Just... go away, both of you. Leave me alone." He waved them away, closed his eyes wearily and bowed his head...

<hr />

Rhiss awoke with a gasp, head jerking up, eyes snapping open in sudden panic. Heart pounding, breathing hard, he tried to recall where he was. The view was still obscured by steam, but thankfully, his eyes could once again register his surroundings with perfect clarity. As far as he could tell, the room was empty but for himself. Strange visitors, both accusatory and pleading, were gone.

Dreamy, indeed, he thought as he climbed slowly out of the pool. Had it been some weird hallucination? Or a strange visitation with an element of reality? He really did feel the two had been in the room. He flexed his arms experimentally, breathed in deeply. His muscles actually felt a little less battered, and his chest no longer quite as though it had been squeezed in a vise. Whatever had been in those herbs... well, he had more than gotten his money's worth there.

Rhiss recalled what the pair had been arguing over. Limits versus possibilities, he thought meditatively; it all boiled down to that. Fear was omnipresent. Fear of failure, fear of getting hurt. Why him? For some unfathomable reason, it seemed there was no one else to do what had to be done. Brother Gavrilos had selected him and no one else. Why that should be, he could not say. The task was overwhelming. But it was his task... if he would undertake it. It was distressing, it was desperately hard to accept, but there it was. Could he do it? In his weakened physical condition, he could not possibly leave the village for some time. Nor could he stay: time was pressing, and dangers were all about. Sighing, he put on his robe and prepared to return to his room.

"I don't know," he said thoughtfully to the empty chamber. "I *really* don't. Truth to tell, I don't feel very heroic — or capable — right now. But maybe after more of these baths... and some rest... and Master Lukarran's ministrations... well, we'll see. After all, as my aunt used to say, things always look better in the morning."

XI

MOOR AND MYTH

"In my hour of need the One shall provide. The Light of the One is my armour and shield. I gird myself with His sword of righteousness. And through the grace of the One, I will prevail over the Servants of the Other. Marvelous are the ways of the One."

The Book of the One, 132:3:8-10
(Cantos 132, Chapter 3, Verses 8-10)

Five days later, Rhiss and Arian finally left Rontha, heading for Pencairn House. He was still not completely recovered and back to full strength, but refused to admit that to Arian, and, in fact, had flatly insisted they leave.

It had not seemed that it would be an easy decision, and in fact, Arian had privately been extremely worried at first that Rhiss would simply give up; the beating he had received at the hands of the thugs had badly shaken his resolve and confidence. But ironically, it turned out that the very thugs who provoked his crisis of confidence also rekindled his determination to move forward and not give up — quite unintentionally, of course, but life is frequently replete with just such strange twists of fate.

They had ventured down to the tap room for evenmeal, as Rhiss finally felt up to being in public. His facial bruises remained visible, but had faded somewhat — perhaps partly from the remarkable healing effects of the bath herbs, and partly from Lukarran's care. And while he was still tired and sore, Rhiss knew he was physically on the mend — although not fully mended yet.

The room was comfortably full without being crowded, and they were served by Othwain himself, who waved off a serving girl and seemed to regard it as his personal task to see to their comfort.

"Now then, young master, it just so happens I had the cook save the ingredients for some of those meat pies you're both so fond of, in the hope you might wish to join us down here tonight. I'll make sure they're made and in the oven in a trice, and meantimes, we'll get you both brown ales, to slake your thirst while you wait."

He bustled off, and Arian turned, smiling, to Rhiss. "There you have the ideal innkeeper and a good man to know: capable, well-informed and well-connected — even if he wasn't able to learn the fate of the Tavnian couple."

"Aye. A mystery, that. I wish we'd been able to learn what happened to them, Arian. It would have made what came afterwards easier to bear if I knew they were safe."

"I know." She sighed. "Still, we can thank the One you have made great strides in your recovery. A few more days, and you will be well enough to ride."

"I'm well enough *now*, thank you very much. Speaking of riding, how have the horses been doing?"

She shrugged. "I have not been over to the stables these last few days, I confess. Having confidence in Othwain, I have confidence in his staff, also. And I may have been preoccupied with other matters." She glared at him meaningfully.

"Arian, stop fussing. I've told you, I feel fine."

"Indeed. You don't look it, my lord, to be honest."

"Nonsense. That serving girl did not run away from me, recoiling in horror, as I seem to recall you prophesying."

She sniffed. "Doubtless only because Othwain has them too well-trained to allow such an unseemly breach of manners."

Rhiss made a face, then glanced around. "You know, I think that, rather than stay here to be the butt of your sarcasm while our food is prepared, I will venture out to the stables and check on our mounts. I'm quite sure that Aralsa, at least, will be glad to see me — regardless of my appearance."

Arian smiled. "Very well. I will not drink your ale while you are gone, but cannot promise the same for the meat pies, if you have not returned by the time they arrive."

Rhiss smiled back, and levered himself into a standing position. "Fair enough," he acknowledged. "Strong incentive not to stay there too long." He turned and walked slowly out to the stables.

Aralsa, indeed, did seem glad to see him, softly whickering at his approach and bending her head down for him to rub her forelock. He spoke quietly to her for several minutes, stroking her all the while, and was pleased to see that she seemed to have been well taken care of. Finally, he said, "Right, lass. I've got to get back, or I'll return to find that Seir-onna Arian has filched my food again. And *that* would be quite unforgivable." He gave her one last pat and exited the stables.

He crossed the yard to re-enter the main building, his mouth watering at the pleasant thought of Othwain's meat pies... only to narrowly avoid a collision with Arian, who was barrelling out the door, face pale.

"Come," she ordered without preamble, and all but shoved him roughly through a different doorway into another room. "In here."

'In here' turned out to be the kitchen, where a serving wench loading a tray and a fat man in an apron simultaneously turned in mute surprise to gape at them. Rhiss turned towards Arian, blindsided by her inexplicable behaviour. "What—?" he began angrily, but she swiftly clapped a hand over his mouth, cutting off his exclamation.

"Hush, Rhissan." She jerked her head towards the tap room. "Can you not hear them?"

Rhiss glared and deliberately lifted a hand to peel hers from his face. She allowed the action, but raised a forefinger and placed it over her own lips. He nodded impatiently, and they stood motionless, silently listening.

It took only a second or two to realize that the timbre of the noises coming from the tap room had altered markedly from when he had left: there was an ugly tone to the voices, and as one in particular rose above the others in drunkenly arrogant, pre-emptory demand, Rhiss turned white, eyes flicking back to Arian.

"It's *them!*" he hissed, and she nodded grimly.

"Aye," she whispered. "Your friends from the other night — all three of them, including Scarmouth. I slipped out as soon as they entered, so as to intercept you before you unwittingly strolled casually back into the tap room."

"But what are they doing *here?!*"

Arian opened her mouth to reply, but before she could say anything, there was the crash of crockery, and a woman screamed. Everything went deathly silent for a moment. Then there were the unmistakable sounds of fists striking flesh, and someone crying out in agony. Another woman screamed.

Rhiss turned instantly and was halfway to the doorway before Arian was able to respond, leaping to restrain him hard in a bear hug from behind. A lancet of pain arced through his battered torso, but he ignored it in a singleminded imperative to confront his tormentors.

"Rhissan, no!" she exclaimed.

He tried to turn on her furiously, a small, rational part of him astounded at the strength of her iron grip. "Arian, let go!"

His body quivered like a taut cable under immense strain, and Arian had no doubt whatsoever: if he had not still been recovering from the thrashing, she could never have restrained him. "You cannot go out there, Rhissan!"

"I cannot stay here!"

"You must!"

"Why?!" The word seemed ripped from his very core.

"Sweet Light of the One!" As he involuntarily halted in shock at her use of the blasphemy, she pressed on, mouth close to his ear. "They'll *kill* you, boy! Think! You are nowhere near your full strength! And even if you were, they are *Sovereign's Men!* In full public view! If you go out there and confront them now, Maldeus will know of it within hours, or sooner! I guarantee it! Do you really seek to throw your life away? Because this is the perfect opportunity, if that is truly what you wish!"

Gripping him, she felt Rhiss draw in a great, shuddering breath, hold it for an endless moment... let it out raggedly... and then the tension drained from him like a flood.

"All right, Arian, you can let go. You've made your point."

She cautiously released him, and as she did so, it seemed the raucous, baying laughter of jackals carried from the tap room, filling the kitchen in evil mockery. Rhiss closed his eyes briefly and winced, as though the very sound was both familiar and painful. Then a door slammed shut, and there was silence.

"Rhissan—"

She was interrupted by Othwain skidding into the kitchen. He cast one startled glance at them, then turned to address the serving girl and the cook, both of whom stood transfixed, as though turned to stone. "Seek out that physician! Hurry!" As if released from a spell, the girl fairly sprinted out the kitchen, and Othwain looked uncertainly at Rhiss and Arian. "Seir-onna? Is all well with you and Lord Rhissan?"

Rhiss remained motionless, staring at the floor, and Arian nodded wearily. "Aye, thank you, Master Othwain. Unfortunately, it was imperative for us to... remain out of sight in here. They were the ones who attacked Lord Rhissan the other night, you see."

"Aye, so I thought." The innkeeper nodded in turn. "You did rightly, then. A bad business — both that night *and* this."

The cook spoke up, voice quavering. "What... what did they do this time, Belan?"

Othwain scowled in contempt. "Accosted one of the serving girls again, then beat up a customer who tried to intervene and stop them." He glanced at Arian. "Fortunately, I don't think we'll be needing your services, Seir-onna. Master Lukarran's should be sufficient. No one in imminent likelihood of going to the One, you see." He made the triune sign, and Arian followed suit. "If you'll excuse me, I must return and see to my customers." He turned and left.

Rhiss had not moved, and Arian gently laid a hand on his arm. "Rhissan?"

He looked up, eyes blazing, and Arian involuntarily took a step back. "Seir-onna, we will leave for Pencairn House tomorrow morning."

She caught his formal tone. "But... my lord, you have not fully recovered your strength. I do not think it wise to tempt the One's providence by departing just yet—"

"Arian," Rhiss said, voice low and icy, "I leave on the morrow. You may accompany me, or stay here, as you choose. This enterprise has been stalled for too long, and I will not waste another single moment more, allowing that despicable Sovereign to remain unchallenged, employing and encouraging scum like these to prey on the innocent and the defenceless. This *cannot* be allowed to stand."

Suppressing strong misgivings, but at the same time oddly pleased by his words, Arian nodded. "Very well, my lord," she replied quietly. "I see you are utterly determined in this. I will, of course, be at your side tomorrow morn."

———◆———

They left separately twenty minutes apart the next morning, meeting several miles outside the village. From Rontha, Arian explained, the road eventually led to Arrinor's northern coastal ports, including Ansby, ostensibly 'Arcan of Follet's' destination. Prior to that, though, it crossed Byrn Moor, then headed into the Eowerth Mountains, a massive, jagged upthrust of land looming forbiddingly against the sea on one side and the interior plains on the other. The Moor itself was a high, windswept plain bereft of trees, although low bushes and bracken were plentiful. It was not a forgiving land, but there was a hard, unspoiled beauty to it that Rhiss found appealing. The only evidence of human intrusion in the wild environment was the road.

They met no one after leaving town, which Arian noted was unusual for a route of such importance. Regardless, both admitted they were exhilarated to be back on the road. "Come, tell me," she said light-heartedly, glad to see his spirits higher after his fey mood of the previous night, "what would that playwright you are so fond of have said in response to your situation at Rontha? What was his name again? Shayspeer? From what you have told me, I'll wager my sword he had something to say, relevant *and* pithy."

"It was Shakespeare, Seir-onna, as I have told you before, and I am not wagering you. Neither of us has anything the other wants, save that I possess no sword, as you noted. But I do not think you would really wager yours."

Arian waved a hand dismissively, inwardly uncertain whether Rhiss would rise to the bait or not. She hoped so. "Shayspeer, Shakespeare. He has been gone to the One for hundreds of years, has he not? So I doubt he will mind. But you mentioned a wager."

"*You* mentioned it."

"Let us not quibble, young man. A wager, a wager... let me see... ah! Grooming the horses. If you have no quote, *you* groom them for... a week, how would that be? But if you can bring to mind a quote both relevant *and* pithy, *I* groom them for a week."

"I am quite sure he was never thrashed within an inch of his life, Seir-onna, so he won't have said anything relevant to my situation."

"I was referring to your crisis of confidence, you thick-headed whelp, as you well know. Come, give me a quote. Don't tell me I have you at a loss."

Rhiss thought for several seconds. "Well... I am not sure I can recall anything this precise moment—"

"Ah ha! I have you!"

Rhiss grinned in ill-concealed triumph. "Unless... 'Our doubts are traitors, and make us lose the good we oft might win, by fearing to attempt.'" He nodded, and winked. "Very true. My gratitude, Arian. Never underestimate a learned man. Remember the way I like Aralsa's mane combed. And any time you wish to wager about 'Shayspeer,' don't hesitate to let me know."

Arian bowed her head, acknowledging his victory, but smiled inwardly, glad to see that he was reachable again.

Aquilea found them half an hour later, flying down in great, swooping glides as she responded to Rhiss calling her with his mind. He did not hide his relief at her arrival, for he was still unclear about the nature of the mental link they shared, and he dismounted to hug her as she landed. She was pleased to see him too, but did not seem to be of a mind to walk. Having tasted the bracingly fresh winds on the Moor, she took off again, but remained close, circling slowly over Rhiss and Arian as they rode. The day was clear, but the wind was cold, from the north, and the sun seemed powerless to warm the land. Rhiss pulled his cloak tighter.

When the sun was overhead, they came across the only landmark on the road: a collection of tall, rectangular stones to one side. They were of various heights, carefully arranged; the smallest was man height, but most were twice that. They were uniformly a smooth and featureless grey, set in a circular formation. In one sense they did not look placed at all, but grown out of the ground where they stood, and had obviously been there a very long time. While the scene was different in several particulars — most notably, no horizontal stones spanned the tops of the vertical ones, and they were not nearly as timeworn — Rhiss was indelibly reminded of Stonehenge back in England, and wondered how these had been positioned. Somehow, they did not look as though erected by humans. The gaps between stones were wide enough to lead the horses through. This they did, dismounting and hobbling the animals once inside. Rhiss stretched gratefully, glad to give his aching body a change. They decided to halt for midmeal, sitting on the ground, gaining the shelter of the stones. The wind from the north blew in through the gaps, but the stones provided a degree of protection. Also, thought Rhiss, from inside, they were not so visible from the moor.

Rhiss felt oddly drawn to the stones, and while Arian retrieved their simple meal from the saddle bags, he wandered slowly around the inner circumference. He estimated the circle to be quite large, some two hundred paces across. As he passed one stone, bigger than many, he halted and eyed it pensively, suddenly experiencing the strangest desire to touch it. Despite feeling foolish, he did so, stripping off his riding gauntlet and closing his eyes, splaying the fingers of his hand to grasp the widest possible area. He calmed and opened his mind, imagining his thoughts extending outwards through his fingers, flowing into the ancient stone and down into the surrounding earth.

Nothing.

The stone was very cold and patchily coarse to the touch from rusty, multi-coloured lichens growing haphazardly over its surface. Rhiss was about to remove his hand when suddenly, he either felt or heard, as from very far away, the muffled sound of a drumbeat. It came again slowly, and, startled, Rhiss was irresistibly reminded of a vast heart beating languidly. Once more it came, and he pulled his hand away, opening his eyes to stare doubtfully at the stone. He cocked his head to one side, but the beating had ceased. He scanned the clearing, but Arian was still preoccupied with midmeal and made no sign she had heard anything out of the ordinary.

Rhiss frowned, moving to the right, directly before the stone. The next thing he knew, ground and sky changed places as he missed his footing, stumbling into a shallow depression at the stone's base. It was a couple of feet deep, hidden by grasses, and he came down hard, sprawling into the depression, which was rectangular, several feet long and at least two feet wide. Involuntarily, he yelped in pain as his injured body sharply registered the tumble.

Arian saw and heard the disturbance and, alarmed, came swiftly. "Rhissan? What happened? Are you hurt?"

Rhiss stood, rubbing his shoulder, which had borne the brunt of his fall. "Nothing much. Calm yourself, Seir-onna. I have simply been careless, paying for my inattention by falling into this hole and banging myself."

He climbed out and they gazed down together. "Curious," said Arian eventually. "Why should there be such a depression here? Are there any in front of the others?"

There were none at the stones to either side. Rhiss did not come across another depression until he had walked a quarter of the way around the circle. There he found another. Arian watched, then walked directly across the middle of the open space to a point exactly opposite the first depression. In the centre, she seemed to shrink suddenly, and Rhiss realized she had entered another dip. Arian said nothing, continuing to the other side. "It is as I surmised," she called when she arrived. "Do you likewise and walk across the circle to the stone opposite. See what may be there."

Rhiss did so, and found, with complete lack of surprise, a depression before that stone also. Arian walked up as he stood. "They are at the four compass points," he observed, and she nodded.

"Aye. And this, at least, is not part of the natural lay of the land. Someone has placed these depressions at specific locations, although to what purpose, I cannot speculate. And as you saw when I crossed through the centre, there is a dip there, although it is circular, not rectangular. Is there anything more to them, I wonder? Could anything be buried there, do you suppose?"

Rhiss shivered, recalling his fall. "I certainly hope not. I fell into one, if you remember." He glanced around again, wondered how to frame his next question. "You, ah... did not hear anything just before I fell, did you? An unusual sound, perhaps?"

The jaundiced expression on her face spoke volumes, but Arian's voice remained carefully neutral. "I heard nothing but wind on the grass. Why? What sort of unusual noise, pray, did you hear?"

"I... I am not sure. Perhaps I imagined it. But it sounded like the beating of a drum... or a heart."

Arian narrowed her eyes. "A *heartbeat*? You fancy you heard a beating heart? Where? In one of the depressions?"

"Well, not really," said Rhiss uncomfortably. "In fact, it was more like it came from... well, the stone I was touching. But it was slow and sounded a great distance away. I could not ascertain the source, whether underground or... somewhere else."

As Arian folded her arms and regarded Rhiss, he felt like a small boy at school, caught under the gaze of a headmistress who had found him telling fibs. He had to resist the urge to squirm with embarrassment.

"Seir-onna, I know it sounds too strange to be true, but..."

"Oh, not at all," Arian corrected dryly. "Even having travelled with you only these few days, I am rapidly learning that the strange and extraordinary seem attracted to you like bears to honey, and 'tis to be expected. While I heard nothing, I do not doubt you did indeed hear the beat of a drum... or a heart." She stopped and regarded Rhiss again, until he felt he must say something to restart the conversation.

"Whence came this circle? What do you know of it?"

Arian looked thoughtful. "They are called Way Stones. There are a number of them throughout Arrinor. They are given little notice and taken very much for granted, although their true purpose and function are unknown. Some say Way Stones are sacred to the One. I wonder..." Her voice trailed off, and she stroked her chin in a way Rhiss already associated with deep thought on her part.

"You were saying?" he prompted.

Arian emerged from her reverie. "Your question made me see them anew. They are not dissimilar in form and layout to a shrine I once visited, long ago and far from here. But there are also differences... hmm. Pray, allow my mind to gnaw on the issue while we gnaw our food. Firstmeal was some time ago."

They sat facing each other, consuming bread and cheese put up by Master Othwain. The horses cropped the grass nearby. Aquilea was nowhere to be seen, doubtless searching for provender on her own. They conversed on several topics as they ate. Rhiss found his mind wandering back to his aged companion in the tap room. The man either possessed an uncanny ability to make shrewd guesses, or had been a spy well-versed with Rhiss and his journey. He said as much, but Arian shook her head.

"I think not. The Sight is well known as a gift of the One. Not a common gift, not by any stretch, but there are those to whom it is given to see events past and future, this we know." She paused, and a peculiar look passed over her face. "Have *you* ever had... dreams that seemed particularly real?" She paused, choosing words with great care. "Dreams that... were strangely out of place, perhaps? Dreams that became reality later?"

Rhiss shook his head, trying to recall. "Well... I think not. Nothing memorable springs to mind. Does not everyone have dreams like that occasionally?" The strange look was still on Arian's face. "Why? Why should I have such dreams, particularly?"

Arian did not answer immediately. She looked out over the southern sky and opened her mouth to speak, but at that moment, Aquilea landed nearby. Rhiss sensed right away something was very wrong. Aquilea cried harshly and quickly approached, highly agitated, closing her beak gently around his sleeve. Tugging, she pulled him to his feet. But she did not release her hold, and kept tugging, compelling Rhiss to a gap in the stones. Arian came also, clearly as puzzled by the gryphon's actions as Rhiss. Then they were on the road, and Rhiss turned his gaze southwards. He suddenly understood her dismay, and his stomach turned sickeningly as he registered the sight.

A roiling wave of dense, grey mist advanced swiftly and silently across the Moor from the south, a wave hundreds of feet high, stretching as far to east and west as the eye could see. Impossibly, it advanced in opposition to the north wind, which blew futilely against it. It was coming quickly, swifter than a horse could gallop, enveloping everything in its path in a silent cloak of leaden ash grey. And it was but moments away.

―――◆―――

Rhiss glanced at Arian. "Should we not retreat into the Way Stones? At the very least, we will be more difficult to spot."

Arian looked grimly uncertain. "I do not know whether 'twill make any difference, especially if the phantom of the moor your friend spoke of is responsible. We cannot outrun it, and I doubt we can hide. I have never heard of fog moving against the wind, and the suddenness of its arising is uncanny."

"That may well be, but I really think we should make use of what shelter the stones provide."

Rhiss expected further argument, or at least debate, but none came. He steered a suddenly, uncharacteristically docile Arian back through the gap in the stones, Aquilea at his heels. Their hobbled horses were unnaturally still, heads erect, ears swivelling tensely, evidently sensing something very amiss, but unsure how to react. Rhiss empathized: he, too, was at a loss.

Before he could do anything, however, the mist was upon them. It did not arrive gradually, but as though someone had thrown a blanket over the land. Visibility dropped immediately to nearly zero, so that seeing one side of the circle from the other became a vague and doubtful perception. The wind sank to a chill breeze, and the air was thick with swirling moisture, a dank, icy dampness settling over all.

Rhiss nervously loosened his dagger in its sheath, very much aware that he was not yet returned to full strength from the beating; and too late, it occurred to him that his insistence on leaving Rontha while still in substandard condition could well turn out to be a fatal error. Would his single-mindedness again be his undoing?

He briefly debated whether to retrieve his bow, but dismissed the idea as impractical in the grey nothingness. There was no accurate sense of distance, no clear perception to sight on. He turned from Arian to gaze around the circle and sighed, murmuring, "Well, at this juncture, I am open to suggestions." But there was no answer, and, frowning, Rhiss turned back to Arian. His next words died in his throat: the priest's eyes were open, but blank and fixed, unfocused. She looked waxy and unreal, a statue almost lifelike, but not quite. Rhiss could not discern whether Arian even breathed. He shook her gently, but was unable to elicit any reaction. Arian's limbs were stiff and unyielding, her skin cold and clammy like the mist rapidly coating all with a slick sheen. When Rhiss felt for a pulse, he could not even find that. Glancing at Aquilea, Rhiss saw with shock that she was the same. He dropped to his knees to check more closely, and found she might as well have been made of stone.

His examination was interrupted by a shrill, far-off howl that might have come from a dog, although no dog Rhiss had ever encountered. It was answered at once by howls at different locations and distances.

Why was he unaffected by the miasma incapacitating his companions? Rhiss looked around wildly, at a loss. He saw the horses several paces away, and ran for Aralsa even as the thought came. Unsurprised to find her as lifeless as Arian and Aquilea, he dug through his pannier bag, feeling for the cold, metallic touch of the Circlet of Araxis. His fingers curled around it, and he lifted it exultantly. Now they would all be safe, as the Circlet blazed forth light, performing whatever mysterious magic was necessary. He raised it to his head, but halted in the act, brows knitting in confusion and alarm.

The striations of colour in the stone's depths were still and motionless, not flowing deep within the gem as they usually did. No light emanated from the stone — in fact, it was as dull, grey and lifeless as the awful mist hanging all about. Rhiss donned the Circlet, hoping the action would somehow activate it, but there was nothing. He took the Circlet off and stared. The stone remained quiescent, and realization hit: the Circlet would provide no rescue. Rhiss felt icy tendrils of fear invade his stomach. His mouth went abruptly dry as dust and he painfully tried to swallow.

There were other howls outside the circle, still far away, but unmistakably closer. Answering in the distance, faintly, there came the sound of a hunting horn, and the howls ceased. Then the dog creatures bayed in answering unison.

Rhiss slumped to the ground by Aralsa, despair mingling with terror. What could he do? He had been so sure the Circlet would save the day. But with it as paralyzed as Arian, Aquilea and the horses, Rhiss felt totally alone, cut off, small and insignificant. Dark thoughts seemed borne on the wisps of the icy dampness, evil tendrils of doubt winding into his mind, smothering his thoughts. It would end there, on the barren moor, in a broken ring of stones, with some dark hunter of men's souls. He was no hero, certainly no fit champion. How had he dared presume to help a king regain his throne? Just as with the vicious thugs in Rontha, he couldn't even help himself. What arrogant nonsense had he been thinking? He was no trained warrior, only a schoolmaster, for goodness' sake, fit only to parse sentences, instructing unwilling pupils, totally unsuited for great tasks. He was a failure, a nought. He was nothing.

Nothing. Now, in the midst of defeat, there was something about that word interrupting the litany of failure to stir a memory, an important memory. Something he should have remembered, but had forgotten. What was it? He strained to recall.

Then, in a flash, it came: the words of Brother Gavrilos. "Without the One, you are nothing, and can accomplish nothing. Put your faith in the One, not in people or things. Call out your needs and desires to the One in faith and humility. With the Light, all things are possible, and help often comes from unexpected quarters."

Rhiss stared at the Circlet in sudden understanding: he had done the exact opposite of what Brother Gavrilos had instructed. Confronted by extraordinary evils, he had put his faith in people and things, expecting Arian or Aquilea or the Circlet to solve his problems. In fact, a moment ago, he might even have looked for Lord Tariel to materialize from the mist. It was a forgivable error, given the nature of the evils encountered thus far in Arrinor. From the Malmoridai outside Tor Linlith to Maldeus of Angramor to nameless things psychically reaching out to find and crush him, and now a hunter of souls on this moor — if that was indeed what was behind the sudden, eerie fog — these were not ordinary malefactors in England *or* Arrinor. But what he must understand was that the Circlet was no panacea, righting wrongs and performing miracles on cue. He did not know everything. Arian did not have all the answers, not at all. Nor did Lady Meranna, or his anonymous friend at the inn. With sudden insight, Rhiss saw that only by acknowledging his own inadequacies and failures, placing his trust in the One, could there be any hope of victory.

Ignoring the howls growing ever nearer, Rhiss stood, placed the Circlet on his head again, stretched his arms above him, and gazed into the greyness. There was no definition, no sensation of distance, just a dizzyingly vertiginous sensation as though he flew into nothingness. He thought back to the day he had interrupted Arian, her instructions on the act of prayer. He closed his eyes, opened his mind once more as he had done minutes earlier, and placed his trust in the power of the Light.

When he was done, he opened his eyes and looked about. Mist and stones remained, no crowds of angelic hosts stood ready to defend him; but he had not expected there to be. The important thing was that he felt more at peace. He would do what he could to defend his helpless friends. As to the rest... well, the will of the One be done.

The horn sounded again, much nearer, and Rhiss turned to make his way back to Arian and Aquilea. There was a sudden, silent explosion of white light from the depressions at the compass points of the circle. Four beams shot vertically into the mist in a gigantic pulse, then cut out as though a switch had been thrown. Momentarily blinded by the intensity, Rhiss blinked several times; then he saw the central depression glowed with a lambent sheen of light.

Fascinated, he walked over in time to see a pillar of light rise swiftly from the depression, extending into the greyness like a silvery spike. As he neared the depression, a deep humming sound emanated from the earth beneath. Whether it came from a mighty chorus of voices or the ground itself, he could not tell, but the humming rose an octave as he reached the depression. Multicoloured spirals of light twisted up the pillar until they coalesced in its centre to form a luminous, glittering object. Eyes widening in utter astonishment, Rhiss beheld what floated there, unsupported and motionless; spirals of light continued to weave around it, shimmering in all the colours of the rainbow.

It was a sword.

Over three feet long, with a jewelled hilt that flashed and glittered as the light played on it, there was an ethereal majesty to the weapon. Tentatively, Rhiss reached out to it, and as his hand entered the pillar of light, the humming noise rose yet another octave. The air inside the pillar was warm, and sent little shocks through his arm, as though charged with electrical currents. Rhiss grasped the grip of the sword, not sure whether to be surprised when his fingers met with solidity: the sword *had* formed from pure light moments earlier. He pulled gently, and the sword came away with only slight resistance, as though stuck in honey. As he slowly removed it from the pillar, the light abruptly died, and the humming ceased. It could all have been nothing more than a fleeting vision... except the sword in his hand was very real, with mass and weighted balance. Rhiss brought it up to his eyes to examine. Made of the same glittering, silvery metal as both Circlet and his dagger, he was unsurprised to see the sword was very similar in design and construction, but on a much grander scale. The same style of lettering was etched near the hilt, an identical sapphire gem in the pommel. There were designs on the hilt, too, but the light was not strong enough to study them closely; nor did he have time. Nothing ever seemed left to chance, he reflected. The sword had to be part of a larger plan, and he was evidently intended to have it... which meant the current crisis was also supposed to occur. Rhiss found the thought oddly soothing.

He hefted the sword experimentally, swinging it through the air. It hissed softly, cutting cleanly through the mist, slicing water droplets. The sword was solid enough, about the same weight as the ones he used practicing with Alistair, but surprisingly lightweight for such a large, lethal-looking weapon. It was extremely well-balanced, and Rhiss found, to his pleasure, he could manoeuvre it well. The drills he had practiced so often instinctively came to mind, and he shifted into a fighting crouch, recalling Alistair's instructions. Despite his soreness, there was something very comfortable in the way the grip nestled in his hand. More than just the physicality of the sword itself — there was a psychological feeling of *rightness* in the way his hand and mind felt connected to the blade.

A horn sounded; chilling howls reverberated in reply, and Rhiss was rudely torn from his reverie. Striding purposefully across the circle, he reached Arian and Aquilea and halted. He glanced around, hope and uncertainty simultaneously crowding his mind. Was the mist slightly lessened? From where he stood, the entire circle was visible, however dimly. And if that was the case, perhaps his new-found sword was not the only weapon at his disposal. He would accept and use the mighty gift gladly, giving thanks for its arrival unlooked for, even though he would be the first to say his skills were insufficient to do it justice. On the other hand, since visibility was improved, if only marginally, his bow might also be of some use...

Rhiss moved to Aralsa to retrieve his great bow and quiver. He hesitated, looking at the sword. There was no scabbard for it, the sword having hung by itself in the vanished pillar of light. Rhiss shrugged, awkwardly fitting it through his belt before taking up bow and quiver. He swiftly strung the bow, took one of the heavy berserker arrows, nocked it, drew the string back part way. Moving beside Arian and Aquilea, he waited, scanning the entire circle to see where the threat would emerge first.

There, to his right: a dim shape coalesced from the murk, and a panicky thrill shot through Rhiss, a feeling he immediately and resolutely damped down as best he could. He sighted, drew the string back full, and waited to see what came.

It was indeed a dog, of sorts. But it was like no dog he had ever seen, or hoped to see: a great, shaggily deformed, hideous mockery of a dog, black as the night, massive, misshapen, slavering lips drawn back in an audible snarl as it caught sight of him and crept forward. Rhiss was revolted to see the beast's eyes redly luminous in the dim light, revealing a dark intelligence that momentarily made him quail under its glare. He swallowed hard, breathed a silent prayer, sighted directly on the red eyes, and let fly.

There was a blood-curdling shriek, abruptly cut off, but Rhiss did not pause to check the results. Out the corner of his eye he detected more movement and swung to face it, smoothly retrieving another arrow and fitting it to the bow in one fluid motion. He waited a fraction of a second to ascertain it was another of the ghastly dog-like creatures and let fly his second arrow. The thing's howl was truncated as it slammed against one of the stones by the force of the armoured berserker arrow, and died.

An unexplainable sixth sense whispered urgent mental warning, and Rhiss spun around, grasping another arrow, to discover a third creature skulking in through a gap behind Arian. Swiftly moving several paces to sight on it better, he loosed the arrow and was gratified to see that shot, too, find its mark. Scanning the circle, however, his elation was quashed as he spotted more creatures in the gaps. The horn sounded again just outside the circle, a different call than before: plainly a command. As one, the creatures crouched, snarling, making no attempt to proceed further. They fell silent, and dread came upon Rhiss. The hairs on the back of his neck rose, and he turned slowly to see a darkling figure on an enormous sable horse enter the circle. A noisome odour of rank decay wafted across on some stray wisp of moving air. There was no doubt as to the new arrival's identity.

A tall, sepulchral figure with robes the colour of dried blood, including the gauntlets gripping the dreadful horse's reins, Moressin the Hunter's face was hidden by an oversized hood completely obscuring his features. The half-light of the circle dimmed momentarily where he passed, and as Rhiss stared in horrified fascination, a dry, scholarly part of his mind was irresistibly reminded of the Masque of the Red Death.

The Hunter reined in and stood in the stirrups, dark folds of the hood moving this way and that, searching. Rhiss realized that while it noted the position of Arian, Aquilea and the horses, halting its scan briefly to study them, it did not seem to spot him. The impulse flashed to shoot an arrow at the Hunter; Rhiss was about to do that when new understanding struck with sudden clarity: the sword at his belt, sent moments earlier, could only have come in answer to his plea. If that was the case, it was undoubtedly the weapon he must use to confront the spectre less than twenty feet away. Carefully, slowly, not taking his eyes from the Hunter, he laid bow and quiver on the grass, and straightening up, drew the sword from his belt. He attempted to do it silently, but the blade rasped momentarily against his belt buckle, a small metallic noise deafening in the stillness. Rhiss winced as he drew the sword clear, and flicked nervous eyes at Moressin, who still stood in the stirrups, surveying the scene.

It was obvious rider *and* horse heard: both heads swivelled in his direction. The rider sat in the saddle, and a voice came from the folds of the hood, a low, grating sibilance, full of malice.

"Alongside horses, two there are, human and beast, who stand, Essences chilled by Hunter's Breath, as should be. But someone has been... *diligent*, yes... very diligent with stinging bow... is there a third, then, responsible for bringing down three of our hounds? Aye... they smell him." The figure paused, considering, and then went on in the same musing manner. "A third, Essence unchilled? How can this be? Will he stand forth, or cower in the mists?"

Desperately afraid, Rhiss swallowed hard, but with the fear, there was resolve to do what he must, resolve that could tamp down the fear. For some reason, the idea came to hold off revealing himself a little longer, and so remaining where he was, he said quietly but clearly, "I am here, Hunter. Look to me if you can. And if you would not share the fate of your miserable curs lying dead, you had best call them off and go back to whatever fell place you come from. While I draw breath, you shall have neither my friends nor me. Come nearer, and I will destroy you. I swear it."

Horrible, creaking laughter issued from the Hunter. "The Hunter is here at his Master's command. Can'st not destroy the Hunter, he whose voice is little more than a youth's. The only one who could is long dead and gone. The Servants of the Other gnaw his Essence, as they will on thine, before the Hunter is done." It raised one arm to point at Arian. "Watch thy friend's Essence wither as the Other claims her."

Rhiss reacted instinctively. He ran forward, halting before Arian. Lifting the sword with both hands, he held it steady and repeated hoarsely, "I warn you again: if you approach, or try to harm them, I *will* destroy you."

Incredibly, the apparition stiffened, holding motionless for an endless moment. There was unmistakable sound of a sharp hiss of breath, and a wild thought blazed through Rhiss' mind, incredulous at first, then certain: the creature was afraid. For some bizarre, unknowable reason, it was afraid. Of what? The man before it? The sword? Rhiss did not know, but felt filled with new hope.

And what had it been babbling about? Arian's and Aquilea's Essences were... aye, chilled, an apt word the creature used. Keeping a wary eye on the Hunter, Rhiss turned and cupped a hand on Aquilea's head, between the tufted ears. *Aquilea,* he thought fervently, *I need you!* Rhiss did not know how to initiate the healing he had brought upon Rhyanna, was not even sure Aquilea's catatonia fell into the category of things that *could* be healed, but...

His train of thought was interrupted and he spun around as the Hunter spoke again: a single word containing both query and exclamation at the same time, a single word infused with hatred... and fear: "Ahrhissian?!"

Astonished, Rhiss made no reply. He had no idea what the creature had said. Ahrhissian? What, in the One's name, was *that*? A name? A curse? Mindless exclamation? But the creature continued, sparing further speculation.

Raising an arm, pointing accusingly, the Hunter hissed, "How comes't thou here, Ahrhissian, and to what purpose? When last we grappled, 'twas long ago. And the sword was lost. How comes't thou by it once more?"

It thinks I'm someone else, Rhiss thought, amazed. *Someone with whom it fought long ago.* What would cause it to make such an error? The sword he held? Miraculous as its appearance was, it could not be that alone. The Circlet? But Moressin recognized Rhiss himself, under the impression he was someone named Ahrhissian. Rhiss realized that could be useful, and decided to bluff.

"Why am I here, Hunter?" he asked, allowing sarcasm to creep into his tone. "Don't you *know*? Think back, if you can: why was I here long ago?"

"To seek Moressin's destruction," came the icy response. "But imprisonment was the best thou could'st achieve. And no prison can hold the Hunter forever, even one fashioned by such a king. The Hunter stands here, now, freed at the will and command of the Lord Maldeus."

The crouched hounds rose as one, as if at some silent signal, although Rhiss saw or heard nothing. Snarling, they advanced slowly. The creature ponderously shook its head beneath the folds of its hood, arrogant contempt creeping into its voice. "The Hunter knows not the manner of thy return to the lands of the living, little lord, but this time, thou art young and bereft of the skills of long ago. We will slowly consume thy Essence, without exhausting it, and so stretch thy torment beyond count of time."

A hound leaped from the mists straight at Rhiss. It had crept, silent and unnoticed, to within a few feet of where he stood. With lightning speed, Rhiss turned the sword to the animal's attack. There was no dodging the thing, and he impaled it on the sword as it bowled into him. The impact threw him to the ground, with the stinking thing limp on top. Rhiss had no idea whether it was alive or dead as he struggled to get it off. He could barely contain his revulsion as he fought against the matted fur, slick with the creature's blood, and its foul stench, aware all the while that other hounds must be closing. Then he pushed the animal aside, realized it was, indeed, dead, and freed his sword.

Rhiss barely had time to absorb that before another hound was on him. It reached him as he struggled to his knees, and, snarling, sank fangs into his right arm. Rhiss cried out at the sudden, icy pain searing his flesh. He dropped the sword and fell on his back, the brute hanging on.

As he flailed his hand in an instinctive attempt to get the animal off, he came in contact with the hilt of his dagger. In one move, he pulled it from its sheath and plunged the blade deep into the dog's side, ripping sideways as he did so. Shrieking harshly, the animal released him, stiffened and died.

Gasping, Rhiss cast around wildly for the sword, finding it as he scrambled to his feet. His right arm was on fire and bleeding freely, and he could not make it help grasp the sword. Holding it only in his left hand, he stood, swaying slightly and casting about to find the other beasts. They crouched, silent and motionless, in a knot fifteen to twenty feet away. Apparently, he thought with exhausted satisfaction, the fact he had killed no less than five of their number gave them pause. He turned to face Moressin. "Now then, Hunter..." he began.

The dark figure leaped off its horse, swiftly closing the distance between them, a long, wicked looking dagger in each crimson gauntlet. Rhiss barely had time to assume a defensive posture before the Hunter was upon him, slashing with both weapons. Rhiss countered with his newly found sword, using every position, every tactic he could recall Alistair teaching him. The exchange lasted perhaps a minute or two, although it felt infinitely longer.

Then, inexplicably, the Hunter disengaged, his weapons slithering off the sword in a raspy metallic clash, and he retreated several long steps back out of range, where he simply stood motionless in some silent speculation.

Rhiss was at a loss to understand why Moressin would cease the attack — he swiftly scanned the circle, paranoid it was merely some devilish ruse to put him off his guard — but nothing new or untoward appeared in the equation. The slavering dog-things still crouched, staring balefully; and Moressin merely... stood there, as though paralyzed by his own Mist. That would have been almost too richly ironic, Rhiss suddenly thought, and had to fight an irrational desire to laugh. Still, as he stood panting, arm on fire, he didn't want to question the creature's reasons: the pause provided much-needed respite.

An angry hiss suddenly came from within Moressin's hood. "Art not Ahrhissian!"

Even though the agony in his arm was growing exponentially worse by the second, Rhiss could hardly believe the exclamation. Of all the things Moressin might have said at that juncture, the comment just struck him as so ridiculously self-evident, so fatuous, that Rhiss felt it kindle a white-hot flame of insane rage within him.

"*Really?!*" he yelled. "It's taken you *this* long to figure that out?! Return to your thickwitted master and beg from him a picture of his enemy! Show him what incompetent tools he commands!" He raised the sword again, held it trembling before him, and shouted exultantly, "I am Rhissan, son of Tovan, you monster, and I will kill you all the same! *Come on!*"

His goading was all too successful. The Hunter leapt at him, their weapons meeting with a clang. Time seemed suspended as Rhiss fought off the Hunter's furious attack. Even in his rage, Rhiss realized that Moressin had the upper hand, using both weapons with deadly skill. Increasingly dazed, barely able to hold his own, Rhiss knew the end was near. He was utterly spent, and the icy fire advanced up his arm. Breathing was difficult. Sweat trickled into his eyes, blurring his vision. He could not continue much longer. The Hunter sensed it, too.

"All is lost, Rhissan, son of Tovan!" it gloated. "Can'st sense defeat? When thou can'st no longer wield thy weapon, thou wilt know the beginning of eternal agony—"

A harsh, screaming cry interrupted him. Startled, they both automatically sprang back from each other to locate the source. Moressin gave no indication what he thought it was. Rhiss likewise had no idea, but was terrified it was the Hunter's dogs, or something even worse, joining the attack — an assault he knew he could not possibly withstand.

But it was not the hounds. Aquilea struck the hapless Moressin like a bolt of lightning, spitting and hissing her fury. She must have shaken off her paralysis at last. The Hunter seemed utterly at a loss how to meet the onslaught, and in that moment, Rhiss saw his chance. Summoning final reserves, he staggered forward and plunged the sword into the Hunter.

A great, shuddering cry rose from the apparition's unseen mouth, echoing over the stones and across the moor before trailing away. As it subsided, Moressin's body became wispy and ethereal. Then, in a soundless concussion of brilliant ruby light, the Hunter vanished, and as the shock wave raced out from the explosion, the dogs howled once in unison before disappearing in like manner.

Knocked to the ground from the force of the detonation, Rhiss lay stunned. Blinking in confusion, he sat up slowly and glanced around: the mist was completely gone, vanishing at the same moment as Moressin's disappearance. The air was clean, clear, crisp and dry, and it was late afternoon, the sun nearly touching nearby hills.

Aquilea had been tossed into the air by the force of Moressin's demise, and she landed beside Rhiss, cheeping with concern, nuzzling him. "Right, lass, it's all right," he repeated over and over, scratching between her ears. He staggered to his feet and found the sword on the ground, unscathed but gore-stained. Unsteadily, he wiped it on the grass before replacing it in his belt. His dagger was a few paces away, and mechanically, he wandered over. It, too, had sustained no damage, and he slowly shook his head in confusion, cleaning it and returning it into its sheath. Aquilea accompanied him while he retrieved his weapons. Rhiss shivered violently. His right arm continued to bleed. It was simultaneously hot and cold, and there was no sensation in it. He felt a growing sense of lethargy, and just wanted to lie down and rest. But there was one more task.

He moved to Arian and the horses. They still resembled statues, but had lost their ghastly, wax-like hue, and now seemed merely asleep, albeit with eyes open. He was certain they would soon recover and be themselves again.

Behind Rhiss, Aquilea cried out in warning. Barely able to stand, Rhiss turned apprehensively to the new threat. Whatever it was, he would be no match for it. Sheer force of will had kept him going this far, but between previous injuries and the new...

"Aquilea..." he began hoarsely, intending to instruct her to protect them, but stopped, staring at the far side of the circle nearest the road.

Someone entered through a gap, a slight figure in a flowing dress of white and tan. A quick series of impressions lodged in Rhiss' rapidly darkening mind: thick mane of long, dark curly hair, youthful, feminine face, mouth creased in quizzical smile — and he realized blurrily that a young woman approached. Aquilea ran to her, relief and joy evident in her thoughts.

Rhiss took an uncertain step forwards, but the ground seemed to heave under his feet, and he stumbled. Not again, he thought disjointedly, as the earth rose to meet him. He landed on his wounded arm, cried out in pain, and heard Aquilea and the woman both respond with alarm. Then it didn't matter: the grass felt altogether cool and comfortable against his burning face, and all he wanted to do was close his eyes and let sleep transport him away from this place, away from aches and hurts, away from the memory of terrible apparitions and hellish hounds. There was residual curiosity — who the woman was, where she had come from, what she wanted — but that swiftly became unimportant and faraway. Rhiss felt the coming of night — or some sort of darkness — and closed his eyes to let consciousness slip away as he surrendered to the silent blackness.

The Man was hurt! The Man was hurt! The Man was hurt! Aquilea's thought patterns cycled endlessly and futilely, locked in a bright bubble of panic. Included in it were large measures of shame and guilt: she had failed in her role as Shield-Protector. The reality that it was in no way her fault did not enter her thinking; like many before and after her, Aquilea unconsciously assumed personal responsibility for something she had not caused, could not have prevented, and had in fact done her best to avoid. Misplaced guilt is a near-universal condition among sentient and usually rational beings.

All she knew was that, in the midst of an otherwise uneventful journey across the barren moor on a sunny day, the Petrifying Mist had abruptly barrelled towards them, and unaccountably, the Sacred Space lacked the Protection it should have provided. Consciousness faded as the Mist enveloped all in slimy tendrils; her thoughts slowed to a glacial crawl. She remembered being cold, so very cold, chilled to the very depths of her Essence, fear at what was happening pricking like needles of ice at the extreme edges of thought; but she could not move, or think to move.

Then came a sudden, unaccountable blast of heat and light exploding through her mind. The Man was calling, and she could hear and respond, limbs obeying her will again. Scanning swiftly, she could see him, sorely injured, strength failing fast: she could see the tide of his Essence ebbing, hurt by the loathsome creatures all around. Some were four-legged like/not-like dogs, and one was a horrifying contradiction: it resembled a human but was not, seemed alive but was not, Essence twisted and corrupted into a horror she momentarily shrank from. But a fresh dart of agony from The Man pierced her mind and fury ignited within her against those who would commit such atrocity.

She launched into the air, then rolled and immediately dived on the Not-Human, rage she had never known before filling the depth and breadth of her Essence. A single imperative was upon her: to rend and tear, bite and scratch, until this... this obscene Thing was no more.

The distraction she provided was enough; it enabled The Man, with last reserves of strength, to thrust at the Not-Human with — by the Light! When and from where had he obtained a metal Stinger? There could be only one source: The One had given The Man a mighty gift, a salvation; it gleamed in the half-light, strange energies plying its surface, a razor-sharp talisman of destruction, as beautiful as it was deadly. In her astonishment, Aquilea nearly forgot her quarry.

But The Man did not. He took his new-found Stinger, and thrust it at the Not-Human. Aquilea had never seen a Stinger sever the connection between Essence and Flesh quite as this one did, even though she had witnessed several human conflicts in her short life. The Not-Human's twisted Essence... exploded into fractured ebon shards of Nothing. Aquilea was not really even sure how to articulate it. She was momentarily ecstatic, before the severity of The Man's injury registered again in her mind, and rational thought dissolved in panic.

Then Aquilea became aware of... another Essence approaching: a cool, clear, calm Essence imbued with gentle hues of violet and palest blue. It was a human woman, but a woman unlike any Aquilea had ever come across in her travels, and she cried out her relief and joy; for The Woman would make all well.

XII

WITCHES AND DISCOVERY

> *"I will pause in the daily rhythm of my labours, allowing the burdens of care and haste to fall from my shoulders like an unwanted cloak. I will stop to hear the sounds of Creation flow through my Essence, and be glad. I will be still, knowing the One is in everything, and all is well."*
>
> The Book of the One, 137:26:8-9
> (Cantos 137, Chapter 26, Verses 8-9)

Sensation returned first: he was on his back, swathed in warm, woollen blankets, coarse and scratchy to the touch. Then came hearing: small, hissing explosions of wooden knots and soft cracklings of a fire nearby, and the gentle drumming of rain on a slate roof. Rhiss recognized the sound from his youth at his aunt's cottage in Wales. But, wait... was this Wales? Surely not. Thunder rolled softly, muted by distance; shards of memory reconnected, fragments arranged and glued together with consciousness returning, a pattern of events and experiences: Byrn Moor... fog... the Hunter and his hounds... appeal and a sword... battle... pain... Aquilea to the rescue... victory... and at the very end, a woman.

Rhiss opened his eyes. Above were large beams, dark and roughly hewn wood, supporting the roof. Shadows from the fire flickered on them, casting weird shapes. He turned his head to the left, and discovered the bed he was in was flush to a whitewashed fieldstone wall. Moving his head the opposite way, he stared with unbridled curiosity at an open room, wondering what strange situation he had landed in. Slowly he levered into a sitting position, noting as he did that his right arm was bandaged in clean, white linen. That brought back a vivid — and unwelcome — memory, and he grimaced, flexing the arm experimentally. It was stiff and a little sore, but there was no pain, and no fever. It appeared he would recover.

A long, dimly lit, rectangular room stretched some twenty or thirty feet, deserted at the present save him. It was filled with skilfully carved wooden furniture: a table and several chairs; another table where food was evidently prepared, set against the wall, cupboards above; stools; a couple of rocking chairs; long, low benches against the walls, upon which reposed a variety of small tools; a huge spinning wheel; and a large harp. Whitewashed stone walls reflected ruddy light from a huge fire pit in the room's centre, currently the only light source. A heavy, embossed metal hood hung over the fire pit like an enormous, dark stalactite descending from the ceiling, providing the means for smoke and fumes to exit. Suspended on an iron spit over the fire, a massive copper cauldron gave off lazy wisps of steam, some concoction simmering gently within. A pile of sawed logs lay on the stone floor by the fire pit, awaiting their turn feeding the ravenous fire. Two heavy wooden doors gave exit: the first was centred along one wall, secured with a stout bar slung across the door's width between two bulky iron brackets; the second was at the room's far end. Several small, square windows were set deeply into thick stone walls, but heavy curtains were drawn tightly closed inside each opening, shutting out the world. All together, the dominant impression was not luxurious, but there was an appealing tidy cosiness.

Rhiss wondered who and where the owner was. Not even Aquilea was present, which he found odd. She was usually perched at his feet when and where he awoke, ready to greet him, and her absence was discomfiting. Rhiss smiled wryly as he realized: *usually* at his feet? Only if "usually" meant the past week or so. How quickly one became accustomed to the bizarre and unusual.

He swung his feet over the bedside, and discovered he was dressed only in the nightshirt from his saddle bag, which hung on a chair by the bed. Rhiss studied the chair thoughtfully. His boots stood beside it, polished and gleaming dully in the firelight; and his clothing, washed and carefully folded, reposed on the chair itself. His shirt, torn when the dog-creature attacked, was painstakingly, skilfully stitched together, looking as good as new. Knife and bow were neatly placed beside the chair, as was his latest acquisition from the Way Stones. Rhiss eyed it carefully, casting his mind back, wondering again at the sword's appearance.

It leaned against the wall, quiescent, shining redly in the firelight, black lettering standing in vivid relief even in the dim illumination. Not for the first time, Rhiss wondered what the inscription said. The quillons, the metal bar forming the crossguard at the end of the grip, appeared interesting, and he leaned over to examine it more carefully. In the centre, in a standard shield shape, a white enamel-like material was vividly inlaid in scarlet with the triune sign of the One. Rich designs were etched over the length of the quillons, culminating in smaller shields at either end. One shield had — of course! — the image of a heraldic gryphon, done, again, in scarlet on white enamel, while the other, similarly rendered in red and white, had... he looked closely... hmm, that was strange: the image was a wolf's head. In many ways — origin, strength, and decoration — a truly remarkable weapon.

He sighed, shook his head, and rose, a trifle unsteadily. While there was no pain, he felt the weakness of someone who had lain in bed overlong. Walking carefully to the warmth of the fire pit, Rhiss wondered how long he had been unconscious, and how he came to be there in the first place. He half-recalled feverish memories of pain, calling out, being hoisted into sitting position as warm broths were poured down his throat, and above all, the soft voices of women.

The floor was mostly covered with woven rugs, rough against his bare feet. Extending hands to the fire, feeling the heat against his palms, Rhiss sniffed the air appreciatively. A delightful aroma emanated from the pot. His stomach growled dismally in response; it was evidently some time since he had last eaten.

Thunder muttered again, and Rhiss became abruptly aware he had no idea of the time. He moved to a window by the door set in the long wall, pushed aside the heavy curtains, and peered out.

It was blackest night: the heavens were lit by neither sun nor moon; in fact the sky itself was completely obscured by masses of heavy clouds discharging watery freight on the land below. A flash of lightning momentarily lit the darkness, and Rhiss glimpsed a bleak landscape revealing, if not Byrn Moor itself, somewhere very nearby. He shivered at the memories and turned away, drawing the curtains tightly to shut out the night. As he did, thunder from the last lightning flash rolled over the moor.

Rhiss walked slowly back to the fire pit, at a loss. He extended his hands again, feeling the warmth penetrate skin and bones beneath, and stared into the fire. The tongues of multi-coloured flame were mesmerizing, intense oranges and scarlets, golds and blues, and Rhiss fancied he could lose himself in them. One could imagine patterns, shapes and images within the flames, images forming and instantly vanishing, only to form new ones which were, in their turn, also destroyed. There... that could have been Aquilea... and there was a horse...

His dreamy musings were rudely interrupted by the far door's opening, and from the corner of his eye Rhiss spied three shapes emerging, quietly at first until one caught sight of him and cried in delight. It was Aquilea, and within seconds, she closed the distance and reared against him, forelegs planted firmly but gently on his chest, butting her head against him, making that strange, rumbling, purring that signified approval. Rhiss staggered under the onslaught of her affection, but grinned broadly, rubbing her head. The exchange continued for several seconds, and he quite forgot the other figures standing by the door in silent observance. Then a smooth, feminine voice spoke in exasperation, reminding Rhiss others were there besides him and Aquilea. He jumped.

"There, now! You've made a liar of me, Prince Rhissan! I *told* Aquilea you'd not miss us if we left for several moments to check my other charges, and she believed me. But we return to find you standing by the soup pot, bold as brass, looking for the world like a penniless beggar ready to sing for his supper!"

Rhiss disengaged from Aquilea, turning his attention to the speaker. It was the young woman who had walked into the ring of stones after Moressin's vanquishing — so he thought, for there had only been time for a fleeting look before all had gone dark, and his memories were a bit fuzzy. She was every bit as pretty as he recalled, but it was oddly difficult to set her age. At first glance in the Way Stones, she had seemed in her teens. Now, she could have been in her twenties — or older — or younger. Eyes the colour of chestnuts radiated both youthful vitality and ancient wisdom. A marvellous cascade of rich brown hair, the colour of milk chocolate, fell thick and lustrous nearly to her waist, contrasted by a plain golden circlet on her brow. She was clad simply in a long, skilfully embroidered grey dress falling to her ankles, and a maroon shawl around her shoulders. Sitting beside her was a very large, roly-poly dog with shaggy dark hair and a tail wagging furiously.

The woman stopped her tirade and smiled a warm, full smile, and Rhiss understood instinctively that, while the words seemed harsh, they were spoken in jest. Nevertheless, he bowed low and summoned as much dignity as he could, considering he stood barefoot, wearing a long nightshirt and nothing else, before a stranger — an engaging young woman at that. Graciously, he said, "My apologies, Lady. I meant no offence. But if it comforts you, I suspect my winged friend here will overlook any imagined transgression on your part."

Abruptly, the fact she knew his name, his full first name, registered, as did her manner of address, and his eyes narrowed. "Prince?" he repeated, shaking his head vehemently. "No, Lady. You do me too much honour, or have mistaken me for someone else." *As did the Hunter*, it suddenly occurred. But it was no time to dwell on that, so he put it aside. "I am no prince, I assure you; merely a bruised and battered traveller who, it appears, owes you a great debt for ministering to me in my hour of need. But my name *is* Rhissan; just plain Rhissan — or Rhiss, if you prefer." He paused and wet his lips, but she did not reply, so he forged on. "You also have the advantage in knowing my name, Lady, for I do not know yours; but then," he smiled ruefully, "if I recall aright, our meeting on the moor was short on introductions."

Her dark eyes sparkled with mischievous glee at his discomfort. "Not a prince, you say?" She sighed in disappointment, but whether real or feigned, Rhiss could not tell. "What a letdown. You fair looked one at Storrenne, I'll say, although aye, rather a battered one." She stopped, eyeing him critically. "But I'm bound to agree you don't look much like one now, and that's a fact."

Her voice had an enchanting, sing-song quality, and abruptly, Rhiss became aware of hanging on her every word. It took a second or two to realize she had stopped, and he hastily gathered his wits, feeling gormless. He glanced down guiltily, as though it was his own fault he was not dressed more regally. And she had still not revealed her name.

"But perhaps I'd be *wanting* to call you a prince," she resumed coyly, bustling to the fire pit and the cauldron over it. "And that's not such a bad thing, now, is it? Letting a poor, lonely maid think she's in the company of royalty?" She picked up a ladle from a low stool and stirred the cauldron.

Rhiss smiled again. "But it wouldn't be honest, Lady. I'm no more a prince than you are a princess."

Her eyes flashed and she stopped stirring, brandishing the ladle at Rhiss like a dagger. "And how do you know I'm *not* a princess? Or even a queen, then? For all you know, I could be a queen brutally cast down from her throne by…" She stopped and pursed her lips, evidently considering what evil force might have been responsible for her sad fate.

"A wicked stepmother, perhaps?" interjected Rhiss with straight face but raised eyebrows.

She scowled in mock exasperation. "Of course not. What blather you spout. Why would you be saying such nonsense? Aren't you the slightest bit afraid you might actually be taunting a queen, then?"

"Well, I certainly hope not. I would never dare taunt a queen, even one who chooses to remain nameless after meeting someone and repeatedly being asked to introduce herself; but eventually, you *must* provide a name I can call you," Rhiss said dryly. "Otherwise, I shall be reduced to calling you—"

"Lowri," she interrupted smoothly, curtseying even as she still held the ladle in one hand. "Lowri of McKraguie will do fine to go on with, Just Plain Rhissan. Or you may call me Mistress Lowri, if you need a title before my name." Her gaze moved up and down his form. "There, now. That's settled, so maybe you'll be wanting to dress, and then we can share this soup. A little late evenmeal, you know, in honour of your rejoining the world. But I'll not sup with someone still in his nightshirt." She gestured towards the bed he had vacated. "Fetch your clothes, Just Plain Rhissan, and take them through there." She indicated the small door at the room's far end, whence she had entered. "I was thinking you might wake, so there's a copper back there full of nice hot water. Mind you empty it into the drain when you're finished. Then you can dress in some privacy, as long as you ignore the other inhabitants. After that, return and I can fancy I *am* dining with a prince."

"Other inhabitants?" queried Rhiss doubtfully, moving nonetheless towards the bed in response to her directions.

"Now, don't mind them, sirrah," she admonished, crossing to a cupboard and withdrawing a bunch of herbs tied together. "Like as not, they'll be more frightened of a great hulking presence like you than you will be of them. Though of course," she gestured at the dog, "they're already used to hulking presences because of my Relamus." She returned to the pot and placed the herbs in, then resumed stirring, glancing at Rhiss. "Stop standing there like a lost puppy. Off you go, now." It was a dismissal. Aquilea padded over to stare at the pot with interest, and Lowri made soft crooning noises at her. Aquilea chirruped in reply, and Relamus flopped down to watch. They seemed to have forgotten Rhiss' presence entirely.

Shrugging, he gathered his clothes. He debated whether to take his weapons, thought better of it, then changed his mind again and took the dagger. As personal accoutrement and gift from Brother Gavrilos, it felt like an integral part of his wardrobe, not something separate, so he picked it up and walked to the far door. Once there, he set his boots down and opened the door with a free hand, peering warily into the next room. Nothing leaped out, so he picked up the boots and went in, closing the door with one foot.

Candles burned in wall sconces, illuminating the room in a soft golden glow, and Rhiss looked around with interest. There were rough cages built in tiers stretching the length of the room, and a work bench with cupboards above. Many of the cages were occupied by small animals. Several had bandages or splints on body parts, while others simply lay quietly in their cages. Rhiss had had cause to visit the veterinary's surgery near Darkton once, and it reminded him indelibly of a rougher, more spartan version.

He spied a fireplace halfway along the room, a great copper tub set before it. Walking down, he found the tub half-filled with steaming water, soap and towels laid neatly beside. Mistress Lowri evidently ministered to humans as well as animals. Carefully, Rhiss placed his clothes on the floor, glanced around, removed his nightshirt, and stepped into the copper, sighing gratefully. His bruises had faded remarkably, as had his muscle aches and pains. A pleasant fragrance emanated from the water, although it smelled more medicinal than perfumed. It didn't matter, whatever it was, for it felt an eternity since the baths at The King's Arms, and even though there was no attendant to provide careful ministrations, the hot water was pure bliss. He wondered whether he should get his bandage wet, which brought the reason for needing one in the first place to mind. After a moment's hesitation, he carefully removed it to peer at the wound beneath. There were dried herbs under the bandage. Some fell into the water as it came loose, and he brushed the remainder from his arm. Then, with great interest, he examined the area where the Hunter's dog-creature had attacked.

Amazingly, little damage was visible. Rhiss vividly recalled the creature sinking fangs into his arm, and the icy pain sweeping through afterwards, but now there was merely slight bruising and a ragged, reddish line where a nasty gash had been. Rhiss did not know whether he had been unconscious for long, or if the herbs had unusual healing virtue — like at Rontha, although even better, it seemed, and without generating bizarre visions — but whatever the reason, he was grateful and relieved to see his arm look nearly good as new. He smiled and slid down into the water, enjoying his chance to soak.

Hair still damp, a fully dressed Rhiss emerged from what he dubbed the 'infirmary wing' into the main room of Lowri's cottage. He was presented with a scene of complete domestic tranquillity.

Singing quietly in a low, melodious voice, Lowri was seated at her spinning wheel, the sound of its soft, rhythmic whirring filling the room as she worked. Aquilea, curled up at Lowri's feet, gazed at her in rapt concentration, plainly absorbed by the singing. Rhiss could not make out the words, or perhaps it was simply that the language was unfamiliar, but it sounded almost Gaelic in pattern and rhythm. He well understood Aquilea's fascination; at that moment, all he wanted to do was also sit at Mistress Lowri's feet, drinking in the words and melody of her song. Relamus, obviously not as enchanted, dozed by the fire.

Lowri noticed his arrival, halting song and work. As the spell broke, Aquilea glanced at Rhiss and chirped a greeting, and Relamus lifted his head, lolling out a long, red tongue. Smiling a rich smile of welcome that unaccountably made Rhiss blush, Lowri stood, tall, dark and fair in the firelight's glow.

"Well, finally I can bid you welcome, Prince Rhissan, to my humble home," she said, curtseying again. "I wondered if you'd melted away in the tub. But in faith, you do look the part of a prince now, not Just Plain Rhissan. Would you be so gracious as to escort a lady to table before breaking bread with her?"

Smiling in return, Rhiss came and offered his arm — his left one, although his wounded one felt completely healed after his time in the bath — and they walked to the table together, Aquilea and Relamus following. Lowri seated him, then made final preparations. Bread, honey, a plate of butter, cheese, bowls, cutlery, a jug and tall earthenware mugs appeared on the table quickly and efficiently. She filled the bowls with rich soup from the cauldron and set them on the table, then halted and sat, looking expectantly at Rhiss. Belatedly realizing she expected him to say grace, he cast his mind back to the one Lady Meranna used at Craggaddon Hall. He made his way through it adequately, and they began their meal. On the floor, Aquilea and Relamus together dug in to a plate filled with various titbits; Lowri had not forgotten them. Rhiss was surprised the two animals got along so well, and said so. Lowri smiled. "Ah, well, Relamus is very easy-going, and quite used to all manner of beasts — although usually nothing as exotic as wee gryphon."

The soup was delicious, if not immediately identifiable, and feeling he had not eaten for a very long time, Rhiss thoroughly enjoyed the food offered.

"What is this called?" he asked between mouthfuls.

"Crumbledown Stew. It's a very old traditional Arrinoran recipe with some rather surprising ingredients."

"It's wonderful," Rhiss declared.

"I'm pleased you like it, but I apologize for serving it to you."

"Whatever for? I told you, it's wonderful."

"Well, it's not really something you would see on the tables of the well-to-do — it's more of a peasant dish, really."

"And what would make you think I'm too good for a peasant dish?" He didn't wait for an answer. "It's a long time since I enjoyed a meal this much."

"I'm glad. And it *will* stick to your insides."

Rhiss grinned. "It certainly does that."

He concentrated on the food then, and was most of the way through his meal before he became guiltily aware of two things: Lowri had evidently finished earlier and now simply watched, smiling; and it dawned on him with shock that Arian had been nowhere to be seen since he regained consciousness.

"Mistress Lowri—" he began, then stopped, not quite sure of the best way to frame his question.

"Aye, Prince Rhissan?"

He frowned. "Lady, I would be very much obliged if you stopped referring to me like that. I have already said I am no prince. You know my name, and I would prefer you use it."

She inclined her head in acquiescence, still smiling. "Very well, Just Plain Rhissan, I'll accede to your request — for the time being, at any rate, but you must return the favour and stop calling me Lady. My name is Lowri, as I also already said. Now, your question?"

"Well, aye... several, actually... and one of some urgency, I fear. When I was in the Way Stones, I had a companion besides Aquilea, a distinguished older woman. She had been rendered... well, I am not quite sure what the word would be. It was almost as if she was turned to stone, but still alive. Did you see her?"

She nodded solemnly. "Oh, aye. In fact, shortly after you fell as one dead, Seir-onna Arian emerged from Hunter's Trance and we rushed to your aid. She assisted in bringing you here, hardly leaving your side." She paused. "She is a good woman, a very good woman, Rhissan; you're fair fortunate to have her as guide and friend, even if it's not been for very long." She glanced down at Aquilea. "As you are to have your gryphon in the same capacities. But it sounds like you had an adventure or two before Byrn Moor."

Rhiss digested this. "Seir-onna Arian? You know her name? Where is she now, pray? I am ashamed to admit it was only as I ate that I realized I had not seen her since I awoke, but..." He stopped and looked at her shrewdly. "You seem to know much about our enterprise. Has Arian told you, then?"

Lowri smiled her enchanting smile. "Aye. She and I spoke at length. We had ample time to do so; it's been two days since we brought you here. When your fever broke late last night and it was evident you were out of danger, she determined to return to Rontha, and left early this morning."

Rhiss was aghast. "What?! You allowed her to go back to Rontha? Alone?"

Lowri looked comically surprised. "I didn't *allow* her to do anything. She's a grown woman, capable of making her own decisions. But aye, she went to Rontha by herself this morning. What of it?"

"But, Lowri... she... she's only a... And she's old! Something could happen to her, travelling by herself!"

Lowri's eyes narrowed, and she wagged an accusing finger. "Now, that's enough of that, Just Plain Rhissan. It matters not whether you be prince or commoner, there's no reason for arrogant rubbish! It's plain you have never seen a Castellar in a scrape, or you wouldn't be spouting such blather. For your information, *my Lord*, they've a thoroughly well-earned reputation for dealing efficiently and ruthlessly with any threat to their persons... and it matters not whether we speak of male *or* female Castellars. So have a care. I don't know how things happen in your country — I'm told it's a far ways from Arrinor — but you'll find in *this* land, many women are just as capable of wielding sword or bow as men. And age has naught to do with anything. I'd wager my Relamus that Arian can defeat most fighting men half her age." She stopped, passion spent. The glare left her face and she grinned impishly. "Besides that... there was no one to accompany her, apart from me. And I had you to mind." She whistled softly. "By the One, Rhissan, it's well you said what you did to me and not Seir-onna Arian. *I* was merely offended. *She'd* have given you a good thrashing if such words reached her ears. So as I said, have a care before you assume she's a doddering old grandmother. You need not fear for her safety — only yours if you treat her as though she's ready to go to the One."

Abashed, Rhiss said sheepishly, "My apologies. You're right, it *is* very different in my land. Most women there are not nearly as independent — or equal — with men as they evidently are here. In fact, much of the time, many are subservient to men."

Lowri shook her head in disbelief. "The One preserve us. Women can be equal with men and yet still delight in being women, distinct from men. And men can appreciate that. Although I'll be the first to admit we're not talking of a universal condition. So... why would women in your land settle for less?"

Rhiss was caught off-guard. "I don't know. It's just... well, it's just how things are... how they've always been." He shook his head in turn. "But it was wrong — my ignorance had me projecting my culture's values on this one. Forgive me."

She smiled. "No need. Only the One is perfect. The rest of us must learn from our mistakes. But if you have any more assumptions, perhaps you'd best mention them quietly and privately to me before trotting them out in public."

Rhiss smiled back. "I will, be sure of it. Thank you. You will be my true, stalwart guide."

Strangely, she seemed disconcerted at that, and her face coloured. She rose quickly and fussed with the pot over the fire, obviously masking her feelings with activity.

After a moment, she paused and, regaining her composure, furrowed her brow in concentration. "Now... where were we before your education about male and female roles in Arrinor? Oh, aye... Seir-onna Arian. She went to secure supplies for the two of you — and me also while she was at it — and to gather what news may be out and about. We've both been curious to see how the destruction of the Hunter has been acknowledged, or whether it has even been understood to have occurred yet." She cocked her head to one side for a moment, gaze becoming serious. "Truly, you know, an amazing feat, Rhissan. Moressin Venator was a terrible, formidable force for evil, vanquishing many over long count of years, including renowned warriors. You can be rightly proud of what you achieved."

Rhiss glanced ruefully down at his arm. "My thanks. But it was not without cost. I don't know how I managed it, really. Aquilea helped. And I am grateful to you for my healing."

She inclined her head modestly. "Aye, well... I have some small skill in healing hurts of both men and beasts. It's nothing quite as dramatic as *your* ability—" she smiled briefly "—but a goodly skill, nonetheless. As for being lucky; ah, now, you were no such thing." She shook her head, correcting him gently. "The grace of the One was full upon you, and well you know it." She gestured to the sword propped against the wall. "Swords like that do not simply appear out of thin air, no matter where you come from or who you might be." She made the triune sign of blessing at it, and Rhiss was sceptical but intrigued.

"What might you know of swords like that, Lowri?"

She raised an eyebrow. "More than you might think, Just Plain Rhissan, so be careful. Storrenne is a right ancient place, full of the One's enchantment, and I tell you that the Hunter was either overconfident or fair desperate to set foot within it as he did."

"Storrenne?" repeated Rhiss. "That's the name of the Way Stones?" She nodded. "What do you know of it?"

"Much also," she answered quietly. "I'll take you there tomorrow if the weather's fair, and you can see and experience it in broad daylight. It's not far: a pleasant stroll in the sunlight — perhaps an hour's easy walk. 'Tis a wondrous place, you see." She looked at him knowingly. "But you already felt that, before the Hunter came, didn't you? Actually, you needn't answer, because I know you did — Arian told me what you said."

Rhiss recalled the heartbeat in the stones, but shivered involuntarily as he also recalled the Hunter and his attack. "I'm not sure I want to return."

"Nonsense," she said briskly. "Why, 'twould be good for you. There's no evil there, I tell you. In fact, far from it — and it's important you understand, so you can also appreciate the Sword you were given to meet his attack with."

"Lowri," said Rhiss slowly, "why were you there? At Storrenne, I mean? Surely you saw the mist."

She nodded, gazing at the fire. "Oh, aye, of course. Hunter's Mist, it's been called for many years. It was often visible from my front door, up on the surrounding hills, even though this house isn't really on the moor itself. You would see the Mist in the distance, and know the Hunter was on the moor again, and he'd either spotted a new victim, or was on the prowl for one." She paused, gaze still on the flames, and added, in a voice barely above a whisper, "Sometimes... I fancied I could almost hear him... his dogs... his victims."

Rhiss was incredulous. "From an hour's distance away?"

She shook her head, still not looking at him. "Well... it's not precisely hearing. Not with ears, at any rate. But I could feel it. Just as I could tell you were out there at Storrenne the other day, as good as alone."

So... why *did* you come?" Rhiss repeated.

She did not answer immediately, and Rhiss could not tell whether she was weighing what to say, or truly at a loss. Then she said softly, almost reluctantly, "Because the Sword came to you. And when I saw, I knew — I *knew* — you were not fated to be yet another poor wretch lost to the Hunter, one more I could not help. I knew you could be the one to do something, perhaps even put an end to him, and you would need me afterwards if you did." She waved a hand. "And you did."

Rhiss stared. "How could you know about the Sword? Even if you did—" he stopped, quickly calculating "—you said this house is an hour's walk from Storrenne. Yet I fought the Hunter, was wounded, destroyed him, saw you, all within... well, ten or fifteen minutes of finding the Sword, I should judge. I don't understand."

She rolled her eyes. "Rhissan, don't be dense. Haven't you heard me? First of all, you didn't *find* the Sword; it *came* to you. Second... how to explain? Here, then... Arian tells me she thinks you have the Sight. Do *you* think so?"

Rhiss was caught off-balance by the abrupt topic change. "Well, I... I'm not sure. It's only happened once or twice... certainly not regularly... not enough to call it an ability I can use or control... No. I wouldn't say I have the Sight. Certainly not as Arian described it."

She sighed in mild exasperation. "May the One save us, sirrah. I suppose next you'll be telling me you don't have the gift of Healing either, because you've only ever done it once. Do you not understand? Even in the short time since coming to Arrinor, you've begun manifesting all manner of abilities that are a clear indication you—" she abruptly stopped in mid-sentence. It was very strange: almost as though she had suddenly heard an inner voice commanding her to break off. "Well, that's neither here nor there right now," she resumed, as though nothing out of the ordinary had occurred. "As Arian said, it's a discussion for later. The point is, you *do* have the Sight, Rhissan, take my word. I can see the signs of it on you as plain as plain." She looked on him with compassion. "I have it, too. The Sight, I mean, though not as powerfully. That's how I knew to come. I saw the Sword come to you, several days ago. So, when Hunter's Mist rose the other day, I knew what would take place, and I made my way as fast as I could. I was just in time to see you victorious over Moressin before you fell like a sack of potatoes. Then Arian and the horses returned from Hunter's Trance and we got you back here."

Rhiss regarded her. He had the firm conviction that, like Arian, she was holding back some of the story. But he was at a loss to understand what it could be.

"All right, Lowri," said Rhiss quietly, "I'm sure you're not telling me something and you omit important details, but we'll leave it for now, because you obviously don't wish to discuss it. But there is one other thing I would know: the Hunter called me by a different name. He thought I was someone else." It was not quite a question.

She said nothing for several moments, gaze wandering back to the fire. "Aye," she said finally. "I can see why he would. But that was a very long time ago, of course."

There was no sound for several moments, as Rhiss silently struggled to understand the nonsensical response. Then a knot of wood in the fire popped suddenly, and Rhiss found his voice again. "What was long ago?"

She roused, interrupted from private reminiscence. "There was a king, many years ago. Your resemblance to him is... well, fair startling, it is. It's really nothing that... nothing we should talk about now, Just Plain Rhissan," she replied in a softly apologetic tone. "You're quite right; there are elements here you're not knowing. I see obviously I can't hide that from you, but... I am fair sorry, and I can say it's for your own protection, your own good at the moment... and I'm asking you not to press me further. Later, when Arian returns, perhaps we can speak on this again."

"Did Arian ask you not to speak of these things?"

She looked at him keenly. "Aye, she did. And just so's you know, I didn't like it; I still don't, but she was... persuasive, so I agreed to abide by her wishes."

She stood. "Now, by the One, you look tired. We'll talk more on the morrow, I promise... more than Arian would like, less than you would desire, how's that for compromise? But it's late, and we need to clear away." She smiled. "Especially since you're adamant you're no prince, just — what did you call yourself? — 'a bruised and battered common traveller?' And since I'm your physician, I can order you around and pack you off to bed. Which is exactly what I'm going to do." She indicated the bed from which Rhiss had so recently risen. "You may have *my* bed for one more night, Just Plain Rhissan, before I claim it back. So let's clear away and get you there quickly."

Rhiss was mortified. "That's *your* bed? I can't take it. Where would you sleep?"

"Back with my charges," she replied patiently. "As I've already done the last two nights, taking turns with Arian while one of us stayed here, watching you. One more night away from my bed is neither here nor there."

"But —"

She raised her eyebrows again. "I'll not hear another word, Just Plain Rhissan. You'll simply do as you're told, and there's an end to it." She grinned roguishly. "See? You should have agreed you were a prince when I called you one, and then I couldn't order you about like a common stable hand. Let's collect plates and cups, and wash them. Then we'll to bed before the night is older."

After tidying up, Lowri banked the fire, then turned and faced Rhiss. "Good night to you, Rhissan," she said softly. "I'm fair glad to see you hale and on your feet again."

She curtseyed low, put her hand out to pat Aquilea's head, and turned on her heel, Relamus following. She walked briskly to the side door and opened it before stopping. Turning, framed in the opening, she smiled mischievously and said, "And... go you with the One... Prince Rhissan," before passing through and closing the door firmly. Rhiss watched her go in bemused but thoughtful silence.

Rhiss awoke next morning to the sound of a bell tolling clearly. For one ludicrous instant, his sleep-addled mind thought it was the school bell, and he experienced an irrational flash of panic, thinking himself late for classes. Then recall flooded in, mixed with relief, and he sat up, listening. There was the sound of a door in the infirmary wing opening and slamming closed, then silence for several minutes until the cottage's main door burst open. Lowri strode in, cheeks rosy from the cold morning air, a heavy cloak swirling around her. Before the door closed, Rhiss got a quick glimpse outside, and saw the day had dawned clear and chilly, the grass still damp from overnight soaking.

"Good morning, m'lord," she said cheerfully, curtseying as she shed the cloak. "Some of us have been up and about a goodly time already, but I see even so sound a sleeper as you cannot ignore an early morning messenger."

"Messenger?" repeated Rhiss incredulously, choosing to ignore the gibe in the title she used again. "Out here? Who would send you a message?"

She snorted and tossed her head indignantly, sending the dark brown cascade of hair flying. "I'll have you know I get quite a regular stream of visitors, Lord High and Mighty Rhissan. Many seek the skills of Mistress Lowri, the Witch of the Ford at White River. Some — like yourself, I might mention, before you get unbearably stuck up — look for healing, either for themselves or their animals. Some look for love potions, or want to know their future, or seek advice on when to sell their livestock.

Some want the fine woollen products I make. But there are a number of people who come by on a fair regular basis, and don't you be forgetting it. This isn't a hermitage I run."

Amazed, Rhiss listened to her tirade, laughing at the end. "'Witch of the Ford at White River?'" he repeated. "Is *that* what you are? I'd not have thought to be left wounded and helpless by Arian in the hands of a witch. Or did you cast some enchantment to make her leave?"

"I did nothing of the sort," Lowri retorted stoutly. "And shame on you for thinking such a thing, her being a priest of the One and all." She smiled and winked. "'Witch' is no title I take for myself, rest assured, for I'd not lay claim to any such blasphemous label. But simple folk see my skills in healing and with animals, and to them it's nothing short of magical." She shrugged. "So that's what they call me, and I've stopped trying to correct them and simply let it be. If nothing else, it fosters respect; and you have to admit a little healthy respect — not to mention fear, at times — can be a useful thing, make no mistake. They use the bell on the pole outside to let me know of their presence — because, after all, they wouldn't want to interrupt the witch in case she's crafting her magic, now, would they? Some don't even wait to talk, but just leave their things at the pole, because they don't want to get turned into a toad from annoying the witch. That's something you'd do well to keep in mind, also, by the way." She tossed her head again.

"Is Relamus your familiar, then?" Rhiss teased.

She frowned. "My what?"

"Your familiar... a witch's familiar." Seeing her blank look, he explained. "An evil spirit in animal shape helping the witch perform her spells."

Lowri looked indignant. "What perfectly awful ideas you have at times! And fair blasphemous, too. I've never heard such a thing before. Is that part of witches' lore in your land, then?"

"I suppose so," said Rhiss, still amused.

"Well, Relamus is my companion the same way Aquilea is yours. Nothing more... although he's very good at protecting a woman living by herself on the moor's edge. Don't let his vacant amiability fool you. He can be fair terrifying when he perceives a threat to me. You're that lucky I had plenty of time to let him know you're a friend."

"All right, Mistress Lowri." Rhiss held up a hand, laughing again. "Let's return to what woke me. What did your petitioner want? You've been too busy defending your good name from my cynically dark nature to tell what came in the crisp early morn."

She held out a letter. "Well, then, we don't know everything, do we? As it happens, it's from Seir-onna Arian. It appears she's sure enough of me to be all right with leaving you under my enchantments a little longer before returning."

Rhiss took the letter eagerly. Written on parchment in a strong, flowing hand, and signed by 'Seir-onna Ardwyad,' it was phrased circumspectly, an obvious precaution against falling into the wrong hands:

The King's Arms, Rontha
June 24th

My Dear Mistress Lowri,

I write to reassure you I arrived safely in Rontha, where all seems much as we left it. The inhabitants seem unaware of the moor personage's demise, although some have gratefully marked the absence of signs of his presence. However, I do not doubt that another with more ability will soon become aware of his destruction and send forces to investigate, which could pose a problem for us. Receiving no messages via Aquilea that developments require me back with your recuperating guest, I assume all is well, and have, therefore, decided to venture slightly further afield in pursuit of other news. Watch for my coming again in not less than four to five days, perhaps more. In the meantime, I trust in the One that your guest is recovering from his hurts and enjoying your hospitality. I shall remain at the Inn tonight in case you would have Aquilea deliver any reports to me, and leave on the morrow.

In haste,
Seir-onna Ardwyad

"Four to five *days*? Or *more*?" repeated Rhiss, puzzled. "So much for a swift ride to Pencairn House. I had the impression she was in a hurry to get there, or at least, to get *me* there. What are we to do for several days while Arian traipses around Arrinor?"

He looked up to see Lowri smiling without guile or design, an open smile of simple pleasure at the prospect of another's companionship. "Well, to start with, Just Plain Rhissan, we'll take a lovely long walk over the heather to a charming spot I know. I believe you have some acquaintance with it, too. Come, let's feed you first, and while I make your oatmeal, you can splash water on your face to rid your eyes of their sleepiness, and dress. There's nothing like a good bowl of oatmeal to stick to the insides of your belly, and, by the One, I can hear yours growling clear across the room. Then we'll wash the dishes, pack a midmeal, and take ourselves on our walk."

The rain had left the air damp and chilled, although in the clear, pale sky, the sun was valiantly attempting to heat the earth. Dew was heavy on the grass as they walked over windswept ridges and valleys. Relamus loped casually along with them, stopping frequently to snuff carefully at each new smell encountered. At Lowri's insistence, Rhiss was fully armed with dagger, sword and bow. Each weapon was there for a different reason: his dagger felt like a part of him, even after so short a time; Lowri indicated she wanted him to take the sword back to where he had received it, although why, she would not say; and the bow, she laughed, was needed in case they spied some tempting morsel for that night's meal, and Rhiss could impress her with his marksmanship.

Rhiss was glad of his cloak's warmth as they passed over the moor, Lowri's arm in his. She was likewise dressed warmly with cloak and gloves over her dress. In her other hand she carried a basket with their midmeal; a nondescript green canvas bag on a long strap was slung across her shoulder. Asking what it contained, he was told it was her "healer's bag," with herbs and various other tools within. She wore the hood of her cloak up, and Rhiss found himself noticing it framed her dark curls and the delicate oval of her face quite fetchingly. He did not have to say much at first, as she chattered continuously, pointing out plants, animals and all sorts of interesting things. Gradually, though, she drew him out; she seemed genuinely interested in his story, and Rhiss found himself opening up about arriving in Arrinor, all that had happened, and his hopes and fears.

Aquilea accompanied them, although she disdained to walk, soaring effortlessly through the air above. Rhiss watched her with detached interest, wondering again about the extent of communication that occurred, or could occur, between them. He mentioned it to Lowri, and she turned in surprise, eyes wide.

"You don't know? Can you not even now hear her joy at being aloft?"

"No," he replied glumly. "She and I have had sporadic communication of sorts, mostly in crises, but nothing meaningful." Then, abruptly realizing what she implied, he asked sharply, "Why? Can you?"

"Aye, of course," she said with quiet conviction, as if it was the most natural thing in the world. She glanced at Aquilea above. "It's not like she actually speaks, you understand, but her emotions are plain as plain. Whether it's actually possible to converse with a gryphon minor, I don't know. Certainly, I can't, and I *have* tried. But I sense her moods and feelings." She turned to Rhiss again, and seeing the frustrated impatience on his face, said softly, dark eyes large and compassionate, "Would you like to?"

Rhiss found his irritation fading away, replaced by a strange feeling he could not immediately label, and could only nod slowly.

Lowri read his expression, and smiled that richly warm smile of hers. She halted and knelt in the grass, drawing Rhiss down too. "All right, then. It's quite simple, really. You need to reach out with your thoughts, and listen for hers. And I mean *really* listen. Most folk either can't, or won't take the time and effort. But they could hear a good deal if they tried. There are animals all around, sending out all sorts of things for people to hear, if they've a mind. It's something I've known for years... injured animals can let you know a great deal about their hurts without ever saying a word. Let's focus on Aquilea, though." She stripped off her gloves and gently placed warm hands against his temples. "Close your eyes, Rhissan, and picture her in your mind," she whispered. "That's right, that's right. See her there, soaring through the sky, proud and free..."

As soon as she understood what Rhiss and Lowri were doing, Aquilea terminated her sky explorations, and swooped down to earth, emitting great cries of excitement. She bounded around them in wide circles as they knelt together on the cold ground. Then she stopped her wild parade and halted before Rhiss, round eyes fixed on him in fierce concentration. Relamus halted his wanderings over the moor, too, and sat watching with complete gravitas.

They spent the better part of an hour at that spot. Lowri seemed oblivious to everything except what she was assisting Rhiss to accomplish. By the end, though, he was trembling and exhausted from his efforts, his limbs aching from the cold seeping up from the earth and lack of movement. However, by the time the hour passed, he felt as though a veil in his mind had been cast aside. The clear, sharp darts of Aquilea's broad feelings and intentions pierced his thoughts in crystalline clarity, and he was absolutely sure she, likewise, felt his thoughts.

Lowri appeared to understand that, too, for she abruptly straightened, took in a deep breath and let it out. She shook herself lightly, like an animal awakening from a dream. Then she stood and smiled down at Rhiss.

"There. That's more like, isn't it, Just Plain Rhissan?"

He swallowed, nodded, and likewise rose, wincing as arms and legs protested sudden movement after such a lengthy period of inaction. "Oh, aye. Indeed, aye, Lowri. What wondrous gifts you have. I can't imagine why Aquilea would want to accompany me when she could be with you."

Lowri rolled her eyes at the heavens and sighed. "Rhissan, you have incredible potential, but I swear, at times you say the daftest things imaginable. Can you not sense the bond between you? It's very obvious to me. And it is a bond liable only to strengthen as time goes by."

Rhiss grinned sheepishly. "You're right, Lowri... not very diplomatic, but right. I treasure your honesty... even though it's probably inappropriate to speak so to a prince."

He spoke playfully, referring to her habit of calling him Prince, but her reaction was surprising. There was a flicker of something almost like guilt in her eyes, and she turned away, making a show of smoothing the folds in her dress and cloak. Then she turned back towards him, cleared her throat, and spoke, tone carefully neutral.

"We'd best be on our way. Otherwise, it'll be nightfall by the time we make Storrenne." She glanced around the hills. "And even with the Hunter gone, the moor is neither the safest nor most hospitable place after dark." She picked up the picnic basket. "Let's be off while we still have the day. I'm that eager for you to see the Way Stones in daylight with your wits about you."

Rhiss nodded thoughtfully, but did not reply. He was wondering what he had said to discomfit her, then realized, if she was indeed keeping something back, expressing how much he appreciated her honesty might have struck a raw nerve. Lowri put her arm in his again, and they began walking together, although she did not meet his gaze. From behind, Aquilea regarded the two humans quizzically a moment, then leapt into the air once more, wings beating slowly but powerfully as she gained height. Relamus leapt after her, barking joyously and running to follow.

Storrenne appeared larger and somehow more majestic when approached on a sunny day, from a different direction, with a winsome lass on his arm, Rhiss decided. The road from the north whence they came crested a small rise, and there were the Way Stones, laid out below. But he was reluctant to enter the ring at first; memories of his encounter with the Hunter were simply too raw, and he had to be coaxed in with Lowri's patient encouraging.

"Rhissan, I beg you," she finally pleaded. "I would have you enter this ring and realize it is not a place of evil, but the opposite. It is sacred to the One. Do not allow your experience a few days ago to taint this place with a reputation it does not deserve. If you will not enter for yourself, at least do so for me. Please?"

Rhiss sighed in resignation, muttering to himself, and stepped through a gap between the stones, moving into the area inside the ring. Lowri left him alone, and gradually, as he wandered the space, he began to understand what she meant. The last time he had been there played itself out in his mind. *There* was the spot where he and the Hunter fought, and with Aquilea's timely assistance, vanquished the creature. And *there* was the stone at which he had heard, or felt, the heartbeat. And finally, *there*... there, in the centre... the pillar of light had coalesced into the Sword even now at his side. A sword materialized from pure light. As the struggle replayed in his memory, he saw, truly, it all was... had been... nothing short of miraculous: confronted by that hellish monster and its servants, crying out for aid, having that call answered in both Aquilea and a Sword beyond all imagining, and to defeat the creature, even though wounded. Then to compound it, Lowri coming to his assistance afterwards... Rhiss shook his head with the wonder. Darkness had been there... but through faith and grace, the Light had come also, utterly dispelling the Darkness. And Rhiss had played a part in it. The conclusion was inescapable.

Lowri was content to sit on a blanket with Aquilea and Relamus, allowing Rhiss to wander on his own while the three of them watched. Eventually she rose and slowly walked over. "You see it, now, don't you, Rhissan?" she asked quietly, answering without waiting for response. "Aye, I can tell. This is a place of great goodness, you know, and you made a difference that day."

"Well, not without help," he hedged, not looking at her. "Not alone. I had help from Aquilea... and Seir-onna Arian... and you... and..." his voice trailed off.

"Aye, maybe so, but you *did* make a difference."

Rhiss shrugged. "If you insist."

"Well, then, say so. Admit you make a difference."

"Oh, come, Lowri," said Rhiss uncomfortably. "Why dwell on this?"

"May the One save us," she sighed. "Rhissan, tell me, why is it so difficult for you to acknowledge your own worth? On the way here, you talked about Brother Gavrilos and Lord Tariel and Seir-onna Arian, implying they were all mistaken, that you didn't see how you could make a difference, and you didn't know how you could help restore a king. You said in your own world, you were just a scholar, and you didn't even think you made much difference there, either. I can't speak to that, because I didn't know you then." She smiled. "Although, even knowing you only a short while, I'm willing to wager you made more of a difference to your pupils than you might think, being the kind of man you are." She paused, then continued earnestly. "As for here in Arrinor... well, look around. I saw your actions with my own eyes in this circle of stones mere days ago, and I tell you, what you did was not the act of a weak, cowardly, or ineffective man. *It was strong, brave, and resolute action.*"

She brought a hand to his chin and gently compelled him to look into her eyes. "And you've already made a difference to many others, as well: think of Lady Rhyanna, who would have died but for you; her mother, Lady Meranna, and her aunt, Seir-onna Arian, who would both even now still mourn that death. And what of the score of men you persuaded to leave the service of Maldeus and find a new life, free from his taint? Or the many travellers who cross this moor, no longer needing to fear the Hunter and his mists enveloping them in white death? Or..." she said, her face colouring, "or people like me, to whom you give a great gift of hope... hope that a tyrant who has long brought terrible evil upon this land may at last be overthrown?"

She stared at Rhiss, eyes filling with tears. "By the One, do you still truly not see what you can do when you set your mind to it? Do you still not understand Brother Gavrilos made no mistake when he sent his portal to you, that the faith Seir-onna Arian has in you is not ill-founded... even that it was no accident this ring of stones, which has lain dark and dormant so long, came alight in a cascade of purity and energy to give you a mighty sword? I tell you it is no accident and no mistake you are here, Rhissan. Now, I do not know whether you will be successful; only the One does. But I do know you were *meant* to be here, and, even as one man, you can make a tremendous difference to countless people. It has already begun. You can no more deny this is your destiny, or turn your back on it, than a young gryphon—" she gestured at Aquilea "—can refuse to take to the air and conquer the skies." She stopped to wipe away the tears trickling down her cheeks, and looked up at him, eyes bright and intense. "Well?" she demanded. "What have you to say for yourself? Have you listened to aught I've said?"

Rhiss felt overwhelmed, and could not immediately find voice to answer. He nodded, swallowed, and pursed his lips together to keep his own eyes from tearing up.

"Is this," he stopped and cleared his throat, "is this why you brought me here today? To lay it all before me?"

"Can *you* think of a better place?" she replied softly, then added wryly, "Certainly, *I* cannot. I doubt the inside of my little cottage would make the point as well."

Rhiss gazed around the ring, the green hills beyond, and the blue sky before nodding again. "Very well," he said, and stopped to take a deep breath. "You're absolutely right in all you've said. I admit it. I don't know why I found it so hard to make that admission, but I have, and I'm sorry — to have upset you, especially."

She shook her head. "There's no need. Modesty is not evil in itself, although too much is as bad as too little. But I don't see you as an arrogant man at all, or likely to become one. But you need confidence in yourself, in the judgement of people you know and trust, and in the One. The rest will follow, I'm right convinced of that." She gripped his arm strongly, then looked around the stones and sighed. "Well, enough talk of great quests and destinies. It's important to acknowledge it all, but not to dwell on it overlong. The day's fair passing, and we came here to enjoy the time together. Come... let's have our little picnic, and then we'll return home — Prince Rhissan." She saw the look on his face, and touched a finger to his lips. "Now, now... today, I *will* call you Prince Rhissan. And what's more, you'll suffer me to do so. It's a title that suits you, whether or no it is justified. And you can pretend I'm the queen we spoke of when first we talked." She smiled impishly. "So come back to the food... m'lord, and let's feast in celebration of... realizations and admissions."

Over the next several days they went on many long walks through the surrounding lands, Lowri showing Rhiss her favourite spots. While out walking on his sixth day at the cottage, her hand again on his arm, Lowri observed they should take to horseback after midmeal, noting Rhiss would do well to regain his riding legs; Arian would doubtless return soon, after which she would be eager to resume the journey to Pencairn House.

Rhiss agreed, but the comment suddenly made him realize, with a pang, that the idea of leaving Lowri and her cosy little home was not a pleasant one. Even in so short a time as he had had with the Witch of the Ford at White River, Rhiss had come to value much about Lowri — her deep, unstinting friendship and faith in him, of course; but there were many other qualities in her as well: her no-nonsense and down-to-earth nature which cut through prevarication, her gentleness with the hurt and wounded creatures she treated, her teasing sense of humour, the various names she called him... all in all, she was a perplexing but utterly enchanting mix of strength and vulnerability.

Sitting in a rocking chair with his feet up on a small stool after midmeal, Rhiss let his food digest and observed Lowri as she made a loaf of bread for their evenmeal that night. Working the dough, she sang quietly to herself, completely unselfconscious of Rhiss or his scrutiny. She was certainly a bonnie lass with many qualities that were very, very fetching. It led him down paths of thought he somehow knew Arian would not approve of. Somewhat guiltily, Rhiss realized he could happily abandon the idea of going forth and restoring kings if it could mean staying with Lowri in her warm, snug home, enjoying a simple but rewarding life with her. There was so much about her that was utterly, absolutely appealing. Rhiss looked at Aquilea, lying beside the work table, gazing up at Lowri with that same rapt expression he had seen on the gryphon before when she was around Lowri, and smiled. Evidently he was not the only one thinking along similar lines.

Lowri looked at Rhiss and smiled warmly, a smudge of flour on the tip of her nose. "You look full of serious thoughts, Just Plain Rhissan, and no mistake, with eyes fair sad for such a beautiful day. What be you a-thinking of, then, lounging there like the lord of the manor?"

Rhiss considered several replies, but made no attempt to match her light tone. "It's coming to an end, isn't it?" he said, his regret clearly tangible.

She put the dough down, taken aback. "And what are you talking about, then? What's ending? It seems to me things are only beginning."

"You know what I mean." He waved a hand vaguely at the cottage. "All this. Our time together. A quiet, peaceful interlude, no malevolent Sovereign's Counsellors or hellish phantoms pursuing me. Just the opportunity to live a quiet, pleasant life for a time with a lovely woman who's already taught me much and whom—" he paused, gathering his courage "—I find more and more attractive in different ways all the time." He swallowed. "But as you said, Arian can't be much more than a day or two away; and when she arrives, she'll want to be off to Pencairn House with all dispatch, won't she? And then... where will that leave us?"

Lowri sat on a stool by the work table. "With memories of fine times, and no mistake," she said, her voice sad. She cocked her head to one side. "Why do you ask? Would you stay, if you could?"

"I... I'm not sure," Rhiss replied slowly, blushing slightly. "I know I find the prospect... extremely appealing." He looked at Lowri, wanting to ask something.

She caught his meaning, and nodded. "Aye. You probably know it would mightily appeal to me, too, my dear." She sighed. "But it's not meant to be, and well you know that, if you're honest with yourself. The eye of the One is full on you, Rhissan, not just His passing gaze. Arrinor has been like an enormous, dark prison locked in the frigid depths of despair these many years, and your coming heralds the arrival of freedom. There are the currents of great events swirling around and through your life now, like warm breezes. And the frozen prison is beginning to thaw and glimmer with the potential of release. I can feel those winds, and I know you can, too. They've been quiet the last few days, perhaps to let you catch your breath, but now you have, they're about to set in motion again. And it means staying here is no option, is it? Your destiny — the choice you made — doesn't include a quiet, rustic life on the edge of Byrn Moor." She paused, then added, in a low, regretful voice Rhiss had to strain to hear, "And I'm that sorry for it, you can be sure. But it changes nothing."

She looked at the floor. Then she sighed again, and looked at him once more. "But there it is. Some few things in our lives we can control, most we must accept. But we can do it without bitterness or lament. So let's not mourn the end of this — what did you call it? — brief interlude, but treasure the time we've had — and may perhaps one day have again, through the One's grace."

She stood, and said decisively, "Come, Just Plain Rhissan. Stop sitting like a bump on a log, looking for all the world as though your best friend just died, and go make ready your horse. When the bread is baked, I'll get my little moor pony, and we'll go for a ride together. Talla is not the equal in size or speed of your mount, but she's a willing little beast for all that, and we can have ourselves a good trot." She indicated Relamus, fast asleep by the fire, and smiled. "And he'll stay here to keep the home fires burning."

Rhiss realized the moment when he might have said anything else was irretrievably past. He nodded acquiescence, wordlessly rising slowly from the chair, and went to do as he was bid.

———◆———

Rhissan! Aquilea could mentally say his name now, savour it, use it, mean it. He was Rhissan, and oh, so very much more. He was Guardian, she was Shield-Protector, and everything was right with the world. His thoughts and feelings were hers, as hers were his, in a relationship transcending mere words. And this was only the Beginning.

It was The Woman who had orchestrated it. Somehow, in a sublime and wonderful manner Aquilea did not comprehend, The Woman had reached in to The Man's — no, she corrected herself — into Rhissan's mind, into his very Essence, and unlocked there a potential lying dormant which Aquilea, in her youth and inexperience, perhaps, had been unable to tap.

Aquilea had known from their first meeting there was something startlingly unusual and beautiful about The Woman; and she was the only other human Aquilea had ever been able to achieve any degree of thought-talk with. But this... she had not dreamed there would be anything like this gift forthcoming. She would be grateful to The Woman for as long as their Essences remained on Arrinor.

Aquilea could not help but wonder... what else could The Woman do to help Rhissan achieve his potentials? He still laboured under the twin spectres of doubt and fear, and was unaccountably reluctant to face both his destiny and his other Gifts. Could The Woman assist him there?

Aquilea intensely desired to find out.

XIII

DARKNESS AND LIGHT

"Blessed is he who comes in the name of the One. He brings healing and wholeness, reconciliation and justice, joy and contentment."

The Book of the One, 141:22:9
(Cantos 141, Chapter 22, Verse 9)

It was a fine afternoon for riding: the sun shone brilliantly, but a cool breeze kept it from being oppressive. Lowri took Rhiss on a gentle ride through the lands north of her home. As they left the moor behind, the land grew markedly less bleak, with undergrowth and actual trees in evidence.

As the afternoon wore on, they saw the mountains beckoning in the distance, tall and snow-capped. Lowri pointed. "Pencairn House is not far inside," she said. "Less than a day's ride, I should say, although I've never actually been there. But you'll not be far from my little cottage, if it's any consolation."

Rhiss smiled at her. "It matters a great deal to me, if that's what you mean. I do not know exactly what Arian will want to do once we're there, but perhaps you can expect a visitor from time to time."

"I'd like that very much," she replied earnestly, "as you well know. But as you say, you'll have to see what Arian has in mind. You may be far too busy to steal off to visit a simple country witch." They both laughed, and Rhiss felt his mood lifting, his earlier melancholy fading in the reality of being with Lowri, riding over the beautiful countryside together.

"Come," she continued. "It's getting on and we should turn for home soon, but, before we do, I want to visit a family who gather herbs for me. Their house is some twelve miles or so from mine, so if we go now, we should be home before evening. As I said yesterday, even with the Hunter gone, we don't want to be out on the moor after dark."

Rhiss found himself light-heartedly curious as they rode side by side. "Why do you keep saying that?" he asked. "What other terrors can the moor hold, with the Hunter gone?"

"Many," she said tartly, glancing sideways. "Don't you be flippant, Just Plain Rhissan. There are many dangerous creatures in the natural world without having to fear undead apparitions. The moor has always been perilous. And don't be forgetting Maldeus is still out there. He won't have forgotten you, count on that."

"Why live here, then, if it's so unsafe?" Rhiss wondered.

She shook her head. "May the One save us. You're always asking the questions, aren't you?"

"How else can one learn?" he countered. "And you haven't answered—"

"Ah, here we are!" she exclaimed, cutting Rhiss off as they rode over a small knoll. In a dip in the land, sheltered from the wind, was a rough cottage and barn. "Now, mind your manners with these folk," she said with mock sternness. "They're loyal friends of mine, if a bit bristly around the edges. It won't be like your grand old Craggaddon Hall and Lady Meranna, but treat these people with perfect gentility, do you understand?"

He was about to agree, grinning, when a swift, chill foreboding swept through him, and the grin faded abruptly from his face. Alarmed, Lowri saw the change immediately. "Rhissan? What's the matter?"

Rhiss scanned to right and left, shook his head, and shivered. "I don't know, in truth. But something's wrong here, very wrong. I can feel it. It just... came over me as we topped the rise." He loosened his dagger in its sheath. Behind him Aquilea landed, waves of agitation and fear emanating from her like physical blows. The sensations were still new to him, and he winced at their intensity. Whatever he had felt, she was also strongly affected.

Lowri looked uncertainly down at the cottage, and started to speak, but before she could get words out, the door flew open and a woman came running towards them. Rhiss tensed and began to dismount, reaching for his bow, but Lowri divined his intentions and held up her hand.

"No, Rhissan," she said urgently. "It's all right. That's Mairi, wife to Jaran. But something *is* amiss here..."

As they neared the cottage, Lowri leaped off her pony and ran to Mairi, while Rhiss got off Aralsa and bid Aquilea to his side. He gathered the reins of both horses and led them towards the women, who had by now met. Lowri listened as Mairi spoke quickly, obviously in great distress, then turned to Rhiss and waved frantically. Rhiss quickened his pace, horses and Aquilea following closely. In a moment, he joined the women before the cottage. Lowri had her arm around Mairi.

"...after it had them cornered, it went for the sheep, and before we knew what had happened, it was upon her," Mairi sobbed. "Jaran saw all from a distance. He said there seemed no reason why it went for Alairra. Then it flew off and he ran to the children and got them back here just before you came."

"There, there, my dear," Lowri said comfortingly. "We're here now. This is my friend, Rhissan," she said reassuringly as Mairi looked up in alarm, "and we'll see what's to be done, make no mistake. Whatever we can do, we will, I promise you that. Where is Alairra?"

"Inside," Mairi said despairingly. "Jaran is at the barn, with the other children. He was preparing to ride to you, even though I told him it was too far and Alairra too sorely wounded... please, Mistress Lowri, make haste to her! That thing... she is badly hurt... I fear she will go to the One unless you can make her well..."

"It's all right, Mairi," said Lowri, moving purposefully to her healer's bag behind Talla's saddle. "It's the One's own blessing we were passing by and decided to look in. I'll go to her now... may my friend accompany me? He can assist."

Mairi turned to Rhiss, bewilderment on her face, and Rhiss realized he did not much resemble a physician's associate. Then Mairi caught sight of Aquilea sitting quietly behind him, and her tear-stained eyes widened.

Lowri touched Mairi's arm, and she jumped. "It's all right, Mairi," Lowri repeated gently. "Explanations can wait until later, but you're among friends. You know that, don't you? For now, we must focus our energies on the child. Rhissan and I will attend her. Go to your husband and wait in the barn. Can you do that?"

Some of the tension left Mairi at those words, and she nodded dumbly. Casting one disbelieving look back, she took the reins of the horses, walking mechanically to the barn. Lowri turned to Rhiss.

"Come, Rhissan. Let's see what's to be done. Or does the sight of blood on others frighten you?"

Rhiss shook his head. "I've seen it before, back in my own land." A thought struck, and he continued pensively, "And, unfortunately, more than my share since coming to Arrinor."

Directing Aquilea to stay outside, they entered the cottage. It was not large; there was a central passage with doorways to rooms on either side. Lowri went swiftly and unerringly to the last door on the right, Rhiss close at her heels. He had a hasty impression of a spartan space: a small window allowing light in from outside, two rough, low beds, a wooden trunk between them. Then he saw the torn, bloody, motionless form of a small child on one of the beds, and all other thoughts faded as they knelt together.

"Hmm," said Lowri, after a quick examination. "There's a mercy. The poor thing's fainted." She began undoing the child's rent and torn clothing to get at the wounds beneath.

Rhiss was sickened. "Lowri, what kind of animal did this?"

Lowri looked grim. "One you have dealt with before, according to Seir-onna Arian," she said. "A Malmoridai."

Rhiss recoiled in shock. "What? Malmoridai? Here?"

"Aye," she said, continuing her examination of the broken body even as she spoke. "Or in the fields yonder, more precisely. Apparently, the children were tending the sheep. Mairi's tale was understandably confused, and she didn't specifically name a Malmoridai, but the description is unmistakable. It seems the monster came swooping by, saw the sheep, and fancied a bit of a meal. Why it went for the poor child, I can't fathom, unless from casual malice. That could well be, from what I know. You can ask the others later, and the father, too. He saw from a distance. But right now, we must do what we can."

Rhiss turned away, a tangle of anguished thoughts swirling through his mind. A Malmoridai, up past Byrn Moor? What was it doing out that way at all? He was reminded of Arian's letter, and a horrible idea occurred: was it seeking him? Was his presence responsible for the horrific attack on an innocent child?

He was brought back to the present by Lowri placing her hand on his arm. He blinked, and looked at her. She shook her head, expression bleak, eyes filling with tears. "She's dying, Rhissan. There's naught I can do," she whispered. "That foul creature batted her around like a cat with a mouse. Her hurts are too terrible, and I have neither the tools nor skill to mend them." She stopped and bowed her head for several moments.

Suddenly she looked up, staring deep into Rhiss' eyes, realization and hope kindling on her face. "But... but *you* do... if you can find it within yourself and summon the ability. Like before."

Rhiss was momentarily nonplussed at her words and gaped, then realized to what she referred. The colour drained from his face, and he gasped. "What are you suggesting? That *I* should try to—"

"—heal this child?" She nodded. "Aye, that's exactly what I'm saying. You have an incredible gift from the One. Why hesitate to use it on a wee child near death who's done no wrong to anyone?"

"But, Lowri, I..." Rhiss sensed panic threatening to overwhelm him. "I *can't*. It happened once, aye. But... I don't know how. I haven't the slightest idea how to—"

He got no chance to finish. She turned on him, dark eyes on fire. "Now, you *listen* to me, Rhissan," she interrupted fiercely, voice low. "I swear by the One, I do not understand why you still have so little faith in yourself and your abilities, but I tell you here and now you must master your insecurities or your presence in Arrinor will be for *naught*. Did I not say only the other day you have abilities to make a world of difference here, abilities straight from the One Himself? Now, I tell you we will not allow this child to die, not here at this time, not when I know you have the power to save her. I made a promise to her mother that we would do everything we could to save the child, and you will honour that promise. Do you understand me?" She grasped his arm, her grip like steel. *"Do you understand me?"* she repeated relentlessly.

Rhiss nodded slowly, mesmerized by her strength of will. "Aye," he said hoarsely. "But I don't know what to do first."

She relaxed slightly, breathing deeply, and released her grip. "Neither do I, but I've thought on it the last few days: try to remember the Lady Rhyanna after she was hurt, how it all began when you healed her, what you were feeling, what you did. You can do this, Rhissan. I *know* you can. But I can't help you as I did with Aquilea. I can't show you what to do, because it is not given to me to *know* how it's done. This is *your* unique gift from the One. It's there, at your fingertips, I'm sure. Have faith in the One, faith in yourself... and know that I have faith in you both."

Resignedly, Rhiss closed his eyes, casting his memory back to the field outside Tor Linlith his first full day in Arrinor. In his mind's eye, he vividly pictured his exchange with the soldiers, arrows hissing from his bow in rapid succession, the wicked dagger slicing raggedly across Rhyanna's throat. He remembered the river of scarlet drenching all as she fell, the desperation he felt on reaching her side, convinced of the futility of anything he might try to save her. As it was futile with this child, lying before him, mauled by another of those hideous creatures that had killed Aquilea's mother? Was that it? Was desperation the key?

No, he decided. It might have worked the first time, with Rhyanna, but desperation was an abysmal catalyst for such a sublime gift. What, then?

Another image came: alone in the ring of stones, Moressin's hounds closing in while he sought for salvation somewhere, anywhere. He had naively thought the Circlet of Araxis would be a magic talisman, only to learn the error of his ways barely in time. He had put his faith in the One. Could it be that simple?

Opening his eyes to view the small form before him, he stretched his hands gently over Alairra's body before closing his eyes again. Allowing himself to touch her with the lightest of touches, he gradually stilled his mind in a deliberate act of will, setting aside all thoughts churning — barely controlled horror at what had been done to this child in casual malice; awful guilt that perhaps the monster had been searching for him and found the child instead; coldly furious anger at those responsible for unleashing Malmoridai in the first place; sick doubt whether he could repeat what he had accomplished at Tor Linlith; and frantic need not to crush Lowri's faith with inability to perform what logic insisted was impossible. All had to be put aside.

When he had achieved that, after a minute or so, he calmly lifted his mind to the One, calling out his need for the child. *Not by my will, or for my glory, but through Yours and for Yours,* he thought silently, and waited, scarcely breathing. In his mind's eye, he could vividly picture the battered, limp little body laid out before him, and he concentrated on imagining the torn and bloody flesh made whole again, terrible injuries washed away by healing energies, as clear running water washes away the grime and grit of a long day's labour.

It began as faint, faraway tingling in the tips of his fingers, a sensation he was not at first even sure was real. But it grew, intensifying, spreading up his hands, into his wrists, up his arms. Heat built in his hands, liquid fire beginning as embers, then flaring into flame, and while he gritted his teeth, it was not as scaldingly painful as he recalled the first time being.

A massive, surging wave of incredible vitality welled up from — from somewhere in his being, although he could not pinpoint quite where — and he opened his eyes. He was just in time, once again, to observe a pair of spectral hands gracefully superimposed over his, and then see that glorious haze momentarily radiating from his hands, bathing the entire room in a gentle golden glow. Then it all ebbed: the inner flame, the glow, the surging wave of vitality, all softly waned.

And the child on the bed was whole again.

She gave a sudden, gasping intake of breath, much as Rhyanna had, and Rhiss stared at the sight, vision blurring with tears of gratitude. He turned to Lowri. She stared back, kneeling beside the bed, mouth slightly agape, weeping unashamedly, shaking her head in dumbfounded wonder.

"I saw," she whispered. "*I saw.* It was... miraculous."

Rhiss nodded mutely, and they looked at each other, overcome in shared awe at what had transpired, until he abruptly slumped back on his heels, exhausted. Lowri reached a hand to steady him, eyes full of concern.

"Are you all right, then, Rhissan?"

He nodded again. "Aye, just rather tired from the... exertions. I'll be right as rain in a minute."

Lowri looked unconvinced. "Are you sure? Arian told me you fell as one dead after healing the Lady Rhyanna, and were unconscious for several days afterwards."

Rhiss nodded thoughtfully. "So I was told. But I begin to wonder if that wasn't shock at what had happened, more than anything else. I don't feel I'm about to lose consciousness now... just weary. But... but it was glorious! The heat, the vitality, welling up within like molten lava, pouring out and into that little girl... it was unbelievable."

"Aye, you're right there," Lowri replied fervently. "I'd have said the same if I hadn't witnessed it with my own eyes."

A thought struck Rhiss. "Did you see a pair of hands over mine? Graceful, strong hands, insubstantial but... very real, nonetheless."

She shook her head. "No... but there was a golden light. And you're right, it *was* glorious. It fair lit the whole room... it came from your hands and spread out, enveloping little Alairra, and... it was like putting a broken doll back together. She just... mended." Lowri smiled at the memory, then roused herself. "I must go and fetch Mairi and the others. They'll be that frantic. Stay here. I'll be back directly."

They stood, and she began to leave. Then she paused and looked at him. She nodded, smiled again and cupped his cheek tenderly in one hand. "You did right well, Rhissan. I'm that proud of you." The door closed quietly behind her. Rhiss looked at the little girl stirring on the bed, then at the ceiling. "Thank you," he said softly.

Only a minute or two later, the family crowded with Lowri into the small room. Rhiss allowed himself to be edged back behind several children and the father, Jaran. Mairi threw herself down by Alairra, face white with shock as she took in the fact her daughter, bloodied and torn only a short while before, was restored and whole. She looked at Lowri, and said dazedly, "Mistress Lowri... 'tis a true miracle... but how—?"

She was interrupted by Alairra's eyes opening. Obviously bewildered, the child's gaze travelled over the crowd clustered around, brows furrowing as she evidently tried to understand how she came to be on her own bed, with many gathered around.

"Mama?"

"There, there, my pet," murmured Mairi huskily, stroking Alairra's face. "'Tis all right now. The bad thing that hurt you is gone, and Mistress Lowri has worked a great magic to bring you back—"

"No, Mama," interrupted the child, struggling to sit up. "Not Mistress Lowri. Where is the man? I want to see him!"

"Man?" repeated Mairi in surprise. "What man, pet? What are you on about?"

"The man with the star on his brow, Mama. He chased the bad monster away and called to me, and then I woke up—" She stopped as the family edged nervously away from Rhiss, belatedly realizing to whom she referred. As they did, he came into her view. "There he is!" she crowed excitedly, pointing. "That's the man, Mama! *He* made me better, not Mistress Lowri. And he said I mustn't worry or be afraid of the monster, he would make sure it could never hurt me or anyone else, ever again. Thank you, sir," she said to Rhiss before frowning and cocking her head to one side in puzzlement. "But why isn't the star on your brow anymore?"

Rhiss was startled by the child's words: it was almost exactly what Rhyanna had said. He involuntarily began raising hand to forehead to check for the Circlet of Araxis. Then, self-consciously, he brought his hand back down, the movement only half completed. He felt deeply uncomfortable as the family turned to him, expressions carefully unreadable. One or two actually made the triune sign of blessing. Lowri came swiftly to his rescue, moving to his side and gazing sternly at the family.

"Now then, there's no need for that. Gather round, all of you. I've something very important that needs saying. Aye, you too, Mairi and Jaran, not just the wee ones. This concerns you all." She waited until they were crowded in a semicircle around her and Rhiss, then knelt by the bed on which Alairra still sat, so she could better make eye contact with the children.

"Right, then," she resumed. "You need to know that Alairra speaks the truth. I had naught to do with her healing. In fact, she was so badly hurt that she was dying, and there was nothing I could do." As Rhiss stood at her side, she put her hand in his, warm and soft. He felt a sudden shock of pleasure, almost missing her next words. "But my friend — *our* friend — Rhissan, here, has been given a great gift by the One, and he performed a miracle, saving little Alairra's life. I saw it happen, right here. Now, there's naught to fear — in fact, quite the reverse, because we witnessed something truly wondrous today, something ordinary folk are hardly ever privileged to see. You all realize that, now, don't you?" There was a solemn nodding of heads around the semicircle as the wariness thawed. One of the youngest launched into a barely intelligible account of the Malmoridai's coming, but Lowri cut him off gently, placing a finger to his lips. "Not yet, my dear. I'm not finished speaking; in fact, I'm just getting to the most important part." He subsided obediently, and she looked around at the family again, making sure she had their complete attention.

"Now, I know your first inclination would be to share such marvellous news far and wide with everyone you possibly can. 'Tis only natural." There was cautiously muted agreement as they waited for her to get to the point.

"*But*," she went on, holding up a forefinger, speaking slowly for emphasis, "I'm saying you *must not* tell anyone. No one must know. My friend — our friend — Rhissan has been sent to fight the evil and injustice plaguing Arrinor. He has just started his work, and so has managed to win only a few to his cause as yet. The forces of darkness arrayed against him are powerful and seek his destruction even as we speak. If they learn of his whereabouts before he is ready to confront them, all could be lost. And if they were to hear of today's happenings, they would know it was he who did this miracle, and they would come to find and kill him. It would put all of you in the gravest danger, too. That is why you must hold the events of this day strictly amongst yourselves. I tell you again, no one must know. Think of it as the price for Alairra's life given back to you by the One. We need you to do this. Can we rely on you?"

There was much nodding, a muted chorus of assent, and then Jaran bowed his head, clearing his throat. He was a tall, thin, clean-shaven man, raw-boned with ruddy complexion. In a clear voice, he directed his words at Rhiss. "Aye. You have my word, and my family's, Lord Rhissan. We'll not breathe a word of what happened today, not to anyone. I swear it in gratitude for my daughter, and all of us. We are deeply in your debt, and if our silence is of value to you, it's the least we can do." He looked around, seeking agreement. "In this we are One."

Rhiss glanced quickly at Lowri, looking to her for guidance, unsure what to say. But she gazed calmly back, eyes radiating confidence, the merest hint of a smile evident at the corners of her mouth. Rhiss licked his lips and inclined his head at Jaran in return.

"My gratitude, sir," he said quietly. "I was only the One's instrument, so be sure to offer thanks where they should be made."

Mairi roused and gently cuffed her husband, shaking her head. "What a great lummox of a man. That's well and good, but we can give more than just our silence." She turned to Rhiss, straightening, and said formally, "May we offer our hospitality, Lord Rhissan? Please say you and your good lady will honour us by sharing our table and staying under our roof this night. All we have is yours. *That's* the least we can do."

Rhiss glanced again at Lowri, and this time she stood, still holding his hand to pull herself to her feet. "We'd be that delighted to break bread with you, dear Mairi. But as for staying the night, I think we'll just be away back home to my cottage after the even-meal, if you don't mind. I've a number of poor, wounded creatures needing attention before tomorrow." She smiled. "Is there aught we can do to help with preparations?"

Mairi clucked disapprovingly. "What? Of course not, Mistress Lowri. You are honoured guests. Jaran, take them through to the front room and see to their comfort while the girls and I make the meal."

"Begging your pardon, Mistress Mairi," Rhiss interjected, "but perhaps I could wash first." He held up his hands, still stained with Alairra's blood.

Flustered, Mairi began stammering an apology, but Lowri said smoothly, "Now, now, no need, my dear. You've had a terrible ordeal, and it's really *we* who should make the meal for *you* while your family gives thanks. However, I know you'd never hear of it, so we'll just take ourselves outside to see to our beasts, and wash from the well. No need to trouble yourselves taking us outside either, I know the way." Turning to Rhiss, she smiled, bowed and said, "If you'll follow me, Lord Rhissan, I will escort you to your ablutions."

Aquilea greeted them enthusiastically, and after making a fuss of her, they tended to the horses. Lowri led Rhiss to a well in the middle of the yard, where there was a crude wooden canopy sheltering benches — evidently a communal washing area. While

Aquilea watched solemnly, Lowri and Rhiss cleansed themselves of the evidence of their toil, although Lowri needed to do very little on her own account. Despite the late afternoon air cooling markedly, Rhiss stripped to the waist and relished washing in the cold water before vigorously towelling dry with the rough cloth Mairi had provided.

"I thought you didn't want to travel over the moor after sunset," he remarked as he put his tunic back on. He gestured at the great orb of the sun, a glowing sphere destined momentarily to touch the horizon and become a semicircle. "At this rate, it will be well after dark by the time we return."

She sighed. "I know, Just Plain Rhissan, and I apologize, not consulting you before refusing their offer of shelter for the night. I know how fair tired you must be from this afternoon's work. Will you be all right to travel, or shall I have to be catching you as you doze off and fall from the saddle?"

Rhiss waved a hand dismissively. "I'll be fine, I already told you. Actually, I'm exhilarated over the experience now, none the worse for wear at all. Riding back won't be a problem. But as I said, what happened to not wanting to be on the moor after dark with things that go bump in the night?"

"Some do a great deal more than that, as I've said before," she said wryly. "But there are several factors. To begin, as you may have noticed, these people have no great wealth and certainly no sumptuous manor to put us up in. They know full well we're not man and wife, so it would mean giving us separate rooms. That, in turn, would require displacing several of them — to the barn, like as not, as it's the only other place with a roof to keep out the weather. They've had quite a day of it and no mistake, and don't need outsiders pushing them from hearth and home. They should be snug together as a family on their own tonight, to reassure themselves they're really all right. And in all honesty, we *should* be back to look in on my charges. Don't forget poor Relamus is by himself, too. As for being on the moor after dark... well," she shrugged and grinned roguishly, "I have a great warrior at my side who will make sure I get home safely."

Rhiss snorted. "I hardly think so, Lowri — unless you refer to Aquilea."

Her grin faded and she shook her head in exasperation. "Rhissan, there you go again with that rubbish. What have I said about having faith in your abilities? You must needs come to terms with that, and sooner than later." She paused. "The last reason why we should go home is less... tangible. I've had a feeling all day that Seironna Arian might return tonight. I keep seeing her in my mind's eye." She stopped, then mused thoughtfully, almost to herself, "And not alone, either... I wonder..." Her voice trailed off.

"What do you wonder?" prompted Rhiss sharply after a moment. "Who else would she bring?"

"I'm sure I don't know, Just Plain Rhissan. It may well be nothing. But I can't shake the feeling somehow she's on her way, and someone's with her. Have you not had that feeling?"

Rhiss shook his head. "Perhaps I repressed it... because... well, because it means leaving..." his voice trailed off.

"Aye, I know what you're about to say," she said, and sighed. "Well, as may be. At any rate, I've given you good reasons not to stay here. Now, if you're finished dressing, we can go in for evenmeal. Mind you be gracious. You've given these people a gift that's nothing short of miraculous, and they know full well in their hearts they can never repay it. So put them at their ease as much as you can, and help them not to feel awkward."

"I will, Lowri. Try to put them at their ease, that is."

Her eyes softened. "I know you will. Like I said, I'm that proud of you over this day's happenings. You're a good man." She raised hands to caress his face, let them stay a moment before dropping them. "Come, let's go in. Bring Aquilea — I can tell they're all dying to see her up close." A mischievous look passed over Lowri's face. "Now, would she be knowing how to do tricks for the children, do you think?"

Evenmeal was plain fare, but served in ample quantities, and Rhiss thought approvingly that it compared favourably with Craggaddon Hall. Jaran gave the blessing, and they initially sat to eat in awkward silence. Evidently they were understandably awed by what they had seen, unsure how to act before a man who performed genuine miracles. Rhiss was also uncomfortable in the hush, and cast his mind about for a way to end it, without success: he had never been particularly extroverted at social affairs. A surreptitious glance at Lowri was no help: her gaze was fixed firmly on her plate.

Then it came to him. Although he had been scandalized by Lowri's suggestion, as she no doubt playfully intended, Rhiss realized that Aquilea performing tricks might be just the thing to ease the mood and provide a little levity. He reached out to Aquilea with his mind as she sat on the floor beside him, outlining in images what he needed her to do, and why. She peered at him with enormous, liquid eyes, and for a moment he was not sure whether she understood — or approved. But she opened her beak silently in what Rhiss swore was almost a grin, and a wave of approval washed through his mind.

Rhiss leaned conspiratorially across to little Alairra. "So, young lady," he said, acutely aware everyone was also listening. "What think you of my gryphon, here?"

"I think she's fair lovely," said the child, so softly it was difficult to hear. "Like something from an old folk tale my mama would tell me."

"Aye, she is, for certain... both lovely *and* like a character from an old tale, that is, but... did you know she also does tricks?" Rhiss continued in the same tone.

The child shook her head, eyes round and huge.

That was all it took. What followed was a hilariously successful time between the family, Rhiss, Lowri and Aquilea. Through a combination of mental commands and physical gestures from Rhiss, Aquilea begged for titbits of food, played dead, and did all the other tricks Rhiss could ever recall performing dogs do — and more, besides. Rhiss was impressed at how Aquilea was prepared to put aside her natural dignity. The children lost their reserve, laughing, shouting and begging her to do her various feats over and over. Mairi and Jaran thawed along with the children, thoroughly enjoying Aquilea's antics. When Lowri stood from the table, also laughing, to say it was time to depart, she did so amid a chorus of protests.

"No, no," she said, holding up her hand for silence. "We really must be off, my dears. I'm sure Lord Rhissan will bring Aquilea to visit when he can, but for tonight we must be away to my own home. Your hospitality has been wonderful, hasn't it, Lord Rhissan?"

The family escorted them out to the yard, where the last rays of twilight had faded into the deep azure of night. One of the older boys held a lit torch. The moon was rising, promising more than mere starlight to ride by. Rhiss and Lowri retrieved the horses from the barn, and as they saddled up, Aquilea flew around the yard, diving at the children, causing shrieks of laughter. Finally, all was ready. At a signal from Rhiss, Aquilea landed, while Jaran motioned his family to be still.

"Thank you again, my lord," he said, bowing respectfully. "We can never repay you for the gift of our daughter's life. Truly, the One is with you. But we will honour you by following Mistress Lowri's command and keeping silent about what happened here. Be welcome in our home whenever you wish."

Rhiss inclined his head in return and gripped Jaran's outstretched hand.

"Thank *you*, Master Jaran," he said. "You should know that you and your family have also helped me. In being allowed... or persuaded," he said with a wry, sideways glance at Lowri, "to be the One's instrument in healing Alairra, I have at last truly begun a journey, I think, to find confidence in myself to master the gifts of the One given me — if I do not fail or falter along the way."

"You will not, Lord Rhissan," said Mairi with conviction. "I know you will not. You are a good man, of a certainty, and the One will guide you, I know." She made the triune sign of blessing, but Rhiss knew it was a benison.

They finished their goodbyes, and with a soft chorus of, "Go you with the One, Mistress Lowri and Lord Rhissan," they mounted and rode slowly out of the farmyard, Aquilea flying along beside. At the crest of the small knoll, they stopped and looked back. The family was still waving in the yard, visible in the torchlight. Rhiss and Lowri gave one final wave in return, then turned their mounts towards the cottage at the Ford at White River.

Despite Lowri's earlier misgivings, the ride across the moor in the moonlight was uneventful, with only a few clouds drifting leisurely across the sky. Rhiss found a great weariness from the day's exertions had, indeed, descended, but it was not unmanageable, and he was never in danger of toppling from Aralsa's back. He found himself reliving the events as he healed little Alairra that afternoon. The responsibility was daunting in a way, but also wondrous. Sensing his mood, Lowri held her peace and stayed quietly in her own thoughts as well. Aquilea soared serenely overhead, her mind a comfortingly peaceful presence that Rhiss could feel distinctly.

Several hours later, around midnight, they passed over a rise at last and viewed the White River, flowing silver in the moonlight, and the Ford, Lowri's cottage nestled snugly beside it. Rhiss was frankly dozing in the saddle, finally submitting to exhaustion, but woke with a start as Lowri halted her pony, and Aralsa stopped also.

"What—?" he began, then looked into the low valley before them, realizing where they were. The next instant, he saw light in the cottage windows, and uttered a startled exclamation, reaching for his sword.

Lowri held up a hand. "Peace, Just Plain Rhissan. Your caution is commendable, and we'll be careful going down, but I feel it's no enemy keeping the home fires burning for us."

They rode slowly and quietly down to the cottage, stopping fifteen feet from the door. Thoroughly wide awake, Rhiss slipped off Aralsa. He retrieved his bow and strung it, selected an arrow and nocked it, but did not pull the string taut. Holding it pointed in the general direction of the door, he looked inquiringly at Lowri, still on her pony. She nodded.

"Who dares enter the house of the Witch of the Ford at White River in her absence?" Rhiss called loudly.

There was a muffled exclamation from within, then silence for several seconds. Finally, a woman's voice responded, "A previously honoured guest, thank you very much, who wonders from where, in the name of the One, the Witch comes in the middle of the night. She was supposed to be caring for a sorely wounded young man, and we have ridden far to see him. But they disappeared, leaving the house empty and forcing the weary traveller to enter and make her own tea. An appalling hostess she is, truly."

The door crashed open and Arian stood there, laughing in the golden light pouring into the night. Grinning, Rhiss threw down his bow and offered his hand to help Lowri dismount. Then he strode to Arian and, disdaining protocol, embraced her.

"Seir-onna," said Rhiss warmly, "it is so *very* good to see you again."

Aquilea found herself well pleased. Under The Woman's tutelage, Rhissan had made significant progress: he now had a measure of understanding of his sublime Gift of Healing (and, equally important, some measure of control — or at least, as much as anyone could have regarding a Gift that obviously emanated straight from the One). Truly, Rhissan was growing by leaps and bounds. It was for that reason she had submerged the affront to her dignity and agreed to his request to be — of all things! — a circus harlequin for the entertainment of children. Normally, she would have disdained even to consider such a mortifying experience. (Although, she conceded grudgingly, the younglings were really quite charming.)

While The Woman's methods could be... somewhat rough on occasion, Aquilea would have agreed wholeheartedly, had she been asked, that desperate times require desperate measures. As her mother had been fond of repeating, younglings cannot be persuaded to leave the Nest and taught to fly through love alone: frequently, it is too comfortable and easy to remain in the bosom of warmth and plenty, and the oft-harsh world beyond the Nest sometimes beckons but little, especially to a fledgling unsure of its own abilities.

And in many ways, Aquilea reflected, Rhissan was amusingly like a fledgling (amusing at times, that was; just plain exasperating at others — very aware that she and The Woman were of like mind on the subject). Rhissan was more than physically ready to make the leap and fly, but he was still emotionally wobbly. Aquilea wondered just what events in his past could have caused him to be damaged so. But for some reason, that part of his mind was still closed to her.

Regardless, he was coming along remarkably well under The Woman's (mostly) patient ministrations, and Aquilea knew well why that was so: clearly, Rhissan and The Woman were deeply drawn towards each other. Their mutual desire for Essence Pairing radiated incandescently from them both, as patently obvious as the stillness that precedes and signals the onset of a summer storm. Aquilea could not understand why they did not simply acknowledge the inevitable and proceed — allowing the love between their Essences to flow around and over each other, joining them together in the union they both so evidently craved. Instead, the silly humans repressed their feelings, pretending no bond existed, as though it could be hidden or denied. It was very strange; Aquilea reflected (a touch condescendingly, perhaps) that her kind had no patience for prevarication or denial of truth, and would neither perpetuate nor condone such a state of affairs. But humans were different creatures, prone to foolish decisions and muddy thinking. Muddy...aye, that was it, she thought: it must be due to their being tied perpetually to the earth, unable to leap into the skies and feel the cool freshness of the wind sweeping away doubt and indecision as one sweeps away the cobwebs around the Nest, observing the world spread beneath like a glorious tapestry woven by the One...

XIV

DISCLOSURE AND DENIAL

> *"It is frequently in the nature of Truth to be painful, for truth is the bright sword lancing through the Other's fog of darkness and deception. Yet such lancings clear away the stinking infection and moral corruption that is worry, doubt, and fear, leaving only calm, certainty and peace in their wake. Do not fear the Truth of the One."*
>
> The Book of the One, 80:22:14-16
> (Cantos 80, Chapter 22, Verses 14-16)

It was wonderfully cosy inside after the night's chill, and Rhiss went directly to the fire pit to warm himself. As she mentioned, Arian had previously made a large pot of tea, and filled earthenware mugs for Rhiss and Lowri. Rhiss was tired and so intent on getting the hot liquid for himself that it was moments before he realized with shock that a *fourth* person was present, sitting in the shadows around the rocking chair, calmly observing the proceedings. Rhiss spun to face the chair's occupant, reaching for his dagger. But the figure, an old man with a scar down his right cheek, anticipated the move and stood, empty hands held out.

"Och, put that thing away, lad," he said mildly. "Ye don't need to be threatening an old man with it, and anyway, it might make me doubt the warmth and sincerity of yer welcome."

Slowly, Rhiss did as he was told, but could only stand, mouth agape, as Arian moved hastily over, handing him his mug. Rhiss took it absentmindedly.

"My lord," she said, "may I present Parthalas of Altmara, one-time Master of Arms of The Knights Castellar. Seir-on Parthalas, Lord Rhissan — although I believe you have already met."

"Aye," said Parthalas, amused, "although it was 'Arcan of Follet' last time, weren't it, lad?"

Rhiss cleared his throat and nodded. "It was, sir. You were in the tap room of The King's Arms in Rontha."

"Aye, that I was, lad. An' ye bought me a drink, and kept company with me. An' here we are."

"You led me a merry — and painful — chase the following day. But I can tell you of that later." Rhiss turned to Arian. "You know each other, Seir-onna?"

Arian smiled and nodded. "Very well. Parthalas is one of the most respected members of our Order — or perhaps I should say 'was,' because we have thought him dead these many years."

"Indeed," Rhiss mused. "I recall you saying something of the sort." He turned to the old man. "My apologies for my initial reaction to your presence, Seir-on. Be welcome with us — although I am curious why you would accompany Arian all this way. What have we to offer that The King's Arms does not?"

"All of ye here, lad," replied the old man, grinning broadly.

Rhiss looked blank.

"Informative as ever, aren't we, Parthalas?" Arian said wryly, but she smiled fondly. "What my dear friend means is he stands pledged to our cause, Lord Rhiss. And thanks be to the One that he is, for he will be uniquely valuable on several levels." She marked off her points on the fingers of one hand. "First, as I already stated, he was once Master of Arms of our Order, and you will not find anyone, anywhere, who can provide better training in weaponry and tactics. Second, he spent time at Pencairn House in days past, so knows it well. And finally, he has great wisdom concealed under that thatch of silver, and can provide much in the way of wise counsel."

Parthalas looked moderately embarrassed. "Well, now, I'm not sure about that last, but the first two are right enough," he allowed, grinning sheepishly. "And The King's Arms, pleasant as it is, doesn't hold much in the way of excitement fer an old man these days — aside from watching the odd brawl, ye know. Havin' spoken at some length that night wi' ye, Lord Rhiss, and then later wi' Arian, here... well, let's just be sayin' that, even at my age, I've been lookin' for a wee bit of adventure — and somehow, I think it's fair to say you and yer cause will supply more than enough. I was pleased wi' much of what ye said the other night — it sounded like Arian has found a proper young choice to... to help put things to rights in Arrinor. So if ye'll have me, as Arian said, I stand pledged to yer cause."

Rhiss looked at Arian beaming at him, then glanced at Lowri on the other side of the fire pit. She nodded and smiled.

Extending his hand, Rhiss inclined his head, replying with heartfelt conviction, "Then surely the One sent you to us, Seir-on. We are honoured to have you join our enterprise — small as it is at present." He raised an eyebrow, then added with a wry smile, "In fact, your addition doubles the number of people accompanying me to Pencairn House."

"Ah, now, that's all right, lad, don't ye be frettin'," remonstrated Parthalas. "Enough drops of water fallin' into an empty bucket eventually fill it to the brim. And I can think of several others who'll be glad enough to join us, and work towards ending the Usurper's reign. We'll get there, lad, you'll see soon enough."

There was silence a moment before Arian broke it. "Very well," she said briskly. "With Mistress Lowri's acquiescence, we will set out for Pencairn House the day after tomorrow, to give Parthalas and myself a chance to rest a bit. With luck, we should reach it the evening of the day we set out. In addition to finding Parthalas, I purchased supplies that should stand us in good stead when we arrive. But now, I think I speak for us both when I say we would welcome a place to bed down for the night." She turned to Lowri. "Before I ask where we may all sleep, I must say in gratitude that you have admirably discharged the task I set: Lord Rhiss has not only been nursed back to health, but obviously glows with vitality, ruddy cheeks and all. Life in your house evidently agrees with him."

Lowri actually blushed. "My thanks, Seir-onna. I think you'll also find Rhissan has had much success in... coming to terms with several of the gifts we discussed."

Arian looked questioningly at Rhiss. "Indeed? It sounds like quite a story wrapped up in that statement."

"Several," admitted Rhiss. "But you will have to ask me, as Lowri would give herself no credit in the telling. She has been... utterly invaluable these recent days, the memories of which I will treasure when we leave. I would have made no progress without her." Their eyes met and held across the fire pit, and then he bowed at her.

"Indeed?" Arian repeated, staring appraisingly with narrowed eyes at Rhiss and Lowri, who had gone an even more delicate shade of rose at his words. Arian seemed about to say more, but Parthalas, whose own gaze flicked shrewdly from Rhiss to Lowri to Arian as he followed the conversation, interjected, "Aye, well, that's grand, lad, and we'll look forward to hearin' all about it tomorrow, won't we, Arian? But for now, if ye could just show an old man where to rest his weary bones, I'd be right grateful."

Distracted, Arian muttered agreement and it was decided Lowri would have her own bed in the main cottage, while Rhiss, Arian and Parthalas would sleep in the infirmary wing. Lowri was dubious, wanting Rhiss to have the comfort of a real bed at least one more night, but Rhiss was adamant he would be fine.

When arrangements were concluded, it was abundantly clear Aquilea wished to remain with Lowri and Relamus; she resisted all entreaties to leave. Parthalas grinned and winked at Rhiss as he shooed Arian into the infirmary wing, pulling the door to. Rhiss turned to Lowri.

"It's all right, Just Plain Rhissan," she said, anticipating what he would say. "I don't mind. Aquilea can stay with me, unless you're unhappy about it."

Rhiss smiled. "I'm not, truly. If she wants to be in here tonight, I don't mind a bit. She's been very taken with you these last few days." He paused and looked at the floor before adding, "As have I." He raised his gaze, licked his lips and continued. "I meant what I said, Lowri. I couldn't have done anything without you. This time here... it's meant more to me than I can say."

Her voice was low and quiet, as she looked steadily into his eyes. "Aye, well... no less to me, Rhissan."

There was more Rhiss wanted to say, but he did not trust himself to say it, so he merely nodded before turning swiftly to go through the door to the infirmary wing. Deep in his own thoughts, he was through before registering the sounds of Arian and Parthalas speaking softly but intensely. They were by the fireplace where Rhiss had bathed his first night. The fire was the only source of illumination, a pool of flickering, reddish light halfway down the length of the cottage, with all else, including himself, deep in shadow. He stopped before shutting the door all the way, surprised to hear real irritation in their voices.

"—ah, fer goodness' sake, Arian, there's no harm to it. They fancy each other, that's clear. And why not? She's a bonny lass, and he's a handsome lad."

"Parthalas, she is *not* suitable to his rank, and well you know it," replied Arian sharply.

"Och, it's not as if they're gettin' *married*, Arian, and we'll be takin' him away from her soon enough. But ye left the two of them alone for a goodly parcel of days. Ye may be a priest, but yer a woman, for all that. Had you no thought they might be drawn to each other? 'Twas only natural, to my eyes. As to his rank: he has none yet — and may never, despite what we hope. Ye know as well as I the odds are against it."

"Nonetheless, it's not something I want to encourage." Arian paused. "My niece would be a far more suitable candidate, if it's marriage and children we're talking of."

Parthalas snorted. "Oh, aye, the daughter of a disgraced earl attainted for murder and treason — who himself died under suspicious circumstances. Now *there's* a likely prospect for the lad. And let's not even get into the story of the brothers."

"*Parthalas!* Those charges were nothing but pure fabrication by Maldeus and his thugs, and well you know it."

"Oh aye, it may be apparent to those of us who know better, but to most, Arian..." Parthalas trailed off, blissfully unaware of the profound shock his words had given Rhiss. "And yer talking *marriage*? And wee ones? Och, give yer head a shake, and then give the poor lad some time, woman. He's only been in Arrinor yet a scant few weeks or so, and when you tell him — which, by the way, I still think ye should have done straight off — he'll have more than enough on his plate."

"You know why I didn't. And my sister and Lowri both agreed with my reasons."

"Oh, aye, but no more happily than I did, I'll wager. Look ye here, Arian: he's a good lad — aye, as yet raw and untrained, but we can both see his potential — and he deserves honesty, especially seein' as what we'll be askin' of him."

"He will have it, my word on that," said Arian earnestly. "But we *must* get him to the sanctuary of Pencairn House first, Parthalas. A few weeks he's been here in Arrinor, barely any time at all, you're right, and just look at the turmoil he's stirred up, the incredible events crowding around him: finding the gryphon as soon as he arrived, killing a Malmoridai — a full grown Malmoridai! — healing my niece; the encounter with Maldeus — perhaps two if you include that very strange event we experienced on the road to Rontha — the destruction of the Hunter, meetings with strange and powerful, mysterious figures — and from what the two of them were hinting just now, even more bizarre happenings. He's like a small boy with a stick, Parthalas, unwittingly stirring up a hornets' nest. I tell you, we *must* get him to Pencairn House and allow things to quiet down a bit while we give him the training he's going to need to survive, or those hornets of Maldeus are going to overwhelm and destroy him."

"All right." Parthalas sounded resigned. "I can see yer convinced of the rightness of yer course. Ye always were stubbornly independent, even all those years ago, when ye were a novice newly under my direction. Sometimes it was to yer own detriment, and ye'd do well to remember that. But ye canna make all decisions on yer own, ye know. Yer not alone anymore, and that'll become even truer as we gather more to the cause."

"I know, old friend," said Arian more gently, "and I *will* consult with everyone working with us, I swear. But you're right; I'm convinced it's best we focus on getting to Pencairn House. Come, enough. The boy should be along any moment, and it wouldn't do for him to hear this." They laid out their blankets and climbed into them.

Rhiss stood by the door, irresolute. Once again, here was that maddening secrecy he had encountered in Arrinor from the very people he trusted — the veiled references to an issue concerning him, but withheld. *What* was it that had to be kept from him? Why *should* it be thus? His first impulse was to go striding to Arian and Parthalas that very moment and demand to know just what the hell they were playing at. He even took a step before halting suddenly, as though a small inner voice warned him to stop. Provoking a confrontation, with emotions already running high, was probably unwise. The secret, whatever it was, could wait until the morrow.

Rhiss sighed, shutting the door to the main room. It clicked audibly, and he moved noisily to where the two priests were wrapped separately in their blankets. Mechanically, he spread his own blankets on the fresh-smelling straw; but his mind was miles away as he considered all he had heard, and sleep came neither quickly nor easily. He lay awake long after curling up in his own blankets, watching the flames leap and dance in the fireplace, listening to Arian's regular breathing and the snores of Parthalas. Remembering the list of events Arian had catalogued, Rhiss reflected on all that had occurred in the last two weeks since his arrival in Arrinor.

Weeks! Was it really only that? It felt strangely as though he had been in Arrinor all his life. Parts were like a fairy tale, or something from the epic poems he had taught... but others were definitely not. The quiet existence as a schoolmaster in a small Lincolnshire village already seemed to belong to someone else. He no longer felt like ordinary Mr. Griffith, the Literature master. He was Master Rhiss, or Lord Rhiss, or — he smiled — Just Plain Rhissan; or even, when Lowri was playful, Prince Rhissan. He had been gifted with truly wondrous abilities, and was learning to use them. He had met all manner of strange people and creatures. And he was on his way to help a king regain his throne. How that was to happen, he was still unsure. However, happen it *would*, he was certain. He was still thinking that as he drifted into deep and dreamless sleep.

Next morning dawned grey and drizzly; low cloud and mist draped the Ford and surrounding moor in a damp, cottony blanket. They rose late, and Arian, it emerged, was much in favour of spending the day by Lowri's fire. Ironically, Rhiss felt unaccountably restless and not inclined to drowse the day away, even with Lowri at his side. Accordingly, after midmeal and recounting their adventures since Arian left Lowri's house, he stood and announced his intention to take Aralsa for a ride in the hills.

"Perhaps I'll see if Aquilea can find us something for evenmeal," he added, only half-jokingly. "She's a pretty fair hunter, you know."

Arian frowned, disapproval all over her features. "Lord Rhiss, I really don't think this suitable weather to be roaming the hills. Look at that mist rolling in! Would it not be preferable to relax indoors, enjoying the comforts of Mistress Lowri's fire and baking?"

Rhiss set his jaw stubbornly, stung by Arian's formal and rather maternal tone. "Seir-onna, I feel the need, as you put it, to 'roam the hills' this afternoon. I think I can handle myself and whatever the moor might thrust my way. If anyone cares to keep company with me, that is fine. If not, I'll ride with my own thoughts. But I intend to go, with or without company. Does anyone wish to come?"

Arian and Parthalas exchanged glances, but Rhiss could not tell their thoughts. Lowri carefully went on sweeping the floor, obviously pretending not to hear. Arian sighed resignedly and rose. "Oh, very well, if you will not be dissuaded, I will—"

Parthalas interrupted from his seat on the other side of the fire. "Ah, fer goodness' sake, Arian, yer like a mother hen. Let the poor lad off the leash, why don't ya? Have ye no' been listening? He's no helpless babe. What between dealin' wi' the Hunter and fixin' the hurts of that wee lassie, Lord Rhiss has shown he's more than capable of taking care of himself. If he wants to get all damp and chilled, with a face full of cold mist for an hour or so, let him. Besides, he's got his gryphon — and personally, I'd not like to be on the receiving end of those talons. She's added assurance he'll not come to grief."

Arian stood undecided a moment before capitulating gracefully. "Very well," she said, spreading her hands. "Enjoy your ride — but do not be too long."

"Aye," interjected Parthalas. "Or the old mother hen'll fret. Never ye mind, lad. Take all the time ye need. We'll make sure the good Seir-onna doesn't cluck overmuch."

As Parthalas had foretold, the ride was damp and chilly, but Rhiss did not mind. He had always found a kind of hushed beauty in rural landscapes shrouded in mist, and he did not count himself alone. Aralsa plodded steadily over the hills and valleys, the quiet thump of her hooves on the turf a soothing, almost trance-inducing background noise. And while Aquilea had snorted in disbelief when he called her from her spot beside the fire, she grudgingly rose when he held out the image of plump, succulent rabbits on the moor, fairly queuing up in their rush to become a gryphon's meal. Now, as he rode, she glided smoothly overhead, not too far above on account of the mist, sharp eyes scanning the terrain for tasty morsels.

In truth, Rhiss found himself glad of no human company, even Lowri's. He desired — no, by the One, he *needed* — to be alone with his thoughts and mull several things niggling just below conscious thought. There were several items to consider: the haste with which Maldeus had marched against Rhiss, to the Counsellor's own detriment; the urgency with which Arian wanted him at Pencairn House; the whispered conversation he overheard last night; and things Arian, Lowri, Parthalas — even Brother Gavrilos and Lord Tariel — had inadvertently said at different times. A number of comments did not make sense, given what he had been told.

Throughout his life, Rhiss had had little tolerance for either prevarication or conspiracy, and he wanted to see what he could arrive at if allowed to sift through the past two weeks while doing something as intellectually undemanding as riding over the moor. Time in Arrinor had raced by at breakneck pace, full of such fantastical happenings that, had he been told them prior to coming, he would have dismissed them as entertaining but impossible fabrications, mere stories from ancient sagas. His ride now gave him the first real opportunity to sift through all that had occurred, put it in perspective, and arrive at some conclusions. All right then; here he was: what *had* taken place?

First, he had been plucked from his life by Brother Gavrilos, a being with incredible powers... after admitting to Alistair only a short while prior that he was not happy with his life and wanted magic in it! Rhiss chuckled, shaking his head ruefully. He had certainly gotten more than his money's worth from *that* wish.

He had been interviewed — there was really no other word for it — by Brother Gavrilos, who had told Rhiss his help was urgently needed by an unnamed king to regain the crown wrongfully taken from him. But who was this king? Could it really be Alistair? And if so, why was Rhiss the ideal candidate to assist in his restoration? Several times in the past fortnight, Rhiss had protested that, as a young, rather ordinary English Literature master from a small rural English school, he did not possess the stuff of which heroes were made. He was no Lancelot, no King's Champion. So why was he uniquely useful or valuable in such an improbable enterprise as aiding an exiled king's return to power?

Well, that was a question he *could* answer, at least partially. Since arriving in Arrinor, he had begun manifesting an ability nothing short of supernatural... in fact, several such abilities, if one thought about it. He had healed people of mortal hurts. He could communicate by thought with an animal long presumed purely mythical — an animal that had, for no particular reason other than that he was present at its mother's demise, adopted him as surrogate parent. And this gift of communication might not be limited to Aquilea... come to that, both Relamus and Aralsa had been unusually responsive to his wishes since Lowri had taught him to be so attuned to Aquilea's thoughts. Perhaps the ability was more generalized than he knew. Both Parthalas and Lowri seemed to think Rhiss had the Sight, as well — some sort of precognition, an ability to foresee events before they occurred. Did it include the means to block the psychic probes of Maldeus or others, as he had apparently done on several occasions? Or was that another, separate ability? Regardless, they were all useful and unusual gifts. But why should these abilities manifest in *him*?

Brother Gavrilos had given him remarkable physical gifts, too, the Circlet of Araxis not the least. And *there* was food for thought all by itself. That the Circlet was no ordinary piece of jewellery was patently obvious — remarkable things had happened when Rhiss wore it. There was also something about the Circlet itself that elicited respect — fear, even — among Arrinorans. Why? Of course, those gifts had been added to by the sword hanging at his belt, the sword about which he still knew little, despite the fact it bore signs of close kinship with his dagger.

The Sword. Vividly recalling how it had come into his possession, it suddenly dawned on Rhiss that he had very credibly fought three formidable Arrinoran antagonists — Malmoridai, Maldeus, and Moressin — against all odds, in spite of not considering himself much of a King's Champion. Vanquishing those foes was more than the exiled king had done, a small, unworthy inner voice noted. Where was this king, anyway? Was it Alistair? Rhiss did not even officially have a name for him — or the Usurper, either. Aye, there was the crux of it: too many unknowns, too much convoluted or contradictory. He had put up with it long enough, and would do so no more. Friends and allies simply did not treat each other like that.

With a brief flash of anger cooling swiftly into grim resolve, Rhiss decided it was high time for answers. He would no longer be content as a mere pawn in the plans of others, buffeted back and forth by the tempests of a conflict he was woefully ignorant of. He would have the truth of what was really going on, or he would have nothing more to do with it — and although key players like Gavrilos and Tariel were unavailable, Arian, Parthalas, or Lowri could supply the answers he sought.

Reaching a decision, he abruptly wheeled Aralsa around and urged her into a gallop, heading back to the cottage. Above, Aquilea cried out her surprise and disappointment at the sudden change in heading — she had not yet found her rabbit — but catching the tone of Rhiss' thoughts, she turned in a smooth arc, following without further argument.

The dim, grey day was fading into twilight as Rhiss reached the house. The fog had lessened and outlines of things were easier to discern, but Lowri had placed lamps in the windows just the same, guiding his return. So typical of her warm and caring nature, the gesture touched him, and he momentarily wavered in his resolve. Then he shifted in the saddle and felt the touch of his sword, sleek and cold against his thigh, and resolve returned.

Rhiss led Aralsa into her stall in the infirmary wing. He gave her a quick rubdown, but left her saddled. He knew he should remove it and her bridle, but was too impatient — there would be time later to attend to her thoroughly, *after* getting the answers he desired. Compromising, he threw a blanket over her, made sure feed was in her box, turned and strode purposefully into the cottage proper.

Parthalas dozed in a chair by the fire, legs outstretched. Stepping forward to greet Rhiss as he opened the door, Lowri somehow immediately sensed the change in his mood. The smile died on her face and she bowed her head, swiftly retreating several paces, eyes downcast, not daring to meet his glance. Arian turned from a window where she stood gazing at the darkening sky. But she was not as astute as Lowri in her assessment of Rhiss as he stood before her, and she did not notice the warning glance Lowri flashed. Arian actually did cluck her tongue in disapproval and annoyance.

"Really, Lord Rhiss. You have been gone a very long time. Now, while I trust your ride was—"

"Arian," Rhiss interrupted quietly but in a tone that brooked no opposition, "I am not interested in your motherly scoldings. I have had opportunity to think, and wish to speak about certain matters pertaining to me and Arrinor. I would have complete and truthful answers to my questions."

Arian blinked in surprise, hearing the challenge. Parthalas likewise heard and came wide awake in his chair, peering at Rhiss still near the door, arms crossed on his chest.

Clearly annoyed, Arian opened her mouth to speak, but the grim expression Rhiss wore caused her to think better of it before uttering a word. Instead, she belatedly made the same assessment Lowri had done as Rhiss entered, studying him several seconds. Then Arian nodded. "Very well," she agreed warily. "What is this about? You do not sound pleased."

"I am not. It is of the King, Arian — the rightful King of Arrinor — I would have us speak. There are several things I wish to know, because regrettably, I have reason to believe none of you here have been honest or complete with me. In fact, I will go so far as to say you have kept vital matters from me."

Reactions to this accusation were swift and amazing: Arian and Parthalas actually paled; Lowri gasped and made the Sign of the One. In a strangled voice, Arian asked, "Have you had... some sort of visitation on the moor? Your elusive Lord Tariel, perhaps?"

Frowning, Rhiss shook his head, puzzled by the question. "No, nothing of the sort. Why?"

Arian waved her hand. "Because I wonder what can possibly have brought this avenue of inquiry to mind."

"The realization, Seir-onna, that in two weeks I have spent much time and effort, at considerable risk to life and limb, fighting this king's battles for him and working for his restoration."

Tension eased palpably, and Rhiss realized he had somehow taken a false turn in his quest for the truth.

"Battles?" queried Parthalas, eyebrow raised.

"Maldeus, Malmoridai, and Moressin," responded Rhiss, listing the names on his fingers. Parthalas nodded slowly.

"And if I am to be King's Champion," Rhiss continued, "I don't want to sound arrogant, but I think it only fair I actually meet this King and ensure he is worthy of my service. Where is he hiding? Why have I not yet met this paragon of virtue?"

The tension returned, although no one spoke. Then Arian sighed, and glancing at Parthalas, said resignedly, "Well, actually, it could be said you *have* met the King. In fact, you know him better than anyone."

"Arian," replied Rhiss in annoyance, "I am tired from today's physical and mental exertions, and in no mood for riddles. Speak plainly. Is it my friend Alistair, then, as I have suspected? And if so, why haven't I met him yet? One would think, as King's Champion—"

"No, Rhissan," Lowri interjected softly, and he turned to her. "I'm afraid you have it wrong, my dear..."

"Lowri!" Arian said warningly.

"He deserves the truth, Arian," Lowri said, eyes still on Rhiss, "and not just because he's that close to it already." Her voice was sad, and she faced Arian. "Friends do not treat friends so. It grieves me that you haven't been true with him. And then, to compound the wrong, you made accomplices of me, and Parthalas." She turned back to Rhiss, and he was astonished to see her eyes bright with tears. "I'm right sorry you weren't told the truth of it straight away, my dear," she whispered. "And I'm that sorry I didn't have the courage to tell you earlier. All I can say in my own defence is I gave my word to Arian, when first we brought you here." She stopped to wipe her eyes. "As I said, you have it wrong, Rhissan. It's not King's Champion you are."

She took a deep breath. "It's King."

There was complete silence in the room for several heartbeats, and Rhiss dizzily felt the blood drain from his face. He stared at Lowri, thunderstruck.

"No," he said huskily, when he found his voice. "You're either mistaken, or mad. I am no king. Nor do I want to be one. You cannot be serious." He turned, and said pleadingly, "Arian. Tell me this is a hideous jest, or mistake. There is nothing to suggest I am a king. I have never made any such claim, never even hinted at such a thing."

Arian shook her head. "Nevertheless, you are," she said quietly. "By the grace of the One, you are rightwise born King of Arrinor, Lord of the Crystal Throne. We knew as soon as you set foot in Arrinor and healed my niece. You might have known too, had you been aware what to look for. Search your memory. There were signs to be read, tokens to identify for those who knew. My sister, for instance, discerned right away, or at least, strongly suspected. That is why she sent for me."

"What signs? What tokens?" asked Rhiss, although he thought he could guess.

"The Circlet of Araxis is an ancient and well-known sign of Kingship in Arrinor. The Sword at your belt is another. It has a name, even though you do not know it: Altanimar, legendary sword of kings of old. Both tokens have been lost for a very long time — until you suddenly appeared with them. And then, you possess the Gifts of the King. They are unmistakable, miraculous, and unique to the King."

"Gifts of the King?"

"That is what they are commonly called: Healing, Seeing and Measuring. The last refers to the ability to measure men's hearts. Only the true king displays all three. All in all, everything about you matched the rumours, long whispered and widely circulated throughout Arrinor, that the disaster which wiped out the Royal Family was no accident — but also that the King's infant son somehow miraculously survived. When you appeared out of nowhere at Tor Linlith, wearing the Circlet, and healed Rhyanna, Meranna was instantly convinced."

Rhiss cast his mind back over the past weeks, realizing what Arian had said could be all too true. In fact, in retrospect, it was blindingly obvious. Still, there was one thing.

"Why was I not told right away? Why was subterfuge necessary?" Another thought struck abruptly. "Brother Gavrilos and Lord Tariel," he whispered disbelievingly. "Even they misled me. Not one of you has been completely truthful with me." He looked around, unseeing and overwhelmed, as the reality sank in. "I cannot... I must..."

"Prince Rhissan—" Lowri began pleadingly, extending her hands, but Rhiss started at the title, shaking his head violently.

"Don't say that!" He stared in fresh realization. "You used that title from the beginning. I thought you were joking, but you weren't! You knew!"

Something within him broke. In frantic dismay at such betrayal, he whirled and ran out the side door, a sole imperative in mind: to get away, to find solitude, to try and make sense of the horrific situation that had turned his entire world upside down in the space of minutes. Stunned, those in the cottage stayed rooted where they were. The outer door slammed, and a moment later a horse galloped away. The sound released everyone from their paralysis. Lowri, Arian and Aquilea cried out and made to follow. But Parthalas surged to his feet and shouted, "Hold, now, both of ye! Hold, I say!"

They halted and turned, Lowri weeping openly. "That's enough. It's done," the old man said sternly. "He knows. And not very surprisingly, 'tis not a good knowing. So while it didn't go well, I don't really know if it could have gone any other way. We have to give the poor lad time to think it through. We have to let him go."

"And if he doesn't return?" cried Lowri, distraught. Parthalas and Arian exchanged unreadable glances.

"He will," replied Parthalas. "He must, or we're lost. But there's nowt good to accomplish running after and hauling him back. He must decide to return, freely." He shook his head. "And fer all our sakes, I hope to the One he does."

———◆———

Rhiss emerged from inner swirling anguish to realize that Aralsa had galloped hard for some time, with no choice but to obey his wild mental imperative to flee. As he slowed her to a walk, sides heaving, Rhiss felt sharp guilt: helpless to resist his fierce will, she might have put a hoof wrong in her mad dash and they both could have died. Fortunately, the mist had lifted, a wan moon providing illumination. Although he had no particular destination in mind, Rhiss eventually recognized their heading: the Way Stones of Storrenne. He did not know why Aralsa had chosen it, but it mattered little.

The night continued to clear; when Aralsa finally brought them over the last rise to Storrenne, the pillars rose clearly against a cold, ebon sky punctuated by countless, glittering points of light. As Aralsa's hooves clip-clopped on the hardpan surrounding the stones, Rhiss halted and dismounted. He led her inside the circle and dropped the reins, not really caring whether she stayed or wandered off.

He walked slowly and aimlessly to the centre, stopping before the central depression where the pillar of light had shone to materialize his sword... what had Arian called it? Altanimar? What a strange name. So it, too, was a token of kingship in Arrinor? How bloody marvellous, he thought sarcastically. He was tempted to chuck the thing back. For two pins, he just might, he thought grimly.

He made his way to a pillar at one of the circle quarter points and leaned against it, listening suspiciously. But there was nothing beyond his own pulse, still beating wildly from his anger, and he did not know whether to be relieved or disappointed. Back to the pillar, he sat and tried to take stock, staring at the sky and the cold, unwavering lights fixed there.

Rhiss had absolutely no desire to be king... could not believe he truly was. It was all pure nonsense. King, indeed! He snorted in bitter derision. How could anyone possibly come to that conclusion based on mere possession of a piece of jewellery and a sword? Although... there was the strange matter of the Gifts of the King. They were unusual, assuredly. Well, a good deal more: miraculous, especially that gift of healing. But confound it, even that didn't make him king! His father had been no king... or had he? Rhiss found his thoughts trailing off uneasily. He had precious few memories of his parents, certainly none of his father, only fragmented ones of his mother, images that might or might not have been born purely in imagination. His mother had died when he was very young, and the aunt raising him had made it plain on numerous occasions that she was not keen discussing his parentage or past. He wondered why that should have been. What caused such reticence? Painful memories? Or... dangerous knowledge?

He shook his head impatiently. There was no way of knowing. The more pressing issue was what to do now. What he *desired* to do was talk to Brother Gavrilos. As the force responsible for bringing Rhiss to Arrinor in the first place, Gavrilos could undoubtedly provide all the answers to his questions. But staring at the dark stone monoliths, Rhiss glumly realized that obliging doorways were non-existent at the moment. And even if a doorway *did* magically appear, and Brother Gavrilos *was* willing to talk, what then? Explanations might be forthcoming... or might not. He could easily visualize receiving a variation of "What is that to me? Follow thou me." Would he be offered the opportunity to retreat down the corridor and re-enter his old life? More to the point, would he even *take* such an opportunity?

Now, *that* was an interesting thought. Rhiss turned the idea over in his mind as he would a new food in his mouth, analyzing its palatability. After a while, he was reluctantly forced to concede he would not.

Even in the span of a few short weeks, he had begun to experience a deep love for this wild, strange land and those who inhabited it. There were creatures like Aralsa, Rhyanna's loyal steed, who had already born him many miles; and of course, there was Aquilea. Neither pet nor servant, she was immeasurably more, even more than companion. He had met Aquilea on his very first day in Arrinor. They had instantly formed a deep mutual bond, orphans in a strange land. She had been constantly at his side... until now, he realized guiltily. There had been no opportunity for her to follow him, and now they were separated... perhaps temporarily... or depending on what he did next, forever.

Then there was Meranna; her daughter Rhyanna; Lowri, Parthalas... even Arian, architect of deception... and in spite of his anger, Rhiss could not bring himself to believe Arian had acted from malice. He still did not know why the deception had been practiced, why no one had told him outright of his status... he had left before Arian had the chance to answer his question.

Rhiss was forced to admit there was something this life offered that his old one did not. Adventure? No, that was ludicrous. It wasn't that. There was nothing glamorous about the prospect of being killed by a purely evil, monstrous thug or his minions, nothing glamorous about being attacked by a hideous creature and coming within a hair's breadth of being slaughtered. What appeal could this life have over his old one? Then it came to him: a sense of purpose, the feeling he was actually helping people, *making a difference*. How had Brother Gavrilos phrased it? 'Working in the service of the Light?' His old life did not have that at all, and he realized he would not want to return to it. It was really as simple as that.

So if going back was neither possible nor desirable, what were the alternatives? Was he to head sheepishly back to Arian in the morning, tail tucked between his legs? Rhiss did not fancy *that* at all. He did not want to be king, and he'd had quite enough of being led unknowingly around Arrinor by the nose.

He *could* strike out on his own, wander through this enormous realm, see it for himself... he could still assist those in need, just not in the role of putative king, having to live up to associated expectations. He could merely live his life as the simple traveller he had tried to convince Meranna he was.

But that didn't seem right, either, somehow. Come to that, was it even practical? The reason they were fleeing to Pencairn House in the first place was to put Rhiss beyond the murderous, grasping reach of Maldeus — a plan which made far more sense now that Rhiss was aware of his true identity. Would Maldeus just give up searching for Rhiss, as the rightful king? Highly unlikely. Maldeus did not strike Rhiss as a live-and-let-live sort. Rhiss placed his head against the monolith and sighed. "I wish," he said to the stars overhead, "I wish I knew what to do... that all was clear and obvious, my path plainly delineated."

The stars glittered silently. Sudden rage boiled up inside him, and he jumped to his feet. "Why is life never simple?" he shouted at the night. "What am I to do?"

There was no answer. His anger spent as quickly as it had come, Rhiss wandered aimlessly to the centre depression, whence the pillar of light had materialized... and the sword. He stepped into the depression itself, removed the sword from his belt, and held it before his face, trying to read the lettering etched in the blade. But it was too dark, and he gave up. In utter frustration at his predicament and the uncertainties associated with it, he gripped the hilt with both hands and on sudden impulse, drove the blade deep into the turf. Releasing his hold, he stepped back, watching intently as the blade quivered from the force of his thrust.

What occurred next was unexpected and disconcerting. A deep subterranean groan sounded, as if the earth itself cried in agony at being stabbed. The stones shivered and swayed, and Rhiss looked up, alarmed, wondering whether any would topple.

Then the convulsion was over as swiftly as it had begun. The grass rustled, and a tall, lean figure stepped from behind one of the monoliths. Full of dark fears, recalling the last time he had been surprised there, Rhiss whirled, dagger in hand.

"Good evening, Prince Rhissan," came a quiet voice. "I have been waiting for you. There is no cause for alarm." Rhiss could not make out the figure's identity, but the voice was familiar. "Nor is there need for shouting or other histrionics. I heard you quite well the first time." The figure bowed, inclined his head to one side, spreading hands wide. "And I should be very much obliged if you would remove your sword from the earth where you most carelessly impaled it."

The figure stepped forward, features becoming visible in the starlight, and Rhiss gasped in stunned recognition.

It was Lord Tariel.

XV

BACKGROUND AND CORRECTION

"There exists need — the need to right a wrong. From that arises awareness and ability — awareness of the wrong and ability to make a difference. From ability arises the will to set things right and restore the One's harmony. That is all required: awareness, ability, and will to do the right."

The Book of the One, 90:6:58-59
(Cantos 90, Chapter 6, Verses 58-59)

"You!" Rhiss exclaimed involuntarily, a small but still rational part of his mind noting even as he spoke that his tone was not at all respectful.

Lord Tariel did not seem offended. "Indeed, young Prince," he replied neutrally. "Your powers of observation are sharp as ever. And well do I understand your dismay. In fact, that is why I have come."

"Why? Because I have been shamefully treated by those I am supposed to count as friends and allies in Arrinor?"

Tariel's eyes narrowed at the sarcasm. "No, I would say rather because you deserve a full explanation, that you might understand. An explanation, I might add, you were already in the process of receiving at Mistress Lowri's prior to your sudden departure. Had you waited... well, you did not, and as a result, we have much to discuss. However, as I asked, please retrieve your sword before we begin. Although you knew not what you did, it should not have happened."

"Why?" asked Rhiss, although even as he spoke, he caught the glint in Tariel's eye, and moved to obey.

"You saw the reaction it produced, did you not?"

"Thrusting a sword into the earth caused such a tremor?" Rhiss said disbelievingly. "Oh, come, my lord, you cannot ask me to believe—"

"Young man," Tariel interrupted sharply, "the wise realize the need to be respectful and open-minded when confronted with things beyond understanding. Only fools prattle on in ignorance. I forgive this impertinence, but solely because of the shock you have recently had."

Abashed, Rhiss understood he had gone too far. Silently, he removed the sword from the turf, replacing it in his belt. "I am sorry, my lord."

Tariel nodded. "Very well. Now, then. As I said, there is much to discuss. Come, Prince Rhissan."

Rhiss frowned. "Please don't call me that," he said quietly.

Tariel shrugged expansively. "It is what you are, like it or not. Denial will not avail you, particularly should you fall into the hands of the Usurper's servants." He turned to go. "Come, young Prince."

Rhiss said nothing, but his exasperated sigh spoke volumes. Nonetheless, he followed Tariel from the hollow. They came upon two flat-surfaced rocks, drawn up like ottomans around a smaller circle of stones obviously meant to contain fire. Puzzled, Rhiss cast his mind back to previous Way Stones visits. He could recall nothing like this. Tariel did not notice Rhiss in his confusion, but glanced around. "Perhaps a little light," he murmured, and raised his arms, spreading them to either side.

Immediately, four clear, white shafts of light rose soundlessly into the blackness from the hollows at the circle's compass points. They were not the same dazzling intensity Rhiss vividly recalled when his sword materialized, but their gentle illumination bathed the entire inner ring in a clear light. Rhiss looked around, awestruck, craning his neck skyward. It was like being inside a cathedral of ice, the beams stretching into the night's infinity. They were not crystal clear, however. Studying them, Rhiss recalled a childhood memory while playing in the front room of his aunt's cottage: watching a sunbeam and the dust particles streaming through it. This was like that; it seemed thousands of miniscule dust motes floated lazily through the depths of the four shafts of light, although there was no breeze to explain their movement. And he was sure the motes were not dust particles — they glittered and sparkled in the light.

He was abruptly brought back from his reverie by Tariel's amused voice. "Pretty, aren't they? Now, sit you down, young Prince, and let us speak together of this fair realm of Arrinor, and her Kings."

Turning his attention back to the surroundings, Rhiss saw Tariel already sitting on one of the rocks, indicating Rhiss take the other. The grey stones were circular and flat, about eighteen inches high and as much around, skilfully carved sides displaying figures and lettering; they were plainly meant as stools. A burgundy velvet cushion reposed on each. Slowly, Rhiss sat, darting a look of disbelief at Tariel.

Tariel seemed to misinterpret the look, for he shrugged apologetically. "Well, perhaps the cushions *are* an indulgence, but there is no reason to shift uncomfortably on cold stone while talking, is there? Speaking of cold—" he stood again, placed his closed fist above the fire ring, then splayed his fingers wide as though dropping something. Rhiss saw nothing fall from the outstretched hand, but immediately, silvery-blue flames erupted from the firewood piled there and leapt up, warm and bright. Tariel sat again with a satisfied grunt.

"There. Much better. Now, is there aught else before we begin? It seems—"

Rhiss opened his mouth to speak, but his stomach grumbled audibly. He blanched and looked guiltily at Tariel, who, incredibly, smiled. "Well spoken, Prince, well spoken indeed. An empty stomach does not invite meaningful discourse, does it? As I recall, you had no time for dinner at Mistress Lowri's." Reaching behind his stone,

Tariel retrieved a flask and metal goblets. Unstopping the flask, he filled one goblet with a deeply reddish liquid. "Aye, you have had this before," he confirmed in answer to the unspoken query. "It sustains and restores. It is *Ruvennar*, the same cordial Brother Gavrilos gave you. Be grateful. It is a drink seldom offered at all to mortals, much less twice."

"My thanks, my lord," Rhiss said with heartfelt gratitude. He swished the fluid inside his mouth, savouring its taste, which was still difficult to pin down. It was dark, full and fruity, sweet but not cloying, hinting of brambles. As he drank, Rhiss could tangibly sense hunger and weariness drop away, as a traveller discards a dusty cloak or muddy boots after a hard day's journey.

Tariel smiled again, approvingly. "Does that ease your dismay, Prince? The physical kind, at any rate?"

Rhiss closed his eyes momentarily, nodding, and Tariel continued. "Good. Then let us speak of what has brought us to this place tonight."

"Lord Tariel—" Rhiss began, then cleared his throat.

"Aye?"

Rhiss paused a few moments, searching unsuccessfully for the proper way to phrase his question. Then he gave up and simply asked. "Please... what are you, really? And what have I stumbled into, here in Arrinor?"

Tariel smiled yet again. "Two astute questions, young Prince, with answers at once both astonishingly simple yet exceedingly complex. So... let us begin with your first question. I am merely a servant of the One — in fact, in many ways, like you."

Rhiss shook his head, eyes on the silvery blue flames before them. "No, my lord, with all respect, we are nothing alike. Your abilities are... miraculous."

"Really? How would you characterize your ability to heal lethal wounds, then?"

Rhiss shrugged helplessly. "Well, aye, but... that is one of the Three Gifts, so Arian says. The Gifts of the King." He stopped. Then, greatly daring but also reproving, said, "Come, my lord. You toy with me. You understand full well my meaning, and the differences in our respective abilities. Let us not bandy words about, I beg you. What of *your* abilities? Do you still maintain we are that similar?"

Tariel gazed back appraisingly, and Rhiss felt the same odd sensation he had experienced with Gavrilos: the very depths of his soul were plumbed by the figure across from him. Then Tariel sighed. "You are right. You deserve the truth, not sophistry and word games." He paused. "Very well, young Prince, while I may not tell all, know this: Gavrilos and I are kin, two of seven in the same Order, high in the service of the One. We are known by many titles; in this world, we are called the Arkos. We are neither mortal nor bound by the mortal world, as you surely have deduced by now, and our... abilities, or gifts, both high — and low—" he gestured at the fire, dark eyes amused, and the flames rose briefly but spectacularly to man-height before settling again "— are bestowed on us by the One, in whose service we labour."

"You are an Arkos?" Tariel nodded. "But... I was told there is no Arkos by that name," Rhiss ventured timidly, hardly daring.

"Tariel is... a convenient name at this time," Tariel replied neutrally but in a manner that somehow did not encourage further questions along that line.

"Are you omniscient and omnipotent, then?"

Tariel looked surprised, shaking his head vigorously. "Of course not. What a strange idea. Only the One sees all possibilities, all ends. As for omnipotent..." he shrugged. "Only the One is."

He raised his arm to wave against the night sky. "As to what you have stumbled into, it is a dark tale: that most ancient of conflicts, the struggle of evil and Darkness to dominate the Light and extinguish it, the struggle to seize the Essences of the Children of the One, delivering them unto the Other. It is a struggle concerning you most directly, here in Arrinor, and perhaps the simplest explanation lies in a sad but true tale."

Tariel paused, marshalling his thoughts. "Some twenty-five years ago, Arrinor was ruled by a good and wise king. His family, of the House of Araxan, had ruled Arrinor well for a long time, through the grace of the One. His wife Riona was a beautiful woman, kind and just, and had recently given him a first child and heir... a son. They named the child—" he stopped and looked sideways at Rhiss, listening raptly, "—Rhissan... an ancient royal name in Arrinor."

Rhiss paled, but said nothing.

Tariel nodded as though Rhiss had verbally responded. "Aye. There was great rejoicing throughout the land at this blessed event... *but*... not by all. You see, Prince, the King had an elder sister, a woman whose Essence was hideously twisted, although she was outwardly a beautiful child, and is even today surpassingly fair. Nowadays, she styles herself Queen Diiderra, a name given her by her chief advisor, of whom I shall speak more shortly."

"What? *Queen* Diiderra?" Rhiss interrupted, thoroughly gob-smacked. "Do you mean to say the Usurper is a *woman*?"

Tariel looked at Rhiss curiously. "Why, of course. Did Gavrilos not tell you?"

"He did not. And I guess in the absence of any mention to the contrary, I just assumed... the Usurper was male."

Tariel looked faintly amused. "Really? Is there no room in either your own philosophy or the history of your adopted country for a strong woman ruler?"

Rhiss recalled at once: Queen Elizabeth of the 1500s, Henry VIII's daughter; a powerful, capable female leader if ever there was one — and she had very efficiently ruled an extremely patriarchal, misogynistic society for decades.

Tariel divined his thoughts. "As I surmised. Diiderra was the name she took on becoming Queen. It is from an ancient tongue not well known, used by the servants of the Other, meaning 'Dark Wild Spirit.' That is not the name she was christened at birth, obviously; what loving parent would name a child so? Yet perhaps the One sought to give prescience of the child's possible destiny even then, for her mother said, much later, in my hearing, she was told to name her daughter 'Rhiamon.' By whom, she never said. But it is doubtful the parents knew the significance of that name either, which in that same ancient tongue I just mentioned, has connotations that are... dark." Tariel sighed, staring into the fire.

"But, my lord," Rhiss suddenly spoke into the silence, "you said she was the elder child. Why did she not become Queen on the death of her father? Why did my — why did her younger brother become King?"

Tariel did not answer immediately. It was several seconds before he slowly replied. "Arrinor's laws of succession are clear: the firstborn child generally stands to inherit the throne... but this is not ironclad and..." he paused. "Advice was given to the Regency Council set up by your grandfather before his death."

"Advice?" Rhiss repeated blankly. "What sort of advice? By whom?"

"Advice on the matter of the succession, of course. Advice suggesting your father, not your aunt, was the better — in fact, the only — choice as next Sovereign. As for the source of the advice, it was... not one the Council felt they could ignore." The look on his face made it again eloquently clear he did not wish to explain further.

Rhiss prudently remained silent, but his own expression was jaundiced, and Tariel rolled his eyes, relenting. "Oh, very well. Look you here. Even as a child, Rhiamon unaccountably could not appreciate the blessings given by the One. All she saw were slights and insults where there were none, opportunities to strike back at imagined injuries, no matter how trivial. She was characterized by cruelties great and small, and grew into a twisted, cruel woman. Few could ever comprehend how a man like your father could have a sibling so much his opposite in so many ways. The two children were like two sides of a coin. It is a great and unfathomable tragedy, but we all choose whom we will serve. However, few could look into her heart and see, etched like a black canker, the true depth of her bitterness and desire to dominate others. Ultimately, I think she craved what her brother had: happiness with spouse and family, of course, but above all, the rule of Arrinor. However, she could never know her brother's happiness, for it was based on love freely given, a concept utterly alien to her. She swore she would possess, at the least, the power denied her when the Crown went to your father."

Tariel closed his eyes, as though his next words pained him. "Rhiamon had already experimented, seeking knowledge she should not have. Meddling with the forces of Darkness, she called out to the Other, who, ever eager to spread corruption, evil and temptation, heard and sent her a counsellor. Now she names this counsellor 'servant,' although she is grossly mistaken, and grievously overestimates her control over him, to the mortal peril of her very Essence. You have met this counsellor already."

Rhiss felt a chill, and for an instant, an icy wind blew into the clearing of the stones, and the silvery blue flames wavered. "Maldeus," he whispered, the name harshly magnified in the darkness.

Tariel nodded, straightened and glanced about. The flames regained their strength, and the cold wind died. "Aye. The very same. Maldeus Falduracha of Angramor."

"You said he is... sent by the Other," Rhiss said hesitantly. "Then Maldeus is—" he did not want to say it.

"—not mortal," finished Tariel. "Correct. He chooses service to the Other, as I choose service to the One."

Recalling the night in the entry hall, Rhiss observed uncomfortably, "You seemed... well acquainted."

"Oh, aye," breathed Tariel, staring into the flames, thoughts elsewhere. "Indeed. Through long ages, we have been adversaries, he and I."

There was a lengthy silence as each reflected. Rhiss finally broke it by saying, quietly but clearly, "Faust."

Tariel roused. "I beg your pardon?"

Rhiss coloured. "Oh... I'm sorry, my lord... I wasn't aware I spoke aloud. I was recalling a story, from my... my adopted land." How strange to call it that, he thought. "The story is of a learned man who falls into folly and calls upon... the Other. In exchange for his... Essence... the Other grants him great powers and knowledge, providing him with a 'servant,' like Maldeus, to assist in the evil he does." He fell silent.

Tariel raised an eyebrow. "How does it end?"

Rhiss looked thoughtful. "There are several versions. In the one I am thinking of, the title character repents of his evil, but it is too late, and he is compelled to join... the Other in the Shadows... eternally, one would suppose."

"Hmm," responded Tariel neutrally. "While we do not yet know Diiderra's end, she would do well to hear this story. It sounds an excellent cautionary tale." He sighed. "Although she would refuse to see herself in it. Your race tends to see only what you wish to see, often at your peril."

"How did Diiderra become Queen?"

Tariel stretched. "She and Maldeus decided, of course, that the rest of the family must die so she could become Sovereign. However, there was a slight impediment to that plan." He looked inquiringly at Rhiss. "Can you guess?"

Rhiss considered, nodding eagerly. "I think so. Seir-onna Arian spoke of the Order of the Knights Castellar. She told me the purpose of its existence was to safeguard the lives of the Royal Family. So we can assume the Order would take a dim view of a plot to commit regicide."

"You are absolutely right. Maldeus and Diiderra had to do something about the Castellars. It is easy to reconstruct their thinking: the most obvious course was to destroy the Order — but that would deprive them of a highly valuable asset in the furtherance of their aims. After all, then as now, the Knights Castellar represented a formidable force for power and control in Arrinor. It would have been a pity to throw that away. So, if one does not want to destroy such a force, what is left?"

Rhiss frowned. "Arian alluded to it, my lord: subvert the organization in question so it will aid, or at the least, not oppose your plans."

"Excellent. And that is precisely what they did. Oh, not so the Order countenanced murdering the Royal Family, of course. They were too subtle for that. But over a lengthy period of time — and they were patient, I grant them that — Maldeus and Diiderra insidiously influenced and corrupted the command structure of the Order so that first, when the time came, it would be malleable to their lead, and second, it would not look too deeply into any tragic 'accident' that might befall the Royal Family."

"Arian made reference to a Coup," said Rhiss. "So I take it Maldeus and Diiderra carried out their plans and murdered the King and his family."

"Aye. Well, they missed one person, of course."

"Me?" Rhiss whispered tentatively, although he was not really asking.

Tariel inclined his head gravely.

Rhiss looked at his feet, then back at Tariel, expression uncharacteristically bleak. "My lord... why was I not told this from the beginning? Brother Gavrilos and Seir-onna Arian have been architects of a conspiracy designed to hide the truth from me, with the assistance, or at the very least, acquiescence, of Lady Meranna, Parthalas and Lowri."

"And you feel betrayed by their actions." There was no doubt in the statement.

"It just does not seem to me how friends should treat with each other, my lord."

Tariel sighed. "If it lessens your bitterness, Prince, Gavrilos and Seir-onna Arian engaged in no conspiracy. They have never met." His eyes flashed. "It seldom occurs, you know — physical contact between your kind and mine."

"By which I assume you mean I should be flattered with the attention I have received from you and Brother Gavrilos. Thank you, my lord, I'm sure. But you must pardon me: it seems, since arriving in Arrinor, I have had 'the Eye and Hand of the One' on me, paraphrasing Seir-onna Arian. And I confess, at times, it is a decidedly mixed blessing."

Tariel's lips quirked into a smile. "No doubt. But is it really much more adventure than you bargained for, Prince? I cannot believe Gavrilos did not give at least a broad idea of what you agreed to in returning to Arrinor."

"He did not tell me I was *returning* to Arrinor at all, my lord," Rhiss retorted. "I suppose, if you mean he spoke in very general terms, sitting in a pleasantly appointed room somewhere between worlds, quietly sipping Ruvennar by a cosy fire — then aye, he gave me a 'broad idea.' But he never mentioned the most important thing — bringing me back to my original question, which I *will* have answered: why was I not told this at the beginning?"

"Spoken like a true King," observed Tariel dryly. "It *does* become you."

A look of desperation crossed Rhiss' face. "Lord Tariel, I cannot be King. I simply cannot."

"Cannot? Or will not?"

"Both. Neither. I don't know. There are many reasons."

"Indeed. Enlighten me."

Rhiss took a deep breath. "Well, to begin... I can barely defend myself. And I have no training in the many skills required of a King."

"Easily remedied if 'twas true," said Tariel dismissively. "But I disagree. While your formal training has been limited, you already defend yourself remarkably well with sword and bow. I know your adversaries of the last two weeks would attest to that — if they could. Some, alas, are no longer alive to serve as witnesses, are they?

Others have helped you, to be sure: for example, it is no coincidence that your friend Alistair had archery and sword-fighting interests, you know, and he taught you well. All those sessions at The Blade and Bow — they served you admirably. But do not dismiss your own skills. Now, regarding your protest that you lack kingship skills: you were a schoolmaster in your other life, were you not?" Rhiss nodded. "Supervising and providing leadership to unruly young charges, I believe? Knocking heads together so you could gain their attention long enough to impart wisdom? Dealing with behaviours from both young and old, who in spite of knowing better, still did cruel, unjust things? Aye, so I thought. Well then, best you understand this now, lest you get grandiose ideas about what it is to be king: the art of ruling is very much like that, Prince." He raised an eyebrow. "People need education, discipline and leadership; that is what a king does. Are there any other objections needing demolishing?"

Rhiss stared into the fire several long moments, struggling to articulate his fears. "I am simply not the stuff of which kings are made," he finally said huskily.

"By which you mean you doubt yourself, your abilities?"

"I do," Rhiss murmured. "I am not ready to lead soldiers into battle, or fight wars, or confront powerful, dangerous enemies; not now, possibly never." He looked up, eyes pleading. "Lord Tariel, how can an accident of birth qualify one for this? I left three people in that cottage tonight; three people already in this land who believe and depend on me and my ability to lead them to victory. Why should they believe? What have I done to justify their belief? How can I ever hope to measure up to it?"

There was great compassion in Tariel's eyes. "You ask excellent questions, Prince, with much humility. Perhaps too much. But there are equally good answers. You speak of an 'accident of birth.' I tell you here and now there is no such thing. In all the heavens above and the worlds below, there are no accidents in the Plans of the One. You were meant for this. You also speak of your fear that people should rely on you — oh, not in so many words, but I see it written on your heart. Know, then, that they — and incidentally, there are already considerably more than three who believe in you — see in you what I, and others, see: a willingness to serve the cause of the Light. You ask *why* should you be King? Because you are capable; because you are needed — more than you know; because you can make a difference; and because it is the right thing to do. No more is required of any king beyond that."

Rhiss looked startled, and Tariel nodded. "Aye, you have heard that before, haven't you? Arrinor is like that small boy in your place of learning, tormented and in desperate need of someone to stand up to cowardly thugs and put a stop to it. *That* is the stuff of which true kings are made... not the highly romanticized tales of legends. You ask how you can live up to peoples' hopes and expectations. The simplest and most compassionate answer is that you cannot, not always, at any rate. You are a Child of the One, meaning, and I say this in all loving kindness, that you are not perfect, and *will* make mistakes. But that is unimportant. What matters is how you deal with those mistakes, and how others see you cope and learn from them."

He paused. "You have witnessed and dealt with much in the past weeks — how did you summarize it? 'Malmoridai, Maldeus and Moressin.' I think we could add the

Gifts of the King as well. Two young women are alive because of the gift of Healing, bestowed on you. I will not waste time asking you how well you coped with those travails, because I know what your answer would be: not well... or at most, adequately."

Tariel smiled faintly. "I begin to understand fair Mistress Lowri's exasperation. You resolved those incidents more than adequately. Did she not scold you on this very point? Modesty is all well and good, but there is a time for realism in appraising strengths — and weaknesses. Your two biggest weaknesses at the moment are lack of experience, and lack of confidence. But you are King, by design, more qualified to be so than you are ready to admit."

"So why was I not told—?" Rhiss began.

"For one very simple reason: you were unready. Gavrilos knew, and later, so did Arian, without needing to be told. Think a moment, boy: after adjusting to the shock of entering the Portal of Gavrilos — a shock you weathered remarkably well, all things considered — what would you said if he had told you what I have related this night? Would you cheerfully, freely have shouldered the responsibility of regaining your Kingship? Agreed to fight against kin you did not even know you had? You know perfectly well you would not — why, I see in your heart you are still not completely convinced, even after weeks of witnessing yourself doing the most remarkable things under the most remarkable circumstances, and doing them very well indeed. No, that Rhissan would have gone back through the Portal to his dreary life, to his everlasting regret. *But you are no longer that man.* Search yourself and realize the truth. You can do this. You already have friends who will help you bear the burden, and more will come." He grimaced. "Besides, your mere presence has set things irrevocably in motion. You recall Moressin the Hunter? And the Malmoridai that savaged the little girl? They were tools of Maldeus, and he has opened the floodgates to even more terrifying creatures in his bid to stop you. Hard as it may be for you to believe... I think he is frightened."

Tariel halted and stood unexpectedly. Startled, Rhiss began rising, but was wordlessly waved back. Tariel stood before the fire, deep in silent thought, staring into it, arms crossed. Then he abruptly turned, blinked, and looked with that soul-penetrating gaze that made Rhiss feel he was made of glass. Tariel nodded, evidently reaching a decision, and said softly, as if to himself, "Aye. There is one thing more in this path of discernment that needs doing. It is the right thing. Gavrilos might not approve, of course, but regardless, it *is* the right thing." He extended a hand to Rhiss to help him stand.

"Come, Prince Rhissan," he said louder. "I have something to show you, something you must witness."

"What is it?" asked Rhiss, getting to his feet.

"Your family's murder." Tariel turned and strode off, leaving Rhiss standing behind, slack-jawed. "And your survival, of course," the Arkos added as an afterthought over his shoulder. Rhiss scrambled after him into the darkness.

XVI

RALLY AND REVELATION

"Fire, death and destruction surround me. Yet even besieged by devastating evil, I will strive to do the will of the One, so that Light prevails. And on the wings of the One comes deliverance and life unlooked for. Marvelous are the ways of the One."

The Book of the One, 138:32: 12-14
(Cantos 138, Chapter 32, Verses 12-14)

Rhiss caught up to Tariel passing through the gaps in the stones. "My family's *murder*?" he repeated, stomach churning queasily at the thought. "But... you said it occurred twenty-five years ago."

"Indeed I did."

"But then, how—?" Rhiss halted, astonished, as they emerged from the circle. Faintly illuminated by stars overhead was a wooden door, apparently built into one of the stones. Under the starlight, elaborate patterns on the door shone in silver tracery like a spider's web.

Tariel turned calmly. "Aye? You were saying, Prince?"

Rhiss found his voice. "I... my lord... this is a Portal."

"Correct. Once again, your powers of observation are breathtaking."

"It does not look like... is this... the Portal of Gavrilos?"

Tariel sniffed. "Certainly not. He has his tools, I have mine. I would not use his Portal for a task such as this. While we share the same goals, and serve the same Power, we do not always completely... agree on methodology." He turned back to the door, surveying it, then faced Rhiss. "Will you do the honours, please?"

Rhiss was fascinated at the hint of discord, but knew better than to ask. He reached towards the door knob, then stopped. "My lord," he said in alarm as he realized, "what of Aralsa? I cannot just leave her wandering aimlessly."

"She will be well cared for, you have my word. The circle is not as deserted as it may seem. There is no need for concern on that score." Tariel gestured at the door. "If you please?"

Rhiss grasped the door knob with the sense of having done this before, but it felt quite different. The door opened — into the stone itself, it appeared — easily and noiselessly into a long, dark corridor, and Rhiss was again struck by the incongruity: if he craned his neck to one side, he could plainly see the stone's rounded back.

As he stepped over the threshold, light flared along the corridor's length. Unlike the Portal of Gavrilos, this corridor was constructed of cut stone, light coming not from candles in strange, elaborate carvings, but from torches held in decorative iron brackets attached to the walls. Rhiss took several steps, but stopped and turned for reassurance at the sound of Tariel closing the door firmly. Tariel merely gestured towards the corridor's end. "If you please, Prince."

Similar to its twin, the way ended twenty feet or so in, opening into a chamber with a large stone fireplace; a second corridor extended from the chamber into darkness. However, the similarities ended there. The Portal of Tariel had a spartan, frankly militaristic atmosphere; the furniture was not nearly as luxurious, and the place had none of the cosy feel Rhiss recalled from the Portal of Gavrilos.

While Rhiss stood surveying the surroundings, Tariel moved to a wardrobe on the room's other side. He flung open its doors and, after a moment's inspection, removed several items. "Come, Prince. We have an appointment, and things need to be done before we rendezvous with the past."

Rhiss crossed the room. Tariel pursed his lips, studying Rhiss thoughtfully before nodding. "Aye. Remove your cloak, tunic and belt, if you please," he said. "Give me your sword and dagger also. We shall leave them safely here, and I will provide you with replacements." He held out items of clothing and motioned for Rhiss to put them on.

Rhiss silently obeyed, handing Tariel his weapons, cloak and tunic before turning his attention to what he had been given: a finely made, sleeveless tunic of creamy white cloth, silky smooth to the touch. Its distinguishing mark was the Sign of the Three on the front, the longest and centremost of the scarlet lines a bold slash twelve inches long. There was also a new belt, cloak and gauntlets of grey. Finished, Rhiss realized in surprise he was now clad almost identically to Tariel, who confirmed it. "Aye. You are dressed as a junior member of my Order — an honour far beyond anything you can comprehend. Remember that. We will do nothing to disguise your features; in the chaos and flames I do not think it necessary, but neither do I wish to draw attention to your identity. Dressing you thus, and not wielding your own Altanimar, we stand to blur the truth of our visit from unfriendly eyes this night. Those who recognize our livery will, we hope, assume you are simply a colleague in my Order. For those who do not know it, we are merely another pair of knights." He handed Rhiss a sheathed sword attached to a belt, which went diagonally over one shoulder to take the sword's weight. The sheathed dagger went on the belt Rhiss already wore at his waist. Like Tariel's weapons, Rhiss noticed that both blades were intricately wrought and had a faintly bluish, metallic sheen. Tariel nodded and motioned Rhiss to follow him down the far corridor, which brightened as their passage triggered the torches.

As they approached the door, Tariel stopped and turned to Rhiss, face grim. "Hear me, Prince, before we step through," he said with quiet intensity. "The events you are about to witness really occurred. When we pass through that door, they *are* taking place, instantly and now. These are not shadows of what was, but real people, solid and tangible, and you are every bit as solid, tangible and *visible* to them. This is no fairy tale where we wander safe and unseen like ghosts. Understand, and keep this thought foremost: *it is all very real.* If you are attacked, you could be injured or killed. You will see flame, and carnage, and innocent people dying. While we both know the night's tragic outcome, I cannot emphasize too strongly that it is not your place to alter its conclusion. Do you mark me? *It happened.* It must be *allowed* to happen. You may defend yourself if attacked, but do not interact unnecessarily with people, or attempt to change what happens. If you do, I will remove you from that night, and we will never have dealings again; you can struggle on alone as best you may. I do this for your instruction, but there is much at risk by taking you into this chain of events, and rest assured I do not undertake it lightly. If it goes ill, there could be grave repercussions for us both."

Thoroughly abashed by the gravity of such stern admonition, Rhiss could only nod mutely, eyes wide. Tariel sensed his mood, clapping him lightly on the shoulder. "Fear not. I believe this necessary, and would not take you through to bear witness if I had no confidence in your ability to comport yourself properly. Just mind you do as I have said. Stay close, and look to me for guidance."

"I will, my lord," Rhiss replied soberly. "You have my word on it."

"Good. Then let us go. Open the door, and step through."

Like the first time he ventured through a Portal, Rhiss did not quite know what to anticipate as he cautiously opened the door, but what waited was, again, curiously anticlimactic: no raging battle, no wanton massacre of innocents, merely another stone corridor, utterly deserted, lit by torches. Confused, he looked at Tariel, who quietly closed the door and joined Rhiss in the corridor.

Tariel nodded in wry understanding. "Not quite what you expected, is it? But rest assured this is the right place and time. We are deep within Tor Eylian, the royal castle in Kilarradine, Arrinor's capital. It is nearly midnight on Midsummer's Eve, twenty-five years ago, shortly before the Coup begins. We are here because I want you to see someone in particular. Come, this way." Tariel walked purposefully along the corridor, Rhiss hastening to follow. He looked back after a few seconds, unsurprised to note that the Portal had vanished.

After several minutes, they stopped before a featureless section of corridor. Tariel looked both ways to confirm no one watched, held out a gloved hand, and after a moment's searching said, "Hmm... aye. I should think... here," and pressed his hand on a plain stone. It was shoulder height and, as far as Rhiss could see, no different from any other. But there was a quiet click, and part of the wall swung noiselessly inwards to reveal a yawning darkness higher than a man and three feet wide.

"This will allow us to observe the Coup's final preparations," Tariel said softly. "Follow, and be absolutely silent, no matter what you see or hear. I will provide a little light — for a while, at least — so you may proceed without fear of stumbling." He looked at Rhiss with narrowed eyes and grunted. "That will never do, boy. Your

Essence burns like a bonfire on a clear night on the moor, and is ten times as visible. We must do something about it, or you will be the ruin of us. Mark carefully what I do."

He laid hands over Rhiss, murmuring something too low to catch. Rhiss felt a very odd sensation come over him, as though he was wrapped in cotton wool; then the whole world seemed... muffled. He tried to commit feeling and process to memory.

Tariel stepped back, looking critically at either Rhiss or his handiwork, then nodded. "It will not last long — your Essence seems difficult to obscure. However, it should shield you from those who have eyes to see. But do not get overly excited, or you will undo the effect." He moved off, leaving Rhiss to wonder how he was to avoid becoming excited.

Behind them, the wall swung closed, and they were in darkness. But he heard Tariel take his sword and scrape it twice along the ground. Two long lines of glowing sapphire light slowly appeared like ribbons on the ground, where wall met floor, extending several feet ahead and behind. The bands of light advanced steadily with them as they moved, providing a dim blue radiance about their feet, enabling them to walk slowly without fear of putting a foot wrong. Rhiss peered around. The dust on the ground was thick and undisturbed, the passage obviously unused for a very long time. As they travelled, the ribbons behind remained lit when the passage turned this way and that, making a safe return route possible.

After several minutes, they reached a dead end. Rhiss had scarce taken this in when, aghast, he saw red eyes in the darkness. He fumbled for his sword. However, before he could do more than begin the action, Tariel turned to Rhiss, raising a finger to his lips, motioning him forward until they stood side by side before the eyes, which turned out to be only two small holes in the wall, five feet off the ground. Tariel put an eye to one, and Rhiss did the same to the other.

Squinting against the brighter light, his first impression was of a large chamber brightly lit. It was the flickering, reddish torchlight that had so alarmed him moments before, and exhaling softly in relief, he studied the room, squirming for a better view.

An octagonal chamber easily a hundred feet across, the room was plainly of some importance. The ceiling was domed and very high, either showing the night sky or cunningly painted to resemble it. Their vantage point was halfway between two massive oaken doors at one end of the room, commanding an excellent view of all that might transpire. The double doors were the primary means of entrance and exit, although there were other, smaller doors around the room. A number of carved stone chairs lined the walls, but the chamber's centre was unencumbered by furniture. Rhiss allowed his gaze to travel to the far end, drawing in his breath as he saw.

On a raised stone dais, sparkling and glittering in the ruddy torchlight, reposed a great throne Rhiss first thought was made of glass. Then, unbidden, he remembered the words Arian used when addressing him, back in Lowri's cottage — "Lord of the Crystal Throne" — and he understood. *This* was that throne; and it was not glass, but a solid block of pure, glittering transparent crystal. He peered into the Throne

Chamber, the seat of Arrinor's rulers. And there was more — someone stood to one side of the throne. Rhiss squinted for a better look.

It was a woman, tall and slim, dressed in a white, flowing dress whose train trailed on the floor behind her. At least, Rhiss assumed the dress was white, although the torches cast strangely troubling, coruscating patterns of ruby light and shadow over her gown. She simply stood there, gazing at the empty throne in private, rapt contemplation. Although he could not have said why, Rhiss felt she waited for something.

The torches flickered briefly but noticeably, as though a gust of wind had blown, and a dark smudge of black smoke was visible fifteen or twenty feet behind the woman. Rhiss blinked, and abruptly, a man was also in the room, standing where the wisp of smoke had been seconds before. It was inexplicable, but he was just... there. Rhiss frowned, puzzled, then started in recognition, shivering as though a dagger's point had been drawn down his spine. It was Maldeus.

Maldeus bowed low and spoke. His voice was not loud and they were not near Rhiss, but through some trick of the room's acoustics or Tariel's intervention, every word was clearly audible.

"My lady?" The voice was as Rhiss remembered, smooth as oil but full of languid, casual malice, and he shivered again in the safety of his dark refuge.

The woman turned, and Rhiss saw her face for the first time. She appeared completely sanguine by the sudden appearance in the otherwise empty chamber, acknowledging his bow with a careless wave of one hand. Her youthful face was coldly beautiful, exquisite pale features finely chiselled like a porcelain doll. Rhiss had seen such a doll once, through the windows of a London shop, and was indelibly reminded of it now. The comparison was apt, for while there was the same unmistakable, delicate allure, the eyes of the woman, like the doll, were dark, cold and impassive, possessing no slightest scrap of human warmth or vitality.

"My Lord Maldeus," she replied, inclining her head, her voice beautiful, low pitched, but haughtily icy. Her words could freeze the very air about her, thought Rhiss — it was a wonder her breath was not visible, even in the chamber's warmth. "You have something to report, I trust."

"Indeed, Lady. All is in readiness. You have but to give the order, and we complete the work we have laboured at so long. Before this night ends, your tiresome brother and his family will be dead, and you will be Sovereign Queen of Arrinor, as promised."

"Dorvanen?" she asked.

"He is in place and ready, with a contingent of hand-picked Castellars who will light the fires and make sure none escape. Then he and I will see that the valiant contingent suffer their own tragic, accidental deaths, fighting the very fires they have ignited. There will be no witnesses to survive and spread awkward tales."

"Except Dorvanen," she pointed out.

"He is too useful a tool to dispose of at present, Lady. We need him in the aftermath of this night to calm and reassure those Castellars not yet turned. But later..."

by all means, he, too, can meet his own unfortunate... accident." He smiled unpleasantly. "All in good time. First things first. Tonight we rid ourselves of your brother, the King."

"*And* his snivelling mouse of a wife, Maldeus. My sister-in-law. Remember the offence she has done me in giving him an heir. Make sure above all: the brat dies first... *as* she watches, so her last moments are as exquisite as possible."

"With pleasure, Lady. Your nephew dies tonight, by my own hand. You have my word on it."

Rhiss listened to the exchange with growing anger, until he nearly exclaimed aloud in outrage. Belatedly recalling Tariel's warning, he clenched his fists and tried to tamp down his feelings.

He was nearly too late. Maldeus whipped his head up like a snake and peered around, dark eyes scanning the empty chamber. In their vantage spot, Tariel glanced sideways and hastily laid a gloved hand on Rhiss, quietly murmuring under his breath. Rhiss felt calm descend and apologetically glanced at Tariel before putting his eye to the peephole again.

"My lord?" the woman called sharply. "What is it?"

"I am... not sure," Maldeus muttered, clearly unsettled. "I felt... I thought... I am not certain." He strode partway along the chamber towards the doors, then stopped near Rhiss and Tariel's concealed spot, still peering around. He said nothing for several moments, and Rhiss held his breath. Then Maldeus shook his head, slowly walking back to the woman, eyes still suspiciously darting from side to side.

"My Lord Maldeus?" she said again, eyes narrowed.

"It was... nothing, Lady." He waved a hand, attempting to sound dismissive. "A strange feeling, that's all."

She looked fleetingly doubtful, then shrugged. "Well... if you are certain. 'Tis time to set our scheme in motion." Seeing him make no attempt to gainsay her, she nodded, confidence returning. "Walk with me, then, and we will bring about the fruition of our plans." The fabric of her long dress swirled as she made an ironic little curtsey to the empty throne, then turned and strode briskly towards the main doors, Maldeus gliding noiselessly behind. The doors opened, swung shut, and they were gone.

Rhiss took a step back from the spy hole, looking aghast at Tariel. "That... that monstrous creature is my *aunt*? We are actually related?"

Tariel inclined his head apologetically. "I am afraid so."

"And Maldeus... what was that about? Could he sense my emotions?"

"I would say rather he sensed your Essence. Your strong emotions unmasked you momentarily. I warned you to be careful about that. Do you recall how I damped your Essence? You will likely have need to do it again when I am not present."

"Aye, my lord, I think I do." Then he recalled the words that sparked his outrage, and stiffened. "Lord Tariel, we must stop them! They are going to murder my parents! I know full well what you said earlier, but we cannot just stand idly by and allow this obscenity to take place. To do so makes us no better than accomplices—"

Tariel raised an imperious hand, cutting Rhiss off. "Enough. I will not stand here and be lectured on ethics by you. I understand your concern, but wonder if you heard me." His expression softened. "Besides, there is nothing in this time or place to be done on that score. I regret to say that your father's murder has already happened. However, if it is any consolation, Seir-on Dorvanen exceeded his orders, carrying it out before being given the command, which I assure you will not sit well with Maldeus when he learns of it. You have witnessed firsthand his treatment of underlings who displease him." He turned and retraced their steps. "In any event, we are not going to 'just stand idly by,' as you spluttered in righteous indignation. Come." He turned.

"What are we going to do?" Rhiss asked as he caught up.

"Appease your conscience. We go to save two innocents from those butchers: your mother... and you." Tariel glanced back to see the look of shocked surprise that came over Rhiss. "Come, boy, hurry. That is one appointment for which we do not want to be tardy."

Emerging from the hidden passage into the corridor, Rhiss already smelled smoke. Tariel caught it also, and nodded grimly. "They waste no time, that is certain."

Rhiss had puzzled over Tariel's words while they strode along. "My lord?"

"What is it?"

"We go to save... my mother and me, you said."

"I did."

"But... I don't understand. I thought you said we were not to change the past."

"So I did. But we are not changing the past, not in any material sense." He looked sideways at Rhiss. "You see, I saved you and your mother twenty-five years ago this night, although you may be forgiven for not recalling it."

"But... how could I... was I not with you before, then?"

Tariel's mouth quirked in a wry smile. "I doubt you would ask that question if you really understood what you ask. Time is not nearly as fixed or linear as you believe, but traversing its convoluted byways can be torturous for mortal minds to comprehend. It is paradox enough to note that you accompany me, assisting in your own rescue. Let us just observe that marvellously subtle and intricate are the ways of the One and have done. This way!"

Tariel led him along corridors and down flights of stairs. Rhiss followed, trying unsuccessfully to conceive how he could possibly come to his own rescue. The smell of smoke all the while became stronger. As they came to the bottom of yet another set of stairs, bells suddenly pealed urgent summons loudly into the night, and shouts rose in answer.

Tariel lifted the latch on a heavy wooden door and they emerged into the open, night air heavy with smoke. Flames leapt up all around, consuming buildings and everything that would burn in the wide square.

The next few minutes were a confused blur. They negotiated their way through a maelstrom of fire and destruction, passing people locked in combat. Some were Castellars, obviously the traitorous contingent Maldeus and Diiderra had spoken of, fighting with those rushing to quench the conflagration and rescue the Royal Household, all the while in deadly peril from the flames. Tariel drew his sword and bade Rhiss do likewise; it was mere moments before they were forced to use them. As they traversed a courtyard near some stables, they were spotted and attacked by nearly a dozen Castellars. The resulting melee was sharp and swift, and Rhiss, at least, was hard put to it.

Instinctively, Rhiss mentally called Aquilea, bidding her to his side. No sooner had he sent the thought aloft than he realized with a sharp pang of regret that Aquilea was separated by an unbroachable barrier, and would not — could not — come hurtling to his aid, a furious, razor-sharp facsimile of death. The realization nearly cost Rhiss his life, for as he hesitated a split-second, he was nearly run through. Only a lightning thrust from Tariel's sword prevented his death. The Arkos gave him a strange, unreadable glance, but said nothing. And although bodies eventually littered the area, Rhiss was quite sure he would have been killed several times over had it not been for Tariel, whose skill was nothing less than incredible.

Breathing hard, Rhiss leaned over. He was sweating, both from the fires' heat and his own exertions. "My lord," he gasped, "under the circumstances, do you not think it would have been wiser for us to be dressed as Castellars?"

Tariel looked about disdainfully, hardly winded. "I would not sully my honour — or yours, Prince — by having us so clad. These brigands are oath-breakers and butchers, and well deserve their fate, banished to the Shadows of the Other."

"But there must be Castellars in the castle who are true to their word."

Tariel shook his head dismissively. "Unlikely by this time. Besides, dressed as the murderers responsible for this, it would be extremely difficult to gain your mother's trust." He glanced at the burning buildings. "Speaking of which, our encounter with this rabble has left me in slight confusion about where and when we are. I will reconnoitre and determine our location. Stay you here a moment while I do. I return directly." His eyes flashed. "Do not let down your guard, especially in futile wishes for help that cannot come! And do not leave this spot!" With those admonitions, he was gone, moving swiftly and lost almost immediately in the reek and smoke.

With an effort, Rhiss raised his sword back to the ready, staring heavy-hearted at the devastation. He wondered how anyone could navigate such conditions, and what the place looked like before such terrible evil. This was — had been — his first home. It was impossible to imagine. With an effort, Rhiss thrust such thoughts aside, undistracted and vigilant to all dangers — Tariel's last words implied all too clearly that he was somehow aware Rhiss had tried summoning Aquilea.

His musings were suddenly interrupted by a woman's screams. Rhiss strained his eyes through the murk to locate the sound. There! Through the arch on the square's far side. He had barely framed the thought before he was running towards it, ducking as flames licked at his head. Rhiss knew full well he was disobeying Tariel's injunction, but he could not ignore those screams and remain true to himself.

Just inside the arch, a man in Castellar robes pinioned a young woman to the ground, intentions abundantly clear. Rhiss stared in shocked disbelief, unable to believe a priest would commit such an act. However, the evidence before him was clear. He shouted in outrage, raising his sword.

The distraction worked. The man jerked around, doubtless thinking it one of his comrades, but his anger at being interrupted changed instantly as he realized that Rhiss was no friend. He snarled defiance at Rhiss standing with sword at the ready, and whipped a small stiletto from within the folds of one long sleeve. Quick as lightning, he drove it up towards Rhiss, aiming for the ribs. There was neither space nor time to dodge the blow; Rhiss reflexively met it with his sword, trying desperately to parry against the smaller, more manoeuvrable blade which was within a hairs-breadth of ending his life.

Against all odds, the gambit worked. The stiletto blade rasped metallically against the sword, slithering harmlessly to one side and unbalancing the Castellar. Rhiss took advantage of that momentary confusion and brought his knee up, hitting the man squarely in the face. There was a crunching sound as the man's nose broke; he gave a croaking scream, slamming back against the ground beside the petrified woman. His head cracked hard against the cobblestones, and his eyes abruptly went glassy in death.

Trembling all over at his narrow escape, Rhiss stared at the dead man before realizing the woman on the ground now gazed at him terrified, obviously wondering whether he would pick up where the Castellar had left off. Rhiss willed his free hand to steady, extending it to the woman, inclining his head, and tried to smile reassuringly.

"My apologies, lady. I did not intend for you to remain lying beside that vermin. Let us get you to safety."

She cautiously took his proffered hand, and Rhiss helped her stand. The movement brought her features closer, and as she stood, he gasped in recognition.

"Aunt Kerian?" he whispered disbelievingly. The face was younger than he had ever known it, but beyond doubt, it was she he had thought his only living relative, the woman who raised him following his mother's death.

She caught her name on his lips, and perhaps the title as well, for she looked doubtful. "Do I... *know* you, sir?"

Rhiss caught himself, again inclining his head to mask his confusion. "No, lady," he said at length. "I thought I recognized you. Your name *is* Kerian?"

"Aye," she breathed. "Kerian of Scallassie, lady-in-waiting to the Queen. How do you know me, my lord?"

It was plain she did not know what to make of him, examining his clothing and insignia. "Are you spirit or flesh? Whom do you serve, that you fight these butchers?"

Rhiss searched for a suitable response, then recalled how Tariel and Gavrilos referred to themselves. "I am but a simple knight in the service of the One... as you see," he replied, gesturing at the Sign of the Three on his tunic.

She looked about, gesturing at the Castellar's body, the fires and destruction. "No, good sir," she said bitterly. "That cannot be. The One is not here this night. He has forsaken all of us."

Rhiss shook his head vigorously. "Not so, Lady Kerian. My companion and I are proof of that. He has gone ahead to seek the Queen's rescue."

Her head snapped up, eyes alight in sudden hope. "The Queen lives? You *know* this?"

"Well... aye," Rhiss replied hesitantly, taken aback by her reaction.

She clutched his arm fiercely. "You *are* sure?" she pressed. "I thought her dead with her husband and son."

Rhiss allowed himself a small smile. "To my certain knowledge, they are alive even now."

She sagged, weak with relief. "Thank the One," she murmured, then looked up. "And your quest is their rescue?"

"Aye, with my comrade. I swear it."

"Then some good may come from this night's evil, after all," she mused. "Your pardon, my lord, for my hasty words earlier. Perhaps you *are* sent by the One."

Rhiss coloured at the praise. "Come, this way. We must rejoin my colleague."

She followed him through the arch and into the square. Tariel was there, gazing about in exasperation and concern. "I was explicit that you were not to wander off, boy—" he began. Then he caught sight of the woman and broke off.

"Lady Kerian, handmaid to the Queen," Rhiss said, introducing them, "My comrade, Lord... uh... a fellow Knight in the service of the One."

She curtseyed deeply. "Pray, do not be angry with him, my lord. He saved my life and raised hope I will soon join the Queen."

Tariel raised his eyebrows. "I see. Well, then, we had best be on our way. Follow, please." He turned.

"One moment," she said, holding up a hand. Tariel swung to face her again. "Do such fair knights have no names?"

Rhiss looked helplessly at Tariel, who said smoothly, "None we care to divulge. For all our sakes, it is best you not know us. If you must have names, refer to me as Lord Altos and your rescuer as Lord Beltor. Now, make haste."

Kerian looked affronted, but said nothing. As they moved off, Rhiss whispered to Tariel, "What names are those?"

"Heroic characters from a famous Arrinoran legend. Some quiet eve, ask Arian for the story of 'The Five Companions.' It is quite an epic tale." He paused, then changed the subject, still speaking in low, conspiratorial tones. "This woman, Prince — are you aware who she is?"

Rhiss grimaced. "How could I not? I *thought* her my aunt who raised me following my mother's death. Now yet again, things are not what they seem. And I regret disobeying your instructions, but I could hardly ignore her screams."

"Of course not. You did rightly. Perhaps more than you can know."

"Really? There is more to this than meets the eye. How is it that the Queen's servant is also my aunt, my lord?"

Tariel glanced at the young woman following in their wake. "It must wait, because things are about to become very busy indeed. But you *have* introduced an interesting complication, I grant you. Keep the lady behind you, proceeding with caution. We approach the climax of our brief sojourn."

The devastation worsened as they advanced. Progress was slower, and unlike Tariel, Rhiss and Kerian were affected by the reek, coughing, choking and eyes tearing. Kerian, in particular, seemed near fainting. Rhiss was about to tell Tariel they could not go much further and must either rest or seek a different route, when a blazing, heavy oak beam crashed before them, shaking the ground, and they cowered in momentary panic. Showers of sparks issued from the beam, borne instantly aloft by a scorching updraft, and all were momentarily blinded. Another gust swept through, temporarily clearing the air, and in the sombre light, Rhiss caught sight of her: an attractive, dark-haired, slim young woman in a long dress of forest green. She clutched a bundle to her breast and seemed paralyzed by the beam's collapse, for even in her extreme peril, she stood rooted, casting desperate eyes this way and that, seeking sanctuary or help. In a dizzying flash of shocked surprise, Rhiss knew he beheld his mother carrying... his infant self. He quickly glanced at Kerian, but she was slumped on the ground, gasping and exhausted, eyes closed.

There was sudden movement beside him. Tariel looked where Rhiss stared, nodding in satisfaction. "Good. We are not too late." The young woman sank to her knees in despair, and Rhiss felt his heart fill with a deep and hopeless ache, an anguished longing to go to her, wrap his arms around her, and give comfort in the hellish nightmare's midst.

Tariel sensed it. "Do you wish to go to her, Prince?"

Rhiss turned to Tariel, panic-stricken. "I, Lord Tariel? I have never even spoken... what would I say?"

Tariel dropped his gaze. "I take your meaning. My apologies. It was thoughtless to suggest it. Remain here, and I will go. Once I have convinced her we are true, I will summon you."

As he strode off, Rhiss watched his mother glance at her bundle, then wearily stand. Tariel reached her at that moment, passing so close to a broken stretch of wall, it must have appeared to the terrified young woman that he materialized from within it. Rhiss saw Tariel stop and extend arms to her. He shook his head and spoke; she replied, although Rhiss could not hear what was said. He merely stood, transfixed. Acutely aware of how short their time in this place would be, he raptly drank in the sight of his mother, a woman he had no real recollection of, committing every part of her to memory.

Abruptly, Tariel turned to Rhiss, and beckoned. Rhiss bent to Kerian, gently shaking her. "Rouse, Lady Kerian. We have found the Queen."

It was a tonic as effective as Ruvennar. Kerian's eyes flew open, and she struggled to her feet, leaning on him for support. "Where, my lord?"

Rhiss gestured, and Kerian stumbled over the rubble. The two women embraced, joyfully cradling the infant prince between them. Rhiss followed slowly, stomach churning at the thought of actually meeting his mother face to face. She turned at his coming, gazing curiously, but he could not meet her eyes.

He stopped several feet away, bowing his head. She called softly, "Well met, sir. My maid informs me she owes you her life. You have her gratitude, and mine."

Unable to reply, Rhiss managed to lift his eyes to meet hers. Surprised, she stiffened slightly, then said doubtfully, "Do I know you, sir? You seem familiar."

Rhiss shifted in consternation; from the corner of his eye he sensed Tariel do likewise. Fighting down panic, he swallowed hard, replying hoarsely, "No, Majesty. We are not acquainted."

Tariel had evidently had enough, and Rhiss could see why: the line of conversation was dangerous. It would not be long before they inadvertently betrayed themselves.

"Come, ladies," Tariel said sternly. "There is no time for idle talk. That murderous rabble still hunts you, and is nearby. We will require the grace of the One to evade them. Follow and stay close." He turned abruptly, walking swiftly, not looking back to see whether they obeyed.

It seemed the women might not, because for some reason, they simply stood irresolute for several seconds, but at a shout from close by, they jumped in alarm, and ran after Tariel, nearly lost in smoke and darkness. Rhiss followed.

Breathing hard, they caught up quickly. Tariel had stopped, peering at the surroundings, head cocked to one side as though listening intently. Suddenly, he turned and headed in another direction, away from the outer walls.

"We must change our route," he called over his shoulder. "I wish to avoid someone nearby."

The Queen frowned. "What?" she demanded, obviously baffled at the nonsensical statement. But Rhiss knew to what Tariel referred: Maldeus was close.

Progress through smoke and flames remained torturously slow, until they arrived back at the wall. The Queen grew more agitated, and looked as though she would speak, when Tariel suddenly pointed at a spot ahead.

"There!" he said, grim satisfaction in his voice, and as the three of them followed Tariel's gesture, the women's eyes went wide with shock.

Embedded in the wall was a Portal door. Whether it belonged to Tariel or Gavrilos was not immediately obvious, but it appeared to be the same door Rhiss had seen and used several times, the dark, polished wood richly carved. As before, it looked firmly married to the wall, betraying no transience. The pearl doorknob halfway up the right side shone redly in the light of the fires.

Tariel turned to the Queen. "Go through yonder door, and leave this place of death. Beyond lies safety and the explanations you seek. Take maid and babe through, and live."

"But where—?" she began.

She was interrupted by triumphant yells of soldiers charging into the area behind them. Tariel muttered under his breath, swung round and calmly drew his sword in one flowing movement; Rhiss followed his example. "Behind us!" Tariel ordered as soldiers fanned out in a semicircle. "Open the door and go through!"

Although the women moved swiftly behind Rhiss, the Queen appeared inexplicably absorbed by the conflict. Instead of grasping the doorknob, she turned to watch, mesmerized, as the enemy soldiers charged and engaged Rhiss and Tariel. Rhiss had to focus on the enemy to the exclusion of all else, but Tariel turned his head and angrily hissed something at the Queen. Continuing to fight, he backed up several steps, a move Rhiss barely noticed in time to avoid being left alone in front.

Half a dozen shuffling backward steps left them squeezed in a knot before the Portal. Tariel motioned with his free hand, but before the Queen could take any action, bowmen poured into the area. Although unhurt, Tariel stiffened as if struck. Then Rhiss felt it too, like a slimy cloak draping his mind in smothering dark, and he understood: Maldeus had arrived.

An archer fired, the arrow striking the Queen's arm; she screamed, and Rhiss turned in panic to see Kerian protectively grab his mother to prevent her from dropping the baby and falling.

Tariel turned angrily. "Open the door! I cannot do it for you. You must choose to do so!"

The Queen started to speak, but Kerian cut her off, gesturing at the baby. "Give me the child, and, for love of the One, do as he says, Majesty!"

Tariel raised a hand, palm out, and swept the area in front in a semicircular gesture. Immediately, the haze intensified and the air visibly changed. Rhiss narrowed his eyes, fascinated at the display of raw power, unable to resist the temptation to lift his sword and test what his eyes told him was there. Several feet in front, his sword tip encountered resistance, as though the very air had thickened like gelatin or the marmalade he used to spread on his morning toast, although the air remained transparent and breathable. Judging from soldiers' reactions, thickened air extended fifteen or twenty feet from Tariel, as he waved his hand back and forth like a fireman spraying water on a blaze. Soldiers entering the zone had their movements slowed to a crawl, as if they struggled through an invisible spider web.

Behind, Kerian snatched the infant from the fainting Queen. Tariel turned and placed a gloved hand on her brow. Silently, he closed his eyes for several moments. Rhiss felt the merest hint of a wave of healing energy passing from Tariel to the Queen. The effect was immediate, and she looked at Tariel with timid awe.

"Who are you?" she whispered. "*What* have you done?"

"Friends, as I said," Tariel replied. "No time for more. Explanations will come once you pass through." He glanced at the soldiers. "The door, if you please! My defences will not last long against the forces arrayed here. Your delaying endangers us all."

Dazed, she finally moved to obey. The doorknob turned smoothly in her hand, the door opened, and candlelight flared in the corridor. Rhiss felt an odd homesickness as he beheld sculpted hand sconces holding the candles: it was the Portal of Gavrilos. Through it he had entered Arrinor, scant weeks — or a lifetime — ago. But the Queen's reaction was understandably different. She turned back to Tariel.

"This is no ordinary door," she said accusingly. "Where would you have us go?"

"To safety," Tariel said grimly. "And quickly. You must trust me. My shield weakens; I cannot maintain it much longer. Choose whether to enter or stay here. However, if you remain, you do so alone, for we will not linger. Then those soldiers will finish what they started, you and yours perishing." He glanced at her wryly. "I grant there is little choice. But I have your best interests at heart, as will a colleague of mine beyond that corridor. Come, my shield is almost spent. Choose."

The Queen stood, obviously undecided, then looked at the soldiers working towards them. The infant Rhiss gave a soft whimper, and she sighed, shaking her head.

"Enough, Knight of the One. I yield, trusting you do not send us to a worse fate."

"I do not," Tariel replied quietly. "Go with the One."

Their eyes met. "Will you not come also? I would not have you meet your deaths here."

Tariel shook his head. "There is no danger of that. But we are needed elsewhere, and may not follow you."

"Will we meet again, sir? There is much I would know..."

Tariel gave one of his wintry smiles. "Who can say? We may meet again, if the One allows. Now, stop delaying. Go."

She nodded. "My gratitude, Deliverers." She looked warmly at Rhiss, and stepped through. Kerian followed, pulling the door. It closed with a very solid bang, melting into the wall. Rhiss had never seen a Portal disappear before. But he recalled his surroundings, and turned. The air suddenly returned to its normal state, to the soldiers' confusion. Tariel raised his sword in scornful salute, smiling humourlessly at Maldeus across the clearing.

"Too slow, as usual," he taunted. "This night's bloody work has failed. Crawl back to that warped creature you have made Sovereign — who naively thinks to be the undisputed conqueror in this — and explain, if you dare, that the seeds of defeat have been sown even in the midst of seeming victory." He lowered his sword, mockingly inclining his head. "Until our next meeting." He turned to Rhiss, whispering, "Brace yourself. This will feel very odd."

Before Rhiss could react, a gust of wind, hot and dry as dust, came out of nowhere, blowing across them both. To the consternation of the watching soldiers, the pair simply wafted away with it, like the many other tendrils of smoke tattered and rent in the confused air of the conflagration.

But to Rhiss, it felt like sand blowing in him, through him. There was a nauseating sensation of being thrust backwards, weightless, against the wall, without impact. All went momentarily dark, and the nausea was replaced by a curious feeling of total disembodiment, of being no more than a curl of stray smoke borne on a hot draught of air.

Then he was himself again, solid and swaying slightly in dizziness, steadied by Tariel, standing... somewhere else. Rhiss looked about, attempting to grasp what had happened. They were still in the castle grounds, just... not where they had been. He turned to Tariel in stunned amazement, eyes wide. "Sweet Light of the One! What did you do?"

———◆———

The soldiers approached the spot where Rhiss and Tariel had disappeared, glancing at Maldeus for guidance. Irritated at their timidity, he brusquely motioned them back even as he strode to see for himself. Reaching the spot where the door had been moments ago, he stopped and extended a hand, feeling the stone surface. But there was nothing. Everything connected to that miserable meddler Tariel had indeed disappeared beyond all finding.

Maldeus sucked in breath sharply. Tariel spoke truth, however unpalatable. The Queen had escaped to Gavrilos with maid and child, and there was no telling where or when he would send them. Aside from the mother's survival, more important was a painful realization: with the infant prince's life spared, the Royal Family's massacre was incomplete. Worse, in fact; it was abject failure. The Prince could surface anytime in the future, threatening to undo all accomplished that night. Maldeus had no intentions of sharing the full story with Diiderra: that would be most undesirable, could even jeopardize his work thus far.

Standing before that blank stone wall, he softly hissed his displeasure, strangely unpleasant eyes gleaming momentarily with an unearthly light all their own.

What to do? Well, he must return to the central keep to report a suitably edited version of the night's events. *She* would expect it. He reviewed the chain of happenings, deciding what to share. But he stopped in the midst of his ruminations, one anomaly suddenly coming to the fore: who accompanied Tariel? It was most unlike him to work with anyone, whether accomplice or apprentice. Vestments notwithstanding, it had not been another Arkos: he knew all the disgusting, servile creatures. Very strange.

Maldeus touched the wall again, casting deeper, looking for traces of the passing or presence of Tariel and his companion. Nothing... blank stone... hold! A faint imprint... like one he had sensed a short while ago in the throne chamber. It was not Tariel's; in fact, it tasted almost... mortal.

Maldeus narrowed his eyes. Stranger and stranger; what could the meddler possibly be up to? Through long ages, Maldeus had come to know that nothing Tariel did was without deeper purpose. There must be a compelling reason for Tariel's consorting with a mortal.

He must know. Spreading his senses wider, further, outward, he would find out — he hissed again, knowledge flooding in: Tariel was *not* gone. He — and presumably, the other knight, the mortal — were still within the castle precincts. Perhaps it was yet possible to pursue and discover what mischief they engaged in. But he would do it himself. Pointless taking the rabble now cowering, awaiting orders.

Without a word to the soldiers clustered at a safe distance, aware of their uneasy stares, Maldeus snapped his fingers and disappeared in a jetting spiral of flame. While it made for a rather flashy exit, the terrified reactions more than justified the theatrics. After all, it was always appropriate to ensure servants displayed a healthy fear of authority. It encouraged discipline and prompt obedience. And of course fear, in and of itself, was *always* a good and useful thing.

———◆———

Tariel raised an eyebrow in mild reproof. "Calm yourself, Prince. There is no need to resort to such language."

Rhiss coloured. "I am sorry, my lord, but I am rather rattled. Did I imagine it, or did we pass through a solid wall?"

Tariel smiled. "Several. And I understand your discomfort. Actually, I commend your restraint, knowing it is nothing experience has prepared you for. But we had to leave swiftly; I did not wish to fight Maldeus with you there."

Rhiss looked about. "Are we still within the castle?"

"Aye. Now we have a moment's leisure, I can summon my Portal to return us to your present. I am sure you have seen enough and are exhausted after what you have witnessed."

"But, my lord—" Rhiss stopped, confused.

"Aye, Prince?" Tariel looked at him impassively.

"I feel as though... we are not finished. I cannot explain *why*, but... must we leave *now*?"

Tariel studied Rhiss with that soul-penetrating gaze. "Why would you have us remain?"

"I don't know." Rhiss felt foolish. "But I am possessed of the strong conviction we have, somehow, not done what we came for."

Tariel shrugged. "I am in no great hurry to return to your present, but if you cannot explain how we profit by remaining, we should leave. We have seen what I wished to show—"

A pair of very different interruptions cut him off. One was physical, a scream of purest agony; the other, a mental bolt of entwined malice and pleasure. Rhiss winced at the intensity of both, and Tariel looked swiftly around, as though he could locate the interruptions through sight alone.

"What is it?" Rhiss demanded. He had a strong suspicion, having felt that mental pulse before.

Tariel held up a hand for silence, then swung to face Rhiss, features grim. "What you *felt* is Maldeus, as you doubtless knew. Unfortunately, he has learned we are still here—"

"How?" Rhiss interrupted. "Have I given us away with an undamped Essence?"

Tariel shook his head. "This is not like the Throne Room earlier. It relies on a... a different skill I have not time to explain. Feel no guilt on that account. But Maldeus *is* coming to investigate. Well, in his rage he intends far more than that." Tariel paused. "As to what you *heard*, it is likely more butchery from his murderous swine."

Rhiss opened his mouth to speak, but sounds of combat and more screams came, and he winced again. "How long before he arrives, my lord?" he asked urgently.

"Less than a minute. Why?"

"Because I cannot stand by and do nothing but listen! It will haunt me the rest of my life if I cannot aid those innocents. Do not look at me like that! I know you said we must not change the past, but I *will* not have their deaths on my conscience. I am resolved to go to their aid. I can make a difference — and it is the right thing to do!" He stopped, glaring challengingly.

Tariel nodded. "Very well. I hear your determination and will allow this. But I cannot assist: Maldeus comes. What would you have me do?"

Rhiss licked dry lips, thinking quickly. "Look you, my lord: can you divert Maldeus away from here?"

"Aye, but... do you propose to single-handedly rescue the nearby unfortunates?" Tariel shook his head vehemently. "You cannot be serious! Much evil has already occurred, and now you propose a course that could result in your death!"

Rhiss shrugged. "What else can we do? I am adamant. I wish Aquilea was here, but she is not, so there's an end. Come, what say you? We waste precious moments."

Tariel looked inclined to argue, but threw his hands up in resignation. "I cannot spend more time debating. Maldeus comes. Farewell, Prince. Once I have dealt with him, I will seek your Essence, hoping to find it still in Arrinor. Go you with the One!" He seemed to turn sideways, then vanished, wafting away like a tendril of smoke.

Rhiss had no time to appreciate the sight, for sounds of combat were very near. He freed his sword from its sheath, and took his dagger in his other hand. Heart pounding, he sprinted towards the noise: he was on his own again, like Rontha, no allies supporting him. Tariel was gone, and Aquilea... would not be born for many years. He ran through an archway into another courtyard and disbelievingly skidded to a stop.

A massacre was in progress, an unimaginably ghastly one even in light of the shocking events already witnessed. The air was heavy with the sickly-sweet, coppery stench of blood, the ground slippery with it. A score of bodies, gruesomely mutilated or dismembered, lay sprawled in grisly disorder. Rhiss realized with dawning horror the victims were *children*, some as young as three or four. Stomach heaving, he nearly gagged, but a child screamed and he forced himself to focus on ending the abomination.

Half a dozen Castellars gathered in a semicircle around the current victim, standing over her, laughing uproariously. One of their number knelt on top of the terrified child, knife out, cutting away her clothes. At least a dozen more children lay petrified, bound hand and foot in a line on the ground.

White-hot rage filled Rhiss, and before he was consciously aware of it, his dagger reversed in his hand and he hurled it at the beast engaged in his hideous sport. It hit the Castellar squarely in the back, and he toppled soundlessly to one side. The child he tormented had just enough presence of mind to roll away as the body came crashing down.

The Castellar's fellows stood frozen in uncomprehending shock for only a second or two, but even that small delay proved their fatal undoing. Rhiss closed the gap between them with a speed that compared favourably with Tariel's abilities, a single thought in mind: to eliminate the vermin who would do such things. Then he was upon them, and two were dead before they even understood they were under attack. The other four scrambled back, out of the way. They reached for their weapons, seeking and appraising the threat.

The Castellar furthest left gaped at Rhiss' darkly murderous expression and the white tunic emblazoned with the insignia of the Three. Not without justification, he thought himself confronted by an avenging angel. "By the One!" he cried. "An Arkos! We are undone!"

As he fell to his knees, his colleague snarled inarticulately and slashed, killing him instantly. The remaining knights launched themselves at Rhiss, but a child on the ground, with amazing presence of mind, lifted bound legs and tripped a Castellar. The man crashed down, cursing and flailing hands in a vain effort to remain upright.

Rhiss was hard put to it as the other two attacked. "No Arkos, only a rash young knight!" one shouted after several seconds, and the other chimed in, "Fatal mistake, boy! Don't you know who we are?"

The tripped Castellar regained his feet and began rushing to the aid of his fellows. Rhiss felt icy clarity penetrate his rage. He was barely holding off two; when the third joined, he could not survive against them all.

A harsh cry thundered overhead, and a mighty downdraft of cold, clear night air smote everyone. There came the sound of huge, rushing wings, and he had a confused vision of gigantic shapes slamming to the ground.

One seized a Castellar in an immense beak and leaped back into the air, still holding the feebly struggling knight. A second slashed enormous, razor-sharp talons at another Castellar, raking his body. The force of the blow spun the man around, and Rhiss saw him go down, the front of his body rent with deep, bloody gashes, his expression in death one of stunned surprise. Rhiss took advantage of the distraction to drive his sword deep into the last Castellar's chest. The man had barely time to gasp before he, too, died, and it was all over.

Rhiss fell on hands and knees, breathing hard. A young child's corpse lay upturned beside him, face still contorted in silent terror, open eyes staring vacantly into the darkness, and this time he could not control his stomach's heaving.

When finished, he spat, tasting sour harshness, then became conscious of being watched. Warily, he sat on his haunches and looked up, wondering what new monstrosity had arrived.

Two enormous, golden eyes, each larger than his fist, gazed alertly, intelligence plainly visible. Beholding the rest of the creature, his jaw dropped in astonishment: sleek body, half-eagle, half-lion, but longer than three or four men laid end to end; wingspan at least forty feet from wingtip to wingtip. It was like seeing Aquilea magnified many times over.

It had to be a gryphon major. Or two, he amended, glimpsing another behind the first, each larger than any flying creature he had ever seen. And even as that registered, a third landed, shaking the ground. They truly were as massively impressive as Tobias had said. Awestruck, Rhiss gazed on them, almost forgetting to breathe. He had once seen a Vickers Vimy bomber at an exhibition after the War and had been firmly convinced it was the very pinnacle of flight when lumbering through the air. But it absolutely paled into insignificance compared with the living spectacle now before him.

The first gryphon opened its beak, a rumbling bass voice issuing forth, unmistakably male. "Who summoned us?"

Rhiss could not find voice. The gryphon waited, cocked its head to one side in a gesture poignantly reminiscent of Aquilea, and spoke again, looking directly at Rhiss.

"Was it you, child of the One?"

"I... what?" Rhiss said huskily. "Did I what?"

The gryphon did not bother answering, but made a deep humming noise in its throat, gazing intently. "A child of the One; a mortal, clad as an Arkos. A son of the House of Araxan, battling the very Castellars supposed to serve him; but Castellars engaged in despicable barbarism, the likes of which I have seen seldom in all my years. And... a human Companion Guardian also, I see. So many contradictions in such a young human... more than usual, even for a mortal. What an interesting youth, to be certain." The creature seemed to be talking to itself; Rhiss was at a total loss as to what, or any, reply he should make. The gryphon solved the problem for him. It shook its head, as though clearing it of all musings, and addressed him.

"Your name, Child of the Light?"

"Rhiss... Rhissan, son of Tovan... Lord of the Air."

A low, reverberating sound, unmistakably a chuckling laugh, emanated from the creature. "I need no title, young one. We do not generally stand on ceremony the way your kind does. I am Angharath; that is sufficient." It paused. "But... Rhissan, you say? *Prince* Rhissan? Of House Araxan?" Rhiss nodded reluctantly, and the creature continued, slowly moving its head from side to side in a hypnotic, almost serpentine manner. "Strange; unsettling. How can a human be at once child newly born *and* a man in the flower of youth? What sorcery is this?"

Rhiss opened his mouth, then closed it in confusion. He was unsure what to say, what Tariel would approve of. But whether the gryphon divined his thoughts, or reached its own conclusion, it suddenly relaxed and chuckled again. "Ah. Not sorcery, I see. But you are clad as the Arkos. Am I to understand one of them works with you this night, and is responsible for this paradox?" Rhiss nodded again, wondering how the gryphon could possibly know. It swept its gaze around the open space. "But not present now? I thought not. They tend to come and go without so much as a by-your-leave, do they not? No doubt he will suddenly return when he feels it convenient, without explanation, either." It laughed a third time, light tone belying the complaint. "And I see the answer to my own question within you. It *was* you who summoned us."

"Me? Forgive me, my lor— Angharath. I did not. Your very existence was unknown to me, much less your presence."

"Of course you did. But not us specifically. You called your own small one, didn't you? And we heard, thinking you called us. Where is your small one?"

"She is... safe, but not here, Angharath."

Angharath glanced about. "It is well *we* heard, then. You seemed in need of assistance when we arrived."

Guiltily, Rhiss realized what he had been doing before the gryphons' coming, and why. "The children! Your pardon, Angharath. I must see to them." He strode quickly to the children, and within moments had them all freed. But they shrank together in a knot, wide-eyed at gryphons towering over them on one side and the tall, grim knight on the other, plainly traumatized at what they had endured, and unsure whether the situation had improved. Rhiss spoke in low, soothing tones, trying to ease their fears. He was successful in the main, for they settled appreciably, some even allowing themselves to be comforted. But appalled at the surroundings, Rhiss decided the children must quickly be removed from the charnel house the castle resembled. How to move a dozen terrified children safely, with fighting still raging? And where to take them, once transport was arranged?

Rhiss wistfully recalled the Portal his mother and aunt had vanished into, wishing for Tariel's return. But minutes sped by with no sign of the Arkos. Where could he be? Locked in combat with Maldeus? Rhiss shivered at the thought. In the meantime, something must be done — but what? He glanced at the motionless gryphons, and sudden inspiration struck. Would Tariel approve? He must. The situation called for immediate initiative, and the Arkos was nowhere to be found. In his absence, Rhiss must decide. He made up his mind, put down a small child who had climbed into his lap for reassurance, and walked to the waiting gryphons.

"Angharath?" he said, nervously licking his lips. "May I make a request? I seek nothing for myself, but am desperate for these children."

The gryphon regarded him levelly. "Ask, Prince Rhissan."

"It is vital to remove them from here immediately. They have been terrorized by what they have endured, and I do not want them to stay another moment, forced to stare at corpses of friends and relatives. But I cannot safely shepherd them through the castle, for renegade Castellar are at large, and this inferno burns unchecked." He paused, taking a deep breath. "Could they... would it be possible to... fly them out... on you?"

The gryphons swiftly exchanged unreadable glances before Angharath turned back to Rhiss. "It is not usually done," the gryphon rumbled. "In fact, 'tis rarely done. But we understand your need, Prince. Always it is the young and innocent who suffer for misdeeds of their elders." Angharath nodded his great head. "And you have taken in one of our small cousins, nurturing her at great personal risk. Very well. We will transport the small ones to safety, if you can persuade them to mount." He looked at the children doubtfully. "But it may be easier said than done."

His words proved depressingly accurate. Many children were so traumatized that the idea of climbing onto the gigantic creatures was too much, even though the only alternatives were burning to death or being murdered by Castellars; tears and hysterics resulted. Keeping a wary eye on the approaching conflagration, Rhiss tried reason and reassurance, to no avail. Despairingly, he cast his gaze to the heavens. It was only a matter of time before death descended, either by fire or at sword point.

He felt an urgent tug on his tunic, and looked down. It was the boy who had tripped the Castellar, likely saving Rhiss from death. "Your pardon, my lord. I think I can persuade them to mount yon beasts."

Rhiss was about to tell him to sit back down, but something in the child's demeanour halted him. He knelt on one knee, the better to study the boy, who was relatively tall for his age, and already possessed a fair but hefty look, suggesting he would be a strong man when grown. He had suffered a nasty cut above one eye for his recent troubles, and having neither time nor energy to heal it, Rhiss had bound it roughly with cloth torn from a dead Castellar's robe. Contrasting sharply with his thatch of dark hair, the white bandage was blood-soaked, the lad's entire face dirty and bruised; but despite the bedraggled appearance, his eyes were not filled with the terrible despair and defeat of many of the children. There was anguish, certainly, but still a spark of vitality — and hope. All in all, Rhiss thought, much promise.

"Indeed?" he queried softly. "Your name, boy?"

"Borilius, sir." The boy squared his shoulders, adding proudly, "A royal page to the King." His expression fell as he suddenly realized what he had said. "Or *was*, before these foul oath-breakers—" he indicated the dead Castellars "—before they..." He stopped, unable to continue, struggling with tears.

"I understand," Rhiss said quietly. To distract the boy from his grief, he went on. "But young squire, at great risk to yourself, you rendered invaluable assistance. Without your aid, we would not be having this conversation. I am deeply in your debt. You have my thanks, and my assurance I *will* remember."

The boy flushed with pleasure. "I did what I could, sir. Not that it looked like you needed assistance, of course."

Rhiss smiled in spite of himself. "I see. How old are you, Borilius the royal page, so sure of yourself that others will do your bidding?"

"Thirteen, my lord." Borilius straightened. "They'll do as I say, wait and see." Sensing explanation was required, he added, "I'm oldest and leader in our games. A royal page, too. So they're used to taking direction from me."

Rhiss nodded, amused, and gestured towards the children, coughing as smoke wafted towards them. "Very well, Borilius the royal page. It shall be as you propose. Introduce me quickly to your charges, then marshal them on the gryphons, and let's be away before death comes calling with flame or steel. The castle is consumed, and we must be gone with no more delay."

Rhiss moved over by the gryphons, letting Borilius take charge. The boy quickly and confidently dispensed a stern word here, a reassuring hug there, and in barely more than a minute, all the children were named for Rhiss, and nearly all were mounted on the gryphons' broad backs; some needed assistance as the smoke thickened and made it harder to breathe. They firmly clutched the luxuriant fur, and even if ill at ease, they were at least stoic. Rhiss was amazed and impressed at the leadership of Borilius.

Apparently he was not alone. Angharath swung his head close and said quietly, so only Rhiss could hear, "Your young apprentice shows great promise, Prince Rhissan."

Rhiss looked around in surprise. The creature's breath smelled faintly of cloves, and was quite pleasant. "Apprentice?" he repeated. "No, Angharath, you are mistaken. I have never met this boy before."

The gryphon continued as though Rhiss had said nothing. "Aye, give him time to reach manhood, proper training along the way, and he will make a fine leader, mark me."

Rhiss wanted to ask about apprentices, but Angharath's remark gave him sudden inspiration. "Tell me, Angharath, do you know a place where that could be managed? A place where these children could grow in a safe, nurturing environment, eventually taking their place and helping right the wrongs done this night?"

The gryphon considered. "Hmm," it rumbled thoughtfully. "Perhaps. You ask much, Prince: a dozen young ones, none ready to leave the nest. They would require much care." It paused. "But there may be a place, or a way. I will think on it and consult my colleagues as we fly."

Rhiss looked around. The last child mounted its gryphon. He moved closer to Angharath, saying softly, "One other thing, my friend. The children do not know who I truly am. No one this night does. It was Lord Tariel's wish we not make ourselves known. I would appreciate you not using my name in their hearing."

The giant creature turned its head sideways, gazing at Rhiss. "I understand, young Prince. It shall be as you ask." It shook its great head. "But mount now. You are the last, and we must be swiftly away. At the least, we will take you to a place of safety. More may be decided later."

Rhiss looked at the devastation all about, shaking his head grimly at the monumental evil perpetrated. One day, he thought. One day, it would be — must be — put to rights. But the time for that was not now, not with the lives of many helpless innocents in his hands. Aye. His first responsibility was to the children, to get them to safety. Wordlessly, he climbed onto the gryphon major's back, and the next challenge.

XVII

FLIGHT AND MENTORS

"The Servants of the One are found everywhere in His Creation. Bidden or unbidden, they are present in every moment, on every mountain top, in every dell, even unto the deep places of the world. Are ye troubled and sore afraid? Seek ye then the Servants of the One."

The Book of the One, 3:36: 41-42
(Cantos 3, Chapter 36, Verses 41-42)

Rhiss settled in the space behind the great wings, where bird's feathers gave way to lion's fur amidst huge, chorded muscles. Although he had seen it in Aquilea, of course, the enlarged scale transition from bird to animal was smoother and less peculiar than Rhiss would have supposed. He clutched a handful of feathers, leaning forward. "Please remember none of us have ever done anything remotely like this, my friend," he called. "And these children have undergone a terrible ordeal already tonight."

The gryphon laughed quietly, cocking its head to one side. "Well do I know that. We will be as gentle as we may. I would not wish the young ones to fall off, but you should know that archers fired on us as we answered your summons and landed. If we must evade their arrows on the ascent, our flying could become a trifle erratic." The gryphon crouched. "But I think you will find it a glorious experience to feel the cool night wind on your face as we soar high over the land, laid out below as though in a child's game." Angharath suddenly leapt into the sky, wings beating gracefully. Rhiss felt a very strange, hollow sensation in the pit of his stomach, and involuntarily gasped. The other two gryphons took their cue from Angharath, likewise jumping aloft.

Rhiss had long thought that galloping on horseback must be rather like flying... floating along in a dreamy fashion... but he swiftly discovered that he could not have been more wrong. He had never in his life flown in an aeroplane — they were almost the stuff of myth until the War, and even afterwards, were not a normal part of the average person's life — and had never been higher off the ground or travelled faster in anything moving than the back of a horse, or seated comfortably inside a train carriage. This... this unnatural climbing hundreds of feet into the sky, unsurrounded by walls, unsecured by any kind of strap or restraint, was nothing short of petrifying. He kept his eyes firmly shut, fighting down the queasy feeling in his empty but deeply unhappy stomach.

But eventually, it occurred to him that, if he was terrified, as an intelligent, rational, grown man, what hysterical alarm must the children be experiencing? Resolutely, he opened his eyes and looked around, prepared to try and give reassurance he did not feel.

Borilius was staring wide-eyed at the lands below, an incredulous smile on his face. He became aware of Rhiss watching him, lifted his face, and gave a whoop of pure delight.

Rhiss felt shame wash over him like a scalding, disgusting skin. A mere boy did not flinch or cower at this marvel, and yet a King was near to mindless panic. He determined to try and master his fear, and gradually, he had to admit that the sensation of flying was exhilarating. They ascended first through smouldering reek and smoke, grim evidence of the Coup. Fortunately, however, they were not fired upon, and in moments they rose above the ash and burning embers, borne aloft on warm thermal currents.

The gryphons climbed in a slow spiral over the city, levelling only when the ground was hundreds of feet below. Rhiss could take in the immense vista afforded him by his perch, and his eyes opened wide with wonder. To his surprise, the moon shone above the clouds, illuminating much of the land in a soft, silvery radiance. To the west lay a huge lake or river or coastline — he was unsure which — foamy white waves contrasting against the waters' inky blackness. And below was the city. It was indeed like looking down on a child's play set, although on a much vaster scale. Kilarradine lay sprawled in a haphazard jumble of buildings and streets, interspersed with green spaces. Then they were over the walls and flying above farmers' fields.

They flew silently for what seemed hours, although there was no way to measure time's passage. The wind grew very cold, and Rhiss was chilled even in his cloak. What the children felt, he could only guess. He turned again to see them huddled behind, two with eyes closed against the night air. Borilius looked at him, weary but resolute, and Rhiss smiled reassuringly.

"Hold fast. We are nearly there," he called, even though he had no idea how much longer they must cling to the gryphon's back. The boy nodded wordlessly, and Rhiss wondered whether he should speak to Angharath. The gryphon had remained mute throughout the long flight, wings beating a slow, steady tattoo against the winds.

But he was spared the necessity. Five minutes later, there was a distinct change in their angle of flight. Together, the gryphons began a slow, gently curving glide downwards to dark forests below. Rhiss strained his eyes in the moonlight to see what they descended towards — there must be a clearing, he thought. Surely they were not going to land among densely packed trees.

They did not. Rhiss had a confused image of coming down fast into a wide, open space fringed by very odd-looking trees, tall, angular and wide, with no visible branches at all. Then the gryphons landed, alighting far more gently than at Tor Eylian when answering the summons Rhiss had unwittingly sent. As he was able to properly see what fringed the clearing, Rhiss gave a sharp intake of breath: they were not trees at all, but a ring of Way Stones, like the ones at Storrenne. In fact, were they not in the midst of a forest, Rhiss would have sworn he *was* at Storrenne.

"Angharath?" he queried, dismounting. "This place looks much like one I have seen before, but that one is located on the edge of a barren moor—"

"Aye. That would be Byrn Moor, as you humans name it." The gryphon turned its great head around to face Rhiss. "Quite a fair distance from here, Prin—" It stopped, and Rhiss realized it had belatedly recalled his request. "What do you wish to be known as, Child of the One?"

Rhiss thought. "Well... Lord Beltor, if you please."

The gryphon's enormous golden eyes widened, and Rhiss thought with brief amusement that had it possessed eyebrows, they would undoubtedly have arched as well. "The name of a valiant warrior from an ancient tale in the mythologies of your race, young human. Do you claim kinship or similar ability?"

Rhiss grinned sheepishly. "Not at all. I am not nearly so vain, believe me. It was Lord Tariel's suggestion, Angharath. A servant at Tor Eylian asked our names, and he introduced himself as Lord Altos and me as Lord Beltor. I do not know the story, but I will hear it when opportunity presents."

"The name is passable, I suppose," rumbled the gryphon, "but among my people, the Arkos are not always regarded as particularly poetic, and I see you are not comfortable being named a hero from ancient myth." It stopped, eyeing him speculatively. "The names *we* bear emanate directly from our Essences, and have little in common with the harsh sounding noises humans use to label each other and the things around you. In recognition of what you have done for these nestlings this night, and for the small one of our kind whom I see in your heart — your love for her shines forth clearly — I would do you honour. I name you—" Angharath paused and trilled a series of musical notes, a complex phrasing causing Rhiss to shiver involuntarily at its beauty. "There," resumed the gryphon. "Among my kind, that is who you are, from now until the End, although even it does not do the name justice. It flows better in the thoughts we exchange with each other. Know that it is a singular privilege, conferred on very few of your race."

Rhiss felt deeply moved. "I am honoured, Angharath," he said, smiling ruefully. "But to my eternal regret, I doubt I could ever pronounce it as you have. Your language sounds marvellously complex and beautiful compared to the harsh crudeness of mine."

"In your tongue, it is pronounced 'Kairconnach-lan.' As you say, when said thus, I fear it loses much grace and charm, but..." The gryphon cocked its head to one side and left the rest of its thought unsaid. Somehow, Rhiss felt as though it had shrugged.

"Why did you choose that name for me?"

"Why, it is who you are." Angharath's tone indicated that the answer was patently obvious. "There *is* no other name for you. I see you before me, and your Essence shines with that one. You could not be anything else."

"Then I accept it gratefully." Rhiss bowed low.

"Very well, Kairconnach-lan," rumbled the gryphon. "You mentioned the stones of Storrenne. Do you know them well?"

Rhiss raised an eyebrow. "Moderately," he responded wryly. "I have had significant experiences there, and would have sworn this place was its twin. Are they of similar ancestry and make?"

Angharath regarded him thoughtfully. "Evidently, your knowledge of Arrinor is limited, Kairconnach-lan. A paradox, but then again, you seem enveloped in several. There are a number of Circles such as this in Arrinor. Those I have seen are practically identical. Storrenne is one. This one, Kirunek, is another. But I do not know how many there be in total, who put them there, or much of their history. It is not something gryphons concern ourselves with, for human affairs are not ours, and we are not eager to meddle. I know they seem connected to the Arkos in some manner. But wherever they are found, the Stones are wholesome places where goodness resides and evil is reluctant to tread, so we make use of them now and again when circumstances make it desirable or necessary. But perhaps you had best dismount the nestlings and see to their needs."

It took Rhiss a moment to realize Angharath referred to the children. "Oh... aye, of course." He turned, and there they were, still huddled together, looking at him wearily but patiently. "Come, Borilius, the royal page," he called. "Assist me in helping the others down, if you please. Our journey is over for a while."

The children clambered down stiffly, and once on the ground, clustered in a group, looking around with wide eyes. Rhiss cast his own gaze about, knowing instinctively that what they needed was a warm fire and a hot drink. But there was nothing in the circle to provide either.

"Angharath? I don't suppose you might have means of making fire, would you?"

Angharath slowly shook his great head. "We are gryphons, Kairconnach-lan, not dragons. We have many useful abilities, but breathing fire is not one of them."

"Hmm." Disappointed, but not really surprised, Rhiss set the children to gathering deadwood on the ground, first cautioning them not to go beyond sight of the stones. Angharath assured him no dangerous animals were in the circle's immediate vicinity, but Rhiss did not want to tempt fate any more this night. Getting the children to procure firewood was really to keep them moving and busy more than anything, although he was determined they should have a fire, even if he must strike stones together to generate a spark. But before he was ready to attempt fire, circumstances changed.

The gryphons noticed seconds before Rhiss. In fact, their sudden uneasy shifting and turning alerted him to something amiss. He strode quickly to Angharath, about to seek explanation, when the outline of a man suddenly materialized from the gloom beyond the stones. Rhiss muttered an oath, fearing the worst, and had his sword in hand at once.

But before he could issue any challenge, Tariel's welcome voice floated calmly through the cold night air. "Lower your sword, young man. I have had quite enough of combat for one night." There was a pause while Tariel approached. "Not to mention that it would frighten the children and puzzle your new-found friends," he said dryly, stopping before Rhiss. "Speaking of which, I begin to understand Seir-onna Arian's chagrin every time she is parted from you, then returns to find you have either made acquaintance with exotic beings or engaged in acts of foolhardy courage. And I continue to be both amused and amazed at your faculty of sewing unlikely new threads in the tapestry that is your life's journey. Had I known you would unknowingly manage to summon a trio of gryphon majors, who just happened to be flying by at that precise moment, then ride them to safety with the children you rescued — well, I do not know what I would have done. Bravo. I would have certainly tried ridding myself of Maldeus sooner, that I might have been present to witness such goings on."

"Then, you *were* able to prevent Maldeus following us?" Rhiss said eagerly.

"Obviously." Tariel turned to the gryphon still crouched beside Rhiss. "Angharath, old friend! A pleasure to see you again, to be sure."

The gryphon bowed its head. "For me also, Glorious Servant. It has been too long since last we met, by the reckoning of both our races."

"Indeed it has," said Tariel warmly. "Tell me, Angharath, is your revered mother still Matriarch of your clan?"

"Alas, no. She has gone to join the One. My sister now holds the Claim."

"Most worthily, beyond doubt," Tariel, inclining his head. He turned to Rhiss. "So, Prince—"

"Lord Beltor, if you please, Lord Altos," Rhiss interrupted, tossing his head meaningfully at the children nearby. "Or if you prefer, Kairconnach-lan."

Tariel's eyebrows arched, and he actually looked faintly impressed. "Indeed? A great honour bestowed upon you. Gryphons rarely name humans in their own tongue. Evidently you made a very favourable impression." He paused. "And I am sure you have things well in hand." His eyes swept the clearing. "Although why are the children cold and unfed?"

Rhiss dropped his eyes, embarrassed. "I apologize for my failure, my lord. I was attempting to light a fire—"

Tariel held up a hand and smiled. "Now, now, none of that, young man. You must learn that even an Arkos can have a sense of humour, and I have been teasing you. No apology is necessary over your conduct tonight. You have performed admirably. May I assist in providing for the children?"

Rhiss sighed in relief. "That would be most welcome."

"Very well." Tariel looked around. "Now, where is the fire ring?" Rhiss looked puzzled, and he elaborated. "All Way Stones have fire rings, Kairconnach-lan, and other interesting features as well, some of which you already know. Others you will become aware of in time, I am sure. For now... ah!" He saw the stones of the fire ring, and strode to it, Rhiss following. It was quite the twin of the one at Storrenne, and Rhiss was again absolutely sure it had not been there moments earlier. As before, Tariel placed his closed fist above the fire ring, splaying his fingers wide. The suggestion of something being dropped was unmistakable, although like last time, Rhiss saw nothing fall from the outstretched hand. However, silvery-blue flames erupted from the firewood, leaping in the ring, warm and bright. As though at a signal, the children all raced over, crowding around, warming themselves, and Rhiss smiled.

"All they need now is sustenance. Is there aught in the pantry that I hope Way Stones possess as well, Lord Tariel?"

"Why ask me? Can you not make provision for them?"

Rhiss was confused. "Well, I could go outside the Circle and hunt, but—"

Tariel interrupted. "No need for anything as crude as that. What would you serve them?" Rhiss looked blank. "What do you wish them to have? Think on it, then recall where your first gift in the Way Stones appeared at Storrenne. You may access the 'pantry' yourself, as you call it. You do not need me."

Rhiss thought. What would he want the children to have? Of course! Ruvennar! The cordial's restorative effects would be perfect. He looked at Tariel, who smiled as though reading his thoughts.

"Aye, indeed," the Arkos said simply.

But Rhiss was still confused. "My lord," he said, brows furrowing, "I do not know where such a thing would be located."

"Of course you do. Where did you find what you needed in the Circle at Storrenne?"

Rhiss thought. *What* had he needed at Storrenne? And *where* had he found it? He did not understand. He had been fighting Moressin at Storrenne, seeking neither gifts nor food. He had been looking for—

Understanding dawned, and Rhiss turned to the central depression. Seeing it, he strode purposefully over.

As though on cue, a soft beam of pearl-coloured light arced from the depression, arrowing straight into the dark towards the heavens. Although he half-expected it, Rhiss jumped; the children applauded, obviously thinking it staged for their entertainment. Tariel and the gryphons showed no reaction, merely watched silently as he walked into the column of light.

Resting on the ground in the depression — not suspended in the air this time, Rhiss noted — were two leather flasks and a collection of small earthenware cups stacked together. Rhiss smiled at the sight, bowed his head in acknowledgement of the gift, and carefully collected all in his arms before retracing his steps. Behind him, the pillar of light faded out. Signalling Borilius to assist, he had the boy take the cups, unstoppered one of the flasks and filling cups two at a time, bade Borilius take them to the children. There were still a couple of cups left when all the children were served. Rhiss halted in puzzlement, but Borilius waited for him to fill them, so he did. Borilius gave one to Rhiss, then took the other to Tariel, who accepted it gravely.

Rhiss looked around, and saw to his surprise that the children just sat, respectfully and expectantly: well-trained at even such young ages, they were waiting for him to give thanks. Regarding the small, ragtag figures, Rhiss felt a surge of emotion well up, making it momentarily impossible to speak. He cleared his throat, paused and raised his cup. "Well, my friends," he finally managed softly, "we give thanks to the One for many things this night: for deliverance from evil, suffering and death; for unexpected allies arrived unlooked for, but welcome beyond imagining." He gestured at the gryphons. "And we give thanks to the One for sustenance, warmth, and life itself."

He raised his cup to drink, but stopped as the clear voice of a young girl piped up from the other side of the fire ring. "And we give thanks for *you*, Lord Kairconnachlan, for our lives. Truly, the One sent you this night. Thank you, sir." She stood up, eyes locked on Rhiss. Her dress was torn and grimy, auburn hair in disarray, face smudged, but there was an oddly grown up, mature dignity in the way she stood, raising her cup to Rhiss. "We will remember this night always. And you, also. We will remember *you* always." She looked at the others and raised her voice. "In this we are One."

A murmur of assent went around and the children repeated the phrase, like a litany. Then, incredibly, they all stood and raised their cups, toasting him; even Tariel joined in. Rhiss blushed. He nodded but could not speak. He drank his own cup empty, then turned and walked slowly to the Way Stones' boundary to gaze out on the night. Behind him, the children sat again and, rejuvenated by the Ruvennar's effects, talked quietly amongst themselves. Rhiss realized Tariel had followed and looked out at the forest.

"Well done," the Arkos said quietly. "You have acquitted yourself admirably tonight, Prince, and I find myself well pleased."

It was not what Rhiss had expected. "You are not angry with me, then?" he asked, hardly daring the question aloud.

Incredibly, Tariel threw back his head and laughed a long, hearty laugh. "Angry with you? Why should I be angry?"

Rhiss considered. "Well," he said slowly, "I cannot imagine this night has gone as you thought it would."

Tariel was plainly still amused. "How so?"

"Do you really need to ask, my lord? There are a host of people alive because of my actions: my mother's maid... these children, rescued with the gryphons' help. They did not survive originally. My contact and interaction with the gryphons — none of it happened originally."

"What is 'originally'? The events you speak of happened. You remember them; I remember them. I do not recall things happening differently *originally*."

"But... we didn't plan them! They must have taken place differently. They occurred simply because I responded to situations that arose — and not heeding your warning that we were not there to change the past."

"Possibly. But you reacted naturally and spontaneously, were true to yourself and the ideals we strive for. You were motivated by compassion and the desire to do right, and I would have it no other way. Marvelous are the ways of the One."

Rhiss sighed in exasperation. "Must you *always* say that?"

"Why not? 'Tis true."

"But you did not *know* these things would happen!"

"Perhaps, perhaps not. But even were that the case, why should it surprise or vex you? Look you here, I have told you, only the One is omniscient. I have also said all things serve the One, that nothing occurs by chance. Our coming to this night has served the purposes of the One, and the events that have occurred were meant to happen. What more needs saying?" He gazed at Rhiss. "And yet, you are still troubled by this, I see."

"Aye. Apparently much more than you, my lord."

"Indeed. Then I say to you, put your mind at rest, Prince; leave me to worry about practical and theological implications. I am not troubled by what we did an hour ago — or twenty-five years, if you would rather think in those terms. Nor do I believe I will be taken to task for this night's work. I admit it was a concern before we left, but my fears are laid to rest, and I would see yours likewise." Tariel drew in a great breath of the cold air. "Now let us return to the fire. We must leave soon to when and where you belong, and our dealings here are not yet concluded. You have an issue still to resolve."

Rhiss opened his mouth, but Tariel spoke before he could say anything. "And by 'issue' I mean the children. I know what you are thinking, but you absolutely cannot take them back to what you think of as your time, nor can you remain with them. Both alternatives are too great a deviation from the plan of the One."

Rhiss shook his head, distressed. "But... then what is to become of them? I did not bring them literally out of massacre and fire simply to abandon them to a slower death in the wilderness."

"I understand. Nor would I propose such a course of action." Tariel cocked his head to one side and paused, studying Rhiss. "What if I were to assure you they will be looked after by other servants of the Light in whom I repose absolute trust to do right by the children?"

"Who are these servants? Are they far away?"

"Some are here even now. Others are on their way, and will arrive before dawn."

"Do you mean the gryphons?"

Tariel shook his head. "No. In the gryphons, you have creatures who are wise, just and venerable. But they are not suitable guardians to raise human children over a long time."

"Then who is here already? What do you mean?"

"I will have them reveal themselves to the children before we leave, and you shall meet those at Storrenne when we return. I think you will not be displeased. Now, come." Tariel clapped Rhiss gently on the shoulder. "This needs explaining to the children, but I know you will do it justice."

Rhiss was startled. "Me, my lord?"

"Of course. *You* are their deliverer, not I, and it is to you they look for explanation, reassurance and leadership. Give your charge to them, and say your farewells. Then leave them and do likewise with the gryphons. While you do that, I will instruct the children about those who will care for them. It is high time we returned to what you know of as the present. Do not fear. All is well."

The children were sprawled comfortably around the fire, looking better than they had since Rhiss first laid eyes on them. But it was no time to play the stern schoolmaster, and he wished Lowri was there: she had a gentle way with children that he lacked.

But she was not, so he must try. He sighed. "Children, hear me. I have something important to say."

They sat up, fixing expectant eyes on him. "My friend and I must take our leave shortly. We must return to — to whence we came. I wish we could take you with us, but that cannot be. However, we will not leave you alone to fend for yourselves. My colleague has summoned trusted friends to care for you until you are old enough to go your own ways. You will meet them before we leave."

Borilius spoke up. "What would you have us do, sir?"

Rhiss smiled as it occurred to him. "I have a simple but important job for you: grow up in honour, discipline, joy, faith in the One and *wait*. Wait for the King — the rightful King. He will come to save Arrinor from itself, and he will need your help when he does. *You* must be prepared to assist him."

A timid voice spoke from the shadows. "How do you know, sir?"

Rhiss looked to see who had spoken. A small, red-haired boy stood at the back of the ring. "What is your name, boy?"

"Petran, sir. Are you sure he will come? I've seen him. He's... only a baby, isn't he? How will he know anything? About what has happened... what he has to do?"

Rhiss smiled. "Well, Petran, you are absolutely right. The King *is* newly born. In fact, my friend and I sent him, his mother the Queen, and a servant to safety a short time ago, just before we came to your aid. And because he is so young, it may take a long time for him to arrive. However, come he will, mark me."

"But how do you *know*?" insisted the boy timorously.

Rhiss stopped, looking at Tariel, who nodded reassuringly.

"Petran," Rhiss said softly, "*I know*. And I swear this to all of you: the King will be made to see and understand he *is* King. He will grow and learn his obligations from those who know him, care about him—" Rhiss stopped and looked Tariel in the eye "—and that he must strive for what is good and truthful; he must seek the Light, and find it, not yielding to the forces of evil always present in the world. I swear to you also he will be made to see he must be King, because he is capable, needed, can make a difference, and because it is the right thing." He stopped and looked around, wondering if they understood any of it. But he need not have worried: they gazed in wonder and grateful comprehension. "Aye," he went on. "He will be made to see all those things, I promise. And he will come to Arrinor. So I charge you to wait, and look to his coming. It may take a long time. After all, as we said, he *is* just a baby. But even if it takes years — even if it were to take as long as twenty-five years — you must keep faith he will come. I have given you my word that these things will come to pass. Do you trust me? Do you believe?"

"Aye, lord," they murmured earnestly but softly. It was as though they felt speaking too loudly would break the spell the moment held.

Rhiss smiled. "No, I think you can do better than that. Are we One in this matter?"

"Aye, lord," they responded, a little more strongly.

"Then let me hear you say it. Mean it."

They looked at each other uncertainly. Borilius stood up. "In this we are One!" he called emphatically, glaring at the children, daring them with his gaze to do likewise.

Several of the children stood. "In this we are One!" they repeated.

"Louder!" demanded Borilius. "All of you!"

The rest jumped up. "In this we are One!" they chorused enthusiastically. Rhiss smiled again.

"Very well, then. Children, I go to thank the gryphons and say goodbye to them. But first I bid farewell to all of you. And I thank you."

Borilius looked puzzled; speaking for all, he said, "Thank *us*? No, my lord, *we* should thank *you*. Why would you thank us?"

Rhiss looked around. He knew he could not tell them the entire truth; Tariel would be scandalized, and beside, the time was not yet right for them to hear it. He paused momentarily and realized how ironic *that* was — *he* was withholding the full story because he did not deem the recipients ready. Now they saw in part; later, with the grace of the One, they would understand fully. But they deserved at least a hint and so, greatly daring, he said, "Because, my young friends, know that you have made a king tonight. As a result, for the first time in a very long while, I have hope that all will turn out well."

Tariel stirred uneasily, and Rhiss understood he had pushed the truth as far as he could. He raised his hand in benediction, making the triune sign. "Go with the protection and blessing of the One. Perhaps, if the One wills it, we shall meet again."

The children bowed their heads. Rhiss looked inquiringly at Tariel, who nodded and stepped forward, motioning Rhiss away. As Rhiss walked over to the gryphons, he heard Tariel speak, but he did not hear what was said.

Angharath gravely regarded Rhiss approach. Rhiss bowed, but before he said anything, the gryphon spoke quietly. "Is it time for you to take your leave, Kairconnach-lan?"

"Aye, friend Angharath. With gratitude for your assistance. Without it, I could never have spirited the children from the castle. Their lives would have been lost, and likely mine, also."

"My heart is gladdened, then. Losing younglings would be tragic — even without their potential."

Rhiss was intrigued. "Potential? What do you mean? What do you sense, Angharath?"

"That you have not seen the last of them, Kairconnach-lan," the gryphon said with what sounded very much like a chuckle. "More than that, I will not say, for Lord Tariel would not approve my being too free with my thoughts."

Rhiss sighed ruefully. "I understand. Lord Tariel can be rather... forceful."

"As may be, Kairconnach-lan, but remember, you are most fortunate to have his presence and counsel. *His* kind does not often appear and work with *your* kind directly or at such length. Your cause is evidently important to him, so be honoured."

Rhiss bowed his head again in apology and smiled. "You are correct, of course, Angharath. I will strive to keep that thought foremost in mind."

"What thought would that be?" said Tariel striding up. Rhiss jumped. He had been so focused on the gryphon, he had not even heard the approach of the Arkos, and did not know what to reply.

Angharath came to his rescue. "A minor point of etiquette, Glorious Servant," the gryphon said smoothly. "Must we say farewell to you, too?"

Tariel gave Rhiss one of those soul-penetrating glances Rhiss knew all too well by now before returning his attention to the gryphons. "Unfortunately, my friend. Much as I would like to remain, I must see Prince Rhissan safely back to his own place in the Master Plan. My thanks for all your help."

Angharath bowed his great head. "Then go with the One, my lords. It has been our honour to assist you this night."

Rhiss looked back at the children. Oddly, the entire clearing seemed alive with light, dancing airborne points of multi-coloured light bobbing and weaving even as he watched. "My lord?" he said disbelievingly. "What is that?"

Tariel looked over casually. "Those are the Sinea-a-Doorn, Prince — the Guardians of this Circle. Do not fear. They are here to protect the children, not harm them."

"May I meet them?" Rhiss made as though to walk back, but Tariel gently laid a restraining hand on his arm.

"Not these ones, or on this occasion. I wish to return you to your own time before you unravel the flow of this one any more than you already have. You will have opportunity to make acquaintance with the ones guarding Storrenne when we return, I promise. They are the same race as here at Kirunek."

Rhiss looked at the circle. It was as though it was filled with fireflies, but whose light was many times brighter, in a profusion of different colours. "Are they alive?" he asked doubtfully.

"They are indeed; take care, Prince, lest you cause offence when you meet. Come, let us go."

"A moment, my lord. Are these the beings who will nurture the children as they grow?"

Tariel lifted his eyebrows. "Indeed not. They are tied to these Circles, Prince, which would not do for those who must bring up the children. They are merely protectors until the real guardians arrive tomorrow. And before you ask," Tariel said, holding up a hand to forestall interruption, "we cannot stay until then." He turned to the gryphons. "However, may I ask *you* to stay with the children, my friends, until Aranell and his forces arrive?"

Angharath looked at his companions as though seeking their approval; although they said nothing, he turned back to Tariel after a moment and nodded. "It shall be as you ask. They arrive tomorrow, you say?"

"Aye," Tariel replied, already gently shepherding Rhiss outside the ring of stones. "Thank you. Goodbye, my friends — until we meet again. Go you with the One."

They were through the stones before Rhiss could stop and turn to Tariel. "Aranell, my lord?"

"A friend, well known to me, but human like you. You and the children were not the only ones to escape Tor Eylian this night. A brave knight named Aranell — Eques Aranell to give him his proper title — managed to fight his way out, along with others. He was a close friend of your father. Unlike the children here, he and his companions are adults. I have summoned them, and they arrive tomorrow. As one result of this night's debacle, they will form part of a resistance that will develop to your aunt. I will say no more at the moment. I realize you feel responsible for the children, but you could not ask for anyone better than the Aranellens to nurture and care for them. One day you will likely meet them — in fact, they may be of great assistance — but that day is not yet."

Tariel paused, fixing his gaze on Rhiss before continuing. "I do not wish to seem I propel you to your own time with unseemly haste, Prince, but the truth is, as you observed, you *have* made several significant alterations from what once was — or may have been. I would rather you make no more this night. As I said, I no longer fear we will be censured for our activities, but they *will* require explanation on my part, and I prefer you not add more paradoxes to the list... including meeting the Sinea-a-Doorn or the Aranellens in this time."

"I see," said Rhiss reluctantly. "Very well, my lord. I yield, if you deem it necessary. How do we return?"

Tariel merely pointed, and Rhiss turned to look. Sure enough, set into the outer face of the standing stone closest to them, looking as though it had always been there, was the Portal of Tariel. Rhiss laughed, a long, loud and clear laugh, moving swiftly to the door and opening it with a flourish.

In the chamber between the two corridors, Rhiss reluctantly removed the Arkos robes and gear. Retrieving his own, he felt glumly that he was just plain Rhissan again — and not as Lowri affectionately used the term.

"Thank you, my lord." He handed the tunic to Tariel. "It was an honour to wear your Order's emblem. I have never felt so privileged to be accorded membership — if only temporarily."

"And you acquitted yourself well in them, Prince. But do not be ashamed of your own House's emblems. They have a long and honourable lineage, and I know you will return glory to them. You *do* realize it *is* your House? You are not merely an 'ordinary traveller journeying through Arrinor' anymore."

Rhiss sighed, recalling all that had transpired the last few hours. "No," he replied thoughtfully, realizing Tariel was right. "You have shown me well why and what I must do, my lord, and who I am. Be assured of that."

Tariel nodded. "Good. That was my goal. As Gavrilos said, never let the truth dismay you. Neither flee from it. Acknowledge it, accept it, and move on. Live your life in the freedom of truth." He pursed his lips. "Now, it is time to return to the Arrinor you know. You have been gone several hours by both your own reckoning and those in the cottage at the Ford at the White River, and you should not worry your friends more than necessary. I bid you farewell — you know the way from here."

Surprised, Rhiss said, "You will not accompany me?"

Tariel shook his head. "I go to... another Place, Prince, to... account for this night. But do not be concerned; I face neither reprimand nor punishment. You will not be alone at the Way Stones of Storrenne. The Sinea-a-Doorn have cared for your horse while you were gone, and you will enjoy meeting them. Remember to be grateful for the attentions they have lavished on it, and then ride to Mistress Lowri's. Your friends there anxiously await you."

"My lord, you said the Sinea-a-Doorn are guardians of the Circles? They are always there to protect the Sacred Spaces?" Tariel nodded. "Well, then... if I may ask... why did they not come to my aid when I fought Moressin? Where were they? If they are guardians, they could have been extremely helpful."

Tariel nodded again. "Be not deceived by appearances when you meet the Sinea-a-Doorn. Many who made that mistake paid dearly for it. They are supremely effective guardians, and would have been able to dispatch Moressin... not easily, but they would have prevailed. And that, I fear, is why they were absent during your combat." He paused. "I ordered them from the Circle prior to your arrival. That is the only reason Moressin dared even enter it — he sensed they were not present. Normally, he would have stayed well clear."

Rhiss was shocked. "*You* sent them away? Why?"

"It was necessary for you to make your own way, Prince, without relying on others. And you did."

"I could have been killed! I very nearly was!"

"But I had faith you would prevail, and sure enough, you did. In fact, you ultimately came through it the stronger." Tariel's lips quirked in a smile. "If you wish, I offer my apology, but take it knowing I would do the same if 'twas to do again."

"Well... did you watch, at least? Would you have intervened in my final extremity?"

Tariel shook his head. "I was not watching, and there is a valuable lesson for you: do not make the mistake of assuming I or Gavrilos or another Power will always be there to catch you if a fall looms. We will not do you that disservice, I promise."

"Disservice?" Rhiss repeated disbelievingly.

"Aye, you heard me rightly. Disservice, I said. Do not look at me like that, boy. If you were to get too used to the idea someone would always be there to save you, too comfortable with it, what would be the point of your doing anything? Your struggles would become as meaningless as those of a puppet on strings. I have told you before, I do not know all ends. Only the One does. But all things serve the One. It *is* possible you may be defeated in your quest. It would be a tragedy, whether we speak of your premature death, or worse. But even that, too, would somehow serve the purposes of the One. Now, I do not say you *will* be defeated; indeed, I hope not: I confess a certain fondness for you. But nothing is certain — nothing except the One's love for you as one of His children; ultimately, all will turn out as He wills it."

"Well... I see," said Rhiss slowly, although he didn't at all. He shook his head. The idea would require some getting used to.

Tariel divined his thoughts. "You will be fine, I know. Much good has been accomplished tonight. And of the many important things done, one stands over all."

Rhiss looked puzzled, and Tariel smiled. "You have reached an understanding in yourself. You *are* Prince Rhissan of Arrinor, rightful heir to the Crystal Throne."

Rhiss nodded. "Aye," he agreed with a rueful smile. "I see that now — in all the ways there are to see it. You have shown me well, and need have no fears on that score, my lord."

Tariel nodded. "I know. And I am glad, for this new understanding is the cornerstone on which all rests. Without it, the entire edifice of your existence here would have—"

"—Come crashing down?" Rhiss interjected lightly.

Tariel looked at him sharply. "Hardly. It could not even have been constructed. Nothing could begin until you acknowledge both your birthright and the responsibilities going hand in hand with it — an acknowledgement you have made."

Rhiss blushed. "Oh," he said, abashed.

"I give you my blessing, and bid you go with the One." Tariel made the Triune sign, and Rhiss bowed his head. "Return to *your* friends, and begin in earnest the task you now acknowledge as yours. You will see me again, Prince, but as I have said, do not look to my coming. It will be when you expect it least."

"Of *that* I am certain," Rhiss said dryly. "Farewell, my lord, until then. And thank you for all you have done this night and others." He bowed and left the chamber, proceeding confidently down the corridor that would take him back to Arrinor and the struggle — *his* struggle.

XVIII

RETURN AND REVITALIZATION

"Child of the One, I say unto you, dwell not on your lot in life, or the part you play on the great stage of the One's Creation. Rather, make peace quickly and quietly, focusing on the vital — indeed, the only — choice given: how you live life in the role offered. Ask what you would do in the time given. It is the Great Gift of the One to His children, so think well and squander it not."

**The Book of the One, 81:14:31-34
(Cantos 81, Chapter 14, Verses 31-34)**

Rhiss emerged from the Portal at Storrenne into pre-dawn's dim illumination, pale streaks of pink beginning to colour clouds on the eastern horizon. The standing stones were dark, shadowy sentinels rearing mutely overhead, forming a protective circle. Rhiss closed the Portal door softly and peered about, wondering where Aralsa was, whether she would be alone, or accompanied by the unearthly points of light — beings, Rhiss corrected himself, living beings — Tariel had named the Sinea-a-Doorn. But all was quiet. No breeze ruffled the grass, which stood heavy and wet with dew. Slender tendrils of mist curled around the stones, and Rhiss took several cautious steps, wondering whether to call out.

There was no need. Before going a dozen paces, the air about him was abruptly alive with thousands of points of light, each no bigger than a sixpence, dancing and jiggling in some frenzied ballet. Rhiss heard multitudes of silvery, bell-like voices chattering and laughing all at once, although he could not discern whether they actually spoke aloud, or if he somehow heard them in his mind. He halted, resisting the strong impulse to draw his sword.

One voice suddenly rose above the others, and Rhiss sensed it came from a point of light directly before him. Clearly female, it sounded youthful, but there was the crack of authority to it, nonetheless. "All right, now! That's quite enough! Look how you've startled him! Give the poor man some peace, all of you! You act like you've never seen a human before!"

The chattering cut off as though a switch had been thrown, although the points of light continued their ceaseless weaving and bobbing. The light that Rhiss fancied had called for silence made an inarticulate exclamation of annoyance, and the other points of light vanished. They winked out of existence in a soundless explosion of light, leaving just the one moving restlessly back and forth before Rhiss.

"I bid you welcome to Storrenne, Prince Rhissan," said the voice eagerly. "You are welcome, most welcome indeed! I am Bold, at your service."

"I beg your pardon?" asked Rhiss, bewildered. He did not know whether the voice had stated a name or behaviour.

"In your tongue, I am called Bold of the Sinea-a-Doorn," clarified the light, speaking rapidly, evidently sensing his uncertainty. "In fact," it continued sheepishly, "I am so named because that is what the others say I am like with those who come within the confines of this ring." It paused. "But please, do not mind them. They did not mean to be rude, I assure you. They are just very excited to meet you at last."

"The... others?" Rhiss said tentatively.

"Why, surely, Prince Rhissan. My kin, of course. They surround you even now, although you may not see them or hear their voices. I have shamed them into silence, you see."

"I can hardly see *you*, either," replied Rhiss truthfully.

"Oh, of course... but that is *easily* remedied!" exclaimed the light enthusiastically. It promptly vanished, as though blown out like a candle. Rhiss scanned the Circle in quick consternation, but there was only the faint light of encroaching dawn, and the eternally silent stones.

"Over here, Prince," came a lilting voice behind him. Rhiss spun around, and there she was, Bold of the Sinea-a-Doorn, sitting on a boulder, knees raised up and arms locked around them, regarding Rhiss gravely and with frank curiosity. Unable to help himself, Rhiss reciprocated.

His first impression was that she was very young, little more than a child, certainly no more than twelve or thirteen. Her features were delicately attractive, the ruddy glow of her cheeks offsetting an otherwise flawless, ivory complexion. Dark, mischievous eyes were framed by a long, shaggy mane of coal-black hair flowing down nearly to her waist. A long, wide crimson ribbon wound its way through the dark curls, imposing a little order on them. She was clad very simply in a short-sleeved, one piece olive-coloured dress that ended raggedly just above her knees. A cloth belt of the same colour as her hair ribbon was tied carelessly around her waist. Her long legs and feet were bare.

But surely the most incredible thing about her was a pair of wings arching from her back. Extending a foot above her head down to her waist and shaped like butterfly wings, they were a dark, velvety maroon. Intricate, lacy, cream-coloured patterns were inscribed on the wings, but it was impossible to say if they were natural or applied. However, there was no doubt the wings themselves were an integral, organic part of her; there was absolutely nothing artificial or contrived about them. Even as she sat at rest, the wings were constantly in slight, lazy motion, back and forth, back and forth, almost like respiration. As he regarded her, there came a twinge from deep recesses of memory, and Rhiss felt a sudden stir of recognition from long ago. He had seen the girl before, perhaps more than once, in circumstances... he could not quite recall. Then it was gone, and he was back in the present.

Rhiss became aware he was staring, mouth slightly agape, and to cover his embarrassment and confusion, coughed several times, bringing a hand to cover his mouth. Bold was not fooled, however. She cocked her head to one side and laughed delightedly, a wonderful sound reminding Rhiss of chimes ringing far off.

"I am not quite what you expected, am I, Prince?"

"I—" Rhiss tried to marshal his confused thoughts. Guardian of the Circle? A mere girl, little older than a child? She looked about as dangerous as the butterfly she inescapably resembled. He checked again. No sword, dagger or bow: she wasn't even armed. Several replies came to mind, but he decided polite honesty was the best policy.

"If you'll pardon my frankness... not really," he admitted.

"Of course not," she agreed cheerfully, lightly rising from the rock and moving quickly before Rhiss. Standing, the top of her ebon curls barely reached his chin. She curtsied, then locked eyes on his, delighted humour still evident in her gaze.

"But you would not wish to see us as we are when called to defend the Sacred Spaces, Prince. Indeed not. You would not find me or my kin quite so—" she stopped and cocked her head to one side again, obviously considering her choice of phrase "—so *delicate*, I assure you. In truth, it would not be pleasant. We are far more capable, far more lethal, than you might surmise, given my current appearance. But we will not speak of that now." She smiled radiantly. "The dawn comes, you have returned safe and sound, as Lord Tariel assured us you would, meaning you were successful, so I am glad." Her eyes took on a knowing look. "And you have changed in the journeying, Prince. Aye, there is something — hmm, different — than when you left with Lord Tariel last night. Aye..." Her voice trailed off.

Rhiss was intrigued. "Different? How so... Lady?"

She laughed again. "You need no titles for *me*, Prince Rhissan. I am simply Bold, as I said. That is who I am, and all I need for name. Even though part of you sees me as a child, you already know in your heart I am not. As for your question..." She paused, considering his query, and looked closely in a way that Rhiss found strangely reminiscent of Gavrilos. "Different..." she mused softly. "Well, you found something within yourself, I see. Something important. And you are more at peace with it than last night." She looked at Rhiss for confirmation, reading it in his surprised glance. Her delight was evident as she beamed. "I see I'm right. Isn't that clever of me?" She looked around as though seeking affirmation, and in response, there was an immediate chatter of the silvery voices. It was odd to hear such a chorus and yet not see their owners, but it lasted only briefly, then stilled as Bold raised her hand.

"Peace, friends!" she called. "In our joy, we forget ourselves and the instructions given us. Make ready the celebration for the Prince's return, and bring forth his mount. He will break his fast with us before rejoining his comrades." She turned to Rhiss questioningly. "Is that satisfactory, my lord? You will not find our company disagreeable, I promise."

"I am honoured." Rhiss bowed.

"Wonderful!" Bold clapped her hands like a small child given the best of all tidings. "Come then, Prince. We will take ourselves out of the way while my friends prepare. I know! You may see your horse while the others make ready our Circle."

She held out her hand quite unselfconsciously, as a child might with a trusted adult, and Rhiss took it. Her skin was soft, warm, and tingled in his grasp, overflowing with an uncontainable exuberance and vitality. It was disconcerting but wonderful.

They walked leisurely to the Circle's far side. Once there, Bold made no audible call, but without warning, another Sinea-a-Doorn stood there with Aralsa. In stature and appearance, he was similar to Bold, except he was obviously male, clad in tunic and shorts, wings slightly larger and darker. In one hand he held Aralsa's reins. As she registered Rhiss' arrival, she whickered softly in pleased recognition, tossing her head.

Smiling, Bold turned to Rhiss. "This is Equlan, Prince. The Sinea-a-Doorn love all the One's creatures, but some of us have gifts with particular animals. Horses are Equlan's especial interest, and he has had charge of yours since you left her here last night. Does her condition meet with your approval?"

Rhiss examined Aralsa swiftly, delighted and impressed. She did indeed appear to have been well cared for in his absence — better, he thought guiltily, than he had been able to manage since leaving Craggaddon Hall. But there was something odd about her. What was it? Rhiss stepped to Aralsa's side, mentally picturing himself mounting. Hmm. It was patently ridiculous, but she seemed larger, more muscular, more full of life than he recalled. In fact... aye... she *was* taller, he would swear it. He glanced sharply at Equlan, whose expression was blandly innocent, and after a moment's hesitation, Rhiss wordlessly returned to his examination. Aralsa's coat was brushed to a glossy sheen, mane combed and plaited with blue and silver ribbons, hooves and saddle oiled and polished, and the bridle was... Rhiss stopped and examined it more closely. It was dark, new leather and bright silver — not the plain and rather worn affair he recalled Arian slapping on at the Hall, but altogether richer, more ornate, intricate embossing skilfully worked in the leather. Equlan noticed him studying it and spoke.

"A gift from the Sinea-a-Doorn, Prince Rhissan," he said, bowing, voice low and pleasant. "Receive it with our blessing."

Rhiss inclined his head, overwhelmed. "My deepest thanks. It is a marvellous gift, and Aralsa looks wonderful. I have never seen her look better. It shames me to see how inferior my care has been compared to yours."

"No, Prince," replied Equlan, laughing. "Be not ashamed. We know you have had much to occupy you since coming to Arrinor. You cared for Aralsa as well as anyone could. It is simply that time was on our hands last night while you were with Lord Tariel. It was no trouble, I assure you."

"And you may be away with her as soon as we have broken bread together," added Bold.

Rhiss realized he was impatient to be off. "Bold, I don't wish to sound ungrateful about your generous offer, but I really should be away. My friends will be frantic. I left them last night hastily, not in the best frame of mind, and they must—"

Bold held up her hand, laughingly interrupting. "Peace, dear Prince!" she said in mock reproach. "Do you think we would knowingly add to their anxiety? Time inside this Circle is ours to control. A day within can be as a minute outside the Way Stones. There is ample time to celebrate your return with us, and yet still be with your friends before the sun has cleared the horizon."

"Oh," replied Rhiss, dazed at this new revelation. "Well, in that case..."

"Take the Prince's horse, and keep her in readiness," Bold commanded. "He will need her shortly." Equlan bowed, leading Aralsa away.

"In the meantime," Bold continued proudly to Rhiss, "see what my comrades have accomplished in the brief time we have been occupied!"

Rhiss turned as she indicated and gasped. He could scarcely believe he was in the same Circle he had come to so short a time before. His first, confused impressions were of light, warmth, tables and decorations everywhere.

Lanterns suspended from wooden poles cast a golden glow throughout the Circle; fires in stone pits roared crimson flames in answer. Flowers of every imaginable variety were present wherever one turned, a riot of colour growing out of the ground, in vases on the tables, and in containers on the Stones themselves. Rows of long tables, draped with creamy white cloths, strained under mountains of foodstuffs. Oak benches, wonderfully carved, stood ready by the tables. Garlands and streamers the colours of the rainbow bedecked everything. The Sinea-a-Doorn were all about, some still bobbing, multicoloured points of light, some in human form. Some danced excitedly around the tables, others laughed and chased each other among the stones, wings blurred with motion in the light of the lanterns. It seemed the Circle was filled with joyous children.

Bold led Rhiss to a seat near the Circle's central depression. Smiling, she indicated his place at the table's head, where an actual carved chair, no mere bench, waited. She nodded wordlessly in confirmation at his startled look, then took a place to his right. He stood waiting behind the chair, but taking his position seemed to cue the assembled Sinea-a-Doorn. They came and stood at their places, waiting.

Simultaneously, they all lifted their hands and held them in front, palms raised to the sky. Rhiss did likewise, for they were obviously about to say the blessing ritual he had become familiar with prior to meals. Was he to say it? He was unsure whether his role was that of host or guest. He looked to Bold for guidance, but her attention was fixed raptly on the predawn sky, and before he could say anything, the Sinea-a-Doorn, as one, began to sing.

Their voices, clear, pure and warm, lifted together in achingly perfect harmony. They used no instruments, simply sang together in a tongue completely unknown to Rhiss. Even in his ignorance, Rhiss sensed the tune was obviously a hymn of praise and thanksgiving directed to the One. The melody was simple, yet exquisitely complex, with countless, interwoven sub-themes. Rhiss stood listening, transfixed by the sheer beauty. He wished it would never end.

An indeterminate time later, of course, it did. As the last clear notes ended, Rhiss blinked as though waking from a wonderful dream. There was a moment's silence, and he became aware, all around, the Sinea-a-Doorn looked expectantly at him. His face coloured as he realized they actually waited for him to sit. He did so very deliberately, and the spell was instantly broken. Everywhere, the Sinea-a-Doorn took their seats, laughing and chattering together. Sprightly music from Sinea-a-Doorn with instruments added to the revelry.

There were no servers. One simply selected from the incredible profusion of foodstuffs within reach. Rhiss found he was ravenous after his night's work, and loaded his plate appreciatively. The food was delicious beyond anything Rhiss could recall, and he ate with a will, the night's weariness dropping away. It was some while before his attention left his food, and he looked up guiltily to see Bold regarding him, amused. As he stammered an apology, she held up a hand, forestalling him.

"No need," she laughed. "I am sure Lord Tariel put you through gruelling labours, and it is our pleasure to see you enjoy our hospitality."

"Do you know much of Lord Tariel?" asked Rhiss, curious.

She smiled and spread her hands. "Of course, my Prince. We are all servants of the One together."

"Does he command the Sinea-a-Doorn?"

Bold shook her head. "Not specifically, but he is high in the counsels of the One, and thus we respect his wishes. Do you ask from idle curiosity, or something specific?"

"Actually, I was thinking of the day Seir-onna Arian and I encountered Moressin in this very Circle."

To his amazement, Bold actually blushed scarlet and hung her head. The music and conversation stumbled, and a brief silence fell. Rhiss looked around, startled. The Sinea-a-Doorn had all halted their activities, gazing at him with large eyes.

"Prince Rhissan, pray accept our humblest, most earnest apologies for that day," said Bold in a small voice. "It was not our wish to withdraw our protection of the Sacred Space. But Lord Tariel commanded it, so of course we did." Bold looked as though she was about to burst into tears. "But we laid aside our guardianship of this Circle, and in consequence, you were sorely hurt. This would never have happened normally. You cannot know the distress and shame this caused us."

Rhiss smiled reassuringly and shook his head. "My friends, do not blame yourselves," he replied, raising his voice for all to hear. "There have been times I, too, have felt the weight of Lord Tariel's commands, and I know well that one ignores them at his peril. He explained the reasons for his actions that day, and I hold you blameless."

There was a collective sigh; tension eased, and the Sinea-a-Doorn resumed their activities.

Rhiss turned to Bold. "But I am curious about something concerning this Moressin. He seemed to mistake me for someone named Ahrhissian."

Bold smiled. "Aye, he might well do so. Your resemblance to Ahrhissian, in looks and temperament, is striking. And not only that." She licked her lips thoughtfully, as though tasting something. "Your Essence is not unlike his, too, in a number of ways. Most interesting, really."

"Who was this Ahrhissian?"

Bold's expression was far away. "A wise and good man, Prince. Like you. He lived long ago, had many adventures, and fell in love with an enchantress. It is the stuff of legends — in fact, your people have composed numerous lays about them."

Before Rhiss could respond, Bold shook herself lightly and turned back to him. "But it is *so* good to have you here. We have looked forward to this ever since first hearing of you." She gestured at the Sinea-a-Doorn across from her. "And I would have you meet..." Bold deftly engaged the Sinea-a-Doorn around her, and they all joined in animated converse with both Rhiss and each other, speaking on many things.

All too soon, the meal was over. Rhiss heard no formal announcement, saw no signal, but suddenly, the Sinea-a-Doorn were rising from tables, whisking plates and trays away — where to, exactly, Rhiss could not discern. He stood and watched, bemused, as decorations, benches and tables all melted away at the hands of the Sinea-a-Doorn. Then the Circle was bare again, with nothing to suggest there had ever been any presence there at all, much less a sumptuous feast. The Sinea-a-Doorn, too, gradually became fewer and fewer, some changing into the brilliant points of dancing light before winking out like candle flames. Within a short time, only Bold remained, smiling as she watched Rhiss study the Circle's transformation.

"Well, my lord," she said, curtseying, "I regret the time has come for me to wish you safe journey and send you on your way. Even the Sinea-a-Doorn are not permitted to hold back the passage of time indefinitely, and as you see—" she gestured gracefully towards the eastern horizon "—the sun rises, and a new day dawns. You have friends who greatly desire to see you, and a task to begin in the role you have freely accepted."

"Very well," Rhiss acknowledged. He gazed at the slight form before him. "Will I see you again, Bold?"

"Of course, my Prince, if you should ever return. My kind dwells in all the Circles in Arrinor. If you enter any of them, you will find us there."

"As may be, but will I *see* them?" Rhiss asked, amused.

Without answering, Bold extended a bare arm. Standing on tip-toe, index finger pointing, she gently reached up. Without knowing what she wanted, he leaned down. She placed a cool finger on his forehead and traced a pattern there. Rhiss felt his skin tingle. "Aye, Prince Rhissan, you will," she said softly, "for I name you Friend of the Sinea-a-Doorn. You will not need the intervention of the Arkos again to move among us. We will do all we can to aid you." She withdrew her arm, seemed about to add something, but thought better of it, and turned with a gesture. "Here is Equlan with your horse."

Rhiss had heard no sound, but suddenly, indeed, there was Aralsa with the Sinea-a-Doorn he had met earlier. He turned back to Bold, bowing low before her. "Thank you, Bold, for your kindnesses. Brother Gavrilos assured me I would find friends unlooked for in surprising places, but you and your kind are among the fairest I have yet encountered."

Bold smiled, but said nothing, merely making the triune blessing at Rhiss. He nodded, returned the gesture, and turned to Aralsa, placing one boot into the stirrup before swinging into the saddle. He grunted slightly and raised an eyebrow, *sure* that Aralsa was slightly larger than last night. He looked down on Bold and Equlan standing at his side. Bold lifted her hand and waved. "Farewell, Prince. Go you with the One."

"You, also, my friends," Rhiss replied, urging Aralsa into motion. She walked slowly until they were through the stones, then of her own volition broke into a canter.

Equlan and Bold remained standing, watching horse and rider progress over the moor. "So young, with so much yet to learn," Equlan murmured after a few moments.

She looked sideways at him. "Aye," she replied thoughtfully. "That is true. But he has much potential, for a mortal. You saw his Essence, as I did. It burns true and clear. If he succeeds, he will do well."

The morning was clear and crisp, the sun rising as a great, molten disk in the east. Riding along easily on Aralsa, Rhiss frowned, trying yet again to recall why Bold seemed so familiar. Like a cool river undercurrent, it had been on his mind while with the Sinea-a-Doorn. He shrugged, dismissing it. Doubtless it would come to him, but at a time of his memory's choosing.

A short while later, they came to a rise, and as they crested it, a clear, still pond was visible on the far side. Aralsa whickered softly, slowing her pace, clearly interested in a drink. Rhiss looked at the sky, measuring their progress against the sun, and decided a few minutes' rest to indulge a faithful companion was not too much burden, although he *was* anxious to return to Lowri's house and see her again. Arian and Parthalas, too, of course.

"Right then, girl," he murmured, as Aralsa tossed her head towards the pool in unmistakable intent. He steered her in that direction, smiling, and dismounted once they reached the water's edge. He let the reins go and slapped her rump gently, motioning her on. Then he flopped down a few feet away, reclining and idly watching as Aralsa moved contentedly into the water, lowering her head to drink. She definitely was taller, he thought. What *had* the Sinea-a-Doorn done?

He wasn't really too concerned. The sun was pleasant, and he closed his eyes, turning his face full towards it, feeling the warmth against his eyelids. After several seconds, he yawned and opened his eyes, looking for Aralsa. There she was, ten or fifteen feet away, no longer drinking — just staring meditatively at the water.

Amused, Rhiss turned his attention to the pond as well, wondering what the horse could possibly find so absorbing. It was easily a hundred feet or more across. The clear water quickly deepened into a dark, ebon hue. There was no wind, and the ripples from Aralsa's entry had completely subsided. The surface was flat as a looking glass.

Curiously, something about that image stirred an ancient memory long submerged, and he frowned. A pool... dark water... Bold... Rothrann...

Without warning, the image exploded into conscious awareness. In fact... *two* separate occurrences dredged from the dim vaults of memory, one long ago, the other recent. Rhiss gasped and sat bolt upright, arms splaying out, banging one hand painfully on exposed rock. He failed to notice, completely preoccupied with the intensity of long buried recollections welling to the surface...

———⸻———

...He was in Wales, a young, sturdy boy of five or six, living in a small cottage in the village of Dinas Mawr with the woman he knew as Aunt Kerian. It was a hot, humid, drowsy summer afternoon, so he slipped away on his own to explore the labyrinth of footpaths surrounding the village, an act his aunt had always strictly prohibited. But of course, that was precisely what made it something to be savoured, for there is no fruit as deliciously tantalizing as one that is forbidden.

At last, after a sticky hour or so, he had come to the Pool of Rothrann, a deep body of water close by the village, all that remained of an abandoned quarry... or mine, he couldn't quite recall which. Bedtime tales parents told local children spoke of a cave at the pool's bottom, with a wondrous treasure guarded by an ogre. Rhiss peered into the depths. The pool was several hundred feet across, utterly still, glassy as a mill pond. The water was reasonably clear, but swiftly faded into inky darkness which made Rhiss shiver. He had been on the point of turning away when something caught his eye over in the shallows. He could not see with clarity what it was, but the shiny, metallic gleam was alluring, just the same. After a moment's hesitation, he carefully removed shoes and socks and splashed over to it, cheerfully oblivious to fears that had been front and centre seconds before.

But when he reached the spot, the object wasn't there. Frowning in puzzled frustration, he looked around, casting for reference points and confirmation. It should have been right there, directly before the great, rotting tree long overturned that now looked like an immense cast-iron pipe or straw through which a giant could come along and suck up all the dark water. But there was nothing.

Shaking his head, he suddenly caught the gleam once more, this time inexplicably further in, where the waters of the pool lost their clarity to assume an ebon flatness. He hesitated, but the siren call of a bright trinket to a young boy overrode all prudence, and he proceeded forward, placing each foot carefully to ensure he did not fall victim to a sudden drop-off.

He recalled being in thigh-deep water, about halfway to his goal, when without warning, several things simultaneously took place. The glint of gold vanished, winking out of existence as though it had never been. He heard an eerie, low, unpleasant sound: a deep, throaty chuckle that seemed to emanate from... everywhere, reverberating across the still water and the dark rocks surrounding. And, most critically, the bottom literally fell out of his world — or to be more precise, the rock he had been standing on, that mere moments before had seemed as solid and firm as Gibraltar, was simply, inexplicably, not there. Rhiss remembered the feeling — not the conscious thought, just the instinctive, icy conviction in the pit of his stomach — of knowing, with absolute clarity, that this was far beyond merely dangerous; for the first time he could recall in his young life, death hovered nearby.

He struggled and thrashed in vain in water that had recently been pleasantly cool in the humid afternoon, but was now suddenly a raw Arctic blast. Its freezing temperature caused him to gasp involuntarily — a deadly mistake, as he sucked a massive draught of water in with it, a torrent that went straight into his lungs.

Feeling suddenly light-headed, Rhiss sank below the surface, struggling in adrenaline-fuelled terror, but with strength ebbing. He became aware of a faraway voice in his head, a panicky voice insisting that slimy ropes were attached to his legs, dragging him down; but it was becoming very difficult to focus on anything. There was no air in his lungs, and the urge to breathe was almost overpowering. The water's surface was a foot away, then two, the sun plainly visible as an unblinking, malevolent eye watching impassively. Blackness tinged with scarlet spots flickered around the edges of his vision, and a deep roaring sounded in his ears. Rhiss felt a growing lethargy, began to feel disconnected from his own body...

Then he felt, rather than saw, a sudden explosion of turbulence: something dove into the water beside him. There was a flash of light and heat, and the ropes on his legs were abruptly gone; not disentangled, simply gone. There was a very real sensation of being lifted by strong arms, bringing him back towards the surface, air and life...

He woke on the bank beside the pool, lying on his back, and the oddest thing was his clear recollection of the moment: instead of a deep realization that he was alive when he should be dead, the irrelevant thought ran through his mind that he was sopping wet and Aunt Kerian would be furious.

He retched, coughed weakly, and rolled onto his side, the better to rid himself of the remaining water in his lungs, and that was when he saw her: a girl, he noted with mild interest, but more interestingly, he did not recognize her. He knew all the village children, but this girl was a complete stranger. He was too young at the time to appreciate it, but looking back, she was attractive, elfin features framed by curly masses of dark, dark hair, more or less like his own in colour, but much longer. She wore a rather shabby-looking dress extending to her knees, a red belt at her waist cinching the dress. His cursory examination took in three more details: she was barefoot; stared with a mixture of wary interest and compassion; and her hair and clothes were as bone-dry as his were dripping wet...

It had been Bold. Sudden awareness of that simple fact knifed painfully through his mind like a lancet, and he gasped at the realization.

Rhiss had forgotten the incident over the years, although at the time, he had long wondered about the identity of the young girl who rescued him. She spoke not a word, just smiled radiantly as he struggled to rise, and when he finally managed to get to his feet, it was only to find she had disappeared as mysteriously as she had appeared.

The thoughts swirled in Rhiss' mind. Bold of the Sinea-a-Doorn... in Dinas Mawr... when he was a child. What had she rescued him from — besides drowning, obviously? Recalling it, not only with adult eyes, but also awareness of who he was, Rhiss was convinced something significant had happened many years ago, something beyond simple childhood misadventure. *Something* deliberately baited him into the Pool of Rothrann. That cheerfully malevolent chuckle, the bottom suddenly falling away... and most especially, the slimy ropes — none of them, he was utterly certain, were just half-remembered imaginings of a terrified child. *Something* with a surfeit of intelligence and malice had lured him, snared him, and very nearly murdered him. The fact that Bold was there, watching over him, lent credence to the idea.

And... there was a second memory, wasn't there? Aye, there was. Triggered by the recollection of the Pool of Rothrann, another memory... gnawing at the edges of consciousness, a far more recent memory... it had slipped his mind, too, in spite of only recently taking place...

...Several months ago, on a grey and damp Saturday, the clouds were low against the verdant English countryside. At The Blade and Bow, Alistair was again patiently instructing Rhiss. That particular day, they had been at it hammer and tongs since early morning, and as a watery sun finally rose to its zenith, Alistair pulled out his pocket watch.

"I should think you must have had enough of losing for a while," he announced cheerfully. "Time to retrieve lunch from the pannier bags on the horses, don't you think?"

Rhiss snorted in derision. "Losing? Me?" he retorted. "I had you fair and square that last bout, and well you know it. If you're worn out and need a rest, all you need do is say so."

Alistair grinned. "All right, I'll go so far as to admit a draw. How's that?" He paused, then added thoughtfully, "You know, I have to say, you're improving markedly, Rhiss. I'm impressed." He rubbed his stomach. "And hungry. Come on, how about it? Go and get the food while I clear away."

Rhiss blushed and bowed his head, trying to mask his pleasure. Compliments from Alistair did not come often, but Rhiss knew they were honestly come by and in earnest when they did.

"All right. In the meantime, try not to fall asleep. I know I must have exhausted you with my prowess."

Feeling quite chuffed with himself, Rhiss walked to the nearby clearing where the horses waited, nose bags attached so they could enjoy a good feed while their masters were occupied. The pannier bags were still in place on Alistair's horse. Rhiss stepped between the horses, murmuring softly lest they take offence at his passage. But they seemed oblivious to his presence, and he was at the bags in seconds.

He was loosening the buckles on one, determining where lunch was, when he froze in the act, hand still in the air as he stood, startled. He could hear a voice. It was Alistair, and it sounded as though he was conversing with someone. "What on earth?" Rhiss muttered. "Talking to himself, then? Daft old bugger. Why, I've half a mind —" He stopped, sheepishly aware he was doing the very same thing.

Rhiss cleared his throat self-consciously and stepped from between the horses, moving across the clearing as quietly as he could. It was his intention to come charging along the path and give Alistair a jolly good scare while he was in the midst of his soliloquy. But as Rhiss crept silently along the path, hardly daring to breathe, he froze in consternation and confusion.

Another voice answered Alistair softly, a youthful, warm, lilting voice, unmistakably female.

What was going on? Was Jennie there? Surely not. Alistair and Rhiss both regarded practice time as sacrosanct; neither would dream of breaking the unspoken pact by inviting an outsider to their sessions. What, then?

Rhiss moved stealthily until he reached the clearing and knelt, watching carefully. Alistair stood with his back to Rhiss, but someone was standing before Alistair, someone much shorter. And Rhiss could discern something very odd peeping from somewhere behind Alistair, something that looked rather like finely made silk, moving in a slow back-and-forth motion. Rhiss frowned and strained to hear the low voices.

"Aye, it's coming very well indeed," Alistair replied. "The bloodline runs true. He has a definite gift, amazing speed and an intuitive grasp of what's needed. I think he'll do wonderfully well, if given half a chance. I've taught him all I know. In fact, you may tell Them our pupil has, to my surprise, begun to surpass me. Truly, he could acquit himself against all but the most skilled masters." There was a moment's pause before Alistair continued. "All he really needs now is to believe in himself and his dexterity. There's still hesitancy on his part to believe he's as capable as he is. I know not why it should be so, but... I have done what I can to erase it."

"He is young, and has yet to meet his greatest challenge," responded the lilting female voice calmly. "But from what you have said, I am confident he will rise to it. All is well, then. I will return and make my report to Them."

"Do you know how much more time we have, or when the moment will come?"

"Soon," was the soft reply. "I regret I cannot say more precisely, but it is not given to me to know. However, the situation worsens. If They are satisfied he is ready, I feel sure They will not hesitate long. He is needed desperately."

Alistair nodded, about to say more, but at that moment, Rhiss felt a sudden white-hot cramp in his leg muscles, and with an involuntary gasp at the intense pain, was urgently compelled to stand, stretching the offending limb. The attempt, hasty and unplanned, resulted in losing his balance and crashing to the ground. Trying to keep his eyes on Alistair and the mysterious visitor, Rhiss had a confused recollection of several images: the ground rushing up to meet him, Alistair whirling in alarm, and briefly — very briefly — the sight of a young, bare-legged girl in a ragged dress, scarlet belt at the waist, masses of dark curls framing a youthful and attractive face in an expression of concern, and, strangely, some sort of gauzy material rising behind her back, like a translucent banner waving backward and forwards. She raised her arms... and there was a soundless explosion of light, brilliant and blinding. Rhiss instinctively closed his eyes against its intensity. Then it was gone, and he cautiously opened his eyes, dark magenta spots clouding his vision...

The young girl's face — he was absolutely sure it had been Bold. Again. Not that Alistair was helpful when he rushed to Rhiss, massaging knots from rigid muscles. In fact, Alistair had been nothing but casually uninformative in answer to the startled, urgent queries Rhiss pressed him with. Yes, of course there had been a girl there. No, Alistair had never met her before. She had introduced herself as cousin to one of his pupils at the school, asking about her relative's academic progress. No, he had not noticed anything especially dramatic or strange about her physical appearance or her departure; the white flash Rhiss described must have been his eyes playing tricks, some bizarre side effect of the muscle cramp. The girl had simply finished her inquiries and left, even as Rhiss had experienced his painful episode and Alistair rushed to his aid.

Rhiss frowned thoughtfully as the memory played in his mind. It was undeniable: a Sinea-a-Doorn had been present with him at least twice. And that might well be only the tip of the iceberg, for if there had been two incidents he *could* recall, there might well be others he did *not*. What did it point to?

Obviously, during the first incident, Bold had saved his life. He had never been quite sure exactly what had occurred that day in the Pool of Rothrann, although admittedly, as a child he had not been eager to analyze the terrifying specifics. In fact, he had tried for years to forget the experience, evidently with nearly complete success. However, a small corner of his mind had always known there had been a terrible presence in the Pool that day. What it was, its origins and purpose, were all things his child's mind shied away from. But it had lured him for — what? His death? Was that presence connected somehow to Arrinor, to who and what he was in this world? It seemed too fantastic to believe. And yet, Bold had clearly been watching over him; had she not, he would have drowned. Of that, he was utterly certain.

Then there was the recent episode with Alistair. If it was Bold, she was not there to save Rhiss from anything that day. But she had seemed interested in gaining news of... some sort of progress. As to whose progress... well, in light of all that had happened since, it was not difficult to guess: she was there to learn from Alistair how his pupil progressed — and *Rhiss* was the pupil, not some nameless child at the school, as Alistair would have glibly had him believe.

But that in turn meant something else, and Rhiss narrowed his eyes at the realization. If Alistair was in league with Bold, he must have come from Arrinor — or been sent — with express instructions to train his charge in the use of weapons. Who had sent him? Gavrilos? Tariel? Someone else entirely? How had Alistair arrived? He must have come through a Portal... or perhaps not. Who knew how many ways there were to enter this world?

Rhiss was forced to concede there were simply too many unknowns, too much he had not been told — even now, after all he had seen and learned, there was still much withheld.

Shaking his head in mixed frustration and wonder, Rhiss realized he could chew on the conundrum all day without reaching any conclusion. But at least he had dredged the recollections he sought from the vaults of memory. He was momentarily tempted to return to Storrenne and query Bold, but doubted she would provide the information he sought. She might not even appear; Tariel would almost certainly have instructed her on the matter. For now, Rhiss realized he must put the issue aside, and return to Lowri, Arian and Parthalas. He looked around for Aralsa, lazily cropping grass fifteen yards away. Brushing dirt from his tunic, he stood and strode to her. Picking up the reins and mounting, he urged her in the direction of the Ford at White River.

Riding easily on Aralsa as she cantered along, for the first time in a long time, Rhiss felt oddly at home. This was Arrinor, and unaccustomed exhilaration rose in his heart at the sights, sounds and smells of the moor. There was a wild beauty to it, completely at odds with the life he had known, but nonetheless compelling. He gave a shout of pure joy, and urged Aralsa into a gallop. Racing across the moor, he glanced up and realized what was missing. Grinning with pleasure, he called Aquilea with his thoughts. He was unsure how far his summons would carry, but it would be useful to discover, and here was an ideal opportunity. Angharath had overheard his inadvertent call, so it would be interesting to see whether Aquilea would hear a purposeful one.

Moments later, he heard an answering call in his mind, crisp and clear as a trumpet's sound. Rhiss halted Aralsa and leapt off, striding several paces before stopping, scanning the skies.

He waited patiently for several minutes. There! A small, black dot appeared on the horizon, rapidly growing larger. Shortly, it was visible as the young gryphon minor, and seconds after that Aquilea landed a stone's throw from Rhiss. Sprinting like the cat she partially resembled, she closed the distance in no time and reared up, placing front legs on his shoulders. She gazed deep into his slate eyes with her own golden ones, great rumbling purr surrounding them like a bass humming emanating from the earth itself. She butted his chest with her head, and Rhiss fell over, laughing. He lay on the ground, and she threw herself down beside him, rubbing her head against him, purring all the while. Her joy and relief were as evident in action as the emotions in her mind.

After several minutes, Aquilea quieted and simply lay beside Rhiss, eyes fixed in trusting adoration. Recalling the previous evening, he felt a pang of guilt.

"I'm sorry I ran off, leaving you on your own, lass," he said softly, scratching her head. "But it had to be done. And I guess if I had to leave you with anyone, Lowri was the best person to do it with." The mention of Lowri's name suddenly brought him back to the present, and he sat up. "But I suppose we'd better get to them, hadn't we? They'll be that frantic. Although your mad dash from the cottage a few minutes ago was likely a clue for Lowri, at least, that I've returned. We'd best be away. Come, girl."

Rising, he sought Aralsa. She was once more calmly cropping the tough moor grasses, quite unfazed by Aquilea's sudden reappearance. Rhiss walked over, took the reins trailing on the ground, and mounted. She *was* taller, he thought absently; there was no doubt. He shrugged, wheeled Aralsa around, and urged her back into a canter. Aquilea launched herself into the air and took up station slightly off to his right, thirty feet overhead. Rhiss looked up approvingly. Finally, all felt complete and as it should be. He glanced down and smiled. Now, *that* was ironic, and no mistake, he thought. Dressed and equipped as he was, with the companions he had — his students would never have recognized their old schoolmaster, riding over the moor like something from Norse legend. It was incredible he should now regard this as normal. But it felt right and natural, somehow. Things had certainly changed in mere weeks. Aye, indeed. He pursed his lips thoughtfully, lightly touching Aralsa's flanks with his boots. She moved into a gallop, and they raced over the moor, Aquilea calmly pacing them overhead.

———◆———

Some time later, with Aralsa long since slowed back to a walk, they topped a rise, and there in the morning light was the Cottage at the Ford of White River. A fluffy curl of smoke rose lazily from the chimney, and the river flowed noisily over its rocky bed. It was odd, Rhiss thought, even after spending so short a time there, he felt he was coming home after being away many years. He smiled. Like Ulysses returning, he thought. Well, not really: it wasn't an apt comparison, as he had yet to see the marvels of this world, and hadn't been away years. And, he reminded himself ruefully, he wasn't coming home to a wife, however much he might wish it were the case.

Down below, a solitary figure stood outside the cottage, scanning the hillsides, accompanied by a large, shaggy animal. Even at that distance, Rhiss could tell without the presence of Relamus that it was Lowri. It was obvious her search was no idle one. Of course — Aquilea had probably streaked from the house when Rhiss called her. Lowri would have understood the significance of Aquilea's hasty departure and what it implied, and come looking for his return. He smiled. At that moment, she caught sight of him, waved madly, and called to those within. Without looking back to see whether she had been heard, she ran towards Rhiss, Relamus on her heels, barking furiously.

Something fluttered pleasantly in his stomach as Rhiss halted Aralsa and dismounted, waiting for Lowri with hands on hips. Lowri closed the distance rapidly, and then she was there. She launched herself at Rhiss, wrapping her arms around him and hugging fiercely. Smiling, Rhiss reciprocated, feeling the strange sensation intensifying in his stomach. At length, they reluctantly disengaged. Lowri scrutinized Rhiss carefully.

"Praise be to the One," she breathed. "You've come back." She noticed something about either his demeanour or appearance, and a different look came over her, a strange look of thoughtful recognition. "And more, it would seem. Aye, I can tell. Don't blush, Rhissan... it makes you look all of twelve." She nodded. "You've made your peace with it, haven't you? I can see it."

Rhiss immediately understood. "Well, not yet, not... not precisely," he replied dryly. "But I think I've come to understand the necessity."

In answer, she stiffened slightly, then suddenly knelt on one knee. "Well, then, I am glad beyond measure, your Grace," she said formally, head bowed, examining the ground.

Appalled, Rhiss gripped her arms and raised her, although she would not meet his eyes. "No, Lowri, no," he whispered urgently. "Never that, I beg you. I am Just Plain Rhissan to you, and will remain so, always, whatever might occur. Please."

She continued staring at the ground. "I cannot. 'Tis not proper. You are Prince Rhissan, in truth, and will some day be King of Arrinor, if the One wills," she murmured. "I am only—"

Rhiss brought his hand up and gently put a finger against Lowri's lips, silencing her before finishing the sentence "—the first person I could legitimately call 'friend' in Arrinor, who nursed me to health when I was injured, who cared *for* and *about* me afterwards, assisted in awakening my abilities, and ultimately helped force me to understand what it is to be king. You cannot go all formal on me with credentials like those, Lowri." He smiled and stroked her cheek. "In fact, if you're bent on making a fuss about my... status... why, then, I order you not to. I need you too much for that, and well you know it."

She smiled in return, at last lifting her eyes to meet his. "Very well, then, my dear," she replied gently, "I guess I have no choice, since you command it." She glanced towards the cottage; Arian and Parthalas had emerged and were striding swiftly up the rise towards them. "But I'm not at all sure Seir-onna Arian will be pleased. There *is* such a thing as protocol, you know."

Rhiss waved a hand impatiently. "We'll deal with that as the issue arises. But I think Arian will not find me quite the same man who left suddenly last night in such distress. That Rhissan was much less sure of himself, more easily manipulated. He left in denial of his destiny, but he no longer exists."

She looked at him thoughtfully, nodding slowly. "Aye, I can see that, plain as plain, and I'm sure it will be equally obvious to them. What's happened, Rhissan?"

He took her hand in his, stooping to pick up Aralsa's reins with the other. "A great deal, dearest, none of it less than extraordinary — as seems the norm here. But let's go meet those two impatient old priests, and I'll tell you all together. Then I won't have to tell it twice."

The reunion with Arian and Parthalas occasioned great rejoicing and relief. Rhiss was surprised by the depth of feeling displayed at his return; and while they were plainly overjoyed to see him back safe and well, possessed of resolve with newly found knowledge, it was evident Parthalas, in particular, had been truly distressed, both for Rhiss and the way they had manipulated him. Apparently, the previous night there had been much anguished speculation amongst the three as to what frame of mind Rhiss might return in — *if* he returned at all. That last had seemed a very real possibility, and they had been full of dark fears about what should happen, for him and for Arrinor.

They were spellbound by the tale Rhiss told of being taken back to the night of the Coup, and his part in it. Was it a new part, or had it always been there? None of them were sure. Did it even make sense? As Lowri adroitly observed, if Rhiss only saved the life of the Queen's hand-maiden last night as an adult, how could she possibly have been there during his childhood to nurture him, becoming the person he knew as his aunt?

He wound up having to tell the tale more than once, or even twice. In fact, they heard it several times down to the smallest detail, turning each development over and over like children examining a new toy. The conversation went into the afternoon, brought to a halt only by a late midday meal.

Plenty of Lowri's good food relaxed everyone and brought a measure of peace. The fire was warm and inviting after midmeal and a pleasant drowsiness lay upon them. The pace of conversation slowed, but with greater reflection and thought. Talk turned to what it might mean, and what plans could be made for the future. It was, as Arian remarked, their first real opportunity to do so since leaving Craggaddon Hall in such haste. It was only days ago, but Rhiss thought sleepily that it felt a lifetime past.

Suddenly, he jerked wide awake. An abrupt silence had fallen inside the cottage, and he saw Arian and Parthalas had nodded off. Rhiss cast his gaze around the room, looking for Lowri, and there she was, standing by the fire pit, hands on waist, smiling. As he started to give voice to his puzzlement, she quickly put a finger to her lips, turned and beckoned him to follow. They went out through the infirmary wing, saying nothing until she gently but firmly closed the door.

"There," she declared, "and about time. I thought those two old hens would never stop clucking. It's all well and good to mull things over, but they just went on and on — and when you do that, productive ideas stop coming and you just rehash the old. So we'll let them sleep a wee while. Meantime, we can clear our heads with a ramble over the moor, if you're willing, Just Plain Rhissan."

Rhiss looked narrowly at her, suspicion becoming certainty in his mind as he spoke. "Did you put them to sleep?"

She looked coy. "Now, I ask you, would I do that?"

"In a moment, if it suited your purposes," Rhiss retorted. "I thought as much. What was it? Did you doctor their drinks?"

She looked scandalized. "Rhissan! I'd not do a thing like that, not to friends, at any rate. They were fair worn out, poor lambs, from all that talking and thinking. I... merely encouraged their inclination to sleep. It's a useful ability with hurt animals, you know, and it works just as well on stubborn people. *They* can have their afternoon nap in peace, *we* can have our walk, and everyone will be the happier for it."

Rhiss looked at her a moment, her lovely eyes opened wide in innocence, then burst out laughing. "Very well, Mistress Lowri. Lead on. But don't you be trying any of your trickery on *me*."

They walked the moor for several hours, arm in arm as they strolled along. Their talk ranged widely over many different topics, some trivial, others deep, and their discourse was broken at times by companionable silences that did not feel awkward, simply natural pauses as each digested what had been said. Aquilea flew quietly overhead, occasionally performing acrobatics, and Relamus loped easily beside them, veering off now and again to investigate particularly tantalizing scents in the wiry grasses. It was all very peaceful, and Rhiss felt he could have gone on in this manner forever. But it was not meant to be, as they were both fully aware.

At length, as the sun was beginning its descent into the nearby hills, Rhiss sighed. "We'd best turn back," he said quietly, looking down at her. Lowri nodded without speaking, the regret in her eyes matching the tone in his voice.

"Besides," Rhiss added, trying to lighten the moment, "remember what you've said several times about the moor after dark. Aren't you afraid of what we might encounter?"

Lowri glanced up at Rhiss, dark eyes unreadable. "Do you toy with me, Rhissan?" she asked softly, then shook her head. "I see you don't," she murmured. "But nothing on this moor can terrify me... not anymore... as long as you're with me." She turned and slowly began retracing her steps. Astonished, he stood still for several seconds, until she cast a sad glance back, holding out her hand. Rhiss came out of his trance and moved swiftly towards her as the sun, a flaming tangerine ball, slipped below the horizon.

When they finally returned, it was fully dark, countless stars glittering coldly in the sky above. Rhiss had extended his cloak about Lowri and put his arm around her as the air grew colder, so they proceeded slowly the final mile or two. As they topped the last rise and saw Lowri's cottage below, the warm glow of firelight visible through the windows, Rhiss stopped to face Lowri. He wanted the moment to last forever. There was so much he wanted to say, and he knew, in all likelihood, there would be no further opportunity to speak to her alone for a long time. She looked up, dark eyes luminous in the starlight, a tiny, knowing smile playing on her face, and he was struck by the nearness of her grace and beauty. A surge of wistful, desperate longing coursed through him, and without speaking, he took her in his arms, leaned down and gently brought his lips against hers in a long and lingering kiss. It seemed the most natural thing in the world to do, and he felt her press against him in response.

Time stopped, and coherent thought with it. An eternity later, Rhiss felt awareness of what they were doing flood his mind like a scalding tide, and he finally broke the kiss. "I... I don't know what came over... I'm sorry," Rhiss stammered.

Her lips quirked into the barest hint of a smile. "For what, dearest?" she asked softly. "For having the courage to give action to feelings we both have, before it's too late? Because once we're back in yonder cottage, I'll wager Arian won't give you a moment alone until you're away. She won't want you having any more time by yourself with a common maid of the moor, you know."

Rhiss shook his head. "There is nothing remotely common about you, Lowri. Even Arian must see that." Then he stopped, recalling the conversation between Arian and Parthalas. "But you're right, as usual. They talked of it only recently. Arian thinks Lady Rhyanna a far more suitable subject for my attentions. She's already scheming on that score."

Lowri shrugged slightly in his arms. "I wouldn't think too harshly of her. 'Tis only to be expected. You're the last of your line. But if it's any comfort, I doubt they'll marry you off right away. Things are still too new and fluid, but it's something that must be planned. And they'll want a legitimate heir from you as quickly as possible, you know, in case things go... badly."

Rhiss was appalled at the implication. "Rest assured I won't be just a royal stallion to service..." he began angrily; but he stopped and with an effort, grimly brought himself under control. "If it comes to that, be aware I will have much to say."

Lowri smiled. "Knowing you, I'm sure you will." She raised a finger to his mouth, traced a line there. "Your lips set in quite a pattern when you're determined, my love."

Rhiss stared, thunderstruck, heart racing. "What... what did you say?"

Lowri tilted her head to one side. "Are you that surprised to hear it from my lips? Let's be honest and admit we shouldn't feel as we do. It would make it easier for both of us. But our feelings are what they are, and there's no shame in that."

Rhiss was silent a moment, struggling with wildly conflicting thoughts. Finally, voice low, he said, "I want you to know... I would turn aside in a flash from the path laid before me, if it meant I could remain with you. I have no particular desire to seek the Kingship, as I said."

"I know, my dear," she replied softly. "And I am glad you do not covet power. But you must seek it, as we are both only too aware. However, there's a small, selfish part of me — well, actually, a substantial part — that wishes with all my heart you did not need to be King. But let me see if I can help make sense of it." She paused. "Do you remember sweet little Alairra, the girl on Mairi's farm mauled by that foul plaything of Maldeus?"

Rhiss nodded. "Of course. How could I forget? Especially—" he smiled, reminiscing "—in light of how you... pushed me to realize what I could do for her."

"Aye, well, I suppose I did. I'm sorry it seemed harsh at the time, my dear, but we really didn't have the luxury to let you sort it through at your own pace."

Rhiss shook his head. "Of course not. You did what had to be done, for all our sakes."

"Aye, well, Arrinor has many like Alairra, young and old alike, innocent and undeserving of the tribulations thrust upon them by your aunt, the Queen and Maldeus. They will continue to suffer her casual — or deliberate — malice for as long as the two of them continue usurping the Crystal Throne. And because *you* are the only one who can change that, you must try. Not for yourself, but for Alairra and those like her. Remember that always, my love."

Rhiss sighed. "Aye, Lowri. I will." A sudden wild idea came to him, and hope flared in his breast. "But of course! It needn't end for us. Come with us! Leave this hermit-like existence by the moor, and ride with us tomorrow."

She hesitated, and Rhiss knew what she would say before she spoke. "I desire that with all my heart, Rhissan... but... a number of things make it impossible."

"What things?"

She looked down. "Well, to start with, can you imagine Arian's reaction to that idea?"

"Arian will do as she's told—" Rhiss began heatedly, but Lowri gently put a hand over his lips.

"No, my love. That's something even a King must learn. You can only override your advisors so often until you stop listening at all and truly become a tyrant. Even a King must bend to the will of his associates at times, or he will find he has none. And although we have disparaged Seir-onna Arian the last few days — to my shame, a thing I should not have encouraged — I spoke at length with her when first we brought you here. She is a good woman, capable and fully committed to seeing you on the Crystal Throne if it is within her power — including giving her life. Such capacity and loyalty are not to be taken lightly."

Rhiss mulled it over glumly, but knew in his heart Lowri was correct. "Well... it seemed a good idea."

"More than that, it was fair wonderful, my love, still is... simply not practical at the moment." She cocked her head to one side. "And I, too, have responsibilities here, to people who depend on me. But that doesn't mean it might not be practical later. You could always come for me once you'd seen the lay of the land. I might be... freer... to come later."

Intent solely on the heartening idea of Lowri joining him, her cryptic last words failed to register. "I suppose I could," Rhiss said slowly. He thought for a moment, then nodded. "So be it. That's what we'll do." He sighed. "I guess we must go down and return to those two old hens." He squared his shoulders and said, in a resigned tone only partially jesting, "Lead on, Mistress Lowri."

Lowri smiled radiantly. "No. We will go down together, my love, hand in hand and arm in arm."

Rhiss smiled back. "What if they see us thus?"

She tossed her head defiantly. "Then they do, and they're welcome to make of it what they please. In the meantime—" she smiled again "—in this we are One."

Arian and Parthalas did not see them enter. Lowri suggested using the infirmary entrance, settling Aquilea and Relamus in the straw before coming quietly through into the cottage proper to see what the priests were doing.

Both were awake; Parthalas sat by the fire, placidly watching Arian pacing like a caged bear. They jumped, startled by Rhiss and Lowri's unexpected dual appearance. Parthalas' obvious relief formed an interesting counterpart to Arian's annoyance.

"By the One! Back at last! How could you both wander off like that? We did not know where you were, why you were gone, or for how long! For the second time today, we wondered whether we should launch a search for you—"

Rhiss held up a hand, forestalling the tirade. "Peace, Seir-onna," he said calmly. "I will try, for your sake, to be more mindful of my safety, but I warn you, I will not pretend to be made of glass, liable to shatter into a thousand fragments at the least mishap. Nor will I be kept tightly on your leash like a hound denied any freedom by its master. Much of what I've read about the institution of kingship suggests it is an awful prison at times, and I tell you, I will not deny myself the occasional opportunity, like the one this afternoon, to find respite from it."

Arian looked as though she might be tempted to argue. She stared at Rhiss, but said nothing, evidently taken aback not only by what he had to say, but by the tone. Parthalas flicked eyes from Rhiss to Arian to Lowri. At length, as the hush grew awkward, Arian nodded slowly and exhaled loudly, a small smile on her lips. "I see a Prince has indeed returned to us, in truth. Very well, my lord. You are correct. But you *should* be mindful of your safety. Much depends on you, and I would be grateful if you keep that uppermost in your mind. In return, I will strive not to treat you like a small child, heedless of danger he puts himself in." She made a small bow, raised a quizzical eyebrow. "Will that satisfy you?"

Rhiss was surprised but not displeased by her sudden capitulation. "Eminently, Seir-onna."

"Good." Arian yawned and looked at Parthalas. "Might we ask, however, what you did all this time?"

"Naught more than a long ramble over the moor, Seir-onna," Lowri replied smoothly before Rhiss could say anything. "Prince Rhissan and I have been on many walks these past days while you were away, talking about all manner of things, so we thought we'd spend a few hours and take a last one before he leaves."

Rhiss glanced sharply at Lowri, wondering if her comments were wise. There was the slightest emphasis in her voice when she mentioned Arian being away, and the implication was abundantly clear: she and Rhiss had forged a close relationship in Arian's absence. Rhiss looked from Lowri to Arian to Parthalas. It was evident from their expressions both had indeed read between the lines: Arian was grim, but Parthalas had a twinkle in his eye, and abruptly put hand to mouth, coughing with unnecessary vigour. Arian glared at him, then returned her gaze to Lowri, who looked back with the innocence of a small child.

"I see," Arian said neutrally. She opened her mouth to say something, thought better of it, and finally said, "Well, then. Perhaps we should make preparations for bed. It has been a long day for all of us, you most especially, Prince, and I would have us leave early tomorrow for Pencairn House, if that is acceptable."

"It is," Rhiss confirmed, although he made no move towards the infirmary door. Parthalas sized up the situation and moved to Rhiss, embracing him. "Well, then, that's that. I'm right glad to see ye and the lass safe and sound, lad, and I'll be off. Good night to ye both. Come now, Arian. We'll let the two young ones tidy up. Rhiss will be along in a moment or two." He moved towards the infirmary door, then turned back to Arian, still irresolute in the middle of the room. "Arian!" he called, softly enough, but with a hint of steel. She started as though wakened from a dream. "Come ye now to yer rest, I say. Rhiss and the lass can tidy up."

Arian nodded, reluctantly moving to follow Parthalas through the entryway, casting a last look back before going through and closing the door.

Lowri began laughing gently the moment the door was shut, and Rhiss turned to her, struggling to keep a straight face himself. "Lowri," he said with mock severity, "that was very wrong of you. You deliberately baited her."

Lowri attempted to look contrite, but the effort failed, and she burst into renewed giggles. "Aye, that I did," she admitted. "Did her a world of good, I shouldn't wonder. She's probably not used to being put in her place, and in just minutes, we both gave her what for. But as I say, 'twas good for her." Deepening her voice in fairly credible imitation, she grandly declaimed, "'I see a Prince has indeed returned to us, in truth.'"

Alarmed, Rhiss said urgently, "Lowri!" in a tone that was genuinely stern this time. He quickly glanced at the door, half-expecting to see Arian storming out, but it remained resolutely closed. Lowri looked quizzically at Rhiss.

"You shouldn't mock Arian," he explained nervously. "She's bound to be in a bad humour without your adding fuel to the fire."

Lowri shook her head, amused. "My dear, show some courage and don't fuss. It'll be all right. Parthalas is on our side, can't you see? I'll wager he's smoothing any ruffled feathers Arian might have even now."

"Parthalas won't have the last word, you can be sure," Rhiss replied grimly, bending to pick up dishes on the table. "And he defers to Arian, anyway."

Lowri shrugged. "As may be, my love. But it's not an issue to be decided tonight, is it? So let's do as Parthalas said. We'll tidy up, and then..." her voice trailed off.

Rhiss became aware of sudden silence, straightening up and looking at Lowri, to find her regarding him gravely across the room with beautiful doe-like eyes. The fire was slowly dying, the cottage full of the interplay of light and shadow. In the warmth of that glow, Lowri stood quietly, hands at the sides of her long, flowing dress, a simple vision of alluring loveliness and grace.

He walked slowly to her, entranced by her beauty, and gazed in her dark, enormous eyes: liquid pools he could fall into and drown in. There was more, too: tenderness, compassion... love.

Without conscious thought, Rhiss put his arms around Lowri, gathering and crushing her to him. Her lips sought his, and they remained there, shadows dancing and flickering around them.

It was Lowri who finally drew back, flushed and trembling. "I think..." she began huskily, then stopped and cleared her throat, holding her hands in gentle warding-off gesture. "I think we had best end it there. Let us not lose ourselves in the moment and do what we would later regret."

Rhiss was immediately conscience-stricken. "Of course," he said, appalled by his lack of restraint. "Lowri, I'm so utterly sorry. I can't think what came over me—"

She managed a wan smile. "I can, my love, because I felt the same. But as I said, let's not risk all we've had together."

"Of course," Rhiss repeated, meaning it with all his heart.

There was a pause. "I'd best go," Rhiss eventually said quietly, moving to the connecting door.

"Wait," said Lowri before he had gone a dozen steps. He halted and turned. She came lightly over and stood on tiptoe to kiss him once more, gently. "May the love of the One shine down upon you. Know that wherever you are, my thoughts and prayers are with you, always."

"I know." He returned the kiss, stroking her cheek. "As mine are with you. Good night, Lowri." He went through the door, closing it softly.

"Good night... Prince Rhissan," she whispered to the empty room. "Go you with the One... my love."

<hr>

Rhissan had returned. Those three simple words were like healing balm on Aquilea's Essence, after an uneasy interval of the Sun's passing.

His abrupt departure the previous evening, Essence in painfully obvious disarray, had deeply distressed Aquilea. But The Woman — who was also distraught — had prevented her from leaving, making it plain Aquilea must allow Rhissan time on his own to sort through the revelation that had so powerfully and painfully shaken the foundations of his world. Aquilea did not like it at all, but since The Woman had thus far been invariably right as regards Rhissan, Aquilea had acquiesced. She did not really understand why the revelation had been so shocking in the first place... was his lineage and destiny not written boldly across his Essence for all to see? But since then, she had begun to comprehend — hard though it was — that it was not given to some of the One's children to see the physical expressions of each other's Essences. Strange idea, but apparently true. How sadly limited the poor humans were in so many ways, Aquilea thought sympathetically.

But then, not long after Rhissan had fled the cottage, and Aquilea was slowly coming to terms with the uneasy feeling of him gone, an even more disturbing development had occurred. The presence-knowledge of his Essence in Aquilea's thoughts — a constant, comforting sensation for, really, only a short time (although it already felt as though it had always been there) was abruptly cut off, winking out of existence like a candle flame extinguished in a breath of wind. Aquilea had been startled, then shocked, then panic-stricken: was Rhissan dead? Was his body even now undergoing the Fire of Cleansing, Essence joining with the One?

The Woman had sensed Aquilea's thoughts and been of like mind, but managed to convey that he had passed beyond their ability to intervene on his behalf, and they must wait: if it was the will of the One, Rhissan would be returned to them. The Woman's thoughts whispered they must have faith in the One, and in Rhissan. Aquilea had understood, but had not found it possible to be sanguine; she had spent the night and most of the next day huddled forlornly at The Woman's feet.

Then, suddenly, in the afternoon, Rhissan's presence-knowledge reappeared in Aquilea's thoughts as precipitously as it had disappeared the evening before. One moment, there was a deep, aching chasm in her thoughts where he should have been; the next, it was filled, and he was there. This time, she would not be restrained, and joyously sped from the cottage to rejoin him, The Woman close behind.

Their reunion — all three of them — was ecstatic. And, Aquilea realized appraisingly, there was new strength, calmness, an acceptance of what he was meant to do, radiating from Rhissan's Essence. The Transcendent Servant of the One had taken Rhissan to... she was not quite sure where. It had been a strange journey, beyond doubt. Some of it even appeared to have taken place long ago, at the time of Rhissan's birth — although that was plainly impossible. The images in his thoughts were extremely confusing... and most strangely, it appeared he had even had close dealings with her kin, the Great Gryphons. (They had verbalized his Essence name, too, although it lost much in the translation from thought to voice.)

Aquilea found she did not really care. After terrible dealings with the likes of the Transcendent Servant, the Dark Servant of the Other, her Great cousins and the Way Stones Guardians — after all that, Rhissan had returned to her.

And once again, it was enough.

XIX

HOUSE AND ACCEPTANCE

"So the Five Companions came even unto Telcharan, that is in the ancient tongue, the Place of Sanctuary. They were sore amazed at the sight greeting them on their arrival, and spoke among themselves, saying, 'How can this be?' But the Servant of the One admonished them, asking, 'How indeed? How can ye ask such a question? Have ye then forgotten that with the One, all things are possible? I say unto you, question not the actions of the One. Rather, rejoice with great gladness at the sight of mighty gifts unlooked for."

The Book of the One, 95:10:47-50
(Cantos 95, Chapter 10, Verses 47-50)

Morning came all too soon. When Rhiss woke, stiff and unaccountably sore, Arian and Parthalas were already up and about, preparing for the journey, and Lowri bustled around the cages, tending her charges.

"Good morning, Just Plain Rhissan," she called over her shoulder, bringing an animal from its cage and gently caressing it. "It's a wonder you could sleep with all this clamour. Come, make yourself ready for the day. Breakfast is on the table, and Seir-onna Arian is anxious to be off. Aye, quite anxious. You've a fair distance to go."

Listlessly, for he was not at all eager to leave Lowri, Rhiss washed and dressed before seeking food. It was indeed obvious that Arian was impatient to be away: she wolfed down her own breakfast, then paced restlessly back and forth while Rhiss tried to enjoy his last meal in Lowri's house. Arian glanced frequently at the plates and bowls, gauging progress made — or lack thereof, Rhiss thought dryly. Parthalas was silent, but winked at Rhiss across the table and matched his eating pace. Eventually, though, Rhiss gave up and rose with a sigh, only partially finished. Packing his few belongings, he was surprised and touched to find two shirts laid neatly beside his saddle bags. Intricately embroidered, they were clearly Lowri's handiwork. Carefully folding them, Rhiss placed them in his bag, only to find there was scarcely room left for the Circlet of Araxis. He held it, wondering what to do. Then he shrugged and placed it on his head. After all, when all was said and done, it was meant for the King. Donning his cloak, he raised the hood to conceal it from Arian, lest she not approve.

Minutes later, Rhiss led Aralsa around the side of the cottage to the front. Parthalas and Arian were already on their horses, and Lowri stood with Relamus at her side.

Arian had a second horse tethered behind her own, laden with boxes of various sizes. The sun was only just peeping above the horizon, but the sky was cloudless. To his annoyance, Rhiss realized the two, sitting silently like stone sentinels, would make his farewell necessarily shorter and more formal than he would have wished.

Lowri sensed his irritation, and with a knowing twinkle in her eye, leaned close to Rhiss and whispered, "Don't fuss, Rhissan. It doesn't matter. A cantankerous old woman can't erase memories we've made the last few days." She winked and pulled back before saying more loudly, "Prince Rhissan, it has truly been honour and pleasure having you in my house; in fact, like having a husband." Arian choked involuntarily, and Lowri smiled impishly at Rhiss. Realizing her statement was a deliberate provocation to Arian, Rhiss could not help returning her smile. He bowed low and kissed her hand, replying, "Lady, my time here has been of healing and instruction that will prove invaluable in the weeks and months ahead. You have my sincerest gratitude." As he straightened, their eyes met and held, with much passing unsaid between them.

"I have a last gift for you, my Prince," Lowri said, suddenly serious. "I have laboured on it, in odd moments, since you first arrived, only finishing last night. Wait you a moment." She turned and went inside. Re-emerging, she brought a long, slender package wrapped in a sheet, curtseying as she presented it.

Bemused, Rhiss unrolled the sheet, then caught his breath at what lay revealed: a beautifully crafted leather and metal scabbard, complete with second belt that looped over the shoulder to support his sword's weight. The leatherwork was superb. Lowri lifted her eyes to smile shyly at Rhiss.

"It's incredible, Lowri," he said softly. "An amazing gift. And the shirts, also. I cannot thank you adequately."

She turned scarlet. "Alairra's father also worked on the scabbard," she murmured. "He's that skilled with leather and metal. Said it was the least he could do, and a great honour."

Rhiss drew his sword and reverently sheathed it in the scabbard, Lowri assisting him to buckle the belts. Rhiss glanced at Parthalas and Arian, unsure of their reaction, but both smiled approvingly.

"A scabbard fit fer a King, in truth," Parthalas declared. "Eh, Arian?"

She nodded. "Indeed. Wear it gladly and with pride, Prince."

Rhiss could not speak, and turned back to Lowri. Their eyes met and held, each reading the other's wistful longing, and she nodded.

"Go you with the One, my dearest," she said, very softly.

"You also," Rhiss managed. He reached out and they clasped hands for several moments, squeezing hard. Then, throwing caution to the wind, he drew her to him in a long embrace and kissed her. Reluctantly disengaging, Rhiss turned and mounted Aralsa, mentally calling Aquilea. She bounded into the yard, nestled briefly against Lowri, and came to sit beside Aralsa.

Rhiss glanced at Arian and sighed, trying to muster some enthusiasm. "Very well, Seir-onna, let us be off, if go we must. I have heard of it so much, I would see Pencairn House at last, preferably before sundown. Lead on, if you will."

Arian inclined her head, first to Rhiss, then to Lowri, but said nothing, and as one, the three reined their horses around, heading for the road. Aquilea leapt into the air. Rhiss glanced back once as they rode, and saw Lowri standing by her house, Relamus at her side. She evidently either saw or sensed him, for she lifted her hand in silent farewell for several moments. Then Aralsa went over a rise and down the other side, and Lowri was lost to view. Rhiss turned in his saddle, grief sharp as a knife, vision unaccountably blurred. From overhead, a distinct wash of sympathy rippled through his mind. Amazed, he squinted at Aquilea, almost remarking on it. He pursed his lips thoughtfully, shifted his weight in the saddle, and tried to focus on the route Arian took.

It was a pleasant day for riding: the sun shone brightly in a sky holding only thin wisps of white cloud scudding briskly overhead. A cool breeze blew, preventing the day from warming overmuch, and Rhiss was glad to keep his cloak on and the hood up even as the sun reached its zenith. The wind blew off majestic, snow-capped mountains, which reared ever higher as they approached. By noon, they were among the mountains, following a wide road which clearly saw regular traffic, although they met no one along the way.

When Arian called a halt for midmeal, they steered their mounts off the road, and Rhiss slid off Aralsa. Sitting on boulders as they ate, he turned to Arian, hoping her mood had improved.

"Seir-onna, I beg you, at last satisfy my curiosity about Pencairn House, before I finally behold it. What manner of place is it, alone and isolated in the mountains, and why is it so unlikely for us to head there?"

Rhiss was relieved: Arian smiled and turned to Parthalas. "What think you, my friend? Should we discharge our young Prince's impatience?"

Parthalas returned the smile, but his voice had a slight edge. "Och, aye, of course. Ye already know what I think of keeping secrets without need, don't ye?"

The smile faded from Arian's face, but she ignored the reproach, turning back to Rhiss. "Very well, Lord Rhiss." She stopped. "I beg your pardon, *Prince* Rhissan. It is hard for me to use your proper title, accustomed as I am in thinking of you as Lord Rhiss."

Rhiss smiled and waved a hand in easy dismissal, although he could not help thinking wistfully of Lowri's titles for him. "Fret not, Seir-onna. I am quite content with either mode of address. In fact, in some quarters, 'Lord Rhiss' might draw less attention. It would certainly be more familiar to me, also."

"Technically," interjected Parthalas mischievously, "the correct form of address is 'Yer Grace,' isn't it, Arian?"

Arian looked at Parthalas sourly. "Aye," she said shortly. "But that title might draw *more* attention, not less."

Rhiss laughed. "I will not stand on ceremony with either of you. But what of Pencairn House?"

"Well," Arian said thoughtfully, "I suppose we *have* kept you waiting long enough, and we can only be an hour or two away." She reached a decision. "Very well. Know that Pencairn House was, at one time, an important establishment of the Knights Castellar. It was a training school for new recruits, and an environment away from the hustle and bustle of daily life, suitable for reflection and contemplation as they sought the guidance of the One in their vocations. As such, depending on how kind time's passage has been since its abandonment, the isolation should be ideal."

Rhiss frowned. "If it was so ideal, why was it abandoned?"

Arian hesitated. "Because... it came to be haunted by an evil spirit," she said finally, eyeing Rhiss to gauge his reaction.

Rhiss raised his eyebrows sceptically. "I beg your pardon?"

"Aye, you heard me rightly. Do not look like that. I assure you I am in earnest. In your short time back in Arrinor, you have already seen things beyond human ken, have you not? I tell you an evil spirit walked the corridors of Pencairn House during the night hours, terrifying the inhabitants until none could remain. Now, bear in mind, Prince, the people were Knights Castellar, brave warriors not subject to childish hysteria. But it was too much, even for those who had experienced carnage and slaughter. It was a truly terrifying sight, this spirit clearly sent straight from the Other."

In spite of himself, Rhiss felt the hairs rise on the back of his neck. "Did it ever... actually *do* anything? Assault or murder people, for instance? Or worse?"

Arian shook her head sombrely. "No need. It was such a dreadful apparition to behold, none could withstand it."

"What did it look like? Did you see it?" Rhiss did not mean to hush his voice, but Arian's words brought up still-fresh memories of Moressin.

Arian shook her head again. "I was not there at the time. But Parthalas was."

They turned to Parthalas, faces expectant. He shrugged, face carefully set. "Well, what can I say, lad? It were a great, horrible apparition, tall, bloody, long flowing robes of black and red, and the commotion it made... howling up and down corridors, 'til no one could either find sleep or dare open their door to run away. Its face... was not to be borne. None could withstand it." He fell silent, recalling events he clearly did not wish to share further.

Arian took up the story. "I well recall the commotion at the time, even though it was years ago. It all seemed too incredible to be true — that such a thing could happen." She shook her head, remembering. "Abandoning the place was an action not taken lightly, I assure you. Parthalas, do you recall Dorvanen's fury?"

"Oh, aye," replied the old warrior ruefully. "Although there was a fair measure of fear mixed in, I can tell ye. He was Grand Master of the Order at the time, lad," Parthalas added in response to the questioning look Rhiss gave. "A hard and intemperate man, not one who fancied abandoning one of the Order's prime training houses, I'll tell ye. At first, he saw conspiracy in it somehow, perhaps with reason. But abandon it he eventually did when it became clear there was nowt else to do." He chuckled. "I can still remember him coming to investigate the reports personally. Spent only part of a night, he did, before out he came a-running in his nightshirt, screaming for all the world like a young girl just shown her worst nightmare."

"Conspiracy?" snorted Arian. "Come now. In the name of the One, how could that possibly be?"

"Oh, I dinna think the One had much to do wi' it," the old man said darkly. "The Other, now, that's a real possibility, though. It was certainly the general feeling, and ye can say what ye like, Arian, but you must admit, it *was* uncanny. A haunting! There'd been no warning or signs of anything untoward until it just up and happened. It seemed totally wi' out cause."

"Perhaps." Arian shrugged dismissively. "At any rate, after it was determined the Order would abandon the place, the buildings were stripped of furnishings and moveable objects. But it wasn't deemed worthwhile to dismantle the structures themselves — the costs would have negated the value of bringing out the lead, timber and stone. *If* a workforce willing to undertake such a task could even have been assembled, of course. So the buildings were simply abandoned intact, and gradually forgotten. As far as I'm aware, no one has been back in many years. At the time, the tale was known far and wide. No one would dare set foot there."

"Many years?" echoed Rhiss. "Just how long ago was this haunting and abandonment? Before the Coup?"

Arian pursed her lips in thought. "No. About fifteen years ago, wasn't it, Parthalas?"

"Aye. Shortly before Dorvanen's mysterious death."

Rhiss was completely nonplussed. "So... what you tell me is that we enter a harsh mountainous environment to find an empty establishment not maintained for years, its last inhabitants driven out by an evil spirit." He paused. "How, exactly, is this ideal? It seems what you have described could hardly be *less* suitable."

"I know not, in truth," admitted Arian. "Nor am I certain what we will find. But I remind you we proceed there solely on Lord Tariel's recommendation. Seeing as he twice saved your life, and in light of the events of the last day or two, I place our trust in him. As I recall, he specifically directed you to say my objections about Pencairn House's suitability were 'no longer valid' — the 'issue had been resolved,' I believe were his words. I do not think he will have steered us wrong. How Pencairn House's suitability problem will be solved, I have no idea. But Parthalas and I agree you move in highly unusual circles, and the hand of the One is upon you. When you related your experiences with Lord Tariel, I was prepared to take this step on faith, and Parthalas concurred."

Rhiss considered. "I see. So, then, you do not expect to find it uninhabitable, physically or spiritually, do you?"

Arian looked thoughtful. "No, I do not. What we *will* find, I do not know. But I am fast learning the unexpected ever seems your constant companion. So, like you, I look forward to seeing what we do encounter upon entering Pencairn Vale."

It was late afternoon, the sun already out of sight behind craggy peaks all around, when they left the main road and took an unmarked, barely recognizable side path that Parthalas assured them was the route. He led the way, followed by Rhiss; Arian brought up the rear. Aquilea still cruised overhead, but lower and closer to Rhiss. Alone, Rhiss would have gone right by the path without a second glance, or even registering that it was a road. Once well-tended, it had obviously not seen use in many years, and was thickly overgrown as the forest slowly reclaimed it. There were several points, indeed, where the path was washed out altogether from spring runoffs, and in such places they were obliged to dismount, leading their horses down into the ravines, then out again.

After a good hour of proceeding slowly in this manner, the cool mountain air had taken on a distinct chill. Rhiss drew his cloak tighter, glancing at the surrounding mountains, wondering when they would arrive. On the summits, there was still much snow, now painted orange by the setting sun. Rhiss urged Aralsa forward, catching up with Parthalas.

"Is it much further, Seir-on Parthalas?"

The old man flicked a friendly sideways glance. "Och, just plain Parthalas will do fine, lad. Ye'll find I'm no' one to stand overmuch on ceremony, until perhaps instruction in weapons and tactics begins... and even then, only in the practice ring."

Rhiss smiled, hearing his own words to Lowri being used by the priest. "Very well, Just Plain *Parthalas*."

"That's better, lad. Not much further, I think. Half an hour, perhaps. The going was faster when this road was in better shape, of course, so I canna be sure. But we'll get there, never fear. Why? Have ye had enough?"

"No, merely curious. But it *is* getting a little nippy as the sun sets. I think anyone with sense would soon want to be inside, tucked away where they can have a fire." Suddenly, Rhiss whipped his head around and stiffened in the saddle: movement had briefly caught his eye.

Parthalas noticed. "Is aught wrong, lad?"

"Parthalas," said Rhiss carefully, "I don't want to alarm you, but I think there was an animal in the brush there." He paused. "Rather a large one. Perhaps even... a wolf."

"What? Where, lad?" Parthalas stopped and surveyed the surroundings intensely, Rhiss pointing to the spot where he had seen the movement. "Hmm. I canna see anything now. Are ye sure of what ye saw?"

Rhiss considered. "Not really," he admitted.

"Well, keep an eye out, and I'll do the same. Like as not, it were a big fox or badger, lad. But in the meantime, we'll keep on our way. As ye said, it *is* startin' to get a wee bit chilly now, and it canna be much further."

Rhiss nodded, unconvinced. Arian caught up at that moment. "Gentlemen? Something of overriding interest? I would like to reach Pencairn House before dark."

"Our young Prince, here, thinks he saw something large in the underbrush. A wolf, mayhap."

Arian raised an eyebrow. "Are you sure? Was it a shadow?"

Rhiss grimaced and did not answer. He mentally called Aquilea to come lower. He sent her the image of what he had seen, telling her to seek it. She cried harshly in assent, climbing again, scanning the area, and they resumed their slow trek.

They saw nothing unusual for another quarter of an hour, and Rhiss began to relax, convinced his mind had been playing tricks. Even the horses sensed nothing out of the ordinary, which reassured him, knowing they could feel the presence of other animals more keenly than humans, particularly hostile ones. If the horses were not uneasy, then probably all was as it should be.

But then, minutes later, not just one, but many long, sinuous shapes were gliding among the trees behind, on both sides, and in front, and Rhiss knew his suspicions confirmed. Inexplicably, they came from nowhere: and they *were* wolves — massive ones. Seeing them, Rhiss again thought absently that Arrinor rarely did things on a small scale.

Simultaneously, Aquilea uttered a warning challenge from above. She remained airborne, flying in circles, crying her alarm, images of what she saw flooding his mind. As if in response to Aquilea's cries, eerie howls rose from the wolves all around.

The horses reacted in an ecstasy of terror. Nostrils flaring, eyes rolling in panic, they whirled, seeking avenues of escape, their riders seeking to bring them under control. Even Aralsa, whom Rhiss had grown to regard as utterly docile and dependable, was not immune to the fear generated by the wolves: she reared in fright, and Rhiss was able to stay mounted only with difficulty. Reining her in, he sought to project calm to all the horses, and Aquilea. As they slowly became tractable, he knew he had succeeded.

Wolves of varying sizes and colours circled, although it was difficult to say for certain exactly how many; movement in the undergrowth suggested more were coming. Rhiss was struck again by the way they seemed to have materialized from thin air. The creatures emerged from the brush and sat in a blockading circle, silently surrounding and regarding riders and horses. The wolves were indeed enormous, far larger than normal, even to the untrained eye. Some were grey, some black, and incredibly, there were even some with distinct reddish-orange overtones like foxes.

The wolves made no overtly threatening movements, but that too seemed unnatural. His experience extended only to what he had read, but Rhiss felt sure that wolves on the attack would not surround their prey, then merely sit and watch. It was as though the riders were penned inside a living barrier fence, ebbing and flowing in the ferns and shrubbery. Rhiss had no doubt their advance would be resisted, should they try to resume riding, and his heart sank. Could they fight their way out? He had his bow, but it was not easy to use from horseback. Swords, then? Three with swords, against... how many? It was difficult to judge, but there must be nearly two dozen. It would be hopeless, even with Aquilea. They would be swarmed by sheer numbers and taken down. Rhiss glanced at Arian and Parthalas, saw from their hard, set expressions they recognized the futility, too.

The largest wolf of all emerged from the forest that very moment and stood directly before him, its lustrous pelt more silver than grey. Larger, sleeker, and with an indefinable air of command, the wolf was clearly the leader, but like the others, made no threatening moves. It merely sat on its haunches, regarding the riders solemnly. After a moment or two, it very deliberately lay down on its belly, massive front paws stretched out like a sphinx, and as if on cue, the other wolves did likewise.

Aquilea chose that moment to stop circling and arrowed down, clearly ready to attack, even though the wolves were all much larger and heavier; but Rhiss stayed her with both gesture and thought. She landed beside him, voicing guttural noises of discontent under her breath. The wolves looked at her calmly, apparently not at all discomfited by the small fury from the sky.

Rhiss regarded the silver wolf thoughtfully for several seconds. An idea arose from... he knew not precisely where. More than an idea, in fact, it was... almost a compulsion. Without thinking, he acted, sliding off Aralsa, dropping her reins to the ground. He walked slowly towards the wolf, palms outstretched, hands well away from his weapons.

"Rhissan?" queried Arian in alarm. "What are you doing? I don't think you should—" Her stirrups creaked as she broke off and began dismounting.

Without looking at her, eyes still fixed on the wolf, Rhiss gestured her to stop. "Hold, Arian. Rest where you are."

"But—"

"I want to approach the silver one. He's the leader, I believe. I don't feel he's dangerous—"

"Have you taken leave of your senses? That is a *very large wolf*— the largest of many. They are *extremely* dangerous. The peril is real!"

"Not so... I have an odd feeling about these wolves... a feeling that—"

"What?"

Rhiss did not answer, but caught the silver wolf's gaze. It watched him steadily from a pair of startling green eyes, and seemed completely unafraid, not moving as he approached. Strange. Unlike most animals, it had no compunction against making eye contact with a human... and maintaining it, too, not taking such contact as challenge or precursor to an attack. It was almost as if... almost as if it was measuring the mettle of the man before it. Rhiss knelt five or six feet away, and realized the entire conclave of wolves was silent, as though collectively holding their breath. To better sense with peripheral vision where the other wolves were in relation to the leader, Rhiss slowly lifted his hands and threw back the cloak's hood, shaking his head slightly as hair fell in his eyes.

The wolf's response was immediate, electric, and completely unforeseen. It reared up, eyes snapping alertly to some point above Rhiss. It did not stand, but shuffled its paws uneasily and whined. Rhiss was taken aback. He kept eyes on the wolf, but involuntarily slipped a hand to his dagger.

"Arian?" he called softly. "What is our friend so intent on? I cannot see what he finds so unsettling and yet engrossing."

"Well, I *can*," she responded in bewilderment, "but it makes no sense."

"What do you mean?"

"Well, *Prince* Rhissan... I see you wear the Circlet of Araxis," she responded quietly.

"What of it?" said Rhiss impatiently. "I could not find space in my saddle bag when we left this morning. What has that got to do with—?" He turned to stare at Arian, comprehension dawning, and he fell silent.

Of course. Lowri's gift filled his saddle bag, and the only place he could put the Circlet... he lifted his hand to his head, felt the cold metal there. He had quite forgotten putting it on.

Arian nodded. "Aye," she said, still in quiet tone. "And it is that, I think, which caught the attention of your furry friend. There is no other explanation."

Rhiss was utterly bemused. "But why would it... no, Arian, that's nonsense. How would it even be aware what the Circlet is, what it represents—?"

"I know not. But somehow, I tell you, the wolf recognizes the Circlet, and seems... well, fascinated by it, I should say." Arian paused, then added, "Clearly, we deal with an animal of some intelligence. Perhaps even as intelligent as Aquilea."

"Lad," interrupted Parthalas, "look ye 'round at the other beasties."

Rhiss slowly stood. Moving silently, the wolves stood left, right and behind the trio. Rhiss was irresistibly reminded of an honour guard he had seen during a parade in London once, when troops of the Household Cavalry held much the same sort of formation around the Royal Family. The silver wolf stayed where it was, but stood and turned, facing the overgrown road leading to Pencairn House. It looked back, the message unmistakable: it was ready to lead them on.

"It just glanced at the others," said Parthalas. "Glanced, and they all moved. Now, what do ye make of that?"

Arian broke the silence. "Well, Prince," she said dryly, "you appear, once again, to have made quite an impression on the situation, even unintentionally." She shook her head, amused. "Travelling with you — we could not merely encounter a pack of ordinary wolves, could we?"

"Thank the One fer that," interjected Parthalas. "If these were ordinary wolves, we'd be dead now, and well ye know it."

"I suppose you're right," she admitted. "Well, Prince, it appears these animals do not want to kill us — at least for the moment. In fact, they stand ready to escort us. Do you trust them to deliver us safely?"

Rhiss nodded slowly. "I think so. I'm not sure why, but I believe they mean us no harm. In fact, they seem almost... respectful."

Arian sighed, whether from exasperation or amusement, Rhiss could not tell. "Then I suggest you mount, and let us ride on with our respectfully unorthodox escort. Just a day's work to you, I am sure, Prince."

Half an hour later, as the light failed at last, they rounded a bend in the path, their silent escort still behind and to either side, and Rhiss had his first look at Pencairn

Vale and the House built there. He halted Aralsa to better focus, and Arian, riding just behind, did likewise, compelling Parthalas in the rear to stop also.

In the middle of the wide valley, framed on both sides by high mountains whose thickly forested sides sloped gently, was a much lower and rounded knoll, its sides likewise forested. Pencairn House was built into the hillside. A clear mountain river skirted the hill, rushing glacial waters from the mountains.

Since first hearing the name, Rhiss had thought Pencairn House would be an ordinary-sized dwelling, capable of sheltering only a few. Although he had nothing to base that on, and should have known better, it still came as a shock to see such an enormous place. If anything, the early evening's failing light only served to magnify the structure's size.

Four imposing, interconnected rectangular stone buildings, each a couple of hundred feet or more in length and several stories high, nestled together on the hillside. Windows were set into the walls at regular intervals. Compared to the cream coloured stone of the buildings, the lead sheeting on the steeply angled roofs looked incongruously like dark felt hats. One of the structures, over a hundred feet tall, towered over the other three. A crenellated wall surrounded all. Rhiss was impressed: it appeared solid, well-built and habitable, with surprisingly little evidence of neglect.

He turned to Arian, unable to conceal his surprise. "*This* is Pencairn House? I had not thought it would be so... grand."

Arian grinned, obviously enjoying his reaction. "Indeed. Our new home... for a while, at any rate. 'Tis in far better condition than I dared hope, eh, Parthalas?"

"Aye," he growled. "Too good, I'll warrant. Who's kept the place up, then? These beasties? Or do they have a master who's been a busy lad on his own, I wonder? Sweepin' and cleanin' and mendin' holes in the roof, by the looks of things. Seems altogether a wee bit too convenient, if ye ask an old man."

Arian shrugged. "Perhaps. At any rate, we'll soon see. The wolves are leading us straight to the main gate."

"Oh, aye," muttered Parthalas. "And what'll we find there? Another beastie who'll invite us in for dinner, I shouldn't wonder? And what's on the menu? I'd be a tad gamy and tough, but our young Prince, here, might give them a tastier time. These wolves aren't the end of the matter, Arian, wait and see. They're not the masters here... something else is."

Arian glanced sideways at Rhiss in wry resignation. "Nonsense, friend Parthalas. Your suspicions are too easily aroused. Have faith in the providence of the One." She paused before adding, "Besides, I don't think you'd be gamy at all. Inedible would be nearer the mark." She winked at Rhiss. "And if we could persuade the wolves to eat you first, they'd have such indigestion, I'm quite certain that they would leave Lord Rhiss and me untouched."

Parthalas said nothing, but his derisive snort seemed an eloquently ample answer to Rhiss.

The path to Pencairn House's main gate wound over a stone bridge crossing a crystal-clear brook, then on up the hillside. As they rounded a last bend before the gate, the wolves appeared to respond to some unknown signal, loping silently ahead as a pack and disappearing around the corner. Parthalas glanced silently at Arian with raised eyebrows. The main gate was open. Like everything else, it appeared in remarkably good working order. They passed through, Rhiss, then Arian and Parthalas.

As they crossed the threshold, a number of torches set in sconces around the cobblestone courtyard were alight, deep orange flames rising into the darkening sky, and they were forced to squint. Then their eyes adjusted to the increased illumination, and they halted, able to behold the courtyard.

A large group of armed people stood there silently. They were fair enough to look upon, well dressed and clean, but their expressions were carefully neutral. There had to be at least thirty or forty, both men and women. Possibly there were more — it was difficult to tell precisely in the shifting torch light. Many had bows, and all had swords. The bows were strung, Rhiss noticed, arrows nocked — although none were aimed directly at the mounted trio. Swords were likewise out, although, again, resting points down. Rhiss thought there was a definite feeling in the air of — hostility? No, that wasn't it. It was watchfulness, he realized in surprise, almost expectancy. He cocked his head to one side. The mood was palpable, at least to him. Another gift of the King? Regardless, it was time to set the encounter in motion.

Rhiss gently nudged Aralsa forward, and they rode another thirty paces, followed belatedly by Arian and Parthalas. Then a man in the vanguard of the group held up a gauntleted hand, and Rhiss halted again; slowly and easily, he dismounted, and they regarded each other closely. The man looked about forty, tall, handsome despite an old, faded scar above one eye. His beard was dark, and there was something familiar to him, though Rhiss could not put his finger on it.

There was silence except for the slight guttering of torches in the breeze. No one seemed about to break it, so after several moments, Rhiss took the initiative. Inclining his head in greeting, he addressed the leader. "Good evening, my lord. I ask your pardon for our sudden, unexpected appearance. We have been making for this place for some time, but did not expect to find it inhabited... or guarded by sentinels of... such unusual size and ability." There was no response, so Rhiss continued. "May I present first my companions? Seir-onna Arian, Seir-on Parthalas, both renowned priests in..." he paused for the briefest of moments, then finished, rather lamely "... in service of the One." He thought it prudent not to mention the Castellars without knowing more about the silent, well-armed group, and where their allegiance lay.

The man bowed. "Be welcome, servants of the One, to Pencairn House," he said formally, straightening and addressing Parthalas and Arian. "It has been long since two such distinguished guests have graced our gates." Despite his courteous words, it was plain they were not the real focus of his interest at all. He turned back to Rhiss, eyeing the Circlet with an unfathomable expression, plainly waiting for the rest.

Rhiss smiled, trying to put the man at his ease. "Aye... well then, as for myself, I am Rhissan Araxis, and..."

His voice trailed off as the crowd murmured. The leader turned, gesturing sharply, and they subsided, but it was clear to Rhiss his words unnerved them. Several actually made the Triune Sign. The man let his hand drop and turned to face Rhiss, eyes wide with a strange mixture of hope and disbelief. "By the One! Can this be true, at last? The Circlet has come. And you, truly—?"

Rhiss became aware of Arian at his side. The priest nodded, smoothly taking charge of the situation. "Aye, my lord," she interrupted in a strong, clear voice, so all could hear. "You have heard rightly. You stand before Rhissan Araxis, first-born son of the late and well-beloved King, therefore rightful King and Sovereign of Arrinor in his own stead. Here—" she gestured at the Circlet "—as you say, is the Circlet of Araxis, emblem of Arrinor's Kings from long ages past." She half-turned to Rhiss, whispering quickly out the corner of her mouth, "Unsheathe your sword."

Rhiss swept the sword from its scabbard and held it aloft. It glittered redly in the torchlight, throwing warm shards of ruby light around the courtyard. "For any needing more evidence," Arian continued in the same ringing tone, gesturing at the sword, "here is Altanimar, long the sword of Arrinor's Kings. Look upon the hand wielding it, know the truth, and be glad." She gazed at the leader, then at the crowd behind, all of whom stood stunned. "Well?" she challenged. "You have seen the tokens. Will you not acknowledge them for what they are, and the man who has been given them?"

The leader went down on one knee, bowing his head, followed immediately by the rest.

"Your Grace," he murmured, looking up, and Rhiss was astonished to see his eyes bright with tears. "Thanks be to the One. Our long wait is ended at last! I apologize for my witless phrases moments ago. I have rehearsed many times what I would say at our meeting, only to have words vanish like autumn leaves in the wind when finally they are required."

Embarrassed by the man's raw emotion, Rhiss did not know what to say or do. He glanced for guidance at Arian, who nodded almost imperceptibly, motioning a hand upwards. Rhiss nodded gratefully, and cleared his throat.

"Rise, my lord; your good people also. And do not be disconcerted about your greeting. Even things long awaited can be startling when they finally, unexpectedly manifest. I know that all too well. But I fear you have the advantage, for we do not know your names."

The man flushed but did not rise. "Of course. I am shamed by my rudeness." He inclined his head in apology, looking up and turning wide, honest eyes on Rhiss.

"Know me, then, your Grace: I am Borilius, leader of the Araxite Community. Our swords are yours to command, and I bid you welcome with all my heart to Pencairn House."

XX

ACQUAINTANCE OLD AND NEW

"What is friendship? It is one Essence reaching out to another. It is delight felt in another's companionship, based not on gain, falsehood, demand, or power; but on truth, giving, freedom, the simple joy of finding a kindred Essence. Why is it so vital a part of the One's Grand Design? Truly, it is neither right nor good for Children of the Light to walk alone in Life's Journey. You were created not to endure isolation, but for community. Therefore, strengthen and lovingly instruct each other; fulfil, complete and delight each other; for you are all Children of the One."

The Book of the One, 90:1:1-5
(Cantos 90, Chapter 1, Verses 1-5)

Even as the man spoke, an icy shock of recognition rippled through Rhiss. He closed his eyes involuntarily and shivered. Borilius! Of course! Rhiss had *known* the man was familiar without knowing why; now it was obvious. The features of the boy who had spoken boldly and been such a help the night of the Coup were the features of the man looking quizzically at him now, blurred by the passage of twenty-five years. For Rhiss, of course, it was only days ago he had last seen those features — on a child's face. He opened his eyes to find Borilius rising and, with Arian, regarding Rhiss with concern.

"My lord?" asked Borilius. "Are you unwell? You've gone quite pale."

Rhiss found his voice after one or two tries. "Your name... is Borilius?" He cleared his throat as the other nodded. "You were..." He stopped, realizing what he was about to say, and tried again more circumspectly. Better not to reveal too much, until he knew the man better. "Were you at Tor Eylian the night my family was murdered?"

"Aye, my lord." Borilius was clearly puzzled at the line of conversation, but swept an arm encompassing the courtyard. "Many you see here were there that night." His eyes took on a faraway look. "We were very nearly all killed — defenceless children, caught squarely in the midst of atrocity and massacre. Aye, we would have died, too, were it not for the resolve of..." It was Borilius' turn to break off as he, too, obviously decided to be careful with his words.

"It was... a brave young knight, unknown to us — about your age — and his older companion, who rescued us and got us to safety." He waved his hand in elaborately apologetic dismissal. "But the manner by which we ended here is a lengthy tale, one better suited to a sleepy evening by the fire with a cup of mulled wine than out here in our courtyard. Time for that later, if the One wills." He smiled an open smile of friendship. "For now, be welcome, and allow us to offer you our hospitality, away from the night's piercing cold. We have much to ask and tell each other."

Rhiss nodded, although he was eager to hear what happened all those years ago after he and Tariel departed. Belatedly, Borilius called to his folk. "Well? Have you not heard? Our honoured guests will enter the House. Halver, Carlus and Fennor, take their horses and make them comfortable, then rejoin us. The rest of you, stop gawking and be about your duties until evenmeal. You will have opportunity to speak with them later."

Three men detached themselves from the group and led the horses away, while the others gradually dispersed, clearly reluctantly. Borilius spread his hands ruefully. "My apologies for their lack of civility. You must think us an uncultured rabble. But they have waited long years for this, and are understandably eager to see and hear all about you." He bowed and gestured them towards a large building. "This way, if you please, to our Great Hall. From there we shall see you settled in; then we would be honoured if you would join us for the evenmeal we were about to begin when you arrived."

As they walked, Borilius glanced at Aquilea, trotting quietly beside Rhiss, eyes and nostrils wide as she drank in sights and smells. "You keep uncommon company, if I may say so — and I do not refer to your human comrades."

Rhiss followed Borilius' gaze, smiled and said dryly, "No more than you. We shall also be keenly interested to learn about your 'uncommon company.'"

Borilius looked confused; then his face cleared and he laughed. "Ah, our four-legged friends who announced your arrival. The wolvans. Aye, fair turnabout. I do not imagine you have seen aught like them before among people, and I'll wager their story is every bit as interesting as yon gryphon's."

Rhiss raised an eyebrow. "Indeed, although that was not to what I referred. What of the other unusual occupant of this House? How do you keep company with it?"

Borilius looked blank. "Your pardon. I do not understand to what you refer."

Rhiss stopped and they all halted. In the gloaming, golden light from torches at regular intervals along the walls gave comforting illumination against the growing darkness. It was difficult to imagine the place haunted by a dreadful apparition.

"Well, then, let me be clearer. Are you not troubled by an evil spirit wandering the halls and corridors of this House? A creature so terrible that even Knights Castellar could not abide it? What of this spirit that sent them fleeing in terror?"

Borilius burst out laughing. "That is one creature we have *not* had to deal with. I know the story well, how it appeared and drove the accursed Castellars out, but we have never laid eyes on this thing, nor has it ever troubled us."

Rhiss turned to Arian and Parthalas. They looked mystified, then shrugged. "Well, that's fine wi' me," Parthalas said wryly. "I'd no pressing desire to see that thing, and that's a fact. Now let's be gettin' on, shall we? Someone mentioned evenmeal, if I'm no' mistaken, and I've quite a hunger. They used to put on a fine table here, and I'd like to see if the new tenants can match the old."

The following week was a whirlwind of activity, especially after the gentle tranquillity of Lowri's house and its brief interlude of shining peace. Rhiss had little time on his hands the first few days. Arian mapped out a training regime in multiple kingly disciplines, physical and academic, and Parthalas immediately began formal weapons practice with him. The old man's age in no way diminished his formidable fighting skills, and Rhiss was pleased when Parthalas expressed unqualified approval at his abilities.

"The lad's a fine fighter, and no mistake," Parthalas declared after several sessions. "A wee bit unschooled in some of the subtler things — and dirty tricks — but someone's given him a fine groundin', definitely."

"Excellent," replied Arian, adding dryly, "I am sure you will teach him *more* than his share of dirty tricks, old friend."

Parthalas shrugged and winked at Rhiss. "Count on it. Kings canna always afford honour, as well ye know, Arian. Remember that, lad. Hit 'em low and hit 'em hard, every time, and *never* waste yer chances bein' noble and courtly and such wi' someone holdin' a knife on ye. T'isn't like some tea party with a fair lass. No point in bein' a dead but honourable king, I always say."

Arian rolled her eyes. "Thank you, Parthalas, for giving our future King the morals of a gutter rat. In the meantime, Rhissan, you and Borilius should be part of our planning discussions, for you are King— or will be, by grace of the One. You should also acquaint yourself with the people of this House — the Araxites, as they style themselves. Their presence is an extreme stroke of good fortune, as we start with a well-trained, disciplined fighting cadre already in existence, dedicated to your cause — a huge advantage when we anticipated just us three. These people will be — in fact, already are — the nucleus of the much larger force we will need. So walk among them, get to know them. They are truly a gift of the One in our need, eager to assist, and we must not neglect to fit them into our plans."

Rhiss tried to do so. As Borilius indicated, the core members were the children he had rescued at Tor Eylian twenty-five years prior. Ranging in age from ten to fifteen then, they were now in their late thirties. But others were much younger, and Rhiss was at first puzzled how that could be. Queries revealed a number of the Araxites were married with children, making it a community in the truest sense. It emerged that the Araxites had recruited on their own over the years, so their original force was bolstered by men and women from places throughout Arrinor, some far from Pencairn House, but all united in opposition to the Sovereign.

Rhiss found it difficult to wrap his head around the fact that mere days ago, by his reckoning, the Araxites were children; now they were much older than he. It strained his sanity a little. He saw many faces he recalled from Tor Eylian, and was impatient to hear how they came from Kirunek to this place, but it was difficult to get the opportunity — there was much to do settling in and assessing the Araxites' strengths and weaknesses. Rhiss also wrestled with how much he should tell of his role in their salvation so long ago. Was it wise to reveal that the younger of their two saviours now walked among them as their future king?

The Araxites' behaviour decided him. While most people were courteous and would talk amiably with him, little groups stared or followed him, sometimes more discreetly than others. If that had been all, he could have put up with it. But there appeared to be a great deal of misinformation going about concerning the actual nature of the Gifts of the King. Some of what he heard, or had asserted right to his face, varied from the merely ludicrous to the disturbingly dark. One tale claimed he could bring people back from the dead; another insisted that he could give life to clay statues, and was making an army of them to defeat Maldeus without anyone else needing to lift a finger. Several times he was accosted by people who seemed to think him some sort of saviour, with the ability to smite down not only Maldeus, but the Other himself. For example, one young man was convinced Rhiss could work miracles for his kin, who lived clear on the other side of Arrinor. Rhiss always found such encounters painful. Each new day seemed to give rise to a fresh rumour, wilder than the last. And it felt like the doubters, the sceptics, lurked behind every darkened corner, not merely downplaying his abilities but denying them altogether. Once or twice, Rhiss heard fairly nasty stories about where Arian and Parthalas had 'acquired' him, so as to make their own lives easier than would otherwise be possible for a couple of aging clerics. Although Pencairn House was larger than Rhiss had expected, its grounds expansive, it seemed there was nowhere he could go without attracting notice. Having led a very ordinary life in England, where no one gave him a second glance, Rhiss was quite unused to being the centre of attention; it was unnerving, and on occasion, distressing.

He sought out Borilius one afternoon, following a practice bout with Parthalas which had gone particularly well. He should have been in high spirits as a result, but an oppressive feeling weighed heavily on him, an oppression Rhiss felt peculiarly sure was externally generated, not some fell mood within himself. It was almost, he decided uneasily, like the oppression he had experienced before shrugging off the dark, questing hand of Maldeus. But there was a subtle difference to this sensation; like and yet unlike. He was still puzzling it through when he finally located Borilius, who was engaged in logistical discussions with two officers as Rhiss entered. They rose and bowed.

"Your Grace," said Borilius warmly. "How may we serve you?"

"I wondered if I could have a word. In private, if you please."

"Of course, your Grace. Immediately? Or would you wish to have our conversation over food? It is nigh to the evenmeal hour."

"Now, if you don't mind."

The other two bowed again and exited, Borilius turning expectantly to Rhiss.

"Is there somewhere away from the main complex we could repair to? Somewhere quiet and private? Or do such concepts not fit the Araxite mould?"

Borilius smiled. "Oh, they do. You are not alone in desiring solitude." He pointed through a window. "Look yonder, near the summit of that peak. What do you see?"

Rhiss peered, frowning. "A house or building on the flank."

"Aye, my lord, but as this place is more than just a house, so is yon construction. What you see, diminished by distance, is Summit's Redoubt: a complex of buildings constructed years ago by those of us recognizing need in a closed community for its members to find somewhere 'quiet and private,' as you so aptly said. A small number of our contingent is always there, although we rotate people through, allowing none to remain permanently. It is a place of contemplation and reflection, but the purpose of our Community is not to produce an army of hermits. Nevertheless, if you find the main House too active, you will find the Redoubt's beauty and isolation appealing. I will take you, and there you may speak. Will that do?"

"Admirably. I am most curious to see it."

"Then let us away to the stables." In answer to Rhiss' questioning look, Borilius added, "The path is at times steep, but broad and easily navigable on horseback. On foot it takes nearly an hour, but horses cut the time substantially."

⸻◆⸻

Summit's Redoubt was all Borilius had promised. Just below the topmost peak was a lower one, connected by a long ridge; it was there that the Redoubt was situated. Located just at the tree line was a small cluster of sturdy stone buildings, fortified by a surrounding wall and gate where the path from the valley wound its way. Rhiss looked to the upper peak, fascinated to see snow glittering even at that time of year.

On arrival, a quietly courteous pair of Araxites took their horses, and Borilius gave Rhiss a tour. It was difficult to imagine the place ever being successfully attacked, and he said as much, but Borilius laughed, saying the Araxites did not believe in leaving anything to chance. Rhiss was impressed. Although all provisions arrived on horseback, Summit's Redoubt could survive on its own for a lengthy period. "The elements alone make that necessary," Borilius concluded. "In winter, the Redoubt can be cut off from the House below for weeks at a time, if weather is inclement."

Finally, Borilius led Rhiss out onto the battlement wall. The view was magnificent: one could see up and down the valley for miles, stunning vistas of natural beauty. The Pencair River wound like an aquamarine thread at their feet. Looking down the mountain revealed Pencairn House proper in the valley's middle, looking like a scale model. On the right, the mountain sheared in a vertical drop many hundreds of feet, leaving Rhiss with a distinctly hollow feeling in the pit of his stomach. At the upper end of the valley was an enormous sheet of white, the toe of the Pencair Ice Field in the mountains above and behind. A cold wind from the glacier blew along the valley, and Rhiss drew his cloak tighter. In all, a wondrous setting. They admired the view silently for minutes before Borilius spoke.

"There, your Grace. If you seek quiet and privacy in our community, I can offer no better place. Now, I have kept my word. What is it you would say?"

Finally given the opportunity, Rhiss was unsure how to begin. "Borilius," he said hesitantly, "you have… been here for some time."

"Indeed. Many years."

"And all that time… you have essentially waited for me," Rhiss mused.

Borilius smiled. "Well… aye. You oversimplify things, but I suppose it does in fact boil down to that."

"And you knew I would come." It was not a question.

"Beyond any doubt." The smile was gone, Borilius completely in earnest.

"How?"

"There were signs. The most significant was that we were told you would come by… an unimpeachable source."

Rhiss looked sharply at Borilius. It was the perfect opening. "Aye. The night of the Coup, wasn't it? A young knight dressed in the raiment of the Arkos. He was alone at first, saving your group from a band of foresworn Castellars. You tripped one, saving the young knight's life while he fought them. Then he spirited you all away on a trio of gryphon majors. Later, he was joined by an older knight, also in the colours of the Arkos. The younger called you Borilius the royal page, and assured you the King would come. *That* was your unimpeachable source."

Borilius stared open-mouthed, his face drained of colour. He swallowed several times before finding his voice. "How could you know these things?" he whispered.

Rhiss smiled sympathetically. "I'm sorry. This is no easier for me than for you." He took a deep breath. "I know because I was there. The young knight… well, 'twas I."

Borilius was not calmed. If anything, he looked even more thunderstruck. "Your Grace! Do you claim to be an *Arkos*?"

Rhiss shook his head, aghast at the misinterpretation, and grasped Borilius by the arm. "No, no, my friend! Far from it, I assure you. Like you, I am no more than mortal man. But I was brought that night by an Arkos. He wished to show me what befell my family and dressed me in the vestments of his Order, that I might blend in better with him. He… was forced to leave briefly at one point, and it was then I heard the Castellars engaged in their abominations against you. I rushed without thinking to your aid, and… the rest, you know."

Borilius stared unseeing at the valley below, reliving long ago memories. "Aye," he finally murmured. "It *was* you. I recall it now." He returned to the present, and stared at Rhiss. "I thought from the first, as you rode in, that you looked familiar, somehow."

Rhiss smiled. "Then you have an excellent memory. It was long ago — for you."

"Aye," Borilius said again. "But such events are not easily forgotten." He frowned. "What do you mean, 'for me?'"

"Well," Rhiss replied slowly, "the memory is much fresher on my part. You see, I lived it mere days ago."

"By the One's Name! That recently? And then, within a week, to see us all twenty-five years older? It must have been quite a shock."

"You have no idea," said Rhiss with feeling. "And I have not been in Arrinor since the Coup, so it was yet another in a long progression of shocks since returning."

"No doubt," Borilius said, and hesitated. "You may wish to wait to tell the Community what you told me, my lord. While it would do them good to hear our paths have crossed before — and that you are responsible for our very existence — we should perhaps allow the shock of your arrival to subside before revealing the miraculous incident of our rescue at your hands. Things seem to have been... unsettled since your arrival." He paused and frowned. "Oddly, much more so than I would have predicted."

Rhiss nodded. "I have noticed that, too, and was unsure as to the best course. That was why I craved your counsel. Do you really think that people's... astonishment... at my coming on the scene is responsible for the—" He stopped, having been about to say "fell mood," but thought better of it. "—strange behaviour at the House?"

Borilius paused in turn. "I... do not know for certain. As I said, the atmosphere of the community as a whole has not been... wholesome... recently, in ways I would not have foreseen. It is disquieting, and I myself have felt a certain... irritability... that I would have said is not usual. Do you know of anything else that could be responsible for all this that we have discussed?"

"It is similar to something I have experienced before," Rhiss admitted slowly. "A machination of the Sovereign's Counsellor... but sufficiently different that I am... not really sure." He shook his head. "I will try to do what I can do to unravel this tangle."

"As will I, my lord. But will you share the tale of your events since coming to Arrinor with me? I should very much like to hear."

"Aye, but first there is something I would like to know." He stopped at the inquiring look Borilius gave. "It concerns what happened after I left. The Arkos I was with said you would be cared for by..." he searched his memory "... a group he named the Aranellens." He looked at Borilius expectantly.

Borilius looked blank. "Aye, my lord?"

Rhiss spread his hands. "Well... who or what are they?"

Borilius' expression cleared. "Ah. You must understand that your not being long back in Arrinor is a new realization for me. If I may make the observation, you seem very much at home and at ease — and quite comfortable with your role."

"It has not always been so, nor is it now, believe me. But I have been helped on that path by friends — not always gently, I fear. I am not always a willing or apt pupil."

Borilius smiled. "I find that difficult to believe. I see in you someone eager to learn, and very capable of doing so."

Rhiss coloured and raised an eyebrow. "The Aranellens?"

"Of course." Borilius laughed. "They are an order of warriors today renowned throughout Arrinor for courage and skill, although not at Court, I fear. They are a proscribed order, your Grace, outlaws. Their leader, Eques Aranell, escaped Tor Eylian the night of the Coup, as we did, and established an order opposed to the Sovereign. They have harried and opposed the Crown since then. They generally keep to themselves, giving allegiance to no one, but they answered the call of the Arkos the night of the Coup, caring for us until we were grown and could care for ourselves, even though they, too, were no more than ragged, homeless refugees at the time."

"Being raised in the company of warriors does not sound a particularly nurturing environment for traumatized children," Rhiss ventured tentatively.

Borilius shook his head. "On the contrary. Your pardon, your Grace, but you are much mistaken. The Aranellens were exactly what we needed after what we had been through. They were kind, supportive, and—" he paused, searching for the word "—well, loving, I would say, in a rather formal manner difficult to describe. They are unique among the people I have met in Arrinor, and can seem stern and distant. Once you see beyond that, however, they are wise, courageous and loving. You will see very soon."

"How so?"

Borilius smiled. "I sent word to them after you arrived. They have always been curious about our prophecy concerning your coming, and they will be vitally interested to meet you, now that you are here, for I have no doubt they, too, will offer their support. Their leader should arrive any day. Eques Aranell, for whom they are named, led them from the carnage of the Coup that dark night, and they have followed him since. He is a leader among leaders, a truly amazing man."

Rhiss was dismayed: another group to hold him against an inscrutable standard, judging whether he was worthy. It had been difficult enough with the Araxites in recent days. Borilius read his thoughts, and said sympathetically, "It is something you must accustom yourself to in the coming months. There are many who will rally to your cause. Some will do so sight unseen, but others will want to see and assess. But they will need to do little more than reassure themselves that in you there is a true King who can liberate them. Even though most do not know what really happened in the Coup, Diiderra and her accursed Counsellor have steadily grown more tyrannical. She is not loved or trusted in Arrinor. Quite the opposite."

"I'm sure you're right," Rhiss replied unenthusiastically.

Borilius brightened. "Come, your Grace. 'Tis not all bad, you know. Tell me of your doings since coming to Arrinor. The afternoon wears on, and I would hear your tale before it is too dark to return to the House."

———◆———

Two days later, Rhiss again felt the need for solitude, but decided to forgo the Redoubt and explore the lands seen from its battlements. He even meant to do a little hunting and hone his archery skills. So on a warm, muggy, afternoon that promised storms before evening, he finally succeeded in quietly slipping away without anyone noticing. Arian had not specifically forbidden him to go out alone, but had been clear he should have people around for protection. "Our hopes rest on you, Prince. If aught happens to you, our cause is lost. You are the last of your line, you know."

Rhiss knew all too well, but felt as if he had been smothered in feathery pillows lately, and a small, rebellious part of him urgently desired to be out on his own, without the whisperings and respectful glances so many Araxites seemed compelled to display whenever he was around.

Consequently, he went on foot. Aralsa's absence from the stables would be noticed, and a man on horseback was in any event more conspicuous than one walking. He also left Aquilea, who sulked when told to remain, but yielded to his will. Rhiss tried to convince her he simply wanted to bring in his own kill, without help; she accepted it, but not gracefully, and actually growled at him as he left, telling her to remain in their quarters. Smiling at her truculence, he left his sword, taking only dagger and bow.

Rhiss tramped steadily through the humid forest with a nameless feeling nagging at the back of his mind for nigh on half an hour before he could identify it: he was being followed. He stopped and listened, extending his senses, eyes closed. There *was* something, he was sure, at perception's very limits. Opening his eyes, he carefully scanned the clearing.

There: on the far side, barely visible. Something resembled an enormous, grey dog. Rhiss felt his stomach do a slow, queasy flip-flop before he blinked, looked harder, and with startled relief recognized a wolvan. He frowned, considering. How strange. Why would a wolvan be in the forest, alone? He was given to understand they were social animals, not solitary by nature.

He walked slowly across the clearing. It was obviously aware it had been discovered, but did not run, remaining where it was, regarding him as he closed the distance. When he was ten feet from it, Rhiss stopped and squatted, just as he had the day they first encountered the wolvans. Like then, it made no effort to melt back into the trees, but merely sat on its haunches, alertly regarding Rhiss while he studied it.

He recognized the creature. It was a large animal indeed, with a glossy, silvery pelt looking so smooth and soft, Rhiss had to fight the urge to go up to it and bury his face in the fur. It was the wolvan pack leader when Rhiss, Arian and Parthalas were waylaid on their way to Pencairn House. Large, emerald eyes regarded Rhiss solemnly, and Rhiss was struck yet again by the plainly visible intelligence.

The two, man and beast, stayed motionless for nearly a full minute. The only sounds were birds in the trees, the breeze through branches of countless fir trees, and a waterfall's distant roar. Rhiss recalled a conversation he had had a day or two previously with Ulcawn, the Araxite wolvan master...

"...The wolvans are exceptionally marvellous creatures," he had been saying with feeling. "They fascinated me from the moment I laid eyes upon them."

"Understandably," Ulcawn agreed mildly. "They are beautiful, strong, intelligent, affectionate and very loyal. Ideal companions, in truth."

"How do you communicate with them?"

The Araxite paused momentarily, looking sideways at Rhiss. "I am told those with gryphon minors often speak in their thoughts. Is that so?"

Rhiss nodded. "It is, although it's not exactly speech. Sometimes, it's feelings, sometimes, it's..." He shook his head wryly. "It's actually hard to put into words. But she and I constantly improve at getting meaning across to each other. One day... it may be words. I'm more and more convinced she has the intelligence."

Ulcawn nodded in satisfaction, his ideas confirmed. "It is much the same with wolvans. In fact, if you have the ability with your gryphon, I would not be surprised if you can extend it to the wolvans, too. If you wish, when opportunity presents, I will assist you in exploring the possibility."

Rhiss looked at Ulcawn with mild surprise. "Really? I would be most interested."

"I welcome it. They are truly elegant creatures."

Rhiss had been struck by a thought. "You sound much taken with them. Is there ever dissension among them?"

Ulcawn laughed. "Not of any consequence. They have minor disagreements from time to time, as all animals do, but are far better than humans at resolving differences."

"What are their disagreements typically about?"

Ulcawn raised an eyebrow. "Status within the pack," he replied briefly, then added dryly, "not unlike like humans..."

Rhiss was brought back to the present as the wolvan opened its muzzle and lolled out a brick-red tongue, breaking the spell of his recollections. The resultant expression so resembled a smile that Rhiss laughed softly. "All right, my friend," he said quietly. "You're out for a walk, too? Looking to be away from the commotion as well? I understand, and you're welcome to either go your way or take mine. All I ask in return is you don't interfere with my hunt. All right? Do we have an agreement?" Expecting no response, he was shocked when the wolvan promptly extended a massive forepaw as though offering to seal the deal. Rhiss slowly reached out and shook the proffered limb, wondering as he did whether the wolvan could hear and understand his thoughts like Aquilea. He stood and retraced his steps. At the point where he had first sensed the wolvan's presence, he looked back disbelievingly. It had not moved: still sat on the far side, watching. Puzzled by the animal's behaviour, Rhiss shook his head and moved on.

Half an hour later, Rhiss was convinced the wolvan was indeed following. It never approached too closely, but several times he looked back and saw its sinewy, low form weaving silently some distance behind through endless trees. Rhiss was not concerned it might be stalking him; he sensed no malice, and knew wolvans were highly regarded at Pencairn House for their strength, intelligence and loyalty to the human community. But it was strange, for all that...

His preoccupation nearly proved fatal. Crossing another clearing, deep in thought, Rhiss suddenly felt like he had been struck squarely in the back by an express train. He fell, getting a split-second view of something black as the night and monstrously huge rush by, carried on by the sheer momentum of its charge.

Then he was lying on the ground, trying to rise, looking wildly around to locate his danger before realizing he was faced with an even more immediate problem. He literally could not draw breath: his lungs refused to take in air. It brought back terrifying memories of drowning at the Pool of Rothrann, except this was on dry land. As he lay gasping like a fish out of water, another massive shape streaked by, lean and silvery, and a small, rational part of him realized the wolvan had just come to his aid.

It felt like an eternity, but was only seconds before Rhiss was finally able to draw a sobbing breath that brought him rolling onto hands and knees. Several more breaths, each deeper and easier than the last, allowed him to shakily gain his feet, looking and listening all the while for attacker and rescuer.

They were on the far side of the clearing. The wolvan weaved around an enormous bear, snapping and snarling as it held the monster's attention. Rhiss instinctively reached for an arrow, but clutched only air. He looked wildly around and saw the quiver, twenty feet away on the grass where it had landed when he was knocked down. He also realized his bow was not even in his hand; another glance revealed it lying in the grass beyond the quiver.

At that moment there was a roar from the enraged bear, followed immediately by the wolvan's agonized shriek. Rhiss pivoted; either the bear was fortunate, or the wolvan was finally not quick enough to evade the vicious claws, which had batted it aside as though it weighed nothing.

There was no time to think, no time to formulate battle plans; Rhiss merely reacted. He shouted and the bear, about to deliver a fatal blow to the wolvan, halted in the act and reared on its hind legs, head weaving from side to side as it tried to locate Rhiss with its poor eyesight. Rhiss found his dagger and without thinking, whipped it out and sent it hurtling at the bear with every ounce of his strength.

Whether it was luck, or the One's providence, Rhiss did not know, but the dagger caught the bear squarely in its massive chest, burying itself to the hilt with the force of the blow. The bear roared in baffled fury, tottering a few steps on its hind legs. Then it dropped to all fours again, weaving its head back and forth in a frantic, futile effort to get at the stinger causing agony greater than anything it had ever known. It caught sight of Rhiss again and charged, deciding he was the cause of its distress. But it only went several strides before it collapsed on its side with a crash that shook the entire clearing.

Breathing hard, unsure whether the beast was dead or merely stunned, Rhiss dove frantically for bow and quiver. He was on his feet right away, arrow nocked, but the bear lay still. He approached it cautiously, ready to fire, but there was no reaction even when he gingerly nudged it with his boot. He forced himself to move around to face it, and immediately saw its eyes unfocused in death, the rictus of a snarl still frozen on its face. What a monster, he thought shakily. He exhaled slowly, releasing the tension on both the bowstring and his body, returning the arrow to the quiver. His legs felt weak and trembling, and all he wanted to do was collapse beside the dead bear and rest.

But there was no opportunity. A low, gasping cry sounded behind the massive corpse, and Rhiss remembered the wolvan which had endangered its life for him. He raced around the bear, dropping his bow to the ground, and found the wolvan beyond.

Pools of blood despoiled the ground, and the wolvan breathed in small moaning gasps. Rhiss knelt, wincing as he saw the jagged tear the bear's claws had made in the wolvan's flank. It was undoubtedly lethal. What to do, what to do? How was he—?

Distracted, Rhiss stopped in mid-thought, a wild idea penetrating his hesitation. His first reaction was profound doubt. Was it possible? Was it even *permitted?* This was, after all, an animal, not a human.

The wolvan decided him. It lifted its head weakly, turning to look Rhiss squarely in the eye. Their gazes met, and Rhiss saw trust, intelligence, calm... and a plea.

Rhiss pursed his lips, nodding. "I'll try," he said hoarsely, as though answering a spoken question. The wolvan seemed to sigh, dropping its head to the grass.

As he had done before, Rhiss collected his thoughts and reached hands out, gently placing them over the wolvan's torn side. Closing his eyes, he willed himself to calmness, mentally calling his prayer for assistance in this most unorthodox case, declaring he meant no disrespect for the miraculous ability he was gifted with, but noting the creature under his hands was also a creature of the One, given the intelligence and ability to choose to render what assistance it could in the service of the Light.

The sensations were similar to prior experiences, but at the same time subtly different in the... flavour... aye, that was the word. Almost like... tasting ginger instead of cinnamon, he decided, although that wasn't really the right analogy at all. It was so very difficult a thing to put into concrete words, or even images.

There was the familiar mounting heat in his hands, the golden flash penetrating even through closed eyelids, and it was over. He opened his eyes, slowly gazing down as he lifted his hands from the wolvan, and aside from the blood matted into its fur, the skin was unbroken. It had worked. Perhaps amazingly, against all odds, it was done. The wolvan looked at him with shining green eyes, and, Rhiss was certain, with gratitude.

Reaction to all that had occurred in recent minutes finally set in, and Rhiss felt an achy, shivering weariness overwhelm him. He lay on the ground, not quite falling, curling into a ball, not caring about any dangers, closing his eyes. The second last thing he felt, as consciousness left, was the distinct sensation of a huge, warm, furry quilt draped around his neck, back and legs. The last thing he felt was an odd rumbling noise, not unlike the sound Aquilea made when she purred, except this was more sensed than heard. Then there was nothing more.

Rhiss woke early in the grey dawn of morning to find rain beating steadily against the windows, a grim-faced Arian sitting in a chair drawn up near his bed. He yawned, stretched and decided the best approach was to speak first.

"Good morrow, Seir-onna. Am I to understand you are now available at all hours to provide spiritual counselling to those in need?"

His tactic worked, to a point. He saw the smallest curvature at the corners of her mouth as she struggled to stifle a smile. But when she spoke, her tone was stern, and she wagged an admonishing finger. "Do not play the innocent with me, you young scamp. I feel like we have been in this situation before. You know well what I have to say."

Rhiss raised an eyebrow inquiringly. "'Young scamp?' I doubt the Araxites would approve of that mode of address. What of 'Prince Rhissan' or 'Your Grace?'"

Rhiss was amused as Arian actually harrumphed. "Unlike our starry-eyed friends, you know perfectly well I am not reticent to speak my mind to you. Your potential position is of no moment. As to 'Your Grace' and such, those are titles reserved for one who is worthy of them." She sniffed. "Not to an irresponsible boy, who throws caution to the winds and wanders into the wilderness alone, telling no one."

Rhiss thought of the wolvan. "Well, technically on that point, I was not alone."

"Aye, so it would seem, and well for you," Arian rejoined tartly, gesturing at the floor beside her. Rhiss pushed himself up on one elbow, peering over the side of the bed. The wolvan lay there, looking up, tail thumping vigorously against the polished wooden floor. Beyond, at the foot of the bed, Aquilea watched alertly. She displayed no expression, but Rhiss could sense her relief and devotion washing over him like warm waves on a summer lake.

"Hmm, indeed," he replied, turning his attention back to the priest. "I remember being very tired, and... did I fall asleep?"

"Hardly. You lost consciousness *yet* again. A search party found you both, man and wolvan, hours later. A fine mist of rain was falling by that time, bitter and chill, and the light was failing when we finally came across you. Aquilea and I were in the group, the latest of several scouring the valley. It belatedly occurred to Parthalas and I that, of everyone at the House, Aquilea was unquestionably best qualified to find you due to your mental rapport. The gryphon immediately rewarded our reliance on her uncanny ability by leading us almost straight to you." She paused. "The wolvan lay curled in a great furry arc around you, sheltering you from the worst of the rain and lending body heat. It would only rise and allow us to approach when Ulcawn, the wolvan master, expressly commanded. Then it followed carefully as we placed you on a rough litter hastily constructed from branches woven together, and slowly returned to the House. Curiously, Aquilea displayed no jealousy or antagonism whatsoever towards the wolvan. 'Tis almost as though the two animals understand each other completely with regards their mutual feelings for you."

"I see." Rhiss took it in thoughtfully. "Arian, I know you're angry with me—"

"Oh, no! I am not angry," she interrupted. "If ever I am truly angry with you, Prince, you will know, rightwise King of Arrinor or not. At the moment I am simply vexed and rather put out — and very relieved we still have a Prince of Arrinor with us. Whatever made you do such a foolish thing? Wandering off alone *again*?"

Rhiss sighed. "Arian, I understand your concerns, believe me, and I am truly sorry for causing such anxiety. But this was not like Rontha. I have said it before: I will not be treated as a porcelain ornament, wrapped in cotton for fear of damage, brought out only on special occasions. I simply felt the need to be by myself, perhaps do some hunting on my own. You can't know what it's been like the last few days. Everywhere

I go here, people gather in little knots, whispering behind my back, or openly cajoling me to perform miracles. I feel like some exotic animal on display in a menagerie."

Her eyes lost their annoyance. "But they do not all act like that, Rhissan. I have seen people treat you as a human being. Even those who gawk and whisper only do it from awe and respect. There is no evil to them."

"Most of them," Rhiss corrected. "There is a group among the Araxites called the Doubters, who think I'm some sort of fraud, you know."

Arian frowned. "Aye, Borilius mentioned them, but does not believe they pose a threat — and he is sure you will win them over." She paused. "In any event, we draw away from the topic. Enlighten me: why was the wolvan with you when you were found? And a dead bear nearby? It was obvious that *you* killed it, not the wolvan."

"How so?"

"Wolvans don't use daggers," Arian replied dryly. "Even ones that associate with you. Yours had pierced the bear's heart. It must have died almost instantly. Unless you were wrestling it, I assume you hurled your dagger. A mighty throw."

"No, a *lucky* throw, an unbelievably lucky throw."

Exasperated, Arian shook her head. "My lord, as a Follower of the One, you know there is no such thing as luck. You denigrate your own skills yet again. I thought Mistress Lowri had broken you of that bad habit."

Rhiss shrugged, and thought back. "Well, whether skill, Grace of the One, or a combination, it was extraordinary," he said slowly. "The wolvan followed me from the House. I don't know why. The bear threw me to the ground as it attacked, knocking the wind out of me. As I lay helpless, the wolvan drew the bear away. Then I recovered and was able to come to the wolvan's aid. But after I managed to dispatch the bear, I found the wolvan mortally injured, so—"

"Injured?" Arian repeated, interrupting. "You are mistaken. It is unharmed, and was when we found you."

"Well, it wasn't *then*. It was gravely hurt by the bear's claws, very badly slashed. I had no choice but to try and heal it, which I did, but then—"

"You did *what?*" Arian demanded in disbelief.

"I... healed the wolvan," Rhiss said hesitantly. "I wasn't sure it was possible... even whether it was profaning my gift, but the wolvan saved my life when the bear attacked, so I had to try. It worked, although it felt much different than healing humans."

For once, Arian seemed at a loss for words. "Well," she said at last, clearly nonplussed, "just when I think nothing else you do can surprise, you manage to confound me. I have never before heard of the Healing gift used on an animal."

"You don't think I did wrongly, do you?" Rhiss asked anxiously.

Arian's gaze softened. "If the One permits it, how can the Healing of any living creature be wrong? No, you did the right thing. You gave grace where it was yours to give. Just make sure you never take your gift lightly or for granted." She smiled. "You appear to have another mouth to feed beside Aquilea, now." She looked at the wolvan on the floor. "It has refused to leave your side since you were brought back. We all wondered why, but now you have furnished the answer."

"I — what do you mean?"

"I think the wolvan — by the way, Ulcawn, the Araxite Wolvan Master, informs me its name is Caylyx — regards itself as your companion, much like Aquilea. Ulcawn says this is not uncommon with wolvans, particularly if a human has saved their life, as you did. Wolvans are social animals, very loyal, apparently even quite affectionate." She wrinkled her nose. "As to their personal cleanliness, I cannot begin to speculate."

Rhiss made a face. "That's unfair. If he has been loyally at my side, as you say, he has not had opportunity to groom himself since we returned."

"On *that* we agree," Arian noted wryly, and looked at Aquilea. "Curious," she mused. "Aquilea has no difficulty accepting its presence. Do you think she understands what is going on?"

Rhiss looked at Aquilea and reached out his thoughts. "*It* is a *he*, Arian. And I am positive she does. Why? Did you think she would be jealous, or possessive of me?"

Arian sighed. "You shamelessly project human emotions on an animal. I am still unconvinced she is capable of some of the things you ascribe to her."

"Perhaps," Rhiss laughed. "But I think we will convince you one day... she and I... and now Caylyx."

Arian stood. "That may be," she replied dryly, and walked to the door, where she stopped and turned, smiling. "But I suggest you be warier while wandering the countryside from now on, lest you find yourself with yet another creature coupling its life journey onto yours. Otherwise, you will ultimately find yourself with an entire menagerie trailing alongside you, and be known not as a king, but as a zoo keeper."

Jealous? Of a large, shaggy and rather smelly four-legs ground-skulker? Once more, Aquilea would have laughed aloud, were she capable: humans really could be so quaintly amusing at times, and the She-Priest, in particular, constantly underestimated gryphons and their abilities. One could feel faintly insulted, if one wished, but it could also be an advantage — Aquilea's mother had often reminded her that adversaries who underestimate each other do so at their peril, for the false sense of security thus engendered can be their undoing. Not that Aquilea regarded the She-Priest as an adversary or threat of any sort — she could see in the old woman's thoughts and actions that Rhissan's ultimate success was every bit as vital to her as to Aquilea, which was really the only important thing.

But Aquilea was also absolutely confident that Caylyx the wolvan would never supplant her. They were united in a crucial bond — a sense of complete devotion to Rhissan and his well-being — and both were very much aware of this mutual bond through the basic thought communication they shared. Aquilea knew Caylyx's mind regarding Rhissan, just as Caylyx knew hers, and that he had been willing to die in order to protect Rhissan was the most compelling argument that could possibly be made to convince Aquilea of the wolvan's good intentions. So Rhissan now had not one, but two Shield-Protectors to watch over him.

With that issue resolved, all should have been well. Indeed it should, Aquilea mused in exasperated anxiety. However, as her mother also said, the Other is devilishly skilled at bringing discord to harmony; there was a new disturbance which Aquilea's ability to Far-See could descry, and it was the source of much apprehension to her; for she was not too young to possess much of the ancient knowledge of her people, and was thus fully aware that the future is always fluid, unwritten and in motion, known with certainty only to the One.

She had Far-Seen a Confluence of Dark events massing like threatening storm clouds on the horizon; some of those events were indeed Small in the Grand Plan of the One, but others were Large, their implications deeply troubling. (And, Aquilea reflected, even Small Troublings could suddenly loom disastrously if cavalierly ignored, as she knew all too well from painful personal experience.) Key in the Confluence, Aquilea could see, were Dark things that might be/would be happening at the Great Stone House where dwelt the Two Women, including the Fair One whom Rhissan had Healed. She was gentle and soft-spoken and kind, and Aquilea hated to think of darkness befalling her — or her mother.

But as yet, the Evil possibilities were too far away and too murky for clarity or definitiveness. Of a certain, they were too vague for Aquilea to lay them before Rhissan, who was only still learning their rapport and the deep ways she could serve him. The Woman might have been able to understand and appreciate Aquilea's fears — but she was, alas, not there, so the benefits of her wisdom were lost for the moment.

With helpless frustration, Aquilea realized she could only watch and wait, and hope for one of two things: either the Confluence would dissipate, as storm clouds admittedly sometimes did under the influence of freshening winds from the West; or she could make Rhissan understand and act when the imminence of that Confluence demanded resolve and instant, purposeful deeds — or risk catastrophe and utter ruin otherwise.

XXI

SCEPTICISM AND FAITH

"He brings healing to the wounded, faith to the doubters, strength to the weak. They will rise up, calling out praise as he puts the Shadows of the Other to flight."

The Book of the One, 137:27:2
(Cantos, 137, Chapter 27, Verse 2)

Rhiss had hoped that the strange stories and rumours concerning him would quiet down, but the tale of 'Caylyx and the Bear,' as it quickly became known, and his amazing role in it, actually made things worse. A couple of days later, he returned to his quarters from a practice bout with Parthalas to find armed Araxites there. They were holding in custody a rather pathetic-looking young woman — not an Araxite, but the daughter of a new recruit — who had apparently been going through his things. She had been looking for relics or talismans — not to sell for profit, but to keep for herself as 'holy icons.' She was clearly unbalanced, and everyone found the incident quite appalling.

The final straw came three days after that, when a fight broke out between a couple of Doubters and a larger group defending Rhiss' status and reputation. No lasting harm was done to anyone, as it was broken up long before things could really get out of hand. But Rhiss was beside himself. His presence seemed to be creating division and chaos, not the unity and strength he had hoped for, and he knew that if a solution could not be found quickly, the community could tear itself apart. How could his presence create such discord? Or... *was* it merely his presence? The suspicion flashed into being... perhaps there was more to all the disharmony than he had thought.

He returned to the Redoubt to think things through on a brisk day marked by a cold wind and dark clouds, riding up alone on Aralsa — Aquilea and Caylyx both deciding they would rather stay by a cosy fire back at the House. Rhiss was glad they seemed to understand that he wanted to be by himself.

Rhiss had always noted that the few Araxites stationed there were different from the ones below, somehow: either Borilius had instructed them, or they were intuitively aware of his need for solitude. Whatever the case, they were always friendly but kept a respectful distance, unobtrusively providing food, drink or anything needed, but otherwise leaving Rhiss to himself.

Arriving at the Redoubt and giving Aralsa into the hands of an Araxite groom, Rhiss went up on the walls, stopping at the place already his favourite: the vantage point Borilius conducted him to his first time at the Redoubt. Rhiss loved the spectacular, sweeping panoramic view of valley below and glacier further up. He wanted a chance to reflect on what needed to be done. He was only there a short while before footsteps sounded, and a familiar voice said quietly, "Good afternoon, Prince."

Rhiss recognized it even as he turned, surprised pleasure on his face. "Lord Tariel! You are welcome, most welcome! I have been hoping you would rejoin us."

The Arkos held up a cautionary hand. "I am here but for a very short time, long enough only to see whether you are doing well. My presence is urgently required elsewhere very shortly."

Rhiss sighed. "Things could be better. I..." He stopped, unable to dive right in, and recalled something else, something far less important, but something he could start with. "I am troubled by a past incident." He paused at Tariel's questioning look. "My lord, what can you tell me of a terrible apparition plaguing the House, forcing the Castellars to abandon it, years ago?"

Tariel quirked an eyebrow. "What do you wish to know?"

"Well... the Araxites have never been tormented by a ghost; whence did it come? What happened to it? They were mystified when I queried them."

"As well they might. It was gone when they first arrived, and will not return."

Rhiss was puzzled. "How do you know?"

Incredibly, Tariel actually smiled. "Because when the apparition accomplished its goal, there was no need to continue the charade."

Understanding dawned. "It was you!" Rhiss breathed. Tariel nodded, looking smug. "As the ghost, you drove the Castellars from Pencairn House so a secure home would be available to the Araxites, who were by then old enough to be independent of the Aranellens. No one would trouble them in such a place."

Tariel nodded. "Bravo, Prince. You are developing a good head for strategy. It will serve you well. It was an amusing task — and ejecting the accursed Castellars was most enjoyable." He paused. "But you said things could be better. I detect more to that statement than might be immediately obvious. What is wrong with the way things are?"

Rhiss exhaled heavily. "The Araxites themselves, my lord. They are splintering into factions over me. It is... distressing. And I do not know how to resolve it. And—"

"Really? I would not have thought that would be a major problem. It would seem to me that—" Tariel stopped and glanced about, frowning, as though he had just noticed an offensive smell. "Something *feels* wrong."

"That has been my thought as well, my lord. Why should my presence generate so much discord among—?"

"No, no, there is much more to it than that," Tariel interrupted. "Something literally feels *wrong*... about this entire place. Almost as though..." He stopped, frown deepening. "You have felt this, too? At least in part? Good, but yet not good enough. Has there been any outside contact with the rest of Arrinor since you arrived here?"

Rhiss gaped. The question seemed so far removed from the discussion, it made no sense. "I beg your pardon?"

"You heard me," Tariel said impatiently. "Think, boy. This could be important. Has anyone left here for the outside since you arrived?"

"I... I do not think so, my lord. Borilius would know with more certainty, but he has said this is a rather insular community. Outside contact is, of necessity, sporadic."

Tariel actually did sniff the air. "You must ask him as soon as you can. And you must search the Redoubt right away. There is something here which should not be here. Something influencing things in the entire valley, including the House below."

"Something? What sort of thing, my lord?"

"It could be any one of several things. The pressing question is, which?" Alarmingly, Tariel actually appeared uneasy. Raising a gauntleted hand, he reached out to Rhiss, touching his temple. Rhiss felt a tingling sensation, his hair momentarily full of static electricity. Then the sensation passed, but a new awareness flared in his being. It was not a pleasant awareness... rather like a niggling toothache, except it was deep within. And... there was a direction attached to it, vague at the moment, but...

"There. You feel it now, don't you?"

"Aye. What did you do?"

"Sharpen your sensibilites to the presence of this... this thing. I cannot remain to help you locate it, but it is imperative you do, and swiftly. 'Tis like—" Tariel stopped. "How to explain? Like a bomb, Prince, a bomb with fuse lit. And there may not be much time before it... goes off."

"A bomb? You mean a real one?"

Tariel shook his head impatiently. "Of course not. Such horrors do not exist in this world. I am simply trying to use terms you can understand." Tariel looked swiftly around the Redoubt, then at the sky, and said a word in some unknown tongue. From his tone, Rhiss was certain it was an expletive, strangely out of character though that would be. "I would assist you in this, but I *cannot* stay."

Attempting to project a confidence he did not feel, Rhiss declared, "I will deal with it, my lord. What am I looking for?"

"A poppet."

"A what?"

"A poppet, Prince — a human-shaped doll, used in sorcery and embodying great evil. An ancient word for an ancient wickedness." Tariel looked at Rhiss' belt. "Are you armed? Aye, your dagger. Find this... this thing, stab it and destroy it. I am unsure where it is exactly, or what it has been put here for, but 'twill be nothing good. In fact, I am sure it is responsible for the recently feral behaviour of the Araxites. Nothing else would account for—" Tariel stopped abruptly, glancing around and repeating the expletive. "I must leave. And someone comes." There was a flash, and Rhiss blinked involuntarily. When he opened his eyes, Tariel was gone. But footsteps could be heard.

Rhiss was deeply disturbed and disappointed by Tariel's sudden departure. The Arkos had been of minimal help; it was almost as though he had fled on purpose.

Rhiss turned and beheld Ulcawn the wolvan Master, who halted several paces away, expression comically surprised.

"Oh, your Grace. Good afternoon." Ulcawn glanced around the walk. "I apologize for my intrusion. I thought I heard voices. Should I withdraw?"

"No. In fact, you can accompany me: I need to... look about the Redoubt for something, but would welcome your assistance as I do so."

As they walked swiftly down the steps, Ulcawn regarded him shrewdly. "If you will forgive my boldness, you seem troubled. Is anything amiss?"

"Aye," Rhiss admitted. "More than you know. I wish I knew—" Rhiss paused, wondering how much to say. The man was Araxite, but... he needed someone to talk to. Arian, Parthalas and Borilius were nowhere near; Tariel had vanished before providing any useful advice. "Well, to start with, we didn't expect to encounter anyone here, you know, so finding you has been as much a shock for us as our arrival was for you." He sighed. "Your comrades... most seem to think I'm some sort of saviour sent straight from the One to deliver them. Some clearly don't know what to make of me. And a few..." he pursed his lips grimly, thinking of a particular Araxite named Petran, "a few think I'm an impostor and fraud." He stopped and looked sideways at Ulcawn. "I'm unsure which group makes me more uneasy."

The wolvan master replied slowly, "You must understand that twenty-five years is a very long time indeed. We have waited all that time, never losing faith you would come. But hope needs something to feed on during such a span, or it withers and dies. In consequence, I fear, expectations can spiral completely out of control." He eyed Rhiss keenly. "I think you need to—" He caught himself, and grinned sheepishly. "Forgive me. I forget myself."

"Not at all." Rhiss waved a hand dismissively and resumed walking, scanning his surroundings carefully as they went. "I welcome your counsel. You have impressed me as a true and honest man. I have noticed in recent days that when you speak, your colleagues listen."

Ulcawn inclined his head, acknowledging the compliment. "What I was about to say is, you ultimately need to convince them you are neither saviour nor fraud, but a man — your own man, not controlled by the two priests. The Araxites need to see a man worthy to be King, not merely through accident of birth, but through ability and deeds."

"How do I accomplish all that?"

"You will find your way, I have no doubt, with both skill and harmony. In fact, although you do not appear to realize it, you have already begun. You did not mention it in your tally, but you should know there is a fourth Araxite group: those recognizing that you have much to learn about the role you are to play, but who also see your enormous potential. We in that group, by the way, are extremely impressed at how you have already begun working with others to realize that potential."

Rhiss blushed, very aware he remained uncomfortable with praise, remembering what Lowri had said about that. "What of the doubters and sceptics?"

Ulcawn frowned. "I do not believe they are a significant number. But tread carefully with them. Petran, in particular, has a reputation for being too impatient and free with his doubts. I fear he has built in his mind a kingly image even the great Ahrhissian would have been hard put to measure up to." He put up a hand, and they both stopped again. "Your Grace? If you do not mind my asking... to what purpose do we pace about like husbands awaiting the birth of their firstborns? I could be of more assistance if I knew precisely what you are looking for."

Rhiss paused, wondering how much to say. "I seek something hidden in the Redoubt, something relatively small, I should think, the size and shape of a child's doll. It is vital I find it without delay."

Ulcawn looked highly dubious. "A *child's toy?* Are you sure? That is most unlikely — children are seldom brought hither. Whatever makes you think a doll is *here?* And why is it so important?"

Rhiss glanced sharply at Ulcawn, his own suspicion spiralling upwards at the man's scepticism. "I have good reason to believe it is no toy, but something far more sinister. We must find it."

Ulcawn gazed around, unconvinced but acquiescing. "Very well, my lord, we shall. I have faith in your judgement. But have you any idea where this thing might be? We could be searching the Redoubt all afternoon."

Rhiss felt his suspicion abruptly drop away, and found it cleared his mind wider to the niggling ache. "Actually, I do. I am fairly certain it is in this very courtyard."

"Then we will find it. There are few places it could be concealed."

As they began making their way around, examining nooks and crannies, Rhiss asked, "Will he cause trouble, do you think?"

Peering into a darkened corner, Ulcawn said, "Who, my lord?"

"Petran."

Ulcawn sighed. "A week ago, prior to your arrival — before we even knew of your coming — I would have said no. But these last few days..." he shook his head. "Had I not heard directly some of the things he has said, I would not have believed. I have discussed this with Borilius, but we are unsure whether speaking to Petran would make things better or worse." He paused. "It is a possibility that Petran may make difficulties. Yet with care, I think he will come to have faith in you. I hope so, at any rate. He is not an evil man. I sense he wants to believe — perhaps too much so. That desire is clouding his better judgement."

"I remember, on that night—" Rhiss stopped, barely avoiding mentioning his part in the Araxite rescue. Ulcawn looked at him curiously, so he cleared his throat and began again. "I recall being told that, even on the night of the children's deliverance by the Arkos, long ago, Petran had doubts and questioned what they said. But I never thought — it never sounded like his words were anything other than a desire for the truth."

"I think that is true. If you approach Petran with that in mind, I am sure you will win him and other sceptics over."

"Hmm," Rhiss grunted, mind elsewhere. Their walk around the courtyard had taken them to the main gate. Rhiss glanced at the path leading down the mountain, and halted, alarmed to see a large group making its way towards the Redoubt — almost at its gates, in fact. "Speaking of Petran," he said, pointing, "is that not him?"

Ulcawn looked and nodded. "So it is." He frowned uneasily. "This is highly unusual. Large groups come here seldom; I can think of no logical reason for Petran to do so, especially at the head of many. I do not like the looks of it. Perhaps you should withdraw and wait. The duty officer and I will ask his purpose."

Rhiss swallowed hard, a queasy feeling in the pit of his stomach. He had more than an inkling what Petran's presence signified, especially given Tariel's unexpected arrival, cryptic words and swift departure minutes earlier. And they had still not found the poppet. Damn, damn and blast, he thought. It was the worst possible timing. He really did not need either the interruption or the confrontation that would all too inevitably follow. But there was no help for it. "No," he replied resignedly. "We go together. I have a fair idea why he's come, and it is not to see either you *or* the duty officer."

Within moments, Petran and his followers arrived, noisily gathered just inside the gate. Ulcawn motioned an Araxite over, the same one who had taken Aralsa when Rhiss arrived. Ulcawn whispered urgently in the man's ear; he nodded and unobtrusively made his way through the crowd and out the gate. Meanwhile, the duty officer, clearly sensing impending trouble, planted himself before Petran, asking him to explain his purpose, especially with a large group at his back.

"I seek this new arrival to the House, the one bearing impressive tokens, the one we are all to bow down to," Petran replied loudly. "There are things I would know. He has not been approachable at the House, but I saw him ride out, heading here, and it is time he answered certain questions."

Ulcawn spoke in a cold voice that carried clearly across the courtyard. "The King's Grace is here, as you know full well, Petran. He is not answerable to you, but for the sake of argument, what would you ask of him?"

Heads swivelled at Ulcawn's voice. Petran looked over and caught sight of Ulcawn, Rhiss beside him. Petran walked slowly and deliberately across the courtyard until he stood less than five paces from Rhiss.

"'King's Grace?'" he repeated disdainfully. "How do we know that, Ulcawn? To many, the man beside you does not seem to fulfil the prophecy, arriving unannounced and unheralded days ago in the company of two much older priests who are obviously his handlers. But what have we seen of kingship on his part, beside tokens that may or may not even be his? I ask you all, is *this* youth the one we have waited twenty-five long years for? I think not. Shall I tell you what I believe?" He did not wait for an answer, continuing relentlessly. "I believe those two old priests are trying to foist a nameless peasant on us — a puppet whose strings they pull, to get us all, in turn, doing their bidding." He turned to the crowd. "They have come with evil intent. Are we then to be led astray by a couple of opportunistic old clerics who seek gullible fools to make the twilight of their lives more comfortable than they could otherwise achieve?"

"This is madness," Ulcawn replied angrily. "Where have these ridiculous fantasies sprung from? They disgrace our calling!"

Rhiss glanced at both Araxites, alarmed. He was astounded at Petran's temerity; nothing he had heard in the last few days would have led him to think Petran would voice mutiny so openly. And Ulcawn... the words were completely out of character for a man renowned for his even temper. Rhiss looked quickly around, disquiet deepening. Unawares, the Araxites were slowly separating into two opposing semi-circles with himself at the centre. Rhiss could actually feel hostility — mindless, irrational, implacable hostility — rising from all those gathered. It must be defused quickly, lest it explode in madness. *Where was that treacherous whorespawn poppet?*

Rhiss shook his head to clear it, raised his hand and stepped forth.

"Peace, Ulcawn," he said in a clear voice. "You also, Petran. What tokens would you seek as proof, if the Circlet and the Sword are not enough? If you doubt the evidence of your own senses, what then could possibly satisfy?" He paused, momentarily at a loss. He looked at the multitude, and saw many whose features jogged his memory of that long-ago night. Some were filled with the same hostility as Petran's; doubt was in others. Children then, they were adults now, older than he, but were nonetheless the people he had saved through impulsive action. He reached a decision. "Petran, it grieves me you are no less impetuous, no more inclined to take things on faith now than you were the night of the Coup."

"The night of the Coup?" Petran sneered. "What were you twenty-five years ago but a mewling babe suckling at your mother's teat? What would you know of such things, save what you have been coached to say?"

Rhiss looked at Petran with narrowed eyes. He had never heard any Araxites, even the Doubters, speak so. What could possibly provoke Petran to such extremes?

"I know because I was there, Petran," he said quietly. "As were many of you." Rhiss looked around again, saw a familiar face, even with years added, searched his memory for the name accompanying it, and pointed. "Maran was there." He pointed at another. "So was Jarella." He moved on, indicating as he said their names. "Norelli, Forgall, Erianthus. They are some of those there that night. I remember them. And you too, Petran. Oh, I remember you very well."

"How?" Petran retorted. "You could not possibly have been there. I say you *were* not there. What sorcery is this? Or is it merely a conjurer's trick?"

Rhiss shook his head, confident now, knowing he had everyone's full attention. "Neither, Petran. For I *was* there, your assertions to the contrary notwithstanding." He licked dry lips. "Do you not recall the younger of the two knights in the raiment of the Arkos? Even then, you were a doubter. You questioned him when he assured you the king would come. Search your memory. That young knight was no Arkos." He paused for effect. "It was I."

A murmur of consternation ran through the crowd. Rhiss nodded and continued. "Aye, 'tis true. I was brought there that night by the Arkos you all saw, the one who arranged for the Aranellens to care for you after we whisked you away from Tor Eylian on the backs of three gryphon majors and arrived at the Way Stones of Kirunek. I was there. I remember it well. Do *you*?" he challenged them.

"No! It's a ruse, I tell you!" Petran's voice was loud and shrill. "Don't you see how he uses trickery and lies to deceive us?" He suddenly spied a loose flagstone on the ground, poking unevenly above its fellows, and pointed dramatically to it. "Like this whorespawn treacherous stone, he seeks to trip us up and then, as we fall, unbalanced and helpless, he will plunge his ornate dagger in our exposed backs, and loom above us laughing as we lie on the ground, bleeding to death!" He kicked the stone contemptuously, and it made a grating noise as it moved slightly.

For the span of several heartbeats, no one moved. There was no sound, save the wind. Then, without warning, Petran shoved those nearby aside, a knife appeared in his hand as if by magic, and he launched himself at Rhiss with an inarticulate cry.

Ulcawn threw himself in front of Rhiss, knocking him sprawling in the process. Rhiss looked dazedly from the ground to see Ulcawn locked in deadly struggle with Petran. It lasted seconds before the two drew apart, although it seemed much longer. Then Petran was standing before him, staring in disbelief at the knife protruding from his breast. Ulcawn stood by, breathing hard. That, too, lasted only a moment, and then Petran choked, turned and collapsed to the ground on his back, narrowly missing Rhiss.

Rhiss rolled to his knees and stood. The tension in the air was suffocating. Some of the crowd lined up facing Ulcawn, while others moved into positions beside the Wolvan master. The cold breeze blew, and the sun moved behind clouds. Rhiss shivered in spite of himself, and gazed at the sky.

His attention jerked back to the scene before him and he looked around, aghast. There was sudden, palpable rage on all there, inexplicable hostility glowing like dark embers in a fire, ready to flame forth on dry kindling. He could feel it. Some were angered over the attack against him, some at Petran's mortal wound, but everywhere was a mindless, irrational rage, waiting to burst forth. Already the crowd was dividing in two. In another moment they would be at each other's throats. How, by the One, had it come to this? It was madness. Absolute, whorespawn, treacherous madness.

His head whipped up in abrupt, astounded realization. Of course! That was it! *Whorespawn, treacherous poppet... whorespawn, treacherous stone.*

Rhiss knew what he must do, quickly, before they all started slaughtering each other. Drawing himself to his full height, and standing in the centre of the crowd, he suddenly called in a loud, clear voice, filling it with all the sense of command he could muster. "Hold! Hold, I say! Your King commands you!"

Startled simultaneously by his voice, its ring of authority, and the audacious claim, the Araxites halted, even as many were moving, everyone's attention fixed on Rhiss. He dove for the flagstone, sensing rather than seeing the sudden swivelling as all eyes turned, focusing on him in incredulous disbelief, their mindless rage momentarily suspended at the bizarre sight of Prince Rhissan hurling himself to the ground.

It was the strangest feeling: everything moved improbably slowly, as though caught in Tariel's gelatinous air — everything, including him. Not only that, it was like he watched himself from ten feet above. Heart pounding, he saw himself dive to the ground, landing immediately before the flagstone — painfully banging an elbow in the process — wrenching at the offending stone, hurling it to one side with more force than he would have thought possible. It narrowly missed a stunned Araxite, but his vision was rudely torn away, back to the dimly glowing cavity suddenly exposed where the stone had been. Like a diabolical maw, a tainted, feeble green light emanated from within, and Rhiss knew, with a mixture of sick dread and grim resolve, that he was going to have to insert his hand to retrieve what he knew with utter certainty lay within.

His hand was in the hole to his wrist... to his elbow...and just before he could go no further, he reached bottom to feel something lying there, repulsively warm and pulsating ever so slightly, as though possessing its own disgusting heartbeat. Fighting nausea, he gasped and locked it in his hand. Then he rolled over on his back, his arm coming up and out the hole. He sat and looked with loathing at the thing in his grasp.

It filled his palm, and was indeed a doll, of sorts. Made with coarse brown fabric and crudely stitched together with enormous black sutures, it was loosely human in shape, the arms and legs mere projections jutting stiffly out from the torso. A mouth was sewn on, twisted in a malevolent leer. The eyes, sewn in great, thick, ropy loops of the black thread, were...

Run, run, as fast as you can! You can't catch me, I'm the gingerbread man!

He jumped. A whispering, obscene voice filled his head. The eyes were...

Taffy! Gog!

No! The eyes were...

Thieving, whorespawn Tavvy!

The eyes were... somehow aware. They glittered with a febrile inner light, an awareness brimming with hatred and cruelty and malice, lying there in some stinking, festering counterfeit of life, and...

Bow down to Me, stupid, worthless Taffy! You cannot prevail—

...gasping, Rhiss...

You witless, miserable Gog! You will never—

...before he was even aware of what he was doing...

You cannot defeat Me, Taffy! I will not—

...had dashed the thing to the ground...

It will all be for naught! Look at you! You are terrified of Me—

...swept out his dagger...

No! You cannot—

...and, not daring to look, blindly stabbed the thing's torso once... twice... three times, resolutely looking up into the sky as he did so...

There was a psychic scream of rage and pain, abruptly truncated, and Rhiss looked down at the doll, grey eyes icy. "Yes," he whispered harshly, "I *am* afraid. But I *will* defeat you, all the same. It is *you* who cannot — *will not* — be allowed to prevail. I swear this by the living Name of the One."

The glittering awareness in those eyes lingered an endless moment longer, and somehow, Rhiss knew with absolute certainty that it had heard him. But it made no response, and with a thrill of hope, as its awareness began to fade, Rhiss saw something else in those eyes... the malice replaced with something very like... doubt.

Then it was gone, and the broken thing was nothing more than a hideous doll, torn and slashed. A green liquid oozed slowly from it, like glue hardening as it is exposed to the air. Rhiss sighed shakily, stood and looked around.

All about... as though caught in Hunter's Breath... Araxites stood motionless, expressions blank, unfocused... and he knew what he must do...

In one smooth moment of decision, he kicked the flagstone back into its proper spot and bent down to pick up the broken poppet. Despite his revulsion, he stuffed it in his tunic, shutting his eyes and grimacing in distate at the feel of it against his skin.

There was a brilliant green flash, visible even through his eyelids. Rhiss opened them in time to notice every person there sway slightly, buffeted by some psychic gale. More importantly, he could literally see the tension evaporate, replaced by bewilderment. The sun chose that moment to come out again. Rhiss glanced up, seeing remnants of the dark cloud tattered away by the wind, and breathed his thanks.

He stood. "There will be *no conflict* in this place," he said in a ringing voice. "Is that clear? We are servants of the One, but if we fight amongst ourselves, we do the will of the Other. I *will not* allow that."

He turned to Ulcawn, who looked puzzled. "We were... looking for something... but I cannot recall... Petran and I had words... did we find it, your Grace?"

"Aye, Ulcawn. We certainly did."

"Your Grace?" called an Araxite. "Come quickly! Petran is near death."

Damn. In the confrontation with the poppet, he had forgotten. Rhiss strode to Petran's side and knelt. The knife was deeply embedded in Petran's chest, blood flowing sluggishly from the wound. Petran's skin was clammy and cold, his eyes half-open, but not really seeing. Shock was setting in and it was obvious he had but seconds to live.

Rhiss gazed down, and for a moment, saw only the face of the child twenty-five years ago, asking his questions. There had been no malice then, and Rhiss felt there had been none minutes ago — just a deep and heartfelt uncertainty, a craving for reassurance in a brutal and uncertain world, and an outside malefic influence all too skilled in taking advantage of that. Rhiss could not find it in himself to condemn the man in the face of such manipulation.

Gently, oblivious to the multitude now crowded around, he reached down and grasped the knife with his left hand. Beneath his touch, it vibrated minutely in time to Petran's ebbing heartbeat. Rhiss hesitated, knowing what must be done, but nauseous at the prospect, needing to steel himself first. He placed his right hand against Petran's chest, making a fist around the knife. Then he breathed in deeply, and shuddering convulsively, swiftly pulled the knife free.

The rasping sound of metal against bone made Rhiss wince and his gorge rise, but he mastered it, throwing the knife aside to clatter metallically against the flagstones. He placed his left hand beside his right, together over the wound from which Petran's life-blood flowed freely. He closed his eyes again, and lifted his thoughts, this time in supplication.

There is no malice in this child of the One; folly, as with all of us, but no malice. But there is also potential for great good, and I would not see him taken from us before his time. Let it be according to Your Will.

As before, it began as a faint, faraway tingling in the tips of his fingers, a sensation at first so soft he could not be sure of its reality. But it was real, and the liquid fire built in his hands, wrists, and arms, until he was engulfed to his shoulders. Even now, the fourth time, it was still painful in part, strangely wonderful in another. Then the vitality washed up through and from within, and he gasped as it spread through his hands and ebbed. This time, he kept his eyes closed, feeling a pleasant lassitude he did not want to end. But he could not fail to see the sudden glow through his eyelids, and knew it was complete. He opened his eyes in time to see the golden haze wash over the courtyard and all who stood there as they watched, rapt and open-mouthed at what had occurred. Rhiss smiled at their collective expressions, bowed his head, closed his eyes again and sighed, mentally giving thanks.

Beneath his hands, Petran stirred and stared at Rhiss, eyes wide with incredulous realization as the full import of what had taken place sank in. Petran slowly brought his hands to his chest, and Rhiss realized his own hands were still positioned over the now-healed wound. Petran laid his hands on top, then lifted Rhiss' to reveal still-wet blood.

"My lord?" he whispered disbelievingly. "What did you…? Why?"

"Because you are no servant of the Other, Petran son of Lochnar, and did not deserve death this day. But I caution you to curb your impetuousness from this time forward. This is not the first occasion it has gotten you into trouble, I am told, but I daresay it has never had such consequences before. Next time, you may not have anyone nearby who is able — or inclined — to rescue you from ill-considered action."

Rhiss stood, extending his hand to Petran, who sat. Petran looked at it, shaking his head. "I am unworthy," he murmured bitterly. "I remember letting doubt consume me without considering what I did. I should have known better. I should—"

Rhiss cut him off. "Aye, you should remember. Enough, Petran. I offer you grace. Take my hand, and rise."

Petran looked at the hand Rhiss offered, took it and stood. His grip was strong, and warm. He looked Rhiss in the eye, then said loudly for all to hear, "I rise, but only to be the first to kneel to our rightwise King of Arrinor, come at last!"

Petran knelt on one knee and bowed his head, an act which galvanized the entire assemblage to follow his action. The only sound was the breeze snapping the standards in the courtyard. Then someone called triumphantly, "In this we are One!"

They took up the cry, repeating it three times. Rhiss looked over the assembled group, tearing up in spite of himself. He cleared his throat, about to bid them all rise, when a familiar voice rang out, "Aye, your King, in truth!"

Startled, Rhiss looked towards the voice. At the gate were four figures on horseback, revealed only now by the Araxites dropping to their knees in fealty: Arian,

Parthalas, Borilius, and another, cloaked and hooded in grey. Rhiss was confused they should be there so soon after Ulcawn sent for them, but relieved; there was also no small measure of satisfaction that they should arrive to see he had the situation in hand without needing their intervention.

Rhiss strode across the courtyard, Araxites parting quickly before him. The riders bowed their heads. "Well met, my friends," he said, pausing to look at the fourth rider, still cloaked and hooded. "I am glad of your arrival, gladder your assistance proved unnecessary." He stopped. "Although I do not understand how you arrived so quickly. The man sent by Ulcawn must have had wings. I would not have thought he could be at the House even now."

"Quite correct, your Grace," Arian responded formally. "But as it happened, we were already on our way, and he met us near here. I, too, am glad to see you had a situation that could have proven dire under control when we arrived." She noticed Rhiss still looking curiously at the fourth figure, and nudged Borilius, who started.

"Oh, aye. Forgive me. Allow me to present Alairra of Telcarre, Lady Marshal of the Aranellens. She responded to my message, riding swiftly to meet you."

The figure nodded. "You are welcome, my lord," came an unmistakably feminine voice, quiet but clear. "We have long awaited the coming of the rightful King to Arrinor." The voice was pleasant, and lifting her head, the figure threw back hood and cloak. Rhiss was doubly surprised: first, hearing the name of the child he had healed from the Malmoridai bestowed on the woman before him; and second, by her appearance, for she was much younger than he had expected on hearing her title. It was a title that plainly bespoke a prominent leadership role, yet Rhiss judged her no older than he.

She was clad in armour, the glittering shine of a silver breastplate enclosing her slim frame offset by chain mail covering her arms. Charcoal grey gauntlets rose up her forearms to meet the chain mail. Long, fine chestnut brown hair, parted in the middle of her head, fell loosely and smoothly to a uniform point just below her shoulders, framing a strikingly attractive face. A golden circlet was on her brow. Grave and unsmiling, she returned his gaze, large, pale blue eyes unreadable above high, smooth cheekbones, narrow lips pursed together, and a long nose lending her an air of gravitas. She looked altogether formidable, and Rhiss uncomfortably felt he was being coolly appraised. He was far from certain in his own mind that he measured up to the critical observations of the very collected young woman, and found it necessary to remember which of them was heir to the Crystal Throne.

At length she nodded again, as though making up her mind, dismounted in one swiftly graceful motion, then followed it immediately with another, an odd combination of curtsey and bow, strangely feminine in spite of the warlike way she was dressed. The chain mail extended from her waist nearly to her thighs, a kind of metallic tunic and skirt. A worn sword scabbard and a dagger were attached to her leather belt. Her legs were covered not with mail, but leather leggings and high, supple boots of the same colour and in the same manner as the gauntlets on her mailed arms. As she rose,

Rhiss realized she was quite tall, nearly his own height — pale, unreadable eyes gazing just shy of his.

"Well met, indeed," she said softly, glancing around the courtyard and seeing the Araxites standing. Her voice had a slightly husky quality. Her gaze flicked from Petran, behind Rhiss, the jagged tear in his tunic very obvious, to Rhiss and his bloody hands. "And miraculous. I am grateful we arrived in time to witness the King's Healing Gift. I have heard of it, of course, but never been privileged to see it."

Rhiss looked down at his own hands, feeling the odd desire to wipe them or hide them behind his back. Remembering Lowri's scolding, he resisted the urge, instead holding them out.

"Aye, Lady," he said dryly. "It is a fairly new experience for me, also."

She made no reply, merely bowed her head momentarily before raising it and locking her icy gaze on him. Silence reigned again in the courtyard except for the wind snapping the halyards, and looking around, Rhiss abruptly realized *everyone's* gaze was on him. He shook his head in exasperation and cleared his throat.

"Very well," he said to no one in particular. It had the desired effect: all stirred as though released from a spell. "There has been more than enough excitement for one day. Perhaps we can remain calm, so the King's Gift is not needed for some time. For the moment," he glanced at Arian, "I think we should return to the House. Accompany me who will. But first—" he looked at his hands wryly "—perhaps someone could bring a basin of warm water. I would prefer not to return resembling an amateur surgeon, or worse, a butcher."

Riding down the hill, Lady Alairra drew her horse level with Aralsa, and leaned over to Rhiss. "My presence at the Redoubt surprised you, my lord," she said in a low voice. "May I inquire why?"

"I was... I expected Eques Aranell."

"My father?" Alairra either did not notice or chose to disregard his surprise. "He is old and very ill, I fear, too ill to travel. In fact, were it not for your coming, I would not have left him. What led you to expect him?"

"Well," Rhiss responded slowly, "I was told the Aranellen leader would meet me. Apparently, I was misinformed."

The icy blue eyes turned full on him. "No, you were not. I lead the Aranellens, and have done for quite some time. My father remains at Tor Aran, our secret refuge. You will find him there, should you ever choose to visit. It is his hope you will. He expressed that to me before I left, saying he would like to see you once more before he..." her voice faltered, then recovered, "...before he goes to the One."

Rhiss felt a pang of sympathy. "I am sorry to hear your father is so ill." Alairra nodded mutely in acknowledgement. "Have I met him before, then?"

"Only as a newborn, your Grace. You would have no recollection." A faint smile played around the corners of her mouth, a smile momentarily transforming her entire being, Rhiss noted. "But he remembers you clearly. A close friend to your parents, no one was more pleased at your birth than he. It is a cruel twist of the Other that the Night of Fire came hard on the heels of that blessed event."

"Night of Fire? I assume you refer to the night of the Coup?"

"Aye. Have you not heard the name?" Rhiss shook his head, and she paused, regarding him thoughtfully before continuing. "'Tis the Aranellen name for the night of the Coup... a terrible, catastrophic night of betrayal, flame, destruction, and death. You were there, but will not remember it, being but newly born." Rhiss shivered involuntarily. Alairra had obviously missed his revelation to the Araxites, but he felt it would be awkward to correct her. He coughed to mask his reaction, but Alairra's features had taken on a faraway look, and she did not notice. "I was not there either, of course, only delivered into this world at the safety of Tor Aran, some months after. But my father, and others who survived, made very sure those of us not present never lacked for the tale, with more detail than anyone could wish. It was *their* duty to speak, they said, *ours* to listen. Theirs to remember, ours to envision. And so we also recall the Night of Fire, though not physically there when it took place. Aye, it is well named, although only Aranellens originally called it thus. But over the last year or two... it is a strange but interesting thing. Crossing the land, I have heard the term whispered among ordinary folk... among those bold enough, of course, when Sovereign's Men are not nearby, and only close, trusted friends to hear. They speak softly of it, then how the true King will come, to rescue Arrinor in her desperate need. I had thought it only wishful fantasy. But now, wondrously, you are indeed come, at last." She stopped and blinked, sapphire eyes losing their remote look as she recalled where she was, and with whom. Transfixed by her story, Rhiss had hung on every word, and she flushed as she became aware of his rapt attention, a delicate shade of rose suffusing her features.

"My apologies," she said brusquely. "I did not mean to bore you with personal trivia. It is of no moment, and I... I must confer with... an Araxite officer before reaching the House. By your leave, your Grace—" she was already in the process of expertly whirling her mount, quite without waiting for permission "—I will see you at evenmeal. Until then, go you with the One." Then she was gone, fled precipitously towards the column's rear. Rhiss frowned in bemusement, twisting his head around to watch her flight, then turned to face forward, shrugging. *Women!* he thought. *What was all that? Utterly incomprehensible, the lot of them.*

──◆──

Arriving back at the House, Rhiss quietly drew Arian aside. "I have grim tidings relating to what just occurred at the Redoubt."

"Grim tidings?" She looked puzzled. "How so? I would have thought the outcome a major triumph — for you, and indeed, for all of us. The release of tension and acrimony is palpable." She smiled wryly. "And the Doubters will have to find a new name for themselves, for they doubt no more."

"True, Arian. But you arrived late and did not see all. There is another reason for that release of tension, which you do not know." He swiftly related his conversation with Tariel and subsequent search, discovery and destruction of the poppet. Retrieving the thing from inside his tunic, he held it out. "You understand, don't you? Someone placed this abomination at the Redoubt — and recently, because the community mood was fine before we arrived. It was our coming that made the poppet necessary. It was cunningly designed to sow anger, fear and dissension among the Araxites, so we might all be destroyed without Maldeus having to lift a finger. And it very nearly succeeded."

She stared at the ruined doll. "Aye," she breathed, aghast. "But who would do such a thing?"

"I do not know. But clearly, we have a traitor in our midst."

"Sweet Light of the One." She sank into a chair as it hit her. "What do we do?"

"We find him... or her. As quickly as possible, before more evil can be loosed on this community."

"Aye," she repeated. "But how?"

"Well—" he began, but was interrupted and held the doll behind his back as Borilius entered. "My lord? I have been searching for you. I have a most important question to ask—" Borilius broke off, studying them. "Is something wrong?"

Rhiss looked at Arian. She nodded, and he repeated what he had told her, adding, "Borilius, has anyone left or arrived in recent days?"

"No, my lord."

"You are confident of that?" interjected Arian.

"Aye, Seir-onna. This is a closed community; contact with the outside world is limited and strictly regulated. Everyone knows everyone else. If someone was missing, it would not go unnoticed — or unremarked."

"You said you sent word to Lady Alairra. Who went?"

"No one, Seir-onna. We used a bearer-bird."

Rhiss glanced quizzically at Arian. "A what?"

"An extremely intelligent species, trained to fly between two points with a message tied to one leg."

"So our traitor is still within the community," Borilius mused worriedly.

"It would seem so," Rhiss replied. "But we may have a slight advantage after the fact, for even if the traitor *was* at the Redoubt during the incident — and we know not whether that was the case — I believe he or she does not recall exactly what transpired at the critical moment."

Arian frowned. "How can that be?"

"After I killed the poppet, everything was motionless for several moments — including all the people. I thought at the time that it was like they were caught up by Hunter's Breath, unaware and unseeing. Then there was a brilliant flash of light, and it was as though they were released from a spell. No one seemed to remember anything from the moment of Ulcawn's conflict with Petran until after I had destroyed the poppet and freed them of its effects."

Arian nodded. "So we may be able to take advantage of the traitor's uncertainty as we conduct our investigation. Whom shall we tell about this?"

"Absolutely no one," Borilius said adamantly, and they turned to him in surprise. "Forgive me, Seir-onna and your Grace, but the traitor could literally be anyone — including Arian and myself, really. But we already know, so there is naught to be done about that. However, no one else should be told. Unfortunately, we can trust nobody."

"So you suggest that just we three attempt to unmask the traitor?"

Borilius shrugged. "What else can we do? And to make the story known to all would be to rekindle the paranoia and hostility we have only just managed to douse."

"A good point," Arian conceded. "Very well. We will begin this investigation immediately — ah, no, by the One, we cannot. There is a banquet and celebration this evening that we cannot pre-empt with a witch hunt. But we can start on the morrow."

Rhiss smiled in spite of himself. "Well said, Seir-onna. Speaking of which, Borilius, what was the important question you came to ask me?"

Borilius' face clouded in confusion, then cleared and he laughed. "I wished to know if there was any food in particular you would like served, your Grace."

Arian laughed too, and held up a hand. "Oh, I can tell you that, Master Borilius, without your even needing to ask. Our Prince has a great fondness for meat pies filled with steak and mushrooms. If you wish to gain his favour, all you need do—"

Rhiss cut her off with his own upraised hand. "Actually, Seir-onna — and Borilius — I rather had something else in mind tonight."

Arian looked startled. "Really?"

"Aye, my lord?" said Borilius expectantly.

Rhiss smiled. "Crumbledown Stew," he said. "I would be obliged if you would make sure it was available for me at evenmeal — and anyone else who wants it."

Arian looked dumbfounded. Borilius blinked in surprise, but was better at keeping his expression neutral. "I... I will make sure our cooks are so instructed, your Grace. If you will excuse me?"

As he strode off, Rhiss steeled himself for the tirade he was certain Arian was readying. But all she said, looking narrowly at him, was, "Crumbledown Stew? You have had this dish before? And *are* aware that it is not precisely high-class food, aren't you? Yet would prefer it to—"

Rhiss smiled. "I have, I am, and I would. Thank you, Arian. I will go now and ready myself for the feast. Until then."

———◆———

Evenmeal was a late but joyful affair, delayed principally due to the Aranellens' unexpected arrival — more than thirty warriors on horseback, many of whom were women, were a sizeable contingent. Their sudden coming necessitated the preparation of additional food. And it was joyful because the news of what had occurred at Summit's Redoubt spread like wildfire through inhabitants and guests alike. Rhiss' healing of Petran left no one in the slightest doubt that the long-awaited King was indeed among them. Although only a very small number of Araxites had disputed the veracity of the claims made about Rhiss, their complete conversion from sceptics to believers transformed everyone and lent a festive air to the evening. It seemed there was food, drink, torches and lights everywhere, music... and following the meal, dancing, Rhiss was mildly surprised to see.

Arrinoran dance seemed a highly structured and tightly choreographed affair, no matter what type of music was played. Some tunes were slow and sad, others quick and lively, but all were characterized by intricate steps in complex formations. It was impressive to watch, in a daunting sort of way. Sitting beside Rhiss, Arian noticed him paying close attention to the goings on, and leaned over, smiling.

"Are you familiar with this sport, my lord?"

Rhiss snorted, shaking his head vigorously. "Of course not, as you know perfectly well. How could I be? The social graces have not been among the things I have learned since arriving in Arrinor. And in my old life, dancing was not a skill I excelled at."

Arian shrugged, a sly gleam in her eyes. "I but wondered if Mistress Lowri took the time to tutor you during those evenings alone. Even if she did not, I wager that in your adopted land, you've danced the night away with many a pretty girl on your arm. In any event, notwithstanding your denials, social dance is a skill you must acquire."

Rhiss looked dismayed, and Arian smiled mischievously. "Come now. Kings, and princes, too, rule not by the sword alone, you know," she said, evidently noting with amusement the discomfiture her words produced. "There is need of the social graces, even among royalty. Perhaps especially among royalty. And are there not comely women here you might care to lead around the floor?" Rhiss sighed, scanning the room. There were indeed, he was forced to admit after a moment's observation. Many attractive women were in attendance, Araxite and Aranellen, not without their respective charms. The Aranellen women, most still in armour and livery, looked very much ready for battle and completely formidable, while the Araxite women were dressed more... softly, that was the word. Their long dresses, whether brightly coloured or more subdued, were far more feminine than the frankly militaristic Aranellens. But even chain mail armour and heavy tunics could not totally disguise the attractions of many Aranellen women.

Rhiss realized he sought one Aranellen in particular, and his face reddened. He willed himself to stop, but curiosity had the better of him. Where was the enigmatic Lady Alairra? She was nowhere to be seen... wait! She stood by the east wall in animated discussion with Borilius. He thought back to their strange conversation earlier.

Arian followed his gaze. "A most interesting woman, wouldn't you agree?"

Rhiss had quite forgotten Arian for the moment, and was taken aback by her question. "I — what? Who do you—?"

"Woman *and* warrior. Am I correct in observing you seem to find that interesting... or unusual... or both?"

"It... no, it did not happen in my adopted land."

"Indeed." Arian raised an eyebrow, ostentatiously looking away. There was much unspoken in the single word, Rhiss thought uncomfortably, and he nearly protested his curiosity was purely academic; but aloof silence was probably the better course.

Pursing his lips, he settled deeper in the chair to hide his embarrassment. He had never regarded himself as the life of the party, but here was another demand that would eventually be made of him, solely because of his position. Fortunately, it looked like no one dared ask him to dance this night. A certain amount of reverential fear of the royal personage was perhaps not a bad thing, he decided.

In spite of his misgivings regarding social dance, the evening could have actually proven highly enjoyable, had there been nothing else on his mind. Unfortunately, though, two highly notable exceptions spoiled things considerably for Rhiss. First, and most importantly, he was deeply, if privately, troubled as he searched the faces in the room. When the day began, he had not the slightest thought that, even with the fractious mood present in the community, anyone there would have actively sought victory for Maldeus and the Sovereign. But now, at day's end, he knew as he scanned those same faces that at least one of them belonged to a traitor, someone who had chosen fealty to Darkness over Light. Potentially, the traitor could have harboured such sympathies for a very long time. Or it could be someone who had only just changed allegiances when he had shown up with Arian and Parthalas in tow. How could anyone possibly think that such a course was either honourable or desirable? It was like Dalys at Craggaddon Hall, in some ways: a trusted servant, nesting like a viper in the midst of people who suspected nothing. And here at Pencairn House, it could literally be anyone. It was an enormously disturbing line of thought, and Rhiss began to realize, with distressing clarity, just how easy it was to see one's natural sense of trust in others eroded.

And then there was Aquilea. She had acted strangely since his return to Pencairn House, Rhiss realized. In the evening, she was extremely restless, first wanting out, then back in, then out again. Her thought patterns were a jumble of golden, chaotic images Rhiss could make no sense of at all, and throughout evenmeal he was hard put to keep her from stalking around the hall. She refused the food Rhiss offered and stared balefully around her, making deep rumbling noises of discontent so those sitting nearby shifted nervously in their seats. As the dancing began, Rhiss finally lost patience. Taking Aquilea through one of the sets of double doors, he bade her fly off her wretched mood. "Come back when you're ready to be civilized, lass," he told her sternly. "I don't know what your problem is. Why can't you be more relaxed tonight? Honestly, I've never seen such a fuss." Aquilea eyed him darkly and disapprovingly, then silently left.

She was gone nearly an hour, returning as the celebration was winding down: virtually all Aranellens, and most Araxites, had retired by the time she came back. Rhiss had been puzzled that people seemed oddly reluctant to leave, even though many were plainly tired. Eventually, Arian quietly pointed out that, according to protocol, guests could not depart until the King himself either left or gave leave for them to do so, and then Rhiss took action. Embarrassed, he had promptly risen, bidding the assemblage to seek rest whenever they wished; there was a slow but steady exodus thereafter. Consequently, there were relatively few left when Aquilea cruised in to land outside the hall. Rhiss sensed her several minutes before she actually arrived. She still expressed the same skittishness, but Rhiss detected a profound shift in her thought patterns that sent him striding swiftly to the entryway. An Araxite spotted her and swung the doors open. She swooped in, landing in a graceless tangle of legs and wings far removed from her usual disciplined alighting, and made quickly for Rhiss, heedless of people between.

Aquilea was not merely restless; she was frantic. No longer annoyed but seriously worried, Rhiss met her and knelt, taking her head gently between his hands, willing her to calm. Aquilea's unorthodox arrival had been noted, and the music trailed off, leaving the remaining revellers around the room to stop and stare in confusion at the sight of Prince Rhissan kneeling silently in front of his obviously agitated gryphon, head bowed.

Sensing something amiss, Arian and Borilius came swiftly over, accompanied by Alairra. They stood beside Rhiss, waiting for him to open his eyes and acknowledge their presence. After several long seconds, he did so, looking up.

"Well?" demanded Arian in a tone far more impatient than respectful, causing Borilius and Alairra to glance at her in surprise. "I have not seen your gryphon act so before. What is it?"

Rhiss shook his head, frowning. "I am uncertain, Seir-onna. But it is nothing trivial. Aquilea is truly upset, and I am still trying to calm her enough to discover the cause. She has seen something to give rise to this fey mood."

"Seen something? Where? Outside?"

Rhiss shook his head again. "I think not. It is not something she has physically seen. This is more like... the Gift of the Sight. She has seen something with her mind."

Arian looked incredulous. "You say a *gryphon* has the Sight? An *animal?*"

Rhiss waved a hand impatiently. "Nothing necessarily as complex as that. But I have learned to have a healthy respect for whatever Aquilea chooses to show me, either physically or in her thoughts." He refocused his gaze on the gryphon agitatedly shifting her front legs. "Peace, Arian, I beg you. I cannot communicate with her *and* you at the same time, not effectively at any rate, and I need to see what has upset her so. She would not act this way without reason."

Arian subsided, and Rhiss closed his eyes, hands again gently cradling the gryphon's head, attempting to understand what Aquilea showed him.

Mist... fog... flashes of undecipherable images. Then... a woman... someone they both knew... Lowri. In frantic distress, looking at someone. Was Lowri in danger? Where was she? Who was she looking at? The image blurred, steadied, and Rhiss saw the interior of the main room at Lowri's cottage, the fire burning brightly in the background. There was a person lying on Lowri's bed, sorely hurt... clothing rent and torn, and some of the dark stains were plainly dried blood. Rhiss willed Aquilea to focus on the figure lying on the bed, urgently desiring to learn who it was.

He gasped as the person's features swam into view, and involuntarily fell backwards, breaking contact with Aquilea as his eyes opened. He looked up in stunned bewilderment to see Arian, Borilius and Alairra clustered around, deeply concerned.

"Meranna," he whispered in anguish. "At Lowri's cottage, sorely hurt. How can that be? What has happened at Craggaddon Hall? By the One..."

Rhiss struggled to his feet, almost angrily fending off the efforts of others to assist. Aquilea stood by quietly, calmer now she knew Rhiss understood. He stood, marshalling his thoughts and reconciling what he had seen. Rhiss knew what must be done — and knew Arian would not approve. But... by the One, was he King or not? It was true what Lowri had said, that even a king must listen to his advisors... but there were also times when it was necessary to overrule those advisors. Rhiss reached his decision, set his mouth in a firm line, and turned to Borilius.

"Have Aralsa saddled, Borilius," he said in a low voice. "I leave immediately."

"What? *Now?*" Arian spluttered, very put out. "The sun left the sky hours ago. The stars now rule the heavens."

Ignoring her, Rhiss raised an eyebrow at Borilius, who looked briefly at Arian, his expression unreadable, before bowing. "At once, your Grace." He turned and left.

Rhiss turned to Alairra. "Lady, I understand that the Aranellens are sworn to me and my cause, and will accept my orders."

The icy, sapphire eyes met his gaze unflinchingly. "They are and they will, your Grace. Absolutely and without question. What would you have of us?"

Rhiss nodded approvingly. "As large and well-armed an escort as can ride swiftly, ready to move out as soon as can be arranged. Will you ride with me this night?"

Alairra inclined her head. "It is both my honour and duty, Prince Rhissan. It shall be as you command. I can have my force ready within the half-hour." She, too, whirled and quickly left without another word.

Arian looked ready to explode, and Rhiss raised a hand to forestall it. "Seir-onna, peace, I beg you."

"'Peace?'" she said incredulously. "Has everyone lost their minds? You briefly commune with an agitated animal, evidently sharing visions of some sort that it has allegedly seen, then abruptly decide to go crashing off into blackest night, and ask me to have peace about it? And everyone leaps to do your bidding in this madness? Would you *please* explain?"

Rhiss shook his head. "It is not madness, Arian. I tell you, your sister is at Lowri's cottage—" he stopped momentarily and frowned "—or will be, I'm not quite clear on the time from Aquilea, as you must appreciate that this is all very new to me. She is — or will be — sorely hurt and alone. How, or why, I do not know, but something is very wrong — I got the distinct feeling from Aquilea that there's been some catastrophe at Craggaddon Hall, one Meranna alone escaped, and only barely. We *must* discover what transpired. Come, walk with me." He was already striding from the hall.

Arian and Parthalas struggled to match his pace. "You would ride out now?" she panted. "In the darkness of night? 'Tis not safe for man or beast." She laid a hand on his arm, and they stopped. "Rhissan, please. If what your gryphon has seen has truly occurred, or will, I am as concerned for my sister as you. But I beg you to consider. You yourself said this — this communication — is very new to you. Perhaps you have misinterpreted what Aquilea saw. What if Aralsa or another horse puts a foot down a rabbit hole in the dark, throwing you or another rider? And there is the... incident... from earlier today."

"Aralsa the Sure-Footed will not put a hoof wrong. And we will not gallop madly in panicked flight, I assure you. I understand the risks in leaving now. But I cannot wait until morning. If I do that, I will pace back and forth in my room all night, like a caged beast, unable to rest. Nor can what occurred at the Redoubt be allowed to interfere with this." He turned his gaze full on her. Uncertainty was in her eyes.

"Arian, this must be done, now, tonight," he said quietly. "You need not worry. I am hardly going alone. I will have Aquilea and the Aranellens as escort... *and* Caylyx," he added, smiling. "All in all, a highly disciplined and formidable force."

"Then we will accompany you."

"No," Rhiss said decisively. "It is my wish you remain here tonight. I want to dispel, once and for all, this image some Araxites have of you and Parthalas as my handlers. But by all means, assemble some of them and follow tomorrow."

Arian looked irresolutely at Parthalas. He shrugged. "It's the lad's lookout, his decision to make. Is he to be King, or no? Ye canna have it both ways... making decisions for him, yet expecting him to lead."

Rhiss suppressed a smile, hearing Parthalas echo his own thoughts. Arian hesitated a moment longer, then threw her hands up in surrender. "Very well, Prince. I can see you are resolute in this. Go you with the One, and my blessing."

Within the hour, Arian, Parthalas and a knot of Araxites watched from the walls as Rhiss rode out, seated on horseback at the head of a formation of Aranellens, Aquilea overhead, Caylyx at his side. The blue and silver Aranellen pennants gleamed in the torchlight before being swallowed up in the dark vastness.

Parthalas shook his head in satisfaction. "Aye, look at him, sittin' regally on that great horse: ye have a young king there now, Arian, in all but name."

"How so?" Arian kept her eyes on the retreating column.

"He made his own decision, and stood up to ye," replied the old warrior, cackling a laugh. "No easy job in the best of circumstances. Yer a formidable old woman, and in all our long years knowin' each other, I recall full-grown Castellars, men who've stared death in the eye wi' out flinching, bucklin' under the weight of yer will... but *he* didna. He listened to ye, weighed what ye had to say, then came to his own resolve. He wasna flustered by ye, and had the Aranellens moving as soon as he snapped his fingers. They could see he was no' to be ignored. There's good potential in the lad, mark my words."

Arian grimaced. "Why? Because he's headstrong and won't listen to reason?"

Parthalas shook his head. "Not at all, and well ye know it, woman. He'll be his own man, not anyone's puppet... not yours, not mine, not the first strong-minded person he comes across who tries bending him to their will. A good thing... and well ye know it, even if ye won't admit it aloud."

"Perhaps." Arian gazed thoughtfully into the night. "What will he find out there, Parthalas? My sister showing up at the witch's cottage... it's almost beyond belief." She paused. "Except the last few weeks with our young Prince have made me realize that *nothing* about him is beyond belief."

"Well, we'll ride after him tomorra, and then, I warrant, ye'll see more than ye've imagined possible." Arian caught something unspoken in the tone, and turned to gaze sharply at the old man. "Aye," he continued, looking into the darkness, "I believe him, whatever he thinks he's seen... yer sister injured, Craggaddon Hall in flames, perhaps... and I think it's begun in earnest. The struggle for Arrinor. The storm is upon us at last." He sucked in a breath and said slowly, almost meditatively, "And, ye know, I fear it'll be long, difficult and bloody. As to whether he'll sit on the Crystal Throne at the end of it... who can say? But I do know this: if nothing else, he'll give that she-demon now on the throne, and her Spawn-of-the-Other Counsellor, a damned good run fer their money."

Here ends

GRYPHON'S HEIR

Book I
The Annals Of Arrinor

The tale continues in

GRYPHON'S AWAKENING

Book II
The Annals Of Arrinor

ANNOTATED PRONUNCIATION GUIDE

In the Arrinoran names listed, the upper-case syllable is where vocal emphasis goes. This is frequently (although confusingly, not always) the second syllable of multi-syllabic words.

Entries are annotated with information either specifically stated or implied by events and characters. Readers are warned that some information may be considered 'plot spoilers.'

A

Admiral Rodney, The – local pub near Darkton School, to which Rhissan and Alistair are fond of retreating after classes

Ahrhissian - (ah RHISS see ann) legendary, ancient king of Arrinor; several people mention that Rhissan resembles him in looks and Essence

Alairra – (ah LAIR ah)
    1: daughter to Mairi and Jaran (friends of Lowri), savaged by a Malmoridai and then healed by Rhissan
    2: of Telcarre, adult daughter of Aranell and leader of the Aranellens

Alistair Bellamy – Rhissan's Darkton School colleague, friend and weapons instructor

Altanimar – (al TANNY mar) legendary ancient sword of Arrinoran kings; Rhiss receives it prior to duelling Moressin at Storrenne

Altmara – (alt MAR ah) the place Parthalas hails from

Altos – (AL toes) heroic character from the Arrinoran epic "The Tale of the Five Companions;" Tariel calls himself this when desiring to conceal his true identity on the night of the Coup

Angharath – (ang HARR rath) gryphon major who responds to Rhissan's involuntary summons of Aquilea on the night of the Coup

Angramor – (ANG gra more) putative place where Maldeus is from; however, given what is known of his true being, the name may be a front to suggest he is mortal

Ansby – (ANZ bee) coastal village in Arrinor, ostensibly the destination of 'Arcan of Follett'

Aquilea – (ah QUILL leah) orphaned young female gryphon who becomes Rhissan's companion

Aralsa – (ah RAL sah) Lady Rhyanna's horse; Arian gives her to Rhissan for his use when escaping Craggaddon Hall

Aranell – (AH ran ELL) knight of Arrinor, close friend of Rhissan's parents; he escapes the Coup, and founds the (renegade) military order bearing his name

Aranellens – (AH ran ELL enz) renegade military order founded by Aranell in the wake of the Coup

Araxan, House of – (ah RACK san) family name of the House of Kings of Arrinor

Araxis, Circlet of – (ah RACK sis) ancient jewellery piece associated with Arrinoran Kings; it contains a gem resembling an extremely large opal, but the gem's colours miraculously appear to move within it; worn by the rightful King, it appears to possess certain powers — or it may act merely as a conduit for the King's abilities

Araxite Community – (ah RACK sight) group of children, rescued by Rhissan during the Coup; as adults, they inhabit Pencairn House, forming the core of a resistance movement against the Crown

Arcan – (ARE kan) stable boy at Craggaddon Hall; later, Rhissan uses the name at Rontha

Ardwyad – (ard WHY add) name given Arian by Rhissan

Arian – (ah RYE ann) lady priest of the One, sometime member of the Castellars, sister to Meranna, who takes charge of Rhissan after his arrival in Arrinor

Arkos – (ARE kose) an Order 'high in the counsels of the One;' Arrinoran Lore of the One teaches there are seven members in the Arkos, but only two are named in *Gryphon's Heir*

Arrinor – (AH rin ore) Rhissan's embattled world

Arrinoran – (AH rin NOR ann) belonging to Arrinor; applicable to people, places and things

B

Belan Othwain – (BELL an OTH wane) owner and proprietor of The King's Arms, an inn located in Rontha

Beltor – (BELL tore) heroic character from Arrinoran epic "The Tale of the Five Companions;" Tariel calls Rhissan by the name when desiring to conceal their identities on the night of the Coup

Berasheathe – (BARE a SHEETH) name Gavrilos gives when Rhissan inquires what the Portal of Gavrilos is called; a private joke of the Arkos

Blade and Bow, The – archery/combat practice area Rhissan and Alistair construct near Darkton; the name is deliberately conceived to resemble that of an inn, so anyone overhearing would assume Rhissan and Alistair were going to a pub

Boar's Head Inn, The – inn situated in the village near Craggaddon Hall; Dalys met his contact there when he had information to pass to agents of Maldeus

Bold – female Sinea-a-Doorn dwelling at the Way Stones of Storrenne

Book of the One – Arrinoran Bible

Borilius – (bor RILL lee us) leader of the Araxite Community; as a child, he saves Rhissan's life on the night of the Coup

Browan – (BROW ann) term used by Parthalas to describe the ale he and Rhissan drink in The King's Arms tap room; it is unlikely 'browan' is actually the drink's name — merely Parthalas referring to its colour ('brown') through his accent

Byrn Moor – (Burn Moor) wild moor located north of Rontha

C

Carlus – (CAR luss) male; member of the Araxite Community

Castellars – (CASS tell arz) Order of the Militant Castellar Servanthood; religious military Order in Arrinor (along the same lines as the Knights Templar in our world), founded for the express purpose of safeguarding the Royal Family; its leadership is corrupted by Maldeus and the Usurper to serve their purposes

Caylyx – (KAY licks) alpha wolvan at Pencairn House, who elects to become Rhissan's companion

Colin Lewis – small boy bullied at Darkton; rescued by Rhissan

Coup, The – event twenty-five years prior to *Gryphon's Heir*, when Arrinor's rightful King, Queen and children (save one) are murdered by the King's sister and her Counsellor

Craggaddon Hall – (kra GAD dun) ancestral seat of the Earls of Tormere; home to Meranna and Rhyanna

Crystal Throne – actual, physical throne of the Kings of Arrinor, fashioned from a single enormous piece of crystal; "Lord of the Crystal Throne" is part of the King's title

D

Dalys – (DALL ees) one-time loyal servant of Lady Meranna at Craggaddon Hall; later corrupted by Maldeus and promised Meranna's daughter for himself

Darkton School for Boys – private school in an unnamed Lincolnshire village in England where Rhissan was an English Literature master

Diiderra – (di DARE ah) Usurping Queen of Arrinor; the name was given her by Maldeus following the Coup

Dinas Mawr – (DEE nas More) Rhissan's Welsh village

Dorvanen – (door VANN enn) one-time Grand Master of the Castellars; corrupted by Maldeus; betrayed the Royal Family and a leading conspirator in the Coup leading to their deaths; later murdered by Maldeus

E

Eowerth Mountains – (EE oh worth) mountain range northwest of Rontha
Eques – (EK wus) Arrinoran word for knight ('Sir')
Equlan – (EK woo lan) male Sinea-a-Doorn dwelling at Storrenne; has a special love for horses, and cares for Aralsa in Rhissan's absence
Erianthus – (airy ANN thus) male; one of the original members of the Araxite Community, rescued as a child by Rhissan on the night of the Coup
Essence – Arrinoran word for the soul

F

Fennor – (FEN ore) male; member of the Araxite Community
Feras – (FAIR az) male; (loyal) member of the group of soldiers accompanying Maldeus to Craggaddon Hall to seize Rhissan
Fire of Cleansing – spontaneous combustion of the bodies of deceased Arrinoran humans or animals who have died in conflict with others; during this process, the corpse is utterly consumed by intense blue flames which do not damage the surroundings; it is evident the Fire of Cleansing does not take place within a specific time frame, as Aquilea's mother's body undergoes the Fire almost immediately following her death, while the body of the Malmoridai destroyed by Rhissan lingers long enough for Tormere household soldiers to examine it and suspect it was brought down by an arrow from Rhissan's bow
Five Companions – protagonists of Arrinoran legendary tale; two of their number were Altos and Beltor
Follet – (FOLL ett) village near Rontha; Rhiss pretended to be from there when introducing himself to inhabitants of Rontha
Forest of Marturin – (mar TURE inn) Arrinoran forest, the intended place of hiding for soldiers who went over to Rhissan's side during his first encounter with Maldeus
Forgall – (FORE gal) male; one of the original members of the Araxite Community, rescued as a child by Rhissan on the night of the Coup

G

Gavrilos – (Gah VRILL oes) member of the Arkos, an Order high in the counsels of the One; the being who summons Rhissan to Arrinor
Gifts of the King – abilities manifested by the rightful ruler of Arrinor. They include the gifts of Healing, Seeing and Measuring, that is, the ability to heal otherwise fatal injuries, the ability to see events that may come to pass, and the ability to determine peoples' inclinations for good or evil

Gryphon Major – larger of two distinct Arrinoran species with the head and forelegs of an eagle and the body of a lion; the gryphon major grows to a very large size, with a wingspan of forty feet or more and a proportional body; they are intelligent and articulate, able to converse in spoken speech with humans, and telepathically with their own species

Gryphon Minor – smaller of two distinct Arrinoran species with the head and forelegs of an eagle and the body of a lion; the gryphon minor grows no larger than a small pony; like its larger cousin, the gryphon minor is intelligent, but seems to rely on telepathic communication; whether they are capable of human speech is unclear in *Gryphon's Heir* — Aquilea does not attempt it during the story

H

Halver – (HAL verr) male; member of the Araxite Community
Hunter, The – name for Moressin Venator
Hunter's Breath – unknown process by which Moressin induces Hunter's Trance
Hunter's Mist – thick grey fog that can move against the wind and suddenly envelop unwary travelers on Byrn Moor; controlled by Moressin, it presages his appearance
Hunter's Trance – catatonic state unfortunate travellers caught in Hunter's Breath/Mist slip into; for some reason, (fortunately) Rhissan seems immune to it

I

'In this we are One' – common Arrinoran saying with dual meaning; first, signifying accord, approval and unanimity within the group; and second, signifying unity with the perceived will of the One
Ilseby – (ILLS bee) village near Darkton School where a dance is held that Alistair attempts to entice Rhiss to attend

J

Jaran – (JAH ran) male peasant, husband to Mairi and father to several children, among them Alairra, the child mauled by a Malmoridai and healed by Rhissan; friend of Lowri's; he assists her in the crafting of a scabbard for Rhissan's sword
Jarella – (jah RELL ah) female; one of the original members of the Araxite Community, rescued as a child by Rhissan on the night of the Coup
Jennie – Alistair Bellamy's girlfriend in our world

K

Kairconnach-Lan – (care KONNACK lann) name given Rhissan by Angharath; it is a vocalization, visible to the gryphon, of the name given off by Rhissan's Essence; as such, the gryphon emphasizes it is only a weak echo of the true name

Kerian – (CARE ee ann) lady-in-waiting to Rhissan's mother, the Queen; after the latter's death in our world, she takes over the care of the child Rhissan, who knows her only as his aunt

Kilarradine – (kill ARE ah deen) port and capital of Arrinor

King's Arms, The – inn located in the village of Rontha

Kirunek – (KEER oon ekk) one of the Way Stone Circles in Arrinor

L

Light, The – a name for the One

Lochnar – (LOCK nar) father of Petran the Doubter

Lowri – (LOWE ree) so-called 'Witch' living at the Ford at White River, so named by neighbours because of her amazing skills at healing wounded animals

Lukarran – (loo CAR ran) itinerant travelling physician staying in Rontha at the time Rhiss is beaten and in dire need of medical assistance

M

Mairi – (MARR ee) peasant woman, wife to Jaran and mother to Alairra, the child mauled by a Malmoridai and healed by Rhissan; friend of Lowri's

Maldeus Falduracha – (mal DAY us FAL du rack ah) Sovereign's Counsellor; servant of the Other, bent on the Sovereign's corruption and advancement of the Other's agenda

Malmoridai – (mal MOREY dye) hideous, intelligent, flying, enormous batlike creatures roaming Arrinor doing the will of Maldeus; one kills Aquilea's mother before being killed in turn by Rhissan; another savagely mauls the peasant child Alairra

Malreck – (MAL wreck) male; leader of a gang of toughs in Rontha who beat Rhiss as he attempts to rescue a young Tavnian couple

Maran – (MAH ran) male; one of the original members of the Araxite Community, rescued as a child by Rhissan on the night of the Coup

McDowell, Mrs. – Rhissan's elderly, formidable landlady and housekeeper

McKraguie – (meck KRAY gie) place Lowri originally hails from

Meranna – (mer ANN ah) mother to Rhyanna, sister to Arian, and mistress of Craggaddon Hall

Moressin Venator – (more RESS inn VEN ah tore) undead apparition roaming Byrn Moor, searching for victims to consume their Essences

N

Night of Fire – name given the night of the Coup by Aranellens; later, the name gains widespread (although surreptitious) use across Arrinor

Norelli – (nor ELLY) male; one of the original members of the Araxite Community, rescued as a child by Rhissan on the night of the Coup

O

One, The – Arrinoran name for God
Other, The – Arrinoran name for the Devil

P

Parthalas – (parr THAL az) elderly, one-time Master of Arms of the Castellar; friend of Arian

Pencair Ice Field – (PEN kare ice field) series of mountain glaciers at the head of the valley where Pencairn House is located; source of the Pencair River

Pencair River – (PEN kare river) glacial river flowing through the mountain valley where Pencairn House is located

Pencairn House – (PEN karen house) originally a training establishment of the Castellar Order; located in the Eowerth Mountain Range; abandoned by the Castellars because of a horrific spirit's appearance; later occupied by the Araxite Community

Petran – (PET tran) male; member of the Araxite Community; sometimes called 'The Doubter,' because he calls into question Rhissan's promise the night of the Coup and, later, his identity as King at Pencairn House; knifed by Ulcawn at Summit's Redoubt, his Healing by Rhissan in full view of many Araxites erases those doubts

Portal – supernatural connection between worlds, used by members of the Arkos; each has his or her own Portal, tailored to individual personality; however, an identical, ornately carved wooden door is the common hallmark of all Portals

R

Relamus – (RELL ah moose) Lowri's dog, a huge, shaggy animal completely devoted to her

Rhiamon – (REE ah mon) birth name of Arrinor's Usurping Queen

Rhissan/Rhiss – (RISS ann/RISS) protagonist of *Gryphon's Heir*

Rhyanna – (ree ANN ah) daughter of Lady Meranna, the first to benefit from Rhissan's new-found Healing ability

Riona – (ree ONN ah) Rhissan's mother

Rontha – (RON tha) village north of Craggaddon Hall; first settlement encountered by Rhissan and Arian after escaping Craggaddon Hall

Rothrann, Pool of – (roth RANN) large, deep pool of water near Rhissan's childhood village of Dinas Mawr; formed after the abandonment of either a mine or quarry — Rhissan is unsure which; an unidentified evil force resides there and attempts to murder Rhissan as a young child, but he is saved by Bold

Ruvennar – (RUE venn are) cordial of the Arkos, it offers amazing restorative abilities to those drinking it; Rhissan finds it has a 'fruity, sweet, full bodied, extremely pleasant and quite unidentifiable' taste

S

Sacred Spaces – another term for the Way Stone Circles of Arrinor

Scallassie – (SKAL lass see) place from whence Kerian, lady in waiting to Rhissan's mother the Queen, originally comes from

Seir-on – (SIR on) title for a male priest of the One

Seir-onna – (sir ONN ah) title for a female priest of the One

Sinea-a-Doorn – (shin NAY ah DOORN) race of beings guarding the Sacred Spaces (i.e. the Way Stones) of Arrinor; they normally appear as human children except for large, butterfly-like wings on their backs, but it is implied they can assume much more terrible form when called upon by Servants of the One

Soran-gar-may – (sor ANN garr MAY) lovely, other-worldly gardens in the Arrinoran epic "The Tale of the Five Companions"

Sovereign's Counsellor – official Arrinoran title of Maldeus; also frequently used by people who would rather not mention his name aloud

Sovereign's Men – thuggish brigands serving as the Usurper's paramilitary army/intelligence service

Storrenne – (store RENN) one of the Way Stone Circles in Arrinor

Summit's Redoubt – collection of buildings constructed high on a ridge below the summit of a mountain above Pencairn House; intended as a place of reflection and solitude for the Araxite Community

T

Talla – (TALL ah) Lowri's dependable little moor pony

Talbot – Head Boy at Darkton School, and the thoroughly objectionable, entitled son of an earl; bullied Colin Lewis before the latter was rescued by Rhissan

Tariel – (TAH ree ell) member of the Arkos, an Order 'high in the counsels of the One.' It is revealed in *Gryphon's Heir* that this is not his real name, but his motive for concealing his true name is unclear

Tar Merida – (tar MAREY dah) one of four daily services to the One, Tar Merida is said (or sung) in the third quarter of the day (between noon and 6 pm)

Tavna – (TAV nah) coastal city-state region northwest of Rontha; once independent, it was forcibly annexed by the Sovereign's forces some twenty years prior to Rhissan's return to Arrinor; Tavna's culture and customs are different from Arrinor's, leading to some discrimination and racial harassment of Tavnians at times

Tavnian – (TAV nee ann) an inhabitant of Tavna

Tavvy – (TAH vee) derogatory name for a Tavnian

Telcarre – (tell CARE) place whence the Lady Alairra is originally from

Telcharan – (tell KAR an) 'the Place of Sanctuary' in the epic 'The Tale of the Five Companions'

Tobias – (toe BYE us) seneschal (business manager and overseer) of Lady Meranna's estates

Tor – (tore) Arrinoran word for castle

Tor Aran – (tore AH ran) secret refuge (castle?) of the Aranellen Order

Tor Eylian – (tore EYE lee ann) Royal castle of the King of Arrinor, located in the capital city of Kilarradine

Tor Linlith – (tore LIN lith) abandoned castle near Craggaddon Hall where the Portal of Gavrilos deposits Rhissan on first entering Arrinor

Tormere – (tore MEER) an Earldom in Arrinor, not a castle, despite the similarity in name

Tovan – (TOE van) Rhissan's father, former King of Arrinor; murdered by his sister and her Counsellor

U

Ulcawn – (ULL kan) member of the Araxite Community at Pencairn House; in charge of the wolvans

Usurper – one title for Diiderra, Queen of Arrinor (not used to her face, obviously...)

W

Way Stones – locations in Arrinor with common characteristics: large, rectangular stones arranged in a circular manner reminiscent of Stonehenge; there are several ground depressions in each circle, through which unexplained events can occur; also called the Sacred Spaces

White River – river bordering Byrn Moor; Lowri's house is located at a ford along its course

Wolvans – (WULL vans) Arrinoran cousins to wolves, but larger and more intelligent; while they can be domesticated, this happens rarely; the Araxite Community maintains an entire pack at Pencairn House to assist with external security, which is unusual and likely due to Ulcawn's skills

ABOUT THE AUTHOR

D.R. Ranshaw has loved reading and writing since childhood, when the printed word's ability to unlock both historical and fabulous worlds became an immediate, lifelong passion. Introduced to fantasy and science fiction at a young age, he began voraciously reading both genres, and it was not long before he was also writing them.

A public school teacher who has enjoyed a long and fulfilling career — unlike the protagonist of *Gryphon's Heir* — D.R. Ranshaw has spent more than three decades in the classroom, transmitting his deep love of literature and writing to his students.

Gryphon's Heir has its origins in the real-life frustrations all teachers occasionally experience. After one particularly aggravating day, the image of a strange doorway from his classroom into a faraway land lodged in the author's imagination and refused to leave. The only recourse was exploring where that door led to and what would happen to anyone daring to cross its threshold. The resulting story rapidly gained depth and complexity and developed a life of its own.

Printed in Canada